Acclaim for E[illegible] and FRENCH KISS

"Eric V. Lustbader has changed directions, from Oriental mysticism to global intrigue. The pace remains...frenetic with sudden transatlantic shifts; violence lurks everywhere, and the most innocuous characters are often the most sinister....

"Lustbader is a master at disguise, constantly tricking his readers with false clues, deadend subplots and fake identities. Just when the outcome appears obvious, a subtle twist of the Kaleidoscope and old allies become bitter adversaries. He also provides a carefully researched background—the ruthless bureaucracy of United States intelligence, the rampant cruelty of the drug network. He throws in several superb mini-travelogs, the mellow pleasures of Nice, the glamorous excitement of Paris, the intense glitter of New York City.

"This is a long, complicated spy novel with continuous action and pages of excellent writing. Lustbader goes beyond the mandatory brutality with clear prose and a precisely logical finale. Here is Ludlum for intellectuals."

Jeremy C. Shea
St. Louis Post-Dispatch

(More)

"Engaging characters, many, many plot twists, and a mystical core."

Daily News

"Fast-paced, intricate and exotic...Lustbader delivers his tale in an almost cinematic/melodramatic onslaught of flash and flourish....As a kinetic descent into sensuality, suspense and exotic heat, it's truly breathtaking."

Chattanooga News-Free Press

"A long, complicated, bloody Oriental thriller. The writing of bestselling author Lustbader is truly magnificent."

Tulsa World

"Eric V. Lustbader has hit the peak of his form with *French Kiss*. The action here sprawls over decades and across continents, as Lustbader pummels the readers with non-stop acton and ingenious plot twists....Lustbader's skill at creating believable characters shines throughout *French Kiss* and brings it an intensity rarely found in thrillers. Even those who fill minor roles are imbued with life."

The Flint Journal

"A fast-paced tale of international intrigue and corruption involving high-stakes drug battles fought among Eastern opium warlords... A powerful and satisfying novel."

Inside Books

"Complicated plots keep the reader moving from one fantastic turn of events to the next."

Magill Book Reviews

"A complex, epic-scale psychological thriller... Also an eye-opener [that] educates the reader about the tumultuous history of Southeast Asia while it entertains."

Rave Reviews

"Fast-paced yet intricate, populated by characters that seem to exist in an exotic, mythical netherworld, part East, part West, part past, part present."

Booklist

Also by Eric V. Lustbader
Published by Fawcett Books:

THE NINJA
BLACK HEART
SIRENS
THE MIKO
JIAN
SHAN
ZERO

The Sunset Warrior Cycle
THE SUNSET WARRIOR
SHALLOWS OF THE NIGHT
DAI-SAN
BENEATH AN OPAL MOON

FRENCH KISS

ERIC V. LUSTBADER

FAWCETT CREST • NEW YORK

A Fawcett Crest Book
Published by Ballantine Books
 Published in the United States by Ballantine Books, a division of Random House, Inc., New York, and simultaneously in Canada by Random House of Canada Limited, Toronto.

Grateful acknowledgment is made to the following for permission to reprint previously published material:

Chrysalis Music, Jones Music America, and Screen Gems-EMI Music Inc.: Excerpts fom the song lyrics, "Aladdin Sane" by David Bowie. Copyright © 1973 by Moth Music, Bewlay Bros. Music, and Fleur Music. All rights for the United States and Canada controlled by Chrysalis Music, Jones Music America and Screen Gems-EMI Music Inc.

Third Story Music, Inc: Excerpts form the song lyrics, "Once I Was" by Tim Buckley. Copyright © 1968 by Third Story Music, Inc.

Warner/Chappell Music, Inc.: Excerpts from the song lyrics, "My Death" by Jacques Brel, Mort Shuman, and Eric Blau. Copyright © 1967 by Rightsong Music, Inc. All rights reserved. Used by permission.

Library of Congress Catalog Card Number: 88-24336

ISBN 0-449-21849-X

Manufactured in the United States of America

First Hardcover Edition: February 1989
First Mass Market Edition: February 1990

ACKNOWLEDGMENTS

A host of people helped in the various aspects of research for *French Kiss*. My thanks to:

Sichan Siv, who was, as always, an invaluable font of knowledge and insight regarding the war in Vietnam, and conditions in that country and Cambodia in 1969. He also provided the Khmer translations, as well as Asian support, especially in Paris.

Brad Miner, for matters pertaining to Catholicism and the Church.

Lu Ban Hap & Armelle, for access into Paris's Porte Choisy and background on the war in Vietnam.

Eliane Benisti, my lifeline in Paris.

Laurine, Michelle, and Mattieu at l'Agence Benisti, for research coordination, translations, and liaisoning in Paris.

Signore Panico, keeper of the blades.

Michael Schochet, for information on bicycle racing and racers.

Lieutenant Colonel Charles Steiner and Lieutenant Colonel Paul Knox (Ret.), U.S. Army Department of Public Affairs (N.Y.), for information on Special Forces training, SOCOM, Vietnam, et al.

Mo Myint, for Burmese translations.

Freddie Khin Maung, for Burmese translations and lore.

Richard Koerner and Hilde Gerst, for sharing their trips to Angkor.

My father, for proofing the MS.

Milt Amgott, Forde Medina for legal research.

Dr. Jamie Stern, Dr. Bertram Newman, for medical advice.

In addition, I'd like to acknowledge M. Mabuse's crash obsession as being insipred by J.G. Ballard's extraordinary novel *Crash*.

Very special thanks to Victoria and Kate, who both worked tirelessly on the MS.

AUTHOR'S NOTE

With the exception of obvious historical figures, all characters in *French Kiss* are the sole invention of the author, and bear no intended resemblance to any real individual living or dead.

Although in every other respect I have been accurate in depicting Tourrette-sur-Loup, there is no church there named Our Lady of Benva, just as there is no Holy Trinity Church in New Canaan.

THIS IS FOR SUSAN, LEONA, AND KATE—
THE OTHER WOMEN IN MY LIFE

CONTENTS

There are only two forces
that unite men—
fear and interest.

—Napoleon Bonaparte

Let us run with patience
the race that is set
before us.

—Hebrews 12:1

SPRING, PRESENT

TOURRETTE-SUR-LOUP, FRANCE/ NEW CANAAN, CONNECTICUT

All spirits vanish with the dawn. That was what Terry Haye thought as he walked across the square fronting the medieval town of Tourrette-sur-Loup.

He had driven his rented Opel up the winding road from Nice during a rainstorm that had driven gray clouds in off the Mediterranean. In the rooftop restaurant of his hotel in Nice, he had had coffee and croissants while looking at the indigo mountains of Haute-Provence below the blue-black sky that presaged sunrise.

Lingering over his coffee, he had wondered whether it was experience or action that destroyed morality. It must be action, he decided, eating the last of his croissant. If he had become a writer, everything would be different now. A writer created only words. A writer was, by definition, a master of deceit; but it was a deceit that had no existence save on the printed page. Morality did not enter into it; a writer could create, but he could not destroy. That was his power—and his weakness. That was why Terry had chosen the other path: action. Action was life; and it was death.

He had watched the first blush of dawn give way to a morning filled with wind and dust as if it were an omen by which he could tell the future. He had walked the streets of Nice with an aimless energy that turned pleasant streets silent and deadly.

Needing company on the drive north into the Loup Valley, he had turned on the radio. *The instant of recognition*, Isabelle Adjani sang in French, *is like seeing the sun at midnight. The copper trees glow in the heat of your eyes. And time falls asleep in your arms.*

Terry thought of black olives swimming in oil and crusty *pain de campagne*, the quintessential Provençal lunch. Five miles out of Nice, he was already hungry. It was just past ten o'clock.

Black clouds hung in the sky, as if pinned to a backdrop. The sun refused to show itself. When the rain came, it did so in thick curtains. Mist, clinging to the low foliage, curled up the ancient stone walls surrounding the village. Tourrette, sitting atop the spinal ridge of the serpentine mountainside, appeared not as a village at all, Terry thought, but rather as the magical horn of a great beast of the earth.

Pigeons scattered in front of him, swooping across the cobbled square. Terry felt the weight of the stainless steel briefcase chained to his left wrist. He felt abruptly conspicuous striding past the children at play, the scattered groups of tourists emerging from their autos like rats from a hole, their faces buried in their green Michelin guides.

A ball the children were throwing bounced toward him. He caught it, lofted it back at them. As he did so, the chain rattled, and the children stared. The ball went bouncing across the ancient cobbles of the square, making the pigeons squawk as they took flight, vanishing like spirits with the dawn.

He passed through the stone portals on the far side of the square, and was transported back five centuries. Ahead of him, narrow, twisting streets sloped downward. He could hear a baby crying through an open window, then a plaintive lullaby sung in a soothing voice. The facades of the stone houses rose up like sheer cliffs on either side. There was barely room for two people to walk abreast.

This early, there was hardly anyone on the streets, save for shopkeepers turning oversized keys in the rusty locks of their storefronts. They smiled at him, and wished him good morning. The smell of baking bread was tantalizing.

He paused to peer through a slivered gap in the buildings. Olive trees, dripping in the misty rain, covered the mountainside all the way down to the hazy lower elevations from which he had come. Within a month or two the lavender would be in bloom, a carpet of fragrance and color for miles in all directions. Terry craned his neck, saw a car ascending on the D 2210 from Vence, the road he had taken earlier. From his vantage point, the rest of the world looked remote, a scene viewed the wrong way through a telescope.

He went left at the first crossroads, then took an immediate right. Down a long, curving flight of stairs worn as smooth as if it had been part of a centuries-old watercourse.

It was darker here. He passed a black, long-haired cat half asleep on a sooty, stone sconce that centuries ago had been used to light nighttime streets. The animal opened its eyes just as Terry passed, staring at him with the intense, dumb curiosity peculiar to cats.

Farther along, he came upon a shop at the corner of a cross street.

Pausing, he looked inside its window. He saw a marionette hung by strings that were invisible against a black velvet backdrop. It was handmade, of exquisite workmanship: a female harlequin. She was dressed in the traditional red and white diamond-patterned suit. A single teardrop was painted on her checkered mask. And then, as Terry peered more closely, he made out a second figure half hidden in the shadows behind her: it was the devil, with a horned head, a beautiful, garish face, and skeleton arms outspread against the black background. Terry stood, transfixed by the marionettes for a long moment. Then, nodding to himself, he turned away.

Down here, the Chapel of Our Lady of Benva stood at the end of a crooked, shadow-laden alley. It appeared as if even at noon the sun would not touch its white stone walls. The enormous, arching wooden doors stood open, their thick ironwork glinting dully.

Inside the church, the air was filled with dust motes and echoes. History pressed inward as if impelled by heaven itself. Terry sensed rather than saw the height of the inner galleries. A small, handwritten sign in French announced that Benva was a corruption of the early Provençal *ben vai*, meaning good journey.

Terry went into the main sanctuary, and stood at the back for a long time. His eyes probed every inch of the gloomy interior. He could not say for certain that he was entirely alone, but he could discern no movement, no other presence. Still, he was vigilant, recalling the biblical verse: "Be ye therefore wise as serpents and harmless as doves."

He walked down the center aisle, past the rows of empty wooden pews, black with age and use. Terry guessed that these were the same seats used when the world was lit only by fire.

He sat in the second row, as he had been instructed to do.

The walls on either side were decorated with frescoes depicting in graphic detail aspects of the Crucifixion and the Resurrection. Terry found the florid and exaggerated aura of pain and torment suffocating. Directly in front of him was a gigantic wooden carving of Christ on the Cross. His head was turned to the side, His crown of thorns had already taken on the aspect of a halo, and His sunken eyes stared out with what Terry could only define as a disturbing hunger. It was as if this Christ was asking a question of all who entered the Chapel of Our Lady of Benva. Though Terry was not religious, he found himself wondering what that question might be.

"*Bonjour*, Monsieur Haye."

Terry turned, saw a man sitting in the row of pews behind him.

"You startled me," Terry said. "I didn't hear you come in."

"I expect not," the man said. "I was already here." His voice was oddly muffled, as if it were being telephoned in.

"And you are Monsieur—?"

"Mabuse," the man said.

Terry peered more closely at the man, but in the dim, dusty light, it was as if the man were part of the shadows. All he could tell was that the man was small. "Surely not," he said. "Are you serious? Isn't Mabuse a name from a classic film?"

"I wouldn't know," the man said, "since I do not frequent the cinema." He had brought out a fan and, opening it, began to wave it back and forth just below his chin.

Terry wanted to laugh. "You're not the man I spoke with on the phone," he said. "That was Monsieur Milhaud."

"Milhaud reaches out his hand for what he wants," M. Mabuse said, "and I close my fist upon it." The portentous phrase was oddly fitting—and powerful—in this setting.

When Terry shifted his position a bit, M. Mabuse moved the fan in response; his face remained a part of the shadows. "Do you need that fan? It isn't warm in here," Terry said, abruptly annoyed.

M. Mabuse seemed to smile from the shadows. "My *gunsen* is always with me," he said. He leaned forward, closer to Terry. "Have you brought the item?" Now Terry could see that the fan was made of metal. It was thickly engraved, and looked heavy—odd for such an object.

"Have you brought the ten million dollars?" Terry asked.

"In diamonds," M. Mabuse said. "As you requested."

"Let's see them."

M. Mabuse continued to fan himself. "Show me what will they buy, Monsieur Haye."

Terry hefted the stainless steel case still chained to his wrist. At the same time M. Mabuse stood, lifted a bulky black attaché case onto the top of the pew.

Terry placed his case beside the other, opened its combination lock; M. Mabuse snapped the levers on his black attaché. Together, they opened the tops. What was inside M. Mabuse's attaché were plastic bags of blue-white diamonds, all, as Terry had requested, between one and three carats. What was inside Terry's case was another matter entirely.

M. Mabuse sucked in his breath at the sight of it. "*La Porte à la Nuit,*" he said.

Terry lifted his case up a bit higher. It was lined in midnight-blue velvet. What lay in its center could only be described as a dagger, but it was like no other dagger in existence. Its gleaming blade, nearly a foot long, was carved from a single piece of Imperial jade. The guard was polished ivory, wrapped with solid gold wire. The hilt was ebony, engraved and acid-etched with incomprehensible runes. At the very end of the pommel was set a single cabochon ruby the color of pigeon's blood. As M. Mabuse had said, the dagger was known as the Doorway to Night.

Terry picked up a diamond at random, put a jeweler's loupe into one eye, extracted a pocket flashlight. In the narrow beam of light he examined the gemstone. He put it back, took another, examined it as well. When he was done, he said, "*La Porte à la Nuit* is what M. Milhaud wants." He shut the lid of his case. "The deal is done."

"One moment," M. Mabuse said. "Milhaud has given me strict orders. I must make certain that this is, indeed, *La Porte à la Nuit*. Please open the case again."

From somewhere within the chapel, prayers had begun. The *Agnus Dei* was being sung, voices drifting down on them, the Latin words like ancient rain.

"What kind of test?" Terry said. "I have told you. This *is* the Doorway to Night."

"Open the case, Monsieur Haye."

"I don't think so. This is not in the—"

"Monsieur Haye, even as we speak, your brother Chris is under surveillance in New York."

"Chris? What does Chris have to do with anything?"

"Just this, Monsieur Haye. If you attempt to cheat us in any way, we will kill your brother. Call it a reminder, if not a warning. Rules must be kept."

Terry saw that M. Mabuse had put aside his attaché case. To Terry's amazement he saw that there was a smaller version of the dagger in the other man's hand. Another piece of the Forest of Swords.

"So it's true," Terry said. "Milhaud has the remaining pieces of the *Prey Dauw*. The Forest of Swords."

"Have a care," M. Mabuse said. "*Les murs ont des oreilles.*" By which he meant, Who can say who might be listening? "The *Prey Dauw* is a trinity," he went on in a hushed tone. "A knife, a dagger, and a sword: the Father, the Son, and the Holy Ghost. One without the others is useless. But, of course, you know that already."

Terry did not care for M. Mabuse's sacrilegious, mocking reference. "You have the knife. Does that mean that Monsieur Milhaud has the third part, the sword, as well?" He was thinking that no matter what the answer, he had found out what he had come here to discover.

Terry did not like this man at all. Despite the money involved, he was already regretting the deal he had made. He was reminded of a line by Victor Hugo, "There are people who observe the rules of honor as we do the stars, from a great distance."

"What Milhaud has or doesn't have," M. Mabuse said, "is no concern of yours." He brought his knife close to Terry's dagger. "Singly, the three weapons have only a monetary value," he went on. "But together . . . they were made to fit against one another to form a single whole: the Forest of Swords, the *Prey Dauw*, as it is known in the Brahman texts. The three together have an entirely different value, one virtually without limit." The dagger in M. Mabuse's hand moved in and out of the dusty light. "I will know if this is *La Porte à la Nuit* when these weapons fit together. The method of their bonding is impossible to see—and impossible therefore to duplicate."

Terry made a sudden decision. He shut the case. "I've changed my mind," he said. "I've decided *La Porte à la Nuit* is not for sale."

"You are being quite foolish," M. Mabuse said. "You need the money to continue your operations. You have been fantastically successful, until a recent series of reverses has put you in a rather nasty vise." As he spoke, he moved into the light. Now Terry could see that M. Mabuse was wearing a mask—a full-head latex mask.

"How do you know all this?" Terry said. Something about M. Mabuse's odd, muffled voice was becoming familiar. In the back of his mind a suspicion began to form. He reached out, and ripped the mask from M. Mabuse's head, exposing a gleaming, grinning skull.

Without warning, M. Mabuse leaned over the pew, swept the knife inward toward Terry, just as Terry instinctively began an evasive maneuver.

"Jesus," Terry breathed in concert with the angelic voices singing the *Agnus Dei*. He used the edge of his right hand, smashing into the other man's collarbone.

M. Mabuse did not even wince. He kept the knife coming in, sweeping it in a shallow arc. Terry's immediate task was to grab hold of the knife's blade. Because its blade was carved from jade, it could not hold an edge. It could also be broken if it was twisted sharply enough, or if it received a hard, oblique blow.

Struggling, Terry wrapped his hand around the small, slim blade. M. Mabuse grunted, gave a great lunge with his shoulder. Terry cried out as the end of the blade pierced his right palm, impaling it against the scarred wood of the pew back.

Now Terry realized that this had been M. Mabuse's intention all along. Grinning, M. Mabuse let go of the knife's handle and, curling his hand around the metal fan, slashed the top edge of it inward at Terry's shoulder.

Terry had never before known such agony. The hellish fan was a weapon! Its pleated steel edges were honed to razor sharpness. *My* gunsen *is always with me*, M. Mabuse had said. Automatically, Terry tried to twist away, but pain exploded up his right arm, emanating from his hand, locked between the wood and the jade blade.

Then M. Mabuse plunged his fist into Terry's sternum, and Terry's body spasmed, his breastbone shattered. He was bent backward over the wooden pew, and his vision was of the crucified Christ, upside down. He saw only those sunken eyes asking their eternal question.

M. Mabuse said, "I'm going to kill your brother, anyway."

As the pain became a river carrying him away to a sea of agony, he tried desperately to move his body. But either the pain or the trauma of his wounds made movement impossible.

It was then that, perhaps as a gesture of his complete control over Terry, M. Mabuse ripped the grotesque skull mask from his face, and Terry saw the true visage of his murderer.

"Oh, my God."

And then he understood everything.

Drowning in his own blood, Terry thought of Chris, and began to pray for his brother's life.

He discovered another kind of urgency inside of himself. To his surprise he felt the proximity of heaven. And, also to his surprise, he found that he very much wanted entrance. He did not know whether he would rise to it, or fall instead into the pit. This uncertainty defined his narrowing consciousness. He began to cry, and as he did so, he saw the image of Christ as if for the first time. It was as if his tears made manifest to him the question Christ was asking. And, as he was dying, Terry Haye answered that question. His lips moved.

M. Mabuse's steel fan whirred, severing Terry Haye's head from his neck.

The *Agnus Dei* had been sung and now, the only sounds inside the church were the distant echoes of Terry Haye's last words, "I have sinned."

Saved.

Saved was the title of this week's sermon. Not that sermons really had titles. But Fr. Dominic Guarda liked to have titles for his sermons. They helped him to gather his thoughts, to arrange what he had to say, to begin at the beginning, as it were. As the Red Queen said to Alice.

Since being assigned to Holy Trinity Church in New Canaan, Fr. Guarda had come to feel much like Alice must have felt in Wonderland. Fr. Guarda had been born and raised in the sweltering Italian ghetto of Manhattan's Hell's Kitchen. His father had been a hod carrier, with a back as strong as Atlas's, and as bowed as Sisyphus's. His mother still lived on Tenth Avenue, in the same rat-infested tenement in which Fr. Guarda and his older brother, Seve, had been born.

And now, Fr. Guarda thought, here I am, thirty-nine years old, an ordained Catholic priest in the middle of the land of milk and honey, where scions are ordained into the religion of wealth.

Fr. Guarda got up from his desk in the rectory, and went to the leaded-glass windows. Everything about Holy Trinity Church, both inside and out, was magnificent. The white stone of its imposing facade, the ornate apses, the groined ceilings, the splendor of its arched rows of stained-glass windows, the enormous, marble images of Christ on the cross, the hooded Virgin Mary in the sanctuary, were all calculated to humble the entering parishioner.

It was impossible for Fr. Guarda to imagine how much money had been spent in the construction of this monument to God. The thought of all that money was disorienting. It was Fr. Guarda's considered opinion that nothing good ever came from money. But it was also a fact of life that the Church needed money to survive.

Fr. Guarda looked out past the flower bed where in June the white peonies with their crimson centers would bow in the warm breeze, past the huge elms overarching the wide fieldstone path that led to the church's front entrance, into the parking lot. It was Holy Week, just days before Good Friday, and the flock was beginning to make its semiannual pilgrimage. What he saw was a sea of gold. He saw the riches of New Canaan's residents like an orchard of fruit trees ready for harvesting. The Mercedes sedans belonged to the older, more conservative members of his congregation. The BMWs and Jaguars were owned by the younger, more upwardly mobile people.

Then there were the old Chevrolet Woodies, the ancient Fords and Plymouths. Fr. Guarda knew each one by heart. As he had been told by the bishop, "Old cars, old money." These people felt no compulsion to display their wealth. Three or four generations of money bred confidence, if nothing else, in its children.

Fr. Guarda watched his parishioners walking into the church. For a moment he wondered what it would be like to be wealthy. Of course he was already wealthy with God's riches. But money—that was another matter entirely. Men, Fr. Guarda knew well, spent their entire adult lives in a quest for money. They destroyed one another for it. They lied, cheated, extorted, all to possess more of it. This was beyond Fr. Guarda's comprehension. God made it so that one was born wealthy with God's bounty: faith. But most people turned away from the riches that faith brought; they turned away from the innate knowledge of themselves that God had provided them.

As, for example, that man at confession yesterday. At Easter, the time of repentance, the Church encouraged the act of confession. During Holy Week, he heard perhaps three times the normal number of confessions. But none had been like this one.

Fr. Guarda could hear the desperation in his voice through the confession screen; it was clear that his guilt was destroying him. Fr. Guarda was certain that he had come to the Church of the Holy Trinity because he wanted to be saved. "Forgive me, Father," he had said, "for I have sinned."

"And how have you—" Fr. Guarda had begun, but the man was already rambling on.

"It's been five years since my last confession. Since that time I have entered hell," the confessor had said. "I have gone to the limits of what man should do, and I have gone beyond those limits. I did so willingly, that I fully admit. Do you suppose that God will forgive me that?" Before Fr. Guarda had had a chance to say, Yes, if you are repentant, God will forgive you any transgression, the confessor had continued. "Others around me, above me, wanted power. I suppose, yes, power. I was driven by greed." The man had spoken in quick, convulsive bursts. It was almost as if he had been living in a locked box for years, and now was getting his first chance to communicate with another human being. "I simply wanted money. And the more money I got, the more I wanted, until it was impossible for me to become sated. I felt like a glutton unable to push myself away from food. The more I ate, the more I called for more food. I could not stop."

His actions, rather than his words, had led Fr. Guarda to see in the man an awareness of the innate knowledge God had given him at birth and, like the flame of a candle flickering dangerously in the night wind, he had sought to nurture that awareness. "Yet you have come here," Fr. Guarda had said. "That is the most positive sign that something within you has changed."

But the man had continued as if he had not heard Fr. Guarda. "For many months I have been consumed. There is a demon in my belly, omnivorous and insatiable. It demanded and I acted. What other choice did I have?"

"You have made another choice," Fr. Guarda had said. "You have come here."

"No. No," the confessor had said. "My hands are already covered in blood." For the first and only time he had responded to Fr. Guarda. "It is too late for me. I am beyond redemption."

"No man is beyond—"

"That is not why I have come here," the man hurried on. "Not for myself. I am already dead. Besides, I have forgotten what life is. I can no longer feel joy or laughter. I have forgotten everything I once knew. The demon in my belly has emptied me of whatever I once had."

By this time Fr. Guarda had become seriously concerned about the man's mental health.

"I am here," the confessor said, "because I have nowhere else to go. There is no one else to trust. I can trust a priest, can't I? Trust is sacred to a priest. I seem to remember that from my childhood." The man had picked up the pace of his speech. Now there seemed to be no pauses between sentences or even disparate ideas. "Even here, I am afraid. I remembered I used to feel calm in a church. Calm and at peace. Now I cannot even recall what those feelings might be like. But there is someone who does, someone you can still help."

So alarmed had Fr. Guarda become at the confessor's seeming instability that he had broken in on the man's rambling. "Stay here," he had said. "I will find you some help."

Immediately, he had heard a sharp rustling from the other side of the screen and, realizing that his words had panicked the man, he emerged from the confessional, ducked his head into the booth on the other side. The man had already disappeared. A small slip of paper was lying on the wooden seat. Fr. Guarda picked it up. It was crumpled and sweat-stained, as if the confessor had been clutching it for some time. On it was written a name and an address.

Fr. Guarda had wondered into the early hours of this morning about how he could have better served the confessor. Which was why he had completed his sermon only moments before he was scheduled to give it.

Now, as he continued to stare out the rectory window, Fr. Guarda heard a discreet cough. Fr. Donnelly, one of his assistants, was summoning him to Mass.

"I'll be there momentarily," Fr. Guarda said. And, still thinking of the mystery surrounding yesterday's confession, he turned away from the elms, the peonies. Who had the man come to the Church of the Holy Trinity to save, if not himself? Fr. Guarda wondered. He took from his pocket the slip of paper the confessor had left. He stared again at the name written there. Then he took a pen from his desk, and wrote the word "Saved?" across the bottom. He quite deliberately emphasized the question mark. Then he shoved the paper back in his pocket because he did not want to forget to follow up on this line of inquiry. He recalled the confessor's words as if they were etched in fire in his mind: *There is someone you can still help*.

The parking lot, now empty of people, was a sea of concrete, filled only with things—the gold of the new land, New Canaan.

And this, too, is God's domain, Fr. Guarda thought as he swept his sermon off his desk and went out the door that led directly into the main body of the church.

"Kyrie eleison, Christe eleison, Kyrie eleison."

Fr. Guarda sang along with Fr. Donnelly and the congregation. He completed the penitential rites, prepared himself while Fr. Donnelly read from the scriptures, Leviticus 26, the blessings of obedience and the punishments of disobedience.

When Fr. Donnelly had finished, Fr. Guarda climbed into the pulpit. He opened the Bible to the place he had previously marked. He read from the First Letter of John, "My little children, I am writing this to you so that you may not sin; but if any one does sin, we have an advocate with the Father, Jesus Christ the righteous. . . ."

Fr. Guarda continued reading the section of the Gospel he had selected, only now thinking that he had chosen it with the confessor in mind.

When he was finished, he put aside the Bible, arranged his papers in front of him. Oddly, he could not recall what he had read.

"The state to which we all aspire undergoes a skillful transmogrification spanning the decades," Fr. Guarda began. He stood with his arms spread, gripping the richly glossed oak edges of the pulpit. Behind him was the image of Christ; in front of him his parishioners sat with uptilted faces. "What we wanted to be when we were in our teens bears no resemblance to what we might want ten years later. And again, what might have made us happy in our twenties must prove shallow and uninviting ten years hence."

Fr. Guarda looked out over his congregation. "Why is this so? Is it true for all human beings? For male and female alike? It would seem universal; as if all thinking creatures continue to grow after their bodies, and even their minds, have matured."

Fr. Guarda made it a point to know every face at Mass, to put a name and, if he was able, an address and other pertinent information to that face. "Perhaps it is the matter of the changing definition of freedom. Here in the land of the free, the concept of freedom is widely discussed, debated, and contemplated. It is also cherished as an 'inalienable right,' according to the founding fathers of our Declaration of Independence."

Fr. Guarda liked to look at the faces of his parishioners while he was giving his sermon, whereas, when he was reading from text, he looked at no one. "Can we then say that we know the meaning of freedom and, therefore, its value?"

This was, he supposed, because he liked to see the effect his words were having on his people, whereas the effect of God's words on them was entirely their own affair. "What we need to know are the parameters of freedom. In the lexicon of human thought there are, perhaps, not enough words to enumerate the *definitions* of freedom, yet we *must* be able to arrive at a set of parameters. Still, freedom may—and often does—exist outside any parameters at all. In this sense freedom is synonymous with chaos."

But now, in his mind, he saw, rising up in front of him like an eerie mist off a swamp, a vision of the man in the confessional. The image was shadowed and ill-lit, yet the pain and despair disfiguring it were as obvious as stigmata. Fr. Guarda could not say how he knew this face in his mind was the man in the confessional, since he had no idea what that man had looked like, but he knew just the same. He was momentarily so startled by his thoughts that he interrupted his reading. He felt abruptly frightened in a way that he had not been since he was in Vietnam. He shook himself, as if to clear his mind, then, pulling himself together, he continued.

"Chaos is death," he said, thinking of the war. "It is the death of the spirit, the death of nature, the death of the natural order of things. It is the death of God.

"Without freedom there is no choice. This is true. But with *only* freedom, choice becomes illusory. Within a world whose only boundary is freedom, there is no landscape, no habitation, no horizon against which to judge progression or regression. There is, in effect, no past—and, consequently, no future. There is only the present, unchanging, ossified."

As he spoke, Fr. Guarda felt a rising panic. He felt as if he were being stalked by an apparition: the spirit of the confessor. But that would mean that the man was dead!

"The calcification of life is the only true Evil," Fr. Guarda went doggedly on. "It did not exist before Satan was cast out of Paradise. It is Satan's only creation. From the calcification of life were formed the so-called seven deadly sins. But Satan did not create these 'lesser' sins; his work was already done. God created the seven deadly sins in order to keep Satan in his place—and to make certain that Satan would never understand the power invested in him through his creation of Chaos.

"There is no danger of this occurring because Satan is Evil. Therefore, he is ossified, unchanging. While God never sits still. God is akin to moonlight as it plays upon the ocean. It dances, sings, caresses, howls, illuminates, grows and shrinks without letup. God is one thing and ten thousand. God is ten thousand and ten million. God is everything—everything except Evil. God allowed Satan his pride because He saw the need for choice.

"When, in Eden, the serpent beckons to Adam and Eve, it is with the lure of knowledge, the siren song of choice: to know what God knows. And this is what they are tempted to learn. But their choice is really one of pride: to put themselves first before God. The serpent's power is in being able to conceal the sin of pride in the guise of freedom.

"Which brings us to Satan—"

And then Fr. Guarda saw him. Scanning the congregation, he had found among the faces he knew one which was not familiar. It was a long, lean face, dark-complexioned; the face of a predator.

"Is Satan to be feared? Is he to be hated? Let us see."

The stranger was watching him with an odd kind of intensity. "Satan is clever, but he is not intelligent. If he were intelligent, he would divine the nature of the incipient power God has given him. He does not.

"God knows this, of course. Otherwise, would he have entrusted the discovery of Evil to Satan? Satan's cleverness lies in his ability to devote his entire attention to detail. Satan has, in effect, a kind of tunnel vision; his focus is exceptionally narrow. This narrow focus is an essential prerequisite for the devising of torture. And torture is, after all, what defines Satan.

"Satan, as God well knows, is the master deceiver. And his first lie—his most compelling lie—is freedom. Freedom from the tyranny of God, the tyranny of Paradise, of the Church, and finally, of faith.

"For, you see, faith is the ultimate parameter. Faith defines the world: its boundaries, its limits, its horizons. Faith puts everything in perspective. Faith shows man his pale in the universe; it differentiates him from the mountains, the trees, the sky, the earth, from man's own creations. Faith is the exalter, and the humbler of man.

"Satan says, 'Hear me, and embrace freedom. Freedom is yours for the taking.' What he deliberately does *not* say is that in embracing freedom, one must give up faith. That is his lie. Satan's freedom is limitless. Therefore it is ossification. It is the antithesis of motion. It excludes change, and it is in changing that we find purpose.

"We must understand that what Satan calls freedom is nothing less than the death of God. It is the unleashing of Chaos."

With the sermon at an end, Fr. Guarda turned to come down from the pulpit. But, now, with the dark-complexioned man staring at him, he found himself almost reluctant to so do.

"We believe in God. . . ." He led the congregation in song while Fr. Donnelly prepared the collection plate. It was passed around, and Fr. Guarda paid special attention as it came to the dark-complexioned man. His eyes opened wide when he saw the man slip a thousand-dollar bill beneath the ones, fives, and tens.

Fr. Guarda poured wine and water into the silver goblet in preparation of the Eucharist. He brought out the wafers and, as he did so, he saw a number of the parishioners getting up to form a line. The dark-complexioned man joined the line.

One by one Fr. Guarda put the Host into the upturned palms of his parishioners while he blessed them.

"Body of Christ."

"Amen."

Then it was the dark-complexioned man's turn. He stood in front of Fr. Guarda and, instead of holding out his hand, he opened his mouth wide. Was there something odd about his face?

Fr. Guarda was obliged to lean over in order to place the Host on the man's tongue. As he did so, he smelled a sickly-sweet scent he could not quite identify. It was coming from the man's open mouth.

"Body of Christ."

Fr. Guarda looked, and was caught by the quality in the man's eyes. A quick surge of memory: a steaming August when he had traded the open fire hydrants of Tenth Avenue for two weeks in a Fresh Air Fund camp. The young Dominic Guarda had come upon a rattlesnake along an Edenic forest trail. The reptile had stared at him, without curiosity but with a kind of myopic hunger that only later, when the boy had grown into a man, was he able to identify as wholly Evil: inimical, monolithic, elemental. Now Fr. Guarda had come across that stare again.

"Amen."

The man had turned away and, with a deep shudder, Fr. Guarda wondered whether he had imagined the whole thing.

It was Fr. Guarda's habit to relax in the sacristy for a time, after he and his assistants had put away their vestments and the sacred paraphernalia of the Mass. The sacristy of the Church of the Holy Trinity was particularly beautiful and spacious. It was filled with many significant religious relics which Fr. Guarda delighted in getting to know in a slow and loving fashion. Besides, Mass was more sacred to him than, perhaps, to many of his vocation, and he needed time alone to decompress from the depth of feeling it engendered in him.

It was always dim in the sacristy. Only one small window was built into the room's outer stone wall, and it was masked from the street by a thick privet hedge perhaps fifteen feet in height. A polished oak bench similar to the pews in the main body of the church was set opposite the window. It was here that Fr. Guarda always sat after performing Mass. The bench was uncomfortable—deliberately so. Rest and comfort were not synonymous in the Church's vocabulary, so that while it was permissible to rest, that is, to cleanse one's mind as well as one's spirit, it was not permissible to be comfortable while going about it.

Fr. Guarda was sitting on the bench, staring out at the green arbor of the privet. There was a wren flitting through the hedge searching for something.

As he watched the bird, Fr. Guarda saw again the triangular head of the rattlesnake. He could see its scales shining oily in the filtered sunlight, the obscene questing of its forked tongue, the black, depthless eyes. Over this unpleasant image was superimposed the open mouth of the dark-complexioned man, his anticipatory tongue, his black, depthless eyes.

Fr. Guarda gave a little start, sitting forward on the bench. The wren was busy pulling something—an insect, perhaps—from within the shadows of the privet. Fr. Guarda watching with a kind of helpless fascination as the predator ate its prey.

When did he become aware that there was someone else in the room? He could not say, so deeply had he been enwrapped in his thoughts.

"Father Donnelly?" His assistant often returned to the sacristy for some item lost within the folds of his vestments.

"Yes, Father."

It was not Fr. Donnelly's voice; Fr. Guarda turned his head. "Who is it?" he asked into the shadowed far corner of the sacristy. "Who is there?"

"Father Donnelly was unexpectedly called away." The voice came from directly behind him, and Fr. Guarda tried to turn around. But something gripped him, firmly, inexorably, restraining him.

"Who are you?" Fr. Guarda said. "What do you want? Money? I have little. Gold? Where could you sell these relics?"

"I am here to call you home," the voice said, so close that Fr. Guarda could smell the same sickly-sweet scent he had caught when he was administering the Eucharist to the dark-complexioned man. He felt the grip on him strengthen. That did not frighten him; in his youth Fr. Guarda had been called upon to take down many a bully. He had been so good at it, in fact, that he had briefly considered a career in the boxing ring before his father had beaten that thought out of his head. Instead, the young Dominic Guarda had enlisted in the army, and had spent a tour of duty in Southeast Asia before, sick at heart and soul, he had sought out God.

Even now, Fr. Guarda continued to have a healthy respect for his body, treating it to highly disciplined daily workouts. Beneath the ecclesiastical robes was a powerful, well-muscled body.

"I *am* home," he said. He willed his body to relax. This man was no different from any of the Tenth Avenue bullies Fr. Guarda had encountered.

"Not just yet," the voice said in his ear.

It was then, as he felt the pressure building on the nerve junction at the side of his neck, that Fr. Guarda understood the extent of the danger to him.

He lifted his shoulders and arms and, as the man behind him shifted to keep his hold, Fr. Guarda jerked his torso downward, and he was free.

He whirled, striking out in a blind blow at the man's face. Felt the impact as he struck the cheekbone, ripped away in a wrenching motion. Heard a tearing sound and, staring down at his hand, he stood stunned, rooted to the spot. A ragged patch of flesh-colored latex was draped across his fingertips; it was greasy with makeup.

Fr. Guarda looked up at the dark-complexioned man. Now he understood what was odd about the face he had seen so closely during the Eucharist: it had no pores. Now there was a rent in the facade; real skin was revealed along the man's right cheek. The man was wearing a lifelike mask.

"Who are you?" Fr. Guarda said again. "Do I know you?"

"It doesn't matter," the man said. What was familiar about that voice? Fr. Guarda asked himself. "I know *you*."

The sound of the steel fan opening possessed a terrible clarity in the tiny sacristy. It had a purity of purpose that reached down into Fr. Guarda's very soul, making him shiver.

Now Fr. Guarda knew with a kind of peculiar finality that he was not merely facing a bully or a street punk. He raised his right hand, made the sign of the Cross. "Bless you. God forgives you." He had to say it twice, his mouth was so dry.

The man with two faces took a step toward him, and Fr. Guarda moved back. The man came on; Fr. Guarda retreated until his back was against the lead sash of the window.

The man with two faces was moving the fan in the air with such speed and dexterity that it made a whirring sound not unlike the whine of a beast.

Fr. Guarda had turned his attention from the weapon. He was, rather, looking into the eyes of the man with two faces. "I *do* know you," he said. "Yes. From long ago."

"And far away," the man with two faces said, almost dreamily. "Yes."

Then the steel fan was flying through the air like a giant bat. Its crenellated edge embedded itself in Fr. Guarda's neck with such force that it slammed his head and upper torso into the window behind him.

Glass shattered, blood spurted, and the man with two faces

stepped away. When he went to retrieve the steel fan, he saw that Fr. Guarda's head lay within the bower made by the privet.

He bent to take the piece of latex out of Fr. Guarda's hand, but the priest's grip was so strong, he was obliged to break two of his fingers to get it. Even then, he had to rip it free.

He stood and, using the thick edge of the closed fan to break out the protruding shards of glass, the man with two faces deftly clambered out the window.

Beneath the privet he squatted and, taking up Fr. Guarda's severed head, bestowed a final kiss upon the blued lips. In a moment he had vanished, and the wren, returning after the explosion of breaking glass, gently brushed its wing against Fr. Guarda's cheek as it alit.

PART I

GOLDEN CITIES IN THE DESERT

SPRING, PRESENT

NEW YORK CITY/PARIS/ NICE/NEW CANAAN/VENCE

Christopher Haye had always wanted to be a writer. But that thought was far from his mind on this leaden, rain-soaked April afternoon. He was center stage, as it were, in a steamy, packed courtroom in the Criminal Courts building on Centre Street, amid the antique jumble of downtown Manhattan.

Standing next to the sallow-faced bear of a man who was his client, waiting for the jury to hand down their verdict, Chris Haye tried to blot out how much he hated being a lawyer. This was particularly difficult for him to come to grips with, since it had taken an awful lot of money and hard work to get him through Princeton and then Harvard Law School. Hard work was nothing new to Chris Haye; it was a commodity he was rich in. Just as his family was rich in the more conventional sense. His father owned a manufacturing conglomerate whose subsidiaries literally spanned the globe. In fact, Chris's father was currently in Beijing with his third wife, negotiating a reciprocal manufacturing agreement for one of his Far Eastern companies.

Chris's hard work at school had not been in vain. His talent had come to the attention of a prestigious Park Avenue law firm still small enough to be hungry for new minds.

Max Steiner, the firm's senior partner who had recruited Chris, was a small, distinguished man in his midsixties. His gray hair was thinning in the precise spot where a monk had his tonsure. He had a large nose that somehow made him look interesting rather than ugly, and wide-apart wary brown eyes that missed nothing. They were wary, he had told Chris, because he was a Jew, and the world hated Jews.

"You understand," he had said on Chris's first day at the law office, "that brilliant though I believe you to be, Mr. Haye, you must first prove your worth to this firm. As a consequence, your early cases may seem, at first blush, quite straightforward."

"What you really mean is that the cases you give all novices are the boring ones," Chris had said. "Perhaps even the inconsequential ones."

Steiner smiled. "My grandfather used to say, 'It doesn't matter whether you spit on a beggar or on a millionaire, it only matters whether you're caught.' " His manner of speaking, slow, accented, often rambling, was disarming.

Chris was undaunted. "What if I tell you that I don't spit," he said.

"We're all human," Steiner had said. "We're all the same."

"Only some of us don't get caught."

Steiner had leaned back in his chair, put his hands behind his head. Though he dressed well, his clothes always looked rumpled, and this, to a large degree, lent him a friendly and forgiving aspect. The first time Chris saw Max in action in the courtroom, he was stunned to see how Max went for the jugular with the speed and precision of a surgeon. "You seem to have something specific on your mind, Mr. Haye. Why don't you tell me what it is?"

"Fair enough," Chris had said. "I didn't come here to handle the leftovers. I came here to build a reputation. I assume that Steiner, McDowell and Fine is no different from any other busy law firm in that there are lucrative cases which it turns away each day. Many of these are dismissed simply because they appear so hopeless that no one in the firm is willing to take them on. Frankly, sir, I think that's wrong."

Chris had pleaded his case for the right of every human being to the best possible defense as eloquently as he had pleaded his hypothetical cases in law school.

"I hope you know what you're doing, Mr. Haye," Steiner had said.

"I think I do, sir. I've given this a lot of thought."

"I must tell you in all candor that there are people here who do not share your egalitarian interpretation of the law."

Chris knew that Steiner was talking about the other senior partners. "There can be no justice without equality, sir," he had said.

Steiner grunted. "We'll see."

For five years Chris had toiled in the trenches of New York's subterranean labyrinth known as "Hell's Circuit." He began with a small but not insignificant case that the firm otherwise never would have taken on. To many people's surprise and subsequent envy, he won it. Soon he was handling successively bigger and more complex cases.

Chris applied himself, determined to work harder still. In a matter of several years he had become so successful that the news media began to follow his cases. Steiner had come into Chris's office on the eve of Chris's first anniversary with the firm, and had said, "You have the gift, Chris. You've got what I call the velvet hammer: the jury believes you. They see you, not the client. They listen to whatever you say."

Chris continued to win case after celebrated case. Soon he was constantly in demand; his time was never his own. That was when he had decided to go out on his own.

Now he had his own prestigious Park Avenue law office, with his own handpicked associates, clerks, and because Max Steiner had insisted, a consulting business with his old law firm, who had let him go with extreme reluctance.

That was eighteen months ago. Then Marcus Gable had walked into Chris's office and everything had been turned upside down.

Marcus Gable was the man standing beside Chris Haye now, waiting for the jury's verdict. A charge of murder in the second degree had been brought against Gable for the death of his wife, Linda. She had been handling a pistol of his for which he had a permit. She did not know how to use the weapon, Gable had said—hated all firearms, in fact. She wanted it, he had said, out of the bedroom, and was removing it from his night table when it had gone off at point-blank range, killing her instantly.

The prosecution had contended that Linda Gable, having discovered that her husband was having an adulterous affair, confronted him. They had quarreled, the prosecution maintained; the quarrel had escalated into a fight, during which Gable had taken out the gun and had shot his wife.

Through a parade of witnesses, Alix Layne, the assistant DA, had shown that Marcus Gable had a ferocious temper, and that, further, it could be easily set off. The prosecution also established that Gable spent a great deal of time during the week at a small apartment he maintained in Manhattan quite apart from the lavish Fifth Avenue triplex where he and his wife had their residence. Through innuendo, the prosecution tried to establish the existence of Gable's alleged mistress.

On the other side of the slate Chris had established with his own phalanx of witnesses that the nature of Gable's high-stakes commodities business made for long and irregular work patterns. Moreover, the overseas nature of the business—especially that sector focusing on the Pacific rim—caused business to be routinely conducted in the small hours of the morning. During the end stages of long and complex negotiations, it was Marcus Gable's habit to conduct his business from his apartment, because his residence and his wife were sacrosanct from the business side of his life.

In the privacy of his mahogany-paneled office Chris had repeatedly asked Gable about the rumors of his affair. He pointed out that if the prosecution could prove the existence of a mistress, or even place in the minds of the jury the possibility that Gable was fooling around, Gable was in trouble.

"I thought I was innocent until proven guilty," Gable had said. "The jury has to find me guilty beyond a shadow of a doubt." He had shrugged his meaty shoulders. "What's to worry?"

"Let me remind you," Chris had said, "of the heinous nature of the crime the prosecution has accused you of. Murder in the second degree is a class A-one felony. The definition of murder in the second degree reads, 'With intent to cause the death of a person, he causes the death of such person.' "

"Intent?" Marcus Gable had shouted. "What intent?"

"The prosecution contends that the act of your reaching for your loaded gun constitutes intent."

"That's premeditation!"

"No," Chris had said. "Subdivision One-twenty-five-point-twenty-five states that intentional killing no longer needs to be a component of premeditation or deliberation. It can, in fact, be the result of an instantaneous decision."

Gable had waved away the legalese. "That bullshit doesn't matter. That's not the way it happened."

Chris had gone doggedly on. "The prosecution will show the jury photos of your wife as she was found by the police. They will drag into court anyone—and I mean *anyone*—who has ever seen you out with a woman, innocent or otherwise."

"Now *I'll* remind *you* that I was the one who called the police," Gable said. "I was there when they arrived. I showed them everything. I let them poke around wherever they wanted."

Chris had gotten to know Marcus Gable well enough to realize that there was no point in telling him that the police had a right to search anywhere they wanted in the crime scene without Gable's permission. But bringing that up, he knew, would only precipitate an argument. Instead, Chris lifted a placating hand. "Admittedly, not the actions of a guilty party," he said. "We're in agreement on that point. However, I am trying to get you to understand that this is not going to be a clean sparring match.

"Fairness and justice, let us hope and pray, will reside, at least, in the minds and hearts of the jury. But until the moment they leave the courtroom to begin their deliberations, anything goes. The prosecution will not back away from dragging you and everyone around you into the pit. I know the prosecutor, Alix Layne, well. The DA must want this case badly; Alix Layne is his best assistant. She's clever and dedicated. She's also headline hungry, and she can smell blood from a city mile off—even when it's not of her own manufacture."

"Hey, listen, I'm a veteran of the Vietnam War," Gable said. "I've got a fistful of decorations, and let me tell you that I put my ass on the line for each one of them; they're all field medals. A lot of guys who came back from that shithole owe their lives to me.

"I expect you to make hay out of that, counselor. I want to see banner headlines, WAR HERO ON TRIAL! That'll shake the prosecution some. And it ain't a lie. Hell, I still have nightmares. One's a doozy. I'm in this steel-lined elevator, see, and I'm going down and down and down. Suddenly the doors open, and I'm awash up to my knees in blood and guts, arms and heads bobbing, dead eyes of my buddies staring up at me, their stiffened fingers beckoning." Gable blew hard through pursed lips, as if to get rid of excess energy. "I always wake up from it with the sound of a little girl crying in my head." He gave Chris a look. "Weird, huh?"

Marcus Gable nodded. "Okay, so it won't be all sweetness and light." He shrugged. "So what is in life? I've been to hell, and come out the other side. So Alix Layne'll give it to us; we'll give it right back to her, in spades. I just want to know when I can get back to my business. This fucking thing is costing me a mint every day I gotta park my ass in that courtroom."

Chris looked at him, a thick-shouldered bantam of a man, with a hard-eyed, combative face, a wide slash of a mouth, handsome if you were generous enough with the term to allow it to encompass the emanation of power. Which, of course, women did all the time.

Especially with this one, Chris guessed. He had the maturity only age could bring, while somehow maintaining the physical attributes of youth. Who knows, Chris thought, perhaps Gable had had a face-lift. He looked more closely at the edges of Gable's face and, sure enough, he found the tiny, telltale scars.

"By 'this fucking thing,' " Chris said, "I assume you are speaking of your wife's death."

"Death has nothing to do with it." Gable had a way of dismissing as contemptible everyone's opinion but his own. "It's this travesty of a trial I'm being forced to sit through."

Chris wondered whether the word "remorse" was one that Marcus Gable would even recognize. Chris suspected that he would, but he was also sure that Gable found remorse contemptible.

"The truth," Chris persisted, "is what I am after, Mr. Gable. If you lie to me about anything, I cannot help you to the best of my ability. And if the prosecution should learn a truth about you that you have failed to tell me, you will most certainly be looking at the inside of a federal penitentiary for the next fifteen years at the minimum, before a parole board will give you a hearing."

"Why are you talking to me about prison?" Gable had said, getting up from the chair he had been sitting in; he had a great deal of kinetic energy. "You're here to make certain I don't go to prison." He was examining a Degas print on the wall. "You know, I bought the original two years ago. I never liked it much, but then I didn't buy it because I liked it. Linda thought it looked good over the sofa in the living room, I think, I don't really remember. Anyway, who cares? I sold it at auction last month, and quadrupled my money. The Japs were sucking up everything in sight." He turned back to Chris. "It was just amazing. Like a bunch of fucking piranha, falling all over themselves to get rid of their overvalued yen while it's still worth something."

"And the truth is?"

Gable blinked his long-lashed eyes. "The truth? The truth is that to me art is like anything else: it's commerce. How much can I get it for, how much will my profit be when I sell it. Color, form, perspective, vision, they don't mean shit to me. Frankly, I doubt whether they mean shit to anybody."

Chris stared out the window at the blue auto haze that wreathed Central Park while he counted slowly to ten. "About this mistress of yours," he said finally.

"That's a lie!" Gable smashed his fist onto Chris's desk. His face had turned into a mask, so hard that Chris had the impression that if he hit it with a hammer, it would shatter into pieces. "I loved my wife. Anyone who says different is a liar, okay?"

Chris had nodded. "Okay. But I've got to warn you that we're going to be in the gutter for the next week or so."

"I'm paying you to do a job," Gable had said, standing by the door. "Just do it. Don't ask for my goddamned permission."

It was then that Chris realized just how much he hated what he was doing. He had always believed in the rights of the individual, as well as in the American legal system. Everyone was entitled to his day in court, a fair trial, impartial judgment by his peers. Upholding this was one of the reasons Chris Haye had gone into law in the first place.

But now, after all his lofty, idealistic debates in graduate school, after his arguments with Max Steiner to take on seemingly unwinnable cases, had come the years in Hell's Circuit, watching the dregs of humanity slither through the noble halls of justice. Chris had soon found that these people often sneered at the law; they hired smart lawyers like Chris Haye to find the ways to get them off. And Chris, believing that everyone's rights needed protecting, had complied. He had simply turned his gaze away from them, as one does from a pretty woman with a wart on her chin. He much preferred to bury himself in his work. Personalities, he had told himself, were for psychiatrists to unravel; they weren't for him to judge.

Now he recognized that in ignoring the kinds of clients he was taking on, he had blinded himself to the kind of lawyer he had become. Without his knowing when it had begun, his absolute belief in the rightness of what he was doing had eroded. Taking on Marcus Gable was merely the last straw. Gable was the instrument through which Chris's doubts and fears coalesced.

Chris remembered Max Steiner's words: *I hope you know what you're doing*. And his own terribly naive answer, *I do, sir*. The sad fact was that Chris had not known anything about what he was getting into. Surely Max had known. Why then had he not stopped Chris at the starting point?

Chris wondered how he was going to reconcile these new—and dangerous—feelings with his innate idealism. He not only abandoned the search for an answer, he also pushed the question out of his mind.

He had swallowed the anger he felt toward Marcus Gable, the disappointment he felt in himself, and had gotten on with the work at hand. He proceeded to counter each of the prosecutor's allegations. He brought in Linda Gable's friends, her former psychiatrist, the doctors at the institution where she had been consigned on more than one occasion for alcohol and Valium addiction. Alix Layne, the assistant DA, seeing Chris's intent, had vociferously objected that the line of testimony was immaterial and potentially misleading; she was overruled.

These witnesses recounted Linda Gable's myriad bouts with depression, repressed anger, and lurid fixation. For example, one of the institution's doctors testified that for six months Linda Gable believed herself to be possessed by a demon.

The result of this rather sordid descent into Linda Gable's very private hell was to reveal another side of Marcus Gable. Formerly, the jury had seen him as a hard-nosed man preoccupied with his business. Now Chris gave them the full war record, evidence showing Marcus Gable to be every inch a patriot, a hero, and a very human husband: patient, kind, forgiving. Chris had taken out his special velvet hammer and had nailed home the case. CHRIS HAYE'S WAR HERO CASE, as the New York tabloids had dubbed it. Not the Marcus Gable case.

The only oddity was that Alix Layne had promised to produce Marcus Gable's alleged mistress, whose testimony, she assured Chris, would damn him. In the end no mistress had been forthcoming and, in Chris's opinion, it was the prosecution's case that was doomed.

"Members of the jury," the judge said now, "have you reached a verdict?"

"We have, your honor," the foreman said, handing a folded slip of paper to the bailiff who seemed to take forever to get to the judge's bench.

The judge took the paper, opened it, and read it. He lifted his head, nodded to the foreman.

"As to the charge of murder in the second degree in the death of Linda Gable," the foreman said, "we, the jury, find Marcus Gable not guilty."

The courtroom erupted in a release of long-pent-up emotion. Through it all Marcus Gable stood silently, stoically. Until, at length, Chris said, "Mr. Gable, are you all right?"

"Yeah," Gable said. He hadn't even blinked. "Let's go split a steak."

As they left the courtroom, Chris shoved a typewritten sheet into Gable's hands, the prepared statement that Chris had written, which Gable read to the reporters who clustered around them in the dim, marbled hallway, echoing with the will of justice.

"That's all, folks," Chris said after Gable had finished. The press was already throwing out questions. "You've heard the full extent of what my client has to say. No further comment."

He propelled Gable through the clamoring throng. At the top of the wide, stone steps, Alix Layne stopped him.

"I'd like a word with you," the assistant DA said.

Chris turned to his client. "I'll be right with you."

Alix Layne watched Gable with cool gray eyes as he went down toward his stretch limo. "I'm amazed to see him walk," she said. "A snake like that should have slithered down those steps." She turned to Chris. "I wish I could say that I admired what you did in there."

"It was my job."

Alix snorted. It brought high color to her cheeks. She had a Pre-Raphaelite face, devoid of angles, that belied the sharpness of her personality. Her reddish-brown hair curled below the nape of her neck. A silver choker was at her throat. "It was your job to see to it that a murderer went free?"

"Watch your mouth, counselor," Chris said. "My client was just exonerated of all wrongdoing."

"He's still a murderer," Alix Layne said. "Maybe the three of us—me, you, and Gable—are the only people who know it. But that doesn't change the fact. And if I'd gotten all the evidence I was promised, the whole world would know it."

"Take some sound professional advice. Shut up," Chris said. He was surprised at how angry he felt, betrayed almost. Could it have anything to do with the fact that he found the assistant DA attractive? How many times since he had met her had he considered asking her out? During their brief conversations in the court hallways between trials he had liked everything about her but her old-fashioned sense of herself. She seemed stiff, as if uncomfortable with her own sexuality. That she disapproved of his way of approaching the law was obvious; that she found him attractive despite her qualms was just as clear. "Accept the fact that you lost. You had a weak case, and the media is going to have a field day picking it—and you—apart. Because I'll tell you quite frankly that if you go on this way, I'll have to press slander and defamation-of-character charges on behalf of my client."

"That would be a laugh, now, wouldn't it?" Alix Layne's eyes were fiery. "God, but I've had it up to here with smug bastards like you who charge a fortune to get slimes like Gable off under the guise of this pious attitude you feed to the press. Everyone deserves the best defense. Oh, yes. You forget to mention when giving interviews that it takes two hundred and fifty dollars an hour to get that defense. It's so spurious, it makes me sick. Tell me, when was the last time you took on a *pro bono* case just because you *believed* in your client? You're not a lawyer, Mr. Haye, you're a showman. You belong under a tent, along with the jugglers, the fire-eaters, and the bottlers of snake oil.'' She gestured behind her at the stone facade of the Criminal Courts building. ''Haven't you figured out yet that you have no place here in the halls of justice?''

Before Chris could reply, she was gone, swallowed up in the throng that was swirling out of the front entrance. He felt depressed rather than angry. It was as if she had peeked inside his head, and pulled out the dirt.

''Shit,'' Chris said to himself as he hurried down the steps, and out into the gray day. It was raining much harder now and, shivering, he made a dash for Gable's waiting limo. He climbed into the car, settled in next to Gable.

''What's with the limp, counselor? I didn't notice it before.''

Chris gave a quick grimace. ''It's the rain.'' He disliked being reminded of the pain in his leg. ''It's nothing. An old hip injury.'' Inside the car it was as dark as a hearse.

''Sports or the war?'' Gable asked. He had already poured himself a glass of champagne from a split that had been ready and cooling in the limo's mini-refrigerator.

''Both,'' Chris said. But he was still thinking about what Alix Layne had said.

''Yeah?'' For the first time since he had walked into Chris's office, Marcus Gable looked at Chris with some interest. ''Hold on,'' he said, and turned to the driver. ''The Grill, Eddie,'' he said. ''And step on it. I'm starving.''

''Yes, sir, Mr. Gable.''

The limo slid easily through the backwater warrens of downtown Manhattan, ancient streets propelled into the atomic age by dreams of making fortunes from palladium, cocoa, and frozen pork bellies.

''Okay,'' Gable said, ''so tell me what happened to your hip.''

Chris looked at him. ''Mr. Gable,'' he said, ''you've just been found innocent of killing your wife. Don't you have any reaction to that?''

Gable squinted. ''What is it you want, a pat on the back from me? Why? All you did was your job. It was what I paid you to do.'' He shrugged. ''Okay. I liked the little speech you concocted for me. Very classy. And it'll make good copy in tomorrow's papers.''

''Are you human?'' Chris said. ''Don't you have any emotions at all?''

''Listen, counselor, whatever emotions I've got, you can be damn sure that neither you nor anyone out there''—he gestured to the world beyond the tinted windows—''is ever going to see them.''

But after three oversized Scotch-and-waters at the Grill, it was a different story.

"What are you," Gable said, "thirty-nine, forty? Sure. I just turned fifty. What does it mean to me? It means that I'm another year further away from the war." They were seated at the best power table in a fashionable Second Avenue steak house. The scuffed white floor was strewn with sawdust. The walls were covered with black-and-white photos of entertainment stars, autographed with self-glorifying personal messages to Don, the Grill's owner.

"The war," Gable was saying. "Sure, I was changed by the war. How could you be over there in that stinking hellhole without being changed? The only way not to be changed by the war was to die. Anyone tells you different is full of shit."

The maître d' approached then; seeing the two men deep in discussion, he discreetly left them alone.

"I'll tell you," Gable went on, "I saw plenty of guys who refused to change. Jesus and Mary, they were goners. You could see it in their eyes. They knew they were in hell, but they wanted no part of it. I'll tell you, the only creatures who survive hell are demons. And y'know what? It was all a matter of power. Those who understood the essential anarchy of the war, made sense of it and survived. Everyone else was, in one way or another, destroyed. Humans withered and died there in those napalm-filled jungles, those booby-trapped rice paddies."

Gable rolled some Scotch around in his mouth before swallowing. "You know, 'cause you were there, that the rice crop depends on the rainy season. Well, one year I was in 'Nam, the rainy season came early. It was red. Blood red, d'you understand? A hundred grunts blown to smithereens, their blood fertilizing the fucking rice." Gable downed the last of his drink.

"One Charlie I captured told me, laughing, that it was going to be a bumper rice crop that year. You can bet the sonuvabitch wasn't laughing when I cut off his dick, and fed it to him." He picked up the menu. "Wanna order? I gotta put something in my stomach."

Chris did not know whether to laugh or to cry. He wondered what to make of this man. From what he had been able to see, Marcus Gable was a fascinating conundrum, a kind of Chinese puzzle in a hideous yet magnetic exterior. Every time you thought you had gotten to know him, another aspect of his personality would pop up like a goblin in an amusement park's house of horrors.

Gable ordered the double sirloin, home-fried potatoes, and fried onion rings. Chris chose the grilled tuna.

"Fish," Gable said when the waiter had left. "It all stinks. I smell fish, and all I smell is blood." He shrugged. "The war again, I guess. After 'Nam, I could never bear the sight of fish. Couple of years ago a buddy of mine invited me out on his boat. He runs it out of East Bay Bridge, one of those places on Long Island. A great, beautiful gray and green sixty-five-footer named *Monique*, after his French mistress.

"Anyway, we went fishing for tuna. I'll say this, he's a helluva sport fisherman. He hooked a quarter-ton monster within twenty minutes. 'Hey, Marcus,' he said a coupla hours later when he was landing the monster, 'come take a look at this baby.' I didn't want to, but Monique was there, so what else could I do? So I took a look, and vomited." Gable began to laugh. "Can you believe it? All over his fucking fish. Jesus."

At that moment, as if on some kind of sadistic cue, the food arrived. Gable was not a man to talk while he ate, so there was silence for some time. He ate quickly, as if there were a board meeting he had to get to. When he pushed his plate away from him, Chris was only half through with his tuna. That did not stop Gable from talking again, or from ordering a double espresso with sambuca.

"So," he said, somewhat more expansively, "tell me what happened to your hip. You get hit in 'Nam?"

"No," Chris said. He had not, in fact, been in Vietnam, as Gable had assumed. He was as ashamed of that all over again as he would have been if he were talking with his brother, Terry. "In Paris."

"France?" Gable stirred the liquor into his coffee. "Hey, come on. Don't tell me you were fighting a war in France."

"In a way," Chris said. "I was in the Tour de France, the bicycle race."

Gable laughed. "You call a fucking bike race a war? Oh, Jesus, that's good!"

"I was part of a nine-man team," Chris said, "that biked nineteen hundred miles in twenty-two days. We started in a town called Roubaix, went into Belgium and Holland, through the French Alps, and ended up in Paris." He was through with his fish. "Believe me, it was a war, all right."

"Not like 'Nam." Gable said it in an odd tone of voice. It seemed to Chris almost as if he were speaking about a woman, or a precious object he considered to be his personal property.

"No," Chris said. "It was very different."

"Like pulling a fucking tuna out of the sea," Gable said. "Hard work, yeah. Like you said, maybe even a war. Well, okay, I threw up all over the fucking fish, like I said. But, hell, it turned out to be worth it, 'cause Monique took me below, licked the sweat off my face, stuck her tongue into my mouth while she opened her bathing suit. The goddamned thing snapped under the crotch. She fucked my brains out while my buddy was wrestling with that big sonuvabitch tuna right over our heads."

Chris could hardly believe what he was hearing. This was the point of Gable's little fish fable? A lesson on how to cheat on your wife while cuckolding your friend? "What about your wife?" he asked.

"What about her?"

"Wasn't she there?"

"It happens she wasn't," Gable said. "But what if she was? She wouldn't have known any more about it than my buddy did."

"You told me that you loved your wife, Mr. Gable."

"Yeah, so what? I told you a lot of things, counselor, and judging by your tone of voice, I'm damned glad I did. You've just confirmed my faith in my own judgment of how to play you. You're a fucking Elliot Ness, you know that?"

Chris was sitting very still. "Are you saying that you lied to me?"

"I'm not saying anything one way or the other," Gable said. "You're the genius here. You read between the lines."

"There *is* a mistress."

"Counselor, I do believe your face has gone white."

"You fought with your wife. It all happened just as Alix Layne contended." He watched with a cold kind of dread creeping through him as the wolfish grin expanded on Gable's lips. "You took out the gun and—"

"Pardon me, Mr. Haye." The waiter had reappeared. "There is a call for you."

"Just a minute," Chris said. He could not tear his gaze from Marcus Gable's terrible face.

"They said it was urgent," the waiter said.

"I said I'd be there in a minute," Chris said harshly.

When the waiter had gone, he went on, "You took out the gun and you killed her, didn't you? You murdered your wife."

"Do you really think I'd tell you that?"

Chris, thinking, What have I done?, leaned across the plate-strewn table. "I just saved your skin, Gable. I think I deserve the truth."

Gable finished off his espresso, wiped his mouth. "Now I'm gonna tell you the way of the world, counselor. You don't deserve shit, and here's why. You're charging me two hundred and fifty bucks an hour and, all things considered, I'd have to say you're worth every penny of it. You send me your bill, and my check will be messengered to you the same day. That's how I do business." He stood up. "And business is all this was."

"Are you crazy," Chris said, "or am I?" And all the time Alix Layne's accusing face hung before him. "I believed you. I wouldn't have taken the case otherwise."

"Oh, come off it, counselor," Gable said. He was grinning as he swept his arm outward. "There's nobody here but us chickens. You can save all that constitutional garbage for the media; you've worked it out, you've learned that's what they eat up. It's why they love you. It's sure as hell why I wanted you to defend me."

"I told you, Gable, that I wanted the truth from you."

"Sure. Sure. I understand. From the beginning I told you all you needed to know. That isn't gonna change now." He threw a couple of hundred-dollar bills onto the table. "Counselor, you're the master when you step inside a courtroom but, otherwise, you don't seem to know shit about anything. You have to learn that in life all questions don't get answered."

Five minutes later Chris took the call, and was told that his brother had died in Tourrette-sur-Loup, France.

Lieutenant Seve Guarda watched the ceiling drool. It was pouring outside, and it was clear that this tenement he was in was in desperate need of repair ten years ago. Now it was no doubt being held up by the grimy buildings on either side of it.

Drip, drip, drip. The drool became a full-fledged leak. Lifting his head, Seve could hear the rats behind the walls, squealing as they scrambled to get out of the way of the encroaching damp.

Seve was in the darkness of the hallway on the topmost floor of this tenement. One foot still on the last stair riser, he clung to the darkness; it was his most trustworthy ally now. Through a window cemented open by decades of city soot, Seve could hear the swift, musical jabber of Cantonese, its broad sentence-ending interrogatives like a song of the sea. Through the miasma of the tenement's urine stink, he could scent star anise and Szechuan peppercorns, roasting pork and drying skate. Seve had once been in Hong Kong on official business, and the confluence of smells here was identical. Outside, beyond a garbage-strewn alley, was New York's Pell Street not Hong Kong's Ladder Street; but, otherwise, he knew, there wasn't much difference.

Seve, his service revolver at the ready, was listening very carefully. He risked a quick glance at his watch. It had been nearly seven minutes since they had had any communication with Peter Chun: given Chun's personality, a dangerous sign.

Seve went over again in his mind the salient facts relating to the situation. Peter Chun—known as Loong Chun, the Dragon, among the Chinese—was at the head of a widespread drug ring. It was said that Chun owned half of Chinatown, and what businesses he didn't own paid him a monthly tithe to remain in existence. Seve remembered the roaring fire that had engulfed three stores on Pell Street late last year. It was never proven, but the consensus among Seve's people was that Loong Chun had used those businesses as an example to others.

Long before that, however, Seve's operation had been in place. He had a mandate from the mayor himself to break the drug trafficking that threatened to strangle Chinatown and all of New York with it. Seve had been chosen because, in part, he had spent eighteen months with the DEA in Hong Kong, Thailand, and the treacherous mountains of Burma's Shan Plateau, tracing the route of the tears of the poppy, as the Asians called opium. He was still connected with the DEA via their InterNat-Link course on the global implications of drug smuggling.

And so he understood from every angle what it would take to burrow inside Chinatown to exorcise the menace represented by Dragon Chun. He also spoke Cantonese fluently, which helped immeasurably. All the Chinese policemen under his command trusted him implicitly. They would follow him into the sea if he gave the command.

But he had been chosen for another, equally important reason. It was well known that if Seve Guarda believed in one thing, it was the line from Blaise Pascal that he had had reproduced on a piece of polished stone. It sat on his desk where otherwise his name plate would have been. It read: "The property of power is to protect."

Seve did not have to look behind him to sense his backup. Two of his men crouched halfway up the stairs in absolute darkness. For an instant the smell of oil from their drawn guns came to him on a moist gush of wind, before being overwhelmed by the other smells of the environment.

Ten minutes since the Dragon had been heard from.

At least everyone else is out of the building, Seve told himself. It had taken a full six months for Seve's people to discover the brothel that Loong Chun frequented, seven more to worm their way inside. Jesus, Seve thought. How many sleepless nights, how many packages of Maalox, how many busted relationships did that represent? He had lost count a long time ago.

Thirteen months of the most intensive work of his career. All in an effort to apprehend one man: Peter Loong Chun. The trap had been set, and was about to be sprung, when a pair of rookie beat cops, their hearts full of zealous duty, had broken into the brothel to make routine arrests. What had they been doing here? Seve asked himself for the hundredth time. They should have been briefed by the precinct duty commander before beginning their shift. This block was strictly out of bounds.

But, in any event, there they were, walking right in on the Dragon, whose bodyguards had shot them both. And when Richard Hu, one of Seve's surveillance team, had killed the bodyguards in rushing the apartment, Chun had shot him.

Christ, Seve thought, three officers. From triumph to disaster in the blink of an eye.

The only thing Seve knew for certain was that the Dragon was still in there with a female hostage, no doubt the woman he had been with when the rookie blues had burst in on him.

Now the objective had shifted. The apprehension of Peter Loong Chun had become secondary, and Seve was concentrating on shifting the focus of his mind. Because it was his job to extricate alive everyone in the brothel. Whoever had been hurt or killed up there was his responsibility. That included the blues. It was his stakeout—he should have seen the rookies and intercepted them before they could get into the building. Somehow that hadn't happened. Seve would find out why; that was his methodical way. But not until the crisis was over.

Now that the rats had gotten away from the wet, it was quiet in the tenement. Still as a tomb. Outside, the dark sky rumbled.

Seve peered into the gloom. He could see the doorway to the apartment. Keeping his eye on it, he slipped along the hallway. He heard his men reach the landing. When he was within arm's reach of the door, it opened inward a crack, and Seve heard a woman's high-pitched scream. This was followed by a stream of Cantonese invective spat out so rapidly that Seve caught only parts of it. Then absolute silence.

The door remained open a crack. From it, brilliant yellow light poured into the hallway, illuminating rain from the open window running along the floorboards.

"Cheng neih maahn maan-gong?" Seve asked. Could you speak slowly?

Another stream of invective. This time Seve understood every disgusting form his mother was supposed to have taken. Seve ignored this; his concern now was for the young woman.

"Ni-go neuih-jai jouh-mat yeh a?" he asked. What happened to the girl?

An evil peal of laughter from behind the door. *"Keuih sin-dai."* She slipped and fell.

"I don't believe you." Playing it straight.

A rustling from behind the door. Then, abruptly, the door was pulled back and a Chinese girl's face was revealed. She was pushed harshly forward so that Seve could see the muzzle of a gun pressed hard against the bone behind her right ear.

Seve had only a split second in which to see the expression on the girl's white face, but it was all he needed. Her terror filled the hallway between them.

"But I'll bet you'll believe *this*," Peter Loong Chun said.

"No!" Seve shouted at the same moment that Chun pulled the trigger. Blood spurted from the place where the girl's right ear had been. She was screaming as the Dragon pulled her back inside the apartment.

Sonuvabitch, Seve thought, watching the blood slide down the walls to mingle with the rain. I've got to get in there. Creeping slowly down the hallway.

"Come any closer and I'll blow her brains all over your clean, white shirt."

The proximity of Loong's voice brought Seve up short. He stood as still as the shadows around him, a part of them.

Keep your head, Seve cautioned himself. "Who else is in there?"

"What do you care? She's the only one who's still alive."

"Give it up, Loong," Seve said, deliberately using Chun's Chinese name. "It's hopeless here. Any way you look at it, you're going down for the count."

"I've heard about you," the Dragon said. "The *loh faan* who speaks." *Loh faan* meant barbarian, which was how Chinese thought of any Caucasian. "I should blow your brains out as well."

Which was all the opening Seve needed. "I'll give you the chance, then," he said. "Me for the girl. A straight swap, okay? She's an innocent, Loong. A victim. Whereas, me, I'm after your guts. Bad *joss* to kill her now for no reason."

"If I kill her, you can bet it'll be for a reason," Loong said.

"But it's no gamble," Seve said. Gambling and sex were two things that Peter Loong Chun could not pass up; Seve knew he was fanatic about both. "She's already hurt. She can't harm you. I can, and I will, given the chance. Or aren't you man enough to handle the ultimate gamble of life and death."

Silence. Rain beating against the open window, gurgling along the hallway. The rats were quiescent, waiting, watching.

"Maybe you've got a point," Loong said at last, and Seve let out a long exhalation. "First, get your goons off the floor."

Seve turned and gestured for his backup to retreat to the staircase. They went reluctantly. He gave them their instructions. "All right," he told Loong.

"Now put your piece on the floor where I can see it."

"What kind of gamble is that?" Seve asked. "I've seen what your gun can do."

The apartment door squealed open all the way. "We'll put them down together," Loong said.

Seve bent slowly, placed his revolver on the floor of the hallway. At the same time, Chun put his gun down in Seve's view.

"Now the girl," Seve said.

"Get over here first," Chun said. "Do you think I'm just going to let her go like that?"

Seve took a deep breath, walked forward until he was at the open doorway. He squinted in the harsh glare of the lights. He faced Peter Loong Chun, a rail-thin man of medium height with the wide, moon face typical of many Cantonese. He had hold of the Chinese girl, and now he came away from the window where he had been surveilling the immediate environment. Seve tried not to look at the girl because that would show weakness, but his peripheral vision showed him that she was near to fainting. Her right side was stained with blood.

"Come in," Loong said.

"Let the girl go first."

"You heard what I said." Loong brandished a switchblade. The steel gleamed in the glare of the apartment's lights.

"We had a deal."

That evil laugh again. "I don't make deals with *loh faan*," Loong snorted derisively. "You think because you can speak you're anything more than a barbarian?" He spat at Seve's feet, threw the girl aside, took a quick step forward. The edge of the switchblade grazed Seve's throat. "I never intended to let her go."

A kind of wolfish smile suffused Loong's face as fully as the sun lights up a drab winter landscape. Its force transformed him. "I gambled on trapping you, and I won."

"Let me at least see to the girl."

"Not a chance, *loh faan*."

Seve immediately understood; Chun fed on power. He was the kind of man—and Seve had encountered many before—for whom a weapon was a drug. Others might be content with money or women, but Loong existed to impose his will on others.

Another time, another place, the Shan, filled Seve's mind for a moment. General Kiu looming larger than life, as he almost always did in Seve's memory; and the scar, the omnipresent evidence of General Kiu's "hospitality," that ran just beneath Seve's left ear down the side of his neck, began to throb.

Like Peter Loong Chun, General Kiu had been obsessed with power. Loong might be the Dragon of Chinatown, but General Kiu had been the Dragon—the high warlord—of Burma's Shan Plateau, in the heart of the Golden Triangle, where the majority of the world's opium was harvested.

Up against Loong now, Seve perhaps understood that he owed his nemesis a debt of gratitude. For it was General Kiu who had taught Seve the value of Sun Tzu's principles in *The Art of War*.

"War is based on deception," General Kiu had said. "Move when it is advantageous, and create changes in the situation." Through the terrible pain that General Kiu had inflicted upon him—perhaps, who knows?, even because of it—Seve had never forgotten those words. And when, months later, he had finally made his way back home, the first thing he did was take out a translation of Sun Tzu's classic from the Forty-second Street Library. He read it so many times that eventually he could recall entire sections at will.

Seve looked Peter Loong Chun in the eye and thought, *War is based on deception. Move when it is advantageous, and create changes in the situation.*

Seve smiled. "What will you do with me?" His eyes held Chun's, and he forced a fatuous tone into his voice. "I've dealt with you Chinese for years. Will you kill me? I doubt it. I am your only way out of this deathtrap. And I know that you want out, Loong."

The Dragon's face twisted. "You don't know anything, barbarian." He drew blood as he slid the blade along the skin of Seve's throat.

"I know what face is," Seve said, mimicking the kind of braggadocio he had overheard on his tour of Southeast Asia. It was, unfortunately, indicative of the American arrogance abroad: a little knowledge made any stupid *loh faan* an expert. "I know that you've got to walk out of here or risk losing your influence in Chinatown." The Asians despised such overconfidence.

"You're stupid," Loong said, feeling more and more that he was getting the measure of this barbarian, and was, thus, on surer footing. "But that's to my advantage, isn't it?"

Loong had the addict's habit of asking questions to which, clearly, he already had the answers. Seve noted this even as he was aware that he was creating changes in the situation.

"I'll kill you, all right," Loong went on, "and no one will know it. Your goons will let me out of here for fear I'll kill you if they stop me." He laughed. "Only thing is, you'll already be dead."

Seve's mask was fear; this—and only this—was what Loong must see and, so, react to. Meanwhile, Seve had effected the change, and it was this: Loong had been afraid when Seve had first confronted him, before Loong had taken full command. Fear was an adversary of inconstant properties. It could engender caution, strength, even resolve. These were all Seve's enemies. He needed Loong to be confident, assured, and thus incautious and vulnerable. Seve, by appearing foolish, had caused Loong's own obsession with control to dissipate his fear.

Loong was having fun with Seve, more fun, even, than he had had with the Chinese girl. That was good, because since Seve had begun the change, the Dragon had not bothered to return to the window to recheck the environment. He did not see Seve's backup team scaling the tenement's back fire escape. He was not even aware of them until they had entered the room through the window.

Then Loong swung around, his right arm up to throw the knife. Seve grabbed the wrist with his right hand, slammed his left elbow against Loong's, bent the cocked arm quickly backward until he heard the sharp crack of the bone splintering.

Loong cried out and, whirling, smashed the edge of his left hand into Seve's shoulder.

Ignoring the pain, Seve delivered a pair of liver kites that doubled Loong over. He collapsed at Seve's feet.

"You okay, Lieutenant?" one of his men asked.

Seve nodded. "How're the blues?"

"Dead," the other man in the backup team said.

"And Hu?" Hu was Seve's man who had gone in after the rookies.

"Gone."

"Jesus." There were tears in Seve's eyes. Richard Hu had been twenty-two years old. Seve had had dinner at his house just last month. Richard had wanted Seve to meet his wife and five-week-old daughter.

"See to the others," he told the backups. "Get the meds up here on the double. I don't know how badly the girl's hurt. And get the coroner and the forensic people up here right away." They scrambled to do his bidding.

Seve knelt next to the girl. Gently, he lifted her up by her shoulders. It was his first good look at her; she could not be more than sixteen, he thought sadly.

Her eyes open, wide and rolling like an animal's. She began to scream, and he said in Cantonese, "It's all right. I'm a police officer. You're safe now." He repeated it in English.

He could hear the sirens now, as the ambulances approached. They'll need a fleet of ambulances to take care of this mess, he thought.

"Younger sister," Seve said, using the familiar form of Cantonese address, "what's your name?"

"Lei-fa." Plum blossom. She had given him her Chinese, rather than her English name. She had laid her trust in the palm of his hand.

Lei-fa clung to him, trembling. "I'm cold," she said.

Seve held her more tightly. He looked up at one of his men. "Where's the goddamned doctor?"

"I'll see," one of them said.

More people were streaming into the apartment now, and Lei-fa began to whimper. Seve stroked her hair. It was matted in places by her drying blood. He had no way of telling how serious her wound was, and this worried him.

When, eventually, the doctor appeared, it was with a pair of paramedics and a stretcher in tow. Seve's man had done his job well.

"Don't leave me, elder brother, I beg you." A whisper was all she could manage. Her head fell back on his lap, and her huge, luminous eyes filled up his world just as if she were his child.

She would not go without him, and Seve kept hold of her hand all the way downstairs. He could feel the tremors rippling through her, and he thought, Jesus, I don't know how she's holding together.

They went through the police barricade, passing before the curious and the morbidly curious, shuffling like an audience restless for the performance to begin. It was odd, he thought, how death brought out the worst in human beings. Was it only because they longed to see the sight of blood or a protruding bone? Or was it, as Seve suspected, something deeper, more sinister? Was the voyeur in people aroused by trauma? Did some dark, centuries-old part of the brain become excited by disaster?

All through the short ambulance ride to Beekman Downtown Hospital, Seve held Lei-fa's hand, leaning over her, whispering in her ear as the doctor worked on the side of her head.

He left her only at the doors to the operating room, and that was because the surgeon would not allow him inside. Lei-fa's slim fingers had slipped from his callused hand as the shot they had given her took effect.

Seve watched that face disappear into the sterile operating room, peaceful now in unconsciousness. But he was seeing her as he first had, with the terror emanating from her, filling up the stinking, dank hallway.

He went to get a cup of coffee, and when he returned, he saw Diana Ming, one of his undercover people, waiting for him. He was somewhat surprised to see her; this was not her beat.

"How you doing?" she asked.

"Okay," he said, nodding. He took a long gulp of the coffee. It had no taste, but that was all right. It was the caffeine he was after. He was very tired.

"That bastard Loong hurt you any?"

"Not much." He looked at Diana. Suddenly he did not want to ask her why she was here.

"Well, you look awful," she said, indicating his bloodstained clothes. "I brought you a fresh shirt."

"Thanks," he said, taking it from her and beginning to strip off his shirt. It was stiff with blood.

"How about we sit down?" Diana said. "I could use the rest, I've been on my feet since three this morning."

They headed for a row of molded plastic seats. Seve offered her his coffee, and she took a swig while he buttoned up his new shirt. She was a good officer, smart and quite fearless. She had just passed her sergeant's exam with the best marks of the group. Seve admired her very much.

"Boss," she said, "I've got some bad news. I guess there's no proper way to tell you."

Seve was watching her.

"It's your brother, Dominic. He's been killed."

Seve thought that the ceiling had fallen in on him. He could not breathe. He tried to say something, but his throat was clotted with emotion. Then, as if through a thick haze, he heard himself asking "What happened?"

Diana told him everything she had been given. "It's not much, I know," she concluded. "I'm here to take you up to Connecticut, to the church. The forensic team is waiting for you there."

Without saying a word, Seve got up. He searched out the men's room, went in, and stared at himself in the mirror. But memories rendered him momentarily blind. He thought of Maggie. What a pair of thighs. How she would wrap them around his neck to pull him into bed, and afterward. But Seve remembered her more for her patience. She never complained when he couldn't make dinner—or anything else later; or when he was dragged out of bed by the phone shrilling at three in the morning; or when he had to cancel that weekend in the Poconos, good God, she had been already in the car, waiting when he had had to tell her, Sorry, no can do.

No, Seve thought, with a great deal of regret, Maggie never complained. But one day she wasn't there. She had changed her phone number to an unlisted one. He had considered getting the new number from the phone company, but then had thought better of it. What would he do once he had it? What did he have to say to her? He knew very well why she had left, and nothing had changed. His job came before anyone else, first, last, and always.

For years Seve Guarda had devoted himself to the law. And for all that time he had been as faithful to its tenets as if he were an acolyte in the service of God.

The comparison was not inappropriate. The law was, indeed, a kind of religion for him, inasmuch as he believed it to be the moral backbone of society—any society. To transgress the law was to allow the encroachment of chaos, it was to hear the trumpets of anarchy blowing, it was to feel the chill wind of the beast endangering all the good that society had wrought over the ages. It was something, in short, that he could not tolerate. It was like a revelation to him, as powerful as the piercing, white light of God striking Thomas Aquinas.

Which was why Maggie, who had sought to touch his callused

soul, had failed to budge him from his moral rectitude. Seve Guarda was a monk bound in the service of a higher calling.

Dominic is dead, he thought, and I'm thinking of Maggie. What the hell's wrong with me? And then, in a flash, he understood. The monk that was Seve was disconnected from the many quotidian normalcies of life—the loves of family and friends had taken a backseat. Without warning Maggie had gone. Now Dominic had been taken from him.

Seve blinked. What he saw in the mirror was a diamond-shaped face with intense features, high cheekbones, and what Maggie had called a cruel mouth. He saw dark eyes, smooth, flawless skin that made it impossible to tell his age. He saw thick, black hair and a powerful neck. He saw brown eyes that stared back at him with a shocked, unbelieving expression. But it wasn't his own face he was seeing; it was his brother's.

He struck out with his right fist. Pain exploded up his arm as the glass and the image shattered. He thought he saw blood spraying. Somehow that made him feel better, but not much.

When he returned, he had some paper towel wrapped around his lacerated right hand. Diana looked at the blood seeping through, but kept her mouth shut.

Seve stood just outside the doors of the operating room. He did not sit down, he did not say another word to Diana. He knew that he should get going. It would be a long ride in heavy traffic at this hour to New Canaan, and there were no doubt many people waiting on his arrival. And later, of course, he would need to see Richard Hu's wife; that duty was his alone. But he could not seem to get himself to move.

Inside, he wept for his baby brother. But that did not change the fact that Dominic was dead; nothing could bring him back. And for Seve it seemed as if time had ceased to have any relevance at all.

"*La Porte à la Nuit,*" Milhaud said. A tall, distinguished man, he held aloft the dagger that had been in Terry Haye's metal briefcase. "The Doorway to Night."

Milhaud had a high, wide forehead, the kind of noble Gallic nose vain Americans tried by surgery to imitate, and a long, deeply cleft chin. He wore his wiry salt-and-pepper hair long enough to affect the look of a mane. While he was well beyond his middle years, he possessed a strength of spirit that easily dwarfed the energy of men thirty years his junior. Overall, one might say that he had the aspect of a great politician or film star, that larger-than-life luminescence that filled whatever room in which he found himself.

"Huph!" Milhaud gave off a disgusted grunt and heaved the dagger across the room. It hit the opposite wall, missing the window by inches, but its blade did not shatter. He stared out the window across the Seine at that part of Paris he loved most: the Parc du Champ de Mars and the École Militaire, on the Left Bank.

"Plastic," he said. "An advanced form of polymeric resin that quite effectively apes the properties of jade." He strode across the room, picked up the dagger. "But it can't shatter the way jade does because it isn't jade."

He walked back to his handmade ebony and partridgewood desk, looking thoughtful. As he did so, he slapped the flat of the polymer blade again and again into his palm. "It's a fake, of course," he said.

"Then it is useless to us," Dante said.

"Not in the least," Milhaud said. "This fake tells us a great deal. For instance, that Terry Haye was far cannier than Monsieur Mabuse gave him credit for."

With this implied accusation Milhaud turned to Dante. "It seems as if Monsieur Mabuse killed Terry Haye prematurely."

"I don't understand," Dante said. "We ransacked Terry Haye's house. I saw to the details myself. There was nothing there, no clue as to what he had done with the real *Porte à la Nuit*."

"However, you *did* find this," Milhaud said. He picked up a postcard from his desk. On the face was a glossy photo of the pre-Alps of Haute-Provence. In typical fashion the colors were so over-saturated that the lavender that covered the slopes was purple. Far in the background, one could just make out the walls of Tourrette-sur-Loup's southernmost facade.

Milhaud turned it over. Its reverse contained a handwritten message. It read:

Chris,

Hope this won't take as long to reach you as it's been since we've been in touch. Hard to believe it's been ten years. Ten years! Tell me, how do two brothers ignore each other for a decade?

Anyway, I hope this finds you well and prosperous. I understand that you have become *le monstre sacré*. I'm sending this on ahead—as a kind of warning, I guess. I need to see you, so I'm coming to New York next week. I wouldn't be doing this if it weren't important, so I trust you'll arrange to be in town. Until then . . .

It was addressed, but unsigned. It was dated the same day Terry Haye had had his meet with M. Mabuse. And the last thing Terry Haye had written on the postcard was "P.S." But his life had ended before he had had a chance to write it. Milhaud wondered what Terry Haye had meant to append to his message to his brother, Chris, *le monstre sacré*, the superstar. He also wondered whether this postcard and the Doorway to Night were in some way linked.

Milhaud went around his desk and sat down. He tapped the corner of the card against his palm as he had done the phony dagger moments before. He hummed quietly to himself. It was the *Agnus Dei*.

I would bet anything, he thought, that Terry Haye has somehow involved his brother in New York in his enterprise. But in what way? As adviser, caretaker, or heir apparent?

M. Mabuse was in New York now on other business. For a moment Milhaud considered having him pay Chris Haye a visit. Then he reconsidered. Instinct told him to move cautiously, following the highly charged events of the past twenty-four hours. There was another way to discover if the real Doorway to Night had found its way from brother to brother. The postcard would be his key, Soutane would be his unwitting messenger. The irony of the situation was not lost on him. Better for the flow of events to show him the course he must now take in order to gain possession of the priceless artifact.

"And what about Mademoiselle Sirik?" he said. He never used Soutane's first name with his people, never gave them any hint that he had anything other than a professional interest in her. "Does she know about us? Specifically, does she know that you have been through Terry Haye's apartment?"

"Je ne peux pas la sentir," Dante said.

Milhaud made the same kind of face he would have made had Dante passed wind. "You can't stand her because she is a Buddhist, and you believe in nothing. Her mind-set is totally alien to you," he said. "I am constrained to point out that this is a failing on your part. I have tried to educate you in the ways of God, but you seem incapable of absorbing the concept of faith." He ran his finger along the false dagger. "Haye's apartment is hers now. It would be well if you kept that in mind."

"She's a bitch."

"You say that because she's Khmer," Milhaud said, looking at Dante's murderous eyes, thinking, Really, you Vietnamese are all alike. "Nevertheless, you would do well to keep in mind that she's very smart. And she wouldn't hesitate to cut your heart out if she ever discovered that you were involved in the death of her lover. We already know how she feels about Vietnamese, don't we?"

Dante grinned.

"That idea really turns you on." Milhaud hid his disgust, his rage at the names Dante was calling her. This is only an animal, he thought, what can be expected of such a poor creature?

"The bitch knows nothing," Dante said. "I made certain of that."

Milhaud nodded. "Good." He handed the postcard to Dante. "See that this gets back into Terry Haye's apartment. And make sure that it's left in a prominent position. The sooner Mademoiselle Sirik finds it, the better."

Dante took the postcard, glanced at his watch. "You have lunch with Monsieur LoGrazie in ten minutes," he said.

And Milhaud thought, Good dog. You're dangerous, to be sure, but you're also loyal. He rose, smoothed down the front of his jacket. "I'm ready," he said.

Mr. LoGrazie was either a wealthy American importer-exporter or a high-level *capo* in the Society of Seven Families—also known as the Mafia—according to how deeply one probed beneath his glossy exterior. Needless to say, Milhaud had probed quite deeply.

M. LoGrazie, Milhaud thought, had that darkly handsome, oily look evinced by the American actors trying to play Italians in *The Godfather*. But they could never be European, since they were defined by the softness and lassitude engendered by their lush country-club existence. Nevertheless, M. LoGrazie felt compelled to emulate them. And, in attempting to appear tragic and heroic at the same time, he managed to be neither.

For all that, even though he was an American, Milhaud liked M. LoGrazie. He tried to look at *la situation en macro*, and not hold it against him.

M. LoGrazie was not only smart, he was clever, a quality Milhaud could appreciate. He—and, Milhaud could only suppose, his superiors for whom he spoke—had an impressive grasp of global politics, which meant that Europeans resided somewhere at the Society's heart.

In addition, Milhaud was pleased to see how well M. LoGrazie dressed, suits by Brioni, shirts and rich Italian silk ties by A. Sulka. He looked as if he wouldn't be caught dead in Brooks Brothers, where, so Milhaud had heard, many modern American corporations kept an open account for their executives.

Mr. LoGrazie was a creature of some culture. He enjoyed talking of Chagall and Modigliani. When he walked—walking exercised his mind, he claimed—he did so often in La Ruche, the *cité des artistes*, where in their day his favorites chose to paint.

Milhaud took lunch with Mr. LoGrazie at various restaurants around Paris, Au Quai d'Orsay, Le Duc, Le Trou Gascon, but most often they met for drinks late in the day at the Club Fleurir.

Milhaud preferred this location because it was beautiful and convenient, so close to his house on the Avenue New York. More important, perhaps, this handsome eighteenth-century building was virtually hidden away on rue Jean Goujon, a discreet tree-lined street in the posh Eighth arrondissement, mercifully free of the traffic congestion that made the Place de la Concorde into a sort of twenty-four-hour-a-day madhouse of tourism and smog which, to Milhaud's way of thinking, were one and the same.

Mr. LoGrazie liked Canadian Club Manhattans, very cold, with a twist. With Milhaud, it varied, according to his mood. Today, as he settled himself against the velvet banquette, he opted for "33" beer. It was a taste he had developed during his trips to Southeast Asia, when he had been known by another name. Milhaud still liked Asian beer and Khmer women best, preferably together.

He watched Mr. LoGrazie with renewed interest. "We have completed the initial phase of Operation White Tiger," he said.

"Successfully?" Mr. LoGrazie asked.

"One hundred percent," Milhaud said somewhat untruthfully. "We have erased the major stumbling block to our joint venture. We are now prepared to step into the vacuum, as it were, that Terry Haye's death created, and assume an unobstructed position in the trade."

"Then you have acquired the Doorway to Night from Mr. Haye," Mr. LoGrazie said.

"Yes." Lying came easily to Milhaud. He had been doing it with great accomplishment all his life.

"Good." Mr. LoGrazie seemed greatly relieved. "Jesus, I can't tell you what a thorn in our side Terry Haye had become.

It's a pleasure doing business with a professional. I will forward the appropriate installment of your fee through our bank in Zurich."

"D'accord."

"The trinity of swords is now complete," Mr. LoGrazie said. "This foolishness—"

"There is nothing foolish about the Forest of Swords," Milhaud broke in. "A great many people—people who control both the product and the pipeline without which White Tiger is worthless—believe in its power. That makes the power real."

Mr. LoGrazie chuckled. "You mean if enough people believe in the bogeyman, he exists? Come on, who's kidding who?" He waved his hands. "Anyway, who gives a shit? The only thing is, after all this, I'd like to get a look at this thing complete."

"That can be easily arranged," Milhaud said expansively. He was feeling quite pleased with himself. "But it will take some time, you understand. It has not even been assembled yet, and that is a delicate procedure."

"Yeah? How long could it possibly take? You've got to ship it off to Asia ASAP. But before it goes, I want to see what I've been paying for."

After M. LoGrazie left, Milhaud sat back, broke open a pack of Gauloises, and lit up. Watching the smoke curl up toward the ceiling, Milhaud wondered what M. LoGrazie would say if he knew that the Doorway to Night that Milhaud had obtained from Terry Haye was a fake. Certainly his payment would not be forthcoming.

The real *Porte à la Nuit* was not yet in Milhaud's possession, but he was pursuing every avenue to obtain it. He knew that it was just a matter of time before he discovered where Terry Haye had hidden the real priceless dagger. The problem was, with M. LoGrazie hounding him, he didn't have much time.

And M. LoGrazie was right, Milhaud could not start up Operation White Tiger without it. Of course, he could rig up a phony, just as Terry Haye had done. M. LoGrazie wouldn't know what he was looking at anyway. But still, the fact remained that Milhaud needed the real Doorway to Night. Not for M. LoGrazie—or for anyone in the Mafia—but for the opium warlords in the Shan.

When the three separate weapons that comprised the Forest of Swords were put together, it would create a talisman so potent that all existing network liaisons between warlords and middlemen would be abrogated. The fiercely independent tribesmen of the Shan Plateau, where the world's best opium was grown, would slay their own brothers if the wielder of the Forest of Swords were to order it.

The *Prey Dauw*, as the warlords called the three-bladed weapon, belonged in the pantheon of their ancient mythology. It was said to have been created by Mahagiri, a rogue monk, a kind of sorcerer who made a deal with Ravana, chief demon in Theravadan Buddhist theology. Yet it existed. Milhaud already possessed two parts; soon he would have the third piece, *La Porte à la Nuit*. Whole, the magic of the Forest of Swords—whether real or imagined—would make its owner the most powerful man on earth.

Milhaud took a long pull on his cigarette, closed his eyes. He allowed his mind to drift toward Soutane. He saw her curled upon a rumpled bed. He saw the slow green river winding like a serpent outside the open window, the cries of the vendors in the passing sampans. He saw her tiny feet bound within pink shoes, her dark, sad eyes upon him.

Soutane Sirik, the subject of Milhaud's yearning, was at that moment staring at a photograph of herself and Terry Haye. They were at an outdoor restaurant, sitting beneath a striped awning, their arms around each other. Terry, wearing sunglasses, was grinning. The edges of the photo were frayed and worn. Soutane had carried it in her pocketbook ever since it had been developed. Through her tears, the figures seemed to take on the dreamlike quality with which the Impressionists invested their finest work. A happy couple; people she knew, or had known, but not well.

Soutane had fled from Nice the day after Terry's death. After she had identified his body, after the police had questioned her, after she had spent a sleepless night in her apartment—her apartment, but Terry's home. Terry seemed to be everywhere she looked, turned, sat, or stood. Not just his memory, but his spiritual presence. She began to feel suffocated by it.

Flight was a primitive response, and Soutane did not question it. When the sun began to tint the sky, she went through her drawers, shoving underclothes, shorts, and tops into a small overnight bag. She needed not only to get away from Nice but to be with family.

Family was very important to Soutane. She was an only child. Now without her mother and her father, she had only Mun, her cousin. His father—Soutane's mother's brother—had been a leader in the Lon Nol regime in Cambodia in the early 1970s, when Prince Sihanouk had been deposed. He had made many bitter enemies. In the ensuing bloody struggle for control of the country, Mun's parents and siblings had been assassinated. Mun had fled to friends of his father's, who, at great risk to themselves, had managed to smuggle him out of the country.

Mun was very important to Soutane, and so it was to his villa in the hills northwest of Nice that she went. She had stayed for three days, living like a baby: eating, sleeping fitfully. She would twitch, stalked by terrible nightmares: a herd of magnificent horses, thundering across a vast, backlit plain, their eyes bloody and streaming. She would start awake, gasping and weeping until Mun came to hold her and rock her back to sleep. Often, he would sing her Khmer lullabies.

At the end of three days Soutane arose from a dream in which she had been a bronze statue of Buddha. She had watched with her bronze eyes as the flesh-and-blood Soutane took off her shoes, washed her feet, and entered the temple where the Soutane Buddha sat. The flesh-and-blood Soutane had knelt before her, praying. Seeing that display of devotion, she wanted to cry, but her bronze eyes would not oblige her. She wanted to speak to the flesh-and-blood Soutane, but her bronze lips were frozen shut. She wanted to reach out and comfort the flesh-and-blood Soutane, but her bronze arms would not move.

That morning Soutane went with Mun to pray, something she had not done for many years. Though she was only half Khmer, she had been brought up with Theravadan Buddhism. This form of the religion is—as the Khmer say—ingested with mother's milk. Basically, the Theravadan Buddhists believe in thirty-one planes of existence into which a human being can be reborn: a wheel called *samsara*. According to them, there is no afterlife, no soul, no omnipotent god. Even Buddha cannot be prayed to directly. Instead, one addressed one's prayers to any number of the thirty-seven *nats*, or saints.

"I take refuge in the Buddha," Soutane prayed. "I take refuge in the Dharma. I take refuge in the Sangha."

The core of Soutane's teaching lay in Gautama Buddha's Four Noble Truths: Life has in it the element of suffering. Suffering is caused by desire. To end suffering one must give up all desire;

to do this one must relinquish all attachments. The way to freedom lies in the Noble Eightfold Path of right intent and right conduct.

When she returned home late that night—last night—she was calmer than she had been since she had received the news of Terry's violent death. Similarly, the house seemed friendly again. She had washed some clothes, put away others she had not used on her trip.

That was when she had discovered that someone had been in the house while she was away. She knew immediately that it had not been the police. She had left them Mun's number, and surely they would have informed her. Besides, they had already been through the house while she was there.

Soutane had opened the drawer in which she kept her underclothes, and noticed that one of her panties—the pink floral one—was missing. At first, she thought she had misplaced it, or had taken it with her. But after checking her overnight case, as well as throughout the house, she could not find it. It was while she was brewing herself tea that she remembered seeing it in the drawer when she had packed to go away to Mun's three days ago. In fact, she could recall pushing it to one side in order to get to another pair she had wanted to take with her. Now the pink pair was missing. Impossible. Unless someone had been in the house and had taken it.

Soutane went methodically through the house, making a meticulous search. That was when she found Terry's unmailed postcard to his brother, Chris, with the postscript still unwritten.

She stared at it for a long time, wondering at the feelings it evoked within her. Terry's handwriting. Chris's name. Then, putting it in her handbag, she finished her search. Nothing else seemed to be missing. Whatever the thief was looking for, he hadn't found it.

She felt a chill creeping up her spine. She felt nauseated by the idea of someone creeping around her home. It was akin to the idea of a stranger putting his hand between her thighs. It was intimate and monstrous at the same time.

Then she pulled herself together. The violated feeling, she knew, came from a sense of helplessness. She needed to regain control of the situation. But it was more than that, she knew. She had spent the past five years—with Terry's loving help—drawing a veil of normalcy over the horrors of the past. Now the violence had returned. There had been great violence in

Mun's past—violence that had almost swept her away. Was this true, too, of Terry's past? The thought that it might be true was almost too much for her to bear.

She realized with a swiftness that took her breath away just how fragile the illusion of normalcy was. Just beneath, like a terrifying shark within dark currents, lurked the knowledge of what she was, what she would now always be. Someone skilled in the art of death.

She turned her mind with a deliberate effort to the present. While she sipped her tea, she thought it all out. When she was done, she got up and turned out all the lights. She stood, then, for a long time, scarcely daring to breathe. Her heart was hammering fast, and it took all her force of will to get to the window.

The curtains billowed against her face. She was very still. Perhaps she was weeping. At last she curled her forefinger around the edge of the curtain, drew it aside just a sliver.

Outside, the Boulevard Victor Hugo was filled with parked cars. Plane trees diffused the streetlights. Shadows drifted along the sidewalks like wraiths as, every so often, a car slid by. She saw nothing out of the ordinary, and was about to turn away when she saw the flare of a match. For an instant darkness vanished from a building's entrance across the street. She waited, breathing slowly. A face, the back of a hand, a figure looking up at her.

Soutane recoiled from the window. She gave a tiny, involuntary cry and, clutching the frayed photo of the happy couple to her breast, whispered, "Oh, Terry. I can't face this alone. Why aren't you here?"

From across the street M. Mabuse watched Seve Guarda standing with Diana Ming in the bright light of the hospital's entrance. He lifted his right arm, pointed his forefinger, and aimed at the spot between Seve's eyes. A sitting duck, he thought.

He imagined the soft cough of the silenced gun, the soft crash of the glass shattering, the soft noise not unlike that of a baby suckling contentedly at its mother's breast as the bullet pierced skin, flesh, and bone.

He imagined the acute motions of the body in trauma, the spurting of the blood, especially the blood, filling the vast industrial vestibule, splashing over the scuffed granite floor, lit up by the brilliant fluorescents, coating the spiky glass shards still in the doorframe so that they sparked and glistened like pink diamonds.

For some reason the thought of blood always brought to mind a certain image: a woman's bare thighs, opened, expectant, dewy with promise. M. Mabuse felt himself growing hard. Sex and death were inextricably linked in his mind, as if they were two sides of the same coin, forever spinning from the darkness into the light.

M. Mabuse shifted in his seat behind the wheel of his rented car. He adored cars in quite the same way he adored sex and death. In fact, he often daydreamed of dying in a car, speeding at a hundred and fifty miles per hour, smashing into a concrete wall or, even better, another car.

The idea had been with him for some time, but it had been given substance by *Crash*, a book he had discovered in a Heathrow Airport bookstall years ago while he was waiting for his outbound flight. Now he never traveled without it, repeatedly reading with greedy intensity its descriptions of erotic car crashes in rain-swept, neon-lit futurescapes.

M. Mabuse was consumed by the notion of death. Often, he wondered why it was he was still living, when a dozen of his brothers and sisters were nothing more than cinders, scattered beneath the soil of Vietnam, muddy with blood, swollen with corpses.

In those moments, like the lucid periods within a high fever, he understood that it was not enough for him to die. Death was simple; it was clean, in its way, the purest experience a human being can have. His *karma* dictated something more for him. But he had as yet to grasp what that might be.

M. Mabuse, watching Seve climb into his car, thought of the death he would mete out to him. The shooting incident was a wisp of smoke, a joke, an amusement he had conjured up to while away the time.

Time was something that M. Mabuse had learned to control. But, then, he had had no choice. Not, that is, unless you considered insanity a choice. When one spent five hundred days incarcerated in the black pit of a Vietnamese prison camp with nothing to eat but worms and insects that one clawed out of the bare earth with one's bloody fingers, one learned to master time.

Or, more accurately, thought. Because if his incarceration had taught M. Mabuse anything, it was that time did not exist. Alone in the darkness and the silence, thought became a monstrous entity. In time it was the only thing that existed. Thought defined one's world and, therefore, one's reality. So M. Mabuse learned to control his thoughts and, thus, to master time.

The skill had had other uses, as when M. Mabuse had been tortured. Even today, had he been asked how much torture he had endured, M. Mabuse would have no way of answering. He simply did not know. While his body was pinned in hell, his mind was reaching for the Void.

Seve's car, with Diana driving, pulled out into traffic. M. Mabuse, gunning his engine, followed. He did not know where Seve was going; it didn't matter. All that mattered was that Seve would eventually come to rest. And when he did, M. Mabuse would be there. Then he would have his fun.

His tongue flicked across his dark, cracked lips. Amid the jabber of the city street, M. Mabuse found silence as effortlessly as he found darkness. His mind was filled with the flowering explosions, the oily napalm running like a monstrous beast that ate his village alive, that flayed the skin off its inhabitants, that devoured the night; this nightmare spread out before him like delicacies at a picnic.

He stopped at a traffic light, just a car's length from Seve Guarda. In the dim streetlight it was just possible to make out a crisscrossing of scars on the inside of his left forearm. Som were obviously old, but others seemed much more recent.

M. Mabuse took out a small stiletto, snapped it open. Then he slid the edge of the blade across a section of his forearm that was free of scar tissue.

The sharp pain of the wound brought him fully awake, as if from a dream, or the thought of a dream. It was very pleasurable.

For what seemed a long time, until the light turned green, M. Mabuse stared at the blood—his blood—creeping along the steering wheel as if it were an animal with a will independent of his own. When, in time with his pulse, it began to drip onto the floor of the car, he got out a handkerchief to stanch the flow.

Two days a week Milhaud worked, inasmuch as one could say he worked at all, at the Académie de l'Histoire Militaire. This was not, however, a school—at least not in the conventional sense—but rather a library encompassing all aspects of military thought, practice, and art.

The Académie was private, wholly funded by the SRGE, the Société Rentrer dans le Giron de l'Église, the Society to Return to the Fold, within whose portals the extraordinary library was housed.

The seventeenth-century French Baroque structure owned by the SRGE, or Le Giron, as it was known among its members, was a glorious affair designed by Jules Hardouin-Mansart, and featured a roofline that bore his name. It was situated in the Place Vendôme which, considering the value of Parisian real estate, bespoke Le Giron's exceeding wealth.

Milhaud was in charge of information acquisition and retrieval for the vast library. At least, this was ostensibly his work for two days a week. In fact, he was a kind of professor at the Académie, tutoring promising pupils in the art of warfare as Le Giron viewed it. This meant presenting a historical perspective, which included the changing theories of warfare as practiced by the acknowledged geniuses of war, beginning with Alexander and ending with Patton.

Then—and only then—did Milhaud introduce his pupils to Sun Tzu, Ieyasu Tokugawa, and Miyamoto Musashi, whose philosophies were both timeless and indispensable.

"Take their lessons to heart," he was fond of instructing his pupils. "The Roman Empire was once the greatest power on earth. Too, the British Empire had its moment of glory. As for America, it peaked as an imperialist nation in 1945. Now it has become the world's largest debtor nation. It is being crippled by its enormous trade imbalance. It is unable or unwilling to house its burgeoning urban homeless population. No one wants its products, even its own people. Americans want to see 'Made in Japan' or 'Made in Germany' on everything they purchase.

"Is it ironic that currently Japan and Germany, who lost the World War, who, forty-five years ago, were on the brink of ruin, have the strongest economies? No. It is a lesson to be learned. All power is fleeting, to paraphrase George Patton.

"As for America, the dying behemoth, it lacks only the *coup de grace* to put it out of its misery. The corruption of ultimate power, the Romans have taught us, comes at the decline of a civilization. Watergate and, most recently, the Iran-Contra affair exhibit those mortal sins of venality and immorality which are the signs of advancing evil.

"So this is where we must begin: the death of America."

His lectures never failed to mesmerize his students, eliciting in them a reverence akin to awe. They saw in him a kind of symbol of the brand of potent radical politics they had been assured was extinct by those in the world outside Le Giron.

But in addition to his seminal work at the Académie, Milhaud supervised many other matters. The most important of these, by far, was running White Tiger.

Operation White Tiger, the creation of a major drug pipeline into the Shan Plateau, was a Mafia code designation, but it was simpler for Milhaud's people to use it as well. For practical reasons Milhaud had delegated much of the responsibility for the actual running of the operation to his Vietnamese hounds, M. Mabuse and Dante. But Mr. LoGrazie, the representative of the Mafia families involved in White Tiger, did not know this.

It was Milhaud's intention never to reveal the identities of his operatives to Mr. LoGrazie. There were myriad reasons for this, most of them basic tradecraft, pertaining to security. But even more important, Milhaud wanted to ensure that the Mafia, whose appetite for selling drugs was legendary, was irrevocably tied to him—and him alone.

Mr. LoGrazie had come to Milhaud, offering him a generous fee plus fifteen percent of the action to handle the logistics of the operation. After all, the Mafia had never had any direct dealings with the opium warlords of the Shan. Milhaud had a decades-long history in the region, and Mr. LoGrazie's people needed his contacts as well as his expertise. Besides which, they would never have been able to deal effectively with Terry Haye.

Milhaud considered the amount of the fee. Ten million dollars plus expenses, in addition to the percentage, made it clear just how important this operation was to the families.

Milhaud had heard how dangerous and treacherous the Mafia could be, but they were in his part of the world now. He held the upper hand. Why, he could even hand over the Forest of Swords to them, and they would not know what to do with it. He almost laughed out loud at the thought.

The telephone rang. Milhaud listened to the voice without speaking a word in reply. It was Mr. LoGrazie calling for a meet—through the automated, dead-drop phone circuit.

Milhaud was curious. It was not at one of their usual haunts, but rather at a dingy tourist restaurant in the business end of the Rue St. Honoré.

Mr. LoGrazie was sitting at a window table, in the shadow of the Ministry of Finance across the street, that rather tedious portion of the monstrous complex that housed the Louvre.

Milhaud ordered an espresso, because the place had no Asian beer. When it came, he sipped it slowly. It was execrable, meant for American tourists who thought the coffee at McDonald's was just fine.

Mr. LoGrazie was drinking a mineral water, which was unusual. "There is a matter I wish to present to you," he said. His voice was odd, tight, full of a springlike coil, and Milhaud was instantly on his guard. What has happened? he thought with a twinge of apprehension.

"Whatever I can do."

Mr. LoGrazie signaled for the check. "It's gotten too close in here," he said abruptly. He threw some bills on the table.

A block away they strolled around the Palais Royal. There were plenty of foreigners around—busloads of Germans, a smattering, here and there, of Japanese, Spaniards, Russians.

"I wonder whether you notice these tourists in the same way I do," Milhaud said. "These days most of them are Germans. That worries us French, because the deutsche mark is so strong, you see. In 1992, all the European borders will come down. Common Market citizens will no longer need a passport or a visa inside Western Europe. Travel will be unrestricted. And not only travel. Anyone will be able to buy property, businesses. We're frankly terrified that the Germans will come in here and do to Paris what the Japanese have already done to New York: buy it wholesale."

"Germans I can live with," Mr. LoGrazie said. "They're good businessmen. It's the Russians I worry about. The worst thing we could do is sign nuclear missile treaties with those lying sons of bitches."

Milhaud wondered if Pavlov ever discovered how much like his dogs Americans could be. It was so easy to gauge their reactions, he believed, because the culture of the brave New World was built on stereotypes: John Wayne cowboy heroes, Black Bart villains. If you rode a white horse or wore a white hat, Americans saw you as a good guy, no matter how your actions might contradict the stereotypical image.

Milhaud was anxious to get back to work. "Do you have something for me?"

Mr. LoGrazie said, "There is a saying in our family: Even small boats leave wakes. We don't want any wakes left at all."

Milhaud watched Mr. LoGrazie, waiting for a clue as to what he was talking about.

"As to setting the groundwork for White Tiger's success," Mr. LoGrazie said, "it seems that there is still a bit more to do."

They turned down a side street, away from the chattering tourists. Mr. LoGrazie stopped in the shadow of a building's arched colonnade. "It's become clear that taking care of Terry Haye wasn't enough. We're afraid that a leak still exists."

They could see, through the windows, a crowd bidding at an auction of French Impressionist paintings. The large room was filled mainly with Germans and Japanese, catalogs clutched in their eager fists.

"Terry Haye had a mistress," Mr. LoGrazie went on. "A French girl with Khmer blood by the name of Soutane Sirik."

Milhaud's bowels instantly turned to water.

Mr. LoGrazie was staring through the windows at the fantastic Monet currently being auctioned off. The bidding seemed quite spirited. "Don't tell me you weren't aware of her."

Milhaud's desperate urge to urinate sent a warning shiver through him. "Well, of course I was. But I assumed that Terry Haye had kept her out of—"

"Wrong." Mr. LoGrazie had not looked at Milhaud for some time. Which was just as well. Milhaud was white as a sheet.

"We want," Mr. LoGrazie continued, "to arrange for the Sirik girl to follow her lover."

"But—"

"But me no buts," Mr. LoGrazie said curtly. "This is not a negotiation. We want you to do it. Period." He turned on his heel and left.

Stunned, Milhaud watched Mr. LoGrazie stride hurriedly off. He was between Scylla and Charybdis. He could not kill Soutane, but neither could he disobey M. LoGrazie's orders.

He closed his eyes, trying to calm himself. Think! he berated himself. What could the Mafia achieve by having Soutane killed? He could not imagine an answer. Therefore, he knew he needed to find one.

He watched the Germans and the Japanese bidding for the Monet, and thought with shame, We French are not, after all, so far from the Americans. Everyone wants a piece of us now.

* * *

It was late in New York by the time Chris Haye was through making arrangements to fly to France. He hung up the phone.

His mind felt like a sieve. Moments in time were grains of sand, slipping through his grasp without either form or substance. He seemed to be existing in a twilight world where all sensation had been banished. His brother was dead. It was as if he had begun breathing in novocaine instead of oxygen. He was numb inside and out.

He found himself staring at a blinking light on his phone. The red glow, like the warning of a lighthouse in dense fog, meant nothing to him. Then he heard the ringing; it seemed to have been going on for a long time. Realizing it was the phone, he picked it up.

"*Bonjour,*" a woman's voice said.

He did not answer.

"*Allô?*"

He cleared his throat. "Yes?"

"*Parlez-vous français, monsieur?*"

"*Oui, madame,*" he said. "What can I do for you?"

"Is Monsieur Haye there?" Soutane asked. "Chris Haye."

"You are speaking to him."

"Ah, *bon.*" Having come this far, she hesitated. Her heart was hammering. "This is Soutane Sirik," she said at last. "I am calling from Nice. France."

Chris sat up straight. "Soutane," he said in a strangled voice, "is that you?"

"Yes," she said. "I am using my mother's maiden name now."

Chris did not know what to say or think; his mind was as numb as if it were encased in a chunk of ice. "After all this time . . ." He almost choked on his words.

"I know," she said. "It must be a shock. You are probably wondering why I'm calling."

There was dead space for so long that Chris said, "Are you there?" Just as if she might be an apparition he had somehow conjured up.

"Yes," she said. "Oh, hell. I'm calling about your brother."

"You knew Terry?"

"We lived together for five years."

God in heaven. His intestines had turned to water. "I know Terry is dead, Soutane," he managed to get out. There was a building crumbling on his shoulders. The weight was killing him. "People at my father's office called me. I imagine the French authorities got his number from you."

"Yes."

"I appreciate your calling." He was having trouble remembering how to breathe.

"What seems odd," she said quickly, "is that I found a postcard he was about to mail to you. It says that you hadn't had any contact in ten years. Is that true?"

He was only half listening to her. "Give or take, I suppose so."

"It also says that he was going to fly into New York to see you next week. He said it was important."

There was silence. Chris found that he was gripping the receiver so hard his hand had begun to hurt.

"Do you know anything about what Terry might have wanted to speak to you about?"

"How could I?"

"I mean, did he send you anything in the past several weeks?"

"Terry never sent me anything," Chris said. "Ever." For a moment he listened to her breathing. Slowly, he came out of his fog. "Soutane, are you in some sort of trouble?"

"I don't know," she said. "It seems that Terry had a lot of secrets."

"That sounds like my brother."

"But these are secrets," Soutane said, "that have survived his death."

Chris considered this. "Look," he said, "since my father is away, I have to take care of the formalities. I'm scheduled to fly into Nice the day after tomorrow. I'll be staying at the Negresco." His heart beating painfully. "Why don't you meet me there for drinks?"

"I have a better idea," Soutane said. "I'll pick you up at the airport. When are you due in?"

He gave her the scheduled arrival time, along with the Pan Am flight number.

"*Bon. Merci*, Chris. *À bientôt*."

Soutane, Soutane. Her name was like the prayers he had said as a child before he went to sleep.

Think of something else.

Terry coming to New York to see him? That would have been an extraordinary occurrence. What could have been so important to impel him to end his decade-long isolation?

Chris wondered if he would ever find out now.

He swiveled his chair around to look out the window. The sound of Soutane's voice hung in his mind long after he had put the receiver down. Blue shadows had stolen across Central Park, engulfing the foliage in blackness. Surrounded as it was by the city's myriad lights, it had somehow become a metaphor for Chris's future: unknown and infinitely malleable.

What's with the limp, counselor?

It's the rain. It's nothing.

Not nothing. Something. Or, rather, someone coming back at him with the force of a boomerang.

Soutane.

He closed his eyes, and compelled his mind to turn to other thoughts. He needed an anodyne. He had been thinking about Alix Layne before the call.

An image of a night perhaps a month ago swam up into his consciousness. He was having dinner with Bram Stryker, a casual friend who was a divorce lawyer. Stryker had a well-deserved reputation as a shark in negotiations. According to the girls in the office, he also had a reputation (well deserved or not, Chris did not know) for taking to bed his female clients. Be that as it may, Stryker had a sharp mind, and Chris enjoyed picking his brains.

On the way out of the restaurant Stryker had said he had an after-dinner obligation to stop in at an open house, and asked Chris to join him.

It happened to be Alix Layne's open house. She lived in a large, dark one-bedroom apartment on West Ninety-third Street. How a place with such high ceilings could be so stifling Chris could not say. Perhaps it was only that there were three times the number of people it could comfortably accommodate.

In any event, Chris was immediately uncomfortable. He was an East Side person in just the same way that residents of Beverly Hills prefer either the flats or the hills. They were two entirely separate environments, and they fit differing personalities.

Chris lost Stryker almost immediately in the smoke-filled mob. The blare of music almost pushed him back into the hallway. He nodded to an acquaintance from a rival firm, said hello to a few more people before he was able to shoulder his way to the bar. Nursing a drink, he spent an uneventful ten minutes talking shop with a Superior Court judge.

By that time he had had it. He went in search of Stryker,

knowing at the outset that in this madhouse it was a fool's errand. He tried the kitchen, but it was so full he could hardly squeeze in.

He went down the hall. In the bedroom he found more smoke, more noise. A second stereo was blasting. The two disparate rhythms created a frisson similar to the one the city emitted each morning at rush hour. People were crawling over the bed. Others had opened the large window and were dancing on the fire escape. Stryker was not among them.

Chris gave it up, went back down the hall. As he was passing the bathroom, its door opened wide enough for him to see inside. There was Stryker with his arms around Alix Layne. It was a moment that, in Chris's memory at least, was suffused with silence.

As he watched them kiss, he was struck by the lack of emotion on Stryker's face, save for a kind of triumph as Alix wrapped her leg around his thigh, clinging to him with a kind of desperation. It seemed as if Stryker was almost laughing at her.

Chris remembered that he had begun to break out in a cold sweat. He wanted to slam his fist into Stryker's face. Chris had never before realized that lust could exist without passion. He had never imagined that the sight of two people kissing could be so ugly. Confronted by that reality, he had retreated in silence.

Chris opened his eyes. Silence must be my strong suit, he thought. I was silent during Alix's diatribe outside the courthouse, too.

He turned off his desk lamp, reached for his jacket, and went out the door of his office. At this hour it was self-locking. The click resounded hollowly in the hallway.

Downstairs, he watched the cabs slide through the rain-slick streets. Rush hour was over, but theater hour was just beginning. So much for trying to hail a taxi.

Chris did not know what to do or where to go. There were so many possibilities. Yet, because his mind was filling up with the jumbled images and emotions of the past, the simple act of choosing one seemed too much to contemplate. He stood beneath the granite and marble overhang of the building, watching colors slip and slide in the wet until the memory he had been suppressing squirted up through the night: Chris at a funeral home across from the airstrip at Dover Air Force Base, watching the soldiers unload the stacks of aluminum caskets fresh-packed from beautiful downtown Da Nang. He was there to make the final arrangements for a friend who, without family, had named Chris beneficiary of his life insurance.

The twenty-year-old Chris Haye shivering in the bright heat of summer, chilled to the bone, the truly horrifying notion sweeping over him that his brother, Terry, the special forces hero, could be inside one of those gleaming caskets, and they had never said goodbye to one another.

The monotony of the steady rain had become overpoweringly depressing.

Chris shook himself. He turned his collar up and, hunching his shoulders against the rain, began walking uptown.

When he got home, he stripped off his soggy clothes, drew on sweat shorts and a sleeveless shirt. In the full-length mirror in his bedroom, he saw himself.

An observer, no doubt, would have been impressed by the ripple of his muscles. He was a tall man, with the broad shoulders and narrow hips of the athlete. His hard muscles possessed that long, lean quality—rather than the bulk of the muscle builder, or the sinewy, almost emaciated aspect of the long-distance runner—that could only come from swimming or biking.

What Chris saw, however, was the young man who had been an aerobic exercise machine, the top prospect to win the Tour de France, that grueling combination of endurance and speed, where cyclists were expected to maintain speeds in excess of twenty-five miles per hour up steep alpine grades. That was in 1969, the same year that Terry had been dodging bullets in Southeast Asia.

That year the race had been dedicated to *la France profonde*, the villages of the country's interior, and to this day, that was the France that Chris remembered and loved with all his heart. *La France profonde*: which had lifted him to the dizzying heights of glory, and then had raised its fist against him, so that he had returned home a different person. The youth of full flower, of unlimited strength and stamina, of what the Italians he met there called *risico*, constant risk taking, of, most of all, life as an ageless present where one was invulnerable, was gone forever.

How much older was he now? Chris wished he knew. If one counted such things merely in years, not much. There were the same blue eyes, curly black hair; there was no fat anywhere on his face or his body, and a minimum of lines. "That's your

Celtic blood, son!'' his father used to say. And, in truth, the young Chris Haye used to imagine himself as a Celtic warrior, armored, sword raised against a horde of Picts swarming over the stone cairns surrounding Stonehenge.

My God, he thought, that seems like ages ago. But Soutane whispering in his ear was only moments past.

At the antique French desk in his bedroom he opened a drawer, drew out a thick sheaf of typescript. The sheets were bound by a rubber band that snapped in two at his touch. The pages were stained and worn. In the upper right-hand corner was an annotation in his hand: *Mougins, 1969*.

He had not taken out this manuscript in years, and reading it now, hating the ineptitude of the sentences, he understood why. With a convulsive gesture he shoved the loose sheets back in the drawer, slammed it shut.

Barefoot, he padded into the small second bedroom that he used for his workouts. A weight rack stood against one wall, next to a rowing machine. In front of the window an exercise bike and an electronic treadmill stood side by side. Chris climbed onto the bike and set off. He looked out the window, down thirty stories at Third Avenue, but there was nothing to see. Instead, images of Thonon-les-Bains, Chamonix, Aubagne, and Digne filled his mind. And for that time he was once again wearing the coveted yellow jersey that only the leader of the Tour de France was allowed to wear.

An hour later he climbed off, and rowed at top speed for forty minutes. Then he threw himself into lifting weights until he felt the delicious fatigue, and the sweat was rolling off him freely. But that did not calm him, and neither did a cold shower. Visions of Mougins, unbidden, filled his mind. It hadn't been only the Tour de France that had happened to him in the summer of 1969.

Dressed, he found himself restlessly pacing the apartment as if it were a prison. In every mirror, in every pane of glass, he saw Soutane's face. He grabbed a lightweight raincoat and went out.

It was not until he was north of Seventy-second Street that he realized where he was headed. He was a block away from Max Steiner's place.

Steiner lived in an old, rambling co-op on Seventy-fifth between Fifth and Madison. The doorman called up, then pointed out the proper elevator; this was one of those buildings where an elevator serviced two apartments on each floor.

Steiner had the door open before Chris stepped out onto the floor. He was grinning, and Chris felt grateful to have such an ally. It had been Max and Chris against the world from the moment Chris had come to work for Steiner, McDowell and Fine; it would always be that way. That was why, Chris realized, he had come here now.

"I hope you've come to gloat," Steiner said, pumping Chris's hand. "You were all over the six o'clock news, you sonuvabitch." Considering Chris's present mood, his enthusiasm was as depressing as the rain outside.

"Max, could we talk?"

"Sure. Sure." Max drew him into the vestibule. The sounds of other voices could be heard behind Steiner. "But later. Come on in. I'm having a little party. Bill and Marjorie Horner, Jack and Betty Johnson, you know them. We've just finished dinner. Have a nightcap, stay awhile. It's almost time for the news at eleven. You can gloat all over—"

"No. No, that's all right." Oh, Jesus, Chris thought. That's all I need now, to put on my professional face and make small talk over martinis and caviar.

"Come on, Chris," Max said. "What? You think you're intruding? You know better than that. Besides, you know all the people here." He laughed. "There are even some fans of yours. They'd eat me alive if they thought I'd let a genuine celebrity like you get away. You'll *make* this party."

Chris realized that he hadn't told Max about Terry's death, and now he couldn't. He could imagine Max's expression as he said, "But you never told me you had a brother." Chris could not face that. He seemed to have to fight Steiner off. "No, really," he said. "I just have a minute. I've got a date, and I'm already late."

Steiner peered at him. "You sure you can't stay for just one drink?"

Chris nodded. In desperation he retreated to the hall, rang for the elevator. "Positive."

"Well, okay." Steiner brightened. "We'll talk tomorrow, yes?"

"Sure," Chris said. "I'll give you a call." Then, blessedly, the elevator door opened, and he got in.

"Hey, Chris, Alix Layne was ready to eat you for lunch," Steiner said. "She asked the DA for your case. I'm damn proud of you."

Chris began to say thanks, but he choked on the word.

Outside, the rain had ceased for the time being, but it had left the city as hot and steamy as an August night. Chris grabbed a taxi.

"Where to, buddy?"

Chris gave the cabby an address, then promptly forgot what he had said. Lost in thought, he watched the city glide by him. It was full of life, stuffed to the brim with movement, laughter, giddy, running feet. Couples strolled down the wide avenues, lovers clung to the shadows between buildings. It was a tapestry, Chris realized with a start, that was complete without him.

They were well into the Central Park transverse when Chris said, "Where the hell are you taking me?"

"To Ninety-third Street, west of Columbus," the cabby said. "You think of a better way to get there? Well, there ain't none."

Ninety-third west of Columbus, Chris thought. Jesus, that's where Alix Layne lives. "I couldn't have—"

The cabby slammed on his brakes and turned around. "You wanna go somewhere else, buddy, all's you gotta do is tell me."

Horns began to blare behind them as traffic began to pile up. "No," Chris said woodenly. "It's all right."

But it wasn't all right. Not by a long shot. He was still wondering what the hell he was doing here when he pushed the button next to her plastic name plate. A screech of static emanated from the grime-encrusted speaker grill. He shouted something into it and, in a moment, the front door buzzed.

The elevator smelled from takeout pizza and cigar smoke. He got off at the fourth floor, went down a narrow, dimly lit hall that had just been repainted. All that had done was to make the bulges in the plaster more apparent.

The door at the far end opened. He could see Alix Layne framed in the light from her apartment. She was wearing a pair of cutoff jeans so old they were almost white, a T-shirt that said "I'D RATHER BE RIDING MY BIKE," and nothing else. She was eating a slice of pizza.

Chris stopped in front of her. "I hope you aren't smoking a cigar."

"What?" She was looking at him in the way people do when the thirteenth clown gets out of the three-foot car in the circus. She didn't quite believe this was happening.

"What I mean is," Chris said, "are you alone?"

* * *

Seve Guarda looked down at the severed head of his brother and thought, What in the name of Christ happened? He and Diana Ming were crouched in the arbor behind the privet in the back of Holy Trinity Church in New Canaan. With them was Harvey Blocker, the supervising detective from the Town Police.

Blocker was a heavyset man with bloodshot eyes. His close-cropped hair was a color somewhere between dirty blond and gray. He had a cold sore at one corner of his mouth that his tongue would not leave alone.

"I never saw anything like this," he was saying now. "The head's here in the garden, and the rest of him's back in the sacristy." He grunted as he shifted his weight from one foot to the other. "As you could see, there was something of a struggle."

"No one saw anyone go into the sacristy?" Seve asked. A lump in his throat was making it hard to breathe.

Blocker shook his head. "We interviewed the lot. Father Donnelly was aware that your brother went into the sacristy after Mass. But that was strictly SOP. Father Donnelly said that your brother liked to be alone for a time, so he thought nothing of it."

Seve had noticed an odd patterning of the flesh at the end of Dom's neck. He stared at it, trying to make sense of it.

"But an hour later," Blocker went on, "when Father Guarda still had not come out, Father Donnelly went into the sacristy. That's when he found your brother, and called us."

Blocker led them around the church, through a side entrance, back into the sacristy. Dominic was lying on his right side. It was eerie, and a bit frightening, Seve thought, to see a body without a head. This is not my brother, he told himself. This cannot be Dom.

"What do you make of this, Detective?"

Blocker pawed his nose with a thick forefinger. "Damned if I know," he said. "Who would want to waste a priest? As far as I can see, it makes no sense."

"A psycho, maybe?" Diana Ming said.

Blocker shrugged. "Could be. Who knows with people these days?" He grunted as he rubbed at his stiff legs; he hadn't liked kneeling in the arbor to take a close look at the head. "Anyway, we've done all we can for the time being. In fact, to be honest,

Lieutenant, I doubt if we'll get anywhere with this investigation. This is out of our league."

Seve was crouched down, staring at the headless body, inch by inch, as a collector might view a specimen. Whatever else happened in his life, Seve knew that he did not want to forget this moment.

Blocker waved the coroner's unit on. "He's all yours now."

"Detective," Seve said, "could I have a moment alone with my brother?"

Blocker pulled at his ear. "Sure." He looked up. "Let's clear out for a moment, boys, huh?"

When he was alone, Seve took a small case from its accustomed place in his hip pocket, unzipped it. Inside was an assortment of tiny metal instruments that he had accumulated over the years—the tools of his trade.

He selected a minuscule tweezers and, reaching out, slipped it into his brother's right side pocket. It had been hidden from anyone standing, but when he had crouched down, Seve had seen a sliver of white. A slip of paper? The tweezers would bring it to him.

In a moment he had it. He stuffed it into his pocket. He was about to put away his kit when he noticed that two fingers on Dom's right hand were bent in an awkward position. He used the end of the tweezers to prod them, saw that they had been broken by a clean, powerful blow.

Then he noticed something else. He peered more closely. From his kit he drew out a small plastic envelope and the kind of brush women use to apply blush. Quickly, he swept bits of debris from Dom's fingertips into the envelope. He pocketed everything, then stood up and went out of the sacristy.

"Detective," he said, "I appreciate everything you've done." He deliberately put his back to the coroner's men doing their work.

"Just my job," Blocker said. "But thanks. No one ever does these days. Thank a cop, I mean."

"I wonder whether you'd allow me to talk to a couple of the priests," Seve said. "I'd like to get their impressions of my brother." He looked at the other cop. "You know . . ."

"Sure," Blocker said. His mind was already on a dinner that was long overdue. "Why not?" He said goodbye to them both, then disappeared around the corner of the church. They saw him driving off with the last of the investigative contingent.

"What was that all about?" Diana asked.

"When in New Canaan, kiss New Canaan butt," Seve said. "As long as, in the end, you get what you want. It's clear that Blocker isn't going to get the job done. You think he cares about Dom? My brother's death has scared him silly. That's why he waited for me to come up from New York. Father Donnelly must have told him Dom had a brother who was a detective lieutenant on the New York City police force."

"Are you crazy? This is Connecticut, boss," Diana said. "You have no jurisdiction."

"Dom makes it my jurisdiction," Seve said. "Anyway, Blocker knows he can use all the help he can get on this one. He's just too big a shit to come out and ask for it."

They found Fr. Donnelly praying before the image of Christ in the sanctuary. They waited patiently until the priest was done.

"Oh." Fr. Donnelly rose, started as he turned around. He looked at the shield Seve held out from him to inspect. "I didn't know there were any more police officers around. I sent the others home."

"That's all right," Seve assured him. He was sure Fr. Donnelly, in his agitated state, did not recognize him. "I'm Dominic Guarda's brother."

"Madonna," Fr. Donnelly breathed. "I'm glad you've come." He was a sallow-skinned man with a naturally dolorous expression. "I am sorry to see you under these circumstances, my son. We all grieve for Father Guarda. He was greatly loved and admired here."

Apparently not by everyone, Seve thought. To the priest he said, "I know. It's been a long day, Father, but I wonder whether you'd mind answering some questions."

Fr. Donnelly nodded. "I will be only too grateful if I can be of some assistance."

"Good," Seve said. "I know that this will be repetitious because Detective Blocker will have asked the same questions. But bear with me. I understand you found my brother."

Fr. Donnelly nodded.

"What happened?"

"Well, Father Guarda always meditates in the sacristy after Mass. But within a half an hour he rejoins us. When he hadn't come out after an hour, I became concerned and went into the sacristy myself."

"And?"

Fr. Donnelly was obviously having a difficult time. Death was hard enough to describe, but this one was devastating. "I saw him—that is, I saw the body."

"How was he lying?"

"I beg your pardon?"

"I mean," Seve said, "was he on his back, his stomach?"

"His right side," Fr. Donnelly said.

So, Seve thought, they hadn't moved Dom until after I saw him. "And what did you do?"

"I went to him, of course," Fr. Donnelly said. And Seve thought, Blocker told me he called the cops immediately. "He was dead. There could be no doubt—" The priest began to choke.

"Go on," Seve said gently, after a time.

Fr. Donnelly nodded, grateful for the respite. "I prayed for him. The Lord's Prayer: 'The Lord is my shepherd, I shall not want.' And the Hail Mary: 'Pray for us now, at the hour of our death.' Then I went to inform the others, the police and the bishop."

"And you did nothing else in the sacristy?"

"No."

"Let's go back a bit," Seve went on. "Tell me, if you would, where you and the other priests were directly after Mass."

"Well, there are no other priests, Detective. You see, in this day and age it's a dying vocation, I'm afraid. So now the Church must employ lay people to do many of the tasks formerly assigned to assistant priests like myself. Here, at Holy Trinity, we have two such lay people, Mr. Dillon and Mr. Reed.

"In any case, to answer your question, I was talking with Mr. Atkinson, one of the parishioners. Fund-raising, you know. Mr. Atkinson often helps us in such ventures. Mr. Dillon was with me. I could see Mr. Reed on the other side of the sanctuary."

"About how long did you talk with Mr. Atkinson, Father?"

"Oh, twenty minutes, at least," Fr. Donnelly said. "There was a great deal to go over."

"I see." Seve was taking notes. "And was Mr. Dillon with you all that time?"

"Yes."

"What about Mr. Reed?"

"He went outside," the priest said. "Out front. One of us always does that after Mass. It was one of Father Guarda's ideas. He felt that some of the parishioners might feel easier about speaking with us outside the church. He was right. As he was in almost everything." There were tears in his eyes.

Seve looked down at his notes for a moment, but he wasn't reading. He said, "Detective Blocker told me that no one saw anyone enter the sacristy while my brother was there."

Fr. Donnelly nodded. "That's right."

"Well, we're standing in the sanctuary now. Are we anywhere near where you and Mr. Dillon were when you were talking with Mr. Atkinson?"

"Just about."

Seve craned his neck. "That's funny," he said, "because I can't see the entrance to the sacristy from here."

Fr. Donnelly looked. "No," he said. "You're right."

"And it's plain that Mr. Reed had no angle at all from the other side of the church. So, anyone could have gone into the sacristy after Mass without being seen."

Fr. Donnelly looked pained. "I'm afraid so."

Seve sighed inwardly. "Did you notice anyone suspicious in the congregation today, Father? A new face, perhaps?"

Fr. Donnelly looked particularly sad. "I'm not very good at faces," he said. "They were Father Guarda's strong suit. He knew everyone by his or her face."

One more try, Seve thought. "Did you see or hear anything out of the ordinary at Mass, Father?"

Fr. Donnelly shook his head. "Not that I can think of." He pursed his lips. "Oh, well, someone put a thousand-dollar bill on the collection plate, but I guess that's not what you meant."

"Not necessarily," Seve said. "Does that kind of contribution happen often here?"

"Oh, yes. This is a wealthy community, and Father Guarda was good at raising funds for the church. But, of course, such gifts are usually rendered by check. I cannot remember another such large cash contribution."

Seve was intrigued. "Who passed around the collection plate, Father?"

"I did."

"Can you remember what this person looked like?"

"Well, he was a man." Fr. Donnelly looked at their faces and said, "That's not a joke. I'm afraid that's about all I can recall. I wasn't paying much attention. And, anyway, I'm—"

"I know," Seve finished for him, "not good with faces."

"The others were busy during Mass and didn't notice him, either. I'm terribly sorry, Detective. I wish I could help you more."

Seve flipped his pad closed. "That's okay, Father." Unfortunately, he thought, this is typical of investigation interviews. If you weren't careful, all the dead ends, the endless paperwork would wear you down before you found the lead that—in Seve's experience, at least—must be there. "You've done your best, I'm sure."

Fr. Donnelly nodded, but his expression said that he was not certain whether he had been of any help at all.

They were almost at the door when the priest called to them. They paused as he hurried toward them. "There is one other thing I remember," he said. "When I was counting the money on the collection plate after Mass, I saw some powder on the thousand-dollar bill."

"What kind of powder?" Seve asked.

"I don't know. That is, I didn't. I wiped it off, showed it to Mr. Dillon later on because I thought it curious. He said it was makeup."

"Makeup?"

Fr. Donnelly nodded. "You know, flesh-colored. Like the kind women wear on their faces."

"You wouldn't, by chance, have kept the powder?" Seve asked.

Fr. Donnelly's face fell. "No," he said. "There was only a trace of it to begin with."

"Nevertheless," Seve said, "I wonder if you would lend me that bill. Perhaps our lab can still pick it up."

While the priest hurried back to the rectory, Diana said, "Face makeup? What are you thinking, that your brother was murdered by a woman?"

"Do you think it's so farfetched?"

"My God, boss, we're talking about decapitation. We're talking some strength."

"How fast can you incapacitate a man?" he asked her.

"A kick in the groin is one thing," she said. "Slicing a head off is another."

He nodded thoughtfully. "Still, it's a mistake to dismiss any possibility before all the facts are in."

Diana took possession of the bill while Seve signed a makeshift receipt he wrote out on a sheet torn from his notepad. "You'll get the thousand back, Father, as soon as my lab crew is done with it. Until then, you have my thanks."

Fr. Donnelly smiled at last. "I'm glad I could help in some

material way. Take care of yourself, Detective. May God walk with you.''

Outside, the street was deserted. The arc lights in the church's parking lot turned the surrounding trees a violet blue. In the car Seve took out the plastic envelope. ''When we get back to the city, give this to the lab, along with the bill. Top priority.''

''What's in there?'' Diana asked, turning on the engine.

''Who knows?'' Seve said. ''Maybe nothing. Maybe a clue as to who killed my brother.''

Diana put the car in gear, and they set off. ''How about some dinner?'' she said. ''I don't think I can last until we get to the city.''

''I know a place near here,'' Seve said, pointing to where she should turn. ''Dom used to take me there when I came up to see him.'' He turned on the interior light. He was looking at the Peter Loong Chun incident report he had written on the way up here, but nothing seemed to make sense. It was as if he held some alien artifact in his hands. All the while thinking, Dom, Dom, who could have done this to you? And, I can't tell Ma, the shock'll kill her. But I can't hide it from her, either.

''I'll drop the evidence at the lab,'' Diana was saying, ''then I'll take you to see Elena Hu.''

Seve nodded, pressed his eyes with the pads of his fingers. I must be getting old, he thought. Eight-thirty at night, and I'm already tired. What time did I come on duty this morning? It was then that he realized that he had been working the Chung stakeout since nine last night. Oh, Christ, he thought, no wonder no one wants a part of me. There isn't anything left to take.

''You look dead on your feet,'' Diana said. ''You need a mommy to tuck you into bed, not a driver to spin you all over the East Coast.''

They both heard the siren at the same time.

Seve looked at the flashing red lights in the rearview mirror. ''It can't be for speeding,'' he said. ''Not with our police plates.''

Diana slowed as the dark blue-and-white cop car came abreast of them.

''Lieutenant Guarda?'' A uniformed sergeant leaned out the window. ''NYPD?''

''That's right.''

''Would you follow us, sir.'' It was not phrased as a question.

''What the hell for?'' Seve asked, annoyed. ''We've got a schedule to keep in the city.''

''Detective Blocker would like to see you.'' The sergeant gestured ahead like Ward Bond on "Wagon Train," and, siren wailing, the cop car sped off into the night.

"And a hearty 'Heigh-Ho, Silver' to you, too," Seve said as Diana stepped on the gas.

If Milhaud was certain of one thing about M. LoGrazie, it was that he could not trust him. And so, he felt comfortable with him. There was nothing like certainty, Milhaud thought, to put one at one's ease. One knew immediately where one stood, and what measures one must take in the course of the relationship.

That was why he had had the foresight to have a listening device planted in M. LoGrazie's residence. Not that the place wasn't swept every day for such electronic bugs, but the maid was in Milhaud's employ, and she had the good sense to remove his bug before the sweep and replace it afterward.

Milhaud opened the wood-paneled door into his armoire, the closet. It was a small back room perhaps, in days past, part of the servants' quarters. It was now bristling with an impressive array of electronic equipment, not the least of which was a six-foot bank of huge-reeled tape machines. At the moment only one was running. Sitting in front of it was a small, sallow-faced man. His earphones made his face look pinched. He saw Milhaud, indicated the machine connected to Mr. LoGrazie's apartment.

Milhaud sat down, put on a pair of headphones. Then he ran the tape back until he heard a tone, indicating the start of the last conversation. He set the machine to Play.

"Well, I must say, I really did not expect to find you here," Mr. LoGrazie said in Milhaud's ear. He possessed the directness of mind typical of Americans. Milhaud viewed this trait much as he would the skill of a New Guinean tribesman, with a combination of admiration and condescension.

"I'm like a spinning penny, I suppose," said an unfamiliar voice. "Heads or tails, it doesn't really matter. Sooner or later I'm going to land. The Old Man knows that. He just took advantage of the knowledge." Old Man, Milhaud had learned, was the term these people used to describe the Mafia's *capo di capi*, its head.

"I hear you were put in something of a bind," Mr. LoGrazie said.

"Yeah, you could definitely say that." The unknown man laughed. "It was fucking uncomfortable, if you want to know the truth. The Old Man really knows how to shrivel your nuts. But, as you can see, everything's turned out all right. Maybe 'cause I'm in the company of angels.'' He laughed again.

''From my point of view,'' Mr. LoGrazie said, ''I'm damn glad you're here. It's an honor working with a legend. Besides, what with all the recent public scrutiny, it's good to know that the Old Man is still gung ho on White Tiger.''

''Never more so,'' the unknown man said.

''Well, you can't blame me for being jittery. What with the squeeze being applied across the board.''

''All the more reason that White Tiger be pushed. The Old Man feels that this operation is the only hope now. The old network out of Hong Kong, which, in any case, is inadequate to our current needs, has become compromised. I don't know precisely how, but I suspect someone along the line has been gotten to by the DEA.'' Milhaud knew he was referring to the American federal unit, the Drug Enforcement Agency. ''As of now, we're shutting down that network. Which means we need to accelerate White Tiger's timetable. Already our street dealers are complaining. We're running out of dope. So we're in a squeeze. That's why the operation has such a short fuse. The Old Man wants me to stress that we cannot afford to let it fail.''

''Full access to Terry Haye's network is one matter; setting it running to our satisfaction is quite another,'' Mr. LoGrazie said. ''There are bound to be fuck-ups. Besides which, everyone experiences difficulty in Southeast Asia. Who can understand those people?''

''Leave Southeast Asia to me. In many ways I know it better than I do my own country. It's one sinkhole of bullshit. You take a step, you're in so deep you need a compass to tell you which way is up.''

Mr. LoGrazie laughed.

''White Tiger means control,'' the unknown man said. ''Control, in this case, means funds—unlimited funds. We will all get what we want, namely our absolute independence, freedom from all unthinking interference.''

''Speaking of control,'' Mr. LoGrazie said. ''What do you want me to do with Milhaud now?''

''Well, first, I have to congratulate you on getting him to ice Terry Haye. Haye had become a real problem. Well, shit, that bastard was always a problem. The Old Man told me it was your idea to get Milhaud to do the hit. No fuss, no muss. That was good, Frank. Very good.''

''You knew Haye in the old days, didn't you?''

"Yeah. We were close, you could say, in 'Nam."

"But something happened, didn't it? I heard Haye fucked you out of—"

"Much as I'd like to stroll down memory lane with you," the unknown man interrupted, "I've got other things on my mind. Such as Milhaud. As far as he's concerned, everything's status quo. We're not gonna cut him out when the time comes. He'll be as useful to us as Terry Haye was destructive."

"I should string him along?"

"In a way. The situation has changed considerably within the last several days," the unknown man said. "DeCordia's been iced."

"That's bad." Al DeCordia, Mr. LoGrazie knew, was one of their key people developing White Tiger through his contacts in high-level international slush funds. He had full access to the entire White Tiger personnel files.

"It gets worse," the unknown man said. "He was decapitated."

"Decap—"

"Read my lips, Frank. The man's head was separated from his torso. Now that means one thing to me: Terry Haye. When Terry Haye was in 'Nam, he commanded a unit assigned to cause havoc among the North Vietnamese. SLAM, they called it.

"Haye came up with the idea of decapitating the SLAM victims. He was smart; it terrified Charlie, because in their minds it interfered with *samsara*, with the soul's endless journey on the wheel of life. Anyway, something snapped in DeCordia after his daughter died last year. Naturally, he had heard of Terry; he had been in Europe quite a lot, setting his contacts in place.

"See, Frank, DeCordia wanted out. I've traced his recent movements. A month ago the poor baby showed up at Terry Haye's place in Nice. He must have given Haye enough to get him moving against us. You can bet that Haye was not happy about the idea of us cutting into his action in the Shan. But something must have gone sour, and Haye had DeCordia iced in his own hometown, no less. New Canaan, Connecticut. That kind of thing is bad for business. It puts our street dealers on edge."

"When was DeCordia killed?"

"Tuesday."

"That was after Terry Haye was killed." Mr. LoGrazie laughed. "What did he do, return from the dead?"

"Ain't no laughing matter," the unknown man cautioned. "The probability is that against explicit orders, Haye let his girlfriend,

Soutane Sirik, in on what he was up to. Logic tells us that she is implicated in the murder. I want her taken care of, pronto."

"Shall I use Milhaud?"

"I—" Here, the unknown man's voice became unintelligible. The conversation continued, and Milhaud strained to make it out. In a moment the sounds of someone else in the room. Milhaud ran the tape back, replayed it several times until he had the volume all the way up and the tape hiss was a blizzard of sound in his ears.

"Merde!" Milhaud wondered what was missing from the tape. With each pass his sense of frustration increased. The voices were there, but he could not make out what was being said. He scribbled a note on the technician's pad to see if that bit could be artificially amplified.

He watched the reels of the tape machine stop spinning. Now he had an explanation for M. LoGrazie's order to murder Soutane. But, on the other hand, Milhaud was certain that the unknown man was lying about her involvement in the murder of Al DeCordia. Soutane killing a man at Terry Haye's behest? It was absurd. What kind of game was the unknown man playing?

He wrote down on another pad what he knew of the other voice. By his accent Milhaud had pegged him as an American. It was clear that he was an expert on Indochina. In that event it was likely that Milhaud would know him or, at the very least, know of him. LoGrazie had called him a legend. A Mafia legend, expert in Southeast Asia? Milhaud racked his brain. Who could he be?

Milhaud did not know. Perhaps when the technician isolated the voice of the other man, and Milhaud heard what he had said, it would provide a clue. But that, Milhaud knew, could take too long. Certainly, it seemed imperative now to learn this man's identity. He'd better put camera surveillance on M. LoGrazie's residence. A long lens would at least give him a face to put with the voice.

That decided, Milhaud took off the earphones, stared into empty space. He felt with increasing urgency that a vise of the unknown man's making was closing in around him.

He picked up the phone and, in a moment, Dante appeared. "I want to know," Milhaud told the Vietnamese, "whether Mademoiselle Sirik knew a man named Al DeCordia. He was an American, recently murdered in the States, in a town called New Canaan, Connecticut. He was part of the Mafia's White Tiger team. Also, find out what you can about his daughter. And while you're at it, see if anyone knows who killed him."

Dante nodded, and left Milhaud alone with the slowly revolving reels of tape.

Alix Layne took her time swallowing the bite of pizza. She regarded Chris coldly. "Why are you here, counselor? Is it to press charges against me for slander and defamation of character on behalf of your client?"

Chris winced. Those were almost exactly his words to her on the courthouse steps earlier today. "I deserved that."

"You most certainly did." Alix stood in the doorway in much the attitude with which a mother bear defends her den; her expression was wary, her stance aggressive.

Chris was abruptly overcome by a wave of fatigue. He closed his eyes as he leaned against the doorframe. "If you won't let me in," he said, "do you think I could have a glass of water?"

"Oh, Christ," Alix said. "Come in."

Shadows in the long, narrow hallway; a pair of racing bicycles were hung on the wall like some kind of modern sculpture. Chris heard the door close behind him, the sound of double locks being thrown.

She led him past the kitchen, into the living room. It was not at all as he remembered it from the party. It seemed larger somehow, and airier. Perhaps that was because there wasn't the forest of people to contend with, or perhaps she had redecorated since then. He sat down heavily on a functional Conran's couch covered in a warm tropical print.

"You look like you could use something a bit stronger than water," Alix observed. "What can I get you, counselor?"

"Vodka. A vodka on the rocks would be nice," he said. He turned to follow her as she went to the oak sideboard behind him. "I'd consider it a great personal favor if you would call me Chris."

"I don't recall owing you any favors," she said, pouring him the drink. Chris wondered what he was doing here; he wondered if Bram Stryker was lurking somewhere about the apartment.

She came around the couch, handed him the vodka. He gulped at his drink and sat back on the sofa. "Won't you sit down?" he said, as if this were not her own apartment.

"Mom?"

They both turned. A tousle-haired boy with the all-out-of-proportion face of the early teens loped into the room from the kitchen. He had a half-eaten slice of pizza in one hand, a can of Cherry Coke in the other. "You coming back?"

Alix smiled, and it made all the difference in her face. That Pre-Raphaelite face. It was like seeing her for the first time. He recalled his reaction, catching a glimpse of her in court, how his heart had beat faster. How strikingly beautiful she was. Perhaps it was because she was out of her professional milieu. She did not have that perfect American face one saw in magazines and on TV. Her mouth was rather too wide, the sprinkling of freckles across the bridge of her nose and her cheeks was a bit too thick, and her nose was slightly crooked. But these were not flaws. They made Alix a beautiful woman in a visceral way, rather than in the one-dimensional manner of the model. Hers, he saw now, was a face to stir the blood.

"In a little while," she said. "Darling, this is Christopher Haye. Christopher, this is my son, Dan."

Chris got up, stuck out his hand. "Hi." Then he realized that both the boy's hands were full, and he let his drop.

Dan took a swig of soda. "Hey," he said, "are you the lawyer? *The* Christopher Haye?"

"If you put it that way," Chris said, "I guess I am."

The boy's face broke into a smile. "Hey, awesome. I did a paper on a couple of your cases last semester. I got Mom to help me on it. It's nice to meet you."

"Thanks," Chris said.

When Dan had returned to the kitchen, Chris said, "Well, I made a hit with him. I didn't know that you were married."

"I'm not," Alix said, "anymore."

"Joint custody?"

"Used to be." She had a very direct way of looking at you, he found. She tapped the crooked bridge of her nose. "Then, one day, his father hit me so hard, he broke my nose. That was when I decided to take an extensive self-defense course. I went back to court and got full custody of my son. My husband can't come near me or Danny now."

"That must be hard. A boy needs his father."

They stood in the middle of the living room. Rock music came from the kitchen as Dan put on MTV.

Chris looked around at the bright curtains cleverly covering the windows dim with ubiquitous New York grime, the cases filled with books, the bleached-driftwood-and-glass coffee table, the dhurrie on the floor, the old, scarred upright piano in one corner with its brass floor lamp. A photograph, faded with age, hung above it of a clapboard country house and its attendant oak tree. A small girl in pigtails—the young Alix, perhaps—sat in a swing set within the oak's branches, staring into the camera with an expression far too serious for a child her age. Behind her, in shadow, was the silhouette of a tall, slim man, standing as ramrod straight as a soldier. "This is a one-bedroom, isn't it?"

Alex nodded. "The bedroom belongs to Dan." She pointed. "You've been sitting on my bed."

"I see the city's still not paying its employees."

She bridled a bit. "I like it here. So does Danny. I'm sure it's tiny compared to your apartment, but it's home."

"It's nice," Chris said, sitting down again. "I like it. I didn't before."

"You were here before?" Alix sat on a chair upholstered in a fabric that coordinated with the sofa's tropical print. "When?"

"Remember your housewarming? I came with Bram Stryker."

"You're a friend of Bram's?"

"We shoot the breeze sometimes," Chris said.

"He handled my divorce. He got me back full custody of Danny when that bastard broke my nose."

"Umm."

"What does that mean?"

Chris put down his drink. He hadn't eaten since his meal with Marcus Gable, and the vodka was taking effect. "It means umm. Nothing." He had to stand up, walk around the room. His stomach was rumbling, and he had an intimation that he was about to say or do something he might regret. "So," he said, "are you and old Bram still hitting the hay?"

Alix jumped up. "You've got a hell of a nerve."

He turned to watch her face. "Yes, well, my father told me the same thing when I discovered he was cheating on my mother." He smiled. He felt like a vessel out of sight of land, devoid of ties, adrift, free. "I told him that she was my mother; that made it my business. I slapped him across the face. Did I mention that my father is Welsh? The Welsh have a saying, 'Let all the blood be in front of you,' which means, my father explained, always face the enemy.

"Well, anyway, six months later he divorced my mother, and within a year she was dead. So, you see, my slapping him had no effect whatsoever. He remarried quite soon afterward. Well, he remarried twice, really. He's on this third now."

"I'm not your mother," Alix said. "What makes this your business?"

Now Chris knew what he was going to say and do that he might regret. "Just this." He came around from behind the sofa, took Alix in his arms, and kissed her hard on the mouth.

She pulled her head away. Her gray eyes watched him. "If you think I'm going to like that," she said, "you're wrong."

"Am I?"

"Don't look so damned smug. Women only melt in the movies. And then it's only when the hero takes them in his arms." Her eyes gazed at him steadily. "You're no hero."

"Not yet, anyway," he said, and kissed her again.

"I was right the first time," she said. "You *do* have a hell of a nerve."

"Well, you were right about one thing. I haven't even thought of taking on a *pro bono* case in a year and a half."

"Umm."

"What do you mean, umm?"

She smiled. "Just that. Nothing."

"You were right about something else as well," Chris said. "I think, now, that Marcus Gable killed his wife."

"Forget it," Alix said. "It's water under the bridge."

"What do you mean, forget it? I'd like nothing better than to nail him."

Alix laughed. "My God, you sound like a spurned lover. So he lied to you. So what? He lied to just about everyone else. What makes you special?"

"I was his attorney."

"Judging by your reputation, it seems to me that was a particularly good reason for him to withhold the truth from you."

Chris looked at her.

"Well, whatever other kind of bastard he might be, Bram is certainly loyal," she said. "He thinks the world of you."

"I always thought he was too busy to notice," Chris said.

"With his female clients, you mean." Alix nodded. "I discovered a while ago that I was one in a long and unending line."

"What did you do?"

She smiled. "I never did care for crowds. But, at my urging, we're still friends. That was a first, too, according to Bram."

"What else was a first?"

She laughed. "If Danny wasn't here, I'd show you." And, putting her hands at the nape of his neck, she drew his head down again. Her lips softened, opened. He felt her tongue probing, he felt her heat against him.

Unbidden, rising like a phoenix from the ashes, a memory of Terry home on leave in his army uniform. Terry, the returning hero, whom everyone despised because he was in 'Nam, where, everyone knew, America should not be. Terry being congratulated by their father, who, remembering Suez, India, and the other global disasters that ultimately crushed the British Empire, appreciated the American military presence in Southeast Asia. Watching him with tears in his eyes as he poured a drink for Terry and then, wrapping his arms around him as he had never done to Chris, kissing his favorite son on both cheeks.

And Chris, looking helplessly on, just returned from his self-imposed exile in France, limping on a damaged leg, all dreams of wearing the yellow jersey into Paris, riding on a wave of emotion too wild to support, destroyed in a moment in the rain, an outsider in his own family.

The Tour de France was a memory he'd just as soon forget. And what else had he from his exile, but in the interstices of his training, bashing at his old portable typewriter, trying to draft the novel, to be the writer he had always longed to be, coming home with a limp and an utterly hopeless manuscript?

Whatever else had occurred in that summer of the Tour de France was surrounded by memories of places and people much too painful to bring into focus anymore. He had spent many years trying to forget, wanting to forget, and finally, succeeding.

You're no hero, Alix had said. Chris thought, She doesn't know the half of it.

Soutane did not know what to do, so she went back to Mun. Her cousin made her feel safe, as Terry had for most of the time she had known him. But she had also been physically involved with Terry and, because of what Mun had taught her, she was aware of how much that form of love could color one's judgment.

Mun lived in a thirteenth-century villa in Vence. It had been a crumbling shambles when he and Soutane had first come upon it years ago, a mere shell of what had once been the magnificent residence of the most powerful bishop of Vence.

She had thought her cousin mad to buy what she saw as a rough pile of stones and mortar. But Mun had seen something else. "I have been witness to so much destruction," he told her as he supervised a small army of workmen he had hired to restore the villa, "that it is important to me that I restore something to lasting beauty."

Slowly, lovingly, Mun had overseen the rebuilding of the Roman stone outer wall. In Tarascon, to the west, he discovered a set of carved wooden gates, depicting the coronation of the Virgin, which he had transported to Vence.

He had the terra-cotta tiles of the shallow Roman-style roof replaced and, within the eaves, the glazed tiles of the *genoise* cleaned by hand.

There was a stand of cypresses to the north of the villa, which protected the building from the direct wrath of the mistral. To the south, white-barked plane trees rose like gnarled, arthritic hands, provided shade in summer, while, farther down the rock-strewn slope on which the villa was set, a copse of ancient lotus trees ensured absolute privacy.

Most people thought Mun and Soutane looked alike. The cousin was a bit taller, his shoulders broader, but every bit as square as Soutane's. The main difference was that Mun's face had a more weathered appearance, as if he had truly become a Provençal farmer.

"You do not look at all well," Mun said. They were sitting in the courtyard around which the U-shaped villa was set. It was filled with pink blossoming almond trees, mimosa, wild roses. The unmistakable scents of wild thyme and marjoram were in the air. Ivy wound like a maypole around a stone fountain carved in the shape of a pair of leaping dolphins, out of whose mouths water clattered onto clear azure tiles.

Sunlight, breaking now and then through slate clouds, fired the treetops as it struck the hillsides of La Gaude, the pre-Alps, rising above the villa.

"I want to know," Soutane said, "what Terry was mixed up in."

Bowls had been laid out on a mosaic table, filled with strawberries from Carpentras, black olives from Nyons, and *calissons*, almond candy, from Aix.

Mun smiled, reminding her of images of Buddha throughout Southeast Asia. He spread his hands helplessly. "Why do you ask me such a question?"

"Do you mean you don't have an answer? Terry often came to you for advice. Did he come for help as well?"

"Help, no," Mun said. "It seems odd to me to remind you that he was a very independent man. He did not like owing anyone anything.''

''You were always adept at answering questions this way,'' she said. ''But I am family. Clever evasions won't satisfy me.''

''Terry's dead,'' Mun said. ''Spirits must have their rest, too.'' By which, she knew, he meant leave it alone.

''I must know, Mun. I *need* to know.''

''He died in a church,'' Mun said. ''I wonder whether that was a terrible thing for him.''

Soutane closed her eyes, and it seemed to her that her mind shuddered. ''Terry may have been killed, but my love for him remains. There is much more, isn't there, that remains.''

Mun was watching her with that Buddha look of his. ''Enlighten me, then.''

Soutane took a deep breath, told him she had found that someone had been searching her apartment when she had returned home that night, how she had seen someone watching the apartment from the street below.

She was curious, as she spoke, at the change that came over her cousin. He no longer looked half asleep, calmly detached from the recent events in her life. He sat on the edge of his seat, alert and stiff as a sentinel.

''You are certain nothing besides your undergarment was taken?'' Mun said after she had finished. ''*Absolutely* certain?''

''Yes. Besides, why else would I still be under surveillance? If he had found what he was looking for, he'd have no more use for me.''

Mun relaxed noticeably, and Soutane said, ''Then you know what he was looking for.''

''No,'' Mun said, but she was not sure she believed him. What was he keeping from her? Soutane had come here to be reassured but, instead, she was becoming more frightened by the moment.

Soutane was staring at her cousin. She decided that, even if he would not confide in her, she must trust in him. She handed over the postcard that Terry had written to Chris, just before his death.

She tried to decipher Mun's expression while he read it. ''Will you please tell me what is happening?''

He looked up. ''Why have you given this to me?'' Blank-faced.

''Stop it!'' she cried. She snatched the postcard from his fingers. It was maddening, this blank wall he was presenting to her. ''I know you think you're protecting me,'' she said.

''Only from yourself.''

"No!" Soutane said it sharply. This was what she had been afraid of. "I won't have you bringing that up! I've warned you about it."

Mun said nothing. He had not moved all this time. The golden light, stealing down from the high slopes, washed the courtyard, extending serpentine shadows along the stone pathways, into the tiled recesses of the villa.

"Still it must come," Mun said at last. "Always it must come."

"I forbid it!" Soutane cried.

"You said it yourself." Mun held his hands in his lap as if he could catch the last of the light. "You come here and beg me to tell you secrets, yet you forbid the ramifications of those secrets. No one lives in a vacuum, Soutane. You must acknowledge that which you are." Mun's voice echoed amid the almond trees, the mimosa, the wild roses.

"What I have become, you mean." Soutane focused on the stony hillside, cool with groves of olive trees. In the space of an instant she had changed. Now there was a granitic core forming beneath her skin, but there was calmness, as well, that was just as striking. "It was you who trained me."

"Those were evil times," Mun reflected. "I did it to protect you from my enemies. Unwittingly, I made you into something you obviously could not live with."

She was quiet for some time, watching the sunlight creep across the ancient stonework. At last she said, "Did you think that I would try to kill myself again, after Terry died?"

"I admit the thought crossed my mind."

"I see," she said. "Well, it was only grief I felt, not self-hatred. I hadn't killed anyone this time."

"You killed my best friend to save me," Mun said. "How can you hate yourself for that?"

"I killed, period," she said. "I have the power. You can't understand it because it was you who gave me that power."

"Both of us have it," Mun said. "Do you think it matters that your father was French? We are family. We are all we have. All that matters."

She cocked her head to one side. "And Terry changed all that, didn't he?"

"I loved Terry," Mun said, watching the water play against the fountain. "We were closer than brothers."

"Because you killed together—you killed *for* each other."

"That was a long time ago."

She nodded. "But hardly forgotten."

"Even the dead, Soutane, cannot forget."

"Ah, damn you." Her voice was just a whisper. Her eyes were wet with tears as she accepted the truth.

Mun took her hands in his, gently stroked the palms as he had done when, as a child, she had been ill or afraid. Soutane could see through the cypress trees a farmer silhouetted by the light. How uncomplicated life must be for him, she thought. He worked, he ate, slept, loved, and worked again. She longed now for that kind of rough simplicity.

"What about that postcard Terry wrote to his brother?"

"It's odd," Mun admitted, "particularly since the two were apparently estranged. Why contact him now? And then there is the unwritten postscript. What did Terry mean to write?"

"Perhaps we'll find out," Soutane said. "I called Chris. I'm to meet him at the Nice airport when he flies in tomorrow to pick up Terry's body."

"Considering your history with him, do you really think that's wise?"

"It doesn't matter," she said. "I don't have a choice. You trained me too well."

"You've been busy," Mun said, "without me."

"It may be nothing. Chris said that he had received nothing from Terry recently."

"So he says. In any event I think it would be a good idea if you brought him here so that I can speak with him."

"Interrogate him, you mean."

"I will not be here when you bring him. Stay, make him comfortable. Wait for me." He caught her eyes in his steady gaze. "Is that clear?"

She nodded. "There is still the man who is following me."

"Yes." Mun had that Buddha look again.

"I don't know what I can do now," she said.

Mun regarded her. "You know precisely what you must do. You knew it from the moment you saw the man watching you from the shadows. You must let him find you."

"No," Soutane said emphatically. "You know where that can lead."

Mun's eyes pierced her, making her shiver. "You brought your suspicions here," he said. "You have already made your choice." He continued to watch her. "You must see that none of this would have happened but for your love for Terry. You cannot renege. You must find out why this man is following you."

The scents of wild thyme and marjoram were stronger now, almost cloying.

"What will I have to do?" Soutane asked with despair.

"Nothing that you are not well equipped to do," Mun assured her.

"I will not kill again!" But she was thinking, It's happening all over again, just like some awful nightmare. Worse, she knew that it was a nightmare from which she could not awake.

"Think of Terry." Mun's eyes were closed. "Think, if you must, of Chris."

The dolphins spewed their sparkling water onto the azure tiles.

They had set up a field of arc lights under the elms because there was no other illumination near the ditch that ran obliquely through the fields. Detective Blocker's face was shiny with sweat. His skin looked like parchment about to peel.

"Goddammit!" he was saying as Seve and Diana came into the field of arc lights. "Goddammit!" The buzz of the portable generator drowned out the drone of the cicadas.

He looked up at the pair's approach. "Will you look at this now?" he said, pointing at his feet. "Will you just look at this?"

One of his men drew the tarp back. A man lay crumpled, belly down in the ditch. The remarkable thing was that his head lay six inches away from the stump of the neck.

"Another one!" Blocker exclaimed with some outrage. "Killed the same way."

"Who found the body?" Diana asked.

"A couple of kids out here to neck. We got their statements and released them. They were shitfaced with fear."

"Have you made an ID yet?" Diana asked. Seve was already sliding down the short embankment. There was blood all over the place but, unlike in the sacristy, here it had seeped into the earth.

"Man's name is DeCordia, Al DeCordia," Blocker said, turning an expensive alligator-skin wallet over. "That's according to the stuff in here—driver's license, credit cards, Blue Cross—Jesus, he won't need that now."

Seve was looking at the neck, noting the same crenellated pattern in the flesh that he had seen in Dom's, as if his brother and this man had been killed by getting caught in the same bear trap. But, of course, that wasn't possible.

"This guy's local," Blocker continued. "Here, look at this." He handed DeCordia's business card to Diana. There was a handwritten note on the back, a reminder DeCordia had obviously written to himself. "Lives down at the end of Lost District Drive, very tony along there, houses go for multiple millions. We haven't had time to notify the family, so, of course, nobody's given us a positive ID yet." Diana was busy taking notes. "Lot of money still in the wallet—over five thousand—so we can eliminate robbery as a motive."

Seve had turned his attention to the fingers. None of them was broken, and there was no trace of powder or any other debris.

"Anyone touch the body?" he asked.

"Photo boys aren't even here yet." Blocker sighed. It looked as if he was never going to eat dinner tonight. "This really sucks," he said to no one in particular.

"If you wouldn't mind," Seve said, climbing out of the ditch, "I'd like you to send me copies of the coroner's report on this one, too."

"Sure," Blocker said wearily, "why not? It's just more paper to push around. I've got the time, haven't I? Don't I look like I've got the time?"

"Thanks, Detective," Seve said as he steered Diana back to their car. "I appreciate it."

He didn't say another word until they were on the highway, heading south. "Whoever killed this guy, DeCordia, also killed Dom. Same MO, same odd markings on the flesh." He closed his eyes. The endless stream of oncoming headlights was giving him a headache. "What the hell could have been used to decapitate them?" He sighed. "Did we have dinner, or did I dream that?"

"You dreamed it, boss."

"Then stop at the next place you see."

It was a diner whose outside was made of fake fieldstone, and whose inside was made of fake marble. The hamburger, french fries, coffee, and cherry cheesecake might have been fake as well, because they felt like they were going to dissolve his stomach on their way to his bowels. He made a mental note to start eating more healthfully, knowing full well he wouldn't.

Back in the car, he popped some Maalox and said, "I want you to stay on Blocker's tail about this. I've got a feeling that the coroner's reports are going to tell us a lot I can only guess at now."

"Do you think this Al DeCordia is tied in with your brother?"

"Maybe. They were killed by the same man, in the same town, though not necessarily at the same time," Steve said. "On the other hand, we could be dealing with a serial madman, which is what has Blocker scared shitless. And he has good reason to be. This guy, DeCordia, has been lying in the ditch a couple of days, at least, so what the connection with Dom might be, if there is any, I have no idea."

The word "connection" set off a bell in his mind and, turning on the car's interior light, he pulled out the crumpled slip of paper.

"I extracted this from the crime scene," he told Diana as he opened it up. "It was in Dom's right pocket. He was lying on that side, and it was hidden from view."

"Not from you," she said. She began to overtake a semi. "I thought you told us not to muck around at the crime scene until the forensic people were through."

"That was before I met Detective Blocker."

It was meant as a joke, but neither of them laughed. Diana was absolutely loyal to Seve. She had, over the years they had worked togehter, put her life on the line for him. She would not hesitate to do so again. And it was precisely because of this loyalty—because she loved and believed in him, in what he stood for, absolutely—that she wondered privately about what had come over him. It seemed to her as if his brother's death had transformed him. He wanted—no, it was far stronger than that, she decided—he *needed* to find his brother's killer.

Sitting next to him, hurtling down the Connecticut turnpike in the dead of night, Diana wondered whether this need would create in him an obsession. Seve had always been a man of the people. The needs of society always came before his own. Now, she suspected, that had begun to change. Not that she could not understand the imperative he must feel. But what if that imperative caused him to abandon his ideals? She had already seen him lie to a fellow officer, cadge evidence from a crime scene out of his jurisdiction, and then withhold that evidence from the officer in charge. Diana had never thought that he was capable of even one of those breaches of procedure.

Beside her, Seve was staring down at the crumpled slip of paper. It contained three lines written in an unknown but odd, backward slanting hand and, below it, one word written in his brother Dom's easily identifiable, cramped writing. This is what Seve read:

Soutane Sirik
67, Boulevard Victor Hugo
Nice, France

Saved?

Chris and Alix, constrained by the presence of the teenage boy in the kitchen, sat on the fire escape outside the wide-open bedroom window. Rock music insinuated itself through the apartment, out into the soft space between them.

"For a long time," Alix said, "I thought of myself as Danny's mother. When you're a woman, it's sometimes difficult to separate your existence from your child's life. At the very least the child takes over your life to such an extent that there just isn't much left over."

There was still some rain and, though, for the most part, they were protected by the building's overhang, here and there drops, like a tiara of diamonds, glistened in her hair. "But, after a time, I came to understand that whatever pleasure he provided—and it was considerable—wasn't going to be enough for me. I was beginning to lose myself in him, which I thought wasn't going to be good for either of us."

"So you joined the DA's office," Chris said.

She smiled. "It wasn't that easy. I had to separate myself from him. There was the bar exam." Her smile faded. "And then my marriage was disintegrating in a slow and painful fashion."

"I'm sorry."

That same smile again, so small yet so transforming. "I never know whether to say 'don't be' or 'thank you.' I suppose I want to say both. It's worked out for the best."

She cocked her head as a song familiar to her drifted through the house. For a moment she sang along in a tentative voice, and it seemed as if all tension drained out of her. She stopped singing. Her eyes were bright, glittery. "And what about you?" she said. "You look more like an athlete than a lawyer."

He laughed at the precision of her eye. Somewhat to his surprise he found that her assessment pleased him. "I used to be an athlete," he said. "A bicycle racer."

"No kidding." She raised her eyebrows. "I love biking. Danny and I ride as often as we can."

"I noticed the bikes in the hallway," Chris said. "They're good ones."

"Where did you race?"

"Oh, just about everywhere," Chris said, looking out into the night. "Mainly, though, I was training for the Tour de France."

"Your family must have been very proud of you," Alix said.

That surprised him. Most people would have asked, Did you win? "No," he said, "they didn't seem to care much one way or the other."

"How awful."

Yes, Chris thought. Awful, indeed. He sighed. "I suppose," he said, "that all I was looking for was a 'well done' from my father. My mother was dead by the time I raced in France. But all my father cared about was my older brother, Terry. Terry, you see, had enlisted in the army and, while I was in France, riding, he was in Vietnam, defending America, justice, and freedom. Everything my father holds dear. I was the runaway, the coward, the ingrate who would not serve the country that had nurtured him." Even now, after so many years, he could not tell anyone what had really happened during the summer. "At least, that's how my father saw it."

"A hawk."

"Superhawk, more like it," Chris said.

"And what happened when you raced the Tour de France?" Alix asked.

"I got hurt." His standard answer, when he chose to give one at all. It was not the truth, either—at least, not the whole truth.

"Badly?"

Yes, he thought. Very badly. He had meant to answer her, but when he spoke, he said, "I'm leaving for France tomorrow night. My brother has been killed."

"Oh, Christopher, I'm so sorry," Alix said.

Christopher, he thought. That's what my father calls me. He saw the concern on Alix's face. I wonder, he thought, if I'm as sorry as she is about Terry? "I don't seem able to feel much of anything one way or another," he said.

"You and your brother weren't close?"

Chris gave a sardonic laugh. "You could say that. We hadn't had any contact for ten years or more. Now I don't know that we knew one another at all."

Alix moved closer to him. "How sad."

He felt her near him, and was stirred. Not in a sexual way but, rather, because when he was next to her he did not feel that black abyss that the news of Terry's death had engendered in him; he did not feel alone.

"For years I blamed my father for that," Chris said. "He was fond of pitting us against each other; he believed that conflict built character. My father is big on character. He comes from stern Welsh stock. 'The Hayes are fighters,' he'd say.

"Well, in those days, when we were young, I suppose my father was the most convenient target. He was strict, often harsh with us. The first kind word I ever heard him speak to either of us was when Terry came home from 'Nam after his first tour of duty. But Terry's death has set me to thinking. If Terry and I never got to know one another, whose fault was it, really? I'm not sure that we, ourselves, ever tried to find out."

"You were right," Dante said. "There was a link between Soutane Sirik and Al DeCordia." Milhaud's heart sank. Could he have been wrong about the unknown man? Had he been telling M. LoGrazie the truth about Soutane and Al DeCordia?

"Apparently," Dante went on, "DeCordia met her when he was over here a month ago visiting Terry Haye. DeCordia's daughter had just died. Her car went out of control in the rain. She was nineteen."

Dante was consulting his notebook. "Anyway, DeCordia formed an attachment to the Sirik girl. Her parents are dead, and she must have seen him as a father figure. DeCordia, it seems, was like that—a people person. The death of his daughter really broke him up."

With his heart in his mouth Milhaud said, "Did Mademoiselle Sirik kill him?"

"Not a chance," Dante said. "She was here in France when DeCordia got hit."

Relief flooded through Milhaud with such intensity that he felt his eyes beginning to overflow with tears. He quickly swiveled away from Dante, staring out the window at the École Militaire and the Parc du Champ de Mars. Thank God, he sighed inwardly. Now I can get on with finding out what the unknown man is really up to.

"Do you know who killed DeCordia?"

"No," Dante said. "I couldn't find out anything about that except that he was beheaded, which is an odd way to go."

Odd is right, Milhaud thought. Odd, too, that the unknown man on the tape would know so much about Terry Haye's Vietnam SLAM unit, more even than he did. Milhaud had not known about the decapitation idea that Terry Haye had come up with in Vietnam. Now someone had used it again to kill Al DeCordia. Why?

But immediately Milhaud realized that was not the primary question. First he had to ask himself why DeCordia had been killed. Since Soutane thought of him as a father figure, it was inconceivable that Terry had had anything to do with murdering him, as the unknown man had suggested.

On the other hand, DeCordia and Terry Haye *had* met a month ago. What did they discuss? They were ostensibly enemies. White Lion, which Al DeCordia was a part of, was set up to cut Terry Haye out of his network. Did DeCordia want out of White Lion, as the unknown man had suggested on the tape? Had he shopped the operation to Haye, the opposition? If so, it was more than likely that the Mafia itself was responsible for DeCordia's death. But if so, then the unknown man, who was a representative of the families' *capo di capi*, would know about it.

Milhaud sat back and contemplated the intrinsic irony of life. He had unearthed the answer to one question, but it had brought him no closer to the truth he was seeking. Now he was faced with an enigma whose implications had already begun to ripple dangerously outward.

The highway was a ribbon of concrete and tarmac, shining like chrome in the man-made sodium light of midnight. M. Mabuse, thinking of death and destruction, idly flicking on the radio, spinning the dial, coming upon Van Morrison singing,

> *Sometimes I wish I could fly up in the sky*
> *Sometimes I wish I could fly like a bird up in the sky*
> *A little closer to home.*

His hand stopped, and it was as if his mind, dark and dangerous, had come to a halt as the words and the haunting melody cascaded over him.

> *Sometimes I feel like freedom is near*
> *Sometimes I feel like freedom is here*
> *But I'm so far from my home.*

Now those words seemed to grip him in a way he had thought impossible. Western music meant nothing to him. Normally, he found it bland and insipid, reinforcing his longing for the plangent melodies, the aching lyrics of the music of home.

But this song was different. It broke through layers of iron and steel to touch with a gentle finger his beating heart.

Sometimes I feel it's closer now
Sometimes I feel the Kingdom is at hand
But we're so far from home.

The highway ribboning out began to blur, the colors to coalesce into a vast swirl of emotion that, welling up inside his chest, threatened to choke him in its intensity.

Sometimes I feel like a motherless child
Sometimes I feel like a motherless child
A long, long way from my home.

He was weeping now, he was certain of it. And, oh, how it hurt him, the scars regressing to open wounds again, and he thought, I cannot stand it. Turned off the radio, the voice dying, silence, the dark spider at his core, weaving its insidious web once again inside him.

M. Mabuse with his foot a bit too heavy on the accelerator, now, as if to escape his own emotions, because the spinning red light blossomed in his rearview mirror like a malevolent poppy.

He slowed, obediently pulling onto the verge, by the side of a steep, grassy embankment, engine ticking like a bomb in the wide breakdown lane in the midst of the purple Connecticut countryside. Beside him his portable library, a stock of government studies, digests of scientific papers, and journals of technological advertising. J. G. Ballard, one of the few authors who interested M. Mabuse, had written that this agglomerate, this "invisible literature," had to a great extent transfigured modern culture. M. Mabuse had decided that was a subject worthy of further study.

He watched the lurid lights set into stanchions by the side of the road, reading the message left for him in their kinetic aureoles. It admonished him for his sins lest he forget the bombings, acid firestorms engulfing entire forests, whole villages, the eerie *whooshing* sound all-encompassing, like *nats*—or saints—grinding their teeth in anguish, downing out whatever last vestiges of human outcry had been made.

He looked up, almost startled to see that he was not all alone with his torment. Mirror-lensed sunglasses dominated a big, beefy face, folds of reddened flesh spilling over the tight, dark blue collar.

"You were over the limit," the cop said. "License and registration." Bending over to peer through the open car window.

M. Mabuse, straining still to hear the cries over the inhuman rushing of the bombs, pulled out his wallet. He flipped it open, drew out the identification that he had laminated into a plastic shell.

He imagined in loving detail the police car parked behind him smashing at one hundred miles an hour into a concrete abutment. He smiled up at the cop as he offered the ID. As the cop reached for it, M. Mabuse's hand accelerated. Flicking out, it drew the edge of the plastic shell across the cop's throat. Blood bloomed, as bright red as the burning light that swung through the car's interior with dull regularity.

The cop coughed, his mouth opening wide in disbelief. M. Mabuse saw his hand fumbling with his holstered gun, drew the man's head and shoulders through the car window until the cop's thick upper torso was pinioned there. Then he leisurely reached up, jamming his stiffened thumbs under the mirror-lensed sunglasses, plunging them deep into the cop's sockets.

The scream was just what M. Mabuse needed to hear, confirmation of the pain human beings suffer as they are dying, beating back for that fleeting moment the eerie sounds of the bombs rushing downward through smoke-filled skies.

In the damp grass, at the rim of the highway, M. Mabuse watched with a manic intensity the ribbons of color pass him by, the endless lines of cars, of humanity, trooping like soldiers to the final battle.

But out where he crouched, alone in the darkness of a midnight that never ended, there was only space, limitless, undefined, an emptiness more terrible by far than death.

Alix Layne was staring at the faded black-and-white photo of herself in the oak-tree swing. She sat on the piano stool, leaning on her forearms, which were crossed over the wooden top.

It was very quiet in the apartment. Dan was asleep, finally, after reading in bed until three. The girl upstairs had stopped her flute exercises and, thank God, the Connors next door had finished their quotidian fight.

The windows were open wide, but even the rush of traffic was subdued. Occasionally, Spanish voices were raised in altercation or laughter, like brief communiqués from another world.

And Christopher Haye was gone.

Alix wondered what to make of Christopher Haye. Or, more accurately, what to make of her feelings for him. After many boyfriends, six or seven love affairs, and a twelve-year marriage, Alix was still waiting for her knight in shining armor. *You're no hero,* she had said to Christopher.

She had met her husband, Dick, in college. He was a radical, wry and gifted—at least when he was focused in on a cause, like the war in Vietnam. She remembered the time he had publicly debated with the college dean on the pros and cons of the war. She had been so proud of him.

But after the war, it seemed, Dick's focus had spun away. While she was working by day and going to law school at night, Dick was trying to write the great American novel that would sum up the state of the nation in the post-Vietnam era.

At first, money was no problem. There was Alix's job at Saks Fifth Avenue, and her law-school tuition and expenses were being paid with a trust her grandfather had left her for this purpose.

But, gradually, it became clear that Dick couldn't or wouldn't write anything at all, let alone the great American novel. Instead, he seemed to take his frustrations out on her, waiting until she got home after classes, exhausted from her dual life, to vent his anger.

Alix, who spent her nights learning the American justice system, coming to appreciate its innate fairness and egalitarianism, had been in no frame of mind to hear this. Nevertheless, Dick persisted.

And so it went. Until he insisted that she have a baby. "We're not a family," he said. "Maybe that's what's wrong with us. We're two separate people, in their own separate orbits. A baby will bring us together. It will bring us peace."

But, instead, the child had fractured what was already a fragile situation. Dan's birth polarized two people who were already slipping away from one another.

For one thing, Alix resented the further burden her pregnancy put on her. Dick still had not gotten a job, though he claimed to be out searching for one every day. "There's nothing out there, I tell you," he would say. "Nothing but laborers' work." Alix, still working behind the Clinique counter in Saks, found this irony tough to take.

But take it she did, because she had thought she loved Dick. She suspected that she would never again find a man who knew what it was she liked, and when. Certainly, she knew that never again would she be able to duplicate the fascinating, complex discussions she and Dick had had on world politics, religion, history, and art. He was not, like her previous lovers, dense when it came to understanding, or to emotion, two things that were of profound importance to her. He was so smart, so knowing, such a good lover, and so tender and patient with Dan.

Staring now at the photo of her as a child growing up in Ohio, she felt tears come to her eyes. How she longed to sit in that swing again, beneath the cool shade of the oak tree. She closed her eyes, could feel the strong, comforting presence of her grandfather. She could smell his warm scent, a little spicy with cologne, a bit musky with tobacco—how she loved it when, laughing with delight, he let her fill his pipe for him!

She could feel the vitality of him as his square, work-roughened hands gripped the ropes, setting the swing to vibrating. "Ready, Princess?" he would whisper in her ear. Then he would give one powerful push, and she would be off.

Why had her marriage failed? Even after all this time, Alix could not stop asking that question. It had not been that they had simply ceased to love one another, as had been the case with so many of their friends from college.

How easy the present would be, Alix thought, if she had discovered that Dick was having an affair. That was like finding roaches in your apartment, it was cut and dried, you knew what to do, get the Black Flag out, and go to it. Had Dick been fooling around, she could have accepted that, a pothole in the road of life, we all have to hit some once in a while. All her friends could sympathize; she was now a member of, as it were, the club. She could hate him, feel confident in that hate, and understand what had transpired to place her in this present.

But life was never that uncomplicated. She remembered a winter when her grandfather had taken her to fish in a frozen lake. Staring down through the ice, she had seen something moving, a shadow, nothing more. And she was unaccountably frightened, not knowing what was down there, and what it portended.

The fact was that Dick had never been unfaithful to her. Even now, she knew from the unceasing letters he wrote her (after she refused to take his calls) that he still loved her, that she was, in his own words, the only woman he ever loved, whom he ever would love.

The end of her marriage was like that gray day on the frozen lake, peering under the ice with a mixture of terror and fascination. Something mysterious and unknown was moving there. Dick simply could not deal with what she had become: a success not only in the world—from Dick's viewpoint that was bad enough ("What happened," he wrote, "to the good, old days when I could always find you smelling good at Saks?")—but in a field of endeavor dominated by men. If only she had wanted to be something else, a therapist or a teacher, perhaps, something feminine—or, at least, unisex—he could have forgiven her those desires.

When it all came out like a torrent of filth from a long pent-up sewer, that was bad enough. But he also succeeded in making Alix feel as if the marriage breakup had been her fault. Her fault that she had wanted to be a lawyer; her fault that she was successful. As if ambition and success were deficiencies.

Which meant that in a way she was still not free of Dick even though they did not live together, she no longer carried his name (though, of course, Dan did, like baggage from another lifetime), and he no longer had visitation rights. If, she thought, I have done such a thorough job of cutting him off, how is it that I still feel the bastard's claws in my back?

With a sigh she got up. Outside, someone was playing on a harmonica a tune, whose name she could not remember, from *Rubber Soul*. She went into the bathroom to brush her teeth, and saw herself in the mirror. She remembered the look in Christopher Haye's eyes when she had laughed. Perhaps—was it possible?—that was the first time he had seen her laugh.

All her life people had told Alix that she was beautiful, but she did not particularly believe it. She would listen dreamily, as if they were talking about someone else, someone in a film. Because when she looked at herself, all she could see were the faults: mouth too wide, nose not straight, the list was too long and too depressing to trot out at a moment's notice. That was saved for when she really wanted to beat up on herself, for those times when she looked at Dan, and thought, as Christopher Haye had said, that the boy needed a daddy, too.

Christopher Haye. Her thoughts kept running back to him, like a river to the sea. She had been aware of him for a long time, aware that she was attracted to him. But she had done nothing about that attraction. And now that he had made the first move, how would she respond? In truth, she did not know. She was tired of being disappointed by men, but she still loved them enough not to be defeated. Never defeated.

In her mind the Beatles song from *Rubber Soul*, plaintive on the harmonica, drifted back through the years. Until she was dancing again with her grandfather, on the wide, warped steps of their house in Ohio, wind shivering the oak leaves, a whippoorwill adding counterpoint to the music, and thick, lemon light cascading over them from the parlor.

Life was so simple then. Alix had been so happy.

What had happened?

Soutane sat down under the striped awning of Le Safari. The restaurant had been a favorite of Terry's, the one in which the photo of them had been taken.

Terry had preferred it because it was at the eastern end of Nice, well past the opera house where the tourists flooded the streets. Soutane liked it because, in the cool beneath Le Safari's awning, one could watch romantic strollers idling away the morning amid the flower stalls of the open-air market on Cours Saleya.

It was late enough now so that most of the shoppers were gone. Many of the stalls were already closed, and those that were still open had little left in the way of goods. Sellers were hosing down their individual areas or leaning on their counters, gossiping among themselves while they smoked or drank a bit of wine.

Soutane had chosen this time, and this spot, after careful consideration. She had returned from Mun's villa in Vence late last night. Which was why she was here now, sipping a Campari and soda at Le Safari. Her unknown shadow had been looking for something in the house—something of Terry's. He hadn't found it. But he obviously needed to find out where it was or, alternatively, who had it. Which was why he was still following her.

Through dark glasses she watched the activity at the flower market winding down. The sun was very strong and, it being overhead, there were almost no shadows. She had chosen this time of day—late morning—because there would be just the right amount of people on the street. If she had come earlier, she would have risked missing her tail in the throngs that clogged the market. Later in the day the street would be emptier. A tail would be more cautious, and she might miss him then, too.

Soutane had no illusions about herself. She knew she was beautiful, and desirable as well, which was not always the case in women. She had golden skin, and features that appeared as much Polynesian as they were Asian. She wore her black hair long, pulled back from her wide forehead in a thick plait. Her only piece of jewelry was a ring of carved red jade that was precious because Terry had given it to her.

She knew that, too, she was far from typical. Her spirit had been forged in the furnace of suffering. She was of French-Khmer parentage, and this had shaped her spirit. It forced her to be strong.

It had been her Cambodian mother's misfortune to fall in love with power. She had married a Frenchman. But the strength this conflict provided—being married to a member of the ruling colonial power in Cambodia—also had its negative side. The often bitter love between her parents, born of her mother's sorrow and anger at what had become of her country at the hands of the French, had hardened her, setting up its own conflict that resonated through Soutane's life. This steellike temper went against her mother's Buddhist teachings, which demanded that she take only meritorious actions.

Thus Soutane's parents had gifted her. Their war—a mirror of history's war—lived on inside their child.

In the ten or so minutes since Soutane had sat down, perhaps three dozen people inhabited her narrow view of the environment. This did not include anyone who was in and out within the span of thirty seconds. No one seemed out of place. A couple of young Frenchmen, giving her the eye, had sat down at a table that would afford them the best view of her long legs. Soutane covered her appreciative smile with the rim of her glass.

The last of the flower sellers in the street had packed up and left. A family of six were eating *poisson* and *pâte au pistou* at the next table. The lanky waiter came out of the restaurant's doorway to serve the two young Frenchmen. When he came by Soutane's table, she ordered another Campari and soda.

The second time the Jesuit priest walked by he caught Soutane's attention. She had marked him, as she had all the passersby, when she had first seen him. He had come down the Cours Saleya from the direction of the opera house, and the odd thing was that when he reappeared, he came from the same direction. That would mean that, rather than returning from some errand, he had circled around. To make another pass?

This time, however, he lingered, pausing beneath the awning of one of the touristy pizza joints down the street. He did not buy anything, which was his second mistake. He got out an oversized handkerchief, and mopped his brow.

Soutane studiously ignored him. The waiter brought her drink. When, after another few minutes, the Jesuit had not moved, she got up and went inside the restaurant, where it was as dark and cool as night. Fresh fruit was piled atop a curved mahogany bar.

She asked for directions to the lavatory even though she knew perfectly well that it was to the right and to the rear.

Back there, it was like being at the bottom of a well. Both light and sound were distorted. Shadows, grotesquely elongated, swept across the walls as if painted with a surrealist's brush. The burst of conversation from diners at the inner tables drifted to her overlaid with echoes created in the tiny space.

Soutane went into the cubicle, pulled the door shut behind her. She stood motionless, seemingly doing nothing. But, in fact, she was listening. At length she heard the soft tread of careful footsteps.

It was very quiet in the close, dank cubicle. Soutane could no longer hear his approach, but she could feel his proximity. She willed her body to relax as she watched the door handle slowly turn. She had not locked the door, and now it began to open.

She turned so that her right side was to the door. As she did so, she lifted her skirt over her hips; she was naked underneath.

The door squealed on its old hinges. She saw the Jesuit standing in the shadows of the threshold. His black robes made him seem somehow sinister, like a raven appearing in a field at noon.

''Oui, monsieur?'' she said.

''Pardon, madame.'' But he hesitated. For an instant, as if magnetized, his eyes were drawn to the patch of curling hair between her thighs.

All the time Soutane needed to jam the rigid tips of her fingers into his solar plexus. The priest doubled over, and she slammed the top of his head against the doorframe, hauled him into the cubicle.

But his left hand was already coming up, she saw the glint of a knife blade. She calmly placed the pad of her thumb along the right side of his nose, pressed inward. He groaned, his fingers uncurling so that the knife clattered to the cracked tile floor.

''Who are you?'' Soutane said. Again, the pressure at the facial nerve juncture. The Jesuit's eyes rolled back into his head.

''Why are you following me?''

And again.

''What did you hope to find in my house?''

The Jesuit's tongue came out. He mouthed silent words, swallowed. Pain filled his eyes like a torrent. ''The For-Forest of Swords,'' he finally managed to get out.

''What?'' Soutane shook him. ''What did you say?''

The Jesuit repeated what he had said.

"I don't believe it," Soutane said. The *Prey Dauw*, Forest of Swords, was, as far as she knew, a myth. It was a three-bladed weapon forged, it was said, to immobilize Buddha. In any event it was a symbol of power, a potent talisman kept alive by practitioners of the *Muy Puan*.

The *Muy Puan* was an outlaw book of Theravadan scripture. Normally the Theravadans taught that four of the thirty-one planes of existence were hells. The *Muy Puan* disputed that teaching. It preached, rather, that there were fully one thousand hells and, further, it purported to describe ways in which one could invoke the devils, demons, and false *bodhisattvas* who were consigned there.

Many younger Khmer, especially in the larger cities, no doubt had never heard of the *Muy Puan*. But the members of the Burmese mountain tribes in the north, the Shan, the Wa, Lahu, and Akha certainly had. They shared with the Khmer a deep belief in Theravadan Buddhism, of which the *Muy Puan* was a part. In their dialect it was known as the *Ta Taun*. Fear of its text ruled their lives. The thought that the *Prey Dauw*, the major talisman of the *Muy Puan*, actually existed was appalling.

The person who possessed the Forest of Swords would wield unlimited power in the Shan State. It would mean an end to the perpetual wars between the opium warlords of the Shan Plateau. It would mean the complete domination of the world's major supply of opium by one person, whereas now there were many who divided up that control. It meant, in effect, that virtually unlimited power, as well as wealth, would be in the hands of a single human being.

"You are lying!" Soutane found that she was shouting. "There is no Forest of Swords! It is a myth perpetuated by the superstitious."

"I myself have seen part of it," the priest said. "I fell upon my knees when I saw it. I could feel the ripples of its power in the room, a cold fire that does not burn. There can be no doubt. It is the knife out of legend, the smallest of the three pieces." He grimaced with the pain that would not end.

"You expect me to believe that?"

"Why not? You must know that it was Terry Haye himself who had the dagger, the middle piece, the Doorway to Night," the priest said. "Now you have it."

"Oh, what a foul liar you are." Soutane did something to the priest that made the pupils of his eyes roll behind his lids. He almost collapsed on her.

"Now," she said, shaking him violently, "tell me the truth."

The priest's eyes focused slowly on her. Pain like a hammer upon an anvil hit him all over again. "Ter-Terry Haye had agreed to sell *La Porte à la Nuit*. Only what he tried to sell was a fake. I have been sent to complete the transaction. To take possession of the real Doorway to Night."

Impossible, Soutane thought. Could this priest be telling the truth? Terry—her Terry—actually had *La Porte à la Nuit*? If so, why hadn't he told her? Surely he must have known what it would mean to her, a Khmer. She wouldn't have allowed him to sell it. She would have insisted it be returned to Cambodia, where it had been forged.

Of course, if he had had a replica made, he hadn't intended to sell the real dagger, either. Then what *had* he intended to do with it? With the whole Forest of Swords in his possession, he could rule the entire Shan. The superstitious warlords who believed in the power of the *Muy Puan* and of Ravana, the great demon, would move heaven and earth to obey the possessor of the Forest of Swords. Failure to do so would surely mean that they would spend eternity with the demon, outside the wheel of life, deprived forever of rebirth. They did not fear death, but this: the destruction of their individual *karma* was too terrible to contemplate.

Again she asked herself, What had Terry been up to? What secrets had he kept from her?

Suddenly Soutane felt as if she had not known the man she had been living with for five years.

Her eyes refocused on the Jesuit. "I still think you're lying. But suppose you aren't." She was watching his eyes. "You said that Terry was going to sell *La Porte à la Nuit*. To whom?"

The Jesuit shook his head. "I cannot tell you any more," he whispered. "I will be killed."

Soutane applied more pressure, until his eyes watered, and she could hear the sound of his teeth grinding. "Then you will die here. Is that what you want?"

"He—he'll kill me." Tears mingled with the sweat rolling down the Jesuit's cheeks.

"Who?"

"Dante." It was almost a sigh. "A Vietnamese named Dante."

* * *

M. Mabuse had been meditating upon the Great Buddha when he saw his quarry draw up in front of the building. M. Mabuse was a block and a half behind. Mechanically, he slowed, but he was still lost within the scene of the Great Buddha.

It was a scene that M. Mabuse not only thought of often, but one which he relived constantly. The Great Buddha, reclining on his right side, his head propped up with the palm of his right hand, had been carved from wood many centuries ago. The scholars sent abroad during the days in which France had stooped to kiss Asia with the condescension and cruelty of colonialism had claimed to have accurately dated it. M. Mabuse had not believed them. Why should he have trusted people whose arrogance caused them to create their own name for his country, Cochinchina?

In any event the Great Buddha lay in a temple upon its gilt-covered base, an eternal symbol of the divine presence in Vietnam. Or so M. Mabuse had believed.

That had been before the war. Before the French, and then the Americans, had brought in their guns and their men and their helicopters and their death rain.

None of them had understood the essential truth—that Vietnam was eternal, that it would resist forever incursions by foreign forces seeking to wrest control from its rightful rulers, by greedy politicians who sought to empty its soul of divinity, by even the frightful death rain that indiscriminately burned humans, dwellings, and forestation alike. For centuries on end the Vietnamese had honed their skills at warfare; who better than they knew the taste of death? Vietnam, like a rabid dog or a soldier too long at the front, could be comfortable only with war.

For M. Mabuse, traveling now through night-shrouded New York, half a world away, that Vietnam was alive, like a coal burning in the center of his being, a flame of suffering, a fire of darkness and death. His sole reason for living—to free himself from the cruel nails that bound him like Christ to his bloody cross.

The Great Buddha. From within his somnolent, peaceful eyes the universe could be discerned. And not only the current universe of man, but the multitudinous planes of existence from which the spirit had come and to which it might one day go, as well as those planes where dwelt gods, saints, demons, and devils.

But at some point, M. Mabuse believed, something must have happened to the Great Buddha; its eyes had turned dim and blind. For the scene that M. Mabuse relived over and over was of himself standing before the Great Buddha.

Weary from constant fighting, he had journeyed more than a hundred miles to return to this holy place in order to cleanse his spirit of the hate and the killing fever that had gripped him for so long.

He could no longer see the multitudinous planes of existence or even the universe in those scabrous eyes. For the vast space before the Great Buddha was heaped with mounds of skulls. Who had killed these people? The Americans? The Chinese? The soft peoples of the south who also called themselves Vietnamese? He did not know. And who were these victims? North Vietnamese? Chinese? South Vietnamese? Americans? It was impossible to say. And in any case, he realized, it did not matter. What mattered was death, and now death was everywhere.

M. Mabuse, his eyes filled with death, pulled into a nearby bus stop and parked.

M. Mabuse had traveled extensively throughout Indochina, gathering as he made his slow, methodical way the essential arts of each region. To M. Mabuse's way of thinking, that meant martial arts.

He had, for instance, spent much time in Sumatra, learning *pentjak-silat*. This was an arcane and exacting discipline that, according to Sumatran legend, had its origins with a peasant woman who had applied principles she had discovered while watching a tiger and an enormous bird battle to the death.

Pentjak-silat used what it called "anatomical weapons," such as the knuckles, fingers, edges of hand, feet, and so on, each against a specific part of the adversary's body. Therefore, its practitioners were always armed, even when they bathed or slept. What set it apart, however, was that it was bound up with the element of spiritualism, as were most ancestral concepts on the Indonesian archipelago.

It was *pentjak-silat* that M. Mabuse had employed to remove the dead cop from his car and to dispose of him in a dry, rock-strewn ravine some five thousand yards away. He had covered the corpse with stones so completely as to ensure that wild animals would not come nosing around.

Then he had turned off all the police car's lights, released the brake, and, one foot on the tarmac, had guided it over the embankment, out of sight of the highway traffic. All this had been accomplished in the space of ten minutes. It had taken considerably more time to remove the last traces of blood from his car's interior.

Now, from across the street, he watched the man he was shadowing go into the apartment building. He wondered now which *jurus* he would use to incapacitate his quarry before the end came. Would it be the folded index and middle fingers to his eyes? The knuckles to his forehead? The fisted four fingers to his solar plexus?

M. Mabuse considered the pain engendered by each blow, at once watching them separately and collectively, like a juggler with his striped balls. He closed his eyes, savoring what was to come, the consequences of his actions rippling outward.

He was such a small thing, blinking at the edge of the cosmos. But what power he wielded!

Almost time, M. Mabuse thought, breathing in the scent of charred flesh as, thrown into the boiling sky, riding the 'copter, he shouted out his anguish to blot out the screams from the burning world below him.

M. Mabuse, watching again the destruction, felt Vietnamese blood like hail, soaking his black pajamas. Darkness, time, and memory, smooth as stones from a riverbed, forever his companions. But were they friends or enemies? M. Mabuse had endured the hell of man's creation to find out. Soon, he thought, I will be one step closer to the answer that I can already feel like an eye, cold against my flesh.

And when he emerged from his car, he was lost against the night.

"You can't go home," Diana Ming said. "Not now."

Seve, head against the car seat, eyes closed, was too exhausted to argue. He had spent a long time with Elena Hu, the widow of his slain detective, consoling her. Actually, Diana had been better at it than he had. Elena had hit him, then had clung to him with a kind of infantile desperation, as if he had the power to erase her husband's death off some cosmic slate.

Diana had had the good sense to make tea, to bring out Oreos from the cupboard, the tiny sounds, the familiar smells in themselves comforting, calming, bringing a sense of reality back into an unreal situation.

It had been Diana who had telephoned Elena's sister, suggesting that they stay until she arrived with her pale, worried face and her overnight bag. Diana, as well, who had to pull him out of the Hus' apartment, shove him, stumbling, back into the car. Which is when she had said, "You can't go home. Not now."

Because home for him was a dark, lonely place that would be, she knew, haunted by his thoughts: how he could have saved Richard Hu; who killed Dominic Guarda and why—too many terrible questions without the possibility of immediate answers.

Seve was asleep by the time Diana pulled up in front of her apartment in Alphabet City on the Lower East Side. She turned off the ignition, listened to the tick of the engine cooling.

Across the avenue Hawaii 5-0 and Nasty Al's were packing them in. The drift of a jukebox's output, the jackhammer explosion of rap music out of a ghettoblaster portable stereo, the snarling of a pair of mongrels pulling apart the contents of a trashcan. A vagrant pushing a steel cart from the A&P piled high with junk kicked the dogs away, then went down on her hands and knees to paw through the wreckage.

Diana let out a deep sigh. She watched the outline of Seve's profile, and thought, I must be out of my mind to bring him home with me. But tonight she was too exhausted to be strong, to give in to her better instincts, to push her love for him into the shadows. I want him, she thought, no matter what he is.

She woke him gently, but even so he started awake. He looked into her eyes, he knew who she was, where he was; he came with her. Up the steep staircase, past the graffiti-strewn walls.

Inside her apartment Diana threw the dead bolt. Seve went straight for the sofa, collapsed onto it. Diana knelt beside him, struggled him out of his jacket. She took off his tie, unbuttoned his shirt, then she spread a light blanket over him. Before she got up, she leaned over, kissed him on the lips.

She went into the bedroom and got undressed. She liked to sleep in the nude, but because Seve was there, she put on an oversized T-shirt. She lay in bed staring up at the ceiling, willing sleep to come. But she could feel Seve's presence like a magnet or an oven, making her body tingle, her muscles tauten.

When she felt the quivering start between her legs, she got up and, in the tiny galley kitchen, brewed herself a pot of jasmine tea. Sipping it, she walked through the living room. She had long ago stopped being embarrassed by her apartment, which looked rather more like the Strand used-book store than it did a home. Books were arrayed not only in rows, but in stacks and ungainly piles. The only decorations were a Japanese kimono and fan which she had hung on the walls facing each other.

Pushing aside some books, she made a place for herself on the windowsill.

Because her eyes kept wandering in Seve's direction, she made herself think about the two corpses in Connecticut. She saw again under the pitiless arc lights the severed heads, the bloody stumps of their necks, ribbons of maroon-flecked skin hanging. Reminding her of . . . what?

Something.

She watched Seve breathing easily, her mind wandering over and over the same ground. What was it? Something dark and sinister crouching in a hidden corner of her brain.

Her gaze fell upon an oversized volume called *Secrets of the Samurai: A Survey of the Martial Arts of Feudal Japan*. The dark and sinister thing began to squirm, edging toward the light of consciousness. She plucked the book off the shelf, began leafing through it with greater and greater speed.

She had many such books on Oriental weaponry, a legacy of a former boyfriend named Ken who had been a knifemaker. "The Japanese blade is almost like a living thing," he had once told her. According to him, the raw steel was softened, then folded and refolded upon itself into ten thousand layers. When it was complete, it was flexible enough to be bent in half without snapping, and its edge was so true that when you looked at it head-on, it disappeared. It could pierce armor or sinew and bone, which made it the ideal warrior's implement.

Diana suddenly looked up, stared at the spread fan on the wall over the sofa upon which Seve slept. It was painted with a scene of a finch amid plum blossoms. She loved that fan, loved that Ken had thought enough of her to send it to her.

Ken had loved his blades more than anything else in life. When Diana had met him, he had already dedicated ten years to trying to learn the Japanese technique of blade-making. Finally, frustrated, he had packed his bags and flown to Japan to apprentice with the last great Japanese swordmaker, a seventy-five-year-old national living treasure.

Ken's love had gradually rubbed off on Diana, who had a small but superb collection of handmade knives. Now, as she leafed through the book, sipping her jasmine tea, something he had said swirled upward with an odd kind of urgency. Most people, even collectors, he had told her, thought only of *katana*, swords, or *tanto*, knives, when they considered Japanese blades. But the fact was that some of the very best work was saved for specialty weapons.

Diana stared at the Japanese fan, its breadth, its width, its design. All of a sudden she felt the tiny hairs at the base of her neck stir. The dark and sinister thing was in the room with her.

"Jesus." Thinking of the odd, crenellated pattern on the two dead men's necks, Diana quickly turned to the section titled "The Art of the War Fan."

She had it! She knew how Seve's brother had been killed!

She looked over to where Seve slept, and thought better of waking him. Exhaustion had made his face gray and drawn. He needed sleep more now than her revelation. She closed her eyes, but for her sleep was still far off.

For Seve, lying so close to her, dreams were like parachutes, lighter than air, taking you somewhere you've never been before or where you've too often been.

He and Dom are together again. The years are like doves, calling from the underbrush, unseen. The two brothers are twenty again, are crazy again, in the midst of the hashish dream of Vietnam's never-ending war. There is blood in air so ashy it has destroyed the sun. Vietnam must be the only place in the world, Seve thinks, where the sky is yellow.

Seve and Dom on a patrol, dressed in the black pajamas of the Khmer Rouge, crossing over from Vietnam into Cambodia. No one knows where they are, even GHQ is in the dark, believing that they are on a routine search-and-destroy patrol. But, then, they don't take orders from GHQ or even MACV, for that matter.

This—not the Viet Cong, not the Khmer Rouge—is very much on the minds of the men in the patrol. It is virtually all they talk about behind the CO's back.

But they have all volunteered; they all want to make this voyage into the unknown, into the infinite. And this snaking, sluggish river they must cross is the dividing line. In Vietnam they can explain virtually any actions they take; this is a lunatic asylum, and anything is condoned if it will help decrease the population of lunatics. But Seve knows that once they cross this river, everything will change. They will be in Cambodia, an officially neutral country, where they have no right to be and where, if the presence of American military forces is detected, they will be summarily executed.

They slide down the muddy bank, clotted with stinking weeds, into the oily, opaque water. It is the color, Seve discovers, that comes over a man's eyes moments after death. The men wade in, wary, nervous, grim. They were told by natives that at this time of the year the river will be swollen and will reach to their necks, but the water never gets above their waists. This is the start, Seve thinks. How will it end?

All of a sudden Dom, who is just ahead of him, slips. Seve

reaches out, grabs his brother's elbow. But his balance is off, and they both go down on their knees. Their chins are in the water. It is as iridescent as peacock feathers. They gasp and spit out river water.

Seve is about to stagger to his feet when a small eddy clears the muck of the slow-moving river, and he sees beneath the surface. Like an iris or a shutter swiftly closing, the eddy brings the opacity back, and Seve stunned, sickened, dizzy, cannot believe what has been revealed to him.

He does not want to but is nevertheless compelled to reach down into the riverbed. Touch confirms what sight has already told him. His trembling fingers do not encounter silt or rock, but rather the drifting tatters of skin, of flesh, sinew, the odd end of bone where the creatures of the river have picked it clean.

Gagging, he stumbles blindly onward, his outstretched hand encountering the same grisly, horrifying deathscape. He is unable to take his hand away.

This is why the river, swollen with water, is still easily fordable. Its bed has been raised by layers of corpses. How many? Seve thinks as he staggers on. Hundreds? Thousands?

He looks bleakly ahead of him. Do any of the others know what it is upon which they walk? Apparently not, for Seve sees no difference in their tense, nervous faces as, at last, they reach the far shore where they can no longer be saved.

But Seve knows, Seve remembers, in dreams such as this one that has parachuted him somewhere he has never been or where he has too often been.

And from a distance too great to recall, he cries out in a voice filled with terror.

Diana threw her book aside, knelt by Seve's side. She pressed her palms against his heaving chest, kissed away the sweat from his forehead. She smiled at him when his eyelids flew open, and whispered, "It was a dream, boss. It was only a dream."

Seve's intense brown eyes focused on her face. "Diana."

"Yes," she said. "Diana. You're here with me. You're safe."

He gave a little sigh, closed his eyes, and was asleep within a minute.

Diana went back to her seat on the windowsill, but she did not pick up the book again. She had wanted to shake Seve awake, to tell him what she had discovered—maybe the break they had been looking for. But he was so tired, had looked so frightened by whatever he had seen in his dream, that she had wanted only to see him sleeping peacefully. Time enough in the morning to tell him everything. She was looking forward to seeing the look on his face when she showed him the *gunsen*, the war fan illustrated in the book.

It was raining again by the time Chris got back to his apartment. He knew that he should be tired, but he wasn't. He felt that somehow tonight he had opened a door, and had entered an entirely new world, though he could not for certain say what that world was.

He watched the rain sliding down the windowpanes and thought of Alix. He went across the room, turned on the stereo. Then he made himself a drink. He pushed off his shoes, curled his toes into the pile carpeting. Then, with a sigh, he sat in an oversized chair facing the window. The rain turned the city's lights into ethereal bursts of color.

> *Dreams are like angels* [a female voice sang]
> *dancing in the light*
> *keeping shadows at bay*
> *keeping love in sight.*
> *Times change*
> *but dreams are like angels*
> *eternal*
> *feeding the flame*
> *of a prayer at night.*

He put his glass against his cheek and closed his eyes, remembering a time when dreams were real, a time when the scents of lavender and bicycle oil were inextricably mixed, a summer in France when anything was possible.

Perhaps he slept or dreamed for a time. In any event when he opened his eyes, a different song was playing. He put down his glass, went into the bedroom to get his suitcase. He found his passport, stuck away behind the box containing his cuff links, tuxedo studs, and dress watch. He'd have to send someone from the office to get his visa first thing in the morning.

He began to pack, methodically, mindlessly. It passed the time. In the bathroom he gathered toiletries together, the disposable razors, the mini-can of shave cream, tiny tube of toothpaste, miniature deodorant, shoved them into his kit bag.

He could hear the music playing softly through the apartment, as if it were a song being sung in another time or place. The apartment was dark, save for a lamp lit beside his bed.

Chris slid aside the mirrored door to his closet. As he did so, he glanced into it. His hand stopped. From this angle he had a partial view down the vestibule to the front door.

Piercing the darkness like a knife, he saw a vertical sliver of light from the hallway outside. As he watched, the sliver of light grew slowly wider.

He was transfixed. He knew that he was watching his front door being silently opened, but it seemed unreal, impossible, unthinkable.

Yet it was happening.

It was happening to him. He did not know what to do. He was consumed by the intimation of acute danger.

The front door was now open far enough so that the light from the outer hallway spilled into his apartment. Chris thought he saw the edge of a shadow in that light, then it was gone, leaving a perfectly clear *V* of light.

He was abruptly aware of the length of his own shadow, thrown by the light of his bedside lamp. It was like a finger pointing directly at him. He stepped into the shadow of his closet, and disappeared.

He stood quite still, listening to the râle of his own breathing. He was aware of how ragged it sounded. His heart was pounding so hard he could feel each double pulse like a shock running through him.

Like many criminal lawyers, he had been threatened more than once, and so had a permit and a handgun. He had never had occasion to use it, but he had taken it to the police firing range several times, where they taught him how to fire it calmly and accurately.

Now, in the darkness of his closet, he fumbled for the drawer that held the gun. He lifted it out, fumbled for the box of bullets, and one by one, loaded them into the chambers. Then he inched out into his bedroom.

He could still see the sliver of light from the hallway, but now it was uneven. He stared at it a moment, trying to make sense of the new shape. With a start he saw that someone was standing in the light.

Silently, he moved out of the bedroom. In the living room, he stopped against a wall and, crouching down in the classic marksman's stance, aimed the pistol at the shape in the doorway. Then he reached up, and switched on the light.

The shape jumped, and he almost fired, saw her face in time, took his finger off the trigger.

"Alix," he said, rising.

Alix, startled by the sudden flood of light, had her hands at her throat. "My God, Christopher! You scared the hell out of me!" Then she saw the pistol in his hand, said, "Oh," in a soft voice.

He was furious, shaking with a mixture of relief and excess adrenaline. "What are you doing? How did you get in here?"

"I wasn't—" She turned her head, closed the door behind her. "I rang your bell. Then I saw that the door wasn't locked. In fact, it was open. You must have forgotten to shut it when you came in."

"Didn't you see the doorman? He should have buzzed me," Chris said.

"I didn't see anyone in the lobby." Alix looked genuinely contrite. "I came directly up. I'm sorry."

He put the gun carefully down on the L-shaped sofa. "It's all right." He took a deep breath. "Really." He smiled, seeing her uncertain expression. "It's okay."

She walked down the hall toward him. "Hello," she said.

"I was just thinking of you," he said, relaxing. He was pleased that she was here. His dark mood was lifting.

She laughed, a soft sound. "I must have heard you."

They watched one another in the semidarkness.

"Were you asleep?"

"For a while," Chris said. "But I've been up."

"I'm glad I didn't wake you." She smiled her dazzling smile. "Were you dreaming of me?"

"I might have been," he said, putting his arm around her.

Her head on his shoulder. "That would be nice."

He led her to the sofa. Her face seemed to glow from out of the room's dim light, the neon and fluorescents from the cityscape outside the window.

"I didn't know what to do," she said, lying in his lap. "I kept thinking of you, and then of you leaving tomorrow." She looked up into his face. "I've never done anything like this."

"Hush," he said, brushing strands of hair away from her face.

She put a hand against his cheek. "Dear Christopher," she whispered. "Am I taking an awful risk coming here?"

He leaned down. Her lips were trembling as he kissed her. "Don't be afraid," he said.

There was in the gray of her left eye a mote of indeterminate color. It was both endearing and mysterious, revealing to him a previously unknown vulnerability and depth.

Her eyes fluttering closed, feeling his open lips against hers, feeling his strength above her, Alix clung to him. Will you love me, she wondered, the way I need to be loved?

She felt his fingers at the buttons of her dress. She wore nothing underneath. She melted at the look on his face when his fingers encountered her bare flesh. Then she gasped, arching up against him. He buried his face in the hollow of her throat and, her heart pounding, she curled her hand at the nape of his neck, stroking. She licked his ears.

Then he broke away from her embrace just long enough to slide down the length of her torso. His hands stroked the insides of her thighs, then his mouth found her.

Alix felt as if she had been thrown into a fire, felt as if her bones were melting. She could not catch her breath. She had never felt such overwhelming pleasure.

There was not even time enough to get fully out of her dress. She pulled him up against her and took him in the palm of her hand, not wanting another minute to go by without him inside her.

Kicked her dress up over her thighs, feeling him quivering at her entrance as she guided him. Then his lips and tongue at her breasts, at her burning nipples, and with a rush that thrust her deliriously against him, he filled her up.

She was already so excited that she was immediately on the brink. She squeezed his muscles, smelled his sweet sweat, felt the pleasure swamping her, and thought that she would faint.

His lips covered hers again. She had never been with a man who kept kissing her all the way through sex. She was aware of his tongue and his penis probing together, and she was thrust into the center of the fire, her body a deep pool of pleasure.

Taken by surprise, shaking and groaning, she jammed her hips in against him until she felt him explode inside her, making her inner muscles spasm, making her come a second time.

Alix awoke sometime later, wondering where she was and whether it had been a dream. Then she saw the shadows on the ceiling, felt the warmth like a special treasure wrapped inside her. She turned over, saw a shadow draped against the couch.

"Christopher?"

His eyes were closed and, putting her hand on him, she could feel tension returning to his frame.

"What is it? What are you thinking about?" Her voice was so soft, so gentle.

Chris turned toward her. "I want to tell you something I've never told anyone," he said. "I was thinking just now about what happened between my brother and me."

Alix was silent, watching him, moving a little so that his profile was limned by the wash of the city's predawn glow through the windows.

"When we were kids, my father used to bring us into his office on Christmas morning so he could see us open our presents. My family always had a lot of money—my father's money, principally—but he was, if not tight, then certainly abstemious with it. 'We had the dirt of Wales when I was young,' he used to tell us. 'That was all, and that was sufficient.' "

Alix could see Christopher smiling a little, and this gladdened her heart.

"Sufficient," he said, "was always one of my father's favorite words." He shifted on the sofa. "Anyway, the one day he forgot about 'sufficient' was Christmas. My father was lavish with his gifts, though more often than not, he presented us with presents he wanted us to have rather than ones we ourselves wanted.

"That was never more apparent than on the Christmas when I was twelve. Terry was a year older, thirteen. My father gave us thirty-thirty hunting rifles, set up some cans for us to practice on, then took us out to find deer.

"Jesus, it was right up Terry's alley. I remember him that year staring at the old hunting rifle Dad brought over from Wales when Grandfather died. 'That's what's left of him,' he used to say to me. 'If there's anything like a spirit, that's his. When I look at that rifle, I see him tall, proud, making his living from the soil of Wales. There's dignity in that, even, yes, a kind of greatness.'

"Terry understood, I guess, what Dad meant; I didn't. I never liked that gun, but Terry couldn't take his eyes off it. Then, that Christmas, when Dad gave us the rifles, Terry was in his element. On the other hand, I didn't know what to make of it. It seemed evil somehow, in my hands, as if it were already full of suffering.

"I didn't want to go—I didn't want to find any deer, because I knew what would happen then. As usual, my father bullied me, shaming me into going. And as usual Terry had no clue as to why I was balking. He was happy, why wasn't I? With Terry it was always the same: Dad likes this, so do I. If you don't, what's wrong with you?

"It hadn't snowed for some time, but it had been very cold. The ground was icy, the needles on the pines as stiff as steel. I remember feeling tired, crawling into a copse of trees to rest. And, looking through the pines, to a clearing on the other side, I saw the deer, a huge, lone buck. He was foraging and, oddly, I recall testing the wind, for Dad had told us to keep downwind of the animals so they couldn't scent us.

"Why did I do that? I don't know. Just as surely as I don't know why I pulled at Terry's shirttail. I know that if I hadn't, he'd have gone right past the deer without ever having noticed him.

"Of course, Terry's first reaction was to tell me to shoot the deer. I can't imagine why that angered and surprised me so. He kept at me. Then, when I refused, he aimed his own rifle. I smashed it against the bole of the tree.

" 'Jesus, Dad'll kill you,' he said, or something like that. And then he did the most extraordinary, the most unforgivable thing. He lunged for my rifle, swung it up until he was pointed at the deer, then he pressed inward against my finger, which was unconsciously curled around the trigger.

"The rifle went off, and the buck went down. I saw its huge eyes rolling, the look in them of bewilderment and pain. He was dying, and he did not understand why. He was no different, I thought, than a human being.

"And then, as Dad came up, I started to cry. I have never felt such despair, such desolation. My God, I thought, staring at the buck, what have you made me do? It was as if I had pulled the trigger, I had killed that life. I felt as if my soul had shriveled and tuned to ashes. And it was his doing. Or, by my tugging at his shirttail, was it mine as well?"

All at once he was crying and shaking. Alix wanted to hold him, to stop his trembling with the weight of her body, the force of her will, but she hesitated, not knowing how he would react. When he had pulled himself together, he said, "I could never find it inside myself to forgive Terry. And now, of course, it's too late."

Without looking at Alix, he lay back down on the other part of the sofa. In time he slipped into an exhausted slumber.

Only after she was certain that he was soundly asleep did she reach out to touch him briefly, lovingly. He had seemed almost to be vibrating with tension while he was telling the story. How sad he looks, she thought, even now.

Light had descended upon his face and, looking at him, she could imagine herself to be Wendy in *Peter Pan*. He's one of the Lost Boys, she thought, a motherless child, a long way from his home.

She wondered briefly what it would be like to hate her sister so completely that forgiveness was impossible. She shuddered, finding the thought unbearable. Poor Christopher. Poor Terry, for that matter.

She stared out the window, into the rain. It was the time when the sky was too pale to be night, too dark to be dawn. Alix remembered a time when she and Dick had gone to Barbados. They had rented scuba equipment, and had descended into the land where it was always night.

In a blue-green shoal the light had been like this, opalescent, translucent, the illumination of a liquid. It had been so quiet that the beating of her heart was the center of her world. She could see Dick floating beside her, the image of herself reflected in his mask. She had felt like a goddess, invulnerable and immortal. She fell back alseep feeling that way again.

And was awakened by the rain rattling against the windowpane. She stared dumbly at it, still half asleep.

A movement from within the apartment caught by her peripheral vision tugged at her. At first she thought that Christopher had awakened. But then she saw him still stretched out on the sofa, face turned into the pillows.

She started, disbelieving. A shadowy shape creeping across the floor. Who? What was it doing? These questions flashed through Alix's mind even as she leaped off the couch.

She had been coiled up, sleeping like a cat. Now, as she sprang, her lithe body stretched, and she landed atop the shadow, digging her knees and elbows into flesh as hard as steel.

Wrapped her left arm around the throat, jerked backward, bending at her waist, using the weight of her upper torso to apply leverage.

But, instead of resistance, she found herself tumbling over backward as her opponent turned her own momentum against her. She hit the floor with an insupportable weight on her abdomen.

Her eyes opened wide as she saw the hideous face of a demon or an animal—not a human face, surely!—on top of her, against her, inside of her.

One arm pinioned behind her back, the breath escaping from her faster than she could draw it in—even breathing took too much effort, too much time, she had none. Made a split-second decision, born of desperation and hope, butting her forehead hard against the terrible face hanging in her vision like a lantern or a moon.

Pain shot through her so thoroughly that she expelled a hard rasp through hard-clenched teeth, the last gasp of an engine before it comes to rest.

But the terrible weight was lifted from her chest, and she sucked in air. She looked up. Rain passing through a prism, turning colors, dripping onto a mirror, no, not a mirror, but shining like metal, crenellated and—

It's a fan, Alix thought, passing from light to shadow and back again. Her only thought now was to warn Christopher. She opened her mouth, but a hand, callused to the texture of hardwood, clamped down with such force that she began to gag.

Fingers like steel rods jammed between her lips, filling her mouth, pushing her tongue down her throat. Alix, terrified, felt the vomit rising, the involuntary spasms racking her.

Used the heel of her free hand as she had been taught, slamming it against the unprotected ear of her foe. Felt the pressure come off her pinioned right arm, brought it up, ignoring the pain, the semi-numbness, began an elementary karate chop, felt with bone-jarring impact the mis-hit.

But it gave her time, now, to roll out from under, escape the attempt to strangle her on her own tongue. Still, her only thought was for Christopher, and she cried out, one short, shrill shout of alarm.

Then the cutting edge of the *gunsen* caught her under the chin, slicing the side of her neck.

Chris awoke to a spray of blood. He shook his head groggily. Then he was fully awake, saw the strange, hunched shadow looming over Alix, in its hand . . . what? . . . a fan?

Lunging for the pistol. Firing point-blank at the rolling, springing shadow that went from its crouch beside Alix, to the hallway, to the doorsill, and was gone.

Chris ran down the hall to the open door, but there was nothing to see. Up or down, he wondered, which way? Then he realized that it didn't matter. With an agonizing wrench he turned back into the apartment.

"Alix."

He knelt beside her. His insides twisted, his heart constricted. There was so much blood. Still, her gray eyes recognized him. Her lips opened, her eyelids fluttered. What was she trying to say?

"Alix." He whispered her name and, in the same instant, pulled the phone toward him, dialed 911.

Chris watching as Alix's life slipped away; he could scarcely breathe. Pain that he could not define emptied him of all coherent thought. He was aware that he was weeping. "Hold on," he whispered into her quiet face. "Don't die, please don't die." It was as if there were a stake plunged into his chest.

Her blood was all over him, her life coating him, drying like a second skin.

WINTER 1968—SUMMER 1969

BAN ME THUOT, VIETNAM/CAMBODIA; MOUGINS/PARIS, FRANCE

When Terry Haye arrives under cover of night in Ban Me Thuot, in the central highlands of Vietnam, his first thought is of a line from Paul Valéry, the great French Symbolist poet: "Power without abuse loses its charm."

When he has been there a week and there is blood on his hands, he is reminded of what another Frenchman, La Rochefoucauld, said: "If we resist our passions, it is more from their weakness than from our strength."

Because by the time Terry Haye gets to Vietnam he is ready to learn how to kill.

"Killing is easy," Captain Claire says, during the first orientation lecture inside the Special Forces compound, "so don't spend time sweating it. You've all heard the horror stories, about kids freezing with their fingers on the trigger. I'm here to tell you those stories are pure bullshit. Anyone can kill; it's a snap.

"You take anyone—and I mean *anyone*—your so-called pacifist, conscientious objector, fucking Martin Luther King himself, I don't care who he is, and you put him in a room with a loaded pistol. Then you show him his wife or teenage daughter being raped, and see how fast he picks up the weapon and kills the motherfucker that's doing his family hurt."

Terry Haye, sitting, one leg casually draped over the other, thinking, What is this, the army's version of a homily?, but part of him certainly wanting—perhaps needing—to believe it in the same way one believes the doctor when he says, Now this won't hurt a bit. Not a homily exactly, just a lie one needs to believe.

"You think it's a big deal under those circumstances, you're in for a rude awakening," Captain Claire continues, " 'cause war is just like seeing your wife or your teenage daughter raped in front of you. Once it happens, you're in it, and you'll find no matter *what* doubts you brought with you, you're gonna kill those motherfuckers out there."

By this time Terry Haye has been through both basic and advanced individual training, OCS, airborne school at Fort Benning, just outside Columbus, Georgia, and Special Forces school at Fort Bragg in Fayetteville, North Carolina.

Terry Haye, listening to Captain Claire drone on about what it means to kill human beings, how the mind perceives it one way while the reality is another way entirely, wonders what all the fuss is about. After all, he muses, man has been killing since the dawn of time, since the first piece of meat or the first female was stolen, since one stone-age tribe encroached on the territory of another. So what?

Terry can't figure what the big deal is. His mind has set none of the traps, illusions of guilt or pity, to which Captain Claire keeps alluding. There is the enemy, Terry thinks, square in your sights. You pull the trigger and, *boom!* he is gone, *finis*, that isn't particularly complex or difficult to understand.

"What you have volunteered for," Captain Claire says, "is the Studies and Operations Group within Special Forces." He grins, a rare and peculiarly ominous expression. "Sounds kind of like you've signed up to be librarians, but that's only army acronese. What you'll be doing first is recruiting CIDGs, that is, for you poor, uninitiated swine, Civilian Irregular Defense Groups. More useless acronese.

"You're going behind enemy lines for sabotage work, laying sanitized antipersonnel mines. Because you'll be in what amounts to uncharted territory, you're gonna need all the help you can get, so the powers that be have authorized use of Khmer Serei, members of the hill tribes along the northwestern frontier and those indigenous to the area of the Mekong delta. Those who are chosen will be given unit designations since Asian names are difficult, at best, to remember. The CIDG recruits will be carefully integrated into your units for use as you see fit, as guides, as sacrifices if need be."

Captain Claire is walking around the room, watching them as he speaks. "Okay, so much for the good news. The bad news is that you're in Asia, and Asia is what can get you killed. First thing to remember is that you'll never understand the place. It's hooked into a different reality, and if you try to make it conform to your Western ideas, you'll wind up causing someone else's death, or worse, be dead yourself.

"The second thing to remember is that death means nothing to the Asians, it's just some kind of process that gets them from one plane of reality to another. So the only difference that counts between you and your enemy is that he doesn't mind dying and you do."

Captain Claire stops. "I see some of you smiling, so I have to assume that you think what I'm saying is funny. The first time you go to help a little girl across the road and the grenade in her armpit blows your legs off, you'll know what I'm talking about." He glares at them. "Or you can get it straight here where all it'll cost you is some time and mental effort."

Afterward, in what passes for the officers' lounge, while Terry is wondering why they need Cambodian, not Vietnamese, guides, Kid Gavilan, one of the new unit, says, "What does it matter anyway? We're here because we believe in America, and keeping the communists out of Vietnam is vital."

Heads nod and there is a general murmur of assent. Terry looks around at the West Point types, strapped into the military ethic at an early age, and wonders what is stirring in their secret minds. Why are they *really* here? Is it straightforward patriotism, an unwavering sense of duty, my country right or wrong, or are there other more personal imperatives being played out among this elite corps of soldiers?

It is not the idle question of the intellectually curious. Quite soon, Terry knows, he might be dependent on any one of these men for his safety, his very life. Knowing their motivations may one day mean the difference between lying facedown in one's own blood and getting out alive.

What, after all, is stirring in Terry's secret mind? He had been a boy who never quite fit in with his contemporaries. He was envied by them because of his exceptional skills in almost every field of physical endeavor. And he, who could run faster, jump farther, think faster than any of them, despised their slow-wittedness, their inability to see solutions which were eminently manifest to him.

Because in high school and college he was so sought after by both athletic teams and girls—for he was exceedingly handsome and magnetic as well—his sense of isolation was heightened. All the girls in one way or another disappointed him, leaving him feeling foolish for having given them so much of his time. He felt constantly besieged, defensive, and exasperated.

Yet he was not, as one would think, lonely. Terry was connected to his thoughts—that is, his thought processes—in the same manner that a city is hooked into its supply of electrical energy. And he took immense pleasure in exploring this unique natural resource, unaware of Francis Bacon's warning that whosoever is delighted in solitude is either a wild beast or a god.

As a boy he had not been given to dreams or imaginings. For as long as he could remember he had known—or he had thought he had known—what it was he wanted out of life. He observed from the proximity only innocence can bring his father's business dealings, divining with appalling swiftness that the only commodity that never decreased in value was power. Power is universal, understood and obeyed in all languages, all ages; it is the golden fleece, the Holy Grail.

He remembers a Christmas morning when his father plucked from under a tree decorated with genuine sugarplums two long, thin decorated packages. "Happy Christmas," he said, handing them to his sons.

Terry was thirteen, Chris twelve. They were in their father's office, where, traditionally, the Christmas tree was put. Terry took his present over to the giant leather sofa. It was set across the office from his father's thick-columned Roman desk, beneath a bay window as long as a ship's side, overlooking a grove of beech trees bare save for a rime of frost. A fire made with hickory logs blazed in an oversized fireplace surmounted by an eighteenth-century French marble mantel carved with sweet-faced cherubim.

Malcolm Haye, tall, mustached, splendidly dressed, stood, grinning, in front of his desk while his sons opened their presents. Terry still remembers the feeling he got when he saw the Remington 30-30 hunting rifle. A little thrill, a little chill moving up and down his spine, making his heart skip a beat.

Malcolm Haye, in bold hunting tweeds, taking his sons out into the countryside, setting up cans on a tree stump, letting them pop away—*spang! spang! spang!*—laughing excitedly, contentedly as Terry's cans, hit through their center, cartwheeled in the frigid air.

But it was not cans Malcolm Haye was after, it was deer. His father had taken him stag hunting in Wales, he told them, when he was only ten. "The old rifle he gave me," Malcolm Haye said, "was longer than I was tall. But I handled it. I handled everything my father gave me."

It was, of course, both reproach and warning. Early on, Terry had learned that his father did not idly tell stories. He always had a point to make. Life, he had said many times, is a series of lessons to be learned. The better one learns them, the more successful one will be. Malcolm Haye greatly valued success, which is why he fell in love with America, the land where success is the royal family; king, queen, and prince.

In the woods, snow, old and crusty, lay here and there in icy pockets. "Look for the hoof prints," Malcolm Haye said. "Search for the spoor, where the bark is rubbed off the tree trunks by their rutting. The evidence is all around you. You'll see. Just remember to keep the wind in your face so the deer won't scent you." He seemed, at that moment, not unlike Terry's private vision of Sherlock Holmes, strong, broad-shouldered, the answer to all enigmas at his fingertips, in control of the mysterious. How Terry admired him!

Then Chris said, "I don't want to look. I don't want to kill anything."

Malcolm Haye stopped in his tracks. He turned, and Terry could see the fire in his eyes. "You'll do as I tell you, Christopher."

"I'll shoot cans off a log," Chris said. "But I won't shoot at an animal."

"You have lessons to learn—important lessons," Malcolm Haye said. "It is not for you to choose among them." He reached out, took Chris by the scruff of his neck, shoved him deeper into the woods. He gestured. "Terry, see that he does as he's been told."

Terry, thankful that he had never given his father cause to turn on him in that manner, loped after Chris.

"What's the matter," he asked his brother, "don't you want to learn how to hunt?" Chris shot him a look, and Terry said, "What's with you, anyway?"

"Let me alone, okay?"

"No. It's not okay, you jerk. Who's gonna protect you from Dad? You really pissed him off back there. The only reason he didn't hit you, I think, is it's Christmas. But you keep on like this and, Christmas or no, you're going to get a hell of a whomping." Malcolm Haye, who had been raised with iron law backed up by a hickory switch, strongly believed that corporal punishment was a major character builder.

"He's hit me before," Chris said. "No one's going to stop him."

"But why do you always have to piss him off? Sometimes I think you do it on purpose."

"You're his son," Chris said. "I must be someone else's."

"Jesus, you're impossible. I don't know why I try to help you."

"Is that what you think you're doing? Helping me?" Chris said. "You aren't. You just want me to believe in all the things you believe in. You're just like Dad, a mirror image, and he loves you for it."

"He loves both of us," Terry said. "The difference is you spend all your time trying to prove you're not like him."

"I don't know whether he loves me or not," Chris said. "But it's clear he doesn't like me. I'm not what he wants me to be. That's too bad, but I don't need his approval."

"You're wrong, kiddo," Terry said as Chris moved off. "Only you're too goddamned stubborn to see it."

Of course, it was Chris who found the deer, a large, antlered buck. They were downwind, within a copse of densely packed pines, excellent cover. Terry was overcome with excitement. The animal was so large. The thought of bringing it down was thrilling.

"Shoot," he hissed at his brother. "Go on, shoot it!"

Chris did nothing but stare at the deer. He said something that Terry could barely hear, It's beautiful, perhaps.

"Well, if you won't," Terry said, aiming his rifle.

"No! This isn't Labyrinth. You're not going to win!" Chris kicked out, and the Remington slammed into a tree trunk, knocking the barrel out of line, rendering it useless.

"Shit," Terry breathed. "Look what you've done. Dad's going to kill you."

Just then Terry turned, saw Malcolm Haye making his stealthy way through the woods. He, too, had spotted the buck. Was he yet aware of the presence of his sons?

Terry threw down his rifle, made a grab for Chris's. "No!" Chris said. "I won't let you—"

But Terry was the stronger, Terry knew what he was doing. He raised Chris's 30-30 until it was pointed at the buck who had moved slightly, standing broadside to the boys. Terry, reaching around, curled his forefinger over his brother's. Pulled the trigger.

The shot was like an explosion, reverberating off the corridors of trees. The buck skidded sideways as if it had slipped on a patch of frozen snow. Then it went down, its forelegs crumbling. Its side was bloody. Its head twisted, searching perhaps for the source of its pain. Then it fell to the forest floor.

Malcolm Haye hurried up. He saw Chris holding the rifle, Terry's on the ground. "Well, Jesus, you've made my day," he said, clapping Chris soundly on the back. "This is one *hell* of a Christmas present!"

Looking over at his brother, Terry thought, Why don't you feel what I feel, the exhilaration? And then, joy turning to anger, I've saved you, you ungrateful idiot, and all you can do is stare at me in hatred while you cry like a baby.

Still, that was not the moment when he gave up on Chris. That came some weeks later. When Chris threw Terry's gift back into his face, Terry promised himself then that he would never put himself into someone else's debt. He never wanted to be weak, in an inferior or indefensible position.

"Always deal from strength," he hears his father saying again, "and the world will be yours."

The team dressed in baggy black Khmer leggings and shirts is inserted by helicopter into an area just outside An Loc. Captain Claire the CO, Terry the looie, second in command. They are barely three miles from the Cambodian border. They wait, crouched in the darkness, while the rising 'copter swirls dust and grit into their faces.

A pair of grim-faced Khmer Serei, the right-wing faction of Cambodian tribesmen, that the team has named Donner and Blitzen guide them through rice paddies and swampy jungle rank with mangrove. A kind of thunder stops them in their tracks. They turn their heads skyward, see beacons passing over them like eerie extraterrestrials. Moments later the earth trembles and the horizon in the west leaps with bright gouts of flame, quick bursts, then a line so brilliant it hurts the eyes.

"What the hell is that?" someone whispers.

Captain Claire says nothing, but privately Terry is doing some quick calculating. He wonders what B-52s are doing bombing targets across the frontier in neutral Cambodia.

Presently, they move on and, within a mile, come upon the perimeter of a Viet Cong encampment. Their guide signals to Captain Claire. The team spreads out. Terry, as yet nicknameless, and Kid Gavilan are assigned to take care of the sentinels.

Terry slings his AK-47 machine gun across his back, takes out a length of wire. At each end he has affixed a piece of dowel with which he can get a firm grip.

He has not yet killed a man, and in an intellectual way he is curious as to what feelings the act will engender in him. He finds his target, little more than an indistinct silhouette amid the foliage. The jungle is buzzing with insect life, the heat and humidity oppressive even after midnight. Terry contemplates the narrow back. How small and light the Viet Cong looks, how puny and insignificant.

Terry wraps the wire around his neck and pulls on the dowels.

Feels the first quick spurt of blood as Charlie's arms whip backward, trying to free himself.

Terry down on his knees, clamping tighter on the handles as death approaches. He becomes aware of its heat, its smell. The Viet Cong dances like a drunk or an epileptic.

Terry feels a kind of bond springing up between them, the taker and the giver, the master and the vanquished, the god and the mortal. He jerks the VC around so that he can stare into his flat face.

What he expects to find there he cannot say, though, perhaps after all it is the hope of a glimpse of the infinite. Instead, he watches eyes as opaque as muddy water stare into his with an expression of such unalloyed hatred that for a moment he is taken aback. The man's cocoa lips part, and he spits into Terry's face.

Terry growls deep in his throat, his brow knotted, his knuckles white with the pressure he brings to bear on the killing wire. There is an awful, fecal stench. Then the man is dead.

Unwinding the wire from the darkened flesh, Terry thinks that he has never before experienced the meaning of power, he has merely dreamed its existence.

He turns, sees Kid Gavilan in trouble with his target. Draws his knife, slams it between Charlie's shoulder blades with such murderous force that the Vietnamese leaves his feet. For a moment Terry and Kid Gavilan stare at each other. Then, bloody face grinning, Kid Gavilan waggles his thumb skyward.

Terry advances over the slumped enemy, unstrapping like the rest his AK-47, firing brief, accurate bursts into the encampment. He sees the giant nicknamed Axman, played guitar back in Red Hook, wading into Charlie, mowing down the enemy. Ten minutes later the team has made its way back to the point set for the rendezvous with the 'copter. It appears, and Captain Claire says, "Right on the money."

They all feel invulnerable as they ascend into the heavens, immortal as if they are Norse gods returning to Valhalla. But Terry, sitting in darkness, with the ether singing past his ears, his weapon across his knees, is thinking of the bombing run about which Captain Claire was silent.

The seventeen-year-old Kid Gavilan, tape cassette player around his neck, slaps Terry's knee and, grinning, says, "That was great work back there. I figure you're Butcher now. Yeah, Butcher." He slaps out a spunky rhythm on Terry's knee. "Hey, man. Everybody agrees."

They are led into the jungles each night for mission runs, but the talk is not about Vietnam. Terry does not see a map of the country or even an update regarding the status of the war in their area. They might be in the Philippines or Guam for all they know of Vietnam.

At other times, bored, filled with dreams he cannot recall, Terry prowls Ban Me Thuot like a vampire unafraid of daylight. Increasingly, in his forays into the tumbledown Coca-Cola-can shanties, Terry is hearing about Cambodia. In between blasts of Jimi Hendrix and the Doors, Terry gleans the morsels of the only history to survive here, the one that existed yesterday.

Terry coming out of a gray-green rain so torrential that he literally cannot see three paces in front of him. Even the ubiquitous motorbike traffic has been temporarily curtailed. It is so hot and steamy that the rain feels warm to the skin. The only good thing about the rain is that it has also temporarily curtailed the ferocious mosquito attacks.

Inside the corrugated-tin shack bar, a neon sign glimmers DRINK COCA-COLA in Vietnamese script. Terry orders a "33" beer. No sooner does he settle on a seat than a swarm of girls in multicolored *ao dais* descends on him, making him think that he would prefer the mosquitoes.

At the next table he hears conversations like music. "All you have to do is look in a fuckin' history book," a pimply-faced former farmhand is explaining to his black buddy. "Don't disappoint me, Fist, you *can* read." A strong-arm man with an upraised fist painted on the side of his scarred helmet. "Sanctuaries have been essential to every successful guerrilla war." In Vietnam every boy is an expert. "The rumor is that COSVN HQ is in one of those sanctuaries in Cambodia." COSVN, Terry has already learned, being the acronym for Central Office for South Vietnam, the legendary nomadic base from which, according to Command, the Viet Cong and the North Vietnamese are conducting the war. "Unless we can find and destroy it, we'll never win this shitty war."

In the days and weeks to come Terry hears this plaint over and over, as if it were a litany or a catechism. A Way to get out of here.

It is always raining, it seems, in Vietnam. Certainly, Terry is soaked each time he enters the rattletrap bar with its DRINK COCA-COLA neon buzzing fitfully, like a bad dream of another time, another place. Another life.

Always there is a blue-bearded bear of a man, sitting in the rear corner of the place where it is dark, hunched over his own bottle of hooch. Like a cowboy from the Old West, he wears a handgun holstered on one hip, a marine KA-BAR knife with a handle carved in the shape of a screaming American eagle sheathed on the other hip. Terry is interested in him because the girls leave him alone, which means that either they know something about him or that he had been incountry since Noah stepped off the Ark.

One day Terry sits down at this man's table.

"Get outta here," the bearlike man says. He's got lieutenant's bars, so it can't, Terry decides, be an order. Nevertheless, with the looie glowering menacingly at him, he whips out a bottle of single-malt Scotch he bought on the black market, puts it on the table next to the man's almost finished bottle of Canadian Club.

The man stares at it. "Get outta here," he says, "but leave the Glenlivit."

Terry laughs, breaks the seal on the Scotch, pours them both hefty shots. "They call me Butcher," he says, lifting his glass.

The bearlike man wraps a meaty hand around his glass, downs the Scotch in an instant. Terry thinks he hears him sigh, though it's hard to tell with Jimi Hendrix singing about kissing the sky.

The man pours another, begins to sip it slowly, lovingly, like a connoisseur. "Name's Virgil," he says.

"Is that your nickname, or is it Lieutenant Virgil?"

Virgil shrugs. "Who remembers anymore. Whoever I once was, I'm Virgil now."

"I'm with the Special Forces SOG," Terry says. "What do you do here?"

"I find things," the looie says. "I hold my lamp high, look into the burning darkness."

"You been incountry a long time?" The Glenlivit is fast disappearing, and Terry realizes he should have bought two bottles.

"It depends," Virgil says, "on how you measure it."

Terry nods. "I know what you mean."

"Nah," Virgil says. "You don't. You're like all these other suckers who don't know why they're here or what the fuck they're supposed to do. Take it from me, pal, this is the most shitfaced excuse for a war that has ever been perpetrated on an unsuspecting public. And the public is us."

"That so?" Terry says, interested. "Well, *I'd* sure like to know what the fuck I'm doing here."

Virgil stares at him for a long time, as if he is an archaeologist holding a vase, wondering what it is made of. "Okay," he says. "You asked for it, you're gonna get the whole nine yards." Pouring more Glenlivit. "These generals here at MACV don't know shit about being here. They think they can take an army essentially trained for heavy tank warfare on the open, rolling terrain of Northern Europe and have 'em adapt to guerrilla warfare in this stinking pesthole.

"Instead of training the South Vietnamese in guerrilla warfare, Command has seen fit to take our own guys—kids whose average age is nineteen—and pit 'em against Charlie.

"Well, let me give you a bit of news, pal. We're losing this fucking war. General Westmoreland's famous 'Search and Destroy' missions against the VC—the linchpin of the our so-called tactical approach to the war—are dismal failures.

"Of course, now that he's gone, Command is either too stupid or too vain to admit to such a monumental blunder. So neutral Cambodia is fast becoming the war's scapegoat."

Virgil takes the last of the Scotch. "See, Cambodia is where the VC is building sanctuaries, arming itself with supplies from the Chinese communists through Laos via the Ho Chi Minh Trail. Now Command knows we won't win it in Vietnam, so they're planning an insane and illegal invasion of Cambodia. And with it, everything—and, pal, I do mean *everything*—is going down the drain."

Virgil watches the girls in the peacock *ao dais* moving through the room. "Y'see, Butcher, Cambodia is the key. If you don't know anything about Cambodia—which most guys here don't—you'll never understand this war. Prince Norodom Sihanouk, Cambodia's leader since 1945, has spent decades treading a damned dangerous political tightrope, holding hands first with the communists, then the French and the Americans, and back again. Sounds stupid, huh? Well, it wasn't. It was just about the only thing that allowed his country to remain free and nonaligned in the battle for Indochina.

"Just as importantly, he kept Vietnam, Cambodia's stronger, age-old enemy, at bay, while receiving aid from both Peking and Washington.

"But, shit, now Cambodia's in for it. Because Sihanouk's allowed the COSVN sanctuaries, Command's decided to go in there. Invade Cambodia."

"You're nuts," Terry says. "What an insane idea. The military'd be pilloried. The administration wouldn't stand for it."

Virgil smirks. "Nixon and Kissinger. Yeah, well, this war's being run by madmen, so what can you expect? Everything's going to come apart in Cambodia, and it'll spread from there. This, Butcher, is the beginning of the end. The fall, as it were, of the American Empire.

"Already there are rumors that the left-wing *maquis*, who Prince Sihanouk calls the Khmer Rouge, are much more powerful than he has led us to believe. Unlike the right-wing Khmer Serei who do our dirty work, we have no control over the Khmer Rouge. They're a wild card in this fucked-up deck, and I think the most potentially dangerous element.

"Anyway, I wouldn't be surprised to see Sihanouk out, maybe assassinated, within six months. And, when it goes down, you can bet one way or another, we'll have a hand in it."

"What do you mean, one way or another?"

Virgil shrugs. "It's not only the armed services are over here, Butcher. Vietnam's become a den of CIA thieves. Who the fuck knows what evil those bastards are up to?"

One moonless night, as the 'copter takes the Special Forces team through cloud-filled skies, Captain Claire speaks to them. This is most unusual. SOP is for the team to receive their premission briefing on the ground just before departure. This time there is none.

Over the heavy vibration, the yammering of the rotors, Captain Claire says, "We're on pretty much of a milk run tonight, a recon ops. Surveille the immediate sector you'll be assigned. As you know, the weather's been lousy recently, so Command needs first-hand confirmation of extent of damage. It sounds simple, and it is."

The team with their heads together as if they are praying before an important football game, Captain Claire shouting to be heard over the din.

"We're essentially picking over a target site of an 'Arclight' bombing run. I don't know if any of you have seen the devastation that kind of a carpet strike causes. Take it from me, it's awesome. Nothing is apt to be left alive. But you're likely to find tarmac roadways, semipermanent buildings, even concrete bunkers. If you do, make immediate note of the number and size."

Terry looking down as the moon slides out from a bank of black cloud, seeing An Loc already to the east, the river twisting by below, shining dully, overhung by slanted trees, ropy vines, knowing now for certain that they are crossing the frontier into forbidden Cambodia, a neutral country where they have no business being. And he thinks, if we're bombing Cambodia—no matter what the cause—then surely we've lost all reason, all perspective.

Knowing this has a peculiar effect on him—it makes him cautious. The aura of invulnerability, the sense of being part of a cadre of male Valkyries being dropped from the skies, abruptly seems to him absurd, an adolescent's wild dream. It occurs to him that the man who seeks power need fear only one thing, the madness of his superiors.

He turns his attention to the other men in the 'copter, sees by the tiny red interior lights their expressions of hungry anticipation, as if by their stares they can melt plastic and steel.

The 'copter dips, banks steeply, circling briefly like a bird of prey. The team, bristling with hardware, jumps from its belly, bastard offspring of the mechanical mother.

Deposited on the dark side of the moon, the team spreads out. They are confronted by a holocaust. Craters, their edges still charred and smoking, pock the devastated area. The clearing has been made by the carpet bombing run. Stumps of trees dot the area. No roadways, structures, or bunkers.

Remnants of supplies litter the ground like a garbage dump. Terry, kneeling, can make out Chinese ideograms as he turns over what is left of the wrappings. These supplies have made their way down the Ho Chi Minh Trail to the VC. So this bombed site has nothing to do with the Cambodians, but with Command's almost monomaniacal quest to destroy COSVN.

And yet, it has everything to do with Cambodia since, in order to appease North Vietnam, Sihanouk has given his tacit consent to allow the VC sanctuaries inside his country's borders.

Cautious, moving slowly on, Terry finds the first of the blasted bodies. Beside him, the CIDG known as Tonto squats, checking faces or what is left of them.

"VC?" Terry asks.

Passing from one corpse to the next, Tonto shakes his head. "Khmer," he says. "Cambodians." He raises his head, and Terry can see his resemblance to those dead faces.

"Not soldiers, surely."

"Where are their weapons? Their ammunition?" Tonto shakes his head again. "These were peasants who never knew of this war, or understood its nature."

Terry says, "Do you know any of these people? Are they family?"

Tonto gives him a slow, sad smile. "My family is far from here. I am not Khmer Serei. I am not tied to your government or to Lon Nol. I am a Cambodian soldier who has spent much time in Burma. My real name is Mun."

The earth shaking, the sky red around the edges, full of whipsawed debris, lethal as bullets. Even the stumps of trees disintegrating between them, the dead killed all over again, joining the living, inundated with a hail of automatic fire.

As he goes down, Terry sees Captain Claire being hit in half a dozen places, his blood exploding along with the bark and flesh of the trees. Kid Gavilan lurching like Frankenstein's monster with half his head blown away. Donner and Blitzen, the team's two Khmer Serei guides, are dead, sprawled facedown in a crater.

"Jesus Christ!" Terry says as he lies half over Mun. "They told us that this was a milk run, a recon, no one left alive after the 'Arclight' carpet bombing."

"What the American army doesn't know about this war," Mun says, "would fill many volumes."

"This is insane," Terry says. "I can't even see a single VC."

The chattering of the automatic cross fire is deafening. Mun closes his eyes and sighs. "Butcher," he whispers, "is this your blood or mine?"

Terry feels between them a swamp, a hot and sticky morass. "I don't feel anything," he says.

"I don't either," Mun says. "I think I've gone numb."

Terry rolls carefully off the Khmer, sees the deep wound in Mun's side.

Quickly, he strips off his black cotton top, makes a crude but quite serviceable tourniquet. The blood stops oozing.

He sees Mun staring at him with his black marble eyes. "Where is it?" he asks. "Will I die?"

"The captain said dying doesn't matter to Asians."

"It matters to me," Mun whispers. "I have my family to think of."

Terry squeezes Mun's shoulder, not trusting himself to answer an unanswerable question. He puts his lips against Mun's ear. "I'm going to find the radio. A signal's the only way we'll get out of here in one piece."

"Assuming," Mun says, "I'm still in one piece."

Terry scrambles away, into the darkness and the death. He creeps from shadow to shadow, from crater rim to the darkened hollow of a charcoaled tree stump. Radio, radio, a child's song rang in his head, who's got the radio?

Axman. He remembers now, the big black guitar player, always doing Jimi Hendrix riffs. Axman, the radioman. Finds what is left of him, clutching the radio as if he had been in the process of signaling for help when the automatic fire tore him in two.

Reaching over, Terry rips the radio out of his desperate grip, sees in the corner of his vision a spark as of a faraway match, hears the familiar *brrraatt!* of Charlie's automatic fire, then the sickening, tearing pain in his side.

He rolls, or lurches or jerks, spasming like a fish. Hurtling into the darkness at the bottom of a crater. Drawing breath is an effort, heat and cold suffuse him, alternating to the beat of his rapid pulse.

Curled in a fetal position, eyes staring upward at the rim of the crater, waiting. Waiting for the inevitable. Waiting for Charlie to come.

Mosquitoes all over him, feeding on the blood, and flies coming, licking up the salt sweat on his face. He dare not move. Dare not.

Until the silhouette, three of them, cautiously hovering at the rim, too far away, but spotting him, coming down, coming nearer, and Terry biting away the pin, throwing the grenade, screaming with the pain it causes him, hearing, or perhaps only imagining the *buurrpp!* of their AK-47s before the world turns white and the earth, appalled at this further abomination, vomits him up.

He lies for a long time, bathed in the sweat of fear, listening to the night chitter and moan. He thinks, This is not the way I thought it would be, not at all what I bargained for. Where's the power here? In death, only death?

There has to be more.

And he thinks of his brother, Chris, flown away from America, from the army, from his duty. In France, the sun shining on his bronzed body, framed by the quaint white Côte d'Azur buildings and the cobalt Mediterranean. A French girl kneeling beside him, oiling his body, relaxing him.

While he, Terry the Butcher, lies here stinking, bleeding, dying of the fear. Is it fair? Terry asks himself. Is it right? To be here so far from France, so far from home? How he hates his brother, Chris, how he envies him, as he always envied the genuine pleasure Chris found in girls, the mundane society of school life that Terry could not help but disdain. But how far that disdain removed Terry from the mainstream of life, consigned to observing it from afar, like a god on Olympus.

Lying here, bleeding, dying of the fear, while Chris, the coward, neatly sidestepping his duty, his responsibility, soaks up sun and sex. How he wishes he was his brother now.

There is a bitter taste in his mouth. A shudder of dread overcomes him. It is far better, he decides, to die than to be dying of the fear. There is nothing, he thinks, worth that.

So he picks up the radio and calls for help, "Nantucket, Nantucket, this is Pequod! We walked into an ambush! We got heavy casualties! Get us the hell out of here, pronto!,'' though he knows that it hurts, coughing up blood in heavy clots, though he suspects that he will be heard by Charlie, now things are different, things have changed, *vita vice*, because he loathes that feeling, that dying of the fear, more than he is afraid of anything else.

You been here a long time?

It depends, Virgil says, *on how you measure it.*

And now Terry knows what he means. Because he is slowly, painfully making his way back to Mun in the night filled with mosquitoes as big as leeches, his skin crawling, everyone out for his blood, which, with every inch, he is leaving in this fetid soil.

Somewhere out there in the chittering darkness Charlie lurks, waiting, patient as Buddha, malevolent as a serpent's bite. But that is not what frightens Terry now. Rather, it is the knowledge that Charlie is inevitable here, is as much a part of the landscape as the blasted trees, the scorched earth. Charlie is inescapable, and he knows that if the chopper doesn't arrive within the next five minutes, he and Mun will either be dead or will take a long time dying in Charlie's cage, somewhere past the river Styx, in the bowels of hell.

He finds Mun, dragging himself through the mud, the pain making sparks fly behind his eyes, in his brain. Mun's eyes are closed but, for a moment, Terry is so exhausted that he lacks the energy to see if Mun is still alive.

He listens to the night, to the insects' chatter, the tree frogs' mating calls, straining for portents, for some sign that Charlie is on the march, closing in. Terry is not yet ready for Charlie, but neither is he ready to die.

Opens his eyes, calls, ''Mun. Hey, Mun.'' Softly, a breath on a breeze stinking of rotting vegetation, decomposing bodies. He is being eaten alive by bugs. ''Wake up, Mun.''

Beside him, Mun stirs. ''Is it the Butcher,'' he says, ''or Ravana?'' His voice is furry, thick as syrup.

''I radioed for help. We'll be out of here soon.''

''Ah, Butcher.'' Mun sighs. ''Then I am still alive.'' He cries out, Terry's hand on his wound.

''Sorry, buddy,'' Terry says. ''But I wanted to check. The bleeding's stopped.'' At least for the moment, he thinks. And then, Where is that fucking chopper?

''I heard an explosion,'' Mun whispers. ''Was I dreaming?''

''I put Charlie to dreamland,'' Terry says.

"What?"

"A grenade in his shorts."

"There's more of them, Butcher," Mun says. "I can feel them out there."

"We'll be gone in a minute," Terry says. "Then let Charlie fuck himself."

"And if the chopper doesn't come?"

"What do you mean? It's on its way."

"And Ravana is on his way," Mun says. "Which one will get to us first, I wonder?"

"Ravana? Who is this Ravana?"

Mun turns his head to look at Terry. "I am a Theravedan Buddhist, Butcher." Terry can plainly see the pain etched into his face. "Ravana is the supreme demon in our cosmology."

"Powerful little devil, huh?"

"So much so," Mun says seriously, "that he can even turn Buddha away from his meditation."

"Well, if he's coming after us," Terry says, "I hope to hell the chopper gets here first."

"But it may not, Butcher," Mun says. "In which case, we must make preparations."

Terry whistles him to silence. He has heard something—what?—a stealthy footstep, the swish of foliage, the brief cessation of the tree frogs' endless sexual dance? All of these, or none? He cannot tell, he cannot fully trust his senses. Pain, like panic, distorts reality, making you miss things, forget about others. It is a dangerous state to be in at any time; in this situation it is absolutely lethal.

Terry checks his AK-47, puts in a new clip. He wishes he was mobile. He feels helpless, totally vulnerable. And, of course, he does not want to fire his weapon unless it is essential, the flame will give away their position.

"What is it?" Mun says after a time.

"I don't know," Terry says. "Nothing." Then, to take his mind off the unbearable tension of uncertainty, "What were you saying?"

"Ravana will not come after you," Mun continues. "He wants me."

"Just you? How come?"

"Because I have something that belongs to him," Mun says. "The *Prey Dauw*. The Forest of Swords."

Up until that moment Terry has not really been paying attention or, if he has, he was not believing any of it, Khmer demons, Buddha, all of that Eastern nonsense. But then he thinks of what Captain Claire said about Asia. *First thing to remember is that you'll never understand the place. It's hooked into a different reality, and if you try to make it conform to your Western ideas, you'll wind up causing someone else's death, or worse, be dead yourself.*

"You're telling me you've got something that belongs to a demon?" Terry says. "What the hell is it?"

"Not the demon directly. A talisman that belongs to Mahagiri, the outlaw priest who was Ravana's disciple many eons ago. With the demon's assistance, Mahagiri composed the *Muy Puan*, a forbidden book of Theravadan scripture that describes the one thousand hells, and how to invoke the evil spirits who dwell there. The *Prey Dauw*, forged by Mahagiri with Ravana's guidance, is the living embodiment of the *Muy Puan*. Whoever wields it controls this entire quarter of the world. This is what my people believe."

"Do *you* believe it?"

"In a way," Mun says, eyelids drooping, "that does not matter. Their belief makes it so."

"How did you get this thing?"

Mun hesitates for a moment and, for the first time, Terry catches a hint of real fear in the Khmer's eyes. "I come from a long line of priests, Butcher. A special line, it is said." He blows out a hissing exhalation. "We do not talk of it, my father and I. And since I am the eldest son, my father told only me. We are the descendants of Mahagiri. It is how my father had knowledge of the *Prey Dauw*'s location. The burial site was passed down from generation to generation.

"No one ever touched the talisman or dug it up—or even dared go near it. Until I did." Mun's eyes are so wide with fear that Terry can see the whites all around the pupils. "Times change and I wanted to make sure that the original burial site would not be compromised. I wanted to move it to a safer hiding place. Or at least this is what I told myself. Then I held the sword in my hands, and I did not want to let it go. I could feel its power, Butcher, like the thunder of a dark river, endlessly flowing. Its strength became my strength. Then I understood fully why it is a symbol of power that Khmer and Burmese alike—all the Theravadan Buddhists—acknowledge.

"I grew frightened, and did as I had meant to do. I buried it again in a safer spot."

Mun is quiet for a time. It is a strain even to speak. But still the fear emanates from him, seeping into the night like a noxious gas.

Terry considers Mun's words. For the first time since they are in this position, the gnawing fear is pushed aside. His mind is hard at work. "Tell me," he says, "is this *Prey Dauw* feared also by the mountain tribes in the north of Burma, in the Shan State?"

"You mean by the opium warlords?" Mun nods. "Oh, very much so. These are highly superstitious men. The Forest of Swords has a special meaning for them; they would kiss the ground on which it lies. But that is of no concern to me, Butcher. If Ravana comes and the Forest of Swords is in my possession, he will devour me. I will be with him and with Mahagiri forever, banned from *samsara*, outcast from the wheel of creation." He shudders.

Now Terry understands Mun's terrible fear. He knows what a hideous fate banishment from *samsara* is for a Buddhist, who believes in the cycle of regeneration. To take the wheel of creation away from a Buddhist is tantamount to condemning a Catholic priest to hell. That is, if one believes in *samsara*—or in hell.

The only hell Terry believes in is the one he finds himself in now. But as Mun has said, the belief of the people created the power of the Forest of Swords. Terry thinks, What I could accomplish with that power!

"Is there anything I can do to help?"

"Yes." Mun is grave. "Now I must will you the Forest of Swords, Butcher. You must accept it of your own free will. You see, you are not Buddhist. As far as Ravana is concerned you do not exist. He will not be able to take me, and the Forest of Swords will be safe from him." His black eyes beseeching Terry's. "You will do this for me?"

Terry, believing it, not believing it. What the hell? Who knows the difference here in the land of make-believe and death? Seeing how agitated Mun has become, how the bleeding has begun again along a ragged seam of the Khmer's wound, says, "Yes," because he wants him calm, he has already lost too much blood. But also because he can already feel the *Prey Dauw* in his hands, can see himself walking up the Shan, the talisman in his hands, the mighty Shan opium warlords kneeling before him like liege knights, giving over their priceless fiefdoms to him to do with as he will. Power! Unlimited power!

But all that will be meaningless unless they can get out of hell. Mun will, Terry calculates, be dead inside of a half hour. And, if Charlie comes now, they will both die before that. Where is that fucking chopper?

"Swear it, Butcher!"

"I swear it, Mun."

Mun begins to speak. Terry sees movement now, definite, voices jabbering in sharp, harsh Vietnamese, quickening on the sodden breeze. Charlie is coming. Not the damned Ravana, not the goddamned chopper; Charlie.

"I buried the *Prey Dauw* in Cambodia. Listen closely. When I tell you where it is, it will be yours, I will be free, Ravana cannot harm me, take me out of *samsara* forever. It is within Angkor Wat. Have you heard of it? The ancient city of the Khmer kings. It is full of spirits, a fitting place for such a talisman to rest. . . ."

Listening to Mun with one ear, memorizing the location of the Forest of Swords, if such a thing truly exists, Terry draws a bead on the moving shadows, is about to fire.

Thwup-thwup-thwup!

The night lights up like New Year's Eve as the chopper, swooping in from the east, turns on its powerful spotlights, automatic fire coming from its open ports, ventilating Charlie, riddling Charlie, exploding Charlie.

Thwup-thwup-thwup!

And Terry, feeling the big wind whipping at him now, sending cinders upward into the night, the tornado about to whisk Dorothy and Toto off to Oz, drops his head on Mun's chest, and thinks, Saved.

"Hey there, you with the stars in your eyes."

And just like that, Terry pops into consciousness. Feels a whirlwind of events–emotions–half-dreams inside his head. For a moment, he is full up. Then it is all gone like a puff of smoke in a conjurer's act, and he recognizes the face hovering over his.

"*Bellum longum, vita brevis,*" Virgil says.

"You look like a bear." Terry's voice is more of a dry croak.

Virgil grins. "The better to eat Charlie with, my dear."

"Where the hell am I?"

Virgil looks around. "This particular bit of hell is the field hospital at Ban Me Thuot."

"Can you find out about the guy they brought in with me? How is he?"

"Ah, the Khmer, Mun." Virgil nods. "Shot up some. Worse than you, they tell me."

"Wait a minute," Terry says. "How come you know his name?"

"He's one of mine," Virgil says, "that's why."

Terry digests this, says, "Will he be okay?"

"He'll survive. Not yet his time to check out of this stinking pit. Yours, either, I see. You had a rough time of it?"

Terry, the recent past rushing in on him like a tidal wave, says, "They're all dead—Captain Claire, Kid Gavilan, Axman, the Khmers, the whole fucking outfit except me and Mun."

"Tough luck."

"You think that's what it is? Luck?" Terry struggles to sit up, is overcome by a spell of pain and vertigo, lapses back onto the pillow.

Virgil shrugs. "In war," he says, "nothing else exists but luck. Shit, Butcher, I'm a hero. Want to see my field decorations? Want to know how many VC I've killed? That was a long time ago. I was older then, I'm younger than that now.

"You're following in my footsteps, son. You'll get a medal for this. We're both heroes now. So how does the army repay your bravery under fire? They ask you to go back and try again to get yourself killed. That's all they really want from you, Butcher. Your life."

Terry is not so groggy that he does not understand what Virgil means. "And what is it *you* want from me?"

"How'd you like to get together a whole new unit? Be in charge, recruit them, be the CO?"

"You can fix that? How?"

"I hold my lamp high, look into the burning darkness."

"In other words, don't ask." Terry looks at the looie. "And what would it do, this unit I would lead?" he asks.

"I'm Virgil now. I told you, I find things. I thought maybe, after this event, you might want to join me in finding things."

"Things like what?" Terry says, thinking, What does he need a Khmer for?

"All kinds," Virgil says. He grins suddenly. "Anyway, what does it matter to you? This is the war, remember? Getting rich sure beats the shit out of dying."

It does not take him long, thinking of the stench of death, of being eaten alive, of, more than anything, dying of the fear, which he has promised himself he will never again feel. Thinking of the madness of his superiors, the madness of those directing this war, the administration. Virgil saying, *That's all they really want from you, Butcher. Your life.*

Considering, too, that with his own unit he will have a chance to get back into Cambodia, to Angkor Wat, where the Forest of

Swords, the talisman of power, is buried. A power more potent, even, than the ubiquitous death that dominates Vietnam.

Studying the looie, wondering what he sees there, good or evil. Or maybe just a Way out, a better Way than trying to find COSVN, trying to find death. "What the hell," Terry says, holding out his hand. "Like you said, war is long, life is short."

Taking Terry's hand, Virgil laughs. "That's the spirit."

Outside, on a white latticework patio, leafy climbing hydrangea grows in dense profusion, its pink flowers perfuming the air. Tendrils, curled and reaching, spread across the weathered boards of the patio, twined around the wrought-iron legs of the chair. In the chair, Soutane lounging, bare feet up, the hem of her blue-and-white summer dress kicked high above her knees, firm tanned thighs crossed one over the other.

Chris Haye can see all this from the rumpled bed where he lies coming slowly to life. His body aches, and he thinks, This is pathetic, I'll never get in shape. Staring at Soutane's long, gorgeous legs, thinking, Jesus, you'll never get in shape that way. But for sure you'll get to heaven.

Abruptly, as Soutane moves, the legs disappear beneath a swirl of blue and white. She comes into the house, and her nose wrinkles.

"*C'est le souk ici!*" she cries. It's like a cattle market in here!

Chris laughs, rises just in time to catch her as she throws herself onto him. "Sometimes, for an athlete," Soutane says, "you're disgustingly lazy."

Chris, his face in the forest of her night-black hair, thinks, That's because, unlike Terry, athletics never came naturally to me. I had to work my butt off for every mile I ran or biked. But sometimes while the body is strong, the mind tires of the constant grind, it craves some rest, wondering what it is, after all, working toward.

Rolling off her, hands behind his head, staring up at the ceiling.

"What do you see there, cat?" Soutane asks. "Only cats see life in shadows."

"The future," Chris says. "The past. Nothing."

She laughs, climbing athwart his naked chest, running her palms down his flesh. "I see this beautiful body coming through the Arc de Triomphe, covered by the yellow jersey." She means the coveted shirt worn only by the leader of the Tour de France, the world's greatest bicycle race. The Tour de France, which has brought Chris to France.

Watching his expression, her laugh fades, and she hits him with her balled fist. "Have I ever told you that you are terrible when you're depressed?"

Chris eschews watching the shadows, instead watches the green motes in her extraordinary brown, almond-shaped eyes. He lifts a hand up, gently strokes her hair back from the side of her face. "Sometimes," he says, "I don't know why I am here. Sometimes I pray it's to win this race."

"Now you are thinking about the war, are you not?"

"I am."

"What precisely are you thinking about the war?"

"Not about the war, really," he says slowly. "About my brother, Terry. He's there, in the war. So I guess I am thinking about the war, after all. I'm wondering if Terry is hurt. Or dead."

"And why you're here in France instead of in Vietnam."

"Okay."

Soutane makes a derisive sound. "You Americans!" she says, as if that, by itself, is a sufficient epithet. "You say 'okay,' and think that explains everything. What does this mean, anyway, 'okay?' "

"This time," Chris says, getting up, "it means, enough."

"I can't," she says, turning to watch him, "beat you as efficiently as you beat yourself."

Chris draws on a pair of shorts, a dark green T-shirt with NANTUCKET silkscreened in faded white across the chest. Out on the patio, the gentle Provençal morning falls across his shoulders. Sunlight, the artist's soul mate, seeps through the stands of sentinel cypresses in, it seems, discrete drops, as if it were, instead, rain, forming ever larger patterns that construct, finally, the whole.

He has rented this small house in Mougins because it is in the pre-Alps, the run just long enough to Digne, a town in the Alps maritime, a crucial stage in the Tour de France. Digne will be, Chris believes, a turning point in the race. Whoever wins the Digne stage will have the best shot at winning the Tour de France. Chris has become intimately familiar, over the past several weeks, with the topography in and around Digne.

This house is on the mountainside facing, like many of the old *mas*—the farmhouses of the region—the valley north beyond which the Alps maritime rise in mysterious splendor. It is a far different view from that which the million-dollar villas face on the other side of the mountain: the breathtaking vista south, down to the curling

Mediterranean. Chris has often seen that view from Soutane's parents' summer villa and, all things considered, he prefers this one.

Sometimes, on perfectly clear mornings, with the sunrise burnishing the Alps, Chris imagines that he can see Digne, lurking in the shadowy mountain pass, waiting.

"What are you painting these days?" Chris asks as he hears her come through the doorway.

"What are you writing?" she says.

She is still in the shadows of the eaves, and Chris turns. "With that body," he says, "you should have been one of *les petits rats*." He means the student ballet dancers with the Paris Opera.

Soutane draws her hands through her hair, making a chignon, the dancer's signature. "I almost took the veil, instead."

"I never believed that story about Soutane being your nickname." *Prendre la soutane* means to enter the Church. "It's just like you to embellish the origin of your name. It heightens the mystique of the artist."

She smiles. "But you'll never know for certain."

"These days," he says, serious again, "I don't seem to know anything for certain."

She comes to him, wraps her arm around his waist. "Except that you'll win the Tour de France." She goes inside, says, "What do you want for breakfast?" Before he can answer her, she has put her favorite Charles Aznavour tape on the portable stereo. Just like her, Chris thinks, but he does not mind. Whatever she prepares he will willingly eat because it will get him through his grueling morning ride, into the mountains to Digne. In the afternoon Soutane will drive up to meet him, and take him back.

Later, as he cycles, building up speed along the twisting rural roads, he thinks of home. Of his father, the proud son of a Welsh farmer who had done nothing more than scratch out a living for his family from the spectacular but unforgiving countryside.

Chris imagines his father emerging from the gray mists of Wales with only a slice of hard bread and a couple of shillings in his trouser pockets. Coming to London for his schooling, joining the Welsh Guards, fighting proudly for the Empire, meeting Chris's mother, an American from Connecticut, a Jew of Polish heritage, not at all the kind of woman Malcolm Haye had envisioned falling in love with. Because of her, and because by then all of Malcolm Haye's family were dead, emigrating to the States.

Enter, one by one, like bullets from a gun, Terry and Chris, the brothers Haye.

Terry. It seems to Chris that he had to struggle for what came so easily to his brother. Terry was born an athlete. He was stronger, faster, more clever than anyone else Chris can recall at school. Chris always struggling, making the second team instead of the first, second string instead of starter, in the shadow of Terry.

And that shadow, stretching, made him try all the harder to equal or surpass his brother's accomplishments. It was an impossible task, which, in a way, was why he felt compelled to take it on. That, sweet Soutane, is what I see when I watch shadows. I see what I should be, and am not, no matter how hard I try.

The one good thing: it led him to cycling, at first a solo event, where he would not be consigned to the second team—he could merely lose. He did that a lot, in the beginning. But slowly, painfully, he worked himself into second-place finishes, then firsts.

By then high school was over, and he and Terry had gone their separate ways. Terry, every bit the Welsh brigadier that Malcolm had once been, had wanted his sons to be. What do you have to possess, Chris wonders as he cycles through sunlight as thick as maple syrup, to be a soldier? Is it patriotism, pure and simple, or, as he suspects of his father and his brother, a kind of burning, personal anger that needs to be assuaged?

He was never touched by that peculiar kind of anger, that need he had observed in some other males to kill. He is a pacifist; that is why he is in France. Or, again, is it as his father claims, cowardice that has sent him here, running with his tail between his legs, running from the dark chaos of war, the possibility of death?

True, this is a war in which Chris does not believe, but so what? Is that enough? "How can you do this?" Malcolm Haye said when he met Chris at the airport. "I still can't believe that you're going to France instead of to Vietnam. Chris, it is your duty to fight this war, to help to keep the communists from overrunning Southeast Asia, to keep alive capitalism and free enterprise, those fundamental policies that make America great." There is no more fervid proselytizer than the man who has adopted, as Malcolm Haye has, his religion. His religion happens to be America.

America, Chris thinks, my country right or wrong? Has he used his pacifism as an excuse to cut and run? Chris wishes he was certain.

"Don't you want me to be proud of you?" Malcolm Haye said just before Chris slipped through the departure gate. "Don't you ever want to learn how to be a man?"

Soutane's father, a distinguished man in his early forties, is much more philosophic. He eerily resembles Charles de Gaulle. All he needs to complete the picture is the kepi on his head. His politics, oddly enough, are quite radical. He is adamantly against the war. He abhors what his country has done to Indochina, Vietnam, and Cambodia. "What we greedily began," he says, "the United States seems intent on finishing."

Odd because Soutane remains untainted by matters of politics or philosophy. She explains, while rubbing him down with liniment, "I had many boyfriends from a very early age. They were, it seems to me now, radicals, revolutionaries, Marats all, rather than Robespierres, irritants rather than reformers. They were too busy being angry to think of reform."

"Like your father?"

"My father is, perhaps, difficult to like. But he is likewise easy to admire." Her talented hands bleeding the aches and pains from his heavily worked muscles. "My father believes that change is the only legitimate path to progress. For him, change begins with freedom from the past."

"History," M. Vosges, Soutane's father, says, "is a manacle. Take Cambodia, for instance. We French made of it a colonial protectorate. While extracting from it her valuable natural resources, we undercut all native industry, driving the country's economy into an inexorable downward spiral. Artisans were forced into poverty, we created no new industry to take the place of the old. At the same time we encouraged in its leaders excesses, gross indulgences, corruption in the furtherance of our own wealth and power. In French manacles Cambodia retrogressed.

"The only way to change this deplorable state is to break the manacles, turn away from a history that holds nothing of value for the Khmer, who are prepared to enter the modern world.

"In short, it is clear that the only way to make Cambodia work is to free it of the past. To start over, wipe the slate clean."

M. Vosges grows excited, rubicund when he speaks in impassioned tones of righting the terrible wrong his country has perpetrated on Cambodia. It is, Chris thinks, as if he views his mission as a kind of jihad, as if he is armed not only with the rightness of ideology, but the sanctity of the Supreme Being as well.

One evening, at a dinner party in the Vosgeses' summer villa, a spectacular white stucco and terra-cotta-tiled estate named Mon Repos, Chris is introduced to a rather roly-poly Khmer in his early forties named Saloth Sar. He is, M. Vosges tells Chris, the leader of Cambodia's *maquis* freedom fighters, the Khmer Rouge. He also happens to be a former student of M. Vosges. "The one," M. Vosges says, "of whom I am most proud."

Saloth Sar shakes Chris's hand, they exchange pleasantries in French; he makes a joke of how much the French radicals have helped him, more even than Marx. When he laughs, he seems jovial and avuncular. But afterward, Chris overhears his comment to a group of dark-suited men, no doubt influential French communists, "Cambodia is already a land of blood and bitter tears." Chris observes a strange, disquieting darkness in Saloth Sar's eyes.

Chris joins the fringes of the group as Saloth Sar goes on, "It is my belief that General Lon Nol, Sihanouk's prime minister, has struck a deal with the Americans, specifically the Central Intelligence Agency. The Americans are notorious for ignoring history, for ignoring the realistic flow of internal events. They are blind to ideological currents."

He has a way of speaking in public that is riveting. His very presence commands attention. But when he speaks he becomes positively charismatic. Chris is oddly reminded of newsreel footage of Adolf Hitler he has seen years before. Of course, he thinks, there can be no comparison between the two, Hitler and Saloth Sar. And yet, their ability to incite and enthrall a crowd seems quite similar.

"It is my belief," Saloth Sar is saying, "that the Americans view Lon Nol as their Chiang Kai-shek, their great white knight against the scourge of communism in Cambodia. If we assume this is so, then we must assume that within a year Lon Nol will be running Cambodia. The people will have exchanged one despot for another. It will still be a land of blood and bitter tears."

"That would truly be a terrible thing for Cambodia," one of the French communists says. "We must do everything in our power to work against it."

Saloth Sar smiles, and again Chris sees that odd, disquieting darkness in his eyes. "On the contrary, my friend. We will do nothing at all to oppose Lon Nol.

"It will be incorrect to assume that nothing will have changed in my country. Following Lon Nol's ascension, we will be one step closer to true revolution. Lon Nol's hard-line policies will further antagonize the people. Their hardships will double, then quadruple. And, out in the countryside, in the mountains and the rice paddies, the Khmer Rouge will be gaining strength. Men and arms will be flowing to us like rivers to the sea.

"We are as inevitable as the monsoons. Our eventual victory is inevitable, too. Why not allow the Americans unwittingly to help us, as they unwittingly helped Mao by backing Generalissimo Chiang Kai-shek?''

Sometime later Chris sees Saloth Sar and M. Vosges standing in a shadowed corner. Above them is the open balcony of the second floor. Curious, Chris mounts the stairs. When he is directly above them, he stops.

''As usual,'' Saloth Sar is saying, ''the Americans are in the process of destroying themselves.''

''You mean the bombing runs inside Cambodia?'' M. Vosges says.

''Precisely. These illegal acts of war are ostensibly to flush out Viet Cong and North Vietnamese strike teams, but over two thousand Cambodian civilians have been killed by these American bombs. You and I both know that the Americans have designs on Cambodia. But they do not—cannot—understand my country. Now, aided by me, anti-American sentiment runs rampant in Cambodia. This, I promise you, will be Sihanouk's downfall.'' That charismatic fire transforms Saloth Sar's face. ''The American imperialists' terrible transgression is the leverage I need to rally more men to the Khmer Rouge cause. It is to our benefit to keep the myth alive that we are a ragtag bunch, in hiding from our own people. Now that the Americans have brought the war to Cambodia, the people see how wrong they have been to ignore the Khmer Rouge. Now they are joining in droves. Within months my army will outnumber Lon Nol's.''

M. Vosges is about to reply, but at that moment a bejeweled woman approaches them, engaging the two men in conversation. Soon after that Saloth Sar slips away.

Outside the French doors the garden of violets and woodbine is lit with candles. Beyond the vine-laden walls, the twinkle of lights in the valley, the glitter of moonlight on the Mediterranean, as far away as a photograph, as close as the soft scent of sea salt.

Celeste, Soutane's mother, dressed in Dior's finest, presses another glass of champagne into Chris's hand. With her copper-colored skin, her almost Polynesian features typical of the Khmer, her commanding height, she is extraordinarily beautiful, but perhaps less exotic than her daughter, who carries the traits of both East and West in her face.

Celeste has a personality that is akin to the calm before the storm, smooth, exquisite without, bands of flashing electricity within. She seems, if possible, even more politicized than her husband, M. Vosges.

She also seems avid to take Chris to bed.

"Don't you think that Soutane will mind?" Chris asks her.

"Anger varies," Celeste says, "with the extent of arousal." She leans over, trails a kiss across his cheek. "Trust me. It will be good for my daughter. I have been trying to get a rise out of her ever since I bought her her first brassiere."

Chris thinks, What would I have done with a mother like this one?

"And your husband?"

"As far as he is concerned," Celeste says, "I am a free agent. He has learned over the years that the only way to hold me is not to hold me at all." She smiles, engaging but not at all ingenuous. "So you see, you have nothing to fear. Quite the contrary."

"You'll have to explain something to me first," he says, deliberately staring into her provocative cleavage. "How do Marx and Dior enjoy inhabiting the same space?"

Celeste laughs. "Well, well," she says, squeezing his muscular arm, "all this and brains, too. Now I really must have you."

"La curiosité est un vilain défaut," Chris says. Curiosity killed the cat. "Do you have an answer, madame?"

She strokes the inside of his wrist, where the twist of the blue veins intrigues her. "You are quite right. Marx would never have understood the importance of a Dior," she says. "I am a radical. But I am not dead. Besides, even for a radical, money has its uses."

Carefully, as he would an octopus's tentacle, Chris disengages her hand from his arm. "I love your daughter, madame," he says.

When Celeste laughs again, there is a flintlike edge to it. "You have so much to learn about life, *mon coureur cycliste.*" She presents him with a smile that he cannot define. "You are still young. You think that you can hold passion in the palm of your hand. You have not yet learned that passion is like sand. It disappears no matter how tightly one tries to hold on to it."

"You're wrong."

"Am I?" Celeste fixes him with an unnerving stare. Then she gives him a smile so radiant it is seductive. "Well, you are still young enough, I suppose, to make foolishness a virtue." She is standing so close to him that when she takes his hand and presses it against her mons, no one can see.

Chris tries to jerk away, but Celeste, unexpectedly powerful, holds fast his wrist. "No, no," she says. "You should know what a real woman feels like." She is hot, pulsing beneath his fingers. It is clear that she wears nothing under the Dior. She moves his hand. "Rub it, rub it." His middle finger begins to disappear in a newly opened fold of cloth, and Celeste's eyelids flutter.

"Haven't you ever wanted to be part of something," she whispers. "Something larger than yourself. The eternal love you think you feel for my daughter is nothing compared to having participated in social change. Upheaval! Manning the barricades! It is our God-given duty to free those not as fortunate as ourselves." Her face twists in a sneer. "Do you really want to live your life as she has chosen to live hers, afraid to commit herself to any cause? How cheap, how worthless life is under those circumstances."

In the heat and the smoke of the party Chris feels abruptly light-headed. He has trouble breathing. Then, as he feels Celeste's fingers close around his hardened penis, he breaks away from her.

Is she laughing as he stumbles away, drunk on her ministrations and her words?

"All my mother really wants," Soutane says later as they dance to the music of a South American band, "is to discover what it will take to corrupt men."

"Does she hate all men so?" Chris says, wondering if he should tell Soutane that her mother has tried to seduce him.

"Oh, definitely," Soutane says, her samba creating a stir in the room. "But only if they are Western. She blames them for what has happened to her country, to Cambodia."

He is thinking of how committed to a cause Celeste is, of how little Soutane wants to contribute. She is, like him, essentially self-involved. "She has reason to hate."

"But not, I think, to do what she does. To my mother, anything that resists politicization is contemptible. Celeste believes in destiny and extremism as if they are canon."

Sweat like jewels springs out on her bare shoulders. She has flung off her shoes. A young, black-haired Brazilian woman sings in Portuguese, "We will be together forever, my love, on the white sand beach, in the blue ocean, my sweet love."

"Are you hungry?" The green motes in Soutane's eyes have grown large in the low light. "Do you want to eat?"

They are near the open French doors, and he pulls her into the garden filled with candlelight and moonlight, warm light, cool light, striping them like tigers.

He leads her running, panting, down ancient stone steps, partially reclaimed by moss and lichen, past tall pilasters, pale and pitted, a sober reminder of how time works.

Behind a hedge, beneath a lotus tree heavy with fruit, they tumble down. The smell of lavender and earth. He can hear the pounding of her heart as he kisses her between her breasts.

He pulls up her tight dress, fumbles until she is bare underneath. Her dress is around her hips, just the lowest edge of her fringe is visible. He begins to lick her voluptuous mound. She opens to his caress, already wet.

"Mon coeur," Soutane breathes, tangling her fingers in his hair. She frees her breasts, pulls his hands up to them. The nipples are very hard, and she moans as he rubs them.

Her marble thighs, strong as oaks, surround his head as, her abandon growing, she lifts them higher. Until, arching up, spasming, she clamps him in a soft, erotic vise.

Kissing him, she whispers breathlessly, *"Mon ange, mon bel ange,"* opening his trousers, enveloping him with her tongue, her lips, the inside of her mouth. She puts him between her breasts.

Chris, watching through eyes slitted with pleasure as she crouches over him, sees the moonlight drape her, burnish her skin, the pools of mysterious darkness between.

When she returns him to her mouth, he is overcome with delight, throwing his head back, closing his eyes, and moaning. Hearing her whisper, as her excitement mirrors his, "Yes. Oh, yes." Then he is engulfed to his very root.

Afterward, they lie together, staring at the molten moonlight pouring through the layers of leaves above their heads. Sounds of the party come to them now and again on the breeze, another sensual samba, a brief gust of laughter, the clink of glasses together.

It is as they are kissing, gently, languorously, that they hear Celeste's voice so close that she must be no more than several paces away.

"I am happy to give you everything you need," she says.

And then, in answer, Saloth Sar saying, "I am pleased to say that I always get what I need at the house of Vosges."

Chris rolls over. Soutane's mother and Saloth Sar must be on the other side of the hedge. Soutane beside him, her hair, wild after their lovemaking, tickling his ear.

"I have gotten Kalishnikovs," Celeste says. "They are absolutely the best weapons available. Better even than the American machine guns."

Saloth Sar laughs. "That is, my dear Celeste, what I love most about you. Your authority in matters that by all rights should be outside your ken."

"Outside the female domain, you mean."

"Perhaps, yes."

"That is how this family works," Celeste says. "My husband covers the theoretical. I manage the practical."

"Such as the procurement of the Kalishnikovs."

"I am good at that. Even the unexpectedly large number you ordered did not faze me," Celeste says without much vanity. "I am good at many things. For instance, I think that we should change your name."

"My name?" Saloth Sar says. "Why?"

"To make you more memorable. More easily recognizable. Names are important, you know. Names of leaders, especially."

"What do you have in mind?"

"I think you should call yourself Pol Pot."

"Pol Pot?" Saloth Sar seems to be rolling it around in his mouth. "It is not a Khmer name. It has no meaning."

"All the better," Celeste says. "You will give it its meaning."

Saloth Sar—or Pol Pot—laughs. "Ah. The family secret is out at last. You are the dominant one."

"Not at all," Celeste says. "Many people have underestimated my husband. None of them are in power now."

"Of course. Between the two of you, your contacts are quite extraordinary. I don't know what my Khmer Rouge would do without your help."

"We have raised quite a bit of money for you tonight," Celeste says. "You are most persuasive."

"The plight of the Khmer Rouge makes me so."

"And what of the other Cambodian people?"

"Well, they are like sheep," Saloth Sar says. "Worse, perhaps, because they have already been corrupted by the imperialists. The intellectuals, the priests all work against the good of the people, the teachings of the Khmer Rouge. This is a grave problem that needs solving."

"What will you do?"

"The only way to rid a host of disease," Saloth Sar says, "is to cut the disease out completely. In order for the balance of power to be truly overturned, we must cut the Americans' legs out from under them. We must cut off their arms. Then we must castrate them so that they will never forget their transgression in Cambodia. To do this, all their contacts—Lon Nol's people, as well as Sihanouk's—must die. The government, the bureaucracy that perpetuates the hideous myth of American benevolence must be eradicated. So, too, the intellectuals and the priests. The new generation of Cambodian must be reeducated as we see fit without interference. 'From the cradle to the grave'—as your husband has taught me. Educate the children properly and the right-thinking adult will follow."

Chris turns to Soutane. He looks into her eyes, finds only despair. He thinks of his conversation with Celeste, how she longs to be a part of something larger. A social change, she said. An upheaval. But what Saloth Sar contemplates is mass murder. It is inhuman, unthinkable.

He motions to her, and they move away from the scheming couple. He whispers in Soutane's ear, *"Elle est le mauvais ange de lui."* She is a very bad influence on him.

Soutane says, "I think that they are very bad for each other."

Chris draws her farther away from the hedge as if it contains poisonous serpents. "We have to do something," he says fiercely. "We have to tell someone in authority."

Soutane looks at him clearly. "No," she says.

Chris is stunned. "What do you mean, no?" He watches her as she rises. "Do you understand what we just heard?"

"I am young," she says. "I am not stupid." The daughter curiously echoing the mother. She begins to walk back to the house, to the South American band playing its seductive music, to the flowing champagne, the acres of cut crystal and silver.

Chris, angry, grabs her wrist, spins her around. "Soutane, Saloth Sar means to gain control of Cambodia, to upset the balance of power in Southeast Asia. Saloth Sar hates the American presence. He'll do whatever he can to drive them out, to eradicate any edge they might now have against the communists there. And if he is successful in getting the American military presence out of Vietnam, he will turn his attention inward. To Cambodia itself. You heard him. He will murder every priest, every intellectual. In order to start over, in the name of the revolution, according to the ideology he was taught here by your father, with the help of the weapons your family will provide the Khmer Rouge, he will commit what amounts to genocide on his own people. Doesn't this mean anything to you? Doesn't it affect you? Or do you see it as tiny and distant, part of another world that cannot affect you?"

Soutane's eyes flash. "Let me go," she says. She bares her white teeth in the moonlight. "He is doomed to fail. I know about the Khmer Rouge. They don't have much support even among their own people."

"They're more powerful than you think," Chris says tightly. "I overheard Saloth Sar and your father talking before. Their weakness has become a myth. Besides, from what I understand, they haven't been well armed before. Now your family is taking care of that." He stares into her stony face, anger welling up in him at her smug and casual attitude. "Anyway, can we afford to take the chance that he will fail? Do you want that on your conscience. That we knew about this intended coup, and kept our mouths shut?"

"I don't care what you say. I want nothing to do with this."

"With you or without you," he says, "I am going to the authorities."

"You fool," she says, "do you expect me to implicate my family? Besides, with their contacts everything will be denied. I doubt that the Americans at the embassy or wherever you plan to go would even listen to such a fanciful story. You will accomplish nothing save embarrassing yourself."

She is right, of course. But knowing this makes Chris even more furious. "I don't care," he says. "I can't stand idly by. I have to do something."

"Don't you understand?" she cries. "If you go, if you try, my father will have you killed."

"You're not serious." But, of course, she is. He knows this with a chilling certainty. Celeste saying, *You have so much to learn about life,* mon coureur cycliste.

He realizes that he is as helpless as Soutane is uninvolved. He realizes that there is after all no difference between them, that he has been a fool to flee here, a frightened refugee from life, trying to escape the war. Because the war has dogged his footsteps, following him all the way to France. It was around the corner all the time, lurking in the shadows to ambush him when he least expected it, a land mine in the gut, tearing away not flesh and bone, but the fabric of reality.

Looking into Soutane's suddenly hard-lined face, he thinks, I could use a little thunder now, a little power at my fingertips, causing some sparks to fly in the night. But he has nothing, he understands, having come here unprepared, as it were, naked.

And now, at last, the truth. He feels not only inadequate to the task of dealing with the consequences of the war, but he finds himself unwilling to face up to them.

He hates himself but, unable to accept that burden, he hates her. He knows that she is right, it is better to remain uninvolved, but he hits her anyway, slaps her so hard across the face that she stumbles and falls.

Soutane is so surprised that she does not even cry out, but lies on the ground, her hand to her hot, hurt cheek, staring up at him.

"Nobody treats me this way." Her voice flicks like a lash. "Get out of here. I never want to see you again."

The countryside, sienna and forest green, slips by, the wind slipstreams past his hunched body. Chris, pedaling, picking up the pace, extending his daily runs, doubling, tripling the distance he managed when he first came to France. Dedicating himself to the Tour de France, focusing all his energy on the race, because it is all he has now; if he lets go of it for even a moment, he is engulfed in a well of despair so black that it freezes his heart.

During the long, grueling days of exercise and practice, amid the spectacular gorge of Haute-Provence, he believes that Soutane is far from his mind, but each night as he slips, exhausted, into sleep, she is there.

He encounters her in dreams filled with dark, Brazilian rhythms that seduce him back to the brilliantly lit house, back to her gray-green eyes, her voluptuous embrace. He reaches for her, with a silent groan he enters her, only to find that it is Celeste, not Soutane, into whom he plunges with such blind, aching desperation.

Always, he awakes from these dreams with an erection so hard, so unfulfilled it is painful. The unpleasant trip-hammer beat of his heart forces him to abandon sleep, instead to embrace dire thoughts in the night until the bitterness in his throat causes him to rise from the empty bed, silently dress, ride his bike into the darkness shimmering with incipient dawn.

He misses Soutane. But that he must deny himself her companionship, her warmth, her affection and love is, as Saloth Sar said about victory, inevitable.

Despite what he said to Soutane that night in the garden, he has told no one of the overheard conversation between Celeste Vosges and Saloth Sar. Much as he yearns for her, he thinks that her absence is hardly punishment enough for keeping it to himself. He does not understand his reluctance to expose himself to danger. He detests its very existence, yet he cannot deny within himself its truth.

It is raining now, the sun, suddenly fearful, has fled behind the protection of black clouds. Chris cycles in the rain, joining his team, the men with whom he will be sharing the victory or the defeat of the Tour de France.

Chris packs his bags. With the team he flies to Paris. They take time off to sightsee the Eiffel Tower, Notre Dame, the Place de la Bastille, the Louvre.

He cannot see these splendid monuments for what they are; instead of inspiring awe, they exhaust him, he feels lost inside them, Jonah in the belly of the Leviathan. But at night he cannot sleep. His mind is abuzz, a hive of unhappy activity. At last he goes to the U.S. embassy. The ambassador is away, the undersecretary is otherwise engaged.

After waiting an hour and a half, Chris is ushered into a room as dark as twilight. It is filled with gross furniture that resembles monstrous children's blocks. Its only view is of a ventilator shaft, so he knows this cannot be the ambassador's office.

He tells his story of Saloth Sar and Cambodia to a sallow-skinned kid who cannot, Chris thinks, be that much older than himself. Halfway through, the kid says, Excuse me, but what did you say your name was? Chris tells him, the pimply-faced kid nods. He holds a pen officiously in his hand, but he takes no notes. Instead, he is drawing a doodle of a woman with big, high breasts.

I want to see the undersecretary, Chris says.

I'm afraid that's impossible, the sallow-skinned kid says in the bored, practiced voice of the professional bureaucrat. He smiles rather absently, drawing in a thigh-high skirt.

Chris gets up.

Is that it? the sallow-skinned kid says.

In his hotel room Chris drafts a letter, rewrites it, sends it to the U.S. ambassador. What else can he do? He can think of nothing more. It is as Soutane said it would be.

The team is waiting for him. They travel northward to Roubaix. As they train, they discuss various strategies, up until the last nervous moments before the start of the race. In the rain, a chill at noon, they begin, jockeying for position through dangerously slick, cobbled streets. Then into Belgium and Holland for two days, riding through immaculately tended urban parks. Recrossing the border, nearing Meziers, climbing long hillside stretches, racing along narrow tree-lined roads, bounded by stone fortresses centuries old, remnants of a time before France was France.

They squeeze water into their dry, open mouths as the killing heat builds up. In the sun Chris sees Soutane, in the rain as well. In fitful sleep, caught each night in a different town, he tosses her image around in his mind, ceding her her time to torment him. With each ache of his muscles, her absence is apparent to him. She, or perhaps what she has come to represent, is a naked sore within him which he cannot stop himself from abrading.

Not first or second, but each day near the front of the pack, keeping the yellow jersey in sight. As the days progress, as the race grinds through its gut-wrenching middle, when endurance, conditioning begin to count, the Tour de France grows in his mind. Winning becomes something akin to attaining the Holy Grail, as if in crossing the finish line first he will somehow have earned a kind of salvation, a cleansing of his sin of omission, forgiveness for the transgression of being here, far away from the mortal danger of the war.

On the final day, beneath a scowling sky, Chris is still within hailing distance of the yellow jersey. Paris, which has been a dream for twenty-two days, over almost nineteen hundred miles, is here.

By the time they leave Creteil, within, as the cyclists say, the petticoats of the great metropolis, the crowds have built until they are in places twelve or fourteen deep. Chris feels the collective breath of the spectators as if it is a wind at his back, pushing him on. Pain flares in almost every place on his body, but the adrenaline, his greatest ally, continues to pump strongly, and he picks up the pace, passing first Troyes of France, then in quick succession, Jurco of Yugoslavia, Spartan of Belgium.

Only Madler and Castel remain. Castel, the Frenchman who has worn the yellow jersey for the past three days, strong, indomitable within his own element. Madler, the tenacious Swiss, who led during the first six stages of the race, has clung to Castel's tail throughout this last, long day.

Though twice more he has come tantalizingly close, Chris has worn the yellow jersey only once. Just outside of Ballon d'Alsace, at the end of the sixth stage, a mechanical failure cost him a crucial eleven seconds—an eternity in this race. From Thonon-les-Bains to Chamonix, the ninth stage, he was close enough to reach out and touch the yellow jersey as he and Castel crossed the finish line one–two, the difference measured in inhuman terms, in hundredths of a second. And setting out from Digne, for the twelfth stage, he was wearing the yellow jersey he had taken from Castel.

None of that matters now, Chris realizes. It is the end, the finish line across the Champs Elysées, that counts. Soutane running her palms down his flesh, saying, *I see this beautiful body coming through the Arc de Triomphe, covered by the yellow jersey.* Oh, God, please let her be right.

From the outset the odds have been weighted against him. Long-distance cycling is the exclusive province of the countries of Continental Europe. His very acceptance on a team caused a bit of a stir, gave him celebrity status in all the prerace coverage. And, then again, as the race went along, and he was able to keep pace with, and even overtake, many seasoned professionals. He did well in the time trials, the sprints, especially in the arduous mountain stages through the French Alps, where it was assumed he would wither and fall back.

Now, on the last day of the Tour de France, he has a legitimate chance of winning it all. By placing first today, Chris will have accumulated enough points to be declared the overall winner.

Who would recognize him? He has lost almost ten pounds. He has had no time to shave, and a reddish-gold beard covers his face. Catching a glimpse of himself in a shop window one morning, mounted, ready to begin the day's stage, he is startled to see the face of the Celtic warrior his father always wanted him to be.

His mind, blurred by fatigue, heightened by the abnormal amount of adrenaline being pumped into his system, concentrates on only one thing: the finish. He is, like the others, beyond exhaustion. Trancelike, in a state of grace, the leaders race toward the heart of Paris, there to make six laps of the Champs Elysées before they hit the tape strung beneath the Arc de Triomphe.

The crowd, the crowd. How they shout, call out the names of their favorites as they flash by. Chris hears his name. Amazing!

Down the wide, beautiful boulevard, Chris finally overtakes Madler, the Swiss champion. He will remember that moment vividly, the look of bewilderment on the cyclist's face.

Now it is Castel's back that Chris sees. He no longer feels his legs. His shoulders, hunched against the wind and the rain, are like concrete. They are on their fifth lap of the Champs. After twenty-two days, there are only minutes, so little time left.

Chris moves up, gradually, inexorably. At the last turn Castel skids slightly on the treacherously slick tarmac, and Chris gains perhaps three, four seconds. His front wheel is almost parallel with Castel's back wheel.

He tries to make up the last several feet between them, but Castel desperately manages to hold him off. Chris can see the finish line now, distant, calling with a siren's song in his head.

Now he knows that he has one more shot, just one. Instead of challenging Castel again, he moves slightly back, so that he is directly behind the leader. Immediately, he feels a lessening of the stiff wind, he gains strength, slipstreaming, riding in the quiet corridor of Castel's wake.

And now, three hundred yards from the end, he makes his move, beginning his drive in the relative calm of the slipstream, building momentum, his leg drive, then at the last instant swinging out into the wind, moving up on Castel's right shoulder, challenging him, gaining, gaining, almost there, and then past the stunned Frenchman, on his way to the finish, to wear, as Soutane predicted, the yellow jersey beneath the Arc de Triomphe.

There is a blur in his vision. So concentrated is he that at first he does not see the dog running out past the policemen lining the boulevard, keeping the crowds back.

It is almost upon him when its shape registers. Even so, in a dry surface he might have been all right, a slight swerve, okay. But the wet tarmac that was so cruel to Castel only moments before once more comes into play.

Chris swerves in order not to hit the dog, his tires skid, losing traction in the rain. Chris slams to the ground, his bicycle falling heavily onto his leg and hip.

Pain sears him, blood begins to run. He hears shouting, an ambulance's high-low klaxon. Sees, from what seems an odd angle, feet running toward him.

He looks up, sees Castel crossing the finish line, back arched, arms held high over his head, fists clenched in victory. He looks down, sees his leg open, blood pumping. Flesh peeled away from the bone. He has never seen anything so stark and white in his life.

He falls back, cradled in someone's arms. He is aware of a great relief from pressure as two policemen gingerly lift his bicycle off him. Then the pain rushes in, and he loses consciousness.

A dog. A lousy, stinking dog. He thinks: I should have hit him, gone right on through. Then he thinks: It would have been the same. I would have gone down anyway.

Another voice says: Who cares? It's over.

He thinks: If I'd hit the dog, I would have killed it. I can't kill anything.

He opens his eyes and, to his surprise, sees Soutane.

"What are you doing here?" *I never want to see you again.*

"I was there," she said, bending over the hospital bed, "to see you win. And you would have."

He thinks: I would have. What exactly does that mean?

"A dog—"

"I saw it," Soutane says. "I broke through the police cordon. I held you while they took the bike off you. I went with you in the ambulance."

He looks at her, wondering what he is feeling, besides empty. It seems he came to France for nothing.

"My leg—"

"Will be fine, the doctors say."

"But not," Chris says, knowing, "as good as new." He sees Soutane look away. "Not, anyway, good enough to bike again in the Tour de France."

"No," she says softly. "That's finished."

Well then, Chris thinks, fuck everybody. He lies back on his pillows and closes his eyes. "Why are you here, Soutane?"

"I thought—" She breaks off. He hears her moving tentatively about the room. At last she says, "You wrote a letter."

"About Saloth Sar, about Cambodia. Yes. I went to the embassy in Paris, but no one would listen to what I had to say. So I wrote to the ambassador, an impassioned plea for the Cambodian people. I'm glad some action was taken."

"Nothing will come of it. The inquiry is dead, as I told you it would be." She stares at him. "You implicated my mother and father," she says. "I warned you not to do anything like that."

"So?" Chris thinks: Fuck Saloth Sar, fuck Cambodia, and most of all fuck Soutane's parents.

"So. You accomplished nothing but you put yourself in jeopardy. You asked, now I'm telling you. That's why I've come. In a few days you'll be able to leave the hospital. As soon as you are released, you must leave France."

Now he opens his eyes, hearing in his mind her say, *If you go, if you try, my father will have you killed.* But he is still so angry. "Or what?"

Soutane is close to tears. "I don't want you hurt." She bites her lip. "I've come. I've done what I can. I've told you what I can, more than I should."

She goes to the door, stands holding on to the steel knob as if without its support she will collapse. "You should have won, Chris," she says. "I'll always think of you in the yellow jersey."

When she leaves, the room seems to shrink down to the size of a cell. Claustrophobic, Chris struggles to breathe. Lying in the bed, sweating with fright.

He hears footsteps coming along the corridor outside. He holds his breath until they pass by. But they do not. They stop outside his door. He imagines a man with a knife, merciless and deadly, about to silence him forever. *If you go, if you try, they'll have you killed.*

Chris, panicked, tries to sit up but, as in a dream, he cannot move. It is too late anyway. The door is swinging open, and a dark-complexioned man pushes his way in.

He smiles at Chris, and says, "I am Dr. Devereaux. How are you feeling today, Monsieur Haye?"

PART II

FRENCH KISS

SPRING, PRESENT

SHAN STATE/NEW YORK/NICE/ PARIS/TOURRETTE-SUR-LOUP

Admiral Jumbo, opium warlord of the Ninth Quadrant of the Shan Plateau, said, "How many Chinese soldiers have we killed today?"

Mogok grinned, revealing the pigeon-blood-red ruby set in one front tooth. "Fifteen," he said, "so far."

The Communist Chinese government was continually sending raiding parties into the Shan in a futile attempt to eradicate the immensely lucrative opium trade.

Admiral Jumbo hefted his machine pistol and grunted. "Not enough. General Kiu has already killed a score of soldiers. One, I hear, is a lieutenant. Very great *joss*."

Admiral Jumbo was not his real name. He was, like most of the most powerful opium warlords, a renegade officer from the Communist Chinese army. Admiral Jumbo was heavy, hence his name. His girth, so he believed, was a sign of great *wa*, great inner spirit. Thus he fostered the dissemination of his nickname. As to his military rank, the "admiral" was a kind of joke, inasmuch as the Communist Chinese had little by way of a true navy; many Chinese disliked the high seas since, out of sight of land, they got violently seasick.

He was a decidedly ugly man, with oversized features and an unpleasantly pockmarked face. He wore canvas breeches, and a sheepskin vest he had no doubt stripped from a dead Russian soldier. He carried scabbarded knives on each hip. His fingers were encircled by ruby and sapphire rings, stones which, other than opium, were the primary source of wealth in Burma. At his throat was a carved circle of jade.

Mogok, a Shan tribal chieftain, now a lieutenant in Admiral Jumbo's opium army, looked at the warlord. In the weeks since her death Admiral Jumbo had not mentioned Ma Ling's name. It was as if she had never existed. "What we need to do is kill some more," Mogok said.

"No. What we need to do," Admiral Jumbo said, squinting into the harsh sunlight, "is to take some Russians. We haven't done that in quite some time. One Russian is worth the *joss* of a score of Chinese."

On the other hand, Mogok thought, since Ma Ling's death, Admiral Jumbo has been obsessed with gaining great face, even to the extent of abandoning his normally conservative methodology. Even Ma Varada, the girl of insatiable desires, whom Mogok had presented to Admiral Jumbo to take Ma Ling's place, had had little effect on him.

"Oh, yes. I myself often think the Russian KGB is more intrusive here than the Communist Chinese army," Mogok said, in an effort to display his grasp of the overall situation.

"Bah!" Admiral Jumbo spat into the underbrush. "Russians smell bad. They stink from a hundred paces. And they are far too stupid for me to worry about." He spat again, a sign of nerves. "Still, General Kiu, I hear, has been stockpiling Russian weapons. I would very much like to know why."

Ah, Mogok thought, now I understand. Admiral Jumbo's basic live-and-let-live approach to territory had in recent days been replaced by a desire to avenge himself against his enemy. Up here, in the hinterlands, revenge meant expansion. Which, of course, meant the Tenth Quadrant, controlled by General Kiu.

"General Kiu is like a piece of poisoned meat," Mogok said. "Better off left untouched."

Mogok did not like General Kiu. In fact, he was quite frightened of the warlord. Weird tales, though twisted perhaps by those with long tongues, of methods of torture for amusement, of the total abasement of women, even of transgressions against holy writ, swirled around General Kiu like mist about a mountaintop. Did these terrifying tales reveal the truth, or obscure it? Mogok did not know; he was not even certain that he wished to find out.

Admiral Jumbo grunted to show his contempt. "Let others stand in cowardly awe of Kiu," he said. "I knew that son of a whore when we were both in the army together. He was well known. His venality was unparalleled in the armed services."

"Then how did he remain in power for so long?" Mogok asked. "Through friends?"

"Fear," Admiral Jumbo said, confirming Mogok's darkest suspicions. "Kiu always knew where the highest-level secrets were buried."

"It is said," Mogok ventured, "that General Kiu still rules by fear. If that is so, there is only one secret here that would be of sufficient interest to him: the *Dah a mya Gyi*, the Forest of Swords."

Watching Mogok shudder, Admiral Jumbo winced. "Why bring that up, Mogok? The Forest of Swords has been lost for centuries. No one knows where it is." He peered out at the winding dirt trail. "But if I knew where it was, if I had it, Mogok, then it would be so easy to make General Kiu pay for his sin. He would watch, helpless, as I marched into the Tenth Quadrant, commandeering all his poppy fields, all his armies, all his network contacts, all his wealth and influence. General Kiu would fall to his knees before the Forest of Swords. And when I touched him with its jade blades, he would shake himself apart with fear."

Now Mogok was beginning to suspect that, if Admiral Jumbo had his way, they would soon be pitted head to head against General Kiu. This was nothing new for the Shan States. The Tenth Quadrant was the most lucrative for harvesting the tears of the poppy. Over the years, since General Kiu had come to power, many warlords had tried to wrest control from him. None had succeeded. It was looking increasingly as if Admiral Jumbo was determined to try.

Certainly, Mogok thought, many would die in such a frightful confrontation. And those who did not? He shuddered. In that event, if the tales about General Kiu were even fractionally truthful, the dead would be the lucky ones.

Mogok crouched down behind a tree trunk, sucked meditatively on a tooth. There was magic here on the high mountains, powerful magic that had for centuries lain asleep, dreaming while it gathered strength. If General Kiu indeed had access to the Forest of Swords, then surely he could unlock that magic, use it against all who were foolish enough to stand in his way of controlling the entire Shan opium trade. For that, truly, was what General Kiu desired. He would be invincible, even perhaps as the *Ta Taun* scriptures say, immortal.

"It is also said that General Kiu was not born of woman."

"What?" Admiral Jumbo looked at Mogok as if he had grown another head.

"Yes." Mogok, seeing the look on Admiral Jumbo's face, thought that perhaps he should not persist in this. But once begun, his anxiety propelled him forward like a driverless jeep, hurtling with increasing velocity down a steep mountainside. "It is said that he had no mother, that he exists outside *samsara*, the wheel of rebirth."

"Huh! That is nonsense," Admiral Jumbo said. "You know better than I do that we Theravadans believe that everyone—man, *nats*, gods, and demons—is bound by *samsara*."

"That is true." Mogok's eyes were bleak. "Except for Mahagiri, the renegade monk who created the *Ta Taun*, the Book of One Thousand Hells. His punishment is eternal, beyond the help of even Ravana, the demon who seeks to destroy Buddha. Mahagiri is immortal, but he has been cut off from *samsara*. He must remain the same, unchanging, forever."

Admiral Jumbo frowned. "What are you saying?"

Mogok swallowed, summoning all his courage. "That General Kiu and Mahagiri are one and the same."

"Mogok, I wonder if you know how foolish you sound."

"Mahagiri cannot die," Mogok persisted. "This is his *karma*. He merely takes on different guises. Well, this is the lore of the Shan. I merely point out that these stories about General Kiu exist."

"Sunlight," Admiral Jumbo said, "clears the mist. Reason is like sunlight in this climate—it dissipates superstition. I advise you to forget these stories, Mogok. Yes, it is true that Mahagiri is immortal, that he returns again and again to this part of the world in order to try to change his *karma*, to lift the curse that makes him the most wretched of creatures." Admiral Jumbo shuddered. "To be outside the wheel of life is indeed to inhabit One Thousand Hells. But whoever Mahagiri may be, he is not General Kiu. I have fought beside General Kiu, and I assure you that he is as much flesh and blood as you or I."

"If you say so," Mogok said, but his voice evinced no conviction.

They heard the sound of a birdcall, and their muscles tensed. Someone had been spotted by one of Admiral Jumbo's sentinels, coming up the trail.

They both checked their weapons, thumbed the safeties off, prepared at a moment's notice to open fire. "Not a Russian," Admiral Jumbo said as the man came into view. "Put down your gun. It's Mun."

Gray light dirtied by the steel mesh over the grime-encrusted window fell across Peter Loong Chun, isolating him from the shadows of the rest of the featureless cubicle.

He sat, like a penitent, hands clasped in his lap, on a steel chair bolted to the floor. He looked neither to the left nor to the right. His left arm was immobilized in a hard cast that reached from his fingers to his shoulder.

"If you want," Seve said, pointing to the cast, "I'll autograph it." There was no response. Seve was standing across the cubicle from Loong, reading the Dragon's dossier, drinking coffee strong and acrid enough to be used as motor oil. "Does it hurt, Loong? I hope to Christ it hurts like hell. I saw Richard Hu's widow last night. Her husband was one of my men. When your bodyguards blew him away, they shut the book on you. Elena Hu thinks you should die. She may be right. I stayed up half the night with her. She may still be crying today, tomorrow, who knows?" Seve gulped at the coffee, feeling it burn its way into his stomach. He continued to read Loong's dossier, updating himself on Diana's continuing surveillance of Loong's sister.

"You're not going to die, Loong, at least not yet. Today I am your protector. Today and forever. I'm going to see to it that you stay alive for every day of the life sentence you're going to get."

At last Chun's head came up. Eyes as depthless as a sheet of plastic stared at him incuriously. "Chinese have a saying. 'When the wind blows, only the weak cringe.' "

Seve came across the cubicle, the idea blooming full-grown in his mind. "Is that what you think I'm doing now, blowing wind?"

Chun shrugged. "I am safe here with the police. I am safe anywhere." There was no expression on his face. "You cannot harm me. Prison cannot affect me. What have I to fear?"

Seve could hear the small sounds of the precinct house from outside the locked door of the interrogation cubicle. He knew that Chun was right. Unless he could find a way to break the Dragon, he had done only half his job.

"A lifetime in prison," Seve said. He bent down so that his face was level with Chun's. "You're responsible for the deaths of three policemen, including one of my men. At any moment a fourth death may be added. I don't care how many lawyers you hire, you won't beat Murder-Two. They would have fried you, in the old days. Now we have to be content with isolating the disease. But before I send you off into purgatory, I want my pound of flesh. I have you; I've won, don't you see. I wanted the pipeline that has been bringing the prime-grade horse into Chinatown. Now I've got you, and you, Loong, *are* the pipeline. At least this end of it.

Without you it's dead, until they can find a replacement for you—and I'll be watching for that, count on it."

Chun's face showed nothing save, perhaps, boredom. He might have been watching a summer rerun on TV. "On the contrary, you have nothing," he said. It was important for face that now at the end he show the extent of his power. "That is because you know nothing. You want the pipeline, but you don't even know one end from the other."

Seve looked across at the Chinese sitting calmly, and thought, I'll squeeze him of everything he knows. I swear it.

Seve was watching Loong closely. "So," he said, snapping shut the dossier Diana had given him, "if you won't talk, I suppose we'll have to get our information from your sister."

Chun did not move, but his eyes turned as opaque as stones. "I have a sister," he said. "She lives in Hong Kong."

"Really?" Seve said. "Hong Kong. Not in the penthouse loft at number one Greene Street in SoHo? Not Ki Shen Song, the artist? At least artist is what she's calling herself this week. Last week it was model, and the week before, dancer. She is—what is it?—a visionary?"

"You have the wrong woman," Chun said in a sullen voice. "My sister Ki lives in Hong Kong. I visit her four times a year."

"Oh, yeah," Seve said, emerging from the shadows, "you travel to Hong Kong four times a year, but the trips have nothing to do with your sister, 'cause she's here, Loong. In Hong Kong you have meets with your drug wholesalers between sleeping with your mistress, Brilliant Kwan."

"Save it for court." Chun sneered. If he was surprised that Seve knew the name of his mistress on the other side of the world, he had hidden it well. "That is, if you can prove anything."

"In court," Seve said, "all I'll have to do is produce Ki Shen Song, because I'm going to link her to your drug trafficking. We found six ounces of cocaine—pure, righteous stuff—in her possession. She'll do the hard time with you, Loong. How do you like that?"

"You shit!" Chun shouted. "My sister has nothing to do with it!"

"She's a beautiful woman," Seve said. "Do you know what prison does to beauty, Loong? It melts it like wax. It corrodes it like acid." He was concentrating hard. This was the first time that he had gotten a reaction out of the Dragon, and because it was a nerve that ran deep, he was determined to use it for as long as Chun would let him.

"What are you telling me?"

"Yeah," Seve said. "I've got Ki Shen Song here at the precinct." He laughed without humor. "But how could that be? She's in Hong Kong, right?"

"You had no right to invade my sister's privacy," Chun said heatedly.

"You're not expecting me to believe you have feelings," Seve said, "are you? Not after you killed three cops."

"They came after me," Chun complained, his tone already changing. "A man in my position must have bodyguards. Those cops were fools. They just broke in, guns drawn. What did you expect? My men were doing their job, protecting me."

"No, definitely not feelings," Seve pressed doggedly on. "Not after you maimed a sixteen-year-old girl just to get at me."

"You'll never be able to prove Ki has anything to do with my business," Loong said, just as if he was not at all concerned.

"See you in court, Loong," Seve said, crushing his paper cup into a bolted-down wastebasket.

Before he could call for the door to be unlocked, Chun said, "Stay away from Ki. You'll pay dearly for bringing her into this."

"Is that a threat?" Seve said, rapping on the steel door. "Because if it is, pal, you just bought yourself a one-way ticket to Palookaville."

Seve left Chun in there to stew for a while. He went into the next room, where Diana had been observing through a two-way mirror.

"That was some bluff, boss," she said. "It was so close to the edge, I could feel my stomach turn over." She followed him to a scarred metal table where something resembling coffee was kept hot. "We don't have anything on the sister. All I saw when I followed her into the dance club's ladies' room was her snorting a couple of rows. There wasn't enough coke left for even a nuisance bust."

"What are you worried about? It worked." Seve took a paper cup from a pile beside the hot plate. "Jesus, did you see him jump! That's a first for that bastard." He poured himself more coffee. "I'm going back in there and finish the job I started on him." He saw the look in her eyes and said, "What?"

"What about Chun's lawyer? He should have been here for this. If he were, he never would have allowed you to—"

"Fuck Chun's lawyer, and fuck Chun three times over. When he murdered my men, when he did that to the girl, he showed his contempt for the law, he said *adiós* to the human race. Any emotion you expend on Loong will be wasted."

"Yeah?" Diana's eyes were fiery. "Well, what about all the emotion *you're* expending on him. You shouldn't be in there with him now. I don't know what's gotten into you, boss."

"Can it," Seve said tightly. "Why aren't you up in New Canaan, goosing our friend Detective Blocker?"

"I've already been on the phone to him." She threw him a look that, had he not been so preoccupied, would have made him wince. "The stuff will be coming in over the FAX wire within the hour."

"Good. I'll be interested to see if the autopsy findings are consistent with the picture of the war fan you showed me. That book of yours could be the key."

"You'd better wrap this up," Diana said. "You've got the last session of your DEA InterNat-Link course in an hour."

Back inside the cubicle with Peter Loong Chun, Seve said, "I just took a peek at your sister, Loong. She don't look too good."

"Bastard." Chun ground his teeth. "What is it you want?"

"Me? Oh, not too much." Seve bent over him. "I just want it all. Every fucking inch of the pipeline. As the godfather of Chinatown, you've got it all up here." He tapped Loong's temple. "You give it to me, and I'll see that the coke we found in your sister's place disappears. *Poof!* Like that. I can do it, Loong, 'cause I'm your angel."

Chun looked up at Seve. "Then maybe I'm already damned."

Seve frowned. "What do you mean?"

"Godfather of Chinatown?" Chun was shaking his head. "I do not have that power. I am merely a caretaker. A gardener, as it were, lovingly sowing like Johnny Appleseed the white powdered poppies as they are shipped into my safekeeping. And for this, as you would expect, I am paid a salary. A handsome one, to be sure, but a salary just the same."

Seve was totally unprepared for this. "But all our information—"

"Was supplied by my network," Chun said. "I believe the government calls it disinformation. It was useful for a time to have you believe in a fairy tale. But now, as you see, I have been revealed as, how would you say?, the Wizard of Oz. A charlatan, of sorts." He looked at Seve. What was in his eyes? "So, now you have me, and you have spent so very many months pursuing me. To what end? You were pursuing a phantom. As we wanted. Now you are further from the truth than when you began, because I am ignorant of the information you desire. I have no idea where the pipeline begins or who actually runs it.''

''Bullshit! You're in Hong Kong four times a year. Who do you meet there, errand boys?''

''Essentially, yes. Oh, these men are quite a bit higher up than that. But they are cutouts, nonetheless. They are pristine from a security point of view, and so am I. Do you still want their names? I'll give them to you.''

Seve felt the anger hot behind his eyes. He wanted to lash out, to grab hold of that smirking face and rip it to shreds. But he did nothing.

Instead, he said, ''I have one question to ask you, and you'd better think long and hard before you answer because your sister's future depends on it.'' Bending over, Seve gripped the arms of Chun's chair. Face-to-face, unblinking. ''If you don't run Chinatown, who does?''

He could see something small and desperate writhing behind Chun's eyes. ''If I tell you, I'm a dead man.''

''Hey, if you *don't* tell me, your sister is history, pal.'' He put his lips next to Loong's ear. ''You've never been inside. You don't know what it's like. Especially for a woman with your sister's looks. She'll last—what?—six months. After that, even you won't recognize her. The women inside are animals, Mack trucks on two legs. They'll take your sister, squeeze her until she's dry. You're calling the shots. Now you condemn her, Loong.''

Seve backed away, saw the tremor in Chun's temple. ''All right,'' Loong said at last. ''But you'll have to spring me for this.''

''No fucking way, pal.''

''It's that or nothing,'' Chun said. ''Where we're going, we've got to go together.''

''Wherever you and I can go, I can take a police team.''

''Think so? Your quarry will be gone before you've left the precinct.''

''What are you saying?''

''You think no one on the outside knows what happens in here?'' Chun said. ''Figure it out for yourself.''

And Seve, feeling uneasy for the first time since he started the interrogation, suspected that Chun wasn't lying.

Milhaud, in the arms of Morphée, dreamed aloud of his wife. Morphée, a Vietnamese woman of exceptional beauty, was used to this post-*amour tristesse* from her client. Young on the outside, inside she was, perhaps, older than he.

Milhaud's wife had been dead for some years, but he had scarcely forgotten what she had done to him or, rather, what they had done to one another.

In those days the name of Milhaud had not yet been invented. He had lived his life nearer to Asia, enmeshed in controversial politics, closer to revolution.

But now, times had changed radically. Asia was a place simply of business, controversial politics was passé, revolution was a part of history. With the internationalization of world economies, even the once great leaders had ceased to dream.

Long before the others, Milhaud had seen the failure of his—and their—policies. The death of his wife had been the last straw, the last link in a previous and outdated life (he and his daughter had had no contact for some time). And so he had ceased to exist. Six months later Milhaud had appeared in Paris with the proper credentials, and had been quickly snapped up by Le Giron, the Society to Return to the Fold.

But his mind was not so easily able to shed his past life. A ceaseless machine, his brain continually dredged up incidents, somber, shadowy, unpleasant, that haunted him during the hours of pleasure or sleep.

Morphée, who knew how to please him in every physical and psychological way, was nevertheless at a loss to stem the flow of effluvia from his past life. After sex, while he lay, half asleep, entwined within her moist thighs, he spoke softly, his words a dark river of misdeeds, small evils, and secret pain. She held his head, kissed his sweat-soaked forehead as she would if he had a fever, recognizing a stream-of-consciousness anger that, growing like a malignant, living thing had, over time, wrecked a family, destroyed several lives.

How many men had Milhaud's wife slept with; how many times had she deliberately let him find her in the act? It was impossible for Morphée to count or to measure the pain Milhaud's wife had caused him. Why, she had often wondered, had they remained together for so long? Once, Milhaud had given her a glimpse of the reason: she had been charismatic, drawing influential people of both sexes to her as inexorably as a flame attracts moths. Therefore, she had been invaluable to him.

It was not surprising that Milhaud occupied her thoughts, for, in her own way, Morphée loved Milhaud, seeing in him the greatness that his wife apparently had not.

Morphée, when she was very young and in Asia, had been used by men. She had quickly seen that if that was to be her lot in life (in truth, she could not conceive of any other), at least she could take her *quid pro quo*.

She had never before been involved with a client, never before had wanted to be, and she found it somewhat terrifying, not to say risky. On the other hand, it was also exhilarating. She loved everything about him, even his pain, because that, too, was part of him, part of what made him what he was.

Within an hour Milhaud ceased to speak, the dark river of words coming at last to an end. Then he slept in the arms of Morphée, while she digested this latest erotic incident where Milhaud's wife had cleverly seduced the mistress of the minister of finance in order to learn the minister's secrets and, in so doing, coerce his support for Milhaud's work in Indochina.

When Morphée fantasized, she dreamed only of Milhaud, finding that she would be happy to be just with him, leading, as she had never before, a normal life.

Milhaud awoke from his sleep within the precincts of Les Portes du Jade as he always did, refreshed. Les Portes du Jade, the house of pleasure, was an eighteenth-century white-stone mansion built around a walled garden thick with roses, violets, and columbine. There was a verdigris fountain in the shape of a mermaid coupling with a dolphin. A single filigreed iron bench was set beneath a chestnut tree.

It was on the Left Bank, three blocks from the Sorbonne, just off the Boulevard Saint Michel. The voluptuous greenery of the Luxembourg Gardens could be seen from many of its apartment windows.

This is what Milhaud looked at while he was dressing. Behind him, he could hear Morphée stirring on the bed.

"Tell me something," he said as he knotted his tie. "What do you think of, dear Morphée, while I sleep?"

"I dream of time," she said.

Milhaud turned to look at her. "Really? I wonder what that is like?"

She smiled her enigmatic smile, what drew him to her over and over. "You would have to be a slave in order to understand. You would have to understand what it is like to have nothing of your own, to be subjugated. I am Asian, so I know what that is like, to have nothing, to see even your own land milked by foreigners.

"But I am also a woman. I am set in a sliver of time like a porcelain ballerina, to be taken out and admired, then put back on a shelf.

"You would have to understand what it is like to be intimate with someone, to accede to their every demand, to kiss them to sleep when they cry like a baby, and then be ignored by them when you pass them in the street or in a restaurant."

She regarded him out of smoky eyes. "For a boxed toy such as I am, the dream of time is the only one worth having."

He came and sat on the edge of the bed in order to touch her. "Is that what you think you are?" He needed to do that every time before he left, to prove to himself that she was real and not a figment of his imagination.

"I know just what I am," Morphée said. "A slave of desire."

"Perhaps," Milhaud said, "that power is what makes you so desirable."

She laughed. "I am hardly that."

"But to create fantasies is to exert the ultimate power."

Morphée followed him with her eyes as he rose, slipped on his jacket. She understood his facility with words. "What would you do if you were with your friends, and passed me in the street? Would you at least smile?" That was the worst moment, the moment of separation. After he was gone, it was all right, she could take care of the ache, dull and throbbing, controlled. But for this moment, this tearing of her reality, she wanted to turn her face away and cry. Instead, she smiled because she knew it was what he loved, what he wanted.

"I would do more. I would stop and kiss you on both cheeks as a long-lost friend." Milhaud, leaving her, thinking with a quickly beating heart, When she smiles I see Soutane, and when I am with her, I imagine I am near Soutane.

Placing the money carefully on the top of the bureau. "*Au revoir*, Morphée."

Chris, sleeping fitfully aboard his Pan Am flight, was dreaming of shadows. He was cycling through the sun-drenched French countryside. Alix was at his side, smiling, matching his pace. Bent over the handlebars, her light, muscular figure was filled with an astounding sexual energy.

Sunlight, moving in and out of the gnarled plane trees that bordered the road, dappled her face, alternately throwing her features into highlight and relief.

She smiled. He saw her even, white teeth just before the shadow overtook her. Chris felt the brush as if from an invisible hand of enormous strength. It shoved him aside so that he wobbled unsteadily for a moment. By the time he had righted himself, Alix was quite a distance ahead.

Chris called to her, but the wind, shrieking past him, bore his words away. He tucked his head into his shoulders, began to race after her, pushing himself so hard that his leg began to hurt. The more it hurt, the more he pushed himself. But the faster he went, the farther away she seemed, until she was nothing more than a speck upon the horizon, gone.

He did not give up, however, merely redoubled his effort, and at last coming upon her, lying with her bike by the side of the road, pinned by a giant fan to the earth dark and damp with her blood.

He awoke with a start as the plane touched down. He blinked, licked his dry lips, and thought of the dream, of the race, of Alix back in the hospital in New York. He knew he was guilty about having left her there, helpless.

He looked out the window at Nice and, beyond, the blue mountains, hazy as from an Impressionist's brush. Inside the terminal, he found that the airline had lost his luggage. He dutifully filled out forms, anxious only to be out of there; he had brought nothing of real value with him.

He saw Soutane on the lookout for passengers emerging from his flight. This is what she was: Terry's girlfriend. He tried to reconcile that in his mind. But it seemed impossible for him to comprehend.

She was even more beautiful than he remembered. Time had heightened the exoticism of her mixture of bloods—Khmer and French. She unwrapped her sunglasses as she saw him.

She wore a linen blouse with thick swirls of forest green, cerulean, and mauve, black form-fitting leggings, short boots of the same color. Her long, extraordinarily beautiful legs still looked like those belonging to *un petit rat*, a young dancer from the Paris Opera Ballet.

Chris stared into the green motes in her brown eyes and uttered her name in a voice filled with an unnamed emotion.

"Soutane."

"Hello, Chris."

It was so prosaic, not at all what he had expected of this moment.

What should they do, embrace? Merely smile at each other? It was so awkward.

She kissed him on both cheeks. As they walked to her car, she said, "This journey can't be pleasant, of course, but I'll try at least to make it less painful."

Chris wanted to ask her how she would do that, but he let it go. He had not eaten during the flight and had awakened entirely unrested; he felt utterly spent.

"Right now," he said, squinting into the brilliant sunlight, "I'd just like to take a shower."

"Of course," Soutane said. She gestured. "Watch your knees. These sports cars never have any space to speak of."

It was a honey-colored Alfa Spider with white leather seats. The cloth top was down, and the air, even when she put the car through its paces at top speed, was as soft as a whisper.

Nice was white and orange, climbing the ascending terrain off the azure Mediterranean with the grace of a dancer. This was a place, Chris thought morosely, to come to on your honeymoon or with a lover, not to pick up the body of your dead brother.

"We'll have you home and in the shower right away," Soutane said.

"Home? Not my hotel?"

"I took the liberty of canceling your reservation," Soutane said. "I thought you'd be more comfortable staying with me."

Chris said nothing, and she took the silence as assent.

"I also thought that you might want some time with Terry's—things."

"What?"

"That is, whatever he left behind. Photos, mementos, letters."

"We never wrote to one another," Chris said. He wondered how he could still be so angry with Terry for that.

She turned to glance at him. "Yes, you told me. Aren't you in the least bit curious, though, about what he kept, what was important to him?"

Chris put his head back against the seat. What I'm curious about, he thought, is how you feel having slept with two brothers. "Truthfully, I don't know. I don't yet understand how my life will change because Terry is dead. I don't even know if it will change at all."

"I've got news for you," Soutane said, putting on speed coming out of a turn, "it's already changed. You're here, aren't you?"

Chris turned to look at her, her high cheeks glowing with a hint of rose, her blue-black hair pulled back in an intricate braid.

"Tell me," he said, "how long does it take you to get your hair like that?"

Soutane laughed. "Over an hour."

"It's worth it."

She nodded, smiling. "Thank you."

Chris remembered Soutane as someone kind, funny, open. Not someone who was the enemy, as, perhaps, Terry had always been the enemy.

Terry's home was not what he expected, either, a bright, high-ceilinged apartment overlooking the Boulevard Victor Hugo, filled with bright flowers, glossy-fingered foliage. The furniture was softer, far less masculine than he would ever have imagined Terry allowing or being comfortable with. And yet Terry had, presumably, been happy here.

"Did you love my brother?" Chris asked, accepting a large, cold mineral water from Soutane.

"Don't you want to take your shower?"

"Do I need one?" She regarded him without answering, and he felt ashamed of himself. "Sorry," he said abruptly, putting down the beaded glass. "You're perfectly right. I *do* smell."

"It's right in that way," Soutane said, pointing. "Through the bedroom where you'll be sleeping."

He went into the bathroom, stripped off his clothes. Now that he had them off, they looked and smelled like clothes that had been worn too long. He dropped them on the bed in the other room, the spare bedroom. It set up all sorts of reverberations in his mind. He took a look around. What had it been used for when Terry was alive? *When Terry was alive.*

He went back into the bathroom, turned on the shower, and stepped into it. He thought about the paramedics, the police arriving at his apartment, the questions, light bulbs flashing ceaselessly as if Alix were a film star or a celebrity. And Chris, wanting only to be with her as she was taken to the hospital, had to endure the frustration of giving his statement to the police over and over again because they seemed to disbelieve several of the details—You want us to buy a woman being attacked by a man wielding a fan? and further incredulous questions from mundane minds who, apparently, could not comprehend the fantastic.

Soaping up, his skin feeling dry and raw, as if someone had tried to flay him to death. Statements to be made, then more questions, forensic specialists creeping all over the bloodstained carpet like a parody of CIA agents. The detective, the black one with the scar on the point of his chin, copying from Chris's itinerary the address and phone number of the Negresco in Nice where Chris planned to stay. Taking down, too, the flight numbers, every scrap of data he could find. How long did you say you'd be out of the country?

Chris had answered everything with, by that time, Max Steiner at his side because it was true, sometimes even lawyers needed lawyers. He did so in a voice dulled by shock and pain, staring at the black detective's scar, a little gray, a little pink, discoloring at a distance the chocolate skin to the color of *café au lait*, as if in that spot someone had stirred in the tiniest bit of milk.

That point of dissonance was somehow comforting, like a bit of rain at night, pattering on the roof, dripping from the eaves, something from which in solitude one could take solace.

They had thanked him in the end. He was not after all a suspect, but merely a witness to something peculiarly urban, particularly wicked.

Chris had said there was Danny, Alix's son, to think of, and the other detective, the white one with weepy, red-rimmed eyes said, Don't worry, pal, we've got all the bases covered. But after they left, Chris took Max with him to the West Side to see to Danny himself, to bring him to the hospital where Alix was in emergency surgery. Jesus, they could perform miracles these days, the papers filled with them, so it was clear that Alix would be all right, oh, dear God, please.

And Chris had not left until he was assured by the attending surgeon that she was out of danger, although she was still in serious condition. But lucky to be alive, sir, she's a real fighter, she'll pull through, all she has to look forward to is, maybe, some plastic surgery. She's a lucky girl.

They wouldn't let anyone in to see her, that wouldn't be possible, the surgeon told him, for another two or three days at least. Chris had left Dan in Max's care and had, with some reluctance, flown out. Arrangements for Terry's disposition could not, unfortunately, be postponed.

Chris, lather sliding off him with the grit, the dried sweat of travel and nightmares, saw a shadow beyond the shower curtain. He washed the soap out of his eyes, pulled the curtain aside.

Soutane was standing in the doorway, the clothes he had dumped on the bed rolled up in her arms. She was looking at him. "It's like a bell, ringing in the mountains," she said. "Your questions, my answers are all filled with reverberations."

She was about to turn away, then changed her mind. "To answer you," she said, "I loved Terry very much." Her gaze dropped to a point somewhere between them. "But, now, I'm not sure what value that had. You see, I never really knew him, either."

The water rushing past his ears, the water taking his stink away, swirling it down the drain along with his life up until now.

"I'll have these clothes cleaned," Soutane said. "There'll be something to eat by the time you're dry. Do you like red or white wine?"

"White," he said. Because right now red would be too much like drinking blood.

When he emerged from the bathroom, he found a fresh shirt and pair of trousers laid out on the bed. He put them on, eerily conscious that they must have been Terry's clothes.

There was a mirror over a bureau. He found a brush, ran it through his hair. He saw the knife when he put down the brush.

He picked it up, the stag-antler scales rough against his flesh and, for an instant, he was back in the snowy forest on that long-ago Christmas morning, Terry's hand over his, forcing him to pull the trigger of the new rifle. The startling crack of the explosion making, it seemed, the bare branches tremble over their heads. The noble beast going down on its knees, its heavy flanks trembling. Its panting exhalations like smoke through nostrils flared in pain. The huge eyes rolling, helpless, as it crashed to the forest floor.

And the next year, again at Christmas time, Terry's present to Chris had been this four-inch folder, whose scales had been cut from that stag's antlers. Chris, of course, throwing it into Terry's face the moment he opened it and saw what it was.

Now, in Nice, Terry dead, Chris turned it over and over in his hand as if it were an alien artifact to which only he had the key. He wiped his eyes. Was it the existence of the knife that made him cry or the fact that Terry had kept it all these years?

Somehow, it was the knowledge that it meant so much to Terry—that it had not, after all, been a cruel joke, but a kind of peace offering—that touched Chris now at his very core.

This knife said more to him about his brother than any volume of eulogies ever could. As he held it tight in his fist he tried to imagine Terry standing beside him. He stared into the mirror, wanting with such longing not to be alone in that strange room, in that foreign country.

After a time he slid the knife into his pocket.

Soutane was sitting on the couch. Wine, cheese, and fresh fruit were on the cocktail table. She was staring at a photo. She handed it to him as he sat down beside her. It was the shot of Terry and Soutane at Le Safari.

"That's the most recent photo of him," Soutane said. "It was taken about a week ago."

He doesn't look any different, Chris thought. He looks just the way he did when he graduated college. But then, as he studied it, he could see something in his brother's eyes, something dark and, perhaps, painful.

With a start he realized that he was seeing Vietnam or, more accurately, what Vietnam had done to Terry. Like some mysterious process, like metal being dipped in acid, a new and wholly different Terry had emerged from that hideous experience. He recalled Marcus Gable saying with vehemence, *How could you be over there in that stinking hellhole without being changed? The only way not to be changed was to die.*

"Chris?"

He found to his dismay that it was painful to tear his gaze away from the photograph. Hand in pocket, he rubbed the stag-antler knife as if it were a talisman.

"What is it? What's the matter?"

"I was just thinking." He sank back into the sofa. "I was wishing I could bring Terry back for just one hour."

"What would you say to him?"

Chris closed his eyes. "You know, it's funny. All the way over here I was wondering about that. There were so many things I would want to say that I just couldn't— But now I don't think I'd say anything at all." He opened his eyes, looked at her. "What I want—*really* want—is to hear him talk. I want to understand him. I want, above all, to know what happened to him in Vietnam."

Soutane got up and, walking across the room, stood looking down with quiet intensity past the curtains at the Boulevard Victor Hugo.

"Tell me," she said, "have you taken any courses in self-defense?"

"I took about six months of aikido when I first got out of law school," he said. "I thought it would be fun, but it was more work than I bargained for. I didn't have enough time. Why?"

She had not taken her eyes from the street. "Part of what you want, at least, can be arranged," she said. "I will take you to meet my cousin Mun. He knew Terry during the war. They fought together. He will tell you about your brother." She turned back to him. "If that is truly what you want."

Chris stared again at the photo as if he could will the image into life. ''It is,'' he said. ''Whatever sin of negligence I committed while he was alive, I can atone for now. I don't want to lose that chance.''

''Are you sure?'' She sat down next to him again. ''There might be, well, areas you'd be better off not delving into.''

''What do you mean?''

Soutane showed him the postcard Terry had written him, then she told him about the priest who had been following her, and what under duress he had told her, including his revelations concerning the Forest of Swords. ''If Terry had *La Porte à la Nuit*, if he was seeking possession of the *Prey Dauw*, then he must have been involved in some manner in the opium trade out of the Shan Plateau in Burma. That is where the *Prey Dauw* is priceless, where it means virtually unlimited wealth and power because every Shan chieftain will blindly follow whoever possesses it.''

''It's impossible,'' he said, stunned. ''Terry would never involve himself with drugs.''

''Chris''—Soutane put a hand on his knee—''Vietnam was a sea of drugs when Terry was there.''

''Yes, but—''

''And you yourself said that you did not know him at all.''

Chris stared at her. ''You loved him. How can you believe this? I mean, trafficking in drugs. That's indefensible, on any level. I cannot—I *won't* believe it of Terry. And, frankly, I'm stunned that you do.''

Soutane's face had changed. It was as if she absorbed his anger. He noticed the sorrow, the sleepless nights bruising her face. ''I loved him,'' she said softly. ''But, it seems, I did not know him.''

''Dammit, where's your faith?'' Chris said.

''Faith dies in the light of evidence.''

''What evidence? That my brother had this sword—''

''It's a dagger.''

''Whatever. Who knows what he was going to do with it? And then you take as gospel the word of some sleazy character who claims Terry sold his boss this dagger? They could have known he had it, and now see a chance to get it for free. It could all be bullshit. I don't care about some mythical triple-bladed sword, which may or may not exist. But I sure as hell want to know about my brother.''

''Do you hate your brother or do you love him?'' Soutane said.

"You've had no contact in the past ten years. He could have been dead all that time, for all you knew of him."

"It was the same for him."

"No. He followed your career. I think he knew every case you worked on."

"That hardly seems possible," Chris said as he watched Soutane open a drawer in a burl desk.

"What do these look like?" she said.

He scanned the newspaper clippings she thrust at him, but he was already familiar with them. They were accounts of his cases.

Chris forced back tears as long-pent-up emotions eddied upward. He was stunned, moved beyond words. "I didn't know," he said.

"Why do you think he refers to you in the postcard as *le monstre sacré*, the superstar?" Soutane closed her eyes for a moment, and Chris saw her swaying just as if she were on a boat at sea. When she spoke, her voice was low. "Now we understand one another. We both loved Terry very much. That's something neither of us should forget. But we have to face the facts.

"Of course, I wouldn't take anyone's word for such a thing," Soutane said. "But I told Mun everything I told you. I saw the look on his face. I saw how he acted."

"What did he say?"

"It's what he *didn't* say that has me really worried," Soutane said. "I suspect that he knows far more about what Terry was up to than he's willing to tell me."

"Maybe he'll talk to me. After all, I'm Terry's brother."

"You don't know Mun," Soutane said. "He is harder than rock. He'll never tell you what he doesn't want to."

"Then," Chris said, "we'll just have to get him to want to."

Over Thai tea, deliciously thick and sweet, they got down to business.

"I have fifty kilos of Number Four," Admiral Jumbo said. "I supervised the cooking myself."

"Fifty kilos?" Mun was puzzled. "You usually reserve one hundred kilos for us."

"We have had a most unfortunate spring—too cold and too dry to suit the poppies."

"But surely the farmers make the most of what harvest they have."

"Ah, the Shan farmers," Admiral Jumbo said in lamentation,

"are there any more lazy than they? I am sorry, my friend. There is nothing I can do."

Ma Varada, the beautiful girl who had served the tea, was pouring more for the two men. In Admiral Jumbo's house she was as much a fixture as Ma Ling had once been. "And how is our friend, Terry Haye?" Admiral Jumbo asked, behind his tiny teacup.

"Terry's dead," Mun said. "Murdered."

Admiral Jumbo's teacup did not move. His eyes, behind it, were as dark and mysterious as a coquette's. His heavy lips formed an *O* of surprise and shock.

"But that is terrible for you. Whatever are you going to do now?"

"I don't know," Mun said, growing more cautious by the moment. Mun did not care for any of Admiral Jumbo's old-woman cluckings after the warlord had clearly pulled the business rug out from under him. Fifty kilos instead of one hundred. The weather might have been bad, but Mun knew just how strong Admiral Jumbo's hold on his farmers was. And wasn't that a new piece of Imperial jade hanging around Admiral Jumbo's fat neck? It was worth in the neighborhood of a quarter of a million dollars. Mun wondered whether it had been a present. And if so, from whom? Admiral Jumbo coveted the rare jade; such a piece would make a perfect bribe. All of a sudden Mun had to face the possibility that Admiral Jumbo had become his adversary. Why? What had happened while Mun was away from the Shan?

"Then perhaps it is just as well that I have only fifty kilos for you, hmm?" Admiral Jumbo was saying. "Perhaps without Terry Haye, the maintenance of the pipeline will prove too great a task. After all, Mr. Haye ran most of the contacts himself." Admiral Jumbo was nodding now, like a parody of a wise Buddha. "Now that I think of it, perhaps you would be better off employed elsewhere. I myself have numerous less, ah, perilous enterprises that could use your skills. Why don't you consider this?"

This remorse, this polite talk—could it be a masquerade? Had Admiral Jumbo already known that Terry was dead? These were questions that were vital to Mun's immediate well-being. Questions that Mun knew only Mogok could answer. But, in the meantime, Mun knew, he must keep the audience going. The more Admiral Jumbo talked, the more he was apt to reveal.

Admiral Jumbo eyed Mun. "It is so sad about Terry Haye," he said. "Do you know who killed him?"

Now Mun struggled with a fundamental dilemma. His answer to Admiral Jumbo's question would reveal whether he would choose to walk away from the situation, from his responsibility to Terry, or to face this new, as yet undefined threat to what was, essentially, Terry's dream. He could say nothing, simply get up, walk out of here, and never come back. That would be the end of it. Or would it? Mun knew better. Terry had been his friend. They had trusted each other as, often, even brothers do not. Mun knew along which path his own *karma* led.

"Possibly."

"Come, come, there is no need to be circumspect with me," Admiral Jumbo said in his most avuncular tone. "You must tell me their names. After all, let us not forget that Terry Haye was also a friend of mine."

"I know who murdered my friend," Mun said. "They are already dead, though they do not yet know it."

Admiral Jumbo's eyebrows raised slightly. Then a broad smile wreathed his face, he set down his teacup and clapped his hands in delight. "You are some fantastic son of a bitch, Mun!" he cried. "I will send some of my men with you. They will return with you, help you avenge the death of your friend, eh? When that is done, they will bring you back here. I will set you up in a new business, a new life. This I will gladly do for you. You and I, we are like brothers. We think alike."

Fixing the Chinese warlord with a stare, Mun said, "True. We never forget our friends—or our enemies."

It was not without misgivings that Seve sprang the Dragon. He had spent so long in getting Peter Loong Chun behind bars, and so many had died in that pursuit that he had to steel himself to sign all the temporary release papers, the personal recognizance bond.

Then there was Diana. She argued vehemently against allowing Chun out of the precinct for any reason. She accurately pointed out the irregularity, not to mention the potential danger to Seve.

"At least take a backup team with you," she said when she realized that she was losing the argument.

Seve shook his head. "The Dragon says it's got to be just him and me."

"It's a setup. Boss, can't you see—"

"Who's he been in touch with since he's been with us?" Seve asked. "No one." He shook his head. "We've got him and he knows it. He's finished, and as long as he continues to believe his sister's going down with him unless he cooperates, he'll be just like a trained pig. She's his family, Diana. You understand. He won't do anything to jeopardize her safety."

"You hope," she said with some exasperation. "You know, you're breaking almost every rule you ever taught me."

"Not breaking," he said with a grin. "Just bending them a little."

But, watching him leave to fetch the Dragon, Diana wondered whether he was aware of how much he had changed. It was as if with the murder of his brother something had come over him. He was, she was certain, not the same Seve Guarda she had known two days ago. What had happened to him? What invisible writing had he seen at the scene of the crime that she had not? She could not imagine, and that frightened her.

For as long as she had known him, Seve had been more than a rock, a foundation: he had been the Law. And the Law, as Diana had come to understand it, was immutable. What now would happen to her world, her concepts of right and wrong, if the Law was transgressed—bent, as Seve had said, but not broken?

Diana wanted to run after him, stop him, shake some sense into him. But, at that moment, the material from the New Canaan Police Department started coming in over the FAX.

Seve took Peter Loong Chun out of the precinct, down the steps, herding him into his unmarked Buick. He immediately handcuffed him to the seat.

"Is that really necessary?" Chun said.

"Don't give me any shit," Seve said, starting the engine. "Think of your sister and what'll happen to her if this turns out to be hot air."

Chun put his head against the seat back. "You'll get what you want," he said in a tired voice. "I just want my sister left alone."

He directed Seve down Third Avenue, until it became the Bowery. As they approached St. James Place, he said, "We should park around here."

Seve swung into a bus stop, flipped down his visor, onto which was clipped a NYPD "Police Business" banner. He uncuffed Chun, but as the Dragon reached for the door handle, he held him back, showed him the service revolver in the shoulder holster under his jacket.

"Remember this is here," Seve said, tapping the walnut grip. "Remember that I'll blow your head off rather than take a chance on letting you escape."

Seve tried unsuccessfully to read Chun's expression. He was all too aware that Chun knew how much he wanted the man who ran Chinatown. That was a weakness he could not hide, and it worried him. Chun was a man who made his living preying upon other people's weaknesses. Seve spent some time wondering how Chun was going to take advantage of his weakness.

They crossed the avenue, went through an arcade reeking of raw fish and star anise, emerging and turning left onto Elizabeth Street. Chun led them right onto Bayard, then left onto Mott, and left again onto Pell just before the Church of the Transfiguration.

At the foot of Doyers, a small, odd street that doglegged to the left halfway down its length, Seve stopped Chun.

"Where the hell are you taking me, in a circle? We could've gotten here directly from the Bowery."

"True," the Dragon said, "but that way I'd never know if we were being observed. During our walk I had ample time to see, hear, and feel the atmosphere. Who could say who might be watching us? This would be reason enough to come alone. There are spying eyes and ears everywhere in Chinatown. We are now ready to proceed. Is this satisfactory?"

Seve, peering hard into the Dragon's face, had no way of knowing if he was telling the truth, or playing some kind of hidden game. Again, he was struck by the essential weakness of his position, and he cursed the luck that had tied him to this dangerous and unpredictable creature.

Not without misgivings, he nodded, and Chun led them down the crooked street. He stopped when they came abreast of a filthy brownstone with a seedy restaurant below street level.

They went through a narrow doorway beside it, up a flight of steep, filthy steps. At the top-floor landing the Dragon paused. Seve listened, but heard nothing save the slow drip of water from somewhere inside the thin walls. There were no sounds of TVs playing, babies crying, adults arguing. None of the basic sounds of human habitation.

"What—"

Chun waved him to silence. "Keep your voice down."

"What's happened to this place?" Seve whispered. "Where are all the tenants?"

"Gone," Chun said in the same hushed tone. "There is only one tenant now." He pointed to a closed door at the opposite end of a landing shabby with stains and peeling paint. He began to walk toward it, but Seve pulled him back.

"Where do you think you're going?"

"In there," Chun said.
"Not without me, you're not."
"Do you want him? The godfather of Chinatown?"
Seve stared at him.
"How much do you want him?" Chun said. "Now we'll find out."
"We'll go together or not at all," Seve insisted.
"Then a bloodbath will be unavoidable. His bodyguards are formidable. They are unconcerned by death. Believe me, you'll never make it back to the precinct. And then what will happen to my sister?"
"What can you do on your own except alert them to my presence out here?"
"My sister's life is more important to me than my own," Chun said. "If you doubt that, then you know nothing of me, nothing of the Chinese, *neh*? I can allay the bodyguards' fears, keep them off guard as you enter. I will make all the difference."
Seve wondered what other choice he had. He pulled out his gun. "Go on," he said. "You have sixty seconds from the moment you walk through that door. Then I'm coming in." He tapped Chun on the shoulder with the barrel of his gun. "And, if you're still thinking of escape, keep in mind that I don't care whether I shoot you from in front or in back."

When M. Mabuse saw Peter Loong Chun emerge from the precinct with Seve Guarda, he knew instinctively where they were headed. It was clear to him, like the red electronic 'scope lines of a bombing run. There could be only one reason why Guarda would risk bringing Chun out in the open: the Dragon was going to lead the policeman home.
On the way downtown M. Mabuse found a public phone that worked and made one call. It was fortunate that he was so diligent, but what would Milhaud say if he knew whom M. Mabuse was calling? He would, M. Mabuse knew, place the muzzle of a gun behind M. Mabuse's head and pull the trigger. He would not understand what M. Mabuse had to do, thinking that M. Mabuse had betrayed him. But he did not know the meaning of the word betrayal; no one did, save M. Mabuse, whose entire country had been betrayed so many times that the sin had become commonplace. Just as death, despair, and suffering had become the accepted norm of everyday life.

Everyday life for M. Mabuse had been seeing the winding brown rivers, the jade-green rice paddies, the gray thatch huts from a raven's perch. M. Mabuse, sitting in the ocher skies with the powerful *thwop-thwop-thwop* of the helicopter in his ears, the American army captain nudging him, shouting in his ear, "Just tell us where Charlie's hidden like you always do. No fuss, no muss."

M. Mabuse could see himself pointing through the open door. The captain's hand on the pilot's shoulder, the 'copter banking sharply. As they swung past a copse of trees and the village came into view, "There."

The chopper swooping down like a greedy beast, the squad ready, the guns chattering into deadly life, the grenades bursting against thatch and skin, throwing up clouds, thick and oily, redolent of frying meat through which the 'copter flew in triumphant arcs.

M. Mabuse's ear to the floor, trying desperately to hear the screams, but any human sounds there may have been were lost in the gunfire, the burst and crackle, fruits of the engines of destruction.

Gaining the roof of the building on Doyers Street, M. Mabuse used the fire escape to enter the top-floor window, which had been left open for him. The office was empty, his call having alerted the occupants who were now far from here, safe from detection. Surrounded only by a scarred wooden public-school desk, a phone, a blotter, three chairs, a sofa against a far wall, two lamps, a threadbare rug. They had been very careful; it looked as if it had barely been lived in. There were, in any event, no papers left anywhere.

M. Mabuse hearing the familiar voice in his ear, *Chun has served his purpose. Silence him before he can cause us serious damage.* Taking him back to '69, to the slow torture of his country, its scars, its agony stretching out below him as he rode the ravenous metal beast, crouched beside the hated Americans, compelled by a cruel fate to aid them before he could begin to destroy them.

M. Mabuse, here now, poised to kill again, the infliction of death his only purpose.

He waited in the deserted office for the door to open, as patient as Buddha. In the shadows that pooled in the room, lived the accusatory faces that haunted him. They whispered his name, not M. Mabuse, which was the name conferred on him so long ago, but the one given to him at birth, the one he kept running from.

He lurched backward as if dealt a heavy blow, sliding down the mildewed wall until he hit the floor. Unable to tear his gaze from the mouths calling his name in the shadows, he clapped his hands over his ears, but the sound, trapped inside his skull, continued to reverberate until he began to vibrate to the dreadful rhythm.

Only the scrape of the door bottom as it began to open broke the spell and, as if blinded by a sudden burst of sunlight, the faces in the shadows withdrew into the walls, the floor, the ceiling.

There.

M. Mabuse, using *pentjak-silat*'s *kebatinan*, the martial arts' spiritual training, cleared his mind. As he did so, he confirmed what he had suspected for some time. Even *kebatinan* was becoming less effective in keeping the spirits of the dead at bay, in keeping open the one last path toward his salvation. And what will I do, he asked himself, when *kebatinan* no longer works at all?

He knew, as he began his silent, headlong rush toward the door, that there was only one answer to that: he would have to be finished with his mission of revenge before that occurred.

Seve was counting to sixty under his breath, not daring to take his eyes away from the door that had closed behind Peter Loong Chun.

Nevertheless, when he heard the sound—the eerie, thin wail that stirred the hairs at the nape of his neck—it was so abruptly cut off, it took him a moment to react.

He sprinted across the landing, putting his shoulder against the door, feeling it give, and compensating on his back leg, he went down in the sharpshooter's crouch, his gun held two-handed in front of him.

Saw Chun's collapsed body, his decapitated head upside down, teeth in a rictus of astonishment and horror, eyes open and staring, as utterly blank as those of a wax dummy. They were staring blindly at the wall on which had been scrawled an image in blood. What was it? Seve wondered. It was vaguely familiar.

And, at the same time, aware of a movement—nothing more than of a gauzy curtain blowing in the wind—at the periphery of his vision.

Broke for the open window, slid, skidding heavily in the blood, slammed against the corner of a desk. Ignored the pain, leaping onto the sill, and out onto the labyrinthine grillwork of the fire escape.

"I see you, you sonuvabitch!" he yelled, scrambling along to the stairs, taking them two at a time, searching all the time for a clear shot at the weaving figure, which was now leaping onto the fire escape of an adjoining building.

Seve followed, heading upward, then downward in a dizzying pattern until, abruptly, he lost the figure. He slowed, trying to catch his breath. Peered between the overlapping grillwork, sure he had spotted him again then, two steps on, realizing that he was staring at nothing more substantial than shadows.

He stopped, and listened for the sounds a running man would make. He heard nothing over the cacophony of the horns from the busy Bowery, the whine of a police siren some distance off, the clash of an argument in Cantonese from below, the seductive lilt of a recorded Vietnamese song coming from a music shop on Pell Street.

Dammit, Seve thought. He's here somewhere, I know it. Counted windows. All of them were shut tight. Scanned the street below. Had he jumped? He scrutinized the adjoining fire escapes. Had he leaped again? People, unmindful, were hurrying by. Unmoving angles. Panes of glass reflecting his image. Nothing.

Then Seve turned his gaze upward. The roof! Holstering his gun because he needed use of both hands, he levered himself up the last eight feet to the parapet of the tenement. Rolling quickly, Seve came down onto the tarmac of the roof, drawing his gun in the same motion.

Where are you? Bastard, I have you now.

Felt the blue, blue sky collapse on him as if the onrush of night drew all air from his lungs.

"God!"

Had he said it or just thought it? He could not say. His eyes were bulging from the pressure being put on his neck. His throat had closed down and, like an epileptic in seizure, he was beginning to strangle on his tongue.

Seve, who was as powerful as a giant cat, felt all the strength pooling in shadow beneath him. He was kneeling, bent over, seeing only the uneven tarmac, and shadows—his own shadow grown grotesquely out of shape by the creature on top of him.

Used his elbows, his heels, his shoulders, anything to get the pressure off, to breathe again, to know that he had more time to live, that this wasn't the end, death on a Chinatown rooftop, killed by an unknown assailant, *finis*.

Nothing worked, nothing he tried dislodged the pressure. There were fireworks behind his eyes, a rushing like a torrent of water in his head. The world turned slowly red, sound like syrup bleeding out his ear holes.

And then he heard a voice, so close against his ear, it might have come from inside his mind.

"Do you remember me, Lieutenant Guarda? I remember you. I know what you've done."

Am I hallucinating? Seve wondered.

"I have come like the wind or the darkness of night for retribution. To repay you for the sins you committed against the people, the land of Vietnam."

I am dying, Seve thought, at the hands of a madman.

"Do you see this?"

A searchlight jabbed into Seve's eyes pushing back, for an instant, the red dye creeping across his vision. His head was wrenched upward; he groaned with the pain.

Not a searchlight, he saw now, but a length of worked metal, catching the sunlight as it spread open.

A fan.

A fan with a crenellated cutting edge sharp as a razor. Dom, he thought. You murdered my brother!

"Do you see this?" The fan waggled until its honed edge was directed at Seve's neck. "This is for you."

Dear God.

Seve struck out, his clawed fingers reaching for flesh but tearing, instead, the cloth of his assailant's shirt. And bared the tattoo. Seve saw the design and, in a flash, the image in blood came into focus. They were one and the same: a *phung hoang*. And he knew who it was who had come for him.

"Freeze!"

Seve, near unconsciousness, recognized, as a drowning man will his rescuer, Diana's voice. His head was jerked again, so hard that the pain snapped him from the edge, it seemed, of death.

Then the sharp crack of gunfire and, as abruptly as a switch being flipped, the pressure coming off, blood running out of his mouth, and he gasped in convulsive heaves the sweet air.

In a moment Diana's gentle hands, her soft voice, "Boss, Boss, are you okay?"

Seve, out of reflex nodded his head, yes, but he knew it for a lie. He spat blood.

"Get him?" he managed to rasp.

"No. He's gone, disappeared. I don't know how."

But Seve knew. Now everything had changed. The past had come rushing back, enveloping him like an open grave in its fetid embrace.

* * *

Milhaud and Mr. LoGrazie met in a tiny two-tiered park at the foot of the Avenue Franklin Roosevelt, where, alongside the Grand Palais, it crossed the Cours la Reine. They were quite near the Pont des Invalides, and the air was infused with the scent of freshly baking waffles from a mobile cart stationed at its foot, across the auto-choked Cours.

Down in the park, where speckled carp hung suspended in a pond, as if in aspic, all they could smell was the traffic exhaust.

Milhaud, facing Mr. LoGrazie, was thinking of the packet of photographs his man with the long lens had delivered to him. Seventy-two hours surveilling Mr. LoGrazie's house, and the unknown man showed himself only once. And then, at three A.M., Milhaud's man had almost missed him. Milhaud had opened the packet. Who was this unknown man who was taking control of Operation White Tiger, who had so much bitter contempt for Milhaud? He was no one. At least he was no one known to Milhaud. A big-shouldered American with the handsome, rugged features of a movie star. He looked like he belonged in Hollywood or on a billboard somewhere, a cigarette stuck in his mouth. A real Marlboro man. Milhaud had felt the disappointment sweep through him. Photo surveillance had proved a dead end. How else to find out who this mystery man was? Continue the audio surveillance.

Milhaud became abruptly aware of Mr. LoGrazie stirring restively beside him. He roused himself. "I'd like to know your sources of information on Mademoiselle Sirik," Milhaud said.

"It's none of your goddamned business. You work for me; you do what I tell you to do," Mr. LoGrazie said in his characteristically abrupt manner.

Milhaud had spent considerable time deciding which way to take this. Basically, he considered the Mafia people to be morons. They had no idea of the true power of the Shan; all they wanted was the opium. For this reason he was especially interested in further playing this Mafia messenger boy for the fool. Toward this end he said, "I have been concentrating on Mademoiselle Sirik. Do you know that she is now with Terry Haye's younger brother?"

"I don't care who she is with," Mr. LoGrazie said. "As long as she dies."

Milhaud watched as Mr. LoGrazie dug out a crumpled paper bag, began absently to feed the somnolent carp. "Then I can assume you don't care that when Al DeCordia was over here talking with Terry Haye, she formed a kind of father–daughter attachment to him,'' Milhaud said.

''So?''

''So daughters don't usually go around offing their fathers.''

''It was business,'' Mr. LoGrazie said. ''Terry Haye told her to—''

''Who do you think you're talking to? What you're telling me is nonsense,'' Milhaud said, taking the plunge. ''I knew Terry Haye. I knew what he was capable of doing. That kind of cold-blooded murder wasn't his style.''

''What the hell is going on?'' Mr. LoGrazie, his hand inside the paper bag, had stopped feeding the carp. ''Are you telling me you won't follow orders?''

''There has already been too much bloodshed,'' Milhaud said. ''The Sûreté continues to nose around. I do not want Interpol into the act as well.''

''That's not relevant. They're all idiots.''

''Idiots,'' Milhaud said, ''can damage the machinery just as easily as geniuses.''

Mr. LoGrazie, feeding the fish again, considered this. ''My source is unimpeachable,'' he said at last.

''Really? Then what do you supposed happened?''

''I don't *suppose* anything,'' Mr. LoGrazie said. The carp stirred just enough to reach the bread crumbs he cast upon the water. ''Just do as you're told.'' His voice was heavy with menace.

They began to walk, heading up to street level. Mr. LoGrazie paused, leaning against the concrete edge of a small bridge that spanned the lower pathway.

Milhaud thought, I've got to turn this around somehow. I can't allow Soutane to be harmed. ''We've got another, more pressing problem,'' he said. ''Terry Haye never meant to sell *La Porte à la Nuit* to us.''

Mr. LoGrazie's head swung around. ''What do you mean?''

''What he sold me was worthless.''

Mr. LoGrazie's countenance turned baleful. ''Your information was that he was in a bind. He needed cash.''

''Apparently, he had other—unknown—financial backing. His need for quick cash was a ruse.''

''A ruse? What for?''

''Terry was beginning to suspect what we were up to with Operation White Tiger. I had already begun luring some of his network people. So this was a kind of retaliation. To make me pay, I imagine, for trying to appropriate his network."

"Vindictive little bugger, wasn't he?"

Milhaud did not want to get into this. What did this lout know about it, anyway?

"It was your information, Milhaud, that got us a worthless piece of metal. We are still no further in finding the last section of the Forest of Swords." Mr. LoGrazie put his heavy hand on Milhaud's forearm and, with enormous strength, pinned him there. "What the fuck happened?"

"I think I've got a line on the real Doorway to Night."

"I said, what the fuck happened, Milhaud."

"I was misled," Milhaud admitted, doing his best not to wince.

"Yeah. Weren't you just." Mr. LoGrazie grunted. "It looks like Terry Haye led you around by the nose. You said you knew him. Didn't you know he was a master of disinformation?"

"Terry Haye wasn't the source," Milhaud lied. Disinformation? So that was how Terry had made Milhaud believe that he was cash poor.

Mr. LoGrazie's grip was fierce. "Who was?"

And Milhaud, feeling light-headed, said, "I used Soutane Sirik. My people ignored Terry Haye's associates. They concentrated on Mademoiselle Sirik's friends." This was all a lie. He knew that he was taking a desperate gamble with Soutane's life. But what choice did he have? He had to try to lift the death sentence M. LoGrazie had placed on her.

He could see the wheels turning behind the American's eyes. Mr. LoGrazie was contemplating the pond from afar. "If you're right, if she was the one who fooled you, then she's in it all the way. It could mean that she's got the real Doorway to Night."

Milhaud shrugged. Inside, he was holding his breath. "If I terminate her, we'll never find out."

Mr. LoGrazie grunted. "I gotta talk to some people," he said. "Until I get their okay, hold off icing her." He took his hand off Milhaud's arm. "I'll let them know that you're advising we pick her up instead. I agree that we need to find out what's what. I think I can get an approval to move on this."

Milhaud felt as if a great weight had been taken off his chest. The sense of relief was almost dizzying. "Good," he said a bit breathlessly. "It's the only way. We need to keep Mademoiselle Sirik alive."

* * *

They were at the northern edge of Admiral Jumbo's camp, where few people came. All the same they had to be careful of the perimeter soldiers, who were on constant patrol.

Mogok's face was pinched, almost as if he were in pain. "Ko Mun, have you brought it?"

"First things first, Daw Mogok." Though the Shan chieftain had addressed him as an equal, Mun was careful to respond with the form used when addressing a superior. "I want to know what has happened since I was last here. Everything's changed. For one thing I've notice a definite tightening of security here. For another, everyone's on edge."

Mogok looked around them nervously. "Admiral Jumbo has made a disastrous decision," he said. "He plans to make war on General Kiu. He wants Kiu dead, and he wants possession of the Tenth Quadrant. But General Kiu is a devil; I am afraid of him. Some say he is not born of woman, that he is immortal. It is even hinted that he is Mahagiri himself."

"Admiral Jumbo has been living side by side with General Kiu for years," Mun said. "What made him decide to attack him now?"

"Ma Ling." Mogok shook his head. "The world will come to an end over a girl."

"Not a girl, precisely," Mun said. "Love."

Mogok snorted. "Whatever you call it," he said, "it is certainly evil. Admiral Jumbo no longer thinks with his brain. He is content to follow wherever his male member leads."

"What happened?"

"General Kiu has set out to destroy us, that's what happened. Through his spies he found out that Ma Ling was Admiral Jumbo's favorite. He had her killed. Now, honor dictates that Admiral Jumbo must have his revenge."

"Then you should already be at war."

Mogok nodded. "True. But General Kiu is far too clever. By the manner of Ma Ling's death, it was impossible to implicate him. We suspect him but we have no proof. We do not even know who murdered her. She was stabbed to death. No one from the outside could even have gotten close to her."

"Then it is clear General Kiu had a spy inside the camp. Tell me, have you found him yet?"

Mogok shook his head. "And he is probably long gone by now."

He dismissed the subject with a wave of his hand. "Enough of this. Now where is the Forest of Swords?"

"I don't have it." How could he tell Mogok that he did not even know where it was?

Mogok cursed in a dialect Mun did not understand. "We are ruined, then. Ruined."

Mun peered into Mogok's face. It seemed pale beneath its honey color. "What is the matter with you?"

"You." Only the clandestine nature of their meeting kept Mogok from shouting his anger. "Our deal is off. You promised the Forest of Swords. With that I would have attempted anything."

"This was strictly Terry's idea, using the Forest of Swords to control Admiral Jumbo, General Kiu, and all the opium warlords," Mun said. "He wanted a kind of peace here, an end to the constant skirmishing between quadrants over territory, manpower, and access routes down the Shan. Just as it was his idea to hire you to keep tabs on our opium, to keep us apprised of any new developments here. We've spent a lot of money on you, Mogok."

"Terry Haye is dead. All that's over with now," Mogok said. "I am through providing you with inside information. Why should I? You have not brought the Forest of Swords. You have not kept up your end of the bargain."

"I want my full one hundred kilos of opium," Mun said. "I don't care what the weather was like here in the winter. Make up the shortfall from someone else's consignment."

"Sorry." Mogok shrugged. "I'm afraid I can no longer help you."

Mun feigned indifference. "If you won't," he said, "I'll find someone else who will."

Mogok scoffed. "I doubt it. This is a closed society."

Mun smiled. "It is also a venal society. It is said that on the Shan a man's loyalty is measured by his monthly pay, eh?"

Mogok would not meet Mun's eyes. "I don't know what you mean."

"What I mean," Mun said slowly, "is that just because I did not bring the Forest of Swords does not mean I don't have it."

"What proof can you give me that you *do* have it?"

"None. You have to trust me."

"I trust no one," Mogok said. "I will not move against General Kiu without the Forest of Swords. What if, as it is said, General Kiu really is the deathless Mahagiri? He would skin me alive, and that would just be for a start."

"Did you know that General Kiu commanded a North Vietnamese battalion during the war?" Mun saw Mogok's eyes open wide in astonishment. "It's true. From November 1969 to May 1974. Then he got fed up, jumped ship—deserted—and came here." Mun spat, a gesture of distaste. "I fought against him in Vietnam," he said. "I saw him kill many men. When a man kills, you discover all you need to know about him. I tell you that he is not Mahagiri."

Mogok stared into Mun's face as if it were the bottom of a cup filled with tea leaves which he could read. It seemed a long time before he made up his mind.

"Admiral Jumbo lied to you. Someone is muscling in on your opium."

Mun felt his scrotum tighten in alarm. He thought, This is a disaster of epic proportions. Terry is dead, and one half of our monthly opium is gone in a puff of smoke—right into an unknown enemy's hands. And who was to say that on his next visit here Admiral Jumbo wouldn't say that he was out of Number Four altogether, So sorry, but the Shan farmers, who are more lazy than they? Talk about being squeezed.

"Who is taking over our shipments?" Mun asked.

"One man, that's all I know. I wasn't here when he came to negotiate with Admiral Jumbo," Mogok said. "I was down the Shan, shepherding a hundred kilos of Number Four when it happened."

"Isn't that unusual? Your captains lead the armed convoys down the mountainside."

Mogok nodded. "It is obvious now that Admiral Jumbo wanted me away from here when he met with his visitor."

"And, of course, you didn't ask about the deal Admiral Jumbo cut with my competitor when you returned," Mun said with some sarcasm.

"But I did," Mogok said. "Without, unfortunately, much success."

"And none of the men here saw who came to the camp?"

"For one thing he did not come to the camp. Admiral Jumbo met him in a clearing in the jungle about a kilometer from here. He took six men with him. They saw the man, of course, but so what? All they could tell me was that he was a Caucasian. And he was big. Handsome like an American movie star."

"*Was* this man an American?"

"It is possible. On the other hand, he gave Admiral Jumbo a gift of the most rare Imperial jade. I do not think that is an American gift."

"Unless it was CIA," Mun mused. "Some of their people are now well versed in local custom and lore."

"This gift had more to do with Admiral Jumbo's personal tastes," Mogok pointed out. "Maybe this man knew the admiral very well."

"Well, we now know several interesting pieces of information," Mun said. "For one thing the man has plenty of power for Admiral Jumbo to give up face by meeting him outside his own encampment."

"I don't see how that is enough to identify him," Mogok said.

"It's not," Mun said. "But we've got to start somewhere."

Mun was beginning to fit the disparate pieces together: Terry is murdered. At the same time someone known and respected by Admiral Jumbo cuts a new deal with him at Terry and Mun's expense. Coincidence? Hardly. Mun would bet every franc he had that whoever had murdered Terry was the one muscling in on Mun and Terry's pipeline.

Mun had to assume whoever was taking over was very powerful, indeed. Because he had not only induced Admiral Jumbo to cut him in on what was normally sacred territory, but he had gotten Admiral Jumbo actually working *for* him. Mun's conversation with the warlord had been scripted beforehand. Whoever Admiral Jumbo was now working for wanted him to pump Mun. This unknown adversary wanted Mun out of the way. He also wanted to know if Mun had any idea who had killed Terry. No wonder Admiral Jumbo had been so anxious to send his men with Mun. They would be there to keep an eye on Mun and, if he got too close to whoever did murder Terry, they would have orders to kill him.

For the first time Mun felt a flicker of fear crawling through his stomach. The power to buy Admiral Jumbo, warlord of the Ninth Quadrant, was, perhaps, not one to be so easily trifled with.

"It seems clear," Mun said now, "that whoever is muscling in on my opium is the same man who ordered Terry killed."

"Perhaps," Mogok said. "But you are asking a question impossible to answer. Leave me out of this."

"You would like to be promoted, Mogok, wouldn't you? Perhaps command your own division of Admiral Jumbo's army?"

Mogok stared at Mun. "What are you talking about?"

All the while they had been talking, Mun had been thinking about the spy General Kiu had inserted into Admiral Jumbo's camp. What he was thinking was this: If no new people had been recruited recently, then General Kiu must have suborned someone *already* inside Admiral Jumbo's camp. A traitor. It also occurred to him that if the spy hadn't been discovered as yet why should he leave? His only value was if he remained in place.

Mun had pondered these matters for some time. Now he said, "How grateful would Admiral Jumbo be if we presented him with General Kiu's spy?"

"He would be beside himself with joy," Mogok said, frowning. "But how could you do the impossible?"

Mun said, "Admiral Jumbo has information that I require. I want to know who came here in my absence. I want to know who killed Terry Haye."

Mogok considered this. "I think Admiral Jumbo will tell you if you deliver the spy. He is consumed by his memories of Ma Ling, and by his hatred of General Kiu." He shrugged. "But on the other hand, whether or not he will tell you is academic. I don't think you can deliver the spy. As I said, I believe he is long gone."

"How much is that ruby in your front tooth worth?" Mun said.

Mogok touched it with a forefinger. "I don't know. Three kilos of Number Four, maybe. Why?"

Mun smiled. "Would you like to bet it?"

Diana brought the information—the files on the murders of Dominic Guarda and Al DeCordia—Seve had requested to his room at Beekman Downtown. "I'll tell you one thing," she said. "I'm damn tired of visiting you in hospitals."

Seve took the plastic oxygen mask off his face. He was sitting up in the bed. "I don't know why I'm here at all." His voice was hoarse, and a bit slurry from his swollen tongue.

Diana contemplated the angry red welt across his throat. "How does it feel?"

"What?"

"Jesus, you're impossible! You had me frightened, you know that?"

Seve seemed almost embarrassed by her admission. "Look," he said, "the captain has already been in, chewing me out because the mayor's office chewed *him* out via the commissioner. I lost a felon in a string of major crimes. That doesn't make me too happy."

"Happy?" Diana echoed. "For Christ's sake, you were almost killed."

Seve tried to smile, but the effort turned into a grimace of pain.

"Almost doesn't count. Which reminds me, what the hell were you doing following me?"

"Someone has to look after you," she said, "since you refuse to do it yourself."

"Meaning?"

"Meaning by circumventing procedure you were looking for trouble."

"I knew what I was doing," he mumbled.

She could have said something then, but she deliberately kept her mouth shut. The truth was, what he had done had terrified her, and she thanked all the gods of her ancestors that she had taken a backup unit after him into Chinatown.

A resident came in, his gum-soled shoes squeaking on the linoleum. He took a look at Seve's chart, said, "How you feeling?" as he examined the welt across Seve's throat. "All things considered, you're very lucky." He was writing on Seve's chart. "You'll notice some noisy breathing for a while, but the change in your voice isn't necessarily permanent. You've got a small hematoma—a blood clot—of the voice box, and I've prescribed an antibiotic, and a steroid to reduce the swelling. That's crucial, which is why the hematoma needs monitoring. If it should grow, it could conceivably block your windpipe, and you'd most likely require a tracheotomy."

He continued to write busily. "It's also likely that you'll be coughing up blood for a while longer. Neck pains and headaches are normal for your condition, so don't be alarmed should they occur. We've done X rays and a CAT scan, and everything's normal. Take your medication, and I'll see you tomorrow."

"When can I get out of here?" Seve asked.

The intern gave him a glassy-eyed smile. "That's difficult to say. For the time being, why don't you just try to relax."

Seve glared at him as if he were a major felon. When he was gone, Seve said to Diana, "I don't need any lessons from you."

She felt bright points of tears in her eyes. For a moment she wondered why she was still here. But she knew how she felt about him, and nothing he could say or do would change that. "Why don't you just admit that your goddamn Latin pride's gotten in the way. You're worried about what the squad's going to say about you being saved by a woman officer."

"Yeah," he said. "Well, I'll bet the jokes are already making the rounds."

"I think that everybody who knows you is simply relieved that you're okay."

"Ah, forget it." But he seemed pleased. "Do you have the New Canaan Police info?"

"Yes." She held it up. "But I'm not supposed to give it to you. The captain told me that you're officially on two weeks' sick leave."

"Yeah," Seve said, "I know." He held out his hand. "Give it here."

"Uh-uh. You know what sick leave means? You leave the job behind."

"I'm not kidding, Diana. Let me have it."

"No. I'm just—"

"That's an order, Detective."

"You're off duty," Diana said. "I don't take orders from you now."

Seve looked at her, knew that she meant it. "Then let me see it as a friend."

"As a friend, I want to see you back on your feet again as soon as possible."

He threw off the sheet, swung his legs over the side. "How about right now?"

"Seve, don't," she said. "Please. Don't you understand that you've been hurt."

"I told you, I'm okay."

"Pardon me if I don't believe you."

He passed a hand across his face. "Christ, all I'm asking is for you to give me a look at the file."

"Give me one good reason why I should."

Seve looked at her, and she was appalled to see the bleakness in his eyes. "Diana," he said, "the man who attacked me is the same person who murdered my brother."

"What? How can you possibly know that?"

"Because I saw it," he said, suddenly weary, feeling the pain more than he had a moment ago. "You were right. It was the iron fan in your book, the fucking iron fan he used to slice Dom's head off. It was what he was going to use to kill me."

Diana stood transfixed to the linoleum floor. She felt dizzy, as if she had just stepped off the Whip she had ridden many times as a child visiting Coney Island.

"Jesus," she whispered. "What does it mean?"

"If you give me that file," Seve said, "maybe I'll be able to tell you."

The fire growing inside him as he took possession of the information, knowing that the present had slipped away, possibly forever, and that he was rushing backward in time, backward to scorched Cambodia, bloody Cambodia, where rivers of skulls crisscrossed the land where once a magnificently conceived irrigation network brought life to dry fields.

The top file was from their own lab and, at first glance, it was disappointing. There had been fingerprints on the thousand-dollar bill the killer had put on the church's collection plate, but they were so smudged that they were useless.

The rest was more promising, however. The latex Seve had pulled out of Dominic's hand was identical to the pliable kind used to construct professional-quality masks. In addition, the trace of powder the lab had found on the bill was consistent with a well-known French brand of women's foundation makeup.

Interesting, Seve thought. He used a mask when confronting Dom. Why? The obvious answer was that Dom knew him, or had known him previously. Yes, Seve thought. In Cambodia.

He went on to the material provided by the New Canaan detectives' unit. There were two coroner's reports, one for Dom, the other for Al DeCordia, the man they had found in the countryside ditch. They confirmed a suspicion of Seve's. One, that Dom and DeCordia had been killed by the same man, using the same weapon. Bruises, the one major wound, the odd, crenellated nature of the wound edges, proved that conclusively.

The only difference was Dom's broken fingers, and the report cleared up that mystery. The coroner had discovered minute particles of latex embedded beneath the fingernails of the broken fingers. That suggested to Seve that Dom had ripped off a piece of his murderer's mask, and that the careful murderer had had to break Dom's fingers to retrieve it.

The report also confirmed that Al DeCordia had been killed somewhere between thirty-six and forty-eight hours *before* Dom had been murdered. Did that mean there was a serial killer at large, or that the two murders were connected?

Seve went back to the coroner's report on Dom, read again the part about the face powder being French.

He looked up. "Diana," he said, "you're an angel."

"Maybe, but right now I wonder whether I'm helping the devil."

"What are you talking about?"

"Boss, you're obsessed by your brother's murder. I mean look at you, you're a mess, but you just won't stop, even for a breather."

"There's no time," Seve said.

"See what I mean?"

"You don't understand." He pointed. "Get me the note I found on Dom's body. It's the handwritten slip of paper in my wallet." If he remembered right, the address on it was in France. A coincidence?

Diana went to the closet, searched through his wallet. "You didn't let me see it. Is this—" She stared at the slip of paper.

"What is it?"

She seemed to have trouble breathing.

"Diana?"

She passed him the slip with Soutane's name and address written on it, along with Dom's scrawled "Saved?" across the bottom. "While you were down looking at DeCordia's body, Detective Blocker was letting me look at DeCordia's notebook. This is the same handwriting!"

Seve stared at the note, feeling as if it had already begun to catch fire. "How can you be certain?"

Diana took something out of her notebook. "Blocker handed me one of DeCordia's business cards he had fished out of DeCordia's wallet. Somehow, in the confusion, he never did ask for the card back, and I forgot to give it to him. I was interested in it because there was a notation on back that rang a bell. Look." She placed them side by side. "You see how back-slanted the script is? DeCordia was left-handed. This script filled his notebook. There's no doubt about it, he wrote this note your brother had."

She's right, Seve thought. Which means that DeCordia had some contact with Dom. There was the connection!

"Did you follow up on the notation?"

Diana nodded. "Look. DeCordia wrote the name 'EastAsia Benevolent Society,' and beside it, here, a phone number."

"So?" Seve said. "Do you know them?"

"That's just it," Diana said. "I never heard of them. There are twenty-seven benevolent societies in Chinatown, Boss, and I know them all."

"Are you saying that the EastAsia Benevolent Society doesn't exist?"

"In a way," Diana said. "The name's phony but the number isn't. It belongs to the phone in the office on Doyers Street that Peter Loong Chun took you to."

Leaves were falling, red and gold and copper, swirling through hazy sunlight. Snow was drifting against bare trees. Alix was half dreaming, in that smoky place between sleep and narcotic daze, where everything seemed razor-sharp and cloaked in meaning.

When she tunneled up for a moment from out of all the dope she had been given, it was like a nightmare she had had once: the all-pervading sense of menace, and wanting nothing more than to shout a warning. Opening your mouth, finding yourself mute.

But this time it was real.

There were bandages, and an overriding pain, as if her face had been dipped in acid. Alix knew she was flat on her back, tubes going into her arm. She was blind and she was mute.

She slept, or thought she did, arriving back in Ohio, as a pigtailed girl of ten, hearing her parents at it once again, voices shouting obscenities, until she could no longer stand the atmosphere of liquor and animosity. Stealing twenty dollars from her father's wallet, running out of the house and, at the depot, taking the bus.

Then the drugs relinquished their hold on her, and once more the recent past came flooding in on her. She was struggling against a powerful, terrifying figure, choking to death on her own blood. She tried to scream.

Convulsed, instead, and someone gripped her hand.

"Mom."

Danny? Oh, Danny! A sense of relief sweeping through her that washed away her panic and her pain. She concentrated only on her love for him.

"I'm not supposed to be in here," Danny's voice close to her, so that she could imagine him, tall and strong and, possibly now, afraid. "No one is, yet."

She held his hand tightly, unwilling to let go of what was so precious to her.

"Chris had to go to France to get his brother. He's okay."

But you're all alone, she thought. She felt a wave of desolation sweep over her. Where was the family she had always cherished?

"I'm staying with a guy named Max Steiner, Mom. He's an old friend of Chris's. A lawyer. Everything's cool. Don't worry about me."

He was so brave. She squeezed his hand. She wanted to know what had happened to her, how badly she had been injured, what she would look like when this swath of bandages was removed. Her throat ached with the questions she longed to ask.

"I just want you to get well."

Oh, yes, Danny. So do I.

"I took my bike out yesterday after school. I went up by the reservoir to, you know, our favorite place. The weather was great, just like June, warmer than it's been for a while. Everyone was out, cycling or running or roller skating. There was music all over, like it was coming from the rocks or something.''

Oh, Danny, I want you to be careful. This is New York, and you're on your own now. Hearing him say again, *Don't worry. Everything's cool.*

Drifting again on a tide of nothingness, sinking through layers of time, on the bus, leaving the urban sprawl of Columbus behind with its eerie intimations of the adult world: her mother's asperity, her father's abusiveness, and between them, leering like a painted whore, the drunken, crashing fights that invariably ended in violence and tears.

Heading south on Route 33, her knees against her chest, the soles of her sneakers against the seat in front, popping gum. Staring out the window at the red and gold and copper leaves swirling in gusts, crushed like exotic pepper in the gutters.

In Circleville she squashed her gum under her seat, alit, walking the last mile and a half, hands stuffed in her pockets.

The autumn wind scoured her cheeks, the sky was so full of clouds it looked like a down comforter. She ran, as she always did, the last thousand yards. Up the rickety steps to her grandfather's house where she was always welcome, where, after the first time—at the age of eight—she showed up unannounced, he never asked the reason why she had come.

The next day he took her to the annual Pumpkin Show where, laughing, she followed a parade of horse-drawn carriages, ate pumpkin pie washed down with fizzy apple cider, observed the judging of pumpkins as big, it seemed, as her grandfather's house.

At night, after he had tucked her in, she drew the comforter up to her chin and watched the moon in the clear night sky, dreaming of a stairway made of stars.

Suddenly awake, aware of the oppressive fist of the present, drenched in sweat, she was overcome by a desire to be a child again, free from daily concerns, from her endless worrying over Danny, from all responsibility. She wanted, instead, to be adrift in the night, on that magical stairway of stars, swaddled, cradled, taken care of.

Was that, she wondered, because she had been trapped into becoming a mother? Did women who consciously made the choice ever feel as she did now, wondering if they had to do it all over again, they would take that one irretrievable step?

But then she felt Danny's strength flowing into her, felt him close and warm beside her and, remembering how he moved while he was curled inside her, how he had looked when he first emerged, small and red and screaming, she thanked God for him, for this miracle of life who was part of her.

She slept again and, when she awoke, was aware of another presence in the room. Who was it? Danny? Christopher? She had forgotten that her son had told her that Christopher was in France.

"Alix?"

That voice. Familiar. She strained to put a face to it.

"Honey? Are you awake?"

So familiar. Who?

"Honey, it's me. Dick." My God, she thought, shaken, it's my ex-husband. "I heard what happened. Christ, I'm so sorry, Alix. I feel like it's, you know, in a way, my fault that you were hurt. If I'd never left you— But that's all over with now. I'm back for good. I'm going to take such good care of you, you'll see. I love you, baby. I see now that I always have."

Seve thought, *War is based on deception.*

"I've got to get out of this hospital," he said.

"Where do you think you're going?" Diana said.

But the war had ended thirteen years ago. In his mind that name: Soutane Sirik, and that address: 67, Boulevard Victor Hugo, Nice, France.

She put a hand on his shoulder. "You're not going anywhere."

I'd better stop kidding myself, he thought. The war never ended. Not for me. And certainly not for *him.*

"You don't get it," he said, shrugging off her attempt to stop him. "I'm not going to find any more answers here. The Dragon's dead. My one lead has turned to dust."

"Sure, Chun's gone," Diana said. "But we've just begun to do the legwork on these two murders. Now that we've got Blocker's permission—"

"Dead ends," Seve said, lurching across the room toward the closet. "Take it from me, from now on running down those murders from here is a waste of time."

Diana watched him dress. "What's happened? What is it you're not telling me?"

Had Dom been murdered because Al DeCordia had told him something? Seve wondered. But why would DeCordia have come to Dom in the first place? And then, one leg in his trousers, half in, half out, he saw it all. His brother writing across the bottom of the note: *Saved?* Al DeCordia had come to make a confession!

He could imagine DeCordia entering the confessional, telling Dom what he could not tell anyone else, unburdening himself of what he could no longer, perhaps, live with.

But had the killer known that DeCordia had given Dom the note? Why would the killer have left it behind, then, after being fastidious enough to wrest the piece of latex from Dom's grip?

"Whatever it is," he said, "doesn't concern you."

With her heart in her throat Diana said, "Whatever concerns you concerns me."

Seve had been buttoning his shirt. He stopped what he was doing. "Diana." He took her hands in his. "I don't know what's in your mind. No—" He put a finger across her mouth. "Don't say anything. Right now, I need you to listen to me. Whatever is happening here is all connected in some way I haven't as yet begun to understand." Is that what had happened, or was this delicate strand of circumstance and coincidence a figment of his imagination? Was Diana right about him? Had he become as mad as Ahab or Captain Queeg? "But the important thing is that it's no longer business. It's personal."

Diana's eyes, so close to his, were large and dark and filled with fear. Seve knew that he had to ignore that, ignore everything now but the war that had never died.

"You see, I know who killed Dom. At least I think I do. Anyway, I've got no choice now but to find out for sure."

And he knew there was only one way to do that.

"He isn't here," Soutane said, walking into the garden around which Mun's villa was built. "He often isn't."

"Where does he go?" Chris asked, watching water spew out of the dolphins' mouths.

Soutane shrugged. "Wherever his business takes him. Asia mostly, I expect. We can never go back to Cambodia; we have too many political enemies. But Mun likes to be near it."

"Do you know where he is?" Chris was anxious to find out all he could about his brother. "Can you call him?"

"Where he goes in Asia?" She laughed. "I probably couldn't even telex him." She came and stood beside him. "Be patient.

You've already taken care of the paperwork regarding the disposition of Terry's—'' Her voice caught, and she turned away to stare into the mountains, blue with haze.

''Chris, I want to ask you a favor,'' she said, after a long time. ''And before you answer, promise me that you'll think about it.''

''All right.''

''I'd like to keep Terry's body in France. I'd like to have him buried here in the place he loved.''

''Soutane, I don't—''

''Please,'' she said. ''You promised to think about it.''

He nodded. He was thinking of his father. What would he say to him? Of course, his father would want Terry to be buried in the family cemetery in Connecticut. But is that what Terry would have wanted had he even contemplated his own death? Being here so near where he had spent his summer of the Tour de France, having gotten to know Soutane even a little, Chris was sure he knew.

''I think it's a good idea.'' He saw the relief flooding Soutane's face, and belatedly realized how difficult her request must have been.

She was so close to him that he could inhale her scent, a bit spicy, a bit musky. ''Who did you call when we first got here?'' she asked. ''I saw your face change. It got dark and hard as rock.''

Chris sat down opposite the fountain. Now that he was here, now that the disposition of Terry's body had been taken care of, he could allow himself to feel how drained of emotion he was. At his core was an emptiness that had begun long before the news of Terry's death. It was, he thought now, as if he had been living a stranger's life, having come in on the middle of a film about someone he knew vaguely or not at all.

''A friend of mine was hurt very badly in New York just before I left. She was attacked. In my apartment, in fact.''

Soutane, concerned, sat beside him. She rolled a fallen chestnut blossom back and forth between her fingers. ''One hears stories about the violence of New York. Are they, after all, true?''

''Not, I suppose, to New Yorkers,'' Chris said. ''I've lived all my adult life in New York. I've never been assaulted or had my apartment broken into.''

''Until now.''

''I don't think this was a burglary, or a break-in,'' he said. ''At least, not of the normal sort.''

''What was it, then?''

''I wish I knew,'' Chris admitted. ''Most of it's a blur. I was asleep. But it seems to me as if my friend, Alix, was injured trying to protect me.''

"Do you have enemies in New York?" Soutane had intimate knowledge of what having enemies could lead to.

Chris laughed. "I suppose. I don't know. But I'm a criminal lawyer, a defender, not a prosecutor, so that seems unlikely."

"Then who would have reason to want to attack you?"

"Not attack," Chris said thoughtfully. "Kill. I'm sure this bastard was out to kill me."

"But why?"

"I have no idea."

Soutane put a hand over his. "How is your friend? She's who you called, yes?"

Chris nodded. "I couldn't talk with her yet. I spoke to her son. She'll be okay."

Soutane sensed something as yet unsaid. "What is it, Chris?"

He sighed. "I also spoke with the surgeon. There was apparently some vocal-cord damage. No one yet knows what the outcome will be. Certainly her voice will change, but that would be the least of all evils."

"And the worst?"

He got up, leaned against the fountain so that the spray from the dolphins' mouths pattered against his hot face. "The worst is that she will lose her voice altogether."

Soutane reached out, turned him to face the sun. "Look over there. These hillsides are so beautiful this time of year," she said. "This part of France is filled with oddities as well as beauty. Do you know that in the sixteenth century, Vence was ruled by a bishop who had been an Italian prince? He eventually became Pope Paul the Third." She lifted her hand to include the countryside. "Why don't we take a walk through history. It's all around us."

Soutane took them through the villa's gates, along a slope, and presently Chris saw that they were walking along a ridge like the spine of some great beast that seemed to be rearing up from the skeleton of the earth.

"We're very near Tourrette-sur-Loup," she said, pointing to a magnificent, ancient walled town built on the center of the spinelike ridge. "Terry was murdered there. In the church." She paused, as if abruptly unsure of herself. "Mun said that must have been particularly terrible, to die in a holy place."

"I don't know. When Terry and I read the Bible, it was in an intellectual context."

"That was a long time ago," she said, "wasn't it?"

They had moved on, and were considerably nearer Tourrette. "Do you hear it?" Soutane cocked her head. "The waterfall is just over there. On particularly still nights you can hear it from the villa."

They were standing on a grassy knoll overlooking the spectacular cascade, the wooded view down into the valley. Above them, the medieval stone village brooded on the crest of the ridge like an owl in a maze of branches.

Soutane stood beneath an olive tree, with her hands together, very white against the dark of her clothes. "Chris, I want you to know something. I never stopped thinking of you. I was so young then. We both were. I did what I thought was right, what I thought I had to do."

"I'm not sure I understand. You thought you had to make sure we'd never see each other again?"

"I was terribly afraid. My father made it quite clear what he would do to you."

"I don't believe you," Chris said. "I knew your father. He wasn't a murderer. He didn't just—"

"You didn't know my father at all," Soutane said. "You were always so maddeningly sure of yourself. I see that hasn't changed either. You never seemed capable of seeing beneath the facade, even if that facade was false. Oh yes, my father was charming, urbane, knowledgeable. But he made his living being engaging to a diverse cross section of people."

"You make him sound like a snake-oil salesman," Chris said. "I remember him being wholly committed to the cause of political revolution. Whereas we believed in nothing but ourselves."

"Let me tell you something," Soutane said. "My father was the most dangerous kind of salesman precisely *because* he believed in the revolution. History is littered with men like my father. Clever people—perhaps even geniuses—who, through their manipulations, thought they had managed to alter the political balance of Indochina. When all they had really done was help replace one tyrant with another.

"But, in the process, they themselves gained great power and wealth. In the end all of them—my father included—were whores to those twin evils. They were sinners in the house of humanity."

"All this anger," Chris said, "and yet back then you refused to help me go to the authorities. But it all happened. With the help of the money and arms your father was able to procure for him, Pol

Pot and the Khmer Rouge wrested power. Pol Pot pulled Cambodia up by its roots, destroyed its past. Then, like the Soviets, he rewrote its history in his own vision. We had in our hands the power to stop him."

"You were wrong then," Soutane said. "And you're wrong now. We had nothing, as you yourself found out. You held what you thought was a genie in your fist, but the moment you opened your hand it dissipated like smoke. You see, my father could move mountains, then. You could not understand that because he never allowed you to see its workings. Just like he never allowed you to see the other side of him, the part my mother and I saw. In any event believe me when I tell you he meant what he said. He would have had you killed had you remained in France."

"And now that I am back in France? How long does your father's memory stretch?"

"My father," Soutane said, "never forgot anything." She shrugged. "But it is of little consequence now. For all I know of him now he is dead like my mother."

"You mean you don't know? How is that possible?"

"He found out what I had done, that against his express instruction never to see you again I went to warn you. He cut me off from himself, from the family."

The view down into the valley, thick with trees and drifting smoke, was spectacular. He could hear the roar of the cascade, though through the trees he could not see it.

"I haven't forgotten what happened that night when we overheard your mother and Saloth Sar," he said quietly. "Often, after the reports of the genocide became widespread, I'd see images of Pol Pot doing just what we overheard him saying he would do: killing the politicians in power, the intellectuals, the Buddhist priests, anyone with an educated brain who stood a chance of defying him. Ten million people slaughtered like cattle, dumped into vast pits. And that wasn't the end of the nightmare. Then the reports on the reeducation camps became public. Children being taught to spy on their parents—learning to betray their own families at the age of ten. I would lie awake at night replaying over and over that scene in the embassy. Why wouldn't anyone listen? Why wouldn't they believe me?"

Soutane watched him. "You look so much like your brother, standing there concerned, a little bit bewildered. He had those qualities, too, but they were part of a darker mix. It was clear when I met him that he had been hurt, perhaps in the same way you had been, but in another, deeper way as well. There was a cruelty about him, but also a pain that might explain it. I saw him in Tourrette one day, and I pursued him. All the way back to Nice, thinking, could he be you?''

''We never looked that much alike,'' Chris said.

Soutane smiled. ''He wasn't you, of course. So I came back here, determined to forget about him.

''And I think I did, until he saw me in Tourrette again, eating lunch. His face, through the windowpane, was dark, brooding, and he possessed that sense of determination I had grown to love in you. That the accident seemed to have destroyed or, at least, damaged.

''He came into the restaurant and sat at the next table. Eventually we began to talk. He was intrigued that I was an artist. He genuinely liked my work when I got around to showing it to him.''

Chris felt the old anger rising in him. ''Did you go to bed with him right away?''

Soutane was curious. ''Does that matter?''

''Yes,'' he said. ''Very much.''

''Oh, Chris. Why do you hurt yourself so?''

''I want to know,'' he persisted.

''Tell me why.''

''Because he was my brother, because you and I were lovers.'' Because, he thought, for a time you were all I ever loved, or could love.

''He wanted to help me,'' Soutane said. ''I needed help.''

''What kind of help?''

Soutane closed her eyes. Chris could see movement beneath her lids, as if she were asleep and dreaming.

''Mun's family—my family as well, if you want to look at it that way—were in power in Cambodia during Lon Nol's regime,'' she said softly. ''They made many enemies—powerful enemies, implacable enemies. When Mun fled here to France, he was afraid that he would be followed. He came to see me—we hadn't seen each other in many years. He did not want to stay long because he hated exposing me to risk.

''I was the one who convinced him to come here to Vence, to create a hideaway for himself. But I found that I did not want to leave him. He was like a brother to me. He was so different from my mother, who I had learned to hate over the years. I missed my childhood in Southeast Asia and, with Mun, I had discovered it all over again.

"But all the time he was terrified that his enemies would find him and kill him. He was obsessed with the notion, to the extent that he made me train with him. He knows many forms of martial arts. His spiritual training is quite astounding, really, like a Tibetan monk who can stand for weeks as if dead or walk upon a mat of fire.

"Of course, it was impossible to teach me these things over the course of months or even a year. But he did teach me how to kill a human being. I fought against it and, once, he threw me out of the villa. 'I don't want you near me,' he told me.

"I came back. I did everything he told me to do. I studied diligently, even though it made me sick to my stomach to learn these things. How many ways there are to kill a human being, Chris!

"The days wore on. The weeks turned into months, and the months into years. No one came to try to kill Mun, but he continued his morbid obsession, insisted that I train even more diligently.

"Few guests were ever invited to the villa. Terry, of course, later on, several of Mun's Cambodian friends living in Paris. A girlfriend, once in a while. Never any business associates. Mun was adamant about that.

"Mun is not monogamous. But there was one girl who came more than any others. She was a Khmer that Mun had known in Cambodia. They had grown up together, played in the mud together, swam in the Mekong together, perhaps even made love so long ago. I remembered her vaguely. I think jealousy was the predominant emotion I felt when I saw her. I remembered how Mun had stared into her eyes.

"On the other hand, she was never less than nice to me. Once or twice I remember she brought me presents when she arrived at the villa for the weekend; she did not want me to feel left out. Her kindness made my jealousy of her even stronger.

"One weekend—it was during the hottest two weeks in August, stifling, really—Mun announced that she would be coming. I was fed up with the two of then, and told him I'd go into Nice for a couple of days. He cajoled me into staying, but when I saw her I wanted to smash her smiling face with my fist. Appalled at what I was feeling, I left.

"It was already dusk, but still terribly hot. My car had been sitting out in the broiling sun all day. I got about a mile from the villa, and the coolant exploded.

"I searched for an open garage or gas station but it was too late. Everything was closed. I took my overnight bag out of the car and hiked back to the villa. No one saw me come in. I used my key at the gate, not bothering to ring inside.

"I found them in the library. Mun's girlfriend—his childhood sweetheart—had put something in his brandy. He was gray-faced, lying on the carpet, unconscious or dead—I didn't know which. She was standing over him, a coil of piano wire stretched between her fists."

Soutane stopped abruptly. Her face was white and pinched, like a patient forced to recall the trauma that has caused her suffering.

Chris put a hand on her but she brushed it away as if her skin were too sensitive to touch.

"What happened?" he asked softly.

"What happened?" Her voice echoed his, eerily hollow. "I killed her. I came at her as Mun had trained me. She did not hear me; she had no chance. I broke her neck. Then I got Mun to the hospital. Then I tried to kill myself."

"Oh, Soutane." Chris was horrified. "Why? You were defending Mun. Defending yourself, for that matter. Don't you think she would have killed you if you'd given her the chance?"

Soutane's eyes blazed. "None of that matters!" Then, just as quickly as it had come, the spark went out of her. "You don't understand." Her voice was dull.

"Explain it to me, then."

"I can't," she said. "Unless you've killed another human being." She looked at him. "But I know you, Chris. You haven't killed anyone. Thank God, you'll never know what it's like."

"So this is what Terry helped you with? Your self-loathing? Your guilt?"

Soutane nodded. "Guilt is one thing you know about." Then she looked up. "I'm sorry. That was cruel."

Chris stared out over the hills, wondering how it was that life had passed him by. So many momentous events had occurred to people he loved while he had been scurrying around the rat warren of the legal profession. "You haven't answered my question," he said at last. "Did you sleep with Terry right away?"

"I thought you would have forgotten." Soutane smiled bleakly. "He reminded me so much of you," she said. "Of the person you had been before the accident."

"I am what I am," Chris said, with a mixture of anger and sadness that her answer had brought him. "You can't bring me back. You can't have what is already gone."

"You talk as if you're dead."

It was then that Chris realized that his desire to discover what had happened to Terry in Vietnam had turned into an obsession. Because that same something—mysterious and elusive—had happened to him, in the rain, in the useless rush of adrenaline, of failed dreams, in the agony of a leg twisted beneath him, and a finish line he would never cross.

"The boy you knew," he said, "*le coureur cycliste*, as your mother once called me. He *is* dead."

"Why? Because you lost one race?"

"I could've won," he said, not wanting to relive it again. "I *would've* won."

"But you didn't, and you still haven't accepted it—even after all these years." She shook her head. "You're more like your brother than you think. He was living in the past, and so are you."

Soutane came away from the tree. She walked in that way dancers have, with her center of gravity low, in her hips and lower belly. *Hara*, the Japanese called it, putting much store in its worth.

What it was, Chris thought, was sexy. Or perhaps it was Soutane who made it so. But then again perhaps it was he who made Soutane sexy.

When she was very close, when he could feel her breath on his cheek, she lifted an arm, using her hand to brush back the hair from his forehead. Her fingertips lingered on his skin.

"Remember when I asked if you knew any self-defense?" Soutane asked. "I'd like to show you something now."

"What for?"

She shrugged. "We don't know what Terry was involved in, but whatever it was, it got him killed. Don't you think it makes sense to be prudent?"

"Maybe we should contact the police, then."

Soutane looked at him. "What will we tell them?"

"Just what you've told me."

"They are policemen," Soutane said. "How do you think they would react to what I've told you?"

She took his right hand in hers. "Make a fist," she said, and when he did, she ran a finger over the first set of knuckles. "In a fight you will tend to hit someone here." Then she elongated his fist so that the second set of knuckles became the hand's leading edge. "Curl your fingers tightly under," she instructed him, "and when you hit, it will be more effective."

She guided his fist to a spot beneath her sternum. "Strike here. Or in the armpit, just here, above the bone." His knuckles against her soft flesh. "These are both lethal places, where the nerve meridians begin. They are, therefore, the source of great power."

He took her hand, held it tightly to stop the shivers coursing inside her. "I remember," he said softly, "when I hit you in the garden. I remember the sound of it, the way your head recoiled, the way your skin reddened, the hateful look in your eyes."

"How you made me hate you, then."

"I wanted that look, I needed you to hate me as much as I despised myself at that moment. Because I had sought out that safe haven, because I had run as far as I could from Vietnam. And Vietnam had followed me all the way here, and I thought that was significant. I thought that I had to find the war.

"Now I think that was the moment—when I hit you in self-loathing, seeing myself in you—when I lost the chance to win the Tour de France. Like me, you were so uninvolved in what were the important issues of the time."

"Who said I was uninvolved?"

"I could see it," Chris said. "You were like me—and so unlike your parents. Self-involved, uncommitted to anything of lasting—"

"Who said I was uninvolved?"

"Your mother," Chris admitted. "We were talking about you."

"You mean *she* was talking about me. Oh, Christ, is that what happened to us? Don't tell me that she was able to so successfully fuck us up."

"What?"

"It was because you wouldn't go to bed with her," Soutane said sadly. "Your morality must have infuriated her. If she couldn't seduce you, she was going to make sure I wouldn't have you for long. She had you sized up in a minute. That was one of her unique talents. She knew which buttons to push."

"Is all this true?"

Soutane nodded. "Unhappily, yes."

"But you had divorced yourself from what your parents were involved in."

"Seduction, procurement, blackmail, murder." She looked at him. "Wouldn't you?"

"Oh, shit."

"It's all over with," Soutane said. "Forget about it. I don't blame you. Your morality made you vulnerable."

"But all that time—"

"Tell me something," she said. "If you hadn't overheard my

mother and Pol Pot that night in the garden, if we hadn't had the fight, if you hadn't hit me. If you'd won the Tour de France, what then?''

''I'd have no secrets for you to steal.'' He could not bring himself to give her any other answer.

She gave him a mocking pout. ''Poor baby, carrying your bruised heart around where everyone can see it.''

''Not everyone,'' he said. ''Just you.'' But he knew that, in a sense, she was right. Just as she had been right all along. The truth was, she knew him better than he knew himself.

''I wonder,'' she said, ''whether you know how much of a manipulator you can be. That, I think, is the only difference between you and Terry. He not only knew how to manipulate people, he was aware of how well he did it.''

Chris thought of what Max Steiner had called his velvet hammer, his ability to sway a jury, to make it empathize with his client's point of view. He shrugged. ''I am what all lawyers are to one degree or another.'' But he knew he was far from sanguine about the way he could so easily manipulate people. It was what the Marcus Gable case had come to symbolize for him: the recognition that he was successful—even, to some extent, a celebrity—in a profession he could no longer tolerate.

''No,'' Soutane said. ''You're something special, Chris. Just like your brother was.''

Chris looked away from her. ''My brother, my brother.'' He was angry. ''Why do you say I look like Terry, I act like Terry?''

Soutane regarded him coolly. ''Even now after he's dead you are still frightened of him.''

Chris was startled. ''Frightened?'' Something hard and cold and unpleasant was congealing in his stomach.

''You always were, Chris.'' Soutane on cat's feet moved away from him. ''I always wondered what it would be like to admire a person so, to idolize them—''

''I never idolized Terry!''

''Of course you didn't.'' She was mocking him again. ''And you never hit me. You never loved me.''

Chris had no answer for her. He went after her until she was so close he could not help but touch her.

''I don't think this is a good idea,'' she said softly.

His arms slid around her. She tried to break away. ''Chris, no—''

When his mouth closed over hers, the years seemed to melt away.

It was as if he was back in the summer of the Tour de France, the rain-slicked Parisian streets, the running dog, the accident existing only in some ephemeral future that might or might not yet occur. He seemed safe and alive again.

"Soutane." He whispered her name. This was, he thought, the moment he had been waiting for ever since he heard her voice on the phone.

He pulled her down to the ground, buried his face in the hollow of her neck. She smelled of summer and sunlight. Or perhaps those were the triggers she set off in his mind.

"Oh, God." She kissed him back, beginning to climb him.

He unbuttoned her blouse, sank lower on her so that she arched her neck, running her fingers through his hair. He remembered what she loved, and what she loved him to do to her. It was like getting on his bike for the first time after the accident: terrifying, pulse-pounding, but so sweet in the associations it brought back, in the recognition of what had been missing in his life, it took his breath away.

Afternoon shadows crept like a host of cats through the glade.

Soutane weeping as they made love in long, slow, ecstatic thrusts. Her back was arched as she rubbed herself against the length of him and, when the pleasure became overwhelming, when her eyes began to roll back in her head, she thrust herself frantically upward, grabbing his hips to keep him hard against her while she shuddered and quaked against him, her breath exploding in little panting bursts on his cheek.

Then, holding him tightly so that he remained at the peak, she slid down him, curling herself around him, engulfing him with her mouth, taking him all the way in until his pelvis lurched, and spasms racked his frame.

The sun, slowly spinning in its arc, set the top of the waterfall on fire, illuminating it out of the darkness that had accumulated like the years at its base.

Christopher and Soutane looked tissue-thin within the precisely ground objectives of the Swarovsky 6×50 field glasses. Dante, lying flat on a rock fifty yards behind and above them, might have been a giant lizard sunbathing in the brilliant noonday sun.

He had picked Soutane up at her apartment where he was observing her movements with a good deal more expertise than had the man dressed as a priest.

Following the last face-to-face with the man he had assigned to keep tabs on Soutane (a defrocked French Jesuit priest who had fallen on hard times), Dante had decided to take over the Sirik surveillance himself. He had found the Jesuit uneasy, unable to meet his penetrating gaze. Dante had had a feeling that something had gone wrong. At first, the Jesuit refused to admit the truth; they could be stubborn, these Catholics. But Dante soon changed that.

Dante had grown up with M. Mabuse beneath the orange skies of Vietnam. They had not fought together in the war until near the end, but Dante had already heard of M. Mabuse's exploits. M. Mabuse had become something of a local legend, and was much revered among his people.

By that time Dante had met Milhaud, who had recruited him, changed his name, his outlook. Milhaud had taught Dante to look beyond his own country, to be a student of *la situation en macro*, to observe the ebb and flow of world politics.

Milhaud, Dante knew, had attempted to do the same with M. Mabuse, but it was already too late. M. Mabuse was like a block of granite. One could laboriously chip away at him, changing, perhaps, his shape, but never his composition.

It took Dante twenty minutes to break the Jesuit down. By then the floor was covered with a dark pool of sweat and blood. Dante was, in fact, just warming up, when the priest began to confess, *Father forgive me, for I have sinned.*

It was not, of course, in Dante's nature to forgive anyone. But he accepted the confession nonetheless, hearing with mounting anger the skein of the Jesuit's sins: the pair of underpants he had stolen from Soutane that had, apparently, alerted her to the fact that her apartment had been searched, her subsequent entrapment of the priest in the Cours Saleya, his divulging everything he knew of the Forest of Swords, of who he was working for, including Dante's name.

Enraged, Dante had slammed his fist into the death point just below the priest's right arm. He had stared, momentarily drained, into the Jesuit's slack face, wondering how he was going to salvage the mess the Jesuit had made. He detested cleaning up other people's messes. He had spent most of the war doing that for the Russians, whom, unlike Milhaud, he disliked as much as he disliked the Americans.

Dante, on mobile surveillance, had followed Soutane to the airport. When he had determined which flight she was waiting for, he had used some of the credentials with which Milhaud had provided him to get a look at the passenger manifest. He was gratified to see Christopher Haye's name on the list.

He had kept track of them all that day, though, now on foot in the countryside, it was becoming increasingly perilous. He was not about to underestimate Miss Sirik. The Jesuit had made that mistake, and it had cost him his life.

As he watched them, he licked his lips. Was it anticipation or simple lust? It was impossible to say.

In his mind all the tortures that had been visited upon him during his imprisonment in Vietnam, were recreated: water dripped endlessly on a spot in the center of his forehead the size of a dime. In his mind he was buried up to his chin; the tropical noonday sun crashed upon the top of his head. In his mind fire-hardened shards of bamboo were driven through the loose skin of his scrotum.

Dante had been incarcerated by the Vietnamese for a year and a half, during the war, out of the reach of even Milhaud. He saw M. Mabuse infrequently, even though they must have been imprisoned near one another nearly all that time. Isolation interspersed with pain, the enemy calculated, would destroy the will as effectively as chemicals stripped paint from a plank of wood.

Layer by layer, Dante had felt himself slipping away, until he had only a dim idea of who he had been, or what he was. He was a heartbeat away, then, from telling the enemy everything they wanted to know, everything he had sworn to keep secret.

But, then, through some miraculous error, he and M. Mabuse were placed together in the darkness of a single holding cell. As they waited for the renewal of pain, M. Mabuse had spoken to him. "Take heart. Another soul is with you."

"Are you angel," Dante said, "or devil?"

"I am you," M. Mabuse said. "We are the same."

"How long have we been here?"

"Take a breath, and let it out," M. Mabuse said. "That is how long."

"I am at the end. I do not even know whether you are real or an illusion."

"It does not matter," M. Mabuse said. "We are here to save one another. Think of me, and I will think of you. Remember this moment. In that way time will pass us by."

The sound of the cell door opening.

Dante blinked. He was back on the wooded ridge overlooking Tourrette. A bead of sweat had stung his eye with its salt. He turned the ring, refocusing the Swarovskys on the twined pair. They were finished.

He had seen their bodies naked. Now he would do the same with their minds.

Seve fell asleep on the plane to Nice reading Billy Mace's report on the assault on Alix Layne. But, because of his injury, he was making so much noise in his sleep that an alarmed flight attendant woke him up.

Billy Mace was a black detective with whom Seve had been a beat cop in the South Bronx, New York City's own choice acre of hell. Up there, the department preferred the ethnic types, blacks, Hispanics, and the like, to take the beat patrols. Still, Billy Mace got in the middle of a gang war, the edge of a stiletto catching him on the point of the chin just before he brought down the Scorpio leader who was wielding it. Billy Mace wore that scar as proudly as he did his badge.

He had dropped off a copy of the Alix Layne report just before Seve had left with the Dragon for Chinatown, and Diana had had the good sense to bring it with her to the hospital. According to the note Billy Mace had attached to the file, there were two reasons he had wanted Seve to see it. One was the fact that "an iron fan" had been mentioned as the assailant's improbable weapon, and two, the incident had taken place in the apartment of a well-known lawyer named Christopher Haye. The last line of Billy Mace's note read, *Didn't you do a tour of duty in 'Nam with a dude named Haye? This the one???*

Seve's mouth was dry, and he had a killer headache. Flying, it appeared, was also not good for his condition. He went back to the lavatory, relieved himself, then splashed cold water on his face. He looked at himself in the mirror. Gingerly, he touched the red welt on his neck. Jesus, he thought, that bastard Trangh got me good.

He downed his medicine, saw napalm exploding behind his reflection. Although he had spent three quarters of his time there, when Seve thought of his tour of duty, it was not Vietnam he remembered, it was Cambodia. The Twilight Zone they had jokingly called it in those days, when rumors were rampant of American undercover units crossing the border into the neutral country. *There's the signpost up ahead. You've just crossed over into . . .* Cambodia.

He got out of that claustrophobic space, hearing his impaired breathing like a grandfather clock gone insane. He squeezed into his economy seat, envious of those in business and first-class. Those with money. Cops, so the saying went, never had money; they had the law.

But, in the end, Seve wondered, what was that worth? With him or without him on the job, the world went merrily on. Would he even be missed while he was in France? He stared out the Perspex window at nothing, an infinity of gray, cold and wet and far away from everything.

He had always felt that the law came first, before personal involvements, before, even, family. Dom's sudden death had forced him to confront his entire orderly universe. With Dom gone, he found himself feeling increasingly divorced from the mundane duties he must perform day in, day out in order to ensure that, at least on his own tiny plot of earth, the law was upheld.

The concept of the law now seemed more abstract to Seve. It had regressed to the mean and impotent state it had been in during the war. The law had not kept Dominic safe. Worse, in the face of his death it could do little but wallow in its own inertia.

What a cumbersome implement the law had become! It was worse than useless.

He turned his attention back to the report. Something tucked into an aside drew him like a magnet. Christopher Haye had left the country several days before to pick up the body of his brother, Terry, who had died in a town called Tourrette-sur-Loup. Christopher Haye did not mention the cause of his brother's death, but he did give an address where he could be reached in the same city as the address on the slip of paper Al DeCordia had given to Dom. Soutane Sirik's address; below her name, Dom had written *Saved?*

Seve was dizzy with the implications. Terry Haye, with whom he served in Vietnam, dies around the same time that Dom is killed. He dies in France, and his brother, Christopher, is staying at the Hotel Negresco in Nice, where he's gone to pick up Terry's corpse. Dom and DeCordia are murdered by Trangh the Vietnamese, who also tries to murder Seve.

How did Terry Haye die? In a car accident? Did he have a heart attack? Did he fall down a mountainside? Or was he murdered? Did Trangh also get to him? And if so, why?

What the hell was going on?

Seve coughed blood into his handkerchief, momentarily closed his eyes against the pounding in his head. He thought of Terry Haye, an odd, introverted character, tough when he had to be, hard to get to know. Still, Seve had liked and respected him. He was sorry he was dead. He wondered briefly what the brother, Christopher, was like. Seve opened his eyes and, marshaling his strength, began to read the Alix Layne file all over again.

Wasn't there another reason why Christopher Haye's name was familiar? Then he had it. Sure. He and Alix Layne were the principal antagonists in the Marcus Gable court case. There had been a lot of speculation at the precinct about whether Gable was guilty or not. In fact, for the last weeks of the trial it was just about the only topic of conversation among the blues.

Seve recalled that Christopher Haye had made a big issue of Gable being a Vietnam vet, even though that potentially could have backfired. In fact, now that he thought of it, why hadn't the assistant DA turned the vet angle around, pointing out how men had learned to kill during the war, knew a hundred ways to terminate a human life? Well, Gable was such a hero, medals up the yin-yang, he suspected Alix Layne would have been taking a hell of a risk in attacking him on that level. After all, how many Vietnam vets had been on the jury?

Seve stared out the window, giving his eyes a rest. Trangh. In Vietnam. He was haunted by Trangh's face. And when he saw Trangh, he was at Virgil's side. There had been a strong bond between those two then; it was possible that there was still a connection. Trangh and Virgil.

When Seve closed his eyes he saw dancing *apsaras*, the immense stone faces of Vishnu and Buddha in the delta of religion, where in the navel of the universe Hinduism and Buddhism commingled. He smelled cardamom and steaming vegetation, felt again the fear of being surrounded by Khmer Rouge while a deal of unknown origin was being consummated.

Virgil's deal. It was always Virgil in the shadows, giving the orders.

He resolved to call Diana as soon as he landed, and have her check Virgil's military background. His real name had been Arnold Toth. Seve, a detective even then, had found that out, though he doubted that Virgil had known that he had.

Seve knew he was being the paranoid detective, seeing conspiracy in every shadow, but what the hell, Diana already thought he had lost his mind.

You've broken every rule you ever taught me, she had said. *Not broken,* he had answered her with some justification. *Just bent.* But he had seen the look in her eyes, and the unspoken reply. *There isn't much difference between the two.*

But, Jesus Christ, this is Dom we're talking about, Seve thought. My only brother. If I don't see that he gets justice, who will?

Chris opened his eyes, staring at the interlaced leaves of the olive tree. He felt Soutane's body warm beside him. The smell of sex was heavy in the air. But the sunshine and the summer were still there, as pungent and distinctive as wood smoke.

"This is what happens," he said, "when you make love to someone you had never hoped to see again."

"What?"

"It's like a dream. Almost as if it never happened. As if your yearning made it so, as if it happened in your mind, in your memory, not with your body."

Her hand stroking his soaked flesh. "Does this feel like a memory?"

"It feels," he said, "like wood smoke and summer." He looked around him at the peaceful countryside. Again, he had the sensation of having come a great distance, far more than the four thousand miles from New York to Vence.

She turned his face toward her, kissed him on the lips. "I never thought I'd ever see you again." Then, pulling back, she saw the introspective look in his eyes. "What are you thinking about?"

"The Forest of Swords," Chris said. "Can it possibly exist? Is that what Terry spent his life in pursuing? Why? What makes it so important? You told me that whoever possesses it can command all the opium warlords on the Shan Plateau. From what I know of the situation up there, I find that hard to believe. First, you'd have to unite them. And I don't think anything on earth can do that."

"Then I think I should tell you a bit more about the *Prey Dauw*," Soutane said. She dressed. She understood that, for now at least, their idyll was over; it was time to get back to the business of trying to find out what Terry was into, and who had him killed. "The Forest of Swords is an ancient talisman which would bestow upon its possessor virtually unlimited power.

"Originally, so the myth goes, the *Prey Dauw* was forged by Mahagiri, a renegade Theravadan Buddhist monk who lived many centuries ago. Mahagiri, an ascetic, wrote the *Muy Puan*, a volume of religious scripture so radical, so revisionist in its tenets that it was immediately forbidden.

"The other monks ostracized Mahagiri. By writing the *Muy Puan*, which was a kind of *abhidhamma*, a reinterpretation of the Buddha's teachings, he had declared himself a *bodhisattva*, a future Buddha. This was intolerable.

"It is said that exile was the worst course of action the monks could have taken. In the desolate, windswept mountains where Mahagiri took up residence, he made his pact with Ravana, the chief demon of our cosmology. Long had Ravana sought to undermine the teachings of the Buddha. In Mahagiri, it seemed, he had at last found the way.

"Using Ravana's blood, Mahagiri forged the *Prey Dauw*. Then they buried it. According to the legend, the sword required thirty centuries in the earth in order to achieve its ultimate power."

"What made the writing of the *Muy Puan* so dangerous?" Chris asked. Clothed, they began to walk past the waterfall, on their way to Tourrette-sur-Loup.

"Theravadan Buddhists believe in thirty-one separate planes of existence. The *Muy Puan* proposes that there are one thousand planes of hell alone where devils, demons, and false *bodhisattvas* dwell."

"So?"

"It also speaks of the Forest of Swords. With it one could open up the thousand planes of hell, and merge them with our own, loosing the scourge of pent-up demons onto the earth."

"But all this is, as you said, myth."

Soutane nodded. "So I believed. Until the existence of the *Prey Dauw* was established."

Chris was smiling at Soutane's intensity in telling this curious fable. "Are you saying you believe that someone can now use this sword to unleash millions of Buddhist demons into our world?"

Soutane was unfazed by his tone. "On the contrary," she said. "I believe that it has already happened."

"You can't be serious," Chris said. "You can't believe all this cosmological mumbo-jumbo."

"I want you to understand me." Soutane said. "I believe in these evil things: devils, demons, and false *bodhisattvas*. The opium trade exists. It makes hundreds of millions of dollars for those who control the growing of the poppy, its refining, and its distribution. It also provides them with unimaginable power. Combine that with the terrible suffering of addiction and you have all the devils, demons, and false *bodhisattvas* in the thousand hells of the *Muy Puan*.

"But others believe in these evils in the literal sense, especially those who control the opium trade in the Burmese section of the Golden Triangle. And they're the ones who count. The *Prey Dauw*, if it exists—and I believe now that it does—gains its power because of these people's belief in it."

They had gone past the roaring waterfall. Ahead rose the outskirts of the town: a rustic restaurant, a *moulin*, an old olive mill. Chickens scratched in the dry earth.

"It is essential for you to understand this point," Soutane said. "The Shan is unlike any other place on earth. It is a place of great power, both man-made and spiritual. Please believe me when I tell you that anything is possible in the Shan for the one who possesses the *Prey Dauw*."

"Which brings us back to Terry," Chris said. "What was he doing with one third of the Forest of Swords?"

"As I said—"

"I will not believe that Terry was involved in the opium trade. It's too heinous, too despicable."

"I'm afraid your belief will not make it so," she said. "What other explanation is there? Terry was desperate to hide something of enormous value. He wrote you the postcard. He was making an effort to see you after a decade of silence. Something of extreme importance had to have prompted him. It was *La Porte à la Nuit*."

"That's something else that bothers me," Chris said. "If it was so urgent that he get in touch with me, why didn't he just pick up a phone and call?"

"It had been a long time." Soutane shrugged. "There was a lot of bad blood between you two. That is difficult to forget—or to face."

"But you yourself said that he was in a desperate situation." Chris shook his head. "I still ask myself, of all the methods of communication he could have chosen, why use a postcard? It's slow, inefficient, and is liable to be lost in the mail." He took it out of his pocket. "Besides, it isn't even stamped."

"That's true," Soutane said. "I hadn't noticed that. It *is* odd."

Chris turned the postcard over and over. "I keep wondering what's special about a postcard. Only tourists buy postcards."

At that moment they crested a small rise, and the village of Tourrette-sur-Loup rose before them. Struck by the afternoon sun, it had the aspect of some mythical place like Camelot or Avalon.

Chris turned his gaze from the town to the postcard in his hand, and saw the same view miniaturized, captured by the camera.

Adrenaline surged through him. "That's it!" he shouted, holding the postcard aloft. "Look, Soutane. Look! Tourrette-sur-Loup!"

He laughed into her bewildered face. "Don't you see it? It wasn't just a postcard Terry left for me, it was a *picture* postcard. A picture of Tourrette." He took her hand, racing along the ridge toward the village. "That's where he's hidden *La Porte à la Nuit*! In Tourrette-sur-Loup!"

M. Mabuse was in chains. Once he was a soldier, fighting on a familiar shore, made alien by foreigners. M. Mabuse, in returning to France, was, by his own estimation, reentering bondage. But it was an imprisonment meant to free him. He did not know, now, whether in fact it would. But this path had been dictated to him, and he must continue to follow it to its end.

It was wholly unlike that other detention he had endured, when the sun seemed harnessed to the trees, when his eyelids were taped open, and he was forced to stare into it until its burning heart was forever imprinted on his brain.

M. Mabuse sitting in his car at the airport at Nice, watching the flow of traffic, the glorious march of sculpted chrome, spangled by the late-afternoon sun. He imagined those flowing lines opening like immense exotic flowers in the high-speed impact of an accident. His mind conjured the stiffening limbs, pale and smooth, draped across the leather-covered steering wheels, the heads, hair glittering with blood and glass, thrust through shattered windshields, tight skirts hiked high on cool thighs, revealing erotic shadows on silken concave surfaces. The sun, that now sparked and danced off the line of automobiles, was always with him then, in the rain, with gray-green clouds seeping across the treetops, at night in the hole, with the darkness so absolute it felt as if he was entombed beneath the earth.

His smirking captors had seen to his imprisonment, as they had deprived him of a place to lie down and sleep, a place to relieve himself. They had starved him, beaten him, urinated on him, fed him animal dung, but they had not broken him.

They had him for eighteen months. It might have been eighteen years or eighteen minutes, depending on whether you could make time your friend, or you allowed it to be your enemy. Surrounded by the enemy, it became imperative to create friends in the empty darkness, in the hideous light.

He had hidden himself within a place as ancient as amber, where no sight, no sound, no human emotion could disturb the ineluctable silence of time. He had taught himself to manipulate time as others, perhaps, used texts or lore to build knowledge. For he had come to see death as neither an end nor a beginning. It was, rather, his ally. And, after all, death was time's twin.

He remembered when he had not yet learned to manipulate time and death. "Sunyata tells us that the world is encompassed by sin," his interrogator said in that utterly lightless place they inevitably dragged him to after pasting the sun to his eyes. "Yet the texts say, that which is sin is also wisdom."

M. Mabuse remembered the feel of his interrogator moving around him like a satellite about the earth. It was like trying with hands tied to scratch an itch.

"Our wisdom," the interrogator said, "or, more accurately, the wisdom of our fathers dictates the extinguishing of the Threefold Fire of Desire, Hostility, and Delusion. Yet I am Kama-Mara, Love and Death, the magician of Delusion." Kama-Mara, M. Mabuse knew, was the last antagonist of Siddhartha, the future Buddha, sent to tempt him as he lay beneath the Bo tree.

"In the extinguishing of all the fires that drive us," the interrogator said, "we attain Nirvana. If we do not want, we do not need. If we do not need, the true nature of the universe unfolds before our enlightened gaze."

The interrogator continued his circling, as a tiger will its prey. "But you still want. You still desire. And as long as that remains so, I know that I will win. I know that eventually you will tell me without exception everything that is in your mind."

M. Mabuse believed him; he had no reason not to. But in that place somewhere between sleep and consciousness, when the mind blinks, and the soul breathes, M. Mabuse was visited by a coiled serpent.

Its flat, oily head lifted as it regarded him. Its forked tongue flicked out. "What is it you want?" it said in a voice that was not human. "What is it you desire?"

And M. Mabuse, knowing that he was in the presence of a god or a godlike creature, said, "I burn with the hate that is the residue of sin. I feel a cold wind in my heart. I want to cleanse my soul."

And the serpent, slithering its coils about him, said, "Show it to me and I will cleanse it."

"But that is my terrible shame," M. Mabuse said. "I have searched, but I cannot find it."

The triangular head weaved in front of his face; the forked tongue touched the tip of his nose. "I have done as you desire," the serpent said.

Keeping his eye on the sinuously crawling line of chrome, M. Mabuse crossed the concrete median and, at a pay phone, slipped a thin plastic card into a slot. He dialed a number, then his authorization code. He listened to the phone ring as he felt himself filling with the sights and sounds of Nice.

He spoke into the receiver when he heard the familiar voice. It made him think of rice paddies, jungles, and napalm coming down in a curtain. "I'm back," he said. "Dominic Guarda is dead, but his brother, Seve, is not. The police were too close. As for Christopher Haye, a woman interfered. Yes, he's still alive." Then he listened, as he always did, to his orders.

At length he hung up, repeated the procedure, this time dialing another number. He said hello to Milhaud. He listened, his eyes protected by dark lenses against the dazzling sunlight.

"Tourrette?" he said. "Are you certain?" In a moment he nodded. "Yes," he said. "I understand completely."

Back across the median, he got into his car and headed north, toward the waiting mountains.

Mun said, "I need a woman."

"That's easy," Mogok said.

"Not just any woman," Mun cautioned. "I need an extraordinary woman."

"And you think this will be more difficult for me?"

"Not in the least," Mun said. "I am merely trying to be as specific as possible."

Mogok laughed, and the ruby set in his front tooth flashed like fire. Mogok liked to laugh, not only because it was in his nature, but also because it showed off his prize ruby. He realized that since General Kiu had murdered Ma Ling he hadn't had much cause to laugh, and that had left an emptiness inside him. It was damn good, he thought, to laugh again. And for that alone he was grateful to Mun.

"I have someone in mind," Mogok said. "Her father owes me a favor. He now makes a great deal of money with Admiral Jumbo, so he will do anything I ask."

Mun nodded. "Get her."

When Mogok returned some twenty minutes later, it was with a young girl in tow. She was perhaps fourteen, though she could easily be younger, Mun observed. All the better, he thought. She was quite beautiful, with dark, smoky eyes, a long, delicate neck, and rapturously thick hair.

"She'll do," Mun said, concealing his pleasure beneath a neutral mask. It was not prudent to let Mogok know how well he was doing. He would then exact a payment from Mun, who, being brought up in Asia, was trained never to pay for something that you could convince someone he owed you.

"What are you going to do?" Mogok asked, watching Mun circle the girl.

"Light a fire," Mun said, "and see who starts to burn." Then he sat the girl down, and had tea brought, then food. She ate ravenously, without artifice, like a little animal. When Mun was satisfied, he had the dishes cleared. Then he set about telling the girl his secrets. He was here, not as a trader in the tears of the poppy, as everyone believed, but as an agent of the Chinese communists.

They had recently become alarmed at the amount of power and arms being amassed by General Kiu and had decided to launch an all-out assault on the Tenth Quadrant to rid the territory once and for all of the warlord. Mun was a kind of advance agent, he explained, searching out General Kiu's perimeter weak points.

When he was finished, Mun had the girl repeat everything he had said. She had not missed a word. Then he sent her into Admiral Jumbo's camp to sow her seeds among the other women, knowing that it would not be long before the traitor, whoever he was, would hear tantalizing bits of Mun's secret. Rumors and gossip were, after all, two of his most important sources of intelligence.

"Now," Mun said, when they were alone, "there is nothing left to do but wait."

Mogok took out a clay pipe, the tiny bowl of which he stuffed with a black, sticky substance. He lit the pipe, took several deep puffs, then passed it over. Mist enshrouded them, creating shifting forms in the air. For a long time the two men smoked, cementing a friendship in a way only Asians could understand.

Alix was crying.

Once I was a soldier
And I fought on foreign sands for you.

Lyrics to a song she remembered from long ago echoed in the

crashing silence of her mind. Without a voice, without mobility, her mind had become a vast stage across which memories appeared like conjuror's tricks. There was no present, no future, only a past made painfully tactile by the absence of any sensory input. Existence had been reduced to the electrical impulses of her brain.

Is that why she had dredged up her flight from her parents, her love for her grandfather, the Circleville Pumpkin Show? Is that why she wanted nothing more than to go back to Circleville? What was so special about it, anyway? Just a cluster of old houses, dusty streets, watery-eyed people.

Once I was a lover
And I searched behind your eyes for you.

But she already knew the answer. It wasn't Circleville itself, but what the town represented to her: freedom. At home with her parents, she felt trapped inside the noisome bubble of their fighting, and her father's alcoholism.

Circleville was everything that made her happy. Time flew by, so that before it seemed she had a chance to turn around, it was time to go home again. Home, where time weighed like a leaden cloak across her slender shoulders, where the atmosphere was so gelid she had difficulty getting through one day. She remembered asking friends to call her each morning, and each evening before she went to bed, to reassure herself that there was a normal world still spinning by outside. Outside: as if she had existed inside prison.

That loss of control over her environment had made life intolerable. It was a prison of the most insidious kind. It was what drove her out of the house, what made her marry Dick. Dick, whom she saw now that she had never loved. She could not even understand how she had managed to live with him, except maybe because for a while at least she had needed to re-create the prison of her childhood in order to escape from it completely.

And soon there'll be another
To tell you I was just a lie.

Now he had come back, unbidden and unwanted, and Alix was weeping because she wanted him gone, and lacked the means of communicating that wish. She was imprisoned in the hospital, swathed in bandages. She could neither move nor speak, and each waking moment her terror mounted. Not only for herself, though she was frightened that her voice had not yet returned. It was for Danny that she worried. She did not want her son spending so much time with Dick. Danny was so trusting, so open. God only knew what garbage Dick was shoveling his way. All she wanted was to protect her son, and here she lay, helpless and afraid that she would never be able to speak again, that her life as a lawyer was over. How quickly life could reduce you. Was it only days ago that she had been healthy, independent, in control of her life? Perhaps this had been an illusion, she could no longer tell. She felt like a bystander waiting for a bus that would never come. Her sense of existence had become distorted, images and incidents exaggerated, intimidating, as if she were viewing everything through funhouse mirrors.

Time crawled by, barely breathing. It was her constant companion, as it had been when she was a child. It mocked her during the day with its slowness, and jolted her awake in a sweat at night. Memories were her only surcease, but soon these, too, became a source of torment, reminding her of what she no longer had, and never would have again.

Oh, dear God. Where was Christopher? How she wanted him here, just to hold his hand, to know that he was watching over her and Danny. But this wasn't Circleville, and her grandfather was dead many years. That kind of protection was gone forever.

But knowing that did not stop her from wishing for it with all her might.

Christopher, where are you now? Are you coming home soon?

And sometimes I wonder
Just for a while
Will you ever remember me.

"The fact is," Chris said to Soutane, "my brother never meant to mail this postcard."

"Then what—?"

The sun had already set in the narrow streets of Tourrette-sur-Loup, leaving the stone facades of the houses in a false twilight. The cobbles were as dark as night.

"It was a kind of insurance for him," Chris said, "and a kind of legacy for me."

Soutane looked at him. "What are you saying? That he knew he was going to die?"

Children, on their way home from school, ran past them, laughing and calling, their backpacks thumping as they coursed down the steeply twisting street.

"Not exactly," Chris said. "But, considering the danger he must have been in, I think he knew it was a possibility. This postcard was a safeguard. See, he knew that in the event of his death, it would find its way to me. Either you'd give it to me—as you did—or the police would."

A mother was calling to her daughter from an open doorway, and the scent of a freshly baked apple tart spiced the air. As they went past her, they could see in a flood of light the spectacular waterfall from which they had come.

"When we were growing up, we were both crazy about puzzles. Terry loved a maze game called Labyrinth. He especially loved to beat me at it. I, on the other hand, preferred more intellectual puzzles, like cryptograms. I always used to leave notes for him in code. It drove him nuts trying to figure them out."

The cascade, now partially in shadow, had taken on a truncated, almost sinister aspect, as if not being able to see clear through to its depths created a danger, dictated caution.

"Then," Soutane said, "the postcard is a puzzle."

Chris nodded. "In a way. Yes."

"But, if you're right, where in Tourrette did Terry hide the Doorway to Night? I don't see any kind of clue on the postcard."

"You wouldn't," Chris said, examining both sides carefully. "Because if you could find it, others could, too, and Terry wouldn't take that chance." There was no mark on the photograph side, no extra lines on any of the letters in his message on the reverse.

"There's also the question of what he was going to write as the postscript," Soutane said.

Chris, looking at the P.S., smiled and nodded. "Exactly. Is there a toy store here?"

"Yes. I think it's down this way."

She gave him a puzzled look as she led him left, then left again. As they went, she glanced in shop windows, but not, Chris saw, as if she had any interest in the goods displayed there. All at once, the street began again to rise. On their left was a shop of handmade children's clothes and toys. They went in.

"Bonjour."

The shopkeeper was a portly, beery-faced woman in her fifties. She smiled at them from her corner perch.

"Bonjour, madame," Chris said.

Chris inventoried the shelves of tiny shirts, trousers, jackets, stuffed animals, and porcelain dolls. Soutane, glancing now and again over her shoulder toward the open doorway to the street, said, "What are we looking for?"

"I don't know. But whatever it is, isn't here." Back in the narrow street he said to her, "Years ago, when dirty words were forbidden and, therefore, fun, I made up a shorthand for the one that excited me the most. I used to use it around my folks, and Terry was the only other person who knew what it meant. I used to say p.s. when I meant pussy."

"Then the P.S. on the postcard was never meant as a postscript."

They began to walk again. "No."

"But what *does* it mean?"

Chris laughed. "It's American slang." He told her what it meant.

Soutane's puzzlement deepened. "I still don't see the connection between the word and where Terry might have hidden the dagger."

"Whatever form it takes," Chris said, "knowing Terry, it's sure to be a joke of some kind." It was odd, but in discovering the meaning of the postcard, in pursuing this quest for a talisman in which he did not even believe, Chris found himself feeling closer to his brother than he ever had while Terry was alive. This both pleased and saddened him. Pleased that he could feel this way at all, sad that it had not happened while Terry was alive.

This connection, he was certain, stemmed in part from the knowledge that all of this was meant for him. Terry had left it in his hands, as if Chris was the only person he could trust to continue what he had begun.

But what, precisely, was that? Chris experienced some fear as he drew closer to the solution to Terry's cryptogram and the recovery of the Doorway to Night. What if Soutane was right, and Terry had been involved in the opium trade? But why? For the money? Terry had never been much interested in money, Chris knew, otherwise he would have stuck close to their father, joining the family multimillion-dollar import-export business.

What else would control of the opium trade provide? According to Soutane, there was money . . . and there was power. But why would someone interested in power willingly allow himself to go to war, to kill, to possibly be maimed or be killed himself?

And then Chris remembered what Marcus Gable had said about the war: *It was all a matter of power. Those who understood the essential nature of it made sense of it, and survived. Everyone else was, in one way or another, destroyed.*

Terry had survived the war. Even more, he had prospered. Had Vietnam warped his sense of morality as it had Marcus Gable's? Had its sere breath even destroyed whatever honor and decency human beings could claim?

Standing now in the center of this ancient town, reminded of a simpler but no less violent age, Chris felt a terrible fear creeping up his spine, threatening to paralyze him. It was not only for his brother—of what he might have become—but for himself as well. For in following this path, limned for him by his dead brother, was he not putting his own sense of morality to the test? What would he do once *La Porte à la Nuit* was in his possession? What if in order to discover what Terry had been, he himself was required to—

To *what*?

Chris had no idea, but he had an intimation that merely finding the Doorway to Night was not an end in itself. Where would it lead? What was he about to become? He had an acute sense of stepping out of one life and into another, the fear vitiated somewhat by a keen sense of anticipation, as if he had been waiting all his life for this precise moment.

"Chris?"

"What?"

"Are you all right?" Soutane said, squeezing his elbow. "Your look was as blank as that black cat's over there."

"I was just lost in th—" He stopped, abruptly. He found himself staring into a display window draped with black velvet. In its center was a female harlequin in red and white. Her head was cocked to one side. Her arms were upraised, her legs, clothed in high boots, seemingly moving, so that in her pose there was a sense of flight. Behind her, the devil, arms opened wide, was poised to engulf her in his dark cape.

"Chris?"

"Wait a minute." Staring at the rhinestone tear stitched to her diamond-patterned mask. And beneath the mask . . . were those whiskers, was that dark fur? Those were triangular cat's ears! Puss 'n Boots! Pussy!

"What is this place?"

"An art gallery," Soutane said. "They're known for their marionettes. Aren't they magnificent?"

Chris laughed, staring at the Puss 'n Boots in the window. "I'm willing to bet that one of them is much more than that."

Inside, at the top of the stairs, a gentleman marionette in medieval dress regarded them with his superbly rendered cock's head. Chris was about to go down the stairs into the gallery when Soutane took his elbow.

"I'm going back outside for a minute."

He saw the concern on her face. "What is it?"

"I want to make sure of something. Improbable as it seems, we may have been followed here."

"I'll go with you."

"That's just what you *won't* do," she said quickly. "Please. I know what I'm talking about. Besides, if *La Porte à la Nuit* is here, you've got to protect it." Then she laughed. "Don't worry. I can take care of myself."

"What does that mean?"

"I'm not afraid of anyone," she said seriously. Then she gave him an all too brief smile. "Don't be so disapproving. You're as much a traditionalist as Terry was."

Chris didn't like it, but what she said made sense. Terry had gone to extraordinary lengths to hide the Doorway to Night.

"All right," he said, "but let's at least agree to meet somewhere."

"Why not the church?" Soutane said. "It seems an appropriate place, don't you think?"

Downstairs, in the well-lighted gallery, he could see that all the marionettes were human figures with animal heads. There was a jolly macaw, a macabre owl, a greedy-eyed pig. But the only cat was the harlequin in the window.

The walls were hung with paintings by two or three contemporary artists. They were oils, richly patterned, deep colored, reminding him of Persian carpets. Their subjects were lush, magnetic, voluptuous.

The middle-aged man greeted Chris as he came down the stairs. There was no one else in the gallery.

"I'd like some information on the harlequin in the window," Chris said.

"Ah, the harlequin and the devil are the two marionettes not made by me or my partner," the proprietor said. "I am afraid there is not much more I can tell you. The artist has told me these pieces are not for sale. They are to display his work only." He gestured, smiling. "Perhaps you would be interested in my macaw or my owl?"

"My interest," Chris said, "is in the harlequin. Is there some way I can get in touch with the artist?"

"Well, normally we don't encourage—"

"Please," Chris said, "it's important."

The man contemplated Chris for a moment, as if he were sizing him up, or estimating his net worth. Then he nodded, and disappeared behind a black velvet curtain behind the corner of the gallery where his desk was.

Chris, alone in the gallery, save for the exquisite marionettes dressed in medieval attire. The owl, arch and forbidding, was mute, but the macaw seemed on the verge of divulging a dark and ironic secret.

Hearing the rustle of the velvet curtain, Chris turned back, expecting to find the proprietor. Instead, he was confronted by a man, slender and pale, with eyes that seemed vague behind black, thick-framed glasses.

"How can I help you, monsieur?"

"You made the Puss 'n Boots?"

"*Oui, monsieur. Je suis Monsieur Asprey. Le artiste c'est moi.* But the harlequin is not for sale. If you want one, it will take—"

"I want *this* one," Chris said.

"*Pardon, monsieur*, but I told you—"

"I'm Chris Haye," he said. "Terry Haye's brother. You made that Puss 'n Boots for him, didn't you?"

The change in the man's face was remarkable. The pale eyes, so watery before, had turned shrewd and discerning. "You have something, perhaps, to show me?"

Chris brought out the postcard. "P.S.," he said.

"Ah, *bon*," M. Asprey said, nodding. "The bill of sale. Now we may proceed."

"—ike—ird—tees—am—"

"*Merde*, can't you do better than that?"

"Sorry." The technician fiddled with a bank of dials and switches. "There must be a magnetic motor of some kind in the room. When they turn a certain way—in this case, I'd say toward the door—the audio dropout at five hundred hertz is appalling."

"Just get it all," Milhaud said, sitting on the edge of his chair. He was about to hear the portion of the taped conversation between Mr. LoGrazie and his unknown companion, and Milhaud could feel the flutter of anticipation in the pit of his stomach.

"Ready," the technician said, punching a button. Through the speakers Milhaud heard the voice of the unknown man say,

"—dislike involving third parties. Look at the damage Terry Haye caused. We have already seen that from a security point of view it stinks."

"In this case I'm afraid it's necessary," Mr. LoGrazie said, through the soupy sea of tape hiss and white noise generated by the maze of filters the technician had used to amplify the voices. Sounds of cutlery striking china, so loud that Milhaud winced, and the technician hurriedly fiddled with the dials. "—you think that we can get into this line of business just by wishing it? We need Milhaud. Only Milhaud has the clout and the organization to muscle in on this territory. He knows it far better than we can ever hope to. And now that Terry Haye has been terminated, Milhaud has provided us with a clear field. In that sense, he has already proven his worth to us. Believe me, this is the only sensible way to approach the problem."

"I make it a habit never to believe anyone," the voice said. "Which is why I have just come from the Shan State. When the Old Man decided that I must return to, as it were, the fold, he made it quite plain to me that I should plunge in all the way.

"In fact, my own theory is that this was why he persuaded me to come back in the first place. You were in the process of being royally screwed by Terry Haye. The Old Man simply had had enough."

"But without Milhaud we will have no access to Admiral Jumbo," Mr. LoGrazie said. "Milhaud's made it plain to me that because he has the Forest of Swords he can—"

"Frank, you aren't listening to me. I have already been to Burma. I have seen Admiral Jumbo. The result is, we're in. As of right now, White Tiger has its product."

Milhaud was in a rage. What did they think they were doing, cutting him out like that? Did these American Mafia bastards think that he was just another amateur like Terry Haye? If so, they were in for a surprise. And furthermore, what was this nonsense about making a deal with Admiral Jumbo? Milhaud knew the situation too well to believe that some Mafia type could just walk up to Admiral Jumbo and get his product at the source that had taken Milhaud years to painstakingly build.

His mind was buzzing. Right now there were too many unanswered questions. Composing himself, he signed for the technician to start the tape machine again.

"Jesus," Mr. LoGrazie said from the speakers, "the stories about you are true. You must be some kind of magician."

"That's what they used to call me. But save the applause until later. You tell me that Milhaud has the *Prey Dauw*. I want it; it's my compensation for starting up White Tiger. Get it from him." The tape machine's reels had stopped spinning.

The technician was grinning. *"C'est assèz clair pour vous?"*

"Clear enough to hear every word," Milhaud said, breaking his stunned reverie. Who was this unknown man? He was in a frenzy to know.

Then Milhaud felt his stomach turn over. Something, lodged in his memory like a pebble, broke loose, rising to the surface. A magician. *That's what they used to call me,* the unknown man had said.

Milhaud had known someone named the Magician, long ago, in Indochina. This could not be the same man. No, he thought. It's utterly impossible. He pulled out the surveillance photos from a drawer, studied again the movie star's face—the unknown man on the tape.

The Magician. Impossible, he told himself over and over again until it became a litany. It's impossible. I do *not* know this man. This *cannot* be the Magician. A hollow catechism disintegrating in the face of Milhaud's mounting terror.

Because, already, at the base of his neck he felt the short hairs stirring.

When Soutane left Chris, she emerged onto the street and, without looking around her, turned to her left. She headed down the steeply sloping cobbles, turning right, then right again. She was, without knowing it, following the path Terry had taken on his way down to the Church of Our Lady of Benva.

Son et lumière, Soutane thought as she descended deeper into the heart of Tourrette. Sound and light are my allies here. The streets were so narrow that any sound echoed off the stone facades of the buildings, and light pouring in obliquely against the walls etched sharply defined shadows. Utilizing both, she could keep track of her tail.

She had spotted him in reflection while she glanced in a shop window. Standing at an angle, the plate glass served as a mirror, revealing the length of the street behind her. Then, again, in the toy shop, a shadow passing too slowly, then backtracking in order to keep her in view.

Who was following her? Not the Jesuit she had confronted in the toilet in Le Safari. Someone higher up? Had the Jesuit confessed his sins, or had he remained mute? Soutane guessed the former, since the Jesuit had not impressed her as having a particularly strong character.

Her shadow was Asian, perhaps Vietnamese, and that worried her. As she had told Chris, she had come up against Mun's enemies before. Betrayal of such an intimate nature had, perhaps, made Mun careless, and that had rubbed off on Soutane.

In killing Mun's lover Soutane had found herself thrust into an ever-descending spiral of self-hatred, culminating in her attempt to commit suicide. Never mind that she had acted to avenge the attack on Mun. She had acted against her innate nature. So, like a madman, the war—and its aftermath—had crept into her life, turning it upside down.

Terry had saved her from herself. Surely she would be dead now but for him. How she had loved him! In caring more about him than she did about herself, she was able to emerge from her self-destructive state. And, seeing the prison of her own making, she could avoid entering its locked gate again.

Now, in her mind, she saw again that grim citadel of her own making, where she had sat, putting the keen knife edge against the blue veins of her wrists, rising up before her, and knew that here in Tourrette was her *karma*. Terry's death had, perhaps, dictated this, as much as the course of his life. Her own fate entwined with his just as if he were still alive.

Echoes, hurrying after her, urging her on at a faster pace. She was in a street filled entirely with shadow. It was chilly here in the blue light, and she shivered, hugging herself.

She was near the Church of Our Lady of Benva. In its stern, overweening facade stone images of suffering and redemption clawed the air like gargoyles whose excesses of human emotion mimicked physical grotesqueries.

Somewhere, a clock was striking the hour. Soutane, listening, pressed herself against the cool stone. She heard footsteps, on the other side, heading away from her. There was no point in staying in the street, but still she waited because she wanted there to be no doubt in her pursuer's mind as to where she was going.

She turned, slipped through the iron-studded oaken church doors. Inside, she felt wind ruffle the hair at the nape of her neck, as if the breath of God lingered here.

It was dim, muffled, except where thick bars of dusty light penetrated arched, leaded-glass windows, and dropped like shrouds to the stone floor.

She saw the worn stone font and, ahead, the nave. Candles flickered before a small altar set into a groined niche to her left. Someone knelt there, head bowed in prayer. Beyond, dim in the dusty light, she saw rows of wooden pews, leading to the magnificent main altar.

The air was dense with incense and prayer. Soutane passed a marble figure of Our Lady of Benva, patron saint of travelers, then, further on, representations of the Madonna and of Christ on the Cross. So much suffering, she thought. So much blood. The sins of mankind seemed hung out here, like wash drying in the sun.

She heard Latin being chanted, a song, a prayer, a sacrament, she could not tell which, and did not know whether, in fact, there was any.

By this time she had taken stock of her environment. She reviewed the possibilities, only briefly wondering where Terry had been when he had been killed, his blood running across the cool granite floor to mix with that of Christ's.

Turning, she hurried back up the aisle until she came again to the statue of Our Lady of Benva. Across the way the penitent was still at prayer. Soutane slipped behind the marble statue.

She felt a chill race up her spine as the damp of the stone wall penetrated her blouse. Her muscles contracted. Squeezed in the interstice, she pressed her cheek against the veined marble so that she would have an unobstructed view of the entrance.

She saw the Asian appear. He was Vietnamese, she was sure now as she scanned his face. There was no spark of human soul there. It was as if he was already dead.

Soutane felt herself shudder, knew that was a bad sign. Her fear would lend him another kind of power, one with which she was less able to cope, and she began mentally to steel herself for the coming ordeal.

He stood in the center of one of the bars of light, sending his lengthening shadow across the stones. It lapped at the foot of Our Lady of Benva like a black sea, curling at high tide.

He did not, as others would, turn himself this way and that as he searched. Rather, he stood quite still. Only his head moved, an owl at midnight, singling out its prey.

His lips were the color of dried blood, and they were slightly parted as if he were tasting the air for her presence. His eyes, like ebony beacons, quartered the interior of the church, and Soutane imagined that they could pierce the marble behind which she was hidden.

Stop it! she thought. You're terrifying yourself. But the fact remained that she *was* terrified of this man, and what he was forcing her to unleash inside herself. She began to hate him for what he was obliging her to do. Gradually, that hate outstripped her fear until, at last, she was ready.

Her body was centered in her lower belly; her mind dwelt in that special Void of being/nonbeing, where thoughts of victory or defeat never entered.

As Dante stood in the dusty light, Soutane uncoiled herself from the safety of her niche. Through the darkness of shadow she leaped, and when she alit, she did so with no sound at all.

Even so, Dante became aware of her. His head swiveled, and his gaze caught her like the talons of a bird.

"Why are you following me?" she said.

"*La Porte à la Nuit* was sold to us." He spoke in a deadly whisper. "Now I have come to claim it."

"Where is the money?" Soutane asked. "Did you pay it?"

"We were deceived," he said. "We were given a worthless duplicate."

"You killed him." Staring now into Dante's face, Soutane was never more certain of anything in her life. "You murdered Terry. Why?"

"I was not present at the transaction," he said in a quite futile attempt to dissuade her. It was not that he did not remember Milhaud's warning about Soutane. It was, rather, that he could not believe that she was quite so dangerous. "I cannot say what happened."

Soutane shrugged, and he, concerned now, tried to read her eyes. "It doesn't matter," she said in an odd, disconnected voice.

Hear my voice, O God, in my complaint; preserve my life from dread of the enemy, hide me from the secret plots of the wicked . . . A Psalm of David, sung in French, enveloped them in sound as vespers was celebrated.

"He's dead."

. . . from the scheming of evildoers . . .

Hands empty. Filled with the Void. Moving closer, saying, "That is what matters now. Not *La Porte à la Nuit*, not your business transaction. A man's life."

"I know nothing of this," he said, preparing himself. "I am blameless."

. . . who whet their tongues like swords, who aim their bitter words like arrows . . .

She used *atemi*, quick, precise percussive blows with the edges of her hands, and her stiffened fingertips. She aimed at his ribs, heart, and liver. But he was prepared, and he was lightning quick, parrying her even as she increased the speed of her attack.

Soutane grabbed his right wrist with her left hand and, as he began to anticipate her *atemi*, she went into an *aikido irimi*, swiveling to her right, using his own momentum to twist his arm back upon itself, as she smashed the heel of her right hand into his chin.

Dante jerked backward, and he almost blacked out from the pain. But he had been breathing from deep in his stomach, and this saved him. For now he drew upon this wellspring of energy, kicking out hard, catching Soutane on the top of her thigh.

It was a nerve meridian, and Soutane's right leg immediately went numb. She stumbled, losing her grip on him as she sought to right herself.

Dante smashed the edge of his hand into her shoulder, and Soutane went down on her hands and knees. She could see him coming, strained to push herself aside, but nothing worked. He kicked her in the ribs, and she gave a strangled gasp.

Reached up in desperation, digging her nails into the cloth of his trousers, just to hold on, to keep his leg at bay, knowing, if only dimly, that another kick would finish her.

She gritted her teeth as another blow sent pain radiating through her shoulder and back. But she would not let go of his leg, strengthening her hold, concentrating her energy, narrowing the focus to a pinpoint, the pain and fear blotted out now, as she fought to survive.

She sought out and found the nerve meridian on the inside of his leg, used her thumb to dig into his flesh just above the knee joint.

The leg gave way, and he was falling, coming her way, his weight like a heat above her, like a great shadow plunging. . . .

She gasped, and rolled. As he hit the stone floor, she jammed an elbow into his sternum, heard his muted grunt of pain, felt his thumbs on her face, near her eye sockets, seeking purchase, wanting to dig in.

No time, had to change her strategy, use the wedge of her fingers just beneath his sternum.

. . . But God will shoot his arrow at them . . .

Plunging in, hearing the cotton fabric of his shirt rip, hearing his little scream, like that of an infant, smelling the quick, nauseating rush of breath from deep inside him.

Because of their tongue he will bring them to ruin . . .

Her hand full of blood; his eyes shouting obscenities at her, his grip on her cheek hard as granite, stiffening, falling away.

Then all men will fear; they will tell what God has wrought, and ponder what he has done.

His eyes fixed on the benevolent countenance of Our Lady of Benva, glazing.

They were in a house three streets away. Chris had tried to talk to M. Asprey at the gallery, but he had raised a cautioning finger. He had brought them here, to a two-story house of low ceilings, stone walls, tile floors. Downstairs, where they were, there was a kitchen, a small living room with a gigantic hearth, and in back a bath.

But, to a great degree, it was taken up with M. Asprey's studio: an artist's easel on which was a blank canvas, a stool with a palette, a wooden box crammed with a jumble of oil and acrylic paint tubes. Below, on the floor, metal cans of turp.

The majority of the space was devoted to a handmade workbench above which hung a galaxy of marionettes in the making. Half in shadow, they stared down at the human inhabitants with peculiar, incurious eyes.

"I have been waiting for you."

There was a devil, a twin of the one who was menacing the Puss 'n Boots in the gallery's window, hanging in a corner of the workshop. He was incomplete, the bones of his skeleton half on, half off. Somehow this conspired to make him even more threatening.

"Monsieur Haye told me that, if he should die, you would come." M. Asprey pulled at some strings, and the devil nodded his partly composed head as if in assent.

There were the remains of a fire in the stone hearth. Chris stared into them as if in their configuration he could, like the Romans who had inhabited this country long ago, divine the future.

"If he told you I'd be coming," Chris said, "he also told you that I'd be asking about a dagger. A very special dagger."

"That's right," M. Asprey said, holding up the harlequin Puss 'n Boots that he had taken from the gallery window. He looked at it as lovingly as if it were his daughter. "This is my first creation," he said, "and, therefore, my most beloved."

He took a razor blade and made one quick vertical incision down the back of the harlequin. From inside it, he pulled out an object. "This is what Monsieur Haye wished to keep safe for you," he said, holding out the dagger. *La Porte à la Nuit.*

Chris took it and examined it in the light. It felt unnaturally heavy, as if it were made of some unknown metal. "Do you know what this is?"

"I know that it was made by a master craftsman," M. Asprey said. "I know that it is very valuable."

Chris nodded. "To some."

On the windowsill outside, a black cat padded slowly by. For a moment it sat staring at them, licking the fur of its forepaws, then it went on. From the open window he could hear the call to vespers, echoing through the walled village, wafting upward from Our Lady of Benva Church. Soon the *Magnificat* would begin.

"The blade is made of Imperial jade," M. Asprey said. "I have never seen a single piece of such size. I could not even begin to calculate its value." He pointed. "Then there is the ruby. Take it closer into the daylight and you will see that it has that special color known as pigeon blood. That marks it as Burmese. It is six carats in weight. Are you at all familiar with gems? A stone of that size is exceptionally rare."

"You seem to know a great deal about this piece."

M. Asprey smiled. "I should. Your brother asked me to make a duplicate of it."

So the Jesuit was not lying to Soutane, Chris thought. Was Terry trying to pull a fast one with the buyers or did he have something more in mind? "The dagger's value is not monetary," he said, "but spiritual."

"I understand." M. Asprey nodded. "It was well, then, that it was hidden so carefully."

"And it must be hidden as carefully again." Chris handed him back the dagger. "Will you see to it?"

The cat on the windowsill had returned. It sat, its back as hunched as a cripple's, bathing in the last of the sunlight. Then it heard something, perhaps far off, and was gone. The distant roar of the cataract as, plunged in darkness, it crashed against the rocks came to him on the lilt of an early-evening breeze.

Chris watching M. Asprey's skilled hands as he returned the Doorway to Night to its sanctuary, and began healing the harlequin.

* * *

Let the righteous rejoice in the Lord, and take refuge in him!
Let all the upright in heart glory!

Sound died away slowly as the echoes painted shadows upon shadows. Soutane's eyes were wild and staring, like those of a mare about to be broken.

Across from her the penitent figure at the small altar rose. He had not heard them at battle, the psalm, that chorus of sweet voices, obscuring all other sounds inside the church.

Now the figure, through with prayer, lifted a burning taper from its sconce and, turning, crossed the stone floor in three strides. Bending abruptly, he thrust the flame into Soutane's face.

"It's not over," M. Mabuse said, grinning. "No. For you it's just beginning."

As Soutane twisted her face from the heat, he grabbed her hair and, jerking hard on it, dragged her back into the thick shadows by the side of the statue of Our Lady of Benva.

Light fled before him; shadow seemed to cling to him as if they coveted his presence. Soutane used her nails, scratching at his cheeks, nose, and forehead.

He hit her hard, and she stopped. He threw her behind the marble figure, stuffing her painfully into the narrow space between the statue and the wall.

She was breathing deeply, trying to regain some of her physical strength and her mental equilibrium. She had killed again, and she felt herself soaking up the self-loathing like a sponge. Emotionally, she was close to the edge of darkness, the place where she had been nothing, wanted only silence and an end to thinking, feeling—to being. Close to the terrible, cold place where the knife edge traced the veins on the inside of her wrists.

Stuffed into that tiny space forced her in on herself. What she saw inside herself was that same black well of emptiness that had made her take the blade to her wrists. Because there was clearly nothing inside of her worth saving, only an open wound, festering and abhorrent.

Time contracted to the wink of an eye, the gleam of reflection on the convex surface of an iris. Above her loomed the face of the enemy, ages old, implacable, insatiable.

Once again she was compelled to fight herself, what she had done, as well as fight for her own life. She felt the cruel pressure he exerted on her, the unyielding stone against which she was being crushed.

She scented from his half-open mouth a stench that nauseated her. He hit her hard on the shoulder, and she cried out. He tried to fill her mouth with the heel of his hand, but she twisted away.

He jabbed at her neck, and the pain made her eyes water. Without knowing it, she jerked her head back toward him, and his hand came down over her mouth like a gag. His powerful thumb was wedged beneath her chin, preventing her from using her jaw and her teeth.

Her neck was exposed and, to her horror, she saw his face filling her vision, his mouth opening, his teeth gleaming like a dog's. She began to shake, realizing that he was about to sever tendons, arteries, nerves with his snapping jaws.

A horror overcame her that transcended even her fear of herself. She balled her hands into fists and, with a hideous strength, she slammed them both into the spot over his heart.

He was staggered just long enough for her to slither out from the damp interstice. With an inarticulate cry she brushed past him, knocking aside his lunge to hold on to her, and ran, breathless, into the depths of the church.

When Mun slept, he did so with his senses wide open. He had learned to do this during the war, had, in fact, been taught the technique by Terry Haye. Where Terry had learned it, Mun had at first no idea. Later, when he got to know them both better, it was clear that Virgil had been the source, as he was the source of so much that flowed out of Terry Haye.

Mun did not understand this until one night in the jungles of Cambodia, after they had crossed the muddy river, the forbidden border from which there could be no turning back, Terry had confided in him.

"Before I met Virgil," Terry said, "I had no idea what this war was all about. It was like someone talking to me in Martian while he tried to blow my legs out from under me.

"Virgil made sense of it all. This war isn't about finding COSVN, it isn't about trying to annihilate Charlie, it's about surviving when the earthquake, the tidal wave, the hurricane all hit at once, and you think there's no place to hide, not the earth or the sea or the sky, nowhere."

Before that, Mun had worked for Virgil, but he had never really understood him. He had thought him a mercenary without a heart or a soul as Mun understood those spiritual things. But from Terry, he saw that neither of these men liked war, or even wanted to be there. They were like Mun, caught up in events over which they had no control.

Terry had seen to the core of Virgil, discovering in him a pathfinder, like a magic talisman, Theseus in the Minotaur's maze, the man who had found the Way out of hell.

Therefore, when Terry taught Mun how to sleep with his senses wide open, Mun absorbed the lesson and, thereafter, practiced it daily.

Because this was how he slept, Mun heard the tread of the traitor as he approached the hut in which he slept. Mun was alone, deliberately so. Mogok had set himself some distance away, in an attitude of patient vigilance.

Nighttime is when the dogs come out. That was one of Virgil's more memorable lines. Virgil had a knack of distilling the chaos of war into tidy thoughts as easy to ingest as capsules. It made those around him feel invulnerable, as if he had special powers, as if he could see in the dark, or exist in a vacuum. Which was, after all, just what the war was: one vast black hole, a vacuum into which the concepts of rationality, morality, life itself were swallowed whole.

Swathed in the darkness, Mun did not move. He barely opened his eyes, for the firelight from outside would surely reflect in them, and give him away. He controlled his breathing so that it was impossible to tell that he had arisen from sleep. It was as if he was hanging in purgatory, neither dead nor alive, but a little bit of both.

As he waited, Mun wondered which of Admiral Jumbo's trusted lieutenants would turn out to be General Kiu's spy. Would it be the sinewy Chao, the fat Pegu, or the elder Kyaik? Chao was the most antagonistic, but Kyaik was the closest to Admiral Jumbo. Besides Mogok, that is. The hidden enemy, Mun knew, sought to cling like sweat. Beneath an adviser's smiling face could lurk the dark heart of the schemer.

The sound could have been that of an insect, but Mun knew better. A glimmer of firelight on the hut's wall of thatch, and the quick drop of a sharp-edged shadow. Mun prepared himself.

The knife came down with great speed and force, burying its point into the mat on which he had a moment before been lying. He reached out, grasping the tensed wrist.

His head snapped painfully back as a booted toe caught him on the point of the chin. Instinctively, he rolled away from the blow to his ribs he could feel coming.

As he did so, he scissored his legs, feeling the body collapse onto the mat. Then he was upon it, flinging the hand away from the hilt of the buried knife. He slammed his fist once, twice into the side of the head, drove his forearm into the throat.

Then Mogok was there, bending over them, a torch held high in his hand. "Buddha!" he whispered, his eyes wide. "*This* is General Kiu's spy?"

Mun stared down at the face of Ma Varada, Admiral Jumbo's concubine. Bruised and bloody though it was, the face was still quite beautiful.

Mogok had pulled an American army-issue .45 handgun out of his quilted jacket. Now he pressed it against Ma Varada's temple.

"Put that away," Mun said.

"No." Mogok's finger tightened on the trigger. "There is only one punishment for a spy."

Mun pushed the gun aside. "She's my ticket to Admiral Jumbo," he said. "It is for him to decide her fate."

She spat in his face. "This is a wild one," he said, keeping her struggling arms pinioned. He risked a glance at Mogok. "How much will Admiral Jumbo pay for this information?"

Ma Varada, looking from one to the other, said, "What do you mean, pay? Pay for what?"

"Shut up," Mogok said, but Mun told her, "For the information that you are working for General Kiu."

She laughed. "I do not work for General Kiu," she said. "You are stupid to think that I would be in the employ of such a pig."

"Yeah?" Mun took her hair in his fist, pulled hard. "Then who *do* you work for?"

She said something in a dialect he did not know. He looked at Mogok.

"She's a liar anyway," he said. "Let me kill her, and be done with it. Admiral Jumbo will be just as pleased with a dead spy as a live one."

But Mun insisted. "What did she say?"

Mogok sighed. "She says she works for a man who calls himself, um, how to translate the word? Magic man? Sorcerer?" He shrugged. "Who cares? I don't know what she's talking about."

But what if I do? Mun asked himself. "Could she mean the Magician?"

Mogok nodded. "Sorcerer, magic man, magician, they're all the same, aren't they?"

Good God! Mun thought. I thought the Magician was dead or,

at least, mad. His insides writhed as if filled with snakes. If the Magician is at work here, then we're all in trouble.

"What's the difference? She's lying," Mogok said. "If I was in her position, I wouldn't admit working for General Kiu, either."

"I've never even met General Kiu," Ma Varada said. Her face was twisted in desperation.

Still, he pulled hard again on her hair. "Describe the man who controls you."

Ma Varada did. They could give the Magician a new face, Mun knew, but his overall body type would remain the same.

"I believe her," he said. He was watching her eyes; no one was that good an actress. She had described the Magician.

"I *am* telling the truth," Ma Varada said.

"I'm afraid she is."

Mun looked up. Mogok was pointing the .45 at his heart. "I am General Kiu's spy."

"You!" Mun was stunned. "But you and Terry—"

"That was a long time ago and, anyway, Terry Haye is dead." He shrugged apologetically. "In any event General Kiu is far too powerful. He will crush Admiral Jumbo and everyone in his army. I saw that coming; it was simply a matter of self-preservation."

He waggled the gun. "Now, keeping hold of the girl, get up. We're going on a night journey." He took them outside, where the firelight was stronger, warming the chill air. "I knew there was someone else running information out of here, but I couldn't find out who it was. Your desire to get Admiral Jumbo in your debt provided a felicitous opportunity for me. I allowed you to do my work for me."

The gun waggled again. "Come. This way. Into the darkness there. You see, I wanted to kill her, to preserve my secret, but you stopped me. Who knows? Perhaps it's worked out for the best, after all. But not for you, certainly."

The jungle waited to swallow them up. "My men are waiting to take you to General Kiu. He'll have some questions to put to both of you. It will be hard, I promise you, very hard. I doubt seriously whether you'll survive. But, by then, I imagine you will be beyond caring."

Chris saw Soutane fleeing down the center aisle of Our Lady of Benva, and took off after her. He had come to the church, where they had agreed to meet, directly from M. Asprey's house. He had the harlequin with him, folded and wrapped in a clear layer of acrylic.

He saw Soutane veer off to the left of the main altar. Atop the rostrum, the silver chalice, where wine and wafer were transformed into the blood and body of the Host, gleamed. Above them the empty choir boxes overhung the side pews. Her face was filled with fear. What devil had she met here in the house of God?

She disappeared through a paneled door of dark, polished oak. When he went through himself, Chris discovered the sanctuary, made of cold stone. Beyond, to the left, was the sacristy. Heavy, red velvet drapery hung from the walls. An ancient cross of worked bronze dominated one wall, bare of other ornamentation. There was a statue of the Holy Trinity and, in a shallow stone niche, a small wooden icon of Our Lady of Benva.

Further on, he passed a tapestry depicting the Harrowing, when Christ ventured into hell to save mankind's first patriarchs and prophets from eternal damnation. Below it was an empty stone bench that, nevertheless, showed a great deal of wear.

He came to a dead end, doubled back into the narrow vestibule separating the sacristy from the main body of the church. He passed oak cupboards on either side, which created a rather narrow defile. Because it was so dark, torches had been lit in their wrought-iron sconces.

He brushed past two priests in starched white surplices. He heard a sound behind him, saw M. Mabuse emerging through the doorway into the church proper. His face was dark, as if engorged with blood. "Get out of here!" he yelled at the priests.

Chris reached up, grabbed the wooden icon, and threw it into M. Mabuse's face.

The priests, fluttering like panicked birds, attempted to restrain M. Mabuse. He shrugged aside their clumsy efforts and raced down the corridor.

Chris ran toward the sacristy, but M. Mabuse caught him before he got there, smashing him backward against the stone. His head hit one of the wrought-iron sconces, and blood oozed down his cheek.

He tried to use his elbow to back M. Mabuse off, but it was immediately pinioned. Chris turned and, remembering what Soutane had taught him, jammed his fist into M. Mabuse's underarm. That freed his elbow, but he was still painfully trapped against the metal.

He reached backward and, grasping the base of the torch,

wrenched it from the sconce. He jammed it into M. Mabuse's chest, breaking free, feeling the heat, the smell of charred fabric filling up the corridor, as M. Mabuse stumbled backward, beating at the flames.

Chris raced into the sacristy, pulling the heavy oak door closed behind him. There was no lock, just a heavy iron latch. Chris closed it, then dragged a thick-legged chair over, wedged it beneath the oversized iron handle.

He looked hurriedly around the room. Leaded-glass windows, aligned like obedient nuns, let in the encroaching shadows of night. Lit tapers in silver candelabra lent the high-ceilinged room an oversized air.

There were more cupboards, a refectory trestle table, a dozen uncomfortable-looking straight-back chairs, a tooled leather trunk beneath one of the windows. Vestments, used no doubt at vespers, hung on thick wooden pegs, along with several black cassocks and a rumpled linen surplice, creating a forest devoid of life.

Beside the cupboards there was a prie-dieu on which a corpulent priest knelt, perhaps in prayer. Except, Chris could see now, he was staring at Soutane, who was pressed against the wall, her chest heaving more with fright than exertion. She gave a tiny scream. The priest's head turned. Then Soutane recognized him.

"Chris—!"

A banging at the door. It began to tremble on its hinges.

"Come on!" He grabbed Soutane and ran. Through the maze of the hanging vestments, onto the leather trunk, and out the window. Into the darkening evening.

The night-lights were lit, the pockets of illumination flickering into the crevices of the stone walls. Along the extreme edge of the village he could see just how formidable Tourrette must have seemed to any would-be attacker.

Built upon the twisted granitic spine of the pre-Alps, the man-made stone walls rose up sheer against the cliffs. He and Soutane were hanging, as it were, in space, suspended on a ledge that ran off into the hazy distance.

Below them the craggy scree plunged down perhaps a thousand feet to the valley floor. One misstep and the unforgiving rock would flay the flesh from their bones faster than the bones could be fractured. The sky was vast, smooth as porcelain above them.

Wind whipped at them. Soutane was so close to him, he could feel the trip-hammer beating of her heart.

"Chris, I found the man following me. We fought, and—"

They heard the door splinter then, and movement like a whirlwind from within the sacristy.

Chris grabbed her around the waist, boosted her up.

"What—?"

"Go on," he urged. "Go up!"

Felt her weight lifting away, then turned, and threw the Puss 'n Boots up to her. Mindful of his step, he found a foothold in the ancient stone face and launched himself upward onto the second story.

Touched Soutane's calf, climbed over her. She was trembling, clinging to the stone with all her might. He moved swiftly, confidently past her until he reached the roof. He felt only a slight twinge from his leg. Then he reached down and, gathering her arms in his hands, pulled her up to his side.

"Let's go!" he said.

"Where?"

"Away from here," he said. "Away from him."

"I don't—" And she screamed. A hand from below had seized her ankle, and now sought to drag her over the side, back into the sacristy.

Soutane stared down at it in horror. She seemed incapable of making a move, let alone an aggressive one. She had already killed once this day; her mind could contemplate no more violence.

Chris, on his knees, tried to pry those powerful fingers loose from her flesh, but they would not budge. On the contrary, Soutane was being inexorably drawn over the roof's edge.

Chris was waiting for her to use her techniques of self-defense. Now he saw that she was paralyzed, and searched his mind for a solution. He dug into his pocket, unfolded the knife that had been Terry's present to him. He reversed it, jammed it point-first into the back of the grasping hand.

The spouting of blood seemed to break Soutane's stupor. She jerked her leg out of the weakened grip, and Chris pulled her to her feet.

They ran through the darkness. The black sky mocking them with the transfiguring beauty of its silver stars, the unattainable sweet safety of its vastness.

Behind them, on the horizon of the roof edge, a black shape humped itself up from below.

Chris heard her breath, smelled the faint odor of her sweat. They were locked together now, in this strange painting that Terry had created. The transformation was complete. He felt an eerie elation, like the triumphant cry of a wolf or the screech of a falcon, its prey clutched in its powerful talons. But, after all, perhaps it was only the adrenaline rocketing through him, propelling them both onward across the rooftops, then down into the street, climbing over one low wall after another, running, crouching, weaving until he was unsure whether they were still being followed.

"Let's get off the street," Soutane, close against him, whispered. "I feel terribly exposed here."

Chris nodded, pushed her down a flight of wide stone stairs into complete shadow. "You're right. This bastard seems to be a goddamned bloodhound."

"Who is he?"

He looked at her. "If Terry was here, he could tell us."

Soutane looked at him. "What are we going to do?"

He looked behind them, but in the gloom he did not know what he was looking at. They were in a short cul-de-sac. Beyond a crumbling, waist-high stone wall, the cliff plunged down onto heath-covered rock. "We'll just have to find out who he is on our own."

"How are we going to manage that?"

Chris was looking around. He saw a faint glimmer, as of metal and, as he moved closer, noticed a door set flush with the wall. It was the knob he had seen shining.

He gripped and turned it, then put his shoulder against the weathered wood panels. There was a sharp squeal as rusty hinges protested movement. A moment later he pushed her inside, closed the door behind them.

They could smell urine and hay but, even so, the space had about it a distinctly abandoned air. Flies buzzed somewhere, trapped against panes of glass. Blue light streamed in from a pair of diminutive windows that overlooked the valley. Dust turned the air as thick as water.

"Where the hell are we?" His voice, though low, echoed eerily in the space.

"An abandoned storehouse," Soutane said. "It was once probably a stable."

The harlequin's face was bright and inquisitive as Chris held it close to his side.

She pointed to it. "What is that?"

"What Terry left for me," he said. *"La Porte à la Nuit."*

"We have it!"

"Not that it'll do us much good if we can't get out of here."

There were the remnants of stalls, some boxes stacked against a wall, a stained tarp half over them. Otherwise the place was empty. They collapsed in a corner.

"Soutane," he said, "what happened to you back there? I've never seen you so frightened."

She looked away.

"I want to help you."

Terry had said the same thing. They were so much alike. "I killed a man," she said. "A Vietnamese who was following me. Chris, it terrifies me that I can do it."

"Did you have a choice?"

"No, of course not."

He looked at her in profile. "So that's not it, is it? Just the killing."

"No." Tears were overflowing her eyes.

"What is it, then?"

She did not answer him for a long time, and when she did, her answer chilled him. "When it happens, when I do it, I enjoy it."

He was silent, listening to the night.

"What are you thinking?" she asked.

There was a ghost in Chris's eyes. Somewhere, in another life, Alix lay in a hospital bed, fed by tubes. She had loved him, she had protected him. How was he to leave her? But, now, she had ceased to be merely Alix Layne but, rather, a symbol of the other life that, more and more, seemed dim and distant, a faded photograph in a tarnished silver frame.

"I am remembering what it was like to be young."

"To be innocent, you mean."

"No," Chris said seriously. "I don't think we were ever innocent."

"We were free of guilt, then."

"It's not the same," Chris said. "Is it?"

He felt as if he had gone back in time. No, that was too simple a concept. This was something far more complex.

Beside him Soutane gave a start.

"What is it?"

"I don't know. I heard a noise."

He could hear the fear clotting her voice. *Don't worry,* she had said in the gallery. *I can take care of myself.* It was clear he could not count on that now.

Chris stood. Now he could hear it, too. He moved a little, nearer the light. The sound was coming from above. He looked up, saw a black shape in the rafters wheeling this way and that.

He came back and sat beside Soutane, closer to her than before. "It's nothing," he said. "A bat."

He felt some of the tension flowing out of her. He took her hand. "I don't know what's happening to me," he said. He wanted to draw her out from her morbid contemplation, but he also meant it.

"Nothing's happened. What do you mean?"

"I've come back to France; I've found you again. It's as if I've entered another life."

"Because of Terry."

He nodded. "But it's more than that. It's as if I'm here in Terry's place, as if through some alchemical change I've *become* Terry."

"No." She traced the line of his jaw with her fingertip. "All your life you've wanted to be him. Now you think you have your chance."

"That's not what I really wanted," Chris said angrily. "And, anyway, we all have our dreams."

"Sure. I always wanted to be a ballerina," she said. "How I envied *les petits rats*. I wanted to be as great a painter as Monet. But I know that I am neither." Her face shone, strained and pale in the light. "You were wrong before. We *were* innocent once, in that summer so long ago, because we were content to dream, then. Now it is no use wishing for these things, because I know what I am, what I am capable of. I'll never be a ballerina, or paint as well as I want."

"That shouldn't change anything."

"But it does," Soutane said, tears running down her face. "Do you still love me, now that you know what I've become?"

"Let's not get into that now."

"Why not? Now is as good a time as any."

"This isn't what I wanted," he said miserably.

"Oh, no," Soutane said. "It's what you wanted, all right. It just isn't what you expected."

"Don't do this, Soutane," he said. "This is as destructive as killing."

"That's what attracted us, initially," she said, ignoring him. "We were never happy with ourselves. That summer when you thought you were running from the war, you were really searching for it." She looked into his face. "Why? Because your brother, Terry, was there. But, so what? What did that have to do with you? Perhaps if you'd spent more time deciding what it was you wanted, and less about what was expected of you, you'd have been happier—or, at least, more content."

"I don't know what you mean," Chris said. "I never had to prove anything."

"Oh, but that's not true," Soutane said. "Despite your differences, you idolized your father. And, as far as Terry was concerned—"

"Let's for Christ's sake leave my brother out of it." He was tired of being reminded of his past; frightened of how much guilt he was carrying.

"That's right," she mocked him, "you don't want to hear any of this." She took his face in her hands. "Don't you see, Chris, it wasn't the war you were running away from. It was yourself. In the end you made me drive you away. That was why. Now it's happening all over again, and I don't want to be a part of it."

She broke away and, before he could stop her, she had risen up, taken a lurching step back the way they had come.

"Dear God."

Chris whirled, coming, too, out of the darkness. And saw what Soutane saw: M. Mabuse loping as light as air toward them.

Deep in the night Milhaud was drawn out of Morphée's arms by memories of his past life. It was as if, like Jean Valjean, he was being stalked by a relentless pursuer from the other side of time, from a life in which he had transgressed once too often or too well.

This struck him as odd, as he sat up, the black satin sheets pooling in his lap, since he believed himself to be a man impervious to guilt. Lines from a Jacques Brel song still drifted through his head, as if he had heard them sung in his sleep.

My death waits among the falling leaves
In magicians' mysterious sleeves.

Outside, the Luxembourg with its thick copses of trees, its inky shadows seemed, somehow, forbidding.

Morphée's soft touch against his side. "There is nothing there." Drawing him down beneath the sheets. "Come back to sleep."

But, in the darkness, the life he had lived lapped cruelly at his feet.

My death waits in a double bed
Sails of oblivion at my head
Pull up the sheets
Against the passing time.

He drew his legs up, then rolled out of bed.

He dressed without a word and left without even a glance backward to the bed where Morphée lay with the covers drawn up to her chin, staring into the emptiness he had created.

At this time of night Paris was dark, as if chastened. All the way back to his apartment, Milhaud again unspooled the film his wife had shown him one night, three weeks after his failure to win vital trade allowances from the minister of the interior. She had presented the film to him at the dinner table, along with the *crème brûlée*, gift-wrapped like a birthday present.

Bach had been playing, the B minor Mass. They had watched the film together, and he remembered the glitter of her eyes as she drank in the changing expressions on his face—disgust, anger, humiliation—as he had, by stages, been exposed to the extent of her depravity. In concert with the sublime music of God's choir, the perverse acts seemed utterly profane. The sexual gymnastics she and the minister of the interior were performing gave way to violent sadomasochism, and Milhaud had ripped the film from the sprockets.

"Why have you done this?" he shouted. His hands were shaking as if he had palsy.

And what had his wife's response been to his rage? "To get you what you want," she had said. "With this I am going to blackmail the minister of the interior into giving you the diplomatic concessions no one else will willingly provide."

And he had groaned, sick to his stomach. "No, I meant why did you give me this? Why did you make me watch it?"

"To teach you your catechism." He would remember her smile until the day he died. "To show you what it is like to be in someone else's control. To make you see what you and your kind have quite callously done to the peoples of Indochina. To prove to you quite conclusively where the seat of your power truly lies."

Images of her bare buttocks, as she stood, legs spread, above the kneeling minister no longer flickered on the screen, but he could not stop them from unwinding in his mind. And he knew that she was right; hers was the power, if not the glory.

He had hit her, then, very hard across the face. Initially, he had only wanted to wipe that gloating smile off her face. But the impact reverberated through his entire frame. Seeing her sprawled on the carpet had felt so good that he did it again, and her lip split; again and her nose shattered. He liked the warmth of her blood.

That was when he had realized what his life had become, and that it required radical surgery if he was to survive.

She had been using him as he had been using her. She had gotten him all the funding, all the protection he could want for his politics, his allies in Southeast Asia. But she did it not because he had ordered her to, but because she enjoyed cockolding him. The price, for him, was too high. In subjugating him, she had robbed him of his self-esteem, of his masculinity.

Bach's glorious Mass had reached the *Ave Maria*; it was a transcendent moment. Milhaud thought of all the explorers, the brave vanguard of modern civilization, rising up in righteous fury at the savagery of ignorance inherent in foreign lands that the word of Christ had not yet tamed. He might be a socialist, a radical, even a subversive, perhaps. But he was not godless. And now he filled like an empty vessel with that righteous anger.

Scooping up the unspooled film, he had wrapped it around and around her neck. Then he had pulled with all his strength. The tighter he drew the noose, it seemed, the more the humiliating images faded. Until they were gone entirely.

There was almost a full reel's worth of conversation waiting for him when he arrived home. He brewed himself an espresso when he entered the electronic operations room because he needed a jolt of something. Licked his fingertips as he dropped a curl of lemon peel into the thick liquid.

By that time the reel had rewound all the way, and he settled himself at the console, the earphones on. He sipped meditatively as he listened.

It was boring stuff, really, as a majority of the surveillance recordings always was. Mr. LoGrazie on the phone with his wife, talking about the new house she was looking at, the new Mercedes she apparently could not live without, the boarding school they were considering sending their wayward son to. Mr. LoGrazie was more tolerant of his son's indiscretions, but his wife was insisting on a military academy. In the end he gave in on the school, but not the Mercedes.

"I've told you," he said, "that we cannot overtly show the wealth we have." Milhaud could imagine his wife saying something akin to, Then what's the use of having it? because, after a pause, Mr. LoGrazie said, "We know it. That should be enough. Who gives a shit what the neighbors think? That's it. I don't want to hear about the neighbors again, Connie."

Hanging up the phone with a crash. In a minute the sound of a door opening.

"You're up late," Mr. LoGrazie said.

"I've been on the wireless with Admiral Jumbo," the voice of the unknown man said. "Anyway, since 'Nam I haven't slept more than an hour or two a night. My need for sleep is apparently one of the things I left behind in Indochina."

"How are you acclimating to being back with us?" Mr. LoGrazie asked.

"Who knows? Anyway, I'm not bored." Sounds of pages turning. "I've been going over the projections the Old Man gave me just before I left Washington. There's a helluva deficit that White Tiger's got to make up for."

Milhaud froze with the cup halfway to his lips. The Old Man, Washington, what the hell were they talking about? It certainly wasn't the price of their imported olive oil. Intimations reverberating in his head like insistent insects.

"Well, of course, that's true," Mr. LoGrazie said, "but only up to a point."

"Why? Besides the Old Man, to whom we all belong body and soul, who the fuck knows we exist? We're all in import-export, right? Our cover's a damn good one. The Old Man saw to that."

"What you say is true," Mr. LoGrazie said. "But we are at least partially dependent on the government for our operating funds because, by extension, so is the Old Man."

The espresso cup crashed to the console, splattering him with hot coffee. He did not even notice. Could he have heard right? Milhaud thought wildly. The Mafia being financed, even unwittingly, by the American government? Did that mean that the Old Man was not, as he had assumed, the *capo di capi* of the ruling Mafia families, but was no one less than the president of the United States? He knew why he kept rejecting the idea, even through the mounting evidence: it meant that his suspicions about the Magician were correct. God in heaven, protect me, Milhaud thought.

He stopped the tape with a hand that shook so much, he was obliged to squeeze it between his knees. He could scarcely breathe. Then it's true. Dear God, he thought, I have been duped. M. LoGrazie is not after all Mafia, but a member of the pernicious American spy apparatus, the CIA!

Tremors racked him. He pulled out a handkerchief, mopped at his brow. Milhaud had had occasion to observe a large number of

CIA operatives in Southeast Asia in the fifties. Those men had been uniformly arrogant, sure that their seemingly unlimited money could make them leap tall buildings with a single bound. They thought their wealth made them invulnerable. Stupider than most other Caucasians, most of them had ended up with a bullet in the back of their heads.

But their number was legion. And their ultimate authority was the government of the United States. For that reason alone Milhaud had felt it prudent to have as little to do with them as possible. But this aversion had now become a detriment, he saw. He had not kept himself up to date with the American spy organization. M. LoGrazie, it seemed, was not in the least bit stupid. And as for the Magician, well, he was a diabolical genius. The very thought that he was still alive terrified Milhaud.

He took several deep breaths, thinking, Now everything has changed. He started the tape machine again.

"But, because we, like everyone else, are constrained by budgetary considerations," Mr. LoGrazie was saying, "we have been hampered in our resources as well as in the scope of our endeavors. So the Old Man came up with the idea of White Tiger in order to fund us over and above all considerations. To free us, as it were, to live up to our ultimate potential."

"Grown-ups can be dangerous," the voice of the Magician cautioned.

"Um, well," Mr. LoGrazie said. "Danger is our stock in trade, isn't it?"

"What I mean is," the Magician said, "the freer from normal channels you are, the more in one man's power you are. What you wind up with is less control, instead of more. Take it from me, pal. I know all about operating outside the law. The law is not made for people like us. We're different. What we do is quite out of the ordinary. Often it puts us in harm's way, so that strict adherence to the law could prove dangerous, if not fatal. America needs to be strong; we need to be able to do our job."

"As you can see, the Old Man is taking care of us."

"That's just what I mean. Look at your faith in yourself. It's overwhelming. But do you ever wonder whether faith has begun to take issue with control. Because let me tell you, buddy, that where the two are concerned, faith is by far the stronger. Faith can move mountains, control is blocked by 'em."

"Faith is for the poor, the needy, the uncivilized," Mr. LoGrazie said. "As far as I am concerned faith is synonymous with superstition. I leave that kind of nonsense to the Asians."

"And you haven't put all *your* faith in the Old Man? I mean, Jesus, he's not infallible. Who is? But what you have to ask yourself is who's in charge here?"

"We're not maverick," Mr. LoGrazie said with some irritation. "Do you believe for a moment that we are operating outside the scope of the Old Man's purview?"

"Not in the least. If he believed that, he'd strike you down like a bolt of lightning. Look what he was able to do to me," the Magician said. "No, I simply mean that the pertinent question is who is the Old Man looking out for—you or *him*?

"You see, unlike in most areas of business, in your trade the deeper underground *you* go, the more likely you are to be discovered. That's why you might consider moving *laterally*, instead of letting the Old Man dig you what amounts to a deeper grave."

"What are you proposing?" Mr. LoGrazie asked, though by his tone it was clear that he knew perfectly well the jargon of innuendo.

"I am wondering whether you are getting your full money's worth out of White Tiger. I am wondering if, in fact, it might be time for you and me to be gathering our own walnuts."

A rustling, as of clothes, of someone leaning closer to ensure confidentiality. "Do you have something specific in mind?"

"I have," the Magician said. "From the very beginning."

The tape machine's reels had stopped spinning.

Now I know how Admiral Jumbo was bought. Milhaud's mind was racing. The Magician was another kind of spy. And only God and the devil knew what kind of operation he had conceived in his mysterious sleeve.

M. Mabuse, his left hand swathed in a makeshift bandage ripped from the cloth of his shirt, advanced across a floor checkered with light. The wound inflicted by Christopher's knife stab had ceased to bleed almost immediately; *kebatinan*, his spiritual training, had seen to that. There was no pain, but a stiffening of the traumatized muscles was inevitable.

Chris and Soutane crouched in the shadows at the far end of the stable. They were behind the rickety line of stalls. M. Mabuse could not see them, but they had no idea where he was either.

Some distance away the oily tarp half covered a stack of crates and boxes. Chris listened, but could hear nothing. That worried him because he was certain that their adversary was on the move.

He got up from beside her and silently crawled to where the tarp was draped. He could see the pale oval of Soutane's face. Her eyes were wide and staring. He wondered which she was most terrified of, the Vietnamese or herself.

Using the knife, he cut through the damp wrapping of a box. His hand encountered bolts of cloth. He went on to the next one, feeling, as he turned, a crawling of his scalp. Where was the Vietnamese?

He discovered hard edges, the cool touch of metal. Implements or weapons? No matter, tools could with ingenuity be turned into weapons. He continued his search, carefully tracing surfaces.

He tried to move his hand, felt it pinioned tight to the damp wood. He whirled, and immediately a hand was clamped over his mouth. Someone climbed his back. He was weighed down as if, having jumped off an ocean liner, he was now sinking down through water, translucent green layers turning to opaque black.

He struggled, feeling an enormous weight coming down into his thighs. If he had not been in such good shape, he would have collapsed beneath the mounting pressure.

"You are stronger than I imagined," a voice whispered in his ear. "I missed you in New York. Must you make me kill you here?"

Chris felt a crawling in the pit of his stomach. It was the man who had invaded his apartment, who had almost killed Alix! What was he doing here? How had he known—

"Your brother tried to cheat Milhaud out of *La Porte à la Nuit*," M. Mabuse went on. "He would have taken our money, and given us a worthless duplicate instead. Many believe he was killed for that sin. I know better. He died in retribution for all the sins he committed in Vietnam."

Who are you? Chris wondered. Part of him was astonished by what he had heard, but another side, the canny trial lawyer, was amassing facts for future reference.

"You will have to contact Miss Sirik," M. Mabuse said, "so I am obliged to take my hand away from your mouth. If you try to warn her in any way, I will kill you. If you will not do as I ask, I will kill you. Is this clear?"

Chris tried to nod; he had seen the results of this monster's grisly handiwork. But he was being pressed so tightly against the crate he could barely move.

"I have come for *La Porte à la Nuit*, and for her. Not finding the one, I will take the other." His lips were like a butterfly's wings against Chris's ear. "Now, when I free your mouth I want you to say, 'Soutane, come over here. I think I've found something.' "

Chris felt the pressure against his lips disappear, and he gulped fresh air. He said softly, "Soutane, come over here. I think I've found something." All the while his mind was working furiously.

He could see Soutane rising, moving cautiously toward him. She was looking around her, rather than at him. She had no idea as to the whereabouts of their pursuer. He peered into the gloom. Was she carrying the harlequin with her? He prayed that she was.

She was almost upon him when he saw it tucked under her arm. He strained backward a little as if he were momentarily off balance. It bought him the bit of room he needed to position himself between his captor and Soutane's left side, where she held the long package. The Puss 'n Boots was his only hope now. If the man behind him saw that Soutane was carrying something of that shape, he'd know immediately that they had found where Terry had hidden *La Porte à la Nuit*.

Now Soutane was close enough for the man to reach her over Chris's shoulder. Once he had her and the harlequin, it would be too late. Chris would be without leverage.

He was almost in position, almost able to touch the package, almost ready to move. But, as if he were able to sense Chris's intention, the man gripped Chris's right arm with such power that Chris's eyes began to water.

"Don't move," he hissed in Chris's ear.

Chris felt overcome by despair. Alix had nearly given her life for him. Now he was consciously putting Soutane in the same position. But what could he do? The painful grip on his arm was like a metal manacle. He was no superman; he had had no special training, except those semesters of aikido so long ago. Did he remember anything of the underlying principles?

"Chris?"

He closed his eyes, conjuring up the image of a circle, the centrism of aikido's energy. Through the darkness he felt his captor reach out for her, and knew all was lost. He was powerless to stop—

And in that moment they all heard the leathery fluttering above their heads as the bat, alarmed by the abrupt movement below, began to batter itself against the ceiling beams. Besides, it smelled blood.

Chris and Soutane, of course, recognized the sound, but Chris's captor did not. His attention was drawn upward. In his surprise his grip weakened, and Chris, using a basic *aikido irimi*, the *ude furi undo*, pivoted away.

It was only a moment in time, less than the blink of an eye, but in that time Chris, freed, snatched the harlequin from Soutane as she was jerked forward against M. Mabuse.

He held her hard against his chest, his forearm across her throat so that he was already half choking her. "I'll have you both," he said, "for supper."

"No, you won't," Chris said, breaking open the harlequin marionette. "You'll turn her loose."

M. Mabuse's laugh was cut off prematurely as Chris thrust the dagger into a shaft of light. "See it?" he said. "It's the real one. This is what you really want, isn't it?" He waggled it, so that the blue light struck the jade blade, darkening it. "It's yours, if you let Soutane go."

"Chris, no!" Soutane was staring at him. "You don't know what you're doing."

"I know, all right," he said, and to the man behind her, "What about it? The dagger for the woman."

M. Mabuse grinned. His greedy eyes drank in the black dagger. At last, he thought. He pushed Soutane forward, closer to where Chris stood.

Chris, retreating, keeping the distance between them.

"Why should I bother?" M. Mabuse said. "I can have her *and* the dagger." And he tightened his hold on Soutane, so that she began to gag with the lack of air. "Give it to me." M. Mabuse's voice was like glass. "She won't last long."

Chris reversed the dagger, held the fragile jade blade between his hands. "If you don't let her go right now," he warned, "I'll snap the blade in two."

"I don't believe you."

Chris had expected this. He exerted pressure, and the blade bent to the limits of its tolerance.

M. Mabuse's eyes nearly bugged out. "No!" he yelled. "You can't!"

"Let her go."

M. Mabuse dropped his arm from around Soutane's neck, and she almost collapsed onto him. She was white-faced, gasping for air.

"Let her go," Chris repeated. "Now!"

"*La Porte à la Nuit.*" M. Mabuse was nearly in a frenzy.

"You'll get it."

"Chris, you mustn't give it to him." Soutane's voice was thin and hoarse.

"Quiet," he said. He was staring at M. Mabuse. "It's a standoff."

"What?"

"I have what you want, and you have what I want. Neither of us trusts the other to make the first move. Besides, I don't know what you'll do after you have the dagger."

M. Mabuse grinned.

"You can't trust him, Chris," Soutane said.

"I don't think I have a choice," Chris said. "I want you safe."

"I'll destroy the dagger," she told him, "before I'll see you let a beast like that have it."

"That's just what Terry Haye thought," M. Mabuse said. "He never had any intention of selling Milhaud *La Porte à la Nuit*."

M. Mabuse dragged Soutane forward into the light, and Chris took another step backward. Soon he would be against the wall with nowhere to retreat. "But now the Butcher is dead." M. Mabuse's voice was eerie in the darkened void of the stable. "That was what we called him in Vietnam."

"We?"

M. Mabuse ignored Chris's interrogative. "Whatever he thought or wanted no longer matters. One way or another I *will* have the sacred dagger. Even if I have to slaughter you both. Do you think it will make any difference to me?" He shook his head. "So many scars inside me refusing to heal, I'll never even feel two more."

"You knew Terry in Vietnam?" Chris asked. "Who are you?"

"My name is Monsieur Mabuse. Or it is Trangh. One and the other, I can no longer tell them apart. My name or theirs, it doesn't matter." He pointed to the jade-bladed dagger. "*This* is what matters."

"Then you must want it as badly as I want Soutane."

"Chris, don't—"

"I told you, Soutane, that I didn't give a damn about your triple-bladed sword. Now you can see I meant it. I care about you; I care about what happened to Terry."

"But don't you see how important the Doorway to Night must have been to Terry? Look at the trouble he took to keep it hidden, to keep it away from these people."

M. Mabuse listened to this dialogue with mounting apprehension. He knew that he was on the verge of getting Christopher Haye to hand him over the dagger. If only the Khmer woman would keep her mouth shut.

Losing patience, he jerked hard on her shoulder, and she screamed.

"That's it. I warned you," Chris said, about to break the jade blade in two.

But M. Mabuse spun Soutane away. Free, she ran to Chris's side. She reached for the dagger. "Put it away now. It's ours."

But Chris would not let her have it. He was staring into M. Mabuse's eyes. "He's still here, Soutane. I've seen what he can do. Besides, we have a deal."

"A deal with a monster like him?" she cried. "You must be mad. He's Vietnamese. No one trusts their word."

"I do." Chris went across the rectangle of light to where M. Mabuse stood, still and watchful. "I have Soutane," he said. His gaze had never left the Vietnamese's eyes. "And now you have the Doorway to Night." He handed over the sacred dagger of the *Muy Puan*.

"Chris, you fool. He'll kill us the minute he has the dagger."

But it was as if, for that instant, she did not exist. Now there was only the two of them. It was clear that there was more to M. Mabuse than he had allowed either of them to see. Chris burned to know his secrets.

Chris could see that like a normal human being M. Mabuse might eat and drink, but he subsisted on hate. In the center of those black eyes a cold flame burned. In other observers it might engender repulsion and fear. Chris felt only sadness, and an odd kind of kinship he was at a loss to explain.

It was as if he confronted a homicidal child. Who was to blame for the damage he might cause? That did not make him any less dangerous. On the contrary, it was obvious that he was quite lethal. But the distinct sense of good and evil one often discerned in human features was not there. Rather, it was as if M. Mabuse's face were a skull, devoid of flesh and cartilage.

Could one divine intention from such a stark and stripped-down visage? Could not one fashion redemption from such primordial clay?

At last Chris backed away from him. "We both have won," he said, "and both have lost."

SUMMER 1969

BAN ME THUOT, VIETNAM/ HINTERLANDS; ANGKOR, CAMBODIA

When Seve Guarda arrives in the smoking pit known as Vietnam, he is overwhelmed by the stench. Brought up in the streets of Hell's Kitchen, he is well acquainted with the stink of poverty: dirt, grime, week-old sweat, month-old garbage, burning rubber, the decay of dead rats. But even this does not prepare him for the miasma of Vietnam.

It is everywhere: in the exploding air, in the blood-matted fatigues he wears, the often unidentifiable food he eats, the watery beer and liquor he drinks. It is the smell of death, and it is inescapable.

Only music mutes the stench of death, only moving to the raw, rock 'n' roll rhythms dulls the senses enough to forget what constantly invades his nostrils.

He hears from the jukebox the familiar beginning bars of the Rolling Stones' "Gimme Shelter." In a moment his surprisingly well-modulated voice sings along with Jagger's.

He dances with a girl he does not know, and can never know, a mysterious atom of the war, a warm body representing a culture lost now amid the debris and the destruction.

It is in this hut made of cannibalized corrugated iron and Coca-Cola cans, this place of a lost civilization, where Seve comes to lose the stench, to lose perhaps himself, that he meets the Magician.

Seve is impressed by the Magician. Seve is not easily impressed; he has far too suspicious a nature for that.

After seven months here Seve has become a kind of anomaly. His nature has been forged in the crucible of war. Here, life is essentially a cut-and-dried affair. Men are sent out to kill one another, and women—well, they are around to bed in between missions.

In such a hellish atmosphere it is not surprising that human beings should lose their value. Life is reduced to a commodity, to be bought and sold, to be possessed or to be terminated. Hearts quickly become so callused that the wretchedness of existence can no longer be perceived.

But somehow, Seve has managed to keep his heart safe from the horrors that the war engenders. As wild as he is in battle, as wicked as he might be roaring drunk in one grimy city after another, he is invariably gentle with his women. In fact, it is an obsession with him. The only way he can be certain that the jungle has not taken everything away from him is when he returns to what the Vietnamese laughingly called civilization, and takes a local girl to bed. There, he can reassure himself that, no matter how many VCs he has killed, how much blood is on his hands, he is still Seve.

A month before he meets the Magician, he gets his brother Dominic assigned to his unit. Dom is an orphan survivor of a Special Forces communications detachment massacred by VC while they were moving field HQ. A week before he meets the Magician, he and Dominic and Captain Bork, their outfit's CO, have gone on a binge, a two-day drunk without parallel. The three of them have taken out a VC vampire patrol—one of those feared, lethal entities that steal through the lines at night, killing soldiers in their sleep.

It is revenge, pure and simple. Half of the original complement of Bork's unit has recently been dismembered by a "Bouncing Betty," a VC-planted explosive device that shot out of the ground when one of the men stepped on its trip-wire. It was odd when it happened, Seve thinks, because this unit, like all the others here, was not shipped over en masse. Rather, its six members were assigned individually. Consequently, no one knew anyone else, there was no camaraderie, no sense of family, of belonging or of protection.

Half the time they sat around drunk on bad liquor or stoned on dynamite grass because they were bored out of their skulls. The other half, they were so terrified they would step on a mine Charlie had buried that they often became paralyzed with dread.

Despite all that—or, perhaps, because of it—Bork wants to do more than destroy the patrol; he wants to make an example of them, to let the enemy know what they are capable of.

They string the eight VCs up by their feet. They hang, mute, staring like rabbits in a trap. Over Seve and Dominic's objections Bork orders them to slit the VC open from neck to pubis, a line of stinking decaying humanity, a testament to the power of human hate and the corruption of the human soul, the true and lasting damage war inflicts on its participants.

Afterward, of course, they are obliged to save themselves—from going mad or, perhaps, from savoring what they have done. Alcohol takes care of that, for forty-eight hours, at least. By that time they are as horny as toads. Executing the release from life precipitates the need for that other release.

Weeping, Dominic soon passes out. Seve is with his girl, a sinuous Vietnamese who might be as young as fourteen. Softly he strokes her thick night-black hair, runs his callused hands over her velvet flesh with such tenderness that she rises off the straw pallet to kiss in gratitude the hollow of his throat.

Seve hears a howl from the next room where Bork is with his girl. Thinking VC, Seve grabs his combat knife and runs to his CO. What he sees turns his blood to ice. Bork has tied his girl with flex so tightly that her flesh bulges obscenely between the strips. Here and there, where the metal has bitten most cruelly into her, she has begun to bleed.

Bork, naked, is beating her with a length of bamboo. His erection stands out before him, red and quivering.

Seve is so incensed that he rips the bamboo from Bork's hand and beats the captain senseless. Then he carefully unwraps the flex from the weeping girl.

"What is happening?" Seve's girl says from the open doorway. "What you doing?"

"What does it look like?" he says. "Look at all this blood."

"It is nothing. It happen all the time," she says. She holds out her hand. "What the matter with you? Come back to bed; it is fuck time."

Seve, with Bork's girl leaning on him, bleeding all over him, stares at this dark-eyed child in the shadows. And he is overwhelmed by an awareness of the utter hopelessness of life.

He needs to forget, so he dances in the Coca-Cola-can shanty the next day, with another child. They are interchangeable, he has found to his utter dismay, these aimlessly drifting atoms of a lost civilization, ghosts who walk through the incinerator life has become.

Sam & Dave shouting their pop-tinged R&B, a funky, chunky piano a wall of sound erected between Seve and the ubiquitous stench of death. In midstep the Magician taps him on the shoulder.

"Go away," Seve says, his face buried in hair smelling of jasmine, only faintly of death.

"Yo, buddy."

"Sing the blues in someone else's ear."

"You're in a heap of shit, so I hear."

Dancing still to Sam & Dave and their Stax piano, better by far than jazz, the true soul of America. Swinging the girl around. "You're right," he says. "This fucking war is the biggest heap of shit I ever hope to step in."

"I'm talking court-martial."

And, for the first time, Seve looks into the Magician's face. "Do I know you?"

"You do now," the Magician says. He gives Seve a wide grin. "Buy you a drink?"

Seve lets the fragrant body go, whirling, an *ao dai*–clothed mote in the dim vastness. The Magician leads him to a corner table, where another man sits slowly sipping a drink.

"I hear," the Magician says, "that Bork the Dork's in the hospital with four fractured ribs, a broken collarbone, wrist, all that good shit."

"Yeah?"

The Magician nods. "Way I hear it, you're responsible."

"That so?"

The Magician leans forward, exaggerating his formidable size. "Hey, buddy, Bork's out for your blood. He's gonna get you fried, if he can."

"I hadn't heard that."

"I'm not surprised," the Magician says. "Maybe I got contacts you don't."

Now Seve is getting the hang of it. "What do you want?" he asks.

The Magician laughs. It is too dark for Seve to see what the other man is doing. "It's more like what do *you* want. Me, I'm doing some recruiting. My name's Virgil, but around here I'm sorta known as the Magician." He hooks a thumb in the direction of the other man. "The Butcher here gave me that moniker and it's stuck."

He takes a swig of beer. "Thing is, the Butcher's getting a team together. A survival unit, you might call it. Our aim is to survive this insanity, and maybe make some bread while we're at it."

"You're not talking about desertion, or anything like that?"

"Hell, no," the Magician says. "You want to kill Charlie, you'll get plenty of chances. We're just gonna make sure we do it on our own terms." He grunts. "If I thought Command had a clue as to how to win this war, I'd be in the thick of it. Christ, you can be dead sure I'd be the first man in.

"But the only thing that Nixon seems to believe in is that clarity weakens power. He's following in Westmoreland's footsteps. To date, the sole consequence of this 'war of attrition' we've been waging is that it's wearing *us* down. I'll be goddamned if I'll die for a man like that."

"But Nixon says—"

The Magician's face twists in a sneer. "Let me tell you about our good president. He has more power than will. Whatever he says is only to squirm out of the messes his orders get us into.

"You remember Fred Allen, the old-time comedian? He once said that success is like dealing with your kid or teaching your wife to drive. Sooner or later you'll end up in the police station.

"Well, Nixon's about to land us there, and I'm not gonna follow him inside. We're into a whole other thing. How's that sound to you?"

It all sounds reasonable to Seve. It is as if the Magician is the only person able to make sense of this inimical environment. "Interesting. But transfers are impossible to get around here."

"Wrong. Piece of cake."

"What about Bork?"

"Leave the Dork to me," the Magician says. "He's no longer your problem, Dancer."

"No wonder they call you the Magician." Seve smiles. It has been so long since he has done that, it feels odd, as if those muscles have begun to atrophy. "But how come you want me particularly?"

"We're interested in a few good men," the Butcher says, coming at last out of the shadow in which he has been sitting. He is a good-looking fellow, Seve notes, quite a bit younger, it seems, than the Magician, though war has a way of distorting time. "I got a first-hand report on what you did at the brothel."

Seve nods. "Fair enough." He sticks out his hand.

Terry Haye, the Butcher, clasps it, saying, "Welcome to the SLAM unit."

Trangh, when Seve meets him, also impresses him, but for other reasons. Seve finds Trangh scary. It is as if he is the inspiration for the unit's name, a golem in the literal sense, a warm, living body without a conscience or a soul. Looking into Trangh's black eyes, Seve thinks, is akin to staring at infinity: you don't understand what you're seeing, you only know you have no business looking in that direction.

But Trangh is the Magician's right-hand man, just as Mun seems to be the Butcher's right-hand man. These Asians, Seve observes, are something more than slaves but quite a bit less than friends. They are, rather, bonded together with their corresponding Americans by some alchemical element that is not in Seve's vocabulary.

He is reminded of his father, proud Spaniard who came to America to make his fortune; poor hod-carrier, so hardworking he is despised by his coworkers, who respond to his heroic fourteen-hour days by calling him "the spic."

Virgil and the Butcher do not call the Asians in the SLAM unit gooks, but to Seve's way of thinking, they could. "Mun and Trangh work for me," he overhears Virgil say to the Butcher. "When I tell 'em to jump, they jump. They owe me, buddy, owe me everything. Whatever you got going with Mun, you better forget it right now. He's mine—all the SLAM mercenaries are—and he always will be."

But one day when it is pouring so hard that even the SLAM unit is stymied he overhears a conversation that changes his point of view.

Trangh and the Butcher are talking while checking their weapons. They appear to be chatting idly, but as Seve nears them it becomes clear that their words bely their appearance.

"Your family anywhere near here?" Terry asks.

"Not near," Trangh says. "Not far. In Vietnam nothing is ever far from where you are." He wipes down the barrel of his AK-47. "Especially the war."

"You must miss them."

"I hardly remember what it was like," Trangh says, "to be with my mother, my family." He shrugs, wiping away. "Like the Mekong that gives life and takes it, the war has swept it all away. It is like a dream now. When I sleep, sometimes, I am back in my village." Checking the action. "But then I wake up, and I am spattered with blood."

"The war," Terry says. "Always the war."

Trangh pauses in what he is doing, stares into Terry's eyes as if he is hypnotized. After a time he nods, says, "Yes."

Seve, also staring at the Butcher, sees again his father's kind eyes, hears his raspy, thickly accented voice saying, "All I ever wanted was for you and Dom to succeed." Lying ill and gray-faced in a dingy hospital room. "For me, it is nothing; for you, it is everything. But now, too late, I know the secret for success. It is belonging."

A month after his father dies, old and broken before his time, Seve quits school and, taking Dominic, enlists in the army, graduates to Special Forces. He wants to make his father proud of them. But, more, he wants for them what his father could never have. He has the mistaken impression that if they fight for their adopted country, when they return home they will be heroes instead of "spics." He believes that they will then belong.

Seve, who does not belong in his own country, who is still uncomfortable around people everyone else thinks of as "Americans," believes he can empathize with the bizarre situation in which Terry finds himself. Despite his nickname, the Butcher is not at all like Virgil. The extent that Seve had believed he was, was due to the Butcher's fine deception. In the beginning Seve was certain that the power lines drawn within the SLAM unit were simple: they consisted of the Magician and the Butcher versus everyone else. Now it seems as if it is the Magician versus Terry, Mun, and Trangh. Seve finds himself wanting very much to learn more about the complex personality of the Butcher.

Under ominous skies the color of almonds Terry Haye and Trangh squat together in the inconstant shade of a burnt-out hut. They eat their salt pills along with their meal. The Butcher looks up when Seve squats down beside them; neither says anything.

The SLAM unit is somewhere in the hinterlands of the country (in a war without a front, Seve has long ago given up asking where in 'Nam he is; it simply does not matter), resting after one mission, even as it prepares for another.

Trangh is busy shoveling rice into his mouth from a cracked bowl held at chin level. The Butcher, though he eats far more slowly, follows suit.

Seve watches them, aware of their clandestine closeness, and is envious of their relationship. "Do you know where we go next?" he asks the Butcher.

Terry shrugs. "Depends."

"On what? The weather?"

"No. On where we can do the most damage." Laughing, he says, "The Magician's in charge of damage prognostication. He whips out his fucking Ouija board or his crystal ball and off we go." He gives Trangh a look as he crunches down on a fish head.

"Don't you have any say in it?" Seve asks. "I thought this was your unit."

The Butcher pulverizes more fish bones between his teeth. "I'm like a Doberman pinscher. The Magician points out the target, and I destroy it. We're all like that in a way, Trangh, aren't we?"

Seve wonders at this. Is Terry joking? He is hardly a dog responding to the Magician's commands. And there was a hard, angry edge to Terry's last comment, almost as if it were an admonition, rather than a joke.

Seve thinks of what is between Terry and Trangh, and wonders if it is more complicated than he knows. It seems to Seve that not only does the Butcher hate Virgil for treating the Asians as he does, but on some level he despises Trangh for putting up with it.

Ahead of them a television crew is hightailing it toward the aftermath of a firefight, cameras grinding away, stirring commentary being composed on the run. Much of the war is like some vast, insane Hollywood set masterminded by Cecil B. DeMille. Often Seve imagines he hears them calling, "Hey, soldier, could we do a retake on that attack so we can get it on videotape?"

The television crew is returning. They dog the heels of the units trudging back from the firefight. Ever since *Life* published photos two months ago of the two hundred forty-two Americans soldiers killed at the week-long battle to take Apbia Mountain, the media—especially television, the most rapacious of news-gathering organs—have descended on the war as if it is a long-lost orphan.

But, sadly, Apbia Mountain has become a metaphor for the futility of the war. A useless objective, Hamburger Hill, as it came to be known, was retaken by the North Vietnamese a month after it ground American troops to bloody meat. Too often in this war this is the ultimate result of American victories.

"One day," Seve says, meaning to be optimistic, "this will all end."

Trangh stops eating; he looks at Seve. "It will never end," he says. "There has been war here, in one form or another, for centuries. You Americans cannot change that; the French couldn't, and neither can the Russians. You seek to crush us, each in your own way, according to the dictates of your ideologies. You think that because you have, now and then, subjugated us that you have defeated us. This is what the French believed when they were here."

He turns and Seve sees on his arm a tattoo of a *phung hoang*, the mythical Vietnamese bird said to possess supernatural powers, including the ability to answer all questions. It is small, but exquisitely rendered by a master artist. It seems to him now an apt symbol of the vast cultural gulf between them.

"You all want the same thing: to teach us. To teach us what? To be better than we already are? To increase our wealth, our health, our happiness? That is what we hear. From the French, from the Americans, from the Russians. But all you really want is to make us in your image."

Trangh stares at the television camera as it closes in on the desperate faces, the wounded eyes of the exhausted boys. "Often I wonder why you are here at all."

Stung, Seve lapses into brooding silence. The Butcher, who is either interested himself or wishes to take up Seve's fallen banner, says, "Why do you put up with this? Do you hate us, then, as much as you hate the North Vietnamese?"

Those black, depthless eyes turn on Terry. "I don't hate," Trangh says. "I burn."

I burn.

For weeks that phrase haunts Seve. For some reason he treats it as if it is a secret talisman, something that binds him directly to the Butcher and to Trangh, for he wishes more than anything to belong to something with more humanity than a SLAM unit that spends the bulk of its time killing. But, in the end, he realizes that he does not understand what it is he has, that he will never fathom it by keeping it locked away.

He turns to his brother, Dominic, who, though younger, is already a scholar, a voracious reader of history, philosophy, and social ethics.

Of all of them, it appears to Seve as if his brother truly has no business being in a war. He has killed, but unwillingly. He has never felt that sudden surge of elation the rest of them do—even despite themselves, little wolves in the wilderness, licking their chops—in the midst of battle. He is not dazzled by the white-light tracers whirring past his eyes, he is not keyed up the the *brrrat!* of the machine pistol's firing. He does not see what the rest of them do in the kill-or-be-killed ethos that pervades the air as thoroughly as the stench of death.

"Of course I understand what he means," Dominic says when Seve tells him of his eerie conversation with Trangh. "But I think you either have to be born here or be a student of history to get it."

They are encamped within a village filled—as these days all of them are—with mistrust and division. As they squat out of the broiling sun, chewing their salt tablets, several village officials, grimfaced, armed with American weapons, are busy canvassing the huts.

"Look, the French came at the turn of the century and fucked this country over. I mean, by and large, they didn't do anything that any colonialist nation hadn't done in centuries past. They started by kicking out all the ruling mandarins, installing French rule, French education, French law, all of which further degenerated a society built on ancient Confucian tenets."

The officials emerge from a hut, dragging a young man in the dust. He is bleeding. His left arm hangs limply at an unnatural angle. In the filth of the street, so that everyone can see, the officials continue their merciless beating of the man.

"Paul Doumer, the former French minister of finance, arrived here in 1897 as the new governor-general. It was ironic, really. His political enemies exiled him for proposing a French income tax. He promptly turned the colony into a money-making proposition."

The man is, ostensibly, a North Vietnamese infiltrator. The officials have been trained by, it is said, the CIA to hunt down communist cadres inside South Vietnam. The problem is that there is a monthly quota the village officials must fill.

"For one thing, the old mandarins had frowned on exporting rice, believing it was wiser to save it to feed impoverished areas of the country. Doumer, however, saw rice as a bottom-line commodity that would go a long way toward getting the colony to pay for itself. By the nineteen-forties, Indochina was the third largest world exporter of rice.

"As a result, millions of dollars flowed into the French coffers, but the other side of the coin was that a majority of the peasants, whose families had owned land for centuries, were dispossessed by French entrepreneurs and wealthy Vietnamese families eager to cash in on a good thing."

One official puts his weapon against the side of the man's head and pulls the trigger. Is the man a traitor or merely a peasant without the means to bribe the officials? Like so many questions in Vietnam it is impossible for the Americans to discern the truth of the answer.

"In fact, this suited Doumer just fine. He used the dispossessed as virtual slave labor in the burgeoning mines, rubber plantations, and the ambitious public works programs he had conceived."

The officials move on, entering hut after hut until they have a line of men and women whose feet are stained with the first man's blood. Dark clouds line the horizon that rises above the jungle.

Sunlight, a rim of fire, behind them is soon gone. The men and women being scrutinized by the officials remain standing, mute as the mountains to the northwest. The officials squat down, eating rice, talking animatedly among themselves.

"But, on one crucial point the French influence on its colony differed. Before the French, opium addiction was not widespread. In fact, it was virtually unknown outside the small Chinese population. Doumer changed all that. Seeing in opium another potential major source of revenue, he constructed a refinery in Saigon. As a result, addiction spread among the Vietnamese at such an appalling rate that soon fully a third of all the colony's revenues came from the selling of the drug."

Dinner over with, the officials rise and, with the rest of the village watching, shoot the detainees one by one.

Dominic's face is as dark and smoldering as the aftermath of a firefight. "The French have since left Vietnam, and one day, God willing, so will we. But opium, and the suffering it causes, will not. This is their legacy in Indochina, the kiss the French bestowed on the people who, Paul Doumer wrote when he arrived here, were ripe for servitude."

"We all bleed on the outside here," Seve says. "They are by now inured to the acts the Vietnamese perpetrate against one another. They have their orders. It would, in any case, be bad for morale to interfere in what is perceived as a vital, American-sponsored anticommunist operation. For all they know, these men and women were, indeed, part of a communist cadre. Your problem is that you bleed on the inside, too. Have you conveniently forgotten the Vietnamese's warlike nature? They continually subjugated less aggressive neighboring cultures like the Khmer."

"We both bleed," Dominic says, "only you're too stubborn to see it. Sometimes, I think all of us must wonder whether Trangh hates us as much as he does the North Vietnamese. The innate nature of the Vietnamese has nothing to do with what the French did and you know it."

"Let he who is without sin cast the first stone, is that it?"

"Essentially, yes." He stares bleakly at the mound of corpses. "Nothing can lessen the burden of this tragedy."

"Tragedy is an understatement when it comes to describing this shitty war," Seve says. "That's a word you use sitting back in your armchair, safe at home musing about world events. When you're here, hip-deep in death and human misery, you goddamn know what hell is like."

The dogs have come now, sniffing the ground where the blood runs freely. The villagers have gone, leaving the animals to it.

"This place has changed me, or rather it's changed the way I see the world," Dominic says. "I have come to understand the good in my being here, the purpose of it. I see the medics scrambling back and forth, trying to patch up the poor bastards who step on a land mine or trigger a grenade in the jungle. But that's all they can do; they can't heal. And that's what a doctor is supposed to do: heal. I want to heal, and this war has shown me the way to do that. These guys who return home after their tours are going to need more than physical rehab. They're going to need spiritual strength, they're going to need their souls healed. Only God can do that.

"There's no faith here, Seve. You can see that as well as I can. God has abandoned this place to Confucius and Buddha. Here is where God died, and was resurrected. Bodies can be knit with sutures and steel pins, but hearts and minds need another kind of healing. The poor bastards who make it out of this hell will need to be saved. I want, when I get home, to help them on that path."

"No one here gets out alive," Jim Morrison sings.

They are "inserted," in military parlance, into "pockets of obstruction." The SLAM unit flying north toward Pleiku and Kontum. The swift Huey choppers deliver them, the emissaries of death, into jungle overripe with vegetation and human bodies.

The Butcher teaches them many things, among them how to decapitate the enemy. "Leave the head beside the body," he says in a matter-of-fact way, "but be sure that all the tendons are completely severed. That way the Vietnamese soul will have no way of escaping, isn't that right, Trangh?"

"The endless wheel of *samsara*, the sacred circle, will be broken," Trangh says without emotion.

"We come not only to kill Charlie," the Butcher says, "but to freak him out. Clear?"

Dominic is shaking his head. "I don't know whether I can do that."

"What is it?" the Butcher says. "Your conscience bothering you?" He is clearly disgusted. "The shitface you kill is the one who planted the fucking mine that blew some poor sonuvabitch's legs to kingdom come. You've been here, how long? nine months? How many times has the grunt next to you tripped a grenade? Think about that while you're doing it."

Dominic shakes his head. "I don't know . . ."

"He doesn't know," the Magician mimics. "Listen, buddy, you better own up to one of life's bitter truths: if we can't be happy being powerful, if we can't be happy preying on others, then we invent conscience and prey on ourselves. There's your choice."

"I—"

But before Dominic can take this further, Seve says, "Don't worry, I'll take care of him."

"Maybe he doesn't belong here," the Butcher says. "I've got the entire unit to think of."

"No, no," Seve says, thinking anxiously that Dom will be safer here, where the Magician in protecting himself will keep them all safe from harm. "I said I'd take care of it."

From Trangh's directions, villages rise up like boils out of the jungle. The team sometimes uses high firepower to blast smoking holes in Charlie's defenses. They brace themselves against the chopper's metal struts and, as it takes them in low, they fire in unison, breaking resistance in an instant, as the chopper looses its payload of rockets.

Alighting on the scorched, burning earth, they continue with short bursts from their AK-47s, "liberated" from former victims, until, surrounded by death, they bend like peasants in the paddies to perform the Butcher's bloody work.

Other times, heading west, following a line traced by Trangh's finger on the topo map, taking lightning "stealth" flights, using no firepower at all, never a shot fired. They creep from hut to hut, slitting throats, severing heads, leaving the grotesque remains for Charlie to see and to fear.

Taking his cue from Trangh's tattooed flesh, the Butcher takes to drawing before they leave a mission site a stylized *phung hoang* in Charlie's blood.

Once, Seve catches Trangh staring at the crude but powerful drawing and, for an instant, sees a splinter of emotion flicker across his face. What, Seve wonders, does he think of the Butcher's invention? Is it inspiration or insult?

Why does he care what Trangh thinks? Is it just because this is his country, and what he thinks, no matter what the American administration believes, *does* matter?

Seve, already the detective in his heart, wishes to unravel Terry and Trangh's essential secret. He believes that when he understands them, he will be able to make some kind of sense of this maelstrom of insanity in which he finds himself.

Most of the boys incountry want nothing more than to go home, get back to school, to forget they were ever here, that this ever happened. Not Seve. He knows that for him at least an elemental truth lurks in the stinking jungles, the dangerous rice paddies of Vietnam. Now he believes that, like the *phung hoang*, Trangh holds the key to that truth.

On a strike far to the north he watches Trangh guide the Huey helicopter above the tangled mass of jungle. Virgil, at his side, whispering, "Just tell us where Charlie's hidden like you always do. No fuss, no muss."

Trangh points, and the Huey banks to the left. A clearing comes into view. A village. "There."

They come in low and fast, guns chattering, rockets *whooshing!* The tree line going down amid a roar, a violent, oily blossoming of death.

Out of the corner of his eye Seve sees Trangh pressing his ear to the floor of the chopper. His eyes are wide and staring, his thick lips moving, as if the noise their weapons are making is erupting like gas from inside him.

As the Huey settles, Seve follows Trangh out. Bent over like old men, crippled by life, they sprint across the blackened clearing, swept of debris by the churning rotors.

Answering fire, bright tracers in the night, makes them dodge this way and that. Seve follows Trangh's hunched back all the way to safety. Crouched, panting, their backs against a pile of rubble still warm and smoking, he is dismayed to realize that he has unconsciously used Trangh as a shield.

Trangh has a haunted look in his eyes, so hollow and devoid of life that Seve is forced to touch him to reassure himself. Trangh's head whips around as he feels the touch and, all at once, Seve is face-to-face with the working end of Trangh's AK-47.

"I was frightened for you," Seve whispers between parched lips. "I thought you had been hit."

The weapon disappears into the darkness. All around them flames leap and dance, crackling and sparking. They remind Seve of himself, the darkness in which they burn, Trangh. They are so close, and so different. And yet, one without the other becomes enervated.

Trangh, his eyes like chips of obsidian, jerks his head. "This way."

They emerge from their sanctuary and, seeing the others pinned down by North Vietnamese fire, make their way in halting, zigzag fashion along the perimeter of the devastation.

Trangh begins to fire and Seve, coming up behind him, follows suit. Together, they rush the last stronghold of resistance. Seve pulls the pin, lofts a grenade behind a hasty barricade of wooden beams and smoldering thatch.

They hit the ground a moment before the darkness turns white with sound and vibration. Then they are up and running, firing still past what is left of the barricade.

They poke through the remains, and Trangh kneels, obediently beginning in expert fashion to slit the throats of those corpses still in one piece.

The others come up, unscathed. The village looks like the dark side of the moon, except flames would not burn on the moon. They begin to mop up, ghostly figures going about their ghastly work like a precision drill team.

Silence, save for the fire feeding itself. Then Seve's head comes up. He stands. He hears the sound again, and the hairs at the back of his neck stand up.

Through the pall of ashy smoke he can make out a figure, stumbling and dazed, coming toward them. Even before his brain identifies the shape, he sees Dom running out to meet it.

"Stop!" the Magician shouts. "Come back here!"

Dom either does not hear him or chooses not to. He continues to run toward the dazed, charcoal-streaked child. It is a girl of no more than five or six. Her long hair lies lank on her head. Her eyes are wide and staring; she is clearly terrified.

Her wailing cries echo through the ruined clearing, tearing at their already raw nerves. She is alternately revealed and obscured by waves of smoke and flame as she wanders amid the rubble of what was once her village. She stumbles, going down on her knees in the ashes, and when she rises, he can see that she is bleeding from a spray of lacerations. The pitiable child seems, to Seve, to symbolize the pernicious amorality that is the direct consequence of war. His heart goes out to her.

As if in slow motion, he watches his brother nearing the apocalyptic vision of a world gone mad. Until the scene becomes something that transcends reality, the charitable hand of a newly resurrected God, reaching out to heal the generation that, in all cultures, is universally innocent.

"Goddammit!" the Magician shouts, and lifting his rifle, aims it at the child.

"No!" Seve screams, lunging for the weapon. But Trangh intercepts him. It seems that the Vietnamese moves only fractionally, but Seve's nerveless arm falls like dead wood to his side.

He watches, helplessly, in horror, as the Magician fires a quick burst into the child's chest. The small figure is thrown violently backward. In midair it bursts apart with a thunderous roar. Dom, near enough to be at its fringes, is lifted bodily.

Trangh releases Seve, who runs to his brother, kneels at his side.

"Jesus," Dom whispers. He is in shock, but otherwise unhurt. "Oh, my God."

"Wired," Terry says, coming up beside them. "It's a common trick. Tape a grenade under a child's armpit, wire it so that when the child is touched . . ." Trangh, looking on, says nothing.

Dom with his head in his hands, shaking as if with a high fever. He begins to vomit. Seve puts his arms around him.

Trangh, a heartbeat away, watches them with eyes that reflect the nearing flames. He drinks in their embrace with an avidity Seve can feel.

"You cannot protect him," Trangh says, "no matter how much you try. This place will take him or leave him as it sees fit. There is nothing you can do."

Seve, his cheek pressed to Dom's wet hair, stares at him. "But there *is* something I can do," he says. "I can love him."

He sees the incomprehension on Trangh's face, and he wonders how it was that he ever wanted to belong here, to be friends with the Butcher and Trangh. The Butcher kills with appalling ease. And Trangh is as alien, as ultimately unknowable as the beautiful young girls in their *ao dais* swinging under pressed Coca-Cola-can roofs to American rock 'n' roll.

"Now you can see it. Why the war will never end." Trangh gestures to take in the burnt ground, littered with mutilated corpses—including what is left of the little girl. "And I am among the lucky ones. Look at the alternative."

But this revelation comes too late; Seve is no longer listening. "Go away," he whispers. "Go away now." But Trangh does not move. He has become a mute observer of their pain and terror, drinking it in as if it gives him as much sustenance as his fish heads and rice.

Dom's racking convulsions have subsided. "Dear Lord," Seve hears him pray, "grant me the strength to get home."

The war grinds excruciatingly on, but not for those in the SLAM unit. Each day, according to Virgil, Nixon brings America closer to ignominious defeat in a land it never bothered to understand.

In Ban Me Thuot, the unit, now seasoned, cohesive, even familial, is on a three-day leave before what the Butcher hints will be its most arduous mission. There are eight of them: Terry, Virgil, Seve, Dominic, and a whip-smart Kansas farmboy named Jawbone, Trangh, Mun, and a Khmer Serei named Chey. They are resupplied, but from where? Seve knows that the Butcher never makes out requisition forms. In fact, he has never seen paperwork of any kind on SLAM.

Curious, he visits Special Forces HQ. Not only have they never heard of a Virgil, major, captain, or otherwise, but they have no record of him, either. No one appears concerned or even interested. Trivia such as this in the face of the war's overwhelming chaos is instantly forgettable.

But it makes Seve think. Who is Virgil if he isn't Special Forces? Maybe he's attached in some way to MACV, General Abrams's Command HQ. From Special Forces HQ in Ban Me Thuot he makes a call to Saigon, and finds, to his dismay, that no one in MACV knows—or will admit to knowing—a CO named Virgil.

Seve is still searching for the answer to his question when SLAM moves out. They are no longer wearing military fatigues but, rather, the black cotton pajamas favored by the Khmer Rouge. They carry Soviet-made AK-47 machine rifles. They have left their dog tags back in Ban Me Thuot.

A matte-black helicopter without insignia of any kind airlifts them northwest, out of the highlands. There has been no briefing, not even a sense of what their mission will entail.

The Magician materializes out of a darkness lit only by the pilot's glowing green instrument panel. "I hear," he says over the yammering of the rotors, "you've been asking around about me. You're a real little detective."

Seve shrugs, trying not to betray the dryness of his throat. "Just trying to get my bearings."

The Magician stares at him for a long time. Seve, feeling a line of sweat rolling down his forehead, prays that it will not go into his eye. If he blinks, he feels, Virgil will think he is lying.

"As long as that's what it is," the Magician says. "As long as we understand one another." Despite the heavy noise in the cabin, there is a silence between them, as uncomfortable and unwanted as an air pocket over the Rockies.

"I don't know about you," Seve says, "but ever since I got here, I haven't known shit about anything."

The Magician laughs. "Yeah, well, I can understand that. It took me some time to find out what was really going on here. That was the hard part." The Huey hits some turbulence and, for a moment, the two men are thrown together. Seve grabs for a strap.

"See," the Magician says, "I don't need to hold on. I'm not gonna die here; I know that. Once you know that about yourself, you'll be okay, Dancer."

The pilot shouts for him, and for a moment he squats down in the lurid light of the instruments. His forefinger stabs out, continuing a route he holds in his head. The pilot nods, the Huey banks, heading due west now, and he turns back to Seve.

"Want to know the single most debilitating thing about this war? Everybody's so busy making sure their ass isn't blown off by Charlie they got no time for anything else.

"Me? I'm stuck incountry for the duration so I know I got to make the best of it. When you step in shit, don't try to scrape it off, go find a sucker you can sell it to."

He leans toward the open door, spits into the wind. "What do I care? Won't hit *me* in the face." He grins. "My orders are to kick Charlie's ass, and that's just what we're gonna do. But if I'm gonna risk my life for Uncle Sam, I figure he owes me." He hooks a thumb in the direction they are flying. "We're gonna make our fortunes out there, Dancer, you can make book on it."

His face, distorted by odd, angular shadows cast by the low-level green glow, has taken on the macabre aspect of a Halloween mask.

"I'll tell you what no one at HQ could or would. You're now part of the Daniel Boone ops. This mission—like those of all the Daniel Boone teams—is classified, strictly Eyes Only. That's why no briefing in Ban Me Thuot, that's why we're sterile—no ID of any kind. Even this chopper flyboy has no idea where we're headed. I guide him as we go along. Our orders come direct from Major Michael Eiland. That clear the air for you?"

Seve nods. "Like I said, I wasn't prying."

Virgil turns away, hunkering down beside the pilot. Seve strains to see the portion of the map they are discussing, but the Magician's formidable bulk is in the way.

They go in low, moving very fast, so that the blurred treetops become a black sea over which they sail like, perhaps, Trangh's *phung hoang*.

Seve, sitting next to his brother, wonders whether it is his teeth chattering or the chopper's vibration that is making him sick to his stomach. He looks at Dominic's face in the almost lightless cabin and curses himself for bringing him into the SLAM unit. He would be far safer back in Ban Me Thuot, Seve thinks. At least there he is an American soldier. Here, in the airless dark, he is nothing, not American, merely a mote in God's eye traveling without identification from point A to point B. If we die on this mission, no one will ever know what happened to us. Which is, he suspects, the idea.

For a while he watches Jawbone telling Mun and Chey one of the long, funny true stories for which he has been named. They sit spellbound by the kid. He wonders how someone nineteen years old has stored up such a seemingly endless supply of tales. He is like a modern-day Scheherazade, keeping the death and the horror at bay by entertaining the others and, Seve supposes, himself.

Sound and vibration, picking up. Seve turns to look out the open door. Overhead, a trio of B-52s pierces the amber cloud cover, overtaking the Huey, then heading on due west. Ten minutes later the first of the explosions blossoms like garish paper lanterns.

Seve cranes his neck, seeing by the illumination of the flowers of evil, the jungle and rice paddies below. And the river, so close, the phosphors are dazzling in reflection, shining like the scales on a serpent's body.

And at last he knows where they are headed. Cambodia.

Low, threatening clouds burst across the Cardamom Mountains far to the west, and the air is so full of moisture that nothing can stay dry. It is the time of the monsoons. In this weather even a minor injury can fester and become gangrenous. A leg wound is a certain death sentence.

Terry Haye watches as Virgil, bringing up the unit's rear, climbs out of the skull-filled river. He wonders whether, just around the bend, Charon lies in wait on his rocking boat. He wonders whether, having crossed the river, the border into Cambodia, they have entered the precincts of hell.

For a moment he feels a twinge of uncertainty at this enterprise. Death waits for them like a panting animal out there in the Cambodian jungles. But the promise of power and riches beyond comprehension draws him onward like a magnet.

They will be a week, perhaps as much as ten days, on their own in enemy territory until, just outside of Angkor Wat, they will be met. In that time they must also hit Charlie, who sits like a grinning ghoul, encamped within the relative safety of Cambodia's neutral territory.

"There's a guy we have to see in Angkor," Virgil told Terry at their private briefing the night before lift-off. "A real important guy. A real fucker." Virgil laughed, downing his Scotch.

"He's a Frenchman. Been incountry a long time, longer than any American." Virgil emptied the bottle. "Thing is," he said, "we can't get what we want by going around him. I want what he's got. I want it real bad. I've lined up some bastards on our side, but he's got his, too. They're all Asians so even if we do the deal who the fuck knows whether they can be trusted. I need some way to tell, see. You're good at this, as good as me, maybe, though you do everything ass backward. The Asians trust you; they're scared shitless of me. I got a feeling this's gonna need some finesse."

"I'll give it some thought," Terry said.

"Yeah. Do that." Virgil lifted his glass. "Only make sure you don't discuss this with your new bosom buddy." Terry knew he was talking about Mun. "You may trust that sonuvabitch, but I sure don't."

Terry is thinking about this conversation as the Magician climbs up beside him on this far shore and says, "Hold on to your hat, buddy. Now it begins."

They hit Charlie at night. The sky is moonless, the countryside utterly devoid of light. It is, at times, as if they are advancing in their sleep or with their eyes closed. The danger is everywhere, as palpable as their heartbeats.

The land unfolds before them, giving grudging way. Now it is Chey, not Trangh, who guides them. He uses a machete, clearing a narrow path for them only when absolutely necessary. "Sound travels in the jungle," he tells them, "as well as in water."

It is so hot, even now, that they must make frequent stops. When that happens, the Asians stand guard, impervious to the humidity that, so it seems to the Americans, sucks the breath out of every living thing. Are they contemptuous of the Westerners' lack of stamina, Terry wonders, or merely indifferent?

The team seems satisfied with the carnage they wreak. They become again blood-spattered slaughterers, but this, after all, is what they believe they have been sent to do. In one fortified bunker, ankle-deep in cindered concrete, they string up the heads of the North Vietnamese on a wire like Chinese lanterns while Terry daubs on the wall the sign of the *phung hoang*.

They sleep by day, fitful catnaps beneath heavy shade, stalked, perhaps, by dreams of what they have become. At one time or another a majority of the unit is up, crowded around Jawbone, eager to hear another story, dropping one by one into a deeper slumber as they are calmed of their inner fears.

At another outpost, where particularly heavy hand-to-hand fighting almost costs Chey his life, they liberate sixteen Khmer children who have been held and tortured by the Vietnamese.

The Magician, enraged, orders a bonfire built. They throw all the severed heads into the fire. The stench of the thick, oily smoke that results makes them gag. Seve watches Dominic out of the corner of his eye, fearful that he will cut and run in the face of this fearful task. Dominic kneels beside the half-starved Khmer children, trying vainly to feed them as they kick the heads of their tormentors into the roaring flames as if they are in on the invention of a new game.

In the gray, stinking morning, while Mun and Chey patrol the perimeter, the rest of the SLAM unit pores through the remnants of the fire and, as Virgil directs them, builds a conical pile of skulls. Then the Magician affixes the figure of an angel he has cut out of paper to the top so that the whole has the appearance of a ghastly Christmas tree.

Standing back to admire their handiwork, the Magician says, "Peace on earth, right?" He gives a harsh, unpleasant laugh.

Trangh watches Terry, who holds a badly burned Khmer child in his arms. There is in Terry's mind an awareness of the obscene juxtaposition between the unholy Christmas tree and the maimed life he holds close to him.

Dominic, his arms around two of the Khmer children, with whom he has slept, tending the worst of them, averts his face, as if he has already taken his vows.

He insists on taking the children to the nearest Khmer village where they can be properly cared for. The Magician says, "That's ridiculous. This is a war."

Terry, still holding the child, strides to the tree, kicks over the skulls. Virgil's mock angel disappears amid the bones. "We're going," Terry says. "These kids need medical attention."

Trangh, staring from Terry to the Magician, feels an odd constriction in his throat. The entire war, it seems to him, hangs suspended in the silent moment before Virgil gives his grudging consent. Then he withers as the Butcher shoots him a look of contempt, as if to say, These are more your people than mine. You should have spoken for them.

At dusk on the third day after their brief detour, Chey returns from recon. There is a North Vietnamese cadre less than a kilometer ahead. It is larger and better equipped than the others they have attacked. It is also commanded by a colonel, "Someone," Virgil says, making the decision to take it, "who might know where COSVN is located."

There is a moon that night but, because of the ominous cloud cover, its light is wan and diffuse. Just after midnight they converge on the cadre in a pincer movement, Terry, Mun, Seve, and Trangh on one flank, Virgil, Dominic, Jawbone, and Chey on the other.

Somewhere in the west it is raining. They can hear the sound of it, rumbling, in contrast to the stillness through which they plod like wraiths about a graveyard.

The cadre is asleep. So far from the frontier, they are confident in the blanket of the neutral territory in which they take refuge. The sentries go down almost simultaneously. Terry uses his wire. It seems almost to sing as he jerks it through flesh and cartilage. Blood at night is like a shadow, seeping into the ground, and soon gone.

Trangh, who broke a sentry's neck with one vicious twist of his hands, volunteers to stay behind, on the edge of their perimeter, to guard their rear. With a whisper that could have come from the encroaching storm Terry, Mun, and Seve enter the compound.

The Magician wants the colonel alive; the unit is instructed to slaughter everyone else. Terry feels at his back the first gust of a wind wet with the deathlike stench of the fetid jungle. They steal from hut to hut, slaughtering as they go. It is hard to know which of them kills with more efficiency or quiet skill. It is hard to imagine how circumstance could fashion from human beings such implacable assassins. What twisted will is at work to multiply death at such an appalling rate?

In order to do his work Terry has already turned blind eyes upon the life around him. He thinks, not unkindly, of Oedipus the King, the blood from his ruined eyes running out of him, taking with it his sins as well as his passions.

One must, Terry thinks, be passionate in order to live, and that in turns brings thoughts of taciturn Trangh, crouching alone in the darkness, who seems to have been born without any desire at all. He seems, instead, to be an image in a mirror who, when you are not looking at him, disappears. He was born for the war. When, finally, it is over, Terry wonders, what will become of him? Will he rise up one day against the Magician or those like him and destroy them? Will he finally come to understand the consequences of what has been thrust upon him? Above all, can he be saved from himself?

He crowds his mind with these and other like thoughts as he busily goes about his grisly labors. Through such elasticity does he remain sane in the midst of utter madness.

Virgil, when they find him, has dragged the North Vietnamese colonel into the center of the compound. He kneels amid the heads of his men. The Magician speaks to the colonel directly, spurning Chey's help in translation.

"Where is COSVN?" he says.

The colonel, expressionless, stares into Virgil's face.

"You know, and you will tell us."

The colonel is unmoved.

Virgil has Jawbone and Chey hoist one of the cadre's mortars. He orders them to place it next to the colonel. He loads it himself so that the colonel can see what is happening. Then he grabs the colonel by his hair, slams his head against the open end of the weapon. One of the colonel's eyes is pressed painfully inside the muzzle of the mortar.

"What will you do now, send me into the clouds?" the colonel intones as if in prayer. "It is of no matter. I am dead already."

Virgil pushes his head roughly away from the mortar. "Death isn't in the cards for you," he says. His hand searches for the hilt of his KA-BAR, but he is not wearing it and, instead, calls for Trangh to hand over his. When Trangh complies, Virgil says, "Life will be your punishment."

Without warning, he smashes the sole of his boot into the colonel's neck, tramps on it hard while he slashes through the uniform trousers at the crotch.

Terry, standing near them, sees Seve grip Dominic's arm as if he suspects his brother will leap to stop Virgil. They exchange glances, and Terry can hear Dominic whisper, "God forgive us all." And he thinks, Isn't God supposed to be dead? Isn't this evidence enough that, if he once existed, he does not now?

The colonel screams more from what is being done to him than from the pain. At least initially, the flesh is self-anesthetized by the trauma.

When he is finished, Virgil takes his foot off the colonel's neck.

The colonel immediately rolls up into a fetal ball, his hands clutched between his thighs.

"Now," the Magician says, squatting down, "where is COSVN hiding?"

"I want to die." The colonel's teeth are chattering.

"No, no," Virgil says. "I told you. A long life is in store for you. That's what I want. You will have so much time to remember what it was like to be a man." His knife crosses the air above the colonel's eyes. "COSVN."

The colonel stares at Virgil from bloodshot eyes. "Will you kill me," he asks, "if I tell you?"

The Magician smiles.

When the colonel has divulged his information, when he is lying headless among his dead men, Virgil rises, saying, "All these heads are the same, eh? So much for power and authority."

According to the colonel's intelligence, they are less than five hours' march from COSVN HQ. "If we start now," Virgil says, "we can make it just before dawn."

They collect Trangh and, with Chey on point, melt into the tangle of the jungle. They are still in the high hill country close to the frontier. Often, the dense foliage gives way to massive gray rock, cracked and split as if with massive lightning bolts or heavy artillery fire. They see much evidence of concentrated bombing and, here and there, the remnants of concrete bunkers, the home of a shadow army.

Chey asks to be relieved from point, and Jawbone has taken his place. The unit winds down through increasingly stony ground. Now mountainous crags rise up on either side of them, making the going even more difficult. The Magician sends Jawbone out of recon. When he returns, there is some discussion about whether to take a looping detour around the rock formation or just head straight on. Chey reckons the detour will add at least two hours to their trek. This would ensure their arrival at COSVN HQ well after dawn, which would necessitate losing an entire day waiting for dark. Chey recommends they head into the rocky defile ahead, and Virgil agrees.

It is so wet the foliage drips moisture as if it were rain. Their feet hurt and everything chafes. Terry wonders whether he will ever be dry again.

They head into the defile, cautious and tense. Terry is uneasy. It is far more narrow than he had imagined. As in a stadium, their position is overhung by tiers of rock galleries, perfect as a perch for snipers. He can see Jawbone up ahead, alert for the same possibility.

One moment Jawbone is there, the next he is gone in a violent explosion. At the same instant automatic rifle fire begins to ricochet through the defile.

From his position, pressed against the rocky ground, Terry can see what is left of Jawbone; it is not much. "God*damn* it," he says.

The unit is helpless, pinned down by the murderous fire. No one, as far as he can tell, has been hit by the erratic automatic fire. But, on the other hand, they cannot move and, logically, it is only a matter of time before they are overrun.

He is closest to Seve, and he signals him now. Together, they squirm their way back behind a pair of boulders. From there, Terry can see that they can make their way up toward where the snipers lie, hidden from them.

Scrambling up the rocky scree, Terry finds himself wishing that Jawbone was there to tell him one of his stories. He does not yet want to think about never hearing them again.

Gradually, they ascend the difficult rock face. Seve puts his mouth against Terry's ear. Even so, the barking of the automatic fire makes it difficult to hear. "Dom thinks that God has abandoned this place. What do you think?"

"If God is life," Terry says, "then certainly he's got no business being here." He points. Up ahead they can see the North Vietnamese snipers at work. Terry pulls the pin of a grenade, lofts it softly so that it bounces at their feet.

They duck down just before the explosion rips through the rock overhang. With a roar, debris crashes into the defile. But now, in their lofty position, they can see reinforcements on the move.

"Let's get out of here," Terry says.

The descent is easier and a good deal faster. Virgil and the rest of the SLAM unit have broken cover, mopping up. Terry tells Virgil what he's seen.

"Shit," the Magician says, "an ambush for sure. The fuckers were waiting for us."

"There's no time for that now," Terry says. "We're not set up for this kind of encounter. Let's split."

But Virgil stands his ground. "An ambush means someone knew we were in the vicinity. No one knew where we were headed beforehand." He looks around. "That leaves only the unit."

"One of us?" Dominic says. "Come on."

The Magician turns to Seve, says, "Okay, Detective, let's see how good your powers of deductive reasoning are. Who's the traitor?"

"You're not serious," Dominic says. He turns to his brother. "Seve, you're not going to play this insane game with him?"

"Who is it, Detective?" Virgil says. "You haven't got much time."

"Who was on point duty through all of this?" Seve says. "Who was on recon, out of our sight much of the time? Who asked for relief just before we got to the defile?"

With an inarticulate cry Virgil grabs Chey by his shirtfront. He spits in Chey's face, then hits him with the stock of his AK-47.

Chey, gray-faced, collapses at his feet.

"For God's sake," Dominic says, "this is no time for revenge."

"He's right," Terry says. "Charlie's coming, and in a big way. Leave it for—"

"There's pieces of Jawbone stuck all over the rocks here," Virgil says, "and this traitor's gonna pay."

"Okay," Terry says reasonably, "but let's do it somewhere else, after we've lost Charlie."

The Magician looks at him and shakes his head. "No," he says. "You still don't get it, Butcher. Charlie's got to know we're smarter than that. Charlie's gonna know we're not gonna be suckered."

He rips off a short burst which, at such close range, almost tears Chey in two. Then he uses his knife to sever the head. He has Mun take up one of the snipers' rifles that has cascaded into the defile from the grenade blast. He sticks it barrel down in the soft earth at the center of the defile. Then he carefully attaches Chey's dripping head to the end of the stock.

"Now they'll know," he says. "Now they'll see."

He leads what's left of the unit back out of the defile, the way they came.

He claps Seve on the shoulder. "You did a good job back there," he says. "You'll be a real detective yet."

"What about COSVN HQ?" Terry asks.

"Fuck 'em," Virgil says. "We've done what we can. They know we're here now, they're already on the move, and I won't jeopardize the rest of the unit."

"You mean the mission, don't you?"

"It's the same thing," Virgil tells him.

The next day they come down from the highlands near the border into flatter, marshy terrain. They move through rice paddies, through the stands of small, shrunken trees, because it is safer there than the roads, which are higher, more exposed. The paddies are barely passable, at that stage that comes each year at the beginning of the rainy season when the monsoons are not yet at their height. The water is high, but not yet flooding the low fields.

Insects swarm in the blistering heat, greedily feeding on the salt sweat. The atmosphere is leaden, with a kind of uncomfortable electric charge that stems from the rumble of distant thunder in the west. They are southwest of Kratie, not far from the Kompong Cham flatlands that extend past the Mekong. The river will be a great challenge for them because of the traffic to and from Prey Veng and Pnompenh.

"Angkor," Terry says to Virgil as they walk. "If that is our destination, we should have been airlifted to the Thai border. From Aranyaprathet it's only a short hike."

"Couldn't," Virgil says. "Our cover story is that we're after COSVN HQ. That's the rationale for getting across the border into Cambodia. It's illegal but that's Nixon's headache now, he gave the okay."

"You haven't even told me what we're doing here."

The Magician smiles. "Well, you don't care, do you, Butcher? You have your own agenda fixed in your mind."

"I don't know what you mean."

"I mean that you're the most amoral sonuvabitch I ever hope to meet. Now me, I know what the law is, and I spend my time circumventing it. I've made it my life's work, in fact. That's okay, 'cause the law's meant for little people. It's good for that; keeps 'em in line. But it just hampers me, so I find ways to subvert it.

"You, on the other hand, haven't a clue as to what the law is. For you it has no meaning. Think of it as a magnet. Now, most people have a polarity, positive or negative, and by that are either drawn toward or repulsed by it. You exist outside the law, totally divorced from it. You, buddy, have no polarity at all."

It occurs to Terry, like a bolt from heaven, that Virgil envies him this. Terry has not thought that Virgil knows what envy is.

It also occurs to him that the Magician still hasn't told him what the SLAM unit's mission is in Angkor Wat. It seems, at first glance, a long way from the war. But then he recalls Virgil telling him that now the war is about Cambodia. Nixon and Kissinger know it, maybe General Abrams does, too, although from what the Magician says that may not be the case.

By the time they near the Mekong, they have already moved away from the low paddy country and have returned to the jungles with which they are more familiar. But now there are other nocturnal predators. This is tiger country.

Their world, brown green, stiflingly dense, seems small, remote, encysted like a pearl within the nacreous body of some terrible beast. They are alone, apart from the rest of humanity, four days and four nights in the hinterlands which, as Dom said, God has already abandoned.

Terry feels the weight of the wilderness through which they trek. Beyond the heat and the humidity there is an oppressiveness that is debilitating. He becomes an orphan, without family or even a modicum of comfort the memory of them can bring. It is as if this place of destruction, this living hell, is not content merely to be, but must, like a vampire, suck the life from him.

Dense growth borders the river. They turn north, paralleling its snaking path until they come upon a creaking pier. Several small boats are tied up, but there seems to be no one around.

They do a thorough recon, then take possession of the boats. They are seven minutes on the river. They dock on the far shore and continue their trek.

They are now no more than three days from Angkor, and Virgil becomes increasingly anxious to avoid any contact with hostile forces. They pass several North Vietnamese and Khmer convoys, but accordingly steer well clear of them.

In the jungle once again. The moon has waned, the monsoon is closer. It gets wetter and wetter, until it seems to be raining all the time. There is no ambient light whatsoever.

Once, Terry hears a growl. He stops them as he listens for the beast lurking somewhere in the maze of the jungle. He scents it first and, confident that they are downwind of the tiger, beckons them on.

While the rest of the unit sleeps, Terry and Virgil talk. "You think any more about the problem?" Virgil asks him.

"Which problem? Staying alive or staying sane?"

"Very funny. I mean regarding the Frenchman, and his Asians."

Terry chews meditatively on a salt tablet. "Maybe one or two things occurred to me. But you haven't given me enough information."

"Don't give me that. You know all there is to know about the Vietnamese."

Terry shrugs. "I doubt that. But, in any case, it's the Frenchman I'm talking about. What's he like?"

"What's it matter?"

"Because, however he forms his strategy will affect his men's thinking and, therefore, their actions."

The Magician looks at him. "I'm an idiot for underestimating you, Butcher." He nods, as if reconfirming his decision. "Okay. The story on the Frenchman is he's so radical that even his own people back in his own country have trouble with him. Many have protested having anything to do with him. He's something of a pariah. But, oddly enough, a powerful one. They ship him over here, periodically, where he's created a real problem."

"How so?"

Virgil grunts. "He's in his element." He takes a swig of water from a canteen. "You've heard of the Khmer Rouge?"

"Thugs, aren't they? Bandits, criminals, and murderers who have been driven out of the cities."

Virgil shrugs. "Yes and no. I guess that's how they started out. But no more. The Frenchman has radicalized them, given them a political purpose, a secure place in the universe from which to safely wreak their destruction while claiming legitimacy. Now they are the left-wing *maquis*, Sihanouk's opposition, the self-proclaimed freedom fighters of Çambodia.

"Or, to put it more accurately, the Frenchman has done this with their leader, one Saloth Sar. He's a dog you don't want to meet with, alone or unarmed."

"The Frenchman or Saloth Sar?"

The Magician laughs. "I was speaking of Saloth Sar, but now that you mention it, it holds for the both of them. They're both highly dangerous. The Frenchman is by far the more intelligent; he's brilliant, in fact. Look what he's created here in these stinking jungles. He has fashioned political power out of shit. But, on the other hand, Saloth Sar has a kind of animal cunning that's truly frightening."

Terry has a faraway look in his eyes. "So I would assume that the Frenchman's people are Khmer Rouge."

"Yeah."

"What's he got that you want so badly?"

"You know what they call it here in the seventh ring of hell?" Virgil says. "The tears of the poppy."

For a long time Terry does nothing but stare into the misty distance. At last he says, "What does the Frenchman want with opium?"

"Not opium. Heroin." Virgil cracks open a melon, begins to carve out conical sections with the tip of his combat knife. "I told you that the Frenchman is brilliant. He's made contacts with the Burmese, so Mun tells me. Through them he has gained control of a network through which he is supplying our guys with smack."

"That's a novel way to kill us."

"Novel," Virgil says, popping a piece of melon into his mouth, "and radical."

Around them the humid day lumbers on like a wounded pachyderm. The incessant dripping of the foliage is a companion who has outstayed his welcome. The two men finish the melon, and Virgil discards the rind.

"You want that network," Terry says. "Is that it?"

"Boiling down all the imponderables, yes."

Terry looks at the Magician. "You've lied to me," he says. "All along you were operating with a false face." There is no rancor in his voice, only a kind of awe. "You aren't Special Forces. This isn't a Daniel Boone operation. Michael Eiland has no idea we're here, let alone having planned this little expedition."

Virgil shrugs, silent.

"Drug trafficking is not part of Special Forces MO. It's not in the plans of *any* branch of the military service I'm familiar with." Like a mountain climber, he is searching the Magician's face for footholds with which to understand the nature of this ascent. "Who *do* you work for, Virgil?"

The stench of rotting vegetation is so strong it seems to coat the insides of the nostrils, the back of the throat with a vulgar film. Eating becomes a chore, rather than a necessity.

"It doesn't really matter."

"But smack matters, Virgil. At least to me it does. It's evil shit."

"I agree. You should be happy to be a part of this mission. You want to know why?"

"What I want to know," Terry says tightly, "is what you're going to do with the network once you get it from the Frenchman."

Virgil puts his head back against the bole of a tree. "You should have been a chess player, Butcher, you know that? I never met anybody who thinks so many moves ahead."

"Answer the question."

"Okay. We're gonna take control of the heroin pipeline and turn it back on itself. We're gonna let the communists consume all that evil smack.''

Terry is quiet for so long that Virgil becomes fidgety. ''I can hear the gears grinding. What're you thinking now?''

''I'm thinking how much money there is in selling that shit.''

''So?''

''So where're the profits going?''

The Magician wiped his hands on his trousers. ''You know your problem? You ask too many questions.''

''I don't want any part of this,'' Terry says.

''What?''

''You heard me. Maybe I believe half of what you told me, maybe I don't believe any of it. Either way it doesn't really matter. I want out.''

Virgil's face gets hard. ''Listen, buddy, when you signed on, you did it for the whole course. There's no midway here.''

''I'm getting the hell out of here.''

The Magician shrugs. ''You want a bullet in your back?''

''Who's gonna shoot me? You? In front of the unit?''

''You ever hear of desertion in wartime, Butcher? You know what the penalty is?''

''You ever hear of a court-martial? Everything will come out before a judicial board. This operation is so top secret you couldn't afford that.''

''True,'' Virgil says. ''But it'll never get that far. Out here in the wilderness, I'm God, Butcher. I hold the power of life or death, and no one in this unit is about to dispute that.'' He grins. ''Seems to me you got no choice. Unless, that is, you got a death wish.''

Terry knows that the Magician is right, but he also believes that he has found a third option that will allow him to live with himself. ''Okay,'' he says. ''You want me in, I'm in. But I'm in all the way. We're partners, Virgil, now and forever. Whatever you're into, you'd better make sure I'm part of, 'cause I'm gonna be the overseer of this pipeline. I'm gonna make sure you've told me the truth; I'm gonna see that no one starts fooling with the profits.''

The Magician stares at him. ''You're serious, you fucker.''

''Dead serious.'' His gaze has moved above the Magician's head. ''Speaking of dead,'' he says in a low voice, ''don't move.''

''What is it?''

''A Hanuman,'' Terry says, his eyes on the small leaf-green snake. ''It's right above your head.'' Its eyes are a bright, primary yellow, broken only by the black vertical slash of the ophidian iris.

"Kill it." Is there a tremor of fear in Virgil's voice? "I've heard stories."

"So have I," Terry says. "Mun says it's supposed to be able to fly, to leap like a monkey, which is why it's named after the fierce monkey god, Hanuman."

"Don't give me a lesson in Khmer lore. Kill it, goddamn you. I fucking hate snakes."

"Slowly, slowly," Terry says. His hand grips the hilt of his combat knife. Out of its sheath, it hangs in front of Virgil's face, light gleaming off it as from a lantern.

All at once it disappears. Virgil hears a *thwack!*—a quick, interrupted hiss. Then, two halves of the Hanuman drop into his lap.

He gives a yelp, springing up. He tramps the creature into the muddy earth where he had been sitting.

"Give it a rest," Terry says. "It's dead."

The Hanuman buried, Virgil takes a deep breath. "Fucking A it's dead." He looks into Terry's face. "You'll help me with the Frenchman's *maquis*? Those fucking Khmer Rouge are inhuman bastards."

"I'll help you till the end of time," Terry says, sheathing his knife, "as long as you're straight with me."

"Deal." Virgil sticks out his hand.

Terry looks at it and, as Virgil did with the North Vietnamese colonel, smiles.

Vishnu, the god, grows out of the jungle. The face is stone, it is faith; it is time itself. Towering upward into the trees, it resonates with a sense of cosmic history.

Trailing vines crown his noble head, curling downward past his all-seeing eyes, his cracked and chipped nose, his thick, lichen-encrusted lips.

"Angkor Wat," the Magician says.

The SLAM unit stands, transfixed. Their exhaustion, born both of physical effort and of fear, dissipates before the Hindu god of the macrocosm. Protean silk cotton and fig trees, as tall as modern buildings, as thickly veined as a weight lifter's biceps, thrust upward from a veritable avalanche of foliage that has advanced upon the mystic city like an avenging army.

Temple walls centuries old are split like a boxer's lip by the voracious roots of trees that have grown atop the stone structures from seedlings carried in the dung of overflying birds.

The jungle is inimical, growing with a celerity unheard of in other parts of the world. It has ripped through Angkor more effectively than machine-gun fire or bombings, devastating the city of temples. Angkor has survived conquests in the fifth century by the Chams, and the twelfth century by the Siamese, but neglect is another story.

The head stands guard beside a *baray*, a kind of reservoir which, along with a network of curved dikes, was built above ground level. In this way the ancient Khmer could even in dry seasons deliver water to their crops, thus reaping several harvests a year instead of one.

In undertaking a monumental project such as Angkor, the Khmer were obliged to incorporate *baray*, canals and irrigation moats, so that the land surrounding this home of the ancient gods would always be fertile and productive.

Angkor, built by King Suryavarman II in the tenth century, is a paradigm of the Khmer universe. The Khmer people, it is said, were so seductively beautiful that many Indian traders arriving in the first century A.D. stayed and were assimilated into the culture. So it is not surprising to see monuments dedicated to the Hindu gods Vishnu, Brahma, and Siva, as well as to Buddha. Accordingly, Sanskrit and Pali inscriptions mingle here in the crucible of a civilization.

But even this powerful pantheon of gods failed to protect their holy temples from invasion, and they, too, passed into dust.

Now, it seems, only the heart of a soulless machine beats here. This is Khmer Rouge territory, and the gods of all religions have, in the absence of execution, been banished. Only their awesome images remain, mute reminders of the monumental changes that have been wrought here over time.

As they approach, the sky seems black and so close it is almost oppressive. Then they see that the darkness is caused not by the storm, but by clouds of bats who have roosted inside the deserted temples.

Heading east, they pass through the main entrance. All the temple entrances save this one face east because west is the direction in which the dead walk. The ancient Khmer constructed Angkor so that coming upon it is akin to approaching life, to being born.

The vast plazas, flanked by bas-relief- and inscription-encrusted walls, are eerily deserted. The rain falls on Angkor with an uncaring persistence. The SLAM unit, in the center of it all, moves cautiously on.

"They're here somewhere, Butcher," Virgil says, "watching and waiting."

"The Khmer Rouge could kill us now, a minute from now, or an hour from now," Terry says, "Why won't they?"

" 'Cause the Frenchman wants what I can offer him."

"Which is?"

The Magician grins. "The deal's already been struck. You're here to ensure that no one decides to double-cross me."

"You mean us, don't you?" Terry says.

Virgil looks at him. "If I were you, I wouldn't be so anxious to go where angels fear to tread."

Terry shrugs. "I'm already here," he says. "What have I left to lose?"

They meet the Frenchman in the Gallery of Creation. It is now roofless. Its major wall, one hundred and sixty feet long, is covered with a bas relief depicting the Hindu myth bringing about the creation of man. Four-armed Vishnu stands at the center balancing, on the right, the half-monkey Hanuman, commanding the gods of light and, on the left, twenty-one-headed Ravana, chief of the demons of hell. Linking them is the great serpent, who, by their opposing efforts, is milked of the magical elixir that will create the world of man.

All this is explained to them by Mun. Gradually, as the myth is spun out, Terry gravitates toward the image of Ravana. The demon's arms are around the five-headed serpent. Around his head small figures dance. Are these, he wonders, the demons of the *Muy Puan*'s thousand hells?

Now that he is here, now that he has come upon Vishnu, Brahma, Buddha, Hanuman, and especially Ravana, he is caught in the web of their myth. Angkor, sitting for centuries in the Cambodian jungles, has not died. As the Theravadan Buddhists know, their gods go through cycles of rule, destruction, and rebirth. In this, they are more closely linked to man than the deities of any other culture.

Here in Angkor, the center of the universe, it seems as if these mighty forces are merely asleep, dreaming of the age that soon will return them to power.

"Inspiring, eh?"

They turn to see a tall man who looks very much like Charles de Gaulle. He is surrounded by men in black pajamas. They are heavily armed. The Khmer Rouge.

"It is all lost now in time." The Frenchman spreads his arms wide. "All forgotten." He is speaking English, no doubt for the benefit of the American unit. "Even by these men." He indicates his bodyguards. "*Especially* by them. I have trained them not only to forget, but to destroy those who wish to remember and keep this alive. I have taught them to revile the decadence of their past, the subjugation they endured at imperialism's callous hand. I have freed them."

No, Terry thinks, you have merely fooled them into exchanging one set of masters for another. It is a painful lesson that man resists learning. Man yearns only for power, and is therefore easily snared by those who promise freedom.

Terry feels an eerie shudder. It is as if he has come upon Satan in the wilderness. Satan who speaks as if he is the friend of man, and is, accordingly, his relentless enemy.

The tall man advances toward them, his hand outstretched. "They call me the Frenchman," he says, pumping first Virgil's hand, then Terry's, "but my name is Vosges."

The Magician introduces himself. "This is Butcher," he says. The rest of the SLAM unit remains anonymous. They stand on one side, as M. Vosges's Khmer Rouge are arrayed on the other. In between, the three principals, enfolded by Vishnu's powerful arms.

"Can we go somewhere," the Magician says, "a bit more private?"

M. Vosges laughs. "My dear sir, what could be more private than Angkor Wat? Who would dare be here besides us?"

"I was thinking of the witnesses," Virgil says. "Yours and mine."

"Ah, but of course." The Frenchman speaks to his contingent of soldiers. He is quite relaxed, jovial even. It makes Terry nervous enough so that as they reach the entrance to a smaller, covered building across the plaza, he excuses himself.

M. Vosges is about to protest, but Terry says, "I got to shit. Sorry. A touch of dysentery."

Virgil takes the Frenchman by the elbow and, together, they disappear into the shadows of the temple entrance.

Terry, keeping the stone walls at his back, circles around until he catches Mun's eye. Mun detaches himself from the rest of the SLAM unit.

"What do you make of these bastards?" he asks, indicating the Khmer Rouge.

"I don't trust them," Mun says immediately. "No one does. Their leader, Saloth Sar, is a dangerous radical. He is not stupid. Far from it. He studied in France, and was a prize pupil there."

"Do you believe they will attack us?"

Mun looks at him with a calculating eye. "What is happening?"

"I don't know," Terry says. "Yet." Only a half lie. "But I've got to find out what their orders are."

"Why don't you ask the Frenchman?" Mun says wryly.

Terry grunts. "I don't speak Khmer well enough," he says. "I won't know if they're lying."

"I am pleased to be of service."

"I will be happy to compensate you."

"That will not be necessary."

"Nevertheless . . ."

Mun grins. "Okay. I want in on whatever is happening here."

Terry is thinking of Virgil having a fit. "After you lead me to where you buried the Forest of Swords."

"Certainly. It is yours."

"Let's go."

As they make their way toward the Khmer Rouge, Mun says, "Listen, the most important thing to know about these bastards is that rank is all-important. Even in a relatively small cadre such as this, the hierarchy is strictly defined."

Terry nods, grateful for the knowledge. "Get me talking with their leader," he tells Mun.

There is no problem in approaching the cadre. The Khmer Rouge are confident here, even expansive. It pleases them that their territory encompasses Angkor, humbled home of their decadent forebears.

Mun speaks to the cadre for a moment. "This is Keo," he tells Terry, indicating a blank-faced individual. He introduces Terry to the Khmer Rouge commander as "the Butcher." Keo gives Terry a wide grin, clacks his teeth together. He holds out a string of human ears, proof of his prowess.

"Charming," Terry says under his breath.

"This man is very powerful," Mun says. "He is the equivalent of a colonel." Keo is talking, and Mun says, "He wants to see proof of your status. He won't talk to you otherwise."

"He wants to see power?" Terry grabs hold of Mun's shirtfront, jerks him forward. "Get down on your knees."

"What?"

Terry hooks his heel behind Mun's, kicks out. Mun stumbles, starts to go down. "Do as I say!" Terry shouts in English loud enough so that Keo grins.

Terry takes out his sidearm, presses the muzzle against the side of Mun's head with such force that the Khmer's neck is bent in a painful arc.

"Now tell him that if he gives the order, I'll blow your brains out."

"You're crazy."

Terry sees with satisfaction that Mun his shaking. He sees that Keo has noticed it, too.

"Tell him!"

Mun translates, and Keo gives Terry a long, hard look. He crouches down beside Mun and stares him squarely in the eye. He is drinking in the situation with the greed of a glutton. For a long time only the screeching of unseen creatures in the jungle can be heard. Then he reaches out, lifts a bead of sweat off Mun's skin.

Nodding to himself, he stands up, says something. "He says as a good commander he cannot condone the execution of an obedient soldier." Mun's voice has regained some of its strength.

Terry holsters his pistol, watches Keo's face as Mun gets up off his knees. He avoids looking at Mun. "Now," he says, "tell him that I appreciate his decision. We are two soldiers who understand the meaning of war."

As Mun is translating, Terry says, "I wonder what a colonel is doing commanding such a small cadre."

"It is a sign of the Frenchman's status," Mun says.

Maybe, Terry thinks. He continues to watch Keo's expressionless face, but he knows that the Khmer Rouge will never willingly tell them the truth. Power, Terry suddenly realizes, is coveted only by those without it. Like Keo. He is only, perhaps, a bandit, elevated by notions of revolution. He is, Terry can see, bewildered by the ramifications of power, and always will be. This is what makes him truly dangerous. It is an ominous sign for Cambodia that its future may be in the hands of such people.

Looking at this criminal, Terry wonders how anyone can believe in revolution. Those ideals are for fools and dreamers. Here is the reality: the unpleasant and frightening future.

"You are strong, indeed," Terry says, addressing the Khmer Rouge colonel, "but I wonder whether it is illusory. Have you the numbers, I wonder, to stand against Sihanouk."

At the mention of the prince's name Keo hawks and spits to show his contempt. "Sihanouk is a dead man," he says. "Justice dictates that he—and all the decadent so-called intellectuals who have for decades bled the peasants dry—must pay for their sins."

Terry shrugs away Keo's bluster. "Sihanouk still rules Cambodia. He commands the army, which can snuff you out."

Keo's face twists. Like all revolutionaries, he is ruled by cant and rigid ideology. "Foolish talk," he says. "The Khmer Rouge is stronger than even Sihanouk believes. We have many, many willing to take up the cause of revolution."

"You're wrong. Sihanouk will swat you down when it serves his purpose."

"My men," Keo says with a sweeping gesture, "are all around you. Do you believe I came here with just this cadre?" He laughs harshly. "Do not mock what you cannot see. M. Vosges is smarter than—"

Terry smashes the butt end of his pistol into Keo's mouth, shattering the front teeth. Then he jams the muzzle between his lips. He looks into the Khmer Rouge's stunned face, forcing himself to ignore the weapons leveled at him.

"Tell your men to put down their weapons. If they don't do it within fifteen seconds, I'm going to pull the trigger."

"Do you think my death will stop them?" It is difficult for Mun to understand him with his mouth full.

Terry's grip tightens, and Keo's eyes open wide. He can see the look on Terry's face; he has seen what Terry was willing to do with one of his own men. He gives the order.

Terry orders the SLAM unit to confiscate the Khmer Rouge's weapons. "Kill them all," he tells Seve, "if they move or make any sound at all. I don't want them speaking to one another. And, for Christ's sake, get them out of sight. There are more of them hidden just beyond the city complex."

Mun stares up at him. "What would you have done," he says, "if this son of a bitch told you to pull the trigger?"

"I would have pulled it." Terry grins at the look on Mun's face. "But the gun would have been in his face."

Then he takes Keo by the hair and shoves him across the stone plaza to the temple into which Virgil and the Frenchman disappeared.

They move through a gallery in which the roofing stones have collapsed. Now the jungle, in the form of vines, moss, and vegetation, has intruded. Here and there Terry can see added support columns, signs of restoration that began in the early 1960s.

He allows Virgil's voice to guide him. The two men are standing in the central sanctuary. The place is overrun by roaches as big as his thumb that have flown in out of the jungle. Their constant movement appears to make the walls ripple.

Virgil looks up when Terry enters, and an unspoken message passes between them. Then Terry shoves Keo into the center of the sanctuary. His mouth is bleeding heavily.

"What is the meaning of this?" M. Vosges demands.

Terry ignores him. "There is a larger contingent of Khmer Rouge commanded by this colonel waiting in the jungle where we can't see them."

The Magician turns to M. Vosges. "Our deal was to be a simple one," he says, slowly and carefully. "We terminate Prince Sihanouk and, in return, you hand over to us your heroin, contacts, pipeline, the works." He cocked his head. "Now what do we have here?"

"I don't know—"

Virgil takes out his combat knife and slits Keo's throat. He looks at the Frenchman, and says, "Well, now you *do* know."

"Christ."

"You're alone here with us, M. Vosges," Virgil says. "We have neutralized your company." He waggles the knife. "I could just as easily slit *your* throat next." The Frenchman takes an involuntary step backward. "But then neither of us would get what he wants. The deal still stands, with the proviso now that you guide us out of here, and accompany us back to Vietnam." He steps up to M. Vosges, places the flat of the blade against his cheek, and draws it down, leaving Keo's blood like stigmata. "It's up to you."

The Frenchman nods.

"But can we trust you, M. Vosges?" Virgil shakes his head. "You've already demonstrated your treachery."

"Killing you was certainly not my idea," M. Vosges says with some indignation. "It was the Khmer Rouge's plan to ambush you. I had no knowledge of the additional forces, and would not have condoned their presence if I had."

"Don't the Khmer Rouge take their orders from you?"

"They take their orders from Saloth Sar," M. Vosges says. "The political imperative of Sihanouk's demise now is, perhaps, lost on them. They believe that they already possess enough power to challenge him. They do not see that the climate is not yet ripe for their ascension. I cannot risk their moving too early, and being destroyed. You have my word that the deal stands."

Outside, Terry pulls Virgil aside. "What is this crap about assassinating a head of state?"

"Can it," Virgil says. "It's none of your business."

"Have you forgotten that I'm in—all the way. I just saved all our lives."

Virgil stares at him. "It is no longer politically expedient for Prince Sihanouk to remain in power. His dubious policies have become a liability."

"To whom?"

"To the U. S. of A., buddy. Who else?"

"What are you giving me? America doesn't murder the leader of a country just because—"

"Haven't you heard," Virgil says with a terrible grin on his face, "there's a war on?"

"I thought you were pro-Sihanouk."

"You still don't get it, Butcher, do you? What I think doesn't matter. I have my orders."

"You hate being a soldier," Terry says.

The Magician is laughing. "I haven't been a soldier in a good many years. I'm what you might call a knight errant."

"Call it what you want," Terry says. "It still stinks. I don't want any part of it."

"You ain't got no choice now," the Magician says. "You wanted in all the way, and that's what you got." He brandishes the bloody knife, twisting the blade until it catches the light. "Here's your alternative."

Terry watching him turn away and, with the Frenchman in tow, take command of the SLAM unit. Terry thinking, What in God's name have I bought into?

PART III

THE NATURE OF EVIL

SPRING, PRESENT

NICE/PARIS/NEW YORK/ EAST BAY BRIDGE/SHAN STATE

When Seve heard the tiny scrape of the key in the lock, he froze. By then he had about had it.

At the Negresco, where he had discovered that Christopher Haye's reservation had been canceled by a phone call from a Frenchwoman, he had been so self-conscious about the welt across his neck, he had been forced to buy a woman's scarf which he had turned into a bandanna.

He had spent a diabolically painful night observing the entrance to Soutane Sirik's home, 67, Boulevard Victor Hugo, scrunched in the front seat of his French rental car, a subcompact which, at the current rates, was all he could afford.

His neck pains were worse and, to top it all off, he had forgotten his pills in the rest room of the plane. By the time dawn had arrived he had felt like he had been swallowed by a snake.

That was when, coming back from his call to Diana, he had said, Fuck it, and had sought entrance into Soutane's apartment. This was one of the things he did very well, picking a lock without scratching the bolt plate, relocking the door when he was on the inside so that no one would know anything had happened. When he was finished, he usually went out a window, but he could also relock the door from the outside. He rarely did it that way because there was more chance of being seen by a neighbor either passing or snooping.

In any event Seve was inside the apartment on the Boulevard Victor Hugo when Chris and Soutane arrived from Tourrette.

They were so drained from their ordeal with M. Mabuse that they stood in the doorway, mute, staring at him.

Chris finally had the presence of mind to say, "I'm getting the cops."

"Don't bother," Seve said in English. He recognized enough of the French. "I *am* a cop."

"Let's see some ID." Chris heard Soutane close and lock the door behind them. He stared down at Seve's shield. "What's a New York cop doing here? France is a little out of your jurisdiction, isn't it?"

By this time Soutane had taken a closer look at Seve. "What happened to your throat?" she said.

Seve put a hand up to the welt. He had taken off the bandanna because it was irritating the inflamed skin. "Some sonuvabitch I knew in 'Nam doesn't seem to like me very much."

"It looks like he tried to kill you," Soutane said, thinking of how Terry had died.

"Yeah. He did his best. Are you Soutane Sirik?"

Soutane nodded.

"You know a man named Al DeCordia?"

"What is this?" Chris interjected. "You break into Miss Sirik's apartment, you start an interrogation—"

"Spoken like a true attorney."

"How do you know I'm a lawyer?"

"I know a lot about you, Mr. Haye," Seve said.

"Listen—"

"It's all right." Soutane raised a hand. "Let him finish. I want to know about Al DeCordia."

Seve looked at her. "Then you *did* know him."

Soutane's face turned white. "What do you mean, did?"

"I'm afraid he's dead, Miss Sirik."

She gave a little shriek, and Chris held on to her.

"Who the hell is Al DeCordia?" he asked.

"How?" Soutane had regained her voice. "How did Al die?"

"He was murdered," Seve said. "By the same man who tried to kill me, by the man who murdered my brother, Dominic."

"Oh, no."

"They were both decapitated, Miss Sirik." He watched her as she slowly collapsed into Chris's embrace. It was time, he thought, to push a little further. "Is that how Terry Haye was killed?"

"That's enough now," Chris said. "What the hell are you talking about, Detective?"

Seve watched him sit her down on a couch. "Ask her, Mr. Haye," he said. "Has she told you yet how your brother died?"

Chris, kneeling beside her, looked from Seve to Soutane. "I—

he was murdered—no, I didn't think—'' He searched her face. "Soutane?"

When she spoke, her voice was soft and low. "I'm sorry. You didn't ask, and I saw no point in telling you. Terry was decapitated."

"Just like my brother and DeCordia." If there was any satisfaction in this, Seve could not find it.

Chris looked up at him. "What the hell is going on here?"

"That," Seve said, "is what I've flown six thousand miles to find out."

Milhaud and Mr. LoGrazie met again in the tiny two-tiered park at the foot of the Avenue Franklin Roosevelt. The day was not nearly so clement as it had been at their last rendezvous.

Mr. LoGrazie was staring at the speckled carp as they dozed in the filthy water. He was in the shadow of an enormous weeping willow. Beyond it, Roman columns rose up into the dense foliage.

"Time is running out," Mr. LoGrazie said in his characteristically abrupt manner as soon as Milhaud came up to him. "I need the Sirik woman to tell us where Terry Haye has hidden the Doorway into Night. When I am done with her, you will dispose of her—permanently."

So, Milhaud thought despairingly, my gamble did not pay off. I have gotten only a postponement of Soutane's death sentence.

It had begun to drizzle, and Milhaud pulled his collar up around his throat. He was still reeling from the way in which Mr. LoGrazie had deceived him. The CIA operative's Mafia cover was so good that it had convinced Milhaud's bloodhounds. That had been meticulous work—not like one of the CIA's usual slipshod ID backgrounds. But, Milhaud was coming to realize, nothing was usual about this situation. Not with the Magician masterminding it. He shivered a little at the thought. He had been ordered to kill Soutane, then been given what had seemed to be absolution, only to have it rescinded. Was this torture the Magician's doing? Did the Magician know who Milhaud was, and was he now tormenting him? That would be just like the Magician's idea of fun: malicious, sadistic punishment.

Mr. LoGrazie shifted from one foot to another, as if he had excess energy that he was unwilling to part with. "In addition," he said, "we have decided that her companion, Christopher Haye, must be dispensed with as well. It is logical to assume that she has told him whatever she knows."

"I'll do whatever has to be done, of course," Milhaud says. "But I feel constrained to remind you that the more we litter the road with dead bodies, the more we invite unwanted attention by a variety of law enforcement agencies."

"You leave that to us, all right?" Mr. LoGrazie said curtly. "Just concentrate on doing your job." He rubbed his hands together. The spring damp made Paris feel more like London. "We speak, you jump. I sincerely hope you haven't forgotten how it works."

"I haven't forgotten."

"Good." He blew on his hands.

"But—" Milhaud took a manila folder out of his coat pocket, handed it to Mr. LoGrazie.

"What's this?"

"Take a look," Milhaud said. He knew that he was being forced into taking ever more desperate measures. But that could not be helped now. The Magician was pulling the strings; he had no other choice.

When Mr. LoGrazie had slipped out the first of the black-and-white surveillance shots of the Magician, grainy from distance and lack of light, Milhaud said, "Obedience was for before, when the rules were clear-cut and I knew which side of the fence I was standing on."

Mr. LoGrazie stood stock still. It was impossible to tell if he was even breathing.

"Now everything has changed," Milhaud said. "Now we must begin all over again to forge a business relationship."

Mr. LoGrazie's face shut down. "This is none of your business." He was studying the surveillance photos of the Magician, one by one, as if in their fuzzy corners he could detect some clue as to their origin.

"Is that so? Tell me," Milhaud said, warming to the topic, "if, by your reckless orders, I get caught in an Interpol action, who will I turn to for help?" He could see the wheels turning behind the American's eyes.

"I told you. You have nothing to fear from Interpol."

"I know that the Mafia is powerful," Milhaud said. "But it is not that powerful. It does not control Interpol."

"So what?" Mr. LoGrazie said at last. He handed back the photos.

"So I want to know who you're really working for. Because right now I'm working for the same people, and I like to know who my employers are."

"Finding the Doorway to Night is your concern," Mr. LoGrazie said brusquely. "Getting us the Forest of Swords is your concern. Firing up Operation White Tiger is your concern. Nothing else."

"Perhaps I am not making myself clear, M. LoGrazie. I'm your expert on the Shan. I'm the only person on earth who can get you the *Prey Dauw*." He waved the photos in the air. "So who have you brought in, and why?"

Mr. LoGrazie glared at him so hard that for a moment Milhaud was afraid that he had given too much away. Then, because he had nothing to lose, he said boldly, "I'm afraid I can no longer help you if you keep me in the dark. And, after all, I do have the Forest of Swords. That is what he really wants, isn't it?"

Mr. LoGrazie was contemplating the pond from afar, and, when he spoke, his voice was as low as if it had come from that distance. "To tell you the truth, Milhaud, I don't know what he wants. His name is Virgil. At least that was the code name the CIA gave him in Vietnam. Some wit gave him the nickname the Magician. It fit. I'm sure you know him by one name or another. He is someone I had heard of, long ago, a legendary figure who, because he had disappeared, I had assumed was dead."

"The Magician?" Milhaud said, feigning astonishment. "Are you certain? I, too, had heard that he was dead."

"Let me assure you that he is very much alive. At first I was elated that he had been brought in. I would, after all, be working with a legend. But that was before I spent time with him. Now, to be truthful, I'm beginning to think that he is a madman."

Milhaud painted his most concerned look onto his face. "Why do you say that?" He was well aware of the difficult ground he was on. He must not, under any circumstances, give M. LoGrazie any hint that he had his residence under audio surveillance.

"Virgil—the Magician is obsessed with death. You raised good points in the matter of the Sirik woman. I made the same arguments. He would not listen. He says he has the full backing of the director in any and all initiatives. The Magician wants Soutane Sirik and Christopher Haye dead."

Mist was swirling, as substantial as dust. It turned the park around them into a ghostly facade filled with sinister shapes. M. LoGrazie ran a hand through his damp hair. "Milhaud, your path must have crossed the Magician's in Southeast Asia years ago. What is your assessment of him?"

"He was a man in love with risk taking," Milhaud said truthfully. He saw Mr. LoGrazie nod in assent. "Like you, I heard a great deal about him. Who knows how much of it was the truth? I had one direct dealing with him, so I know his face, which is more than you can say for most people who knew of his existence."

"As you saw, you won't recognize him now," Mr. LoGrazie said. "His own family, if he had any, wouldn't know him. He spent six months with a team of plastic surgeons. From what I gather, they broke his face apart, and put it back together in a whole new way."

"That may be," Milhaud said, "but they didn't touch his brain. Inside that new face he's the same person. And if that's the case, you have real cause for concern."

Mr. LoGrazie turned his back on the pond, which, at this distance, appeared as gray and opaque as the illusion of water on a model-railroad setup. "You are correct in another assessment. I am not Mafia. I am CIA. So is the Magician. He wants to leave the Company. He was coerced back into it by the director, and now it appears that he hates it. Who knows? Perhaps he always has. In any event he wants me to break with the CIA as well, to come along with him. I don't know what to do. It is suicide to join him. But I am afraid that the Magician will kill me if I refuse."

"What will you do?"

"I admit that I haven't any idea. But I don't have much time to make up my mind." Mr. LoGrazie's eyes were bleak.

"Report him."

Mr. LoGrazie's smile was a bit frightening in its lack of warmth. "You do not understand the high esteem in which the Company holds him. He would deny everything, and I would not be believed until it was far too late."

"Do you know what he plans?"

"Not yet." Mr. LoGrazie brushed drops of rain off his face. "He won't tell me until I've agreed to join him."

Milhaud's heartbeat picked up. Perhaps this was just the opening he had been praying for. A chance to squirm out of the vise the Magician had created for him, and to pay him back for the torment he was putting Milhaud through. "You know, he could be planning to kill you whether you join him or not." His mind was racing eight and nine moves ahead. He had to find out what the Magician was up to, and he thought that now he had found the way. "With that in mind, there is a third course you might consider," he said.

Mr. LoGrazie's head swung around. "What is it?" He spoke so

quickly that Milhaud actually felt sorry for him. He was clearly a drowning man.

"Pretend to go along with him. It would give you some breathing room and allow you time to prepare a report to your people that would surely condemn Virgil by his own actions rather than by your words, which might, as you say, be suspect."

Mr. LoGrazie nodded. "That could work. But I don't think I'd be able to do this alone. I'd need help."

"But, of course," Milhaud said, feeling the chains that had bound him in servitude ready to fall away. "You have me."

Mr. LoGrazie stuck out his hand. "If you're serious—"

"I am." Milhaud shook it.

"In that case you must take care of the Sirik woman and Christopher Haye immediately," Mr. LoGrazie said somewhat breathlessly. "We must satisfy him in this, as well as with the *Prey Dauw*."

"Leave it to me," Milhaud assured him.

"Yes?" He could see that it was sweat, not rain beading Mr. LoGrazie's face. "I have no wish to die."

"Al DeCordia," Soutane said over coffee and cake, "came over here recently, a month or so ago. He spent some time with Terry on business."

"Do you know what kind of business?" Seve asked. He was in heaven; he had never tasted such good coffee.

"No." Soutane stirred another spoon of sugar into her cup. They were sitting in the dining room. Bright sun streamed in. The windows were open to the street and, occasionally, the throaty *brrrt!* of the motorbikes passing below punctuated their conversation. "For better or worse, I never got involved in Terry's business. I think, now, that was a mistake."

Seve, seeing Chris's hand cover hers, said, "Go on, Soutane." It had not taken them long to get onto a first-name basis.

"Al was only supposed to be over here a week, but he stayed three. He liked it here—and we . . ." She broke off, staring down into her coffee.

Seve said nothing, giving her time to deal with an obviously highly emotional subject. But the silence went on so long that he decided to give her a nudge. He took a slip of paper out of his pocket, slid it across the table.

"Look at this," he said. "It's got your name and address. It's how I found you."

"How did you get it?" Soutane asked. She was staring at the word: *Saved?*

"Just before he was murdered, Al DeCordia came to see my brother. Dominic was the priest in DeCordia's parish in New Canaan, Connecticut. Apparently he was more concerned with your welfare than his own." Soutane was staring at him. "It's obvious from this that DeCordia wanted you saved. The question is, from what?"

Soutane cupped the paper in her hands as if it were a cherished photo. In a moment her fingers enclosed it entirely. She took a deep breath. "When Al arrived here," she said, "it was clear he was hurting. Perhaps I reminded him of his daughter, I don't know. She had just died in a car accident. That was horrible enough, but the autopsy said she had been mainlining heroin. She had hit up with some bad stuff."

She ran her hands through her hair. "Now I blame myself. I knew Al wanted out of his business, though I never suspected that his business could be drug running.

"I told Terry, and he got very excited. He and Al went off for an entire afternoon. I have no idea where. But after that Terry was different. Happier, as if he'd suddenly had a weight lifted from his back."

Soutane sighed. "If I'd been smart enough, I would have realized that the reason Al was so broken up was because that was the business he and Terry were in."

"Jesus, you're being too hard on yourself," Chris said. "How could you have guessed?"

"Wait a second," Seve interrupted. "Are you telling me that Terry Haye was mixed up in drug running?"

Soutane nodded.

"I don't believe it," Seve said. "I served with Terry in 'Nam. I knew him. It's impossible that he—"

"That's just what I told her," Chris said. "But there is mounting evidence that he and Soutane's cousin Mun—"

"Your cousin's name is Mun?" Seve said.

"Yes," Soutane said.

"Did he serve with Terry in the war?"

"Yes."

"Dear God." Seve ran his hand through his hair. "Everyone I ever knew in the SLAM unit has come back to haunt me." Briefly, he told them of the formation of the SLAM unit by Terry and Virgil, what they had been involved in.

When he mentioned Trangh's name, both Chris and Soutane jumped as if he had hit a live nerve. Chris told Seve of his encounters with the Vietnamese, including the background on the *Prey Dauw*.

"The attack in your New York apartment I already knew about," Seve said. "But this other information makes it clear that he thought you had the *Porte à la Nuit* or knew where Terry had hidden it."

"Can you backtrack a minute?" Chris said. "What were you doing in Angkor during the war?"

"We rendezvoused with a Frenchman," Seve said. "He commanded a unit of the Khmer Rouge. Very scary guys. Terry and Virgil spoke with him. We never knew what the deal involved."

"Now we know it was drugs," Soutane said. The misery was visible in her face.

"Maybe," Chris said. "But if so, why? Terry never coveted money. Our family had more than he could ever spend."

Seve was considering all this. "If he did become involved," he said, "it must have been for a damn good reason."

"Like what?" Chris asked. "What could be so important that he'd sell his soul for it?"

Seve stared out the window. "I don't know," he said. He was thinking of General Kiu, and a line from Sun Tzu's *The Art of War*: Nothing is constant. None of the five elements is always the strongest; at times, the nights are long, at others, the days. The seasons change. To the diligent comes victory. "But I think our only course now is to find out. What do you say?"

Chris nodded. "I'm for it."

Seve deliberately did not look at Soutane. He was not as sure about her as he was about Chris. Chris had surprised him. He was not at all like any of the criminal lawyers Seve had met. Interestingly, aspects of his personality reminded Seve of Terry's wild, almost primitive determination. He had the energy and spirit of the adventurer. Nobody could be more relentless than Terry Haye when he had set his mind to it.

Seve pushed his cup away and rubbed his head. The pain was worse than ever. "Well, at least now we know why DeCordia was iced. His daughter's OD death did it for him. He wanted out. Someone found out, and set Trangh on him. He knew it, too. That's why he went to Dom. To confess, and to try to save Soutane. At least in that he was successful."

"But you said that this Vietnamese, Trangh, killed your brother," Chris said. "And he tried to kill you. You and I are linked together, Seve. Is it just through Terry, I wonder?"

"It's *La Porte à la Nuit*," Soutane said. "That's all Trangh ever wanted from you, Chris. Seve's right. Trangh was sure Terry had given it to you."

But Chris was already shaking his head. "Not true. He came after us to get the dagger, yes. But he wanted you as well."

"Me?" Soutane was stunned.

"Yes."

"But why?"

"I don't know," Chris said. "But it was the reason I gave him the dagger. It was the only way I could think of to save you."

"You're Mun's cousin," Seve said to her. "And Mun's involved in this snakepit up to his eyeballs. Ten to one Trangh's masters would like a word with you."

"But I don't know anything."

"*They* don't know that."

"Who do you think Trangh's masters are?" Soutane asked.

Seve shrugged. "My first choice would be the communists. But I wonder if the Magician is still alive—that's what Terry used to call Virgil."

"I thought Virgil and my brother were partners."

"They were—for a while," Seve said. "But something happened to bust them up. I never did find out what. By that time I didn't care. I was on my way home."

"Trangh is not working for Virgil," Chris said, "and he's not working for the communists. At least not anymore." They were both looking at him. "He told me who his master is. A man named Milhaud."

"Now where have I heard that name before?" Seve's face furrowed in concentration. Something had clicked in his mind, a sliver of information gleaned in his DEA InterNat-Link course. Wasn't Milhaud a senior member of Le Giron? "Either of you ever heard of the Society to Return to the Fold?"

"The SRGE," Soutane said. "Sure. It's some kind of small political organization with headquarters in Paris, isn't it?"

Seve nodded. "It's small, all right, but it's very powerful. It's ultra-radical, ultra-reactionary. And, so some believe, much of its money comes from the international drug trade.

"This man Milhaud is a prominent member of Le Giron. If

Trangh works for him, then the odds are we'll find them in Paris. At least Paris is where we have to start.''

"Even saying you're right about this,'' Chris said, "what do you propose we do when we find them?''

Seve got up from the table, looked out the window at the boulevard. "I'd like to talk to Mun but, as you know, Soutane's tried calling the villa several times, and he's not back yet from Asia. There's no sense waiting for him.'' He was thinking again of Sun Tzu, who wrote that in taking the offensive one should, if possible, defeat the enemy by destroying his strategy. It was clear that Trangh was the chief instrument of the enemy's strategy.

Seve turned to them, "We've got to use the weapons available to us.''

"Is that a joke?'' Chris said. "We have no weapons.''

"But we do,'' Seve said. "We have Soutane, and we have you.''

They both stared at him as if he had sprouted gills, and he laughed. He sat down at the table. "Look, we know that Trangh came for Soutane. Milhaud wants her. We also know that for some reason he has acted both rationally and honorably with you.''

"What are you suggesting?'' Chris asked, although he thought he already knew.

"Our only real lead is Trangh.''

"No,'' Chris said immediately. "Absolutely not. I won't permit you to use her.''

"Stop it!'' Soutane cried. "I'm sick of the two of you holding a conversation about me as if I were not here!''

"Soutane, he wants to use you as bait.''

She turned to Seve. "Is this true?''

"Only long enough for Chris and me to get close to him,'' Seve pointed out.

"If it's all the same to you,'' Chris said, "I'd rather not get within a hundred yards of Trangh again.''

"Yeah?'' Seve looked at him. "That's funny. I would have thought you'd want another chance at your brother's murderer.''

"What?''

"Look, Terry devised this idea of decapitating all the SLAM unit's victims. Trangh took Dom's head off; you can be sure it was he who did the same to Terry. He's killing the remaining members of the unit using the method the SLAM unit employed. Sounds to me like some kind of screwed-up idea of revenge.''

"But you killed North Vietnamese and Viet Cong in 'Nam,'' Chris said. Something about Seve's explanation just didn't add up.

"If you guys were using him, Trangh is *South* Vietnamese. He hated the North Vietnamese more than the Americans."

"Well, he would," Seve said, "*if* he was South Vietnamese. I mean, he claimed to be from the South, and I guess his credentials checked out because he was one of Virgil's men. But, off and on, the unit encountered mysterious difficulties." He told them about the ambush inside the Cambodian border. "Virgil asked me, and I fingered one of our Khmer Serei soldiers. Because of some convenient circumstantial evidence, he seemed the logical choice at the time. Now it occurs to me that maybe it was *too* logical, too convenient. I think Trangh set him up. After Virgil executed the Khmer Serei, we never worried about a traitor again."

"Didn't this Khmer Serei offer some defense?" Chris asked.

"Nobody gave him the chance," Seve said. "It was war. We were in enemy territory, under enormous pressure. There was no time for the niceties of due process."

"This is monstrous," Soutane said.

"I agree," Seve said. "This bastard Trangh used an innocent Khmer as his scapegoat."

"That's not what I mean," Soutane said. "I'm talking about what's happening here. Look at the two of you, plotting murder, revenge. You're going down the same path that destroyed Terry."

"I want to get at the truth," Seve said. "That's my job. Chris's, too, when it comes to it."

"Are you deliberately missing the point?" Soutane's eyes flashed. "Are you willing to sell your soul, like Terry did, to get at the truth?"

"Don't you get it?" Seve said. "This guy has got to be stopped. He's a madman. He's already killed my brother, and yours, Chris. He's killed Al DeCordia. Aren't those reasons enough?"

"No!" Soutane was shouting now. "Those lives are already lost, but they don't have to be meaningless deaths. Learn from them, for God's sake! These people are still fighting the war. It doesn't mean you have to. Save yourselves!"

Seve was shaking his head. "It's too late. We're too near ground zero. This storm already has too much energy. We're inside it, and either we'll destroy it or it will destroy us."

"I'm afraid he's right, Soutane," Chris said.

She looked from one to the other. Her expression was bleak. "You're both hopeless." Then she lashed out. "Goddamn you!" she cried. "Why did you come here?" She collapsed at the table, her head on her arms. "Dear God, you're all madmen."

* * *

Following Seve's orders, Diana Ming had gone as far as she was able with background on Arnold Toth, the man Seve had asked her to track down. Pieced together from information provided by the department computer, as well as those of the IRS, the New York State Tax Commission, school and military service records, and the like, his history proved standard in every way. He was born in a poor suburb of Chicago, had a public-school education through high school. His grades were marginal, at best.

He had spent a year at University of Michigan before dropping out to go into the container-manufacturing business in Maryland. In November 1963, the year Kennedy had been shot, he had enlisted with Special Forces. His remains had returned from Vietnam in an aluminum coffin.

Dead end, and Diana had thought, This is a waste of time. But she had been trained to be thorough, so on her day off, she had flown down to Fayetteville, North Carolina, arriving in the early afternoon at Fort Bragg, headquarters of SOCOM, the U.S. Army Special Forces First Special Operations Command.

She identified herself and was treated with a great deal of courtesy by the commander, Captain Connolly, a rather young, bronze-skinned giant with a disarming Madison Avenue smile and hard, calculating eyes. He had his adjutant fetch the file on Arnold Toth's service record. In the meantime he kept up a continuous line of patter while appraising her with a stony gaze. Diana had the impression that if she ran into him on the street ten years from now he would not only remember her but would also recall every detail of her visit.

Connolly's adjutant, a sergeant with a blunt face in his fifties named Jaegger, returned with a thick, buff-colored file. He handed it to Connolly, then, with a brief glance at Diana, left.

Diana watched Connolly leaf through the folder, looking, she supposed, for classified information. With a flick of his wrist he skimmed the file across his desk. She picked it up, stared at a black-and-white photo of a square-jawed man with short, bristly hair, large ears, and a bull neck. Something in the stark face implied the heavily muscled bulk of the unseen body.

Toth's military record was anything but standard. He had come to Vietnam with the Fifth Special Forces Group (Airborne), First Special Forces in August 1966, and had been immediately involved in Project OMEGA, ostensibly set up to provide in-depth long-range reconnaissance and intelligence of tactical enemy movement. OMEGA was composed of eight Roadrunner units to track VC route networks, the same number of recon teams engaged in high-saturation patrols through enemy-held territory.

Apparently not satisfied with the original OMEGA mandate, Toth had sought and gained permission to create a clique of three commando companies employing, as the army put it, "elements of local ethnic and religious minorities trained in unconventional warfare skills."

Toth's commando companies were apparently employed in the "extraction of compromised teams," infiltration behind enemy lines, and "emergency situations." It was in this capacity, as company commander, that he got his nickname, Virgil.

In the performance of his duty Toth had garnered every field medal it was possible to receive, as well as receiving two field promotions, both times for taking charge when, under fire, his superiors had been killed. He was clever, resourceful, and brave: the quintessential soldier. He was killed while on a Roadrunner mission north of Pleiku in December 1969.

Diana closed the file. Whatever Seve was looking for wasn't connected with the late Arnold Toth. She thanked Connolly and got out of there. She had a wait at the airport. After a bite to eat she bought a couple of magazines, took them back to the gate where her return flight was scheduled to depart.

That was when she saw Jaegger. Connolly's adjutant was standing by the check-in counter, smoking a cigarette. He saw her, and sauntered over.

He came up to her, and something in his gait told her he had been waiting here for some time. His wide face was as dented as a thirdhand car, and as used up. "Don't you think your leaving is a bit premature?" he said.

"I doubt it," Diana said. "I got what I came for."

"Did you?" He flicked ash on the floor. "Well, I guess that depends on whether you came to praise Caesar or to bury him."

"Haven't you got that the wrong way around?" She was wary. The smell of an ax grinding turned the air sharp.

He gave her a wintry smile. "You still have some time before your flight. Why don't we take a walk?"

She wondered whether she should. If Jaegger had a grudge against Toth, whatever information he was selling would be suspect. On the other hand, he might have a lead and she could not in good conscience walk away from that possibility. She would just have to be careful.

She shrugged. "Why not?"

"I don't know what you came for," Jaegger said, "and to tell you the truth I don't think I want to know. But the fact is, what Connolly showed you is bullshit through and through."

"How much of it?"

"Just one item. But it might as well be everything." Jaegger lit another cigarette from the butt that was not yet finished. "How does that grab you?" He flicked the butt into a chrome ashtray.

"How do you know?"

"Because I served in the Fifth Special Forces Group, Airborne, First Special Forces, and I knew Toth." He lifted his left hand, and Diana could see that it was made of plastic. "I lost this in an OMEGA Roadrunner mission in sixty-seven. I spent six months in rehab. I should've been sent home. My CO had already cut the orders, but I got them rescinded. I didn't want to go home. There was nothing waiting for me there except people who would stare at my ruined hand while giving me excuses why they couldn't give me a job.

"I wangled a transfer to the Fifth's records section, and within eight weeks I was running the office, meaning I knew by heart every sonuvabitch in the Fifth down to the size underpants they wore, and I can tell you categorically that Toth didn't die."

Outside, a jumbo jet heaved itself into the ether. The scream of its takeoff was numbing even through the thick windows of the terminal.

"Do you know what happened to him?"

That wintry smile again, and because he made her wait while he lit another cigarette, she knew they were getting to the nitty-gritty.

"What's it worth to you?" Jaegger said.

"I didn't come down with cash," Diana said. "This little meeting wasn't yet on my dance card."

"Not what I asked." He exhaled the words along with the smoke, squinting at her.

And Diana suddenly had an insight. "You're enjoying this, aren't you?"

"I gotta admit the Vietnamese were right. Patience is the sole possession of the wise man." He picked a shred of tobacco off his lip. "What I didn't know in those days would have astounded you. But at least I wasn't an asshole like Arnold Toth."

"You hated him."

"As they say, I was so much older then, I'm younger than that now."

Diana watched him, wondering whether he was serious or was just trying to make a fool of her. But then she remembered the anxiety he had held within his gait as he had approached her.

She wanted to ask him why after all this time he still hated a dead man, but instead she said, "What happened?"

Which made Jaegger laugh. "I like that. You knew right away that something *did* happen." He wasn't crazy, and he did not think she was a fool. Where did that leave her?

He nodded and, turning, stared out the immense plate-glass window at a 767 taxiing down the runway. "Like I said, I had been in OMEGA, so I thought I had seen it all. But I was wrong.

"We had an emergency situation—this was in February of Seventy—up in Pleiku. VC put on a real blitz, began overrunning our positions. We had heavy, heavy casualties, even among our more elite Roadrunner units. Military Assistance Command, Vietnam, ordered me to come lend a hand, since I had been a former Roadrunner and knew the score. Even so I guessed things must be coming apart because with me they were for sure scraping the bottom of the barrel.

"Anyway, I came by helicopter into a town whose name I can't remember. Maybe I'm getting old, or maybe I just don't want to think about it anymore. It was chaos. The dead—our dead—were piled up, still smoking from the attacks." The 767 was poised, trembling. The sky behind it was filthy with fuel, dancing with heat.

"When I get on the ground, I see a group of Americans, skinny, you know, and young—mostly they looked like pimply kids, except that they've got their heads shaved, and they're wearing VC black pajamas and are armed with Soviet weaponry, AK-47s and the like.

"I gotta tell you these were the scariest dudes I'd ever seen. Mean looking, mean spirited, and mysterious, keeping to themselves, staring down anyone who walked within five feet of them.

"One of them was Arnold Toth, alive and well three months after he had been officially declared dead."

Diana felt a tremor go through her, and her level of concentration increased. The 767 rushed off with a percussive roar, lifting, thrust from the runway with a mighty burst of power.

"When I got back to HQ, I ran these guys down. Turned out this was a SLAM company. They were part of MACV's Studies and Observation Group, which was a joke of a title. It was a cover which hid units who were out there engaged in highly classified 'Jump' missions.

"You wouldn't know what SLAM means. Most army guys wouldn't either. SLAM's an acronym for Search, Location, and Annihilation Missions. These included sabotage, assassination, and psychological cross-border operations. Know what that means? Their work was not only in Vietnam, but in Cambodia, where Charlie had dug in. Cambodia was a neutral nation, which was why the SLAM companies were highly classified."

"That's what Toth was into?" Diana felt her initial excitement dissipating. "Then it's simple; that's why the army declared him dead."

"It's not simple, and the army had nothing to do with it," Jaegger said, " 'cause the army doesn't work that way. We may screw up paperwork just like any bureaucracy, but we don't deliberately declare live guys dead."

"Well, somebody did it," she said. "Who?"

"Same people who set up the Studies and Observation Group," Jaegger said. "The CIA."

"SOG was a Company show?" She was aware of her heartbeat picking up.

"All the way."

"Did the men in SOG know it?"

"Are you kidding? They didn't know shit except how to kill the enemy. In those days, especially, what with all the unrest and protests at home, the CIA felt the need to keep an exceptionally low profile."

"What about Toth?"

Jaegger mashed out his cigarette. "I think Toth was different," he said. "He must have been on the inside. Or—more accurately, maybe, climbed into it when he got himself 'killed,' transferred into MACV-SOG. See, Toth didn't exist inside SOG, he never did. He was already 'dead.' "

"But you just told me you saw him alive outside Pleiku."

"I saw him, all right," Jaegger said, "but he sure as hell wasn't Arnold Toth."

"Who had he become?"

Jaegger shook out another cigarette, stared at the end of it as if there was something there of interest. "How badly do you want to know?"

"Whoever he is," Diana said, "he may be implicated in three murders. Do you still want to withhold the information?"

"No," Jaegger said. "I never did." He lit up, blew out a rush of smoke. "Toth was for many years real bad news for the VC. But I saw him indiscriminately murder too many Asian women and kids to think about shielding him. As far as Toth was concerned, if you were Asian you weren't any better than the shit he scraped off his boot soles."

Diana was interested in that. "Apparently that didn't stop him from using them in his commando units."

Jaegger nodded. "That was it. See, he seemed to get a kick out of seeing them slaughter their own brothers. Also, he got off on their savagery. He taught the Vietnamese how to survive the advent of the American army, and they taught him how to make the enemy eat his own private parts."

"Christ." Diana turned away, momentarily sickened.

"I won't apologize," Jaegger said. "I told you that for a reason. Now you know as much about Arnold Toth as you ever need to know."

"He's very bad news," Diana said, recovering.

"If he's still alive and operating," Jaegger said, "you can bet on it. But by the same token he'll be protected, do you understand me?"

Diana nodded.

"Okay. That said, we can finish this," Jaegger said. "Arnold Toth became someone named Marcus Gable."

"That's just crazy," she said. "Gable was recently on trial. Photos of him were all over the newspapers, the newsweeklies, and TV. The two men don't look anything alike."

"I can't help that," Jaegger said.

"When was Gable's tour of duty over?"

"He was pulled out of 'Nam near the end of seventy-two. But the interesting thing is that SOG had already been deactivated months before."

"When he was discharged, where did he go?"

"Impossible to say because there are no transit records for him."

Diana wore her skepticism on her face. She was about to walk away from him, and he knew it because he waited until the last possible instant to hand her a small manila envelope. "Do me a favor," he said. "Wait until you're in the air to open it."

She did as he asked. The captain had turned off the NO SMOKING sign when she shook out the contents: a pair of Xerox prints from two military records. They contained fingerprints. One set belonged to Arnold Toth, the other to Marcus Gable. They were identical.

At dawn the mist began to writhe.

Mun, goggle-eyed, watched as a slender figure materialized out of the mist. The odd thing—the truly frightening aspect of this—was that the morning was perfectly clear. No cloud or mist was in sight. Except that which curled and writhed between the trees as if willed up from the crust of the earth itself.

Mogok and his escort of soldiers had dumped Mun in this clearing before taking Ma Varada away. Mogok told him that if he moved, he would be shot, and Mun had no reason not to believe him. Especially after he had heard the click of a machine pistol's safety catch when, once, he walked to the periphery of the clearing to relieve himself.

He had spent the remainder of the night shivering on the damp ground, listening to the nocturnal sounds of the numinous forest.

As the night sky gave way to oyster-shell gray in the east, the mist had begun to rise.

"Welcome, Mun," General Kiu said, with the mist enshrouding his legs. Sunlight, pink as a baby, struck his head and shoulders, presenting him with a palpable aura.

All at once Mun recalled the tales Mogok told of General Kiu's origin: that he had no mother, that he was not born of man but, rather, was an incarnation of immortal Mahagiri, disciple of the chief demon Ravana, banished for eternity from *samsara*, the wheel of life.

General Kiu laughed, and held out his hands. "I see my entrance caught your attention. Good. I must say that this mist never fails to engender a certain degree of awe." He grinned. "It's quite an expensive piece of hardware, you know, although it cost me nothing."

General Kiu was delighted with Mun's slack-jawed expression. "I am pleased with the effect it has on someone like you—well educated, with one foot at least in the Western world. You may be a believer, but you are not ignorant like the Shan. Even the best of them, like Mogok, are born with terror in their hearts. The supernatural is a specter ever hanging over their shoulder."

He bent down, flipped a switch. The mist began to dissipate. "Belief in the supernatural is akin to faith, don't you agree?" He took a step down. It was clear now that he had been standing on a platform of some kind. "And faith exists to be exploited. It is, as far as I can determine, a weakness that, once understood as a strategy, can be turned back upon itself in order to manipulate its adherents."

Now all the mist was gone. Mun stared at the machinery beneath the plywood platform.

General Kiu laughed. "It is a smoke machine," he said. "It was a present from an American rock star. I saw him use it in his show in Bangkok, and I was impressed.

"The very next day his tour became stranded. It had run afoul of the law. Drugs, I believe." He made a clucking noise that made him sound like an old lady. By his expression Mun knew that General Kiu had caused the tour to be detained. "I interceded with the local constabulary, who, as you are no doubt aware, are on my payroll. The rock star was so grateful, he gave me what I wanted. Of course, I had to buy a larger generator, but it's proved worth the expense. Do you like it?"

"It's—I'm stunned," Mun managed.

"An excellent choice of words," General Kiu said. He was an extraordinarily handsome man, with glossy skin and long, sleek hair that resembled an animal's pelt. It was altogether black, though his beard and mustache were quite white. His face was dominated by high Mongol cheekbones and wide-apart eyes that viewed everything in his vicinity with a mixture of curiosity and amusement. It was as if he believed the whole world to be his plaything.

"Well, get up off the ground, man," General Kiu said. "You look so damned uncomfortable there, you're making my back ache."

Gingerly, Mun rose, poking himself here and there, taking inventory of his small pains.

"Are you well?" General Kiu asked.

"This isn't . . . what I expected," Mun said.

General Kiu swung around. "No?" He grinned. "Oh, you mean all that talk about torture?" He grunted. "You know Mogok. He often gets carried away. He's useful, I suppose, because he takes his role as spy exceedingly seriously. But, as you can see, that can sometimes present, er, distortions in zealousness."

Mun was having difficulty believing any of this. Wasn't General Kiu the enemy? Wasn't this the same General Kiu who, in years ago, had refused to deal with him and Terry, who had, in fact, tried several times to kill them? He said all this.

General Kiu waved away his words. "That was a long time ago," he said. "Furthermore, the current climate here has shifted dramatically. Sun Tzu counsels that to be master of his enemy's fate, the successful general must be both resolute and resilient."

"You must be talking about the deal Admiral Jumbo made with the Caucasian."

General Kiu pulled at the end of his mustache. "Everything changed here when that happened. Admiral Jumbo's greed will destroy us where even the Chinese army cannot."

Mun, watching the warlord, felt his guard slipping. Was this what General Kiu intended, or was he being honest and straightforward? He was as yet reluctant to mention the Magician's name. He told himself that if General Kiu confided a secret which he, Mun, could verify—such as the identity of the Caucasian—he could be trusted. Mun felt as if he had a weight in each hand, and though they both felt equal, he was being forced to decide which one was the heavier. How was he to do that? "Do you know who killed Terry?" he asked.

The startled look in General Kiu's eyes told Mun a great deal. "Terry Haye dead? I had not heard. This is something Mogok did not relay to me. You say he was murdered?"

"If I read the situation correctly, the same people with whom Admiral Jumbo made the deal for the opium killed Terry."

General Kiu nodded. "That is a logical deduction."

"Does that mean you know who is muscling in on my territory?"

"Come," General Kiu said. "Let us take a walk along the Shan."

Mun heard the whimpering long before they came upon Ma Varada. General Kiu's men had tied her to a rough wooden cross, inverting it so that her head was not more than six inches from the ground.

It was not until he was quite close that Mun noticed that her eyelids had been taped back so that she could no longer blink. Mun was so repulsed by the sight that he was brought up short.

"Why are you upset?" General Kiu said. "She is a spy and, as such, is no longer your concern."

"She is still a human being."

General Kiu was looking at him shrewdly. "I see it is good I had you brought here," he said. "I am beginning to get a measure of you. I think now that I understand what motivated you and Terry to burn the tears of the poppy you bought from Admiral Jumbo."

"What are you talking about?"

"Did you think *nobody* knew your secret, Mun? I am the only one who suspects. Do not be alarmed, it is as safe with me as a newborn baby is on my knee." He folded his hands across his chest. "I admit that I had thought you two mad, beyond any understanding. What you did was like swallowing the best rubies, turning them into shit. What could be the purpose, I asked myself, except madness?

"Then, for a long time, I suspected you of working for the Communist Chinese. I thought they had discovered an innovative method of destroying us. Next, I feared, you would pay Admiral Jumbo to burn his crops. But when that never happened, I began to get curious. What if you weren't mad? And if you weren't working for the Chinese, then what?"

"What Terry and I did is our own business."

General Kiu shrugged. "But Terry is dead, and perhaps so, too, will you be."

"Then it will no longer matter to anyone."

General Kiu was somber. "In that you are wrong, Mun. It will matter to me. You see, the Shan is my world. It may not have been my cradle, but it has become my mother. Surely, it is my god. I cannot allow anything or anyone to destroy it, or change it in any way.

"That is why I tried to kill you and Terry Haye. I believed that you wanted to destroy us."

"And now?"

"Now I am not so certain of that. Now I find myself increasingly of the mind that you and I are not so far apart in our goals."

Mun glanced at Ma Varada and shuddered.

"You have been too long in the West," General Kiu said. "You have forgotten that here life is cheap."

"Cheap," Mun said, "but not unimportant." He shuddered again. "Cut her down. There must be another way to get what you want."

"But you must know there isn't," General Kiu said. "Everyone in the area needs to know what she is, and to see her inevitable fate. It is a valuable lesson to be learned."

"Didn't Sun Tzu write that it is better to capture an enemy than to kill him?"

"Yes, but here we are talking about a spy."

"Didn't Sun Tzu advocate turning an enemy spy so that he spied for you?"

General Kiu regarded Ma Varada. "She is a woman and, therefore, untrustworthy. Furthermore, she despises me because of certain of my, er, sexual preferences with women."

"But she does not hate me," Mun said. "Let me retrain her and set her back on her master."

General Kiu pulled at the corner of his mustache. "An interesting idea," he said after a time. "It requires further thought."

Mun did not think so, and in any event it was time to begin testing General Kiu's intent. He crouched in front of Ma Varada and carefully removed the tape. She blinked rapidly several times until her eyes began to tear. She focused on him.

"Mun?"

"Be calm, be patient," he said softly so that only she could hear.

Then he got up and turned around. General Kiu's reaction now would be critical.

"Were you born compassionate?" General Kiu said wonderingly. "Or did the West do this to you? Compassion, you know, is an unsafe emotion to indulge. It can be the death of you."

"Whether you cut her down," Mun said, coming up beside him, "is entirely your decision." He did not want this to become a matter of face. No one but General Kiu would ever know what he had done. "Use her or destroy her at your will."

But because he had invoked Sun Tzu, he hoped he knew what General Kiu's decision would be—if he had been telling Mun the truth and not, as Admiral Jumbo apparently had, one version of a lie.

"You know," General Kiu said, "in many ways, the Shan is like Shangri-la or Eden. It stirs the world around it while being absolutely isolated from it. It is a universe in and of itself, with its own laws that encompass even creation and destruction. It is as if time—the clock by which all men calculate life—does not survive here. And if magic exists anywhere in the world, surely it is here, because I have fashioned it out of superstition and fear."

They walked on through leafy glades. Mun was content to let General Kiu continue talking, knowing that the more he spoke, the more he was likely to reveal of his true motives.

"Into Eden comes the devil," General Kiu continued. "The fast-talking Caucasian with decades of contacts, ready to take up where he left off years ago."

"Then you *do* know who Admiral Jumbo made his deal with."

"As I said, the devil." General Kiu looked out over the mountainside. "A man once called Virgil. Now he has another name, another face. But, inside, the same venom runs through his veins, threatening to poison everything he possesses. And what he wants to possess now is the Shan."

* * *

Diana was waiting for a callback from Dick Andrew, her contact at the CIA's main office in Washington. Sitting at the computer, its glowing green letters reflected in her face, she was staring at the sum total of a life. It stared blankly back at her, revealing nothing.

Back in New York, after a rotten night's sleep missing Seve, she had come into the office an hour early so she could run a computer check. Returning from Vietnam in May 1974, Marcus Gable was soon into transshipping cargo to and from Asia. By that time he had settled in New York City, where he met his wife, the former Linda Starr. He had no brothers or sisters, no children.

But the curious thing was that Jaegger had said Gable had been pulled out of 'Nam at the end of 1972. That left a gap of eighteen months. Where had Gable gone, and what was he doing during that time?

Diana had begun her current line of inquiry with the FBI and CIA.

She had drawn a blank with her contacts at the first agency, which came as no surprise to her. She was waiting for a callback from Dick Andrew at CIA when her captain summoned her into his office.

"What's this I hear about your extracurricular activity?"

"Sir?"

He took off his reading glasses. Joe Kline was a shiny-cheeked, clean-shaven man in his midfifties. He was well dressed, and was often seen on the network news shows, which meant that he knew how to play the game from the commissioner's point of view as well as television's. He was at once avuncular and articulate. Anyone seeing him on TV could not help but feel that the city was secure. The mayor thought him invaluable.

"Don't play dumb with me," Captain Kline said. "Leave that attitude for the slobs who look at you and see only a girl in blue."

"Yes, sir."

He waited a moment, rubbing the frames of his glasses across his wide forehead. "You're a pain in the ass, Ming, do you know that?"

"I'm sorry you feel that way, sir."

"No, you're not," he said. "Otherwise your loyalty to me would supersede your loyalty to Seve."

"You are my captain, sir."

Captain Kline sighed. "Sit down." He put aside his glasses and stared at her. "Now would you kindly tell me what the fuck you're doing that I should get a call from Washington?"

"I don't understand, sir."

"Why the squeeze?" He meant the investigation. "Marcus Gable's a hero of the war, for chrissakes."

"Is that the call you got from Washington?" Thinking about what Jaegger had told her, that if Gable was still inside the Company, he'd be protected.

"They're very conscious down there about the image of Vietnam veterans. They've spent a lot of time and money cleaning things up, changing public perception. It's a mandate left over from the Reagan days, and they don't want any problems."

"I wasn't aware that I was presenting a problem, sir."

He squinted at her. "Sometimes," he said, "I have the feeling by your tone that you're laughing at me."

"Completely erroneous, sir."

He sat back, hands locked behind his head. When he spoke again, his tone had changed. "You know, Diana, I'm not ignorant of what goes on around me. I know that some of the blues call me 'Live at Eleven' Kline. They see how far off the street I am, and it galls them that I'm chosen to speak for the department. But I don't think they realize the heat I take off them. Contrary to popular notion, I serve a legitimate purpose around here."

Diana said nothing. She was wondering about the call he had gotten.

"Have you heard from Seve?" he asked suddenly.

"Yes," Diana said, and immediately regretted it. This was what he was really good at. Maneuvering. That was what she got for allowing her mind to drift.

"He's on leave, Ming. I thought I made that plain." Captain Kline slipped on his glasses. "You have, I imagine, legitimate police business to occupy your time. If your workload is inadequate, I will be happy to add to it."

"That won't be necessary, sir," she said, sliding out of the hot seat. At the glass door to his cubicle she paused. "Sir?"

"What is it?"

"Who did that call come from?"

"Morton Saunders at State."

"The State Department? Not the CIA?"

"Are you asking me for verification?"

"No, sir," she said, about to swing out the door. She had to contact Seve right away. "Thank you."

"Ming." His voice held her one last moment. "If your first loyalty isn't to Seve Guarda, how come you don't call *me* boss?"

"Put it together."

A room, lit solely by bars of light filtered through bamboo shades. Outside, beyond the winding Seine, the École Militaire and the Parc du Champ de Mars.

"What will happen when the pieces are fit together? Will there, I wonder, be lightning and thunder?"

M. Mabuse hunched over Milhaud's desk, his deft fingers pressing metal against metal.

"I have never seen the three swords together," Milhaud said.

"Perhaps Terry Haye and Mun are the only ones who have," M. Mabuse said.

"Imagine. This priceless artifact was once buried right under my nose. It would be amusing if it weren't so infuriating."

M. Mabuse's head came up. "Why infuriating?" he said. "You have the *Prey Dauw* now."

But not for long, Milhaud thought, if the Magician has his way. I must outfox him as once he outfoxed me. The Magician's genius, he knew, was in utilizing the talents of those around him. Milhaud knew that he had been bested in Angkor by Terry Haye. That moment in time, he had some years ago realized, had marked the waning of his own power.

Once, he had been as strong as Alexander. His influence had stretched throughout Southeast Asia, from Burma to Vietnam. He had educated the Khmer as he saw fit, manipulating their schooling much as a single-minded parent would, to create his offspring in the image he had envisioned for them.

Then the Americans had come with their arrogance and their wealth. There was not an American on the face of the globe, Milhaud suspected, who did not, in adolescent fashion, equate money with power. That was America's secret, its strength and its hubris. It was young, brash. It had not yet been humbled as France had been by the invader's boot.

Despite all its recent posturing it did not see Vietnam or Cambodia as a mirror to its own rotting soul, but rather as an object lesson in which several men in their zeal overstepped the authority of their office. But had they transgressed the law? America was still undecided on that count.

Like the Roman Empire, America was blind to the rot festering in the decayed facade of its culture. The stink of decadence was like a graveyard.

It seemed unfair to Milhaud, as he watched M. Mabuse fitting the three swords together, that for so many years he had been bound to the Americans as if to a wheel. He had been nothing more than their chief—if unwilling—pawn. They had ordered and he, craven and in servitude, had obeyed.

Now that he was free, now that he was able to manipulate them as they had for so long manipulated him, he could look back upon the past and see it for what it was. But, oddly, his newfound freedom did not lessen the bitterness of those years. If anything, the complete understanding of his enslavement—which had come upon him like an epiphany, as it had to St. Paul, struck down by God's white light in the dust of a country road—enraged him all the more. Now he saw that it was this rage, formed from the acrid core of his enslavement, which would provide him with the energy he needed. He would make it the cynosure for all his subsequent actions.

Yet he could not help but wonder whether his rage would be enough to overcome his fear of the Magician. He knew Virgil far better than M. LoGrazie ever would, but he did not see this as an advantage. Quite the contrary; because he knew what the Magician was capable of, it fed his terror like a stoker fed a fire.

Excess and irony were two elements Virgil could be counted on to weave into all his schemes. He was a genius of a rather perverse sort. It was not so much his intelligence, but his sheer leaps of reasoning, defying logic and order, that made him so dangerous. If he were merely—as Milhaud believed Terry Haye to have been—amoral, it would have been bad enough. But the Magician was more. He was Chaos anthropomorphized.

Milhaud thought of Morphée, alone in her black bed. For the first time he realized how cleverly she had constructed her own private oblivion, surviving everything, in a place beyond pain and fear, beyond even time. For a moment he envied her this bastion constructed by her persistent introversion. She had protected herself from even the chaos that was Virgil.

Then he saw her world for what it really was, and knew with a fleeting melancholy that she had merely exchanged one prison for another.

How he hated the Americans! They were like lepers, these perverted sons of Midas, altering everything they touched with the promise of unlimited gold. First the Arabs, then the Germans and the Japanese, flush with inflated currency, emulated the Americans.

Their philosophy was anathema to him; he equated true freedom with equality. The guiding spirit of the French Revolution lived on in him, though it was either ridiculed or—worse!— forgotten by his countrymen.

The winds of change had stranded him, along with the rest of humanity, on this bleak shore. Mankind's only hope now lay with Le Giron, the Society to Return to the Fold. Only the swift, unsparing scalpel applied to the disease spreading across the globe. Soon France, as Indochina had once been, would be stripped of its treasures by looters too greedy to see the nature of their actions.

M. Mabuse, almost finished with his task, nevertheless hesitated. Although the *Prey Dauw* was not of his culture, he was intimate with its legend. Many times he had scoffed at its power, feeling smugly superior to those primitives who believed in its sovereignty.

Yet now that he had all three blades together, now that he was about to link them into one, into the true *Prey Dauw*, he nevertheless felt a shudder of intimation. His fingers manipulating the ivory pins just below the shanks of the jade blades felt abruptly swollen and clumsy, and he almost dropped the talisman.

Milhaud, in the darkness on the other side of his desk, his fingers steepled as he sat lost in thought, did not notice. To him the *Prey Dauw* was simply a means to an end. What could he know of centuries of power, sleeping like a beast alien to the new world grown up around it.

Stop it! M. Mabuse admonished himself. Milhaud is right. There is nothing here but a triple-bladed sword. People's belief in it is all that gives it its power, nothing more.

And yet . . .

"It is done," M. Mabuse said from out of the semidarkness. He rose, holding the triple-bladed sword in both his hands.

"The *Prey Dauw*," Milhaud breathed.

M. Mabuse was immersed in shadow. He felt the darkness creep over him like the coming of an eclipse. He gripped the hilt of the *Prey Dauw* with an almost preternatural strength born of despair, and thought, What is happening to me?

He felt cold, hearing in his mind the chittering screams of the dead. He lived now with their breath constantly on his face. Soon he would join them, when his mission was done. But through what ritual of purification he could not imagine.

His spirit was black with the grime of sin. Like scoria, it seemed the inevitable by-product of his inner burning: not a purging, but a desire so strong it must be called lust.

A chill wind pressed against his cheek, like the back of a corpse's hand. The room in which he was standing had not changed. Or had it? All at once M. Mabuse had the vertiginous sensation of the walls ballooning outward, collapsing, disintegrating into the infinite blackness not of space but of time. His spirit grew, elongating until it was the size of a river of infinite length.

He stared into the dark mirrored face of the *Prey Dauw* and saw, at last, the object of his lust and the oblivion waiting for him, patient as a praying mantis.

His mind had long ago erased it from his memory. But the power of the *Prey Dauw* was such that it extracted his oblivion from its prison like a painful scream from a locked throat.

Her name was Luong . . .

The link between sex and death is forged in M. Mabuse's mind when, some time after the SLAM unit returns from Angkor, he goes back to his home in the north.

For months he has thought of little else. He has been frightened to see it again, but it is a magnet, a kind of lodestone that he feels as a weight inside him, and he knows that he will not sleep until he does. Now he knows why. The devastation is complete. Nothing remains of his village. Almost a hundred villagers have been killed by the American 'copter attack, untold others are maimed beyond anything but a temporary surcease provided by opium.

M. Mabuse arrives toward dusk. He wanders around the charred wreckage as if he is a vessel lost at sea. He wants to remember, but it is as if the chopper raid destroyed his past when it leveled the village. Casting his mind back in time to when he lived here, he encounters only a formless void into which he can insert no idea or image.

"Trangh?"

An old man has appeared. He is already adept at picking his way through the morass of ash and rubble, as if he accepts this now as his way of life.

"Trangh, is that you?" He peers up into M. Mabuse's face. "It is I, Van Ngoc. Do you not remember me from the old days? My daughter and I are the only ones left. All the others are dead or dying."

In shock M. Mabuse nods. "I remember you." It is his worst nightmare come to life. He wants nothing more than to turn and run away from this sea of death as fast as he can. But the old man's hand holds him fast.

"It is good you returned," Van Ngoc says. "It is good to have a native son here where no other will see the light of another day."

He leads M. Mabuse to a makeshift shelter before which a small fire is burning. It is tended by a young woman whom M. Mabuse does not recognize.

"My daughter, Luong," Van Ngoc says. The young woman bows, averting her gaze. She is quite beautiful. She has a strong, open face, eyes deep with the mystery of intelligence. "You must be hungry, Trangh. Let us feed you. You can tell me of your own fortune, and afterward we will sleep."

All during their meager dinner Van Ngoc asks questions about M. Mabuse's exploits with the Americans in the war. Out of the corner of his eye M. Mabuse sees Luong watching him, but every time he turns his gaze in her direction, her eyes are always cast down at the wooden bowl in her lap.

The old man and his daughter eat little. Whatever pathetic foodstuffs they possess are for their guest. M. Mabuse has no appetite, but to refuse the food or to leave any scraps would be an insult. He eats everything, tasting nothing.

"You are a great hero, Trangh," the old man says. "It is a measure of your greatness that you have returned to a place filled with nothing. You honor us here with your presence."

M. Mabuse is uncomfortable with Van Ngoc's praise. "I am unworthy of such words, or of such hospitality," he says, meaning it.

Van Ngoc grins, his yellow teeth gleaming in the firelight. "Nonsense. This was woefully inadequate. I assure you that in the old days you would have been treated to a harvest of food." He sighs. "We were well off then. The bounty of the land and *abhidhamma*, the teachings of Buddha, nourished us." His head bows, whether in fatigue or acceptance, M. Mabuse does not know. "Then the communists came with their ideas of death and destruction. No god, no family, no hope."

Van Ngoc shakes his head. "The priests shrivel inside when they see the communists. The beast marches south, and Buddha turns his face away. The Catholics, who preached the word of Jesus, are long dead, but I suppose you know that, Trangh. The beast is unyielding. It takes away everything, and in return provides us with nothing."

His eyes are large in the firelight, glittering with incipient tears.

"It is the worst for the youngsters. At least I recall my teachings. Buddha remains in my heart. But the children have not yet had time to learn. Now they absorb the poison of the beast and are turned into beasts themselves. Now hate is our prime commodity, Trangh. Won't you help us?"

M. Mabuse stares into the fire. His tongue feels attached to the roof of his mouth, and for a long time he remains mute.

The old man says, "That was unforgivable of me. Please accept my humble apologies. You have done more than a score of men have to help us." He looks toward his daughter. "Luong will provide whatever else you might require. You have only to ask. She will stay with you tonight."

"That is hardly necessary."

"Should the prodigal hero sleep alone? Would you have me shamed?"

It is dark by the time they are finished. Van Ngoc is already dozing. In the near distance fires have been lit as if on a vast empty plain. It is an eerie sight.

M. Mabuse has never felt so alone. His isolation clamps his heart in its icy embrace. If only I could remember, he thinks, what it was like here before the communists. But my mind is blank. It is as if I was born when, as Van Ngoc said, they marched south.

What is Jesus, or even Buddha to him? Words, only, contemptible and devoid of meaning. The old man might have been a Martian espousing a philosophy alien to M. Mabuse. Faith is a word he cannot even pronounce.

He sees the firelight dancing across Luong's cheek. Wordlessly, she rises, takes him inside the makeshift hut. It is constructed of old American army field jackets, tin cans, cut and pressed flat, even a piece of animal hide, black and still smelling strongly of incomplete tanning.

M. Mabuse has not been with a woman since long before the Angkor mission. His mind, locked tight within its own agony, does not remember what to do. But his body does.

Luong's luxuriant hair covers him as if with a silken web. Her dexterous fingers unbutton his clothes, their tips stroking his flesh as she goes.

When he is naked, she undresses in a manner he finds utterly arousing in its innocence. He stares down at his erection with a stunned expression as Luong encloses it with the palms of her hands and draws him down to where she lies on a rough mat of straw. She encompasses him in a softness so exquisite the breath hisses out of him.

Her thighs open to darkness, and her small belly rolls inward, her hips canted backward in unmistakable invitation. Her small breasts with their pointed nipples are thrust toward his mouth, their erotic movement urging his lips to open and take them, one by one, inside, as she had moments before done with him.

Her hot breath on his cheek, her dusky skin, burnished like silk in the wavering firelight contacting his like electricity, her heat transmitted to him like a fever, and finally, her dewy wetness eliciting from him an unconscious groan.

Their mating is intense, furious with pent-up emotion. M. Mabuse believes that old Van Ngoc wants his daughter with a hero's child. It is little enough to give back, he supposes. And, for a moment, he is actually happy, conscious of what he is doing. It has never before occurred to him that he can make someone else happy. Pleased at the efficiency of his work, yes. But happy? That is another matter, entirely.

Then, as he nears orgasm, he feels Luong's finger grip his shoulder. His eyes fly open, and he is staring into hers. Her look of utter hatred turns his saliva bitter.

He sees the knife blade then, the flash of its swift movement. But he cannot believe this is happening. It must, he thinks, be a dream.

Then she is arching up against him, her face convulsed with a beatific pain. He feels the wetness creeping along his belly, heating his crotch. He rolls off her, sees the blade buried to the hilt in her side.

Her fist encloses the hilt. He knows that once she draws the blade out, she will bleed to death within seconds. He looks into her face. Her eyes are clear and lucid and, in a moment, he understands what she has done. Her expression of contempt tells him everything.

"I know about you," she whispers. "Who you really are, and what you have done." She is not, he suddenly realizes, like her fatuous father, who believes in the spurious legend of the hero. She knows the truth.

"How?" His voice a croak of disbelief.

"I have met the man who like Buddha knows all about you." Luong laughs. "You will dream of it now, won't you?"

"I wish you had plunged the knife into me, instead," M. Mabuse says.

She is smiling. "I know."

And then he understands the nature of her contempt, the completeness of her triumph. He is undeserving of a simple death such as this. She wants him to live with the knowledge of what he is, of what he has done. Her death is the agent.

Seeing the expression on his face, Luong's smile broadens just before, with the last of her strength, she pulls the knife out of her side, and her eyes close for the last time. . . .

"Tell me about Mademoiselle Sirik," Milhaud said.

"What?" For a moment M. Mabuse could not distinguish Milhaud's voice from the cacophony of those within his spirit. Stunned by the vision emanating from the *Prey Dauw*, M. Mabuse stood, shaken, the void inside him so long lifeless vibrating with agonizing tintinnabulations. "What of her?" His voice was thick with emotions he had long forgotten were his. "As I told you, there was a stalemate of sorts. Christopher Haye threatened to destroy *La Porte à la Nuit* unless I handed over Mademoiselle Sirik. He was not bluffing. I felt that I had no choice. He has proved as clever as his brother. In fact, I found it eerie confronting him."

"How so?"

"It was as if I had never killed Terry Haye, or that he had come back from the dead. I saw Terry Haye again as clearly as I see you now."

"Foolish talk."

"Of course," M. Mabuse said woodenly. Because the *Prey Dauw* in his hands told him otherwise. And, at last, he understood the nature of its power. He could see beyond the petty concerns of humans. He was dazzled by the cosmic design, even as he glimpsed the moment of his own death. He recognized the power he now possessed but, simultaneously, knew that it was not for him. His desire for oblivion was too strong.

Neither was it for Terry Haye. Terry Haye, whose desire for power was too strong.

The *Prey Dauw* was for someone who, as the Theravadan Buddhists believed, was cleansed of all desire, and like Siddhartha was thus ready to tread a higher path.

Terry Haye, whom M. Mabuse had misunderstood and, in so doing, had come to loathe. It was Terry Haye, so M. Mabuse had been told, who, having discovered his infiltration of the SLAM unit, had sold M. Mabuse out to the South Vietnamese. The prison pit, a degradation that each day had made M. Mabuse long for death.

Now, from the depths of his own memory, via the power of the

Prey Dauw, had come the truth. M. Mabuse had been traduced, not by Terry Haye, but by the Magician.

Luong *had* told him, but not in words. In remembering with such sickening clarity what he had fought for so many years to suppress—the moment of Luong's death, the moment she had bound him to this limbo of lifelessness—he had recalled in perfect details the knife she had used: the unique KA-BAR with the carved hilt. The Magician's weapon. M. Mabuse remembered that the Magician did not have the knife on their mission to Angkor. When he had castrated the North Vietnamese colonel, the Magician had used M. Mabuse's knife.

Now M. Mabuse understood everything. He saw that the Magician was the only man who knew who he was, and who could have told Luong.

The revelation hit him with the force of a thunderbolt. He staggered, bracing himself against the edge of Milhaud's desk with the heel of his hand, reluctant even now to relinquish his grip on the *Prey Dauw*. A hollowness in the pit of his stomach, where he had thought nothing could touch him ever again, expanding. He thought of Kama-Mara, his interrogator during his imprisonment. *Day is night*, Kama-Mara had said, *and night is day. When you have admitted that black is white, then you will be on your way to reclamation.* Now, truly, day had become night; white, black.

Was it the power of the *Prey Dauw* or his own mind that had shown him the truth? This particular bitter truth had been locked away inside of him all this time, just as he had locked a part of himself away.

Milhaud was staring hard at him. "Foolish, indeed. Especially since Christopher Haye will be dead soon," he said. "I want you to kill him."

For a long time M. Mabuse said nothing. He seemed to be staring at the center of the *Prey Dauw*. At last he said in a neutral voice, "What about Mademoiselle Sirik?"

"I want her taken."

"Dead or alive?"

It was a simple question, but it caused Milhaud to fly into a rage. He ran at M. Mabuse, pressed the jade blades across his throat. "Alive, you cretinous animal! Does everything have to be defined in terms of life or death? Bring her to me, but make it look like a death. Her death. Do you understand me? You *do* understand simple French?"

M. Mabuse, bent backward over the desk, stared impassively up into the face he knew so well, yet would never know at all. He and this man could have been born on different planets for all the understanding there was between them.

It was then that M. Mabuse saw through the lens of the *Prey Dauw* that he had gained more knowledge of another human being in the short tension-filled moments he and Christopher Haye had stood facing one another in the abandoned stable in Tourrette than in all the years he had served the Frenchman in faithful duplicity.

And he understood finally what it was that drew him to Christopher Haye. There was unfinished business between M. Mabuse and Terry Haye. Terry Haye might be gone, but a spark of his spirit lived on in his younger brother. This is what fascinated M. Mabuse so completely.

Not merely the doorway to oblivion, but the promise of peace for a spirit too long consigned to the nightmare of a tormented purgatory. The death of nihilism. The precious gift of faith, regained.

They were in Paris by nightfall. Soutane kept the accelerator to the floor all the way, the Alfa Spider eating up the miles as they took the A7 north through Lyon and the chateaux country.

She did not say a word to either of them. Her expression was as grim as if she were on her way to a funeral, and Chris began to worry about her. He tried to talk to her when Seve went off to deliver his rental car and, again, during dinner, but she refused.

But when Seve returned from speaking with Diana, he forgot about her mood.

"Chris, what can you tell me about Marcus Gable?" Seve said, sitting down. He had not finished his meal, but he seemed to have lost all interest in food.

Chris shrugged. "Nothing," he said. "He was a client of mine."

"I know that," Seve said. "I followed the trial like everyone else at the precinct. But my interest is not in whether Gable was really guilty or innocent of murdering his wife."

He told them what Diana had discovered in Fayetteville. "So it appears," he wound up, "that Marcus Gable and Arnold Toth are the same person. He was Virgil, the Magician, the mysterious topkick of my and your brother's unit. Now, it seems, he's CIA, still active in some manner. I think we've got to consider the probability that he's involved with Trangh."

A cold lump had been developing in Chris's stomach. Now he

felt compelled to push his plate away from him. "Then it was no accident that Gable sought me out."

"I think not."

Chris felt sick. "What does he want? What's he up to?"

"I don't know," Seve confessed. "But I've got a feeling that if we find Trangh, we'll be a giant step to finding out." He paused a moment. "Do you still feel the need to invoke the client–attorney privilege?"

"It's not a question of what I want," Chris said. "There are ethics involved."

"Tell that to Terry, if you can wake the dead," Seve said bitterly, "and I'll do the same with Dominic."

Chris stared into his wineglass. While it was true that whatever Marcus Gable had told him in confidence concerning the death of his wife was inviolate, there were other off-the-record conversations that Chris could certainly repeat. If they would be of any help. He thought back, trying to piece together Gable's words.

"Look, I don't know what I'm looking for," Seve said, "but it's becoming increasingly clear that if Gable and Trangh are working together, then Gable ordered the hit on Al DeCordia. We already know that DeCordia and Terry were involved in some way in smuggling opium out of the Golden Triangle. Does that help you? I mean, Gable may have let something slip. Even something small, something offhand."

Chris, exhausted, pressed his fingers against his eyes. He shook his head. "There's nothing I can think of."

Later, in his hotel room, Chris watched the closed door to the bathroom, hearing the water running for a long time. He closed his eyes, thought of Terry and Marcus Gable, once partners—in what? Then, perhaps, bitter enemies. He thought of Gable bringing heroin into the States. How would he do that? Through his business? He was in import-export, the perfect cover. Except that Chris, having had some contact with his father's company, knew the enormous risks associated with putting a company in such jeopardy. He recalled a spot check by U.S. Customs on one of his father's planes. They knew to look in places Chris would never have thought of.

If Gable was prudent, he would have found another path to bring the drugs in, and if he was really smart, he would have found a third party to take the brunt of the risk.

Then Chris sat up in bed and, heart pounding, dialed Seve's room. "I just remembered something," he said into the mouthpiece. "It may turn out to be nothing, but . . . Gable was bragging to me one day, about how he'd cuckolded his friend. The thing that sticks in my mind now is that this friend had a pleasure boat that sailed out of East Bay Bridge or Montauk on Long Island. A lot of drugs still come in that way, don't they?''

''Sure do.'' Seve's voice was crackling with excitement. ''Gable's friend have a name?''

He didn't mention it,'' Chris said. ''But the boat's called the *Monique*. According to Gable, it was named after his friend's mistress.''

''Got it,'' Seve said. ''Thanks, Chris.''

When Soutane came out of the bathroom, she immediately turned off the lights. He felt her get into bed beside him. Her body was as cool and smooth as marble.

''Soutane—''

She turned on her side, away from him.

He had been about to tell her what he had remembered, but now changed his mind. He wanted to find some way to break down the wall she had built between them. ''How is it,'' he said, ''that I never heard of your cousin Mun before this?''

''I'm tired,'' she said. ''Can we not talk?''

''We've been not talking since we left Nice,'' he pointed out. ''It's not very pleasant.'' He waited a minute. ''It also serves no purpose.''

''Chris,'' she said softly, ''I already lost you once. Twice would be too much to bear.''

''It would be nice,'' he said softly, ''to know a little more about Mun.''

''Mun.'' She stirred beside him. ''In those days,'' she said, in that faraway voice she got when speaking about the past, ''he was still in Indochina, working for his father. It was a source of friction between my parents, no doubt because Mun's father was part of Lon Nol's regime. That was what caused Mun's father and his family to be murdered. Mun was never mentioned at home.''

She turned onto her back and because, like moonlight on water, he could see the glitter of her eyes he did not feel as emotionally distant from her. ''Mun and I grew up together. I was born in Indochina, you know. No, I guess I never mentioned that before. I spent the first eight years of my life in Pnompenh and Bangkok.''

Soutane held her hand up where Chris could see the spade shape she made with her pressed-together fingers. She touched him with it, in a spot just above his Adam's apple, and he could not breathe.

He gasped, trying to suck air into his lungs. "That is just one of the things Mun taught me."

She rolled over, stared at the ceiling but, really, her eyes were turned inward. "The thing about Mun—the thing he never wanted anyone to know was that he never knew who his real parents were. He was an orphan. The people who raised him—my aunt and uncle—never knew where he came from, either. He just appeared one day, on their doorstep. It is a mystery of his life that has never been far from his thoughts. And, in a way, that unanswerable question of where he came from has shaped his personality. When his adopted family died, he was rootless, without even the sense we all have of a starting place in life."

"He has you," Chris said.

"Yes, he does. But I am female, and in Asian society that makes all the difference in the world. Mun could never confide in me the way he could with Terry. And, always Mun is terribly alone. He always has been. I think that is why he and Terry were so friendly. They both saw themselves as outcasts of some kind. Their relationship was so close that in some ways it served as a family substitute for Mun. Terry's death was especially hard on him."

There was a silence for some time. Chris was aware of their breathing, aware that a kind of barrier had risen between them.

"How did you and Mun lose touch?" he asked.

"At some point my mother determined that it was important for me to have a proper French education as she and my father had. She despised the schools in Indochina. Besides, she found her métier here in France. She was adept at soothing the ruffled political feathers that my father's radical philosophy created.

"But she also grew bored at the relatively sedentary life here. Life in Asia is very different, and she had a hard time adjusting. My father was away in Indochina, often for long stretches of time. She was soon having an affair with a government minister who had come down from Paris for a weekend visit.

"My father found out about it, and there was a terrible row. Until she told him about the minister's unusual sexual habits. This set my father to thinking. He had discovered that she was also good at finding out which skeletons were in whose closet."

"He encouraged her to have adulterous affairs?" Chris said. "What kind of a man was he?"

"I told you before that my father was an exceptionally dangerous man. He was a radical in spirit as well as in form. I think that, in the end, is what doomed my parents' marriage. My mother was simply not the zealot my father was. She did what she did for the sake of it. She *enjoyed* everything about her infidelity: the sex, the power over others it brought her, the ill-concealed jealousy it engendered in my father, even the fact that she was, in a way, still working for what they both mistakenly thought of as Cambodia's freedom.

"For her, my father's radical politics was a convenient beast upon which she rode for personal pleasure. In the end I think that realization destroyed the marriage for him."

Her eyes closed for a moment, and he imagined her fighting the painful image. "You know, I'm certain my parents in their own way loved one another. But my father's single-mindedness doomed them. It was his deeply abiding beliefs that made him unstoppable. It is possible for a mercenary like my mother, for instance, to be bought off or turned around. But not my father. He was different. He was special."

"Did you love him," Chris said, "or hate him?" echoing the question she had once asked him about Terry.

"For a long time," she said in a dreamy voice, "my father defined my world. 'This is life,' he said, and I saw it through his eyes. What other choice did I have? My mother bore me, but she did not raise me. A succession of nurses took care of me while she was out with my father. At night it was he who shooed the nurses away so that he could spend time with me, especially when I was ill. Then he would tell me stories of saints and sinners, Christ and the devil, while he fed me water to cool my fevers.

"And it was he who punished me. With my mother it was entirely different. It took me a long time to understand that she had immediately seen me as a threat. I was younger, more exotic, if not more beautiful than she. At first she did her best to ignore my presence in the household. When that was no longer possible, she treated me with scorn."

She looked at him. "Did I answer your question?"

"That depends," he said, "on your point of view."

She laughed. "Yours or mine?"

"I don't have any," he said. "And you have too many."

He cupped her breast.

"Chris."

"Ah." He felt her respond.

She put her hand over his. "We may be in Paris, but are we really any closer to Trangh? How in God's name will we ever find him here? I hope with all my heart we never do. Oh, Chris, I'm so afraid!''

''Tais-toi!'' he admonished, covering her lips with his. ''In the dead of night, even serious matters must sleep.''

She wrapped her arms around him and, arching up, pressed her breasts against him. His flesh tingled at the feel of her pointed nipples. He bit her shoulder, and she made a sound deep in her throat.

He spread her thighs with his until they encompassed his hips, and he lifted her off the bed. Surprised, her eyes flew open, and he saw himself reflected in their convex surfaces. He pushed up into her, and she shuddered, grabbing hold of him.

''Chris, I love you!''

Her hips made a circular motion, and they were as close together as two human beings could get. In the Parisian night, with the city lit like a chandelier just outside their window, they watched the changing expression on one another's face, as if with an artist's brush they were imbuing color, line, and perspective with the divine grace that summons from the depths of the individual the special warmth of memory.

In the night the floodlit Seine flowed silently by, supporting languid boats filled with lovers staring starry-eyed at each other, while they floated by the Eiffel Tower, Notre Dame, and the Musée d'Orsay.

Chris let out a deep groan as he reached the peak and Soutane, her eyes fluttering closed, began to spasm above him, breathing at the exhausted end one word into the spangled darkness, the warmth of memory.

''Terry.''

Dick Andrew at the CIA never did return Diana's call, which was decidedly odd. She phoned him several times and was told that he was in a meeting, out of the building, or unavailable, depending on who answered.

That was when she decided that DEA would be her best bet. Brad Wolff, director of Eastern Seaboard Operations, was already in her debt. Wolff had been Seve's boss when Seve had been on loan to the DEA some years ago. Seve had advised her to drop off everything they had accumulated in the massive Peter Loong Chun file, which she had done the day Seve had left for the airport.

Within twenty-four hours, Wolff had called to thank her personally for the drone work she and the rest of Seve's unit had done on the case.

It was to Wolff she had gone with the information Chris had provided Seve. She knew she had neither the authorization nor the time to search for the *Monique* on her own. And after Kline's warning, she was not inclined to ask him for a favor.

It was late in the day when Brad Wolff called. She was already on her way out of the office and was not at her desk when she took the call.

"We've got to meet," he said. "Right away."

She responded to the tight, flat tone of his voice, wondered what had happened. But she was too well trained to ask over the phone. Instead she said, "I'm hungry," and gave him an address.

They met at a restaurant in Chinatown that Diana had discovered. It had become Seve's favorite because it served the best seafood in New York, and walking into it without him was a depressing experience.

Diana suspected that she had made a mistake, not in falling in love with Seve, because one could hardly help that, but in persisting in loving him. She knew that he cared about her as deeply as he could care for anyone, but she did not think that would be enough. It was folly to love a priest, let alone to want to marry one. And Seve, she knew, was more priest than police officer. He and his brother, Dominic, merely differed on the method they had chosen to carry out their life's work.

How could so much pain be wrapped up in loving someone? she wondered as she spotted Brad Wolff. He was sitting at a corner table in the rear of the bustling restaurant, facing the entrance. There was humiliation in giving of yourself so unselfishly, and getting so little in return. She might have been angry at Seve for enslaving her so mercilessly were she not intelligent enough to realize that it was she who had done the imprisoning.

"Hello, Diana." Wolff smiled, rising and extending his hand. "It's good to see you. I haven't been here since the night you and Seve and I finished the Delloria stakeout." He was a short, dark, dynamo of a man with a sharp, watchful face. Though he was in his late fifties, he had the lean, muscular body of a man twenty years his junior.

Diana recalled the Delloria stakeout well. She had seen Brad Wolff stand perfectly still for close to four hours, then break into a sprint that overtook a Colombian cocaine runner.

He poured her some tea. "We're still sifting through all the reports,'' he said. ''I think you've compiled a treasure trove, especially the recent information on Chun.'' The waiter dropped stained menus on the table, and he swept them aside. ''It could not have come at a more opportune time. The newest info you turned up was right on the money. We've just bagged fifty kilos headed for Chinatown—slated for Chun's network.''

''Where did it come on shore? Montauk?''

''East Bay Bridge,'' Wolff said. This was a major breakthrough, Diana thought. So why wasn't he in good humor? ''Nice place,'' Wolff said. He poured them more tea. ''Settling down now. Used to be a resort, filled with day-trippers. These days it's become more of a second-home situation for the new rich, the super-rich, as well as the wealthy.

''Anyway, we've had a team in place for nearly eight months, running a fishing boat out of Montauk and East Bay Bridge. Real yahoo types who look like they've got nothing between their ears but hair.

''All that time we got nothing. Until your tip. Just before dawn they caught up with the pleasure boat named the *Monique*. It was captained by a woman of the same name, French, no less.''

''What has she given you?''

''Zip.'' Wolff fiddled with his cup.

''Why not?''

He let out a long breath. ''She was dead before she could be questioned.'' He would not meet her gaze. ''And don't ask me what happened, because I'm still trying to find out.''

''There was a shoot-out?''

''No.'' There was a pained look on his face. ''The team took her in intact.''

She stared at him, digesting the implications of what he was saying. ''You mean she died in DEA custody?''

''Yeah.'' Wolff shook his head. ''At first it looked like she had a heart attack, but I just got the coroner's report. She was poisoned. Very sophisticated stuff. The lab had to run it through several times to be sure of what they had.''

''Poisoned by who, one of your men? Why?''

He looked at her at last. ''You tell me. Something's up. Something bad. And I don't know what it is.''

Diana ran her fingers through her hair. ''Maybe this isn't a good time to ask for a favor.''

''Shoot,'' he said. ''I owe you a big one. I told you the info you dropped off was a treasure trove, but I didn't get into details. Remember the EastAsia Benevolent Society which had its offices in the building on Doyers Street where Seve was attacked?"

Diana nodded.

"Well, it's a corporation, set up by Al DeCordia. He was a lawyer, with a high degree of practice specialization in international finance. His particular genius, it turns out, was in knowing—and sometimes circumventing—international import-export laws. He could get any product you could name from point A to point Z faster, for the least amount of money, and with the least number of people knowing than anyone else we've ever come across.

"Turns out that DeCordia arranged the EastAsia Benevolent Society as a shell holding company. It leases everything, so it has no fixed overhead; it owns nothing outright, so it has no assets. The investigation is going exceedingly slowly, but that always happens when you get near the shit."

He waved his hands. "So ask, my child, and you shall receive."

Diana outlined the resistance she was encountering with the investigation into Marcus Gable's background.

"Looks like you've run afoul of the CIA," he said thoughtfully when she had finished.

"Not the CIA," she corrected him. "The State Department."

"Oh, but who do you think blew the whistle to State? Morton Saunders is the department's liaison to the CIA."

"What about Dick not returning my calls?"

"Dick Andrew is a grunt, a soldier in the trenches," Wolff said. "He's been ordered to stay away. This is obviously way out of his league."

"Can you help? I have to tell you that Gable's CIA, and active with a capital *A*."

Wolff still had that thoughtful look on his face. "Maybe we can help each other. Even before Monique died, I had a gut feeling that the boat wasn't hers. I mean, it's registered in her name, all right, and she had a captain's license. But something didn't smell right."

"There's definitely a male involved. Friend of Gable's. You think it was a setup?"

Wolff shook his head. "I don't think so. More like a front, maybe. But after what happened to Monique right in my wine cellar, I'm reluctant to continue the investigation with personnel from my unit, because if her murder wasn't an inside job, I'm as Chinese as you are. I've got a real problem."

He picked up the menu, perused it. "Aren't the crabs and tofu here terrific?"

"You remembered," she said. "Not to mention the steamed sea bass, and the stir-fried octopus."

"Done." He put the menu down. "How about I give Joe a call, see if your captain will give you a temporary leave of absence?" He looked at her. "You work for me on this, and I'll follow up with DEA resources on the Gable thing. What say?"

Diana thinking about the long skein of events: of Peter Loong Chun, of heroin trafficking, of Seve's mysterious Vietnamese killer, of Al DeCordia's headless body, of Dominic's head in the bower behind the sacristy, of Seve's brush with decapitation, and his subsequent interest in the Alix Layne–Christopher Haye assault file Billy Mace had brought him.

I've got a real problem, Wolff had said. She did not think he knew the half of it. None of them did yet. But they were getting closer, she could feel it.

"Order me a Tsing Tsao," she said, feeling happier and freer than she had since her confrontation with Seve in the hospital, "and let's get started."

Mun was on the mountainside with Ma Varada and Mogok. Ahead of them was a jungle so dense even the shadows were green.

"You want Virgil because he has designs on the Shan," Mun had said to General Kiu, "and I want him because he ordered Terry's death." But he had wondered as he had laid out the deal whether that was in fact the situation.

"Ma Varada is the key," he had continued. "She works for Virgil, but if we play it right, if she is convinced that I've saved her, I can turn her. Surely that is a more economical use for her than as an example to future spies."

General Kiu had allowed Mun to cut Ma Varada down. The balance of Mun's afternoon was spent tending to her, feeding her mind as well as her stomach.

General Kiu had insisted that Mun take Mogok along as guide until they were off the Shan. He did not want to involve any of his soldiers, since even a party of three was more conspicuous than he deemed wise. "The borders are already filling with Admiral Jumbo's men," he told Mun just before they left camp. "His alliance with the devil has propelled him from his lethargy."

Mun, armed with a Russian Kalishnikov that was a twin of the one Mogok carried at the ready, took Ma Varada by the hand and plunged into the thicket.

It was dense and moist within the vast triple-canopied jungle. Already, since they had descended from the highest plateaus upon which the opium lords made their camps, the temperature had risen more than thirty degrees.

Mun considered General Kiu and thought that, perhaps, he had missed his true calling. With his ability to turn preposterous rhetoric into logical justification he would have been a natural as a missionary. As it was, he was content in his demagogue status. That was because as far as proselytizing was concerned, the two were synonymous.

Outside the Shan Mun could realize that to call it Eden or even Shangri-la was absurd, unless one imagined these places to be akin to enormously wealthy feudal kingdoms ruled by cruel despots, feeding off the pernicious fruits of their starving vassals' labors. And yet, Mun had to admit that General Kiu had made that absurdity believable.

Was he any better—or worse—than Admiral Jumbo? Perhaps—if, as the evidence indicated, Admiral Jumbo had cut a deal with the Magician. But the explanation had been entirely General Kiu's, and Mun distrusted that. He particularly distrusted General Kiu's magnanimity in letting him and Ma Varada go.

As if to underscore Mun's concern, Mogok tapped him on the back and said, "We're being followed."

Mun turned his head, but could see nothing through the welter of trees, vines, and underbrush. "Who are they?"

"Soldiers," Mogok said. "But whether they are General Kiu's or Admiral Jumbo's I cannot say."

Enfolded within the gigantic cathedral of the jungle, they were motes, like cast-off detritus riding an endless sea. The threat, unseen and unheard, lurked behind every scarred bole, every insect-laden vine.

Had Admiral Jumbo, through a spy, discovered what Mun and Mogok were up to? Or had General Kiu been lying to him all along, and had now ordered their execution?

They picked up their pace, which was difficult enough because of the density of the foliage. Now Mun could hear the distinct sounds of pursuit echoing through the forest. He saw the fright on Ma Varada's face and pushed her onward down the Shan.

She stumbled over a root, arched out of the ground like an old man's arthritic finger. Annoyed, Mun bent to pull her up, which was when the firing began. Perhaps, he thought later, this clumsiness on Ma Varada's part had saved his life. Bark on the tree near which he had been standing shredded as the fusillade of bullets struck it.

Stretched full-length on the jungle floor, flung over Ma Varada's body, Mun turned his head long enough to see Mogok just behind them. He was crouched, firing in short bursts into the dizzying green layers of the jungle.

He waved them on, following as he methodically sprayed the area behind them with fire. They were heading into a particularly dense pocket of foliage, and the air sat in their lungs like seawater.

To their rear the gunfire had increased. Mogok turned, crouched within a clump of ferns that reached over his head. He moved, to get a better shot, aimed. Then he was flung to the side, his head and torso ripped open by the massed machine-gun fire.

Mun turned, put his Kalishnikov to his shoulder. But the trigger wouldn't work. The gun had jammed! Sweat broke out under his arms, along his spine. He was utterly defenseless.

He pushed Ma Varada down into the ooze of the jungle floor, then snaked his way toward where Mogok's body lay sprawled. He waited, listening for the smallest sound. Had they seen him? Was he even now within their sights? It did not do to dwell on such matters, he knew. Without Mogok's weapon they were dead anyway.

Cautiously, he reached out, pulled the AK-47 back toward him. When he had it, he scrambled back to Ma Varada, dragged her to her feet, and headed off through the thick, clinging underbrush.

The gun he had been given had proved useless. *Karma.* Or had it been deliberately disabled to make his execution that much easier?

No time to attack the puzzle now. Ferns and branch tips flicked by his face as he ran through the jungle. He could hear Ma Varada's panting breath in his ear.

He took them along a zigzag path of his own making, hearing now and again a crash through the foliage behind them. Then he began to hear noise on either side of them and knew that the soldiers were trapping them like game in an ever-narrowing net.

No wonder there is so much noise from directly behind us! Mun thought. Those soldiers are the beaters, meant to push the quarry forward so that we can be picked up by the true hunters.

With this in mind, Mun brought them up short. Thinking, No step taken in vain, as Sun Tzu has written, he began to lead them back the way they had come.

"What are you doing?" Ma Varada whispered. Her face was pinched and filled with lines. She was clearly terrified.

"Quiet," he said. "If you do not want to die, you will follow me silently, and do as I say without question."

Now he used the sounds of the beaters to guide him. He checked his Kalishnikov; there was ample ammunition.

"They are so close!"

He ignored her tremulous voice in his ear, pressed on from tree to tree until he saw the first of the beaters. Then he pushed Ma Varada down against the thick bole of a tree before stationing himself in good position against a scabrous tree trunk.

When he had a clear shot at the beater, he squeezed the trigger and brought him down. Immediately, he was up and running to another position as automatic fire broke out from the hunters farther down the mountainside. They had not seen him, he knew, but were responding to the shots.

Two more beaters appeared, and he fired again, watching with satisfaction as they spun off into the underbrush. He was moving again, listening for the beaters. He did not know precisely how many soldiers had been assigned this task, but he could not imagine a commander utilizing more than four or five of his complement in this manner.

Three down, he thought, as he spotted the fourth and dispatched him with a short burst as he was still on the run.

Crouched against an outcropping of rock, Mun rechecked the Kalishnikov's ammunition. He had been deliberately abstemious, wanting to give the hunters as little clue as possible as to his location.

He listened for further evidence of the beaters, heard none. He signaled for Ma Varada to join him. He would have preferred to wait longer, but knew they could not afford such luxury. All too soon the hunters would figure out what had happened, and would be after them.

He took her hand and crept from the protection of the rock face. And was brought up short by a harsh voice shouting, "Stand where you are!"

Mun began to swing his Kalishnikov toward the voice.

"Stop or I'll cut you off at the knees."

The fifth beater was very close. He was grinning, and Mun could see that the only reason he had not already shot them was that he was enjoying the situation too much.

"Did you think you were clever?" the beater said. "You were stupid."

Mun could see his finger tighten on the trigger. The muzzle of the AK-47 loomed as large as the mouth of a mortar. He calculated the odds of him being able to aim and shoot in time. The machine gun was a clumsy weapon at this range, and Mun knew that he would be dead before he could even get his weapon into position. There was nothing he could do. He imagined the spew of bullets, the tearing pain, the cessation of life, and prepared himself.

"Why should I kill you now?" the soldier said, and threw a short length of cord at Ma Varada's feet. "Tie him up, bitch. I want to see his face while I play with you. I haven't seen a body as fine as yours in months. I want some diversion before I kill you both."

The beater turned his attention to Mun. He was gloating. Then his eyes opened wide, and he said something imcomprehensible. Mun had been aware of a blurred motion from beside him, and now he saw the hilt of the knife protruding from the beater's neck as he realized that Ma Varada had thrown it.

The man staggered, fumbling for the trigger of his machine pistol. Mun swung his weapon up, got off a short, reflexive burst into his chest that threw him deep into the underbrush.

Ma Varada ran to where the beater knelt, folded like a marionette, and, placing her foot against his chest, extracted her knife.

"Don't forget his machine gun," Mun said, and as they took off into the jungle, "Where did you get the knife?"

"I stole it from Mogok," she said. "As it turned out, he didn't need it, and we did."

"Karma," Mun said with a good deal of admiration.

"Karma," she agreed, accepting his oblique compliment.

But they had not gone fifty yards when he spotted the forward patrol. The soldiers saw him at the same time, and rushed toward him.

He took Ma Varada by the hand and, lurching heavily to the left, veered off in that direction. He heard the firing begin behind him and knew that the soldiers were gaining. Still, there could be no question of turning to face them. They knew where he was, and that he was armed and dangerous. He had no illusions. He had been successful against the beaters because he had taken them by surprise.

He was about to ask Ma Varada about the terrain when he felt a tearing in his shoulder, as if it had been caught by a branch. Then from out of nowhere blood seemed to explode. Ma Varada screamed, and he turned to see blood covering her face and side. She had been hit!

Slowly, because she was staring at him with a horrified expression, he realized that it was he who had been hit. He looked down, saw his side drenched in blood. Abruptly dizzy, he stumbled.

Ma Varada wrenched her hand from his and, putting the AK-47 at the ready, turned on their pursuers. She hastened through the trees, firing off short, accurate bursts.

Mun saw one, then another of the soldiers fly backward beneath the fusillade. Then he was down on all fours, his vision blurry. His head shook back and forth like a wounded animal's, and when he heard his name being called, he blindly brought his machine gun up.

Ma Varada pushed it out of the way and slapped him across the cheek. Slowly, his vision cleared.

"Can you get up? Can you walk?"

"The soldiers," he breathed.

"Come on. I have bound your wounds," she said, grunting as she put her arm beneath his. "Try now. We are almost out of their territory. Almost off the Shan Plateau. Almost safe."

Mun gritted his teeth with the effort. The natural anesthetic of trauma was beginning to wear off, and the pain was appalling. With her help he rose and, together, they began to stumble down the mountainside.

Mun closed his eyes. *Almost safe*, she had said. Perhaps from Admiral Jumbo or General Kiu, whoever was the liar. But not from Ma Varada. He hardly knew her. He certainly did not trust her. Yet now he was utterly dependent on her for his life and well-being.

His pain made him helpless. He was obliged, in order to have a chance of surviving, to do what she ordered. He knew that he could die. His wounds might not be simple ones and, in this primitive land, if infection set in, he was a dead man.

He knew that he did not want to die, that if the end came without having reached the Magician, he would weep. He thought more about Terry now than he did about himself. Terry was why he had returned here; Terry was why he had done what he had done in the Shan. Without having a chance to avenge Terry's death, Mun knew his life would have no meaning.

With these thoughts in mind he clutched at Ma Varada all the harder. He needed her to protect him. *Karma* had transformed her from a dupe into a goddess. In her presence he felt mortal and vulnerable. Now she had the power of life and death over him, and

Mun, for the first time since he had left Vence, found himself praying.

Because he knew what the goddess was capable of. Her power was paradoxical: it nurtured, protected, and annihilated.

Morphée stood before the full-length mirror so that Milhaud could see all of her naked body at once.

From behind her, on the bed, he said, "Now get dressed slowly, one item at a time."

She did as he bade, by the delicate motions of her hands, making love to her body as she knew he wished to do. When she reached a certain point (it did not take long), she heard him get off the bed. A moment later he was against her. She felt him hard and hot between her legs, and her eyes closed. She raised her arms over her head and, shuddering, pressed her damp palms hard against the mirror.

The newly created engine heated the room like a furnace.

"What is it like," Milhaud said sometime later, "to dream of time?"

Morphée's eyes were closed. In that state she seemed to him as mysterious as time. "You are French," she said. "Even if I were to tell you, how could you possibly understand it?"

They were curled up on the bed, and he rolled her around so that he could better see her face. The light from the city seeped like excess energy through gaps in the velvet curtains. It struck her face in such a way that she appeared to be an *apsara*, one of the celestial dancers carved into the facades of Añgkor's ancient temples.

"Why must you talk down to me," he complained, "as if I were a child or a member of an inferior race?"

"On the contrary," Morphée said, caressing him, "I speak to you as I do because you are a member of a *superior* race."

Milhaud recoiled as if she had struck him. "If that is a joke, it is a bizarre one."

"But it is no joke," she said. "That was the lesson you French taught us in Indochina. This was your particular talent: to rape us while assuring us of our inferior status in the world."

"Not *my* talent, certainly. I never condoned such a philosophy."

"Not *you* individually, darling," she reassured him. "I meant you as a people."

Milhaud lay back in the bed, suddenly depressed by the conversation. Morphée rose up on one elbow, looked down at him. She put a hand on his chest, feeling the beating of his heart. "Now I have upset you."

"It's not you," he said, realizing it was the truth. What she had said had hardly come as a revelation to him. He had spent much of his life trying to atone for the sins his countrymen had committed in Indochina. No, his black mood was due to the Magician. It terrified him that his nemesis was out there, that, like the devil, he knew of Milhaud's existence—his former life!—and was using him to his own, malefic purpose. All of a sudden Milhaud had begun to wonder whether he was deluding himself. Was he really free of the CIA's influence? He knew that he could not be until he discovered what the Magician's plan was. Only the possession of that knowledge would make him truly free.

Morphée kissing him gently, lovingly on the lips. "What is it you wish to know, darling?"

Milhaud stared past her to the ceiling, where reflections made by the traffic lights illuminated the ornate scrollwork, artistry of another century. "I want you to tell me," he said slowly, "how you have freed yourself from the past."

"I'm not sure that I can," she said. "First, you would have to understand what it is like to be Asian."

"To have been a prisoner or a slave, you mean." He was thinking of how much a prisoner of the Americans he had been and, in a sense, still was. How he hated that humiliating position! "I know what that is like."

"I don't disbelieve you," she said, "but you are mistaken."

There it was again, that knowing tone. He could not bear it, so he told her everything. "I have been a slave to a group of Americans," he began. "They ordered, and I obeyed. Now I think I have found a way to be free of them, but I cannot be sure. There is one American who still haunts me, who has, I suspect, tracked me like a bloodhound. He is the only person I am afraid of."

Morphée stroked his forehead. "He will destroy you," she said. "You can see that he has already tried."

"What do you mean? He hasn't tried to harm me."

"Oh, but he already has," she said. "You have only to see how much you hate yourself to know to what extent he has succeeded."

He stared at her, thinking about what she had said. Is the truth always so painfully obvious when it is spoken? he wondered. And for the first time he understood the depth of her power. "You can help me," he said. "What am I to do?"

"First, you must reject hate," Morphée said. "Hate and fear are two sides of the same coin. When you hate, you fear yourself. Hate imprisons you in time. It is like a disease that turns minutes into hours. Once you let go of hate, all else follows. You are free of time, and of the past."

"You make it sound so easy."

"Do I? I'm sorry. It is very difficult."

Milhaud rolled over, so that he was looking at her bare body. "It must take a great deal of discipline," he said, "not to hate, not to feel fear."

"Discipline, yes," she said. "But also emotion."

"Emotion?"

"One must learn how to love even one's enemies, *especially* one's enemies." She took his face in her hands. "That is what you taught me, darling, when I fell in love with you."

"Then I have been more to you than a lover. I have been a teacher."

"A teacher," she said, "and an enemy."

Milhaud was startled. "You thought of me as your enemy?" He watched her face with a growing realization. What a fool he had been to treat her with such contempt. Hadn't he done to Morphée what his countrymen had done to Vietnam and Cambodia? He had taken possession of her body over and over without any conscious realization of what he was doing, of who she was. He had, to use her own words, raped her while assuring her of her own inferior status.

She was only a whore, so that when she had spoken he had listened with half an ear as one does to a lovable but querulous child. Outside of that he had dismissed her. No wonder she had asked him if he would speak to her if he met her on the street. He decided, then, that he would indeed like to be seen in public with her.

"You are the devil, my darling." She kissed him. "You have entered me, and I have loved you. You have ignored me, and I have loved you."

He looked at her uncomprehendingly.

"I have given you your answer," she said. "This is how I am free of time, and of the past. I embrace you, and feel only love."

"But what do you get in return? How do you know that I don't secretly hate you or, worse, care nothing about you?"

"Do you?"

"No," Milhaud said with something akin to awe.

Morphée smiled, content at last.

* * *

Chris dreams of entering Paris in triumph. Wearing the coveted yellow jersey, he feels renewed strength as he approaches the finish line. The day is bright and sunny. The road is dry and firm and there is no reason why he will not finish first.

The crowd, beside itself with delight, surges against the sawhorses and the gendarmes. Many spectators are waving tiny American flags, urging him on, the first American to win the Tour de France.

Nothing can stop me now, he thinks in elation.

Then he sees Alix emerge from the excited throng. The gendarmes who guard the raceway do not see her. Chris calls out to her but she does not hear him or see him. Instead, she is running directly into his path.

She is so close and his speed is such that even if he swerves he knows he will strike her. Suddenly, as he is upon her, she turns and sees him.

She smiles . . .

And Chris woke up, drenched in sweat.

It was already after noon. Sunlight crept through the thick curtains. He turned, saw that Soutane was gone. He went into the bathroom to relieve himself. She was not there.

Back at bedside he dialed the States, got the hospital. Alix was stable, the floor nurse told him, but she was still apparently unable to speak. Surgery was scheduled for the next day, but she could not give him any specific information about it. When he had called last evening, the hospital had given him the number of the surgeon's office, and he had called there. The doctor had been in surgery, he learned, and would be there all day.

''Shit,'' he had said, slamming down the receiver. The whole world, he had thought, is built of secrets.

Max Steiner's secretary had been happy to hear from him, but said Max was at a meeting outside the office. Chris had left a message for him to find out what kind of surgery Alix was facing and get back to him. He had left the hotel's number.

Now he called down to the front desk, but there was no message from Max or from anyone else. ''Shit,'' he said again. He went in to shower.

With the hot water cascading all around him, he wondered what it was like to have your lover call out your brother's name while the two of you were making love. It had happened, and he didn't know how he felt. Angry? Hurt? Betrayed? All of the above, or any?

It seemed odd to him that his brain had reacted by dreaming about Alix—or, more precisely, what he was doing to her by being here. Would anything be different if he had been by her side all along? he asked himself. She would still be facing this operation tomorrow.

Idiot! he thought. There would be someone, other than her son, to hold her hand. There would be a presence close by on whom she could rely. Instead, he was six thousand miles away trying to hold water in his hands.

He had just finished dressing when Soutane came in with Seve. They were laughing, talking about something inconsequential, and Chris felt his stomach contract.

"I see you're finally up," Soutane said. She held up a paper bag. "Coffee and croissants, courtesy of the café around the corner."

Chris opened the bag. "Aren't you two hungry?"

"We already ate, at the café," Seve said. "Not surprisingly, we all slept late, but I woke up feeling like I'd just gone fifteen rounds with Mike Tyson. Soutane went with me to the pharmacy. I had to fill the prescriptions the hotel doctor wrote for me."

Chris sat down at the writing desk. While he ate, Soutane said, "I've decided to do whatever I can to help."

Chris looked at her. "You're no longer concerned about selling your soul? Don't you want to be saved?"

She grinned. "I've got you two angels beside me. What could happen to me?"

Chris stared at Seve and wondered what he had said to her to make her change her mind. Objectively, he knew it did not matter, the result was what was important. He also knew that what he was feeling was unhealthy. It occurred to him that his jealousy at the easy friendship that had sprung up between Soutane and Seve was somehow wrapped up in his guilt at abandoning Alix. It was clear to him that when he did not like himself, he did not much care for anyone else either.

"In any case," Soutane went on, "we're going down to Porte de Choisy later in the day. That's Paris's Asia Town. Seve and I have decided that's the best place to start. I'm fairly familiar with the area, and even if Trangh doesn't live there, he's bound to be around at some point to at least hear from friends that I'm there."

There it was again, a squirmy worm in his gut. Chris let out a breath. "It seems a little obvious, don't you think?" He drank the last of his coffee, crumpled the wax paper around what was left of the croissant. "Trangh is smarter than that."

"Sure." Seve shrugged. "But it seemed the best of the possibilities. Unless, of course, you've come up with something we haven't thought of."

Chris admitted that he hadn't. "But, on the other hand, I haven't given it much thought."

"Well, why don't you think about it while we take in the Musée d'Orsay," Seve said.

Soutane nodded. "We'll go to La Coupole for dinner afterward and talk strategy. It's going to be tricky with Trangh knowing all of us by sight."

"The museum, then dinner? What the hell are you two thinking of?" Chris said angrily. "We've got to find Trangh as quickly as possible. He's our only lead to the Magician."

"That's true enough," Seve said. "But, as Soutane pointed out to me, the Asians—at least the kind we're interested in—don't come out in Porte de Choisy until nightfall. Then the gambling joints are going full tilt, the whores are active. During the day, there's nothing there but old men and mothers with baby strollers."

"I'm sure you two can handle it," Chris said. "Why don't you go on without me. I have some things to take care of."

Seve shot Soutane a look, and she said, "Chris?"

"It's okay, Soutane. Really. You go on with Seve. Have fun. I'll see you later." He did not want to confront her now, although the truth was he did not want to confront himself. His conflicted feelings were all of a sudden too complex to contemplate unraveling. "Go on now."

There was, of course, nothing he had to do, and when he was alone in the room, he felt the void with the acuteness of pain. He wondered what Soutane felt at calling out Terry's name. He wondered if, as he was, she was thinking about it.

He stared out at the street below. He saw Soutane and Seve crossing the street, heading in the direction of the Seine. They were near enough to the museum for them to walk.

There was still time, he knew, for him to catch up with them. Knowing Soutane, he could guess their route. She would cross to the Left Bank via the Pont Alexandre III, her favorite of Paris's myriad bridges, then stroll along the Quai d'Orsay to the Quai Anatole France.

He watched them disappear around the corner, but made no

move. He wished that he could turn back the clock. He wished that she had never uttered that one name.

But as soon as they were out of sight his mind, switching gears, turned again to Trangh. Ever since their confrontation in the stable at Tourrette, his eyes had haunted Chris. That he was Terry's murderer seemed oddly, frighteningly irrelevant.

How could that be?

Seve was committed to tracking him down, and Chris had agreed. But, inside, all Chris wanted to do was run. It was difficult to admit his fright, disappointing to realize that he was not the hero he had begun to imagine himself to be. He was not, after all, his brother Terry. But neither was he the Chris of old. What, then, had he become?

He did not know, but sensed with the vestiges of animal instinct that one person held the answer.

Trangh.

He got up, threw the dregs of his meal into the wastepaper basket. Then he put on a jacket and went out of the room.

When he got onto the street, he went toward the Champs Elysées and the métro station. He had never heard of Porte de Choisy, but he found it on the métro map, at the extreme southern periphery of the city. He traced the route to the station, saw that he would have to change at Chatelet for the number-seven line to Mairie d'Ivry.

He bought a second-class ticket and, inserting it, went quickly through the turnstile.

Diana had no difficulty in finding Monique's house. It was perhaps four miles outside the village of East Bay Bridge, on a spit of land between the ocean and the bay. It was not a typical East End house with the exaggerated multisloping rooflines, the cedar boards weathered a dead gray.

It had, rather, neoclassical lines, with generous gables, a slate roof, and siding stained bright white. Brad Wolff had provided her with the key, as well as instructions, so she had no difficulty with the police locks.

At this time of year, during the week, the area appeared deserted. The posh houses were still closed from the long, cruel winters out here near the end of Long Island.

There was no traffic along the road, save for the occasional fisherman's Jeep or Blazer.

Inside, the house was not what she had pictured. It was heavy with thick, Persian rugs, dark woods, and richly patterned curtains. It looked more like a home in the city than a beach residence.

She pulled aside the drapes, shivering at the damp that had begun to creep in with the cold. Outside, a wooden walkway went across the dunes to the wide expanse of beach beyond. There were dark patches on the walkway, where the winter winds had scoured away the stain. The metal rims of the light fixtures set into the wood were corroded by the salt.

Diana wondered what the upkeep on such a place might be, and shuddered. On a cop's salary it was not prudent to consider such things.

Everything was oversized in the place, as if its occupants' needs encompassed areas with which Diana was not familiar. What did one do, for instance, on a twenty-foot sofa that one couldn't on a piece of furniture one third that size?

The big-leafed plants needed dusting and, in the kitchen, she found a half-eaten bowl of cat food but no cat.

After a tour of the house she went back into the master bedroom because, after all, she was here to discover signs that someone else also lived here, someone, if Brad Wolff was right, for whom Monique was fronting. Marcus Gable's friend.

Taking up an entire wing, the bedroom was lavish, heavy, sensual. Besides a circular bed, there was a floral chintz-covered settee. One wall of mirror-doored closets revealed rack upon rack of women's clothes and, below, a staggering array of shoes. Despite herself, Diana found envy rising up inside her. When you're a cop, she thought, it took a great deal of mental discipline to be poor.

To the right were shelves filled with accessories: necklaces, bracelets, earrings, bangles, and the like—all costume, but well-made and not inexpensive.

Diana checked the clothes and shoe sizes, determining they belonged to one woman. As for the accessories, it seemed clear they were the product of a unified taste. She could find nothing of a man's wardrobe anywhere in the bedroom, either in the closets or in the massive French armoire filled with Monique's coats, jackets, and jumpsuits.

As for the night tables, one held a box of tissues, a sleep mask, a jar of Oil of Olay night cream, a small vial of prescription sleeping pills, two paperbacks, one a thriller, the other a copy of Marcel Proust's *À l'Ombre des jeunes filles en fleurs*, the second volume of his *Remembrance of Things Past*. The drawer in the other night table was empty, but not dusty.

In the enormous bathroom the medicine chest contained the usual assortment of bottles, boxes, and jars. More prescription vials, one for Benzedrine, the other for Valium. Nothing out of the ordinary. The soap by the side of the whirlpool tub was from Caswell Massey. She smelled it; jasmine.

It would be too easy, she thought, suddenly to come across a bottle of men's cologne or a jockstrap. Still, she had the feeling that Brad Wolff was on the right track. Perhaps it had been the sight of the night-table drawer, empty and clean, as if someone had recently cleared it out.

With that in mind, she returned to the bedroom, went through everything again. She riffled through the pages of the paperbacks, in desperation a detective in a book, hoping to find a cleverly secreted clue such as a note written in the margins. There was nothing.

She was about to close the night-table drawer when her eye fell on the sleeping-pill vial. Then, disbelieving, she picked it up. It was not Monique's! The name on it read: Reed Parkes. Now who in the hell—

Her head came up. She sat very still, listening for a repetition of the sound she had just heard. When none was forthcoming, she pocketed the vial, drew her service revolver.

She got off the bed, circled around until she was pressed against the wall beside the door. It was open to the hallway and the rest of the house.

She risked a quick glance. It was a sunny day, but the thick drapes were drawn, and wide swaths of shadow obscured the interior as if it were a forest.

Diana, holding her gun with both hands, stiff-armed at the ready, moved cautiously into the hallway. Her eyes darted back and forth, trying to probe the gloom of bedroom doorways, as well as the farthest reaches of the hallway.

Her ears strained for a sound. What was it that she had heard? A footfall? She was certain she had locked the front door when she came in. But, of course, the police locks had to remain open. Did that mean someone with a key to the house was inside?

She went through one bedroom after another, one bathroom after another. Darkness and dust filled up the corners. The kitchen was open via a pass-through to the dining area, and that, too, was deserted. She heard the ice-maker at work inside the refrigerator, its brief whirring exaggerated in the silence. Could this be what she had heard?

Out in the living room the great sofa loomed as large as a wall. She moved swiftly behind it, aiming the gun. The empty space mocked her.

Beyond the kitchen, the hallway, interrupted by the main section of the house, began again, leading off to a gym, a media room, and a den-library, as well as another bath.

Keeping her eye on the hallway, Diana crept to the front door. The bolt had not been thrown; the door was unlocked. Then someone *had* come in while she was there.

She heard the sound and simultaneously saw the shadow. The gun swung around, and she almost blew the cat's head off. It mewed into the maw of the weapon, then yawned, padding away into the darkness.

Diana was sweating. She had begun to tremble with the sudden release of adrenaline. It had nowhere to go, so her muscles jumped and popped with useless energy.

In the hallway she strained for a hint of any sound. Then she froze. In the semidarkness of the gym she could see a figure crouched and waiting. She smiled to herself, edged forward, keeping to the deepest shadows of the hallway.

When she judged the angle to be right, she rose, holding the figure in her sights. "Freeze!" she yelled. "Police!"

Then she crashed into the doorframe. Bright lights exploded in her head, and her service revolver went skidding across the polished floorboards of the gym. Was it then that she realized that she had been staring into a floor-length mirror, and that all she had had in her sights was a reflection?

It must have been, because in the next instant she had plunged into a darkness where only thought dwelled.

At what point had he made the decision not to give the Forest of Swords to the Magician? Milhaud did not know precisely, although he suspected that it had come at the moment when he realized that whether or not he gave the *Prey Dauw* to the Magician, the Magician wanted Soutane dead. No doubt he also wanted Milhaud himself dead. But not so quickly. That was not the Magician's way.

So the knowledge that the decision to keep the Forest of Swords might well cost Milhaud his life did not deter him. Not that he wasn't frightened of dying. He most certainly was. But he was more frightened of what he saw as mortal sin.

In this way he had begun to understand his terror of the Magician.

It was a mortal fear because of the hate in his heart. Morphée had seen this. With her help Milhaud had discovered in the workings of the Magician all the exploitation, greed, and lust of the Westerners—both French and American—in Indochina. In other words he recognized in the Magician the dark side of himself.

The existence of the Magician was like a mirror held up to his face. In it he could see reflected his exploitation of his wife, of those he had used so unscrupulously in Vietnam, Cambodia, and Burma. It had all been, he had told himself, in the furtherance of his dream to free Indochina from Western influence, to return it to the pristine state it had once enjoyed.

But in that mirror was also reflected the cruelty of Pol Pot, the genocide of the Cambodian people, and their eventual enslavement by Vietnam and, by extension, the Soviet Union, who, in turn, controlled Vietnam.

In wanting so desperately to purge Indochina of the disease of exploitation, he had only helped to spread the contamination. Because of him, its own people now carried the radical ideals he held dear, had sought to teach with such loving care, and in the process, had twisted them to their own ends.

This occurred to him, perhaps, after returning home from his most recent rendezvous with Mr. LoGrazie.

"I told him," Mr. LoGrazie said breathily, "that I would join him." His face had that highly colored aspect of the persistent drunk. He was dressed in evening clothes beneath his ubiquitous trench coat. The two did not go together. They gave him the air of someone who was in a hurry.

"What did he say?"

They were standing in the shadow of the opera house. The wide Boulevard des Capucines was dense with jostling tourists. The structure's eclectic Second Empire facade, with Carpeaux's justly famous sculpture *La Danse*, was lit up, so that the opera house became a beacon for blocks around.

"He did not seem surprised."

"That's not what I meant," Milhaud said. "What did he tell you of his plan?"

"It involves the heroin pipeline out of the Shan State," Mr. LoGrazie said. "It involves both Admiral Jumbo and General Kiu."

"But that is impossible," Milhaud said. "The two are the bitterest of enemies."

"I don't know about that," Mr. LoGrazie said. "I only know that Virgil needs money—lots of it."

"What for?"
"I don't know."
"Press him," Milhaud said. He was so close to knowing the Magician's secret he could hardly bear it. "You and he are partners now. He has to tell you."
"It's not that easy. I don't want him to become suspicious."
"Just do it!" Milhaud said, overcome by his desire. "It is essential that we know what he has in mind. We cannot destroy him otherwise."
Mr. LoGrazie had nodded. "I understand."
But Milhaud, staring out at the night from his study, knew that M. LoGrazie understood nothing. Only he and the Magician understood the nature of creation and destruction. It was proof that in Asia as well, absolute power corrupted absolutely. But what did it say, he wondered, about his own complicity? If he had it to do over again, would he knowingly provide Pol Pot with arms? He knew the answer. Yes, if there was even one chance in a thousand that the Cambodian would use them to free his country of outside intervention.
What others might recognize in him as selfishness, Milhaud saw as determination. Enlightenment was useless, he had taught—so successfully, it seemed!—if kept to oneself. The cardinal imperative of the gospel after understanding it was spreading it.
But what did one do with those who, once having been taught the holy scripture, abased its tenets to serve their own ends? Surely, God, as Milhaud understood Him, would strike them down. Yet there must either be another God or He must have another face, one with which Morphée was thoroughly familiar.
Retribution is impossible without hate, she had said. *Hate is impossible without fear.*
"Tomorrow night at ten, come to the park where we always meet," Mr. LoGrazie had said in his terse phone call of a few minutes ago. "I think I will have your answers by then."
He remembered the great sculpted wall at Angkor Wat. He recalled its depiction of a Hindu creation myth. Ravana and Hanuman, gods of the darkness and the light. Between them, mediating the balance of power, stood Vishnu.
But what would happen if Vishnu was somehow toppled, if the two lesser, venal gods were allowed full rein? There was only one answer: Chaos.
Milhaud, sitting in his darkened study, stared out the window and tried to think of the Magician without terror.

* * *

Mun said, "If I die, there is a place I wish to be buried."

"You will not die," Ma Varada said.

"How can you be sure?"

"The blind man has made you a potion. You have been drinking it for three days now. You are still alive, your high fever has abated. The worst has passed."

The evening was alive with the tintinnabulations of bronze gongs, silver cymbals, and the copper bells rung by orange-robed monks from whose temples, monasteries, and pagodas this never-ending music emanated.

"The bullet?"

"Passed through the flesh of your left side, just beneath your ribs and above your hipbone. I suspected as much, since you were able to walk even while in pain. The major problem was seeing that you did not lose too much blood."

"Karma," he said.

She smiled. *"Karma."*

They both knew what broken ribs or a fractured hip would have meant. The potion would not have worked. And he would never have recovered.

He closed his eyes for a moment. The smells of water buffalo and frangipani came strongly to him. "Where are we?"

"In Sagaing, just outside Mandalay." She was fussing with his bandages, and he felt some pain. "I have had a difficult time evading the notice of the authorities." She was wearing a traditional *longyis* of a brightly patterned cotton, knotted above her breasts. "It is dangerous to stay here for any length of time."

Sagaing had been, after the fall of Pagan in the beginning of the fourteenth century, the capital of a separate Shan kingdom. Now it was the center of the Buddhist faith in Burma. It was here that mothers sent their sons for *shin-pyu*, the initiation into Theravadan Buddhism. Perhaps one in a hundred decided to renounce the world of man and embrace Sangha, the order of monkhood. The monk, or *pongyi*, possessed only eight articles: three robes, a razor for shaving his face and head, a needle for sewing rents in his robes, a strainer to ensure that he would eat no living creature, a belt, and a wooden alms bowl. This last was the font of his subsistence, for he stayed alive by begging.

"You mentioned a blind man," Mun said. "Who is he?"

"One of the Magician's people."

"A Buddhist monk?"

She smiled. "Is that a joke? No." She was finished with the dressing. She had been both careful and gentle. "I haven't had a chance to thank you for saving my life."

"You paid me back by saving mine," Mun said.

She looked at him seriously. "No one else, I think, would have gotten General Kiu to cut me down."

"He is definitely a flawed human being."

If she got the joke, she gave no sign of it. "There is rice and mango," she said. "Are you hungry?"

"Only for knowledge. Tell me about the Magician."

She handed him a rough-hewn bowl. "Only if you eat; only if you are good." He heard the cotton *longyis* rustle as she settled more comfortably beside him. "I loved him once. He came to my village to recruit men into his organization, and he saw me. I was sixteen, then, and northern Burma was my world.

"He showed me how mistaken I had been. He made love to me, and he taught me . . . everything. Or so I thought. He showed me the world, and told me how it would be his one day. In my naiveté, I laughed at him. It was the last time I thought of him as foolish."

Mun was abruptly annoyed. "What do you mean, he's turned into Ming the Merciless?"

"I don't understand."

"Ming the Merciless was a comic-strip character determined to take over the world. Nobody took him very seriously except Flash Gordon."

"I think you should take the Magician very seriously," Ma Varada said.

"Listen, even governments haven't been able to take over the world. Do you think I'll believe that one man can?"

Ma Varada stared at her hands in her lap. "Well, I imagine that depends on how you define taking over the world. If you mean by either force or coercion, no. But if you mean by amassing capital, the gradual infiltration of national and multinational conglomerates by accumulation of stock and leveraged buyouts, I know that he has already gained powerful footholds in a majority of the industrialized nations of the world."

Mun stared at her as if she had suddenly begun to breathe fire. "Where did you learn all that?"

She smiled. "Where do you think?"

He grunted. "The Magician was never given to sharing anything, especially knowledge."

"That's true enough," she said. "I suppose he saw me as different. I was unformed, an ignorant child when he met me. He took me away, and became my father, my teacher, my mentor, my god. He liked that. He found, eventually, that the more he taught me, the more he confided in me, the more godlike he became.

" 'It seems,' he told me once, 'that I have been waiting all my life for this opportunity.' I think what he meant was total control of a human being, to form from living clay an individual wholly in his own image."

"And now you will betray him," Mun said, not at all certain that she was telling him the truth, or all of the truth which would be, in its way, even more lethal.

Ma Varada shook her head. "I am betraying nothing, least of all the Magician. To him I am a thing, I always have been. Like a marionette, he pulls my strings and I move. I hear his whispers in my head the way you hear the wind in the trees. It is always there.

"I want—I *must* have my freedom. Already, I do not remember my name. Varada is the name the Magician gave me. All that you see of me is his. He gave me existence, but he could not invest me with life. Now I want that more than anything else. I will do whatever I must to possess it."

Mun wondered what to do. He had to get out of Burma. Once in Thailand, it would be relatively easy to get to Bangkok, and home to Vence. But to do that he needed Ma Varada. He had to trust her with names, places he held sacred.

The hypnotic droning of the monks at prayer hung in the foothills, instilling the afternoon with an aural haze that penetrated into every corner of Sagaing.

The prayers hung like incense in his head, opening up doors he had sealed so many years ago. It was as if the monks were telling him what to do.

"It was here I came when I could no longer stay in Cambodia," Mun said, wondering, even as he spoke, why he was confiding in her, someone who could wield total mastery over him. "I entered a *kyaung* to study Buddhism. Eventually, I lived at the Kaunghmudaw Pagoda. You know, the one with the hemispherical pagoda which, legend says, is a mirror image of the perfectly shaped breasts of King Thalun's favorite wife."

"It is difficult to think of you as a monk," Ma Varada said.

"I have transgressed many times the precepts of faith," Mun said. "It makes me sad to be here again, in the cradle of Buddhism.

It makes me realize how far I have strayed from the Noble Eightfold Path."

"You were whole, once," she said, "and did not even know it." Her eyes seemed to glow, even in the shadows of dusk. "You lost what I so desperately long to be. You are neither a fool nor a madman. Yet you turned your back on life. Can you tell me why?"

"Rage," he said, understanding it himself for the first time, "and despair."

"And is it over?" She placed the palm of her hand over his heart. "Has the fire burned itself out?"

The prayers, emanating from the houses of the holy, made of the air food and wine. All the sustenance of the cosmos was here in this place, and Mun despaired that he had ever left. Anger and despair had turned his spirit restless and, in the process, had blinded him to the deep stillness that brings peace. He had allowed himself to become involved in the war, used by both the French and the Americans, and thus had left the one place that was for him nourishing.

"The fire is gone," he said with some wonder.

Ma Varada smiled, and kissed him. "Then you can help me be whole. I have come a long, long way to end up here."

Mun watched her, thinking thoughts that were perhaps already half prayers. "I know people here," he said, making the decision. "Go to the Sun U Ponya Shin Pagoda. Gain an interview with the *sayadaw* there. Tell him where I am, and that we need help. He will do the rest."

But as she rose to do as he asked, he stopped her. "How is it," he asked, "that you brought me here to Sagaing?"

She shrugged. "It was part happenstance, and part deliberate. It is close to the Shan, a natural staging area on the way to and from the plateau. It is also filled with Buddhist monks who have no love for the socialist regime."

It was also the one city in central Burma where he had friends and, privately, Mun wondered what he had said while he was burning with the high fever. Had he been delirious? Had he spoken about his pact with General Kiu to turn Ma Varada against the Magician?

Thinking of the blind man, he said, "It is also crawling with the Magician's people."

"The blind man is the only one here," she said. "But even if he weren't, I have you with me. I cannot use my normal conduits."

Mun let go of her and, closing his eyes, resigned himself. Whatever the truth, he lacked the strength now to alter events. He was still helpless, still bound to her. If she was faithful, he would survive. But what if, like Admiral Jumbo, she had something else in mind?

Diana awoke with a head full of sand. She felt a rocking beneath her and knew she was on a boat. She opened her eyes into such utter darkness she knew what had happened. She was blindfolded.

"Ah, you're awake." It was a pleasant male voice, deep and confident.

Diana felt around her, was surprised that she was not bound.

"And you're alert," the voice said. "That's very good for what I have in mind."

"Why don't you take this blindfold off," Diana said. "I'd like to see what you look like, Mr. Parkes."

"Oh, yes. Reed Parkes. I'd almost forgotten that alias. But, then, I remembered the prescription I'd needed, the one that Monique had started to use. That's why I came back to the house. I'm meticulous that way."

Diana, in trying to stand, crashed into a seat front. She came down hard on her elbow and hip.

"Hum. Perhaps you *do* need some help."

She felt herself lifted off the deck, pressed down until she was sitting on what felt like a bench. She raised her hands, to remove the blindfold, and he hit her so hard she crashed to the deck again.

She was immediately hauled back onto the bench. "Don't do anything you aren't told to do," Parkes said. "That's the first rule."

Diana sat with her back straight, her hands at her sides. Her face hurt so badly that tears had come to her eyes and, for a moment, she was glad of the blindfold. In hostage training she had been taught that it was important not to reinforce in any way the captor's sense of power. This was, after all, what drove him. Increasing his control of the situation by creating pain or fear was, in the end, his only weapon.

"Who are you, and what were you doing in my house?"

"I thought it was Monique's house."

"The second rule," he said, "is to answer my questions."

"Drop dead."

She heard Parkes laugh. "Okay, fair enough. We're gonna have us some fun now." Then her head was drawn back as he pulled harshly on her hair. "The third rule is, Don't resist."

Her wrists were placed in her lap, then crossed one over the other, before they were tied tightly with rope. Then she was led like a mule to a railing.

Without warning, she felt a powerful push at her back. She cried out, tried to maintain her balance with her arms. But with her wrists tried, this was impossible, and she went over, spinning into space, hitting the frigid water with a heavy *smack!*

Salt water filled her nose and mouth, and she began to choke, half swallowing, half retching, as she struggled to come up from the depths. But every time she broke the surface of the water, she felt his hand on the top of her head, pushing her down again.

There was no time to breathe, let alone to think.

Classroom theory and real life, Diana was learning, were two very different situations. Despite her training she felt the first queasy tendrils of panic snaking through her as she flailed about, trying desperately merely to survive.

She had powerful legs, and these worked to keep her near the surface. But this proximity to air, light, and life merely contrived to increase her panic because it kept her within Parkes's control.

Repeatedly, she tried to swim away from him but, as he would a swordfish or a mako, he kept a tight rein on the rope to which she was bound, drawing her inexorably back to the spot where his outstretched hand waited to keep her just beneath the water's surface.

Her lungs were burning, and there was a roaring in her ears. She heard a familiar voice shouting and realized it was her father, blowing up at her on the day she had announced she had signed up at the police academy.

Not that he wasn't always blowing up—the antithesis of the archetypal calm Chinese. But this time was different. Not because of him, but because of Diana's mother. She had made no attempt to shield her daughter, as she always had before, from her husband's wrath.

"She never learned what it means to be a female," went his by-now-familiar plaint. "All she thinks of is being a man, doing men's work, what's the matter with her, is her brain fevered, where is her sense of yin and yang?"

Because her mother said nothing this time, Diana knew that she was in her way as upset as her father by what Diana had done, and that had broken her heart. But it had not stopped her from graduating from the academy first in her class.

Screaming hard and long as her head was pulled from the water by her hair. She hung there, feeling as if the roots had been set on fire, gasping for air, too involved in that primitive reflex to struggle for freedom.

Dimly, she heard Parkes saying, "Who are you? What were you doing in my house?"

"I—I'm a New York cop."

"That's what your ID says, sure." Parkes shook her, so that she screamed again. "Do you think I'm stupid enough to believe that? What's NYPD doing out in Suffolk County? No, your ID's as phony as your story."

And down into the water she dropped, the salt shooting up her nostrils, and she was back struggling to stay alive. The intense cold sapped her strength. But now she was tiring, not only physically, but emotionally as well. The panic, combined with the relief of being held—however painfully—in the open air, instead of underwater, had weakened her resolve.

Now, she realized, appalled, he was keeping his hold on her hair, not just to keep her under, but to stop her from sinking too far down.

Drop dead, she had told him, and meant it. Now the thought occurred to her that if he dropped dead she would, without sufficient strength to save herself, sink like a stone into the blackness below her. Absurd as the notion was, it frightened her, which should have given her an inkling as to the desperateness of her plight.

Parkes, an experienced fisherman, sensed that she was at the point of breaking. He drew her up for one ragged gasp of air, before plunging her back into the water.

Then he hauled her back into the boat and ripped off her blindfold, stared into her face.

Diana blinked. She saw a hatchet-faced man in his midforties with the lined, leather face of the outdoorsman. He had prematurely silver hair, which he wore as long as a rock star's, and a close-cropped, salt-and-pepper beard. She was sure she had never seen him before.

"Welcome to the real world," he said.

She had already begun to shiver, not only from the cold, but from shock as well.

Parkes nodded. "Now," he said, "we're getting somewhere."

"I'm cold." She had trouble speaking, her teeth were chattering so hard.

"Who are you?"

She told him her name.

He grunted, pulling hard on her leash, so that she was jerked up and, stumbling, hurled against the railing. He came at her, and she knew he was going to throw her over the side again.

Staring down into the water, she knew she could not bear another moment underwater. She turned, and told him everything—who she was, that she had been on assignment for Seve via Brad Wolff at DEA, that she had discovered the dual identity of Arnold Toth/Marcus Gable. It did not seem like such a terrible thing to do. It was more like a lump of poison she was ready to spit out.

But when she was done, a wave of self-disgust swept over her, and she collapsed, sliding down the railing into a heap. She began to cry, in anger and humiliation, feeling that she had betrayed everything she had ever held in importance.

As for Parkes, he had already turned away. Inside the cabin he was dialing a number on a portable phone.

Diana stared at his back. At that moment the only thing she hated more than herself was Reed Parkes. And it was that hate that gave strength to her exhausted mind and body.

In one motion she rose and hurled herself on top of him. He must have felt her coming, because at the last instant he had begun to turn, and so he hit the deck with his shoulder, not his chin.

Even so, Diana had struck him across the throat before he was fully facing her. He kicked, striking her just above the kidneys, but there was no force behind the blow, and she brought her knee down, her full weight behind it. His ribs gave way, breaking through muscle and skin.

"Bitch!" Parkes screamed at her.

Which was when she slammed the edge of her hand into his throat with such force she broke his windpipe. She watched, panting and shaking all at once with the adrenaline rushing through her, as he died. And it was only after the light faded from his eyes that she became aware of the enormity of what she had done.

Reed Parkes—the only lead—was now literally a dead end. He would never be able to tell her who he really was, or what his involvement in the drug pipeline had been. She had forgotten one of the cardinal rules of any red-zone situation—leave your emotions at home.

Parkes had broken her all right—in more ways than he would ever know. Because of him she had ceased to be an officer of the law. At last she understood what Dominic's death had done to Seve. Parkes had caused her to become, as Seve had, an agent no longer bound by the law. But the law was sacred, so what did that make her? She did not know. She was only aware that she was now a prisoner of what she had done here. That utter despair that comes only when the human soul is in utter eclipse took hold of her, and she began to shake as if with a high fever.

It was then that she saw the red LED display on the overturned portable telephone unit. Ten sparks of light in the shadows of the cabin. Runes glowing in the darkness.

She crawled over, and stared down at the number that Reed Parkes had dialed.

M. Mabuse sat inside the smoky interior of Desiropolis. He was drinking whiskey, staring at the wall of sound the club had erected all around him.

The atmosphere of Desiropolis was self-consciously straight out of *film noir*. Dark, thick-bladed fans in front of white flood lights turned the air as grainy and colorless as black-and-white cinema from the forties.

Women in short skirts, Robin Hood hats perched atop sinuously elaborate hairdos, paraded legs encased in seamed stockings. Young men in balloon-legged trousers vied with others in American-style baseball jackets for their attention. Current rock music caused hearts to beat faster.

But this prodigious wall of sound was, to M. Mabuse, like white noise, a screen on which to view the noisome remains of his past. When he had returned from what had once been his village, he had thought of nothing save what Van Ngoc's daughter, Luong, had done to him. He had spat on her, carving out the dead eyes that had sentenced him, the tongue that had convicted him, but he had been unable to break her hold over him. Yet her curse remained intact: an indictment from the collective souls of his people—the tens of thousands who had died, so many because of him. Her curse told him that they knew of his perfidy, and were damning him because of it.

He was now, he knew, like Mahagiri, condemned for his sins to exist outside of *sámsara*, the wheel of life, forever forbidden from being reincarnated.

He was damned to the one thousand hells of the *Muy Puan*. He was the son of no woman, he would be the sire of no progeny. He was already nonexistent. All that remained was to die.

And yet. And yet, he burned with a fire not recognizable to man. He was aflame with the lust of retribution. His eyes, not Luong's, were gouged-out pits wherein dwelled the restless, tormented souls that plagued him. His tongue, not Luong's, crawled with the unspoken epithets of innocents fried in the caldron of the war.

Only in his imprisonment was he visited by angels who, in the utter blackness of the pit, could tolerate his presence. Only in these sublime moments of ecstasy when within merged with without, when past-present-future were fused by the flux of his mind, did he see a reason to keep his life intact.

He had thought that by giving himself up to the enemy, he could break Luong's curse. If he could not kill himself, let the enemy do it.

But he found to his dismay that he no longer knew who the enemy was. Was it North Vietnam or South? His mind refused to remember what had been, or even to speculate about what was now. And that was when it occurred to M. Mabuse that he could give himself over to either camp, and it would be the same. They were both the enemy.

Passionate bright young things. Takes him away to war—don't fake it, sang a female voice over the charismatic clangor of massed guitars. A bass line loud enough to jar loose fillings wrapped itself around the room. *You'll love Aladdin Sane.*

The lights at Desiropolis possessed great power. They broke down the barriers between reality and fiction. If you danced there, you did so in order to imagine yourself in another time, another place. If you came there at all, it was because the past held out promise as well as secrets.

M. Mabuse's interrogator, who had, over the months, become Kama-Mara, Love and Death, the magician of Delusion, had interpreted his dream concerning the serpent, though he could not remember telling Kama-Mara that he had dreamed it.

"The serpent," Kama-Mara had said, "did not cleanse your soul. The serpent is an illusion, but your sins are not. Now you expect me to say that if you tell me everything I want to know, I will cleanse your soul. But I will not lie to you. You and I have become too intimate for that. Have you ever had such a close friend as I am? Someone on whom you can place all your trust? Someone who will care for you, who will never betray you no matter what he learns about you? The truth is, no one can cleanse your soul. You are beyond redemption."

Motor sensational, Paris or maybe hell—waiting.

"But I can offer you something that no one else will," Kama-Mara had said. "I can offer you release. I can offer you the end."

Clutches of sad remains, waits for Aladdin Sane.

Cinema would call for a fade-out here, but M. Mabuse was in no such privileged position. His life, an endless ribbon of smoking flesh and fused glass, went on and on.

The women who came to Desiropolis all wanted something extreme. They were creatures who, it seemed, existed only during the glitter of night. As they were whirled across the dance floor by their self-involved escorts, their faces slipped into a glassy-eyed ecstasy so mindless it turned M. Mabuse's curiosity into despair. But, of course, this was why he came here. Because all hope had been bred out of its habitués by the modern world, he felt, if not comfortable, at least at home here.

The cinematic light revealed previously dark corners of his past; the sinuous movements of the dancers, more erotic than kinetic, exposed sudden, startling nuances.

He could say that in all probability he had come to love Kama-Mara, if one expanded the definition of love to include absolute dependency.

In the black hole of the South Vietnamese prison-hell, M. Mabuse had come to master time so that his captors could not break him with the utter solitude that made other prisoners throw themselves against the walls. But, in the end, he had come to cherish the time he spent with his interrogator. He never saw his face or even his full silhouette. In the minuscule interstice between light and dark afforded him during his sessions with Kama-Mara, M. Mabuse glimpsed only a rare curve, a partial outline at best. All he had to go on, to cling to, eventually, was the voice.

And it was the moment when he realized that the voice was his lifeline that he snuffed it out.

"Your mistake is in contemplating your escape from this camp," Kama-Mara said. "You assume that you are a prisoner here. But the reality is that it is your own filthy, inert body within which you are imprisoned."

It was Kama-Mara's habit to circle M. Mabuse during the interrogation sessions. When he paused, as he often did, behind where M. Mabuse sat naked on an upright cane chair, he clamped M. Mabuse's shoulders between his fingers. "It is only logical. The body is subject to maiming, to disease, and to death." As he spoke in this manner, he began to knead M. Mabuse's flesh. "Your body is impure, and this impurity contaminates your mind until it, too, is impure. To achieve Nirvana you must disgorge your body.

The first step on this enlightened path is to empty your mind of all its stored feculence."

That day—or night, he never knew which, let alone the actual time—M. Mabuse reached upward and back, clamping his hands over Kama-Mara's face, plunging his thumbs into the soft eyes as he felt his interrogator react.

Slowly, he brought Kama-Mara's head down to his level while the body jerked and spasmed as if exposed to an electric current. Covered in blood, his hands full of the flesh, he kissed those cool lips.

Then, dressed in his interrogator's uniform, he walked out of the prison. But, as if in retribution for killing the man he loved or depended on completely (whichever your point of view), his eyes were never the same. Without dark glasses sunlight burned his brain, and spotlights blinded him.

"Forgive me if I'm late."

M. Mabuse turned his head slightly as the figure slid into a chair at his small table.

"There is nothing to forgive."

The man, deep in shadow, gave a slight bow with his head. Red and purple light struck him obliquely, delineating his handsome features, his glossy skin, shiny and poreless as wax. "Are you well?"

M. Mabuse stared through the monument to plastic surgery at the Magician, seeing the man as he used to be. "Well enough. And you?"

"Me? I'm doing what I love doing," the Magician said. "Breaking balls." He gave the waitress his drink order without asking M. Mabuse if he wanted a refill. "Which is what you should be doing," he continued when they were alone. "A question has begun to concern me. I keep asking myself why you haven't killed Christopher Haye yet."

"I have to find him first."

"I thought you would have killed him in New York as I ordered. I thought, failing that, you would have killed him in Tourrette. Isn't that what you indicated to me when you called me from the airport in Nice?"

"Yes. But circumstances changed. He had *La Porte à la Nuit.*"

"I trust you got it from him."

"Yes."

"You could have killed him, then." Light fell on the Magician's face as it would upon granite, illuminating sculpted ridges and hollows that under close scrutiny had little to do with natural human anatomy.

M. Mabuse shook his head. "He would have destroyed it had I killed Soutane Sirik or attacked him. We made an exchange."

"You should have killed him then."

"I gave my word."

"Your word?" The Magician's laugh echoed, bleeding into the rock music, turning it discordant, as unpleasant as the look on his handsome face. "Since when has your word been worth a damn?"

"I question whether he knows anything that could damage us," M. Mabuse said. "I question whether he should be killed."

The Magician cocked his head, looking at him quizzically. "Since when is it your place to question what you are ordered to do? I threatened Terry. Maybe that was a mistake—it gave him time to formulate a plan. Certainly your killing Terry before he could tell us where the real Doorway to Night is was a serious miscalculation. But because of these events, we must assume that Christopher Haye has become involved. How much he knows will be of no concern to me once he is dead. I trust that is clear enough for you."

"I will kill him," M. Mabuse said. He was sitting stiffly.

"Do that," the Magician said, downing his drink in one great swallow. "And then get the *Prey Dauw* away from that idiot Milhaud. Now that you've retrieved the long-lost dagger, I want it all."

"That has been our purpose all along."

"But it has become so much fun to torture Monsieur Milhaud," the Magician said. "I had LoGrazie order him to kill Soutane. Don't you find that funny?" He peered at M. Mabuse's stony face, then said, "Something happened to you in America. You lost your sense of humor."

"Milhaud told me to bring the Sirik woman to him. He told me to make it look like she had died—but not to kill her."

"A charade for my benefit, no doubt," the Magician said. "I see that he still has a bit of imagination left."

"I don't understand," M. Mabuse said, "why you ordered Milhaud to kill Soutane Sirik when you knew he could not possibly do it."

The Magician gave an unpleasant laugh. "Like a worm on a hook, I wanted to see him squirm."

M. Mabuse stirred. "Should I do as he asks?"

The Magician smiled. "Yes," he said, "and no." His smile widened into a grin. It was like a tiger baring its teeth at its prey.

"Do the faked death as he suggests. Bring Soutane to Milhaud. And then kill her in front of him."

M. Mabuse was stunned. "That will mean the end of me with Milhaud. He will know that you have ordered this; he will know I have been secretly working for you all the time he has employed me."

"Oh, yes." The Magician nodded. "His understanding of how thoroughly I have controlled him is part of what I have planned for him. Before that happens, though, there will be more surprises for him. Milhaud needs to be educated. Morphée is first to die. Then Soutane. Only when everyone he holds dear has been destroyed will the end come."

"I would have thought that you would want to kill him yourself," M. Mabuse said.

"What I require from you now," the Magician said, "is an act of loyalty. Killing Milhaud is it."

"But Milhaud can still be useful to us," M. Mabuse said.

"Not anymore." The Magician rolled his glass between the palms of his hands. "We have suffered something of a setback in the States. That end of the pipeline will have to be reinvented. I am in the process of sealing off loose ends. And Milhaud's end will be the most entertaining one."

M. Mabuse watched the Magician weave his way through the crowded club, thinking he had learned to walk with the kind of ominous swagger filmic cowboys employed. He closed his eyes briefly, as if to rest them from having too long stared into a fierce light.

Who'll love Aladdin Sane
Millions weep a fountain
Just in case of sunrise
Who'll love Aladdin Sane . . .

M. Mabuse, watching the dancers leaning on one another's hips as sad songs drifted like dreams through the loudspeakers, thought again of his brief encounter with Christopher Haye. *You could have killed him.* He had meant to kill him, as he had killed his brother. What had stayed him?

Some dark force had trapped him as it had deep in the prison pit in Vietnam. Some savage instinct for survival within himself had responded to a current eddying in the center of Christopher Haye's eyes. M. Mabuse imagined himself locked there, tried to break away, and failing, surrendered to it.

And when he did, he understood in a moment of revelation so powerful he shuddered, that he was not considering merely the promise of survival.

When he was with Christopher Haye, he had been in the presence of freedom.

"I don't know," Seve said over an indifferent dinner at La Coupole, "maybe I'm too stupid, but I didn't get any of it."

Soutane, who had been pushing her *andouille* sausage around her plate, said, "Get what?"

"The art."

She shrugged. "Don't worry about it. It is the peculiar ability of the French to make everyone else feel inferior through our art."

They were surrounded by perhaps the most famous columns in Paris. On them were paintings and drawings by Picasso, Chagall, and Léger, Parisian artists who were penniless more often than not. In this city of light their art had been their only wealth. With it they ate and drank and, here, passed the time in each other's splendid company.

He sipped his beer. "What did you think of it?"

"Well . . ." It was at that moment that Soutane realized she could not remember one piece of art they had seen. For that matter, she couldn't recall what the interior of the Musée d'Orsay looked like.

The afternoon had not gone as planned. Having gained the Left Bank, she had made them turn around. But, returning to the hotel, they had not found Chris, and he had left no message with the desk as to where he had gone.

It was already dinnertime when they had emerged from the museum. Soutane had phoned the hotel, but Chris had not yet returned.

"What's up?" Seve said, pushing his plate away. He didn't know whether it was the headache or the pains in his neck, but he had no appetite. "In Spain they say it is easier to talk to someone who hasn't shared your life."

"Is that where you're from? Spain?"

"Where my brother and I were born, yeah." He shrugged. "I don't remember it, though. My folks came to the United States when I was two. I think it was the best thing they ever did." He had that pride in America all immigrants shared. He looked over at her plate. "Are you gonna eat those?"

"No. Do you want them?"

"Absolutely not," he said, calling for the waiter. "It's just that the smell is making me sick. What part of the pig are they made from?"

Soutane laughed. "In your state you're better off not knowing." With the table cleared, they ordered coffee.

She saw him looking around at the spacious room with its clusters of brass-rail-topped booths, crammed with diners, and said, "What are you doing?"

"Aren't there always celebrities here?"

"There are, but don't look for them. What is most important at La Coupole is maintaining *le snobisme*. When Giacometti would spend rainy afternoons here sketching on napkins, no one stared. When Beckett and Buñuel and Josephine Baker sat down to eat, no one pointed them out. One observed them out of the corners of one's eyes."

"Those are names from long ago."

She shrugged. "The same holds true for Catherine Deneuve or Jean-Paul Belmondo."

"It's not the same," he observed. "Once there was Fitzgerald, Modigliani, and Man Ray."

She nodded. "Nothing's the same. You should know that."

"In a cop's world," he said, "everything stays the same. Don't you know that's how we catch criminals? In the end they can't help repeating themselves over and over. It's pathetic, really."

He went off through the gold and red glow to try calling Diana, but had no luck. When he returned, he said, "Seriously, what's the matter? You didn't eat a thing."

"Neither did you."

"I've got an excuse. I've got more aches and pains than an eighty-year-old, and God alone knows what these pills are doing to my insides. What's your story?"

Soutane stirred sugar into her coffee. When she had watched the spoon revolve long enough, she said, "Last night, in bed, I called out Terry's name."

"Yeah? So?"

"I was with Chris at the time."

"Ah."

She licked the spoon, put it aside. "Now there's a cogent statement."

"Well, I didn't know—that is, it hadn't occurred to me that you two—"

"And now that you do?"

"I wonder what it's like to sleep with two brothers."

Soutane almost threw the coffee into his face, and he knew it. Nevertheless, he did not move.

Soutane said, "Unless you're gay, you'll never know."

"Brothers, sisters, what's the difference? You know what I meant."

"Oh, I know, all right." She was very angry.

"It's only natural to wonder about it. I'll bet Chris was thinking the same thing just after you said 'Terry' in his ear."

"Nonsense." But she could see the peculiar look on Chris's face when they left him in the hotel, and she knew Seve was right.

Seeing her expression, Seve said, "I'm a stranger, see. I figure if you ask a question, I can tell you the truth." He downed half his coffee. "By the way you showed commendable restraint there when you kept your coffee in your cup."

"How is it you can make me laugh even when I'm angry at you?"

His grin widened. "It's something my old man taught me. He told me it was a survival trait. That and carrying bricks was all he knew."

"Chris left a girl behind in New York."

"Yeah, I know."

"You do?"

"Only from the police file. Her name's Alix Layne. She was severely injured when Trangh broke into Chris's apartment. She's an assistant district attorney. Do you know what that is?" Soutane shook her head. "A prosecuting lawyer for the city of New York."

"He's been trying to get through to her in the hospital."

"Well, I think that's a lost cause," Seve said.

"Why? How badly was she hurt?"

"Bad enough. Trangh slit her throat."

"Oh, God." Her spoon clattered against the side of her cup.

"It was a mess, all right." He was looking at her shrewdly. "What are you thinking, that Chris will go back to her because of what she's been through?"

"Right now I don't know what to think, except that I wish this were all over. I wish Trangh were dead."

"You and me both, lady."

She put her head in her hands. "But he's not. Somewhere, he's out there. We've got to find him and stalk him so that we can get to the Magician."

"Listen," Seve said, "you don't have to do anything. You can walk away right now, and forget Trangh ever existed."

"Do you think I can forget that Terry ever existed, or what Trangh did to him?"

"It's not the same."

"Why? Because I'm a woman?"

"Because you're not a cop."

"That wasn't what you were going to say and you know it."

He looked down into his coffee cup. He tried to imagine Diana tracking down Trangh, if Trangh managed to kill him. He could not. He didn't think she could. "You're right," he admitted. "Being a cop—having a cop's mentality is part of it. But the truth is I don't think a woman's got either the fortitude or the single-mindedness to see this kind of manhunt through to the end."

"I suppose you think a woman will stop to have a baby or two and then, maternal instincts rampant, will forget all about it."

He smiled a little at her facetiousness. "Women always seem to have more on their minds than death. Let's just say that Jack the Ripper could not have been a woman, and leave it at that."

"I'll find Trangh," Soutane said, "and I'll kill him."

"Don't do it on my account, lady."

She snorted. "I wouldn't worry about that."

He grinned, and she saw that it had all been a ruse to keep her in the hunt. What did he know about Porte de Choisy, or Paris, for that matter? He needed her, as bait and as a guide.

"What would you do without me?" she said.

He drank his coffee. "All female bravado aside," he said, "I don't want you tackling Trangh alone. You've done that once before, and we know the result."

Her face went white with rage. "That bastard Chris. I told him in confidence."

Seve nodded. "Maybe so. But the situation's changed radically. He told me out of concern for you. He—"

"I don't care why he told you."

"I don't believe you. It would take someone inordinately stupid or ignorant to feel that way, and you're neither."

"You think you know it all, don't you?"

"I am a seeker after truth," he said. "My profession demands that knowledge be the most valuable commodity." He pushed his cup around on its saucer. "To answer your question in a less oblique manner, I know what I see and hear, nothing more."

"When I see Trangh again," she said, "I'll kill him. You're a fool if you don't believe that."

Seve shrugged. "I don't doubt that you'll want to try, and that would be a shame, because right now Trangh will eat you up. According to Chris's account, you're far too frightened. Is he wrong?"

Soutane turned her head away, but remained silent.

"It would be unnatural for you *not* to be terrified of Trangh," Seve said gently.

"It's not Trangh I'm scared of," she said. "It's myself." She told him of how she had been trained, of how Mun had taught her how to kill. But she stopped short of telling him that she had killed someone. That part was too private, too painful—she had already questioned the wisdom of telling Chris. His knowing about the murder, and how her subsequent remorse had caused her to try to take her own life, made her feel weak and vulnerable. Seve had a disturbing way of making her feel that way as it was.

"It sounds to me like Mun had the right idea in training you."

"That's a simplistic way to look at it."

"Yeah? I think it's realistic."

Soutane cocked her head. "How does your wife react to your lack of emotion?"

"I'm not married."

"Your girlfriend, then." She looked at him. "You do have a girl back in New York."

"A girl?" he said, thinking of Diana. "I don't know."

She laughed. "What kind of answer is that, you don't know?"

"There is someone," he said tentatively, "but I'm not sure—"

"About her, or about yourself?"

He finished his coffee. "Let's go. This place is too crowded, anyway."

"Just like New York, isn't it?" She put a hand over his. "Sit down. Please. Didn't you say that we were both strangers? There isn't anything we shouldn't be able to say to one another." She laughed. "Besides, you don't know me well enough to be offended by anything I'll say. And I don't know you well enough to feel I have to lie to protect your feelings."

Seve settled back down. In the wooden booth next to them, a woman in a black raw silk Chanel dress and a leopard-skin hat pinned to her blond hair with a diamond brooch was busy eating oysters. She hadn't bothered to remove her opera gloves.

"This isn't at all like New York," Seve observed. When more coffee had been brought, he told her about Diana, winding up by saying, "I've never been good at relationships. My job takes up too much of my life."

"That must be convenient."

"What?"

"I mean, it must make it easy for you to get out of relationships when they start to get too serious, or too uncomfortable."

"Hey, you've got it all wrong. It isn't like that at all."

"No? Don't you like your bachelor comfort?"

"A cop—especially one like me—doesn't know the meaning of comfort. More often than not, I spend all night in the front seat of my car. I eat cold, greasy french fries, and coffee so thick you could use it as lampblack."

"I wasn't talking about your job," Soutane said. "I was talking about *you*. I think serious emotions from anyone who is close make you uncomfortable."

"Jesus, I don't even know what serious emotions are," he said.

"Stop kidding yourself. Everyone knows. The only question is whether they choose to acknowledge them."

"How come you know so much about this?"

"I'm surprised you have to ask," she said. "I love two brothers, and it's tearing Chris up inside."

A group of teenagers came slouching through the glass doors and, at the behest of the maître d', threw themselves into a booth. Within moments there was enough cigarette smoke around them to start a funeral pyre.

Seve seemed to stare at them or at nothing, for a long time. At last he turned back to Soutane. "The truth is, I'm frightened."

"Of getting involved? Everyone is."

He shook his head. "That's not it, or at least not the important part." He looked around. "I want to order a drink." He asked for a whiskey, and she watched him swallow it in one gulp. "What I am afraid of is death."

"But that's ridiculous," she said. "Look at what your profession is. You should have become a bookkeeper or a librarian."

"Maybe. But I wouldn't have been able to live with myself."

"So you became a cop to prove to yourself that you weren't afraid."

He nodded. "In a way." He thought of his father. Maybe it was to prove it to you, Pop, he thought. "It was why I enlisted in the army, anyway. After I got back home, it seemed the logical thing to continue to protect and serve."

"And your girl?"

"It's bad enough, this fear, with just me. But with a family . . ."

"Maybe a family would make the fear go away," Soutane said. "Did that ever occur to you? In a way, a family is the continuation of life, even after death."

Seve felt the warmth of the liquor still burning in his chest. The woman in the Chanel dress was finished with her oysters. Now he could see, sitting beside her, a curly-headed miniature poodle, quiescent and trusting, its eyes filled only with her.

On the other side of the room the teenagers in the booth were lost in a Gauloise haze. Two of them—a pair of girls in sleeveless tops and skirts like sagebrush—were dancing, taking turns twirling and being twirled down the aisles. The white-jacketed waiters sidestepped this apparently dangerous missile with admirable sang-froid. They had seen it all before.

He closed his eyes. "Can we go back to the hotel? My head hurts."

When Alix opened her eyes, she saw an unfamiliar face. The last she remembered was a vague feeling of motion as they had wheeled her, already half out, into the operating room. An impression of white and stainless steel, a womb run by a gigantic engine, throbbing with the double beat of a heart.

And then a dream of falling, endlessly falling. The farther she falls, the more terrified she becomes because the more certain she is that she will never survive the end of the descent. Because the deeper she goes, the faster she falls, and the closer she is to the end.

Then, in the dim, subterranean light she sees Dick standing on a ledge. She calls out to him, he turns his head to grin at her as she flashes by.

She screams.

And below her, sees Christopher standing on another ledge. He holds out his arms, and she knows that he has the strength and the courage to catch her. He is not afraid, as she suspects Dick was, of her weight and momentum flinging him off the ledge.

He smiles as she nears his outstretched arms, and she knows she is saved. Until, at the last instant, he snatches his arms away.

No! she screams. *No!*

Falling.

Faster and faster, until . . .

"Alix, can you hear me?" Max Steiner said.

Alix blinked, searching her memory for a name to go with the face. "Do I know you?" she said.

She saw etched on his face an expression somewhere between concern and elation.

"My God," he said, "I've got to get the doctor. You can speak!"

She reached out tentatively. She was going in and out, nothing seemed real. Part of her, having been betrayed by Dick and Christopher, was still falling. Grabbing onto his sleeve made holding on to consciousness that much easier. Still, it taxed her. She was very tired.

"Don't go." Her voice, more a blistered croak, sounded odd. But good. So good!

"My name is Max Steiner," he said. "I'm a friend of Chris's."

"You're taking care of my son."

He nodded, happy to be having a conversation with her at all. "He's a fine boy, Alix."

"Is he all right?" Her eyelids were drooping. She lacked the energy even to keep them open. But there was so much she wanted to say, so much she needed to tell him. First and foremost about Dick. She wanted Dick out of there. She wanted Max to keep him away from Danny.

But she was falling, faster and faster, into night.

"Jesus, look at you," Brad Wolff said. His men, coming off the launch, were all over the boat. They were better than bloodhounds.

He beckoned, and a tall, bespectacled man with thin hair and liver spots on the backs of his hands cracked open an old-fashioned doctor's bag. "Give her the once-over," Wolff said.

Diana, wrapped in a coarse blanket, was sitting up against a bulkhead. She thought that Wolff had responded to her call in record time. No wonder Seve trusted him.

She gave Wolff the ten digits. "Run it through the phone company and see what you get," she said. "It was the number Parkes was calling when I got to him." She winced as the doctor got to the area where she had been kicked.

"Nothing broken." The doctor seemed to be talking to his liver spots.

Wolff, staring at Parkes's body through the forest of forensic specialists, said, "You didn't get all your training at the academy."

Diana gave him a little smile, then immediately bit her lip as the doctor hit another sensitive point. "I had some private lessons."

"With what, a Mack truck?"

Now she did laugh. "Ow. No. Someone a bit more refined."

"There's nothing refined about what you did to Reed Parkes."

"He was going to kill me."

"Hey." Wolff swung around. "That wasn't a rebuke. I'm damn glad I sent you and not another operative who would have been less qualified to handle this monster."

"Still, I killed him. He was our only lead. From what he said, you were right. Monique was fronting for him."

"You got the phone number, anyway." Wolff shrugged, then, unthinking, squeezed her shoulder in reassurance. "Sorry," he said, as she winced. "Maybe you got us the wedge we need."

"Whatever way it goes," Diana said, "I want to be there."

The doctor nodded, and Wolff, extending his hand, helped Diana to her feet.

"Her body is marvelously elastic," the doctor said, packing up. "I should only be so lucky." He sauntered over, a victim of professional curiosity, to take a look at the corpse.

After Diana gave her report Wolff handed her a cheap vinyl overnight bag. "I brought you some clothes. Maybe they're not the most stylish—"

She leaned over and kissed him on the cheek. "Doesn't matter. I'd be just as happy to step into a potato sack." She had turned to go into the cabin to change when Wolff took her wrist.

"Diana," he began, "I want you to know that I appreciate what you've done."

"Thank you."

He held her tight, staring into her eyes. "That's only part of it. I want to be sure that *you* also appreciate what you've had to do."

"You mean what I've been through."

Wolff nodded. "That, too. I want you to have the time to absorb it. To think it all through."

"I have."

"I wonder." He led her to a bench inside the cabin where they both sat down. "I want you to know that as far as I am concerned you did your duty. You aren't a spy. You aren't supposed to bite a cyanide bullet rather than divulge information to the enemy. There should be no guilt involved."

She gave him a brittle smile. "Chinese don't feel guilt."

"You know, it concerns me that through all this there hasn't been even a hint of a crack in your armor. It isn't natural."

Her gaze was steady. "I meant what I said. I want to be in on it. Sitting home and brooding isn't going to do me any good. I want—I need—to work."

"Don't worry. I have no intention of pulling you off this assignment. I just want to know you're okay."

"I'm fine—"

"But?" He was studying her face.

She put her head down. She was certain she was going to cry, and felt ashamed. She remembered how her father had hit her when, as a child, she had cried. She had twisted her ankle running from a flock of teasing boys, and did not know whether her tears were from pain or humiliation. *Chinese do not cry,* her father had said in the stern voice he used to frighten her. *Chinese show no emotion, especially to* loh faan, *barbarians. The* loh faan *will never know the pride of composure that, as civilized people, we Chinese enjoy.* Obeying her father and her ancestors, she had never cried after that. "But I wish Seve were here," she conceded.

Wolff sat back against the salt-stained bench. "Christ, you two ought to get married and be done with it," he said. "The best thing for Guarda would be for you to give him a son."

"Thank you very much," she said with mock sarcasm. Inside, she was very pleased. And grateful to Brad as well. The time for tears had passed.

"Be the best thing for you, too, Diana. Kids are the original fountain of youth. And what they can do for a boring afternoon! Take it from me, I've got three of them." Wolff grinned. "Now, come on, we've got a lot of work to do."

Chris found Porte de Choisy at once fascinating and depressing. It was a roughly triangular section of perhaps three square blocks, dominated by two features unusual in Paris. One was the clusters of ugly, concrete, government-sponsored high rises which were already passé since the city had several years ago outlawed any new such constructions. The other existed, as it were, between the sentinel buildings: a pair of gargantuan indoor-outdoor malls within which one could, it appeared, subsist indefinitely without emerging.

Restaurants of all sizes coexisted with fresh meat and produce markets. Down fluorescent-lit corridors, or vast central avenues, rows of tiny, brightly painted shops dispensed Vietnamese and Cambodian clothes, records, audio and video cassettes, books in Khmer, as well as *plats à emporter*, Southeast Asian fast food of every description, to go. The variety was endless.

Chris spent hours wandering through the malls, scanning the Asian faces. He looked in through plate-glass windows at shoppers and diners alike. With the larger restaurants such as L'Oiseau du Paradis, Rang Phuong Hoang, and Le Tikoc, he went in because from outside it was impossible to see all the tables.

Did he really believe that it would be so easy to track Trangh down? Yes, it was true that Soutane had said that, sooner or later, all Vietnamese in Paris came to Porte de Choisy, if only to buy music cassettes or to eat a familiar meal. But even so, what were the odds of Trangh and Chris being here at the same time?

All of a sudden he felt as if he had come on a fool's errand. He did not know this area as Soutane obviously did. There must be other places—gambling dens, to name just one—hidden from the outside world, where Trangh could be secreted. Trangh could be on the same block, and he would never know it.

He felt like an idiot for not having spent the day with Soutane and Seve. And for what? Because she had, in a moment of release, used his brother's name. He felt in his pocket for the folding knife. He rubbed the rough stag scales as if the knife were a talisman.

His feelings for Soutane were like a fire that, once started, were impossible to extinguish. It seemed odd that he might want them to end. Didn't he love her? What about Alix? Didn't he love her, too? But how could he love two people at once? It seemed impossible, contradictory. He felt shredded into a million pieces, unable to find his own center.

And then it occurred to him that perhaps Soutane was feeling precisely the same things. She, too, loved two people—they just happened to be brothers. Was that such a terrible sin? It would be, he thought, if both he and Terry were still alive. How would she choose between them? *Whom* would she choose?

That choice had been taken out of her hands. But what about *his* choice? What was he to do? How was he to find his way?

All this time he had not stopped looking for Trangh. He seemed compelled to press on, even when, in his heart, he did not believe he had a chance to stumble across him in this labyrinth of three square blocks. After all, if he was here, he could be in an apartment in any one of the high rises to which Chris had no access.

None of that mattered, for some element in Trangh's face had already burned itself into Chris's soul. Was it anguish or recklessness? Anger or despair? Certainly, it had not been hatred. If he did not think it out of the question, he would suspect that he had glimpsed the same kind of vulnerability that Soutane claimed she saw in him.

But how could a human being be at once vulnerable and capable of such hideous acts of violence? Trangh had murdered Terry and Seve's brother, Dominic. He had maimed Alix, and had killed Al DeCordia. The war was one explanation for such aberrant behavior, but it was clear that Trangh had not been broken by the war. He functioned with frightening efficiency, and Chris had found him rational, even honorable. What else could the war have done to him?

That seemed the central question. Whatever the war had done to to him was what Chris had seen in his eyes, it was what had touched Chris's own spirit. It was why Chris had come to Porte de Choisy on this obvious fool's errand. He was motivated by more than curiosity. Despite his protestations to Seve, he felt impelled to come closer to the flame that burned so dangerously behind Trangh's eyes. He needed to discover the source of that bright light. For in its nature he suspected that he would find himself.

By the time he arrived at Angkor Vat it was dark, and he found that he was very hungry. The restaurant was faced with dark red plastic and, beneath its name, it said, SPÉCIALITÉS ASIATIQUES.

It was steamy inside. He wandered through the room, settling on a table in the rear. He sat with his back to the wall so that he had a clear view of every table.

It was then that he saw M. Vosges. Soutane's father. He was older, to be sure. His hair was longer, though not necessarily whiter. But that face, so much like Charles de Gaulle's, was unmistakable. He had come in with a stunning Asian woman. They sat down across from one another at a table in the center of the restaurant.

For a moment Chris's mind went numb. When he had recovered sufficiently, he slurped down some tea, in the process scalding his tongue and throat. He was struck by a bolt of paranoia, and he almost choked. Perhaps M. Vosges had seen him strolling through the mall and had followed him in here. Hadn't Soutane said that her father never forgot anything? At one time he had wanted to kill Chris.

M. Vosges and the Asian woman were smiling at one another, and Chris could see that beneath the table their legs were entwined.

Then, in the mirror that ran along one wall, he caught sight of himself, and relaxed. He had been just a kid then. He doubted that M. Vosges would even recognize him now.

Still, it was disconcerting to run into him this way, a goblin springing out of a closet at night.

Chris could see that M. Vosges was known to the restaurant, for the manager, a small, dapper Vietnamese, personally brought the couple's tea and menus.

A moment later Chris was sitting as rigid as stone. His mind was aflame, and he could scarcely breathe.

In greeting Soutane's father the manager had said, "Good evening. How are you tonight, Monsieur Milhaud?"

While Brad Wolff went off to run the phone number through R&I, Diana phoned the office. As she suspected, there was a message from Seve. She dialed the number he had left and spoke with him for some time. It was already late in Paris. He sounded as if he had died and no one had let him know it. With no little anger, she told him so.

Wolff returned, saw she was engaged, and occupied himself with paperwork, of which he had far too much.

When she was through, he threw down his pen, said to her, "What do you know about this Marcus Gable that you're not telling me?"

Diana looked at him quizzically. "I don't understand."

"Okay, then. Why are you so hot to run him down?"

She shrugged. "Seve asked me to."

He sat on the corner of his desk, slapping a folder against his free-swinging knee. "That it?"

"Do you mean does Seve suspect him of running the heroin pipeline out of the Golden Triangle into Chinatown? You mean do we think he's the real godfather of Chinatown? Who knows?" There was an offhand tone to her voice, an aftermath of her ordeal, perhaps, but more, anger and frustration at Seve being six thousand miles away, off-duty, and giving her cryptic orders.

Brad Wolff nodded, as if he had read her mind. "The reason I ask," he said, "is that Marcus Gable doesn't exist."

"What?"

"Let me amplify." Brad Wolff came down off his desk, sat on a chair next to her. "Marcus Gable exists now, in the real world, but as far as the CIA is concerned, he does not."

"They're covering up."

Wolff shook his head. "No, they're not. He did work for them from 1968 through 1972. Then he picked himself up, and left."

"To do what?"

Wolff shrugged. "Presumably doing what he's doing now: import-export."

"Drugs, you mean?"

"Diana, there's no direct evidence that Gable was involved in what the *Monique* was up to. We—and you—don't recognize guilt by association. Nobody's linked Gable to Monique or Reed Parkes in any business sense."

"Only because Monique was murdered before she could say anything."

"All that may be true," Wolff admitted, "but we've still got no proof."

"If Gable's no longer CIA, then who is protecting him?" Diana sighed. A wave of fatigue washed over her. She closed her eyes for a moment. "How did you get this stuff on Gable?"

Wolff grinned. "That was simple. But only because I made it so. Couple of years ago we busted a fairly high-level coke ring. They were quite creative, stuffing corpses with bags of shit to get it into this country via Mexico.

"Anyway, I recognized one of the ring. He was the son of someone I knew at the Agency. It turned out that he had come up with the corpse idea while high on coke. I hustled him out of there before he could be booked, and he and his father and I had a long talk.

"The upshot was the kid went into a voluntary drug rehab program in D.C. I keep an eye on him because he won't listen to his old man, and from time to time his father responds to, ah, requests I make of him."

"This kid's father is a CIA spook?"

"Nah, they don't know which way their belly button's screwed on, those Company guys. Charlie Karnow's a computer operator with A-level clearance. He's tapped into even more than the secretaries."

Diana laughed. "It's not who you know," she said. "It's who you know."

"Right. It's the drones of the world, not the CEOs, who're plugged into Information Central."

Diana ran her hand through her thick hair. "Well, we've still got the number Reed Parkes was going to call."

Wolff nodded. "We'd better hope that leads us somewhere, otherwise we're up against a wall we're just not going to get through simply with good intentions."

"We've got more than that, haven't we?" Diana said. "We've got the law. I was always taught that the law was everything: the light, the Way, the truth."

Wolff sighed. "Now you know the real truth, Diana."

"No!" She shook her head. "I won't accept that, as officers of the law, we're helpless. That's what you're telling me, isn't it?"

"I'm not telling you anything," Wolff said. "It's the situation that's dictating—"

Then the phone rang, and he snatched up the receiver. "Yeah? Hold on." He reached for his pen. "All right. Give it to me." He scribbled something down, then hung up. He looked at Diana. "The address of the number Parkes was dialing just came in. I think we'd better get over there right away."

"I need to stop off at the ladies' room first."

"Go on. It's the second-to-last door on your right at the end of the hall," he said. "I'll wait for you here."

On her way she passed Randy Brooks, Wolff's assistant. He didn't see her because he was in a sweat. He hurried up to Brad and, curious, Diana turned to watch.

"Jesus, Brad, there's been another incident down in detention," he said. "I think you'd better—"

"On my way!" Wolff said, jumping up. He followed Brooks down the corridor toward the bank of elevators.

"Brad!" Diana shouted, but he had already stepped into a waiting elevator. When she returned to his office, she went behind his desk and called the office to see what messages, if any, were waiting for her.

She was in the middle of the first of them when she saw Randy Brooks running back down the corridor. He was white-faced and out of breath.

"Is everything all right?" she asked him, but he was already past her. She saw him signaling to several other people on the floor and now, as she looked past him, she saw a commotion near the bank of elevators. Hurriedly, she hung up the phone and ran up to Brooks. "What is it?" She thought of gunshots, and Brad lying on the detention-room floor. "What's happened?"

Randy Brooks's head swung around, and she could see his eyes were opened wide. He was trying to control his breathing. "Miss Ming, not now," he said. "We're trying to determine—"

"What?"

"A situation of unknown origin."

"My God, will you just tell me! Has something happened to Brad?"

Brooks nodded, as if now that she had broached the subject it was permissible to tell her. "I was on the fifteenth floor. I ran all the way up here when I heard. There's been a terrible accident."

"What kind of accident?"

His face was pinched, and he was holding a walkie-talkie that kept crackling like a live wire. It was black where he held it, as if smudged with ink or soot. "The cables holding Brad's elevator broke."

"What do you mean?" Her stomach contracted painfully. "We're twenty stories up!"

"The car went all the way down to the basement."

"But how could it? What about the emergency brake?"

"Truthfully, I don't know."

"No," she said sharply. "There must be some mistake."

They were running side by side. Men brushed past her. They were shouting, and somewhere an alarm was sounding.

Terror filled Diana's heart as she rode down with them. No one would look at her. The elevator stank from sweat. Randy Brooks was speaking into the walkie-talkie. She strained to hear the replies to his repeated questions, but everything sounded garbled with static. Numb and in shock, she prayed for Brad, and hoped that he was still alive.

In the basement lurid blue light arced from acetylene torches. Everyone was sweating from the confinement and the heat. They were already working on getting the body out of the crushed car, but she could see that however long they took, it wouldn't matter. At least not for Brad Wolff.

She wanted to see, anyway. She ignored their protestations and, dropping down into the grimy pit, peered over their shoulders into the interior of the elevator. She had seen an accident years ago when she was just out of the academy where a semi, skidding on a slick highway, had plowed into an auto at eighty-five miles per hour. The inside of the car had been so severely foreshortened, the metal had sliced the passengers in two.

"God in heaven." She turned away, stumbling over a torch canister. Randy Brooks caught her before she could fall headlong onto the oil- and blood-stained concrete. Someone, noticing that she was weeping, lifted her up out of the light and the heat.

It was only later, when she had returned to Brad's office after giving her statement both to DEA internal security and the NYPD detective team, that she went looking for the address of the number she had read off Reed Parkes's mobile telephone.

It wasn't there.

At nine-thirty Milhaud paid the check. Fifteen minutes later he and the Asian woman got up to leave the restaurant. That was when Chris saw that they were being followed. A slim, rat-faced Vietnamese in blue jeans and chambray workshirt reached for a baseball jacket emblazoned with L.A. DODGERS and went out the door moments after them.

Intrigued, Chris trailed behind. But when Milhaud and the woman stepped into a Renault, and their tail got into a waiting black BMW, Chris was abruptly at a loss.

He ran out into the Boulevard Massena, looking for a cruising taxi, but couldn't find one. For a moment he had a crazy notion to flag down a passing car and, as he had seen in countless films, commandeer it. But reality intruded. The idea had a low probability of success. Besides, there wasn't time. The two cars were disappearing into traffic.

So Chris did the only thing he could do: he stole a bicycle.

On a highway or in the dead of night, he would not have had a chance; the autos' speed alone would have defeated him. But traffic slowed the cars and, after all, as long as there were no steep hills to negotiate, he could maintain speeds of thirty-five miles per hour or more for extended periods of time.

It felt good to be back on a bike, pushing himself—his legs, his knee, his stamina. It was like the old days. The familiar exhilaration began to fill him, pumping adrenaline through him. Now and again he felt a twinge in his knee, but he chose to ignore the pain, wanting very much to work through it. He was determined not to let it get in his way.

Chris had one bad moment, when he thought he was going to lose them. At the Place d'Italie, the cars began to move on the cusp of the traffic light. The rest of the traffic had come to a halt, the intersection was clearing of pedestrians. Suddenly Milhaud's Renault jerked forward and, with it, as if tied by a chain, the black BMW. Chris, taken by surprise, was now against the changing traffic light.

Ahead, he saw the cars disappearing up the Avenue des Gobelins and, hunched over the handlebars, he put on a sprint. Horns blared and brakes screeched. He was forced to veer to the right in order to avoid hitting two cars. Then he was past the intersection, racing after his quarry. They were bogged down in traffic, and he caught up to them as they were turning onto the Boulevard de Port Royal.

As he pedaled, Chris began to think again of what Seve had said about Trangh killing the remaining members of the SLAM unit because of some screwed-up idea of revenge. That had not sounded right to him when he heard it, and it had been gnawing at him ever since. Why? Trangh had decapitated Terry and Dominic Guarda. Terry had been part of the heroin pipeline, and Dominic had heard Al DeCordia's confession. But Trangh also decapitated Al DeCordia because, it seemed clear, DeCordia was about to go to the authorities with what he knew of the pipeline. That meant that Al DeCordia's death had been a sanctioned murder. Which meant that Trangh was working for someone high up in the pipeline network, possibly even the head man.

So far, so good, but something was still bothering him. What? Some loose end that did not so neatly fit this scenario. He thought of Alix, lying in the hospital. What kind of operation—?

Alix. Of course! Trangh had tried to kill Chris, too! Alix had gotten in the way, and Chris had saved her from being killed by Trangh. But why me? Chris asked himself. I was neither in the SLAM unit or involved in the pipeline. I am the anomaly. I don't fit into Seve's theory. Which means that either Seve is wrong or Trangh is working for someone else, someone with a different—as yet hidden—agenda.

They went north along the Boulevard Raspail, turning left onto the Boulevard St. Germain, heading toward the river. They crossed over the Pont de la Concorde, onto the Right Bank.

Lights set the city ablaze. The Eiffel Tower glittered in the haze accumulated over the course of the long, industrial day. It hung above the river, a pendant suspended against the throat of the world's most superb woman.

Along the Avenue New York. The black BMW was nowhere to be seen. Milhaud's car stopped in front of a building with an ornate white stone facade midway along the first block. He and the Asian woman emerged.

Chris, getting off the bike, saw her holding Milhaud's hand. He was just across the street, in the shadows cast by several large chestnut trees. The light from oncoming traffic rose and fell across the Asian woman's face as she spoke to Milhaud. They kissed. Milhaud turned, heading on foot back the way the cars had come.

Suddenly the Asian woman's face was thrown into sharp highlight. The black BMW had reappeared. Caught in the double yellow beam of its headlights, the Asian woman stood as still as a deer trapped on the middle of a highway. Milhaud, startled, turned back toward her, and Chris began to run.

Chris saw the BMW's smoked side window roll down; he saw the glint of the gun barrel. He leaped without thinking. His shoulder slammed into the Asian woman's right side just as the gun was fired. The explosion roared in his ears.

The two of them tumbled to the sidewalk, and another shot spattered shards of concrete into Milhaud's face.

Then Chris was up, pulling the unharmed Asian woman with him. "Come on," he said urgently to both of them.

Milhaud stared at him even as he began to follow him at a run. "Who are you?"

"Someone you hate," Chris said, turning a corner. He made sure they kept to the thickest shadows. "Someone who just saved your life."

Diana sat waiting in a cab. The meter was running, and the driver had his nose stuck in the *New York Post*. Mike Tyson was fighting somebody for the undisputed something or other of the world.

Diana, shivering, pressed into the corner of the cab, staring at the entrance of the DEA offices. She was waiting for Randy Brooks to appear.

He had told her that he had been down on the fifteenth floor at the time of the accident. *I ran all the way up here*. Yet she had seen him ushering Brad into the doomed elevator. He must have used some excuse to stay out of that elevator car. In any event he had lied to her. The walkie-talkie he had been using was smeared with what at the time she had assumed to be ink or soot. Now she suspected it to be grease. Cable grease.

She could hear Brad saying to her, *After what happened to Monique right in my wine cellar, I'm reluctant to continue the investigation with personnel from my unit, because if her murder wasn't an inside job, I'm as Chinese as you are. I've got a real problem.*

Now Diana thought she had found the problem, the inside man. Randy Brooks. But whom did he work for? The CIA, the State Department, or both? She had no idea, but she had come up with a plan—a dangerous one—to find out. She had used the phone in

Brad's office and, waiting until Brooks was within earshot, said into the mouthpiece, "But why did he say he was on the fifteenth floor when I saw him, when Brad stepped into the elevator on the twentieth?"

There had been nothing on the other end of the line save a dial tone, but, of course, Brooks hadn't known that. Diana had been improvising, looking for a way in. Seve might not have approved, but these were rapidly becoming desperate times. The manner of Brad's death told her that they had been coming close. This was the moment to take a chance, not to go by the book.

She had figured that Brooks would react in one of two ways: either he would come after her directly, or he would head to his contact in order to get emergency instructions.

Privately, she had banked on the second scenario. Brooks did not seem the type to run her to ground on his own initiative. He'd need help, both physical and moral.

It was looking more and more as if she was right.

She saw him now, coming out of an elevator in the lobby, stopping to talk to a young woman, nodding, smiling. Coming through the outer doors and down the granite steps. He had obviously called a car service, because there was a gray Lincoln waiting at the curb, a short way down the street from the entrance. Brooks nodded to the driver.

Diana leaned forward and tapped the cabby on the shoulder. "Time," she said, and he put the cab in gear without picking his head up from the Tyson story.

Here we go, she thought.

But before the taxi had a chance to pull out into the street, there was the screech of burning rubber. Diana watched in horror as the Lincoln lurched forward and, accelerating with appalling rapidity, jumped the curb.

Its gleaming chrome grille struck Brooks full on, twisting grotesquely even as it threw him high into the air. He crashed headlong into a fire hydrant even as the big car, rocking on its shocks, shot down the street.

Diana threw herself out of the taxi and, running, pushed her way through the gathering crowd.

"Police officer! Police officer!" she shouted, brandishing her badge. Within the inner circle of gawkers she stopped, staring at the limp, bloody form of Randy Brooks. She saw a man with a handkerchief over his mouth. That didn't stop him from staring at what was left of Brooks's chest.

Diana went quickly through Brooks's pockets, but found nothing of value to her. An address book would have been nice, she thought as she stood up. But that would have been too convenient, not to mention bad security on Brooks's part. He may not have been a leader type but he was far from stupid.

She shouldered her way out of the throng and was about to go into the DEA building when she reconsidered. It was still, strictly speaking, a red zone. She did not know who she could trust there, and which phones were tapped. She turned around, ducked into the taxi.

She had the cabby stop at a public phone. It took her three tries before she found one that worked. Using a credit card, she called Seve in France and told him everything that had happened. She became aware that her forehead was pressed against the metal side of the booth, and her eyes were closed. She felt slightly dizzy.

"Jesus," he said when she was finished, "we must be awfully close if they've taken out Brad and Randy Brooks. Brooks was obviously their contact inside the DEA. They must be planning to move fast now."

"Whoever *they* are," Diana said.

"You can bet Arnold Toth knows it all."

"You'd better get to him fast, boss. Or there won't be any of us good guys left on this side of the Atlantic."

"I'll get him," Seve said. "Now take yourself out of it. You've done more than your share. You sound all done in."

"I'll be safe at the precinct."

"No you won't," Seve said, thinking of Loong Chun's warning of an inside man in the precinct. "Go to ground—some neutral spot like a hotel—and stay there until this is over. They already got Brad. You can be sure you just made the endangered species list."

It was only then that she realized how frightened she was. "Oh, Seve. I wish you were here."

"To tell you the truth, I wish I was there, too," Seve said, thinking of Soutane saying, *How does your wife react to your lack of emotion?* Was he really emotionless? He thought he had just been doing his job. He resolved to ask Diana that question when he saw her.

"Seve, what are we doing at opposite ends of the universe? We should be together now."

"I know," he said. "We'll be together soon, Diana. Now do as I've told you."

She was familiar with that tone of voice, and knew she could not possibly win an argument with him. "Okay. I know everything's going to be fine," she said. "Don't worry."

She had the taxi take her home. It waited for her while she changed. She loaded her spare service revolver, checked the action, jammed it into the wafer holster at the back of her waist.

Back in the precinct house she checked in with Kline, who was just on his way out. Then she did two things. She made a call to R&I and looked through the Manhattan phone book. Charles Karnow lived on East Eighty-second Street. When she got the callback from R&I, she memorized the information. Then she took her coat, went downstairs, and signed out for an unmarked police car without even considering taking backup. Seve was either going to recommend her for a medal or bust her down to patrolman. That is, if she lived that long.

"I don't think we should go to Porte de Choisy tonight," Soutane said to Seve. The hotel doctor had just gone.

"Finding Trangh—"

"Seve, the doctor was *very* angry." She sat on the bed, next to him. "Your French is rudimentary, so you missed most of it. He said that you should never have been released from the hospital. In fact, I had to talk him out of checking you into one now. He says because you haven't been taking your medicine there is a real danger of infection."

"He's an alarmist," Seve said, getting up. "I'm fine. We're going to Porte de Choisy as planned."

That was when the phone rang. Soutane watched him, scarcely able to breathe. Seve put down the phone, said, "That was Diana. She was calling from a phone booth in New York. She's shaken the tree back there far harder than I thought she could. All hell has broken loose. From what she tells me, I think we've just about run out of time."

Soutane put her hands together. She walked to the high windows, stood with her back to the panes of glass. He could see that she was having trouble breathing. "Seve, you were right about me," she said in a strangled voice. "I won't be able to go through with this. I'm scared to death." She had that kind of sad, broken beauty one reads about in fiction, certain that such an ephemeral quality never could exist in real life.

"It's natural to be scared of someone like Trangh."

Soutane said nothing.

"I'll make sure Trangh doesn't get near you, Soutane. And, in any case, from what you tell me, you're well trained."

"You do not understand," she said miserably. "I do not want to use what Mun taught me."

"Tell me something," Seve said. "Would you use your skills at hand-to-hand combat if Chris was being physically threatened? Or if I was?"

"Of course I would," she said. "But that isn't the issue. Not for me, at least. You and Chris are alike in one way: you always think you're right. You're arrogant and that makes you shortsighted."

Seve turned his head so that the left side of his face and neck were exposed and, with them, the old scar that began beneath his ear and ended at his collarbone.

"Do you see this?" Out of the corner of his eye he was aware of her moving into the light. "I am going to tell you how I got it. I've never wanted to tell anyone what happened, but I want to tell you. I was in Hong Kong years ago, on assignment for the DEA, the American Drug Enforcement Agency. From there we went into Laos and Burma. Into the Golden Triangle, searching for the source of a particularly lucrative heroin pipeline."

Soutane came nearer and nearer to him, her eyes on the twisted line of glossy flesh.

"There were four of us originally," Seve said. "One died in an ambush in the Laotian mountains. The second broke a leg on the trek into Burma.

"Two of us made it onto the Shan Plateau, but my lone companion was buried in a rock slide caused, I think, by the torrential rain. I'm still not sure. Perhaps the rocks were given an assist by human hands.

"In any event I was alone when I slipped inside General Kiu's territory. I see now how insane that was—to continue under those circumstances. What could one man alone do against the army of an opium warlord? But that's why I could not turn back. There had been too many deaths, too much misfortune. I thought that if I abandoned the hunt, those men would have died for nothing, and I would be giving in to the misfortune."

Soutane was very close now, peering in the lamplight at the pale flesh that ran like a moonlit river along his neck.

"It is clear now, in retrospect, that I had no chance, that right from the outset none of us had had a chance. General Kiu was so well connected, he had been getting hourly updates on our progress. He was very pleased with us, he told me later. We were more entertaining than a radio program or a film shown on cassette.

" 'I should kill you,' he told me when I had been brought before him, 'as I have killed all the agents of the East and the West who have come to me seeking either my opium or my death. American or Russian, Chinese or Burmese, it makes no difference to me. I am a nondenominational executioner.' He laughed. He was a man who, like all evangelists, was in love with his own voice.

"And that is precisely what General Kiu was. An evangelist who preached a philosophy that was, in its own eerie way, just as much a religion as Buddhism or Christianity, complete with gods, a heaven, and a hell. 'In the beginning,' he told me, 'there was Eden. And it was the Shan.' Then he would laugh again.

"While he spoke, I was hung upside down on a rough-hewn cross of timbers. I was not fed, and I had nothing to drink. The sun was very strong and it hurt my eyes. When it rained, someone would come to tape my mouth shut so that I could not drink.

"When I was so disoriented that I no longer knew whether I was conscious or not, General Kiu had me cut down. He fed me water himself, using a teaspoon so that I would not get sick by gulping down too much at once.

"I lay on the ground, and watched the moonlight on his legs and feet. I slept, and when I awoke, he was sitting beneath a tree, as the Buddha had done in the incarnation of Siddhartha.

"I was weak, and he fed me, as if I was his sickly son. 'If you die now,' he said to me, 'you will disappoint me greatly.' As I gained in strength, he read to me from Sun Tzu's *The Art of War*. This was his bible, and he adhered to its tenets with the fierce orthodoxy of the righteous.

"But because I had been so near death, my recovery took some time. When General Kiu wasn't with me, a young boy of perhaps thirteen took care of me. His name was Win, and he was already an opium addict, smoking with the serenity of an eighty-year-old, which was eerie in someone so young.

"Over the days we became friends. You've never been to war, so you wouldn't know. But when your life is constantly at stake, a peculiar closeness springs up between people sharing quarters that is hard to describe. It happens not only among guys in an outfit but, curiously enough, between a prisoner and his interrogator.

"In any event this is what happened to Win and myself. He spoke English very well, but often we would converse in the dialect of his tribe, which he seemed pleased to teach me. And I, in turn, taught him about morality and the law.

"These conversations were my sole pleasure, and I looked forward to them. But they were also a source of great sadness, for I saw in Win an expression of all the failed potential, all the unlimited evil that opium caused.

"As my love for him grew, so did my hatred for the tears of the poppy. I knew that I had failed in my mission. Worse, I understood that I had never had any chance for success. But in this boy I saw, well, I guess you could call it my salvation. I became convinced that if I could save him—just one individual—from his addiction, I would have turned defeat into victory. I would have beaten General Kiu at his own game.

"So I planned my escape and, one night I moved out. I had not been bound since the day General Kiu had me cut down off the cross. I could see Win sleeping not ten feet from me. I took him up in my arms, and he came awake. He asked me what I was doing, and I told him. I wanted him to live, I wanted him to be free from his addiction.

"And that," Seve said, running a forefinger down the scar, "is how I got this. Win drew a knife from his belt and cut me under the ear, all the way down to here. I bled so much I became frightened. I dropped him, and fell to the ground.

"Which was where General Kiu found me. He squatted over me, and while his people worked to stanch and clean the wound, he said to me, 'Now you know why I haven't killed you. That would have been too easy.

" 'You want to leave and take the boy with you. Because you believe in your arrogance that you know what is best for him. You believe that you know what he needs and what he is. But, barbarian that you are, you know nothing. And now you understand that you know nothing.

" 'Win does not want to leave here. He does not hate his life. Here he is already a man, a fact that you can neither believe nor comprehend. Here he has a man's responsibility, a man's rewards. He has killed, and he has been injured. He is wealthy even by your standards, and he has proven his courage.'

" 'You've spent all this time speaking for Win,' I said. 'Let him speak for himself.'

"I turned to Win and he spat in my face.

"General Kiu laughed. 'What you believe you see in him is purely a product of your mind, your culture,' he said. 'You have created an illusion. But this, too, I do not expect you to comprehend. All Westerners, I believe, are self-delusory. You cannot help it. Pity. It is in your nature.'

"As soon as I recovered sufficient strength, he let me go. He sent an escort of his soldiers with me down the mountainside, to protect me through dangerous territory, and to make sure that my wounds did not become infected."

Seve turned his head and the old scar fell into shadow. He watched Soutane. "General Kiu was right," he said softly. "I knew nothing. I was arrogant, thinking I knew black from white, that I knew what was best for these people on the Shan. But General Kiu proved to me that white was black, and black was white, and I've never forgotten that lesson."

Soutane touched him on the shoulder. "I'm sorry," she said, "for all the nasty things I said."

"Forget it." He looked into her eyes. "Ready to go?"

She nodded.

"Okay, then." Seve went to the door, turned the knob. Then a wave of vertigo made the floor ripple. It came up and hit him on the side of the head.

Milhaud ran across the Avenue Franklin Roosevelt, following Morphée and his unknown savior; everything began to fit into place: M. LoGrazie's fear of the Magician, his indirectly asking for Milhaud's help, the last rendezvous at the park. It had all been a setup. It had all been part of the Magician's plan.

While Milhaud had been celebrating his so-called freedom from the Americans, they had been playing with him as a tiger will a mouse. How the Magician must have savored these last few days!

"Watch out!" Milhaud's companion called as a black BMW came careening down the street from the direction of the Avenue New York. "That car's been following you all the way from Angkor Vat!"

Milhaud, taking his cue from the man with him, ran across the sidewalk, ducked into a shadowy doorway on the corner. The BMW screeched to a halt, and two Vietnamese bolted from the back seat.

Milhaud hugged Morphée to him. He felt a tug on his sleeve, and he and Morphée followed his companion around the corner, down the Rue François I. "Who are you?" Milhaud asked again. "What is your name?"

"Don't you recognize me?" The face, vaguely familiar, kept

appearing and disappearing as they raced through the pools of lamplight along the street. "I'm Christopher Haye."

"My God!" Milhaud reeled, momentarily lurching into the wall of a building. The past, for so long carefully hidden from the world at large, had suddenly come rushing at him with a speed he could not handle. Chris reached out, pulled him along.

"Move it!" Chris said to them both. The echoes of their footsteps hurried after them. Morphée had wisely taken off her high heels. She ran barefoot, trembling still, hearing the whine of the bullet as close as a bee near her ear.

"This is not possible!" There was a pounding in Milhaud's chest. Had Christopher Haye said that he had been followed from the restaurant? He had been betrayed on every side. "Why are you here?"

"I came to bring my brother Terry back to the States. I stayed to find out who murdered him and why."

"But where are you taking us?"

"To the only place I know is safe. I'm taking you to see your daughter."

"Can the computer lie?"

"No. It's only a machine, and machines are incapable of lying."

"But it can be fed false or misleading information."

"Not this computer. This is CIA."

"Let's see."

"Okay," Charlie Karnow said. "I can access anything from the central computer right from here." He tapped the keyboard of the computer terminal. "Naturally, no one knows it, and I'd kind of like to keep it that way."

"I have no problem with that," Diana said.

They were sitting in Karnow's library, drinking brandy. He had taken the news of Brad's death very hard. "Brad was a helluva guy," Karnow had said as he poured them drinks. He was a small, gray-faced man with the yellowed mustache and fingers of the inveterate smoker. "You only had to see what he did for my son to know that." He had brought the glasses to where Diana sat. "Now with Brad gone I don't know what will happen to him. Jeff listened to Brad."

He scrubbed at his thinning hair. "I don't know. After my wife died, my family just seemed to fall apart. I guess I never had any practice keeping it together. I left that to her." He sat down heavily in front of the computer terminal. "It was the Company first, last, and always. I never thought there was anything wrong with that until she—" He took some brandy, swallowing quickly. "Ah, well, what the hell. It's all old news now." He looked at her. "I'd do anything for Brad."

Diana nodded. "Then find out where Marcus Gable is hiding."

"What do you mean?"

"He's CIA, but he's not CIA. He's active, but he's not CIA active. He's being protected by a shadow network, but it isn't CIA. There's pressure coming from the State Department, but it isn't originating from CIA."

Charlie Karnow was already hunched over the keyboard, his fingers punching in long series of codes. "Who at State?" he said.

"Morton Saunders," Diana said. "The CIA liaison."

"Watch the screen," Karnow said.

Diana did as he asked, seeing the data come up on Morton Saunders. "He's not CIA liaison."

"Not anymore." Karnow's fingers were still dancing. "He was, as they say in the vernacular, 'appropriated by a third party.' "

"Meaning?"

Karnow shrugged. "It could be any one of a myriad entities in the intelligence community. Let's see if we can find out which."

The doorbell rang, and Karnow looked up. "Must be the repairman," he said, scraping back his chair. "My phone's been on and off all day long."

Diana was staring at the glowing screen, reading, "SECURITY CLEARANCE BREAK AXEL NINE REQUIRED FOR FURTHER INFORMATION." Still, she said, "Ask for credentials and check them through the peephole before you open the door."

Karnow nodded as he called out, "Coming!"

Diana could hear him at the door, asking who it was. She wondered what security clearance Break Axel Nine was. She saw Karnow put his eye to the peephole just before the heavy explosion blew the peephole point-blank into his face.

The percussion was so great, Karnow flew back the length of the hallway. Diana was up, her service revolver drawn as the front door crumpled inward, and she thought, they've found me.

She could see Karnow sprawled on the floor. There was very little recognizable left of his face. She thought, Charlie's CIA and they've killed him. Who the hell are they?

In a crouch she fired two shots before ducking down behind an upholstered chairback as a shotgun blast shattered the room. It was then that she understood how little protection the law provided her.

Even as her ears were ringing, she rolled out from behind the tattered chair, and was up and running. She knew she had no chance staying in place.

In the bedroom she yanked on the window, but it was locked. She groaned and, using the butt end of her revolver, smashed the pane. She tapped the remaining sharp shards with the gun's barrel, then slipped through.

She found herself on an old-fashioned iron fire escape, and immediately headed down. She had no desire to get trapped up on the roof with nowhere to turn. Her breath came hard and hot, and there was the metallic taste of fear in her mouth.

On the second floor she did not bother with the ladder, but jumped from story height. When she landed, her left ankle buckled over, and she felt a pain like a lightning bolt race up her leg.

"Damn!" The breath whistled through her clenched teeth. She heard a noise above her and dropped into a crouch, rolling across her shoulder. When she came up, she fired at the figure on the fire escape, heard a satisfying grunt. She heard a clatter, metal on metal, but did not stay around long enough to see if it was, as she suspected, the sound of a gun falling onto the grid of the fire escape.

She limped to Second Avenue, flagging down a cab. The driver turned around, staring at her disheveled state. He said, "I don't know, lady—"

"Yes, you do." Diana flashed her shield and gave him her home address.

She sat for a full minute, staring at her own doorway, after the cab reached her apartment building. Her first instinct had been to return to the precinct, but Seve had warned her against that. Peter Loong Chun had intimated that his organization had cops inside the station house on its payroll. But he had been murdered before he had had the chance to identify them.

"Lady?" The cabby was staring at her. "This is it."

Diana leaned her head back against the seat, closed her eyes. She was so weary that waves of dizziness threatened to overwhelm her.

"Lady? Hey, lady, c'mon already."

She had been so close to the heart of darkness surrounding Marcus Gable, so close to being able to give Seve everything he wanted. She longed to do that so badly. She remembered what Brad Wolff had said: *The best thing for Guarda would be for you to give him a son.*

Now the precinct was a red sector, and she realized the same went for her apartment. If they knew who she was, they'd know where she lived. She stared up at her darkened windows. Someone could be crouched there, waiting for her to turn the key in the lock. Diana shuddered. She had to get out of here.

"Lady, have a heart, willya? I gotta make a living, even if you don't."

Diana gave him the address of a midtown hotel, all the way on the west side, off the beaten path, quiet, anonymous. It was one she was familiar with because the city often used it when sequestering juries.

Standing on the sidewalk as the taxi drove off, she felt terribly exposed. The feeling of vulnerability drove her off the street. She hurried into the hotel and, thinking security, asked for a room on the top floor.

Locking the door behind her and fastening the chain, she stripped off her clothes and stood beneath a steaming shower. Her legs were shaking so hard she was obliged to hold on to the tapes with both hands. Soap took away the sweat and grime, but not the fear.

She dressed and took her service revolver from its holster. She lay down on the bed. Beside it was a cheap wood-grain melamine night table, a black phone, a hideous metal reading lamp, an ashtray. In the drawer was a Bible.

Diana closed her eyes, listened to the sound of her own breathing. She must have fallen asleep because when she next opened her eyes she saw the door with its broken chain and the figure at the same time. She fumbled for her gun, heard a voice, "Say good night, Gracie."

The shotgun blast drove her off the bed and against the wall. She felt nothing. The sound was the loudest she had ever heard. Abruptly it, and everything, was gone.

Milhaud pulled Chris back against a building's facade. "We can't leave here yet."

"What are you talking about? These people are trying to kill you and your friend."

"That's just it," Milhaud said, His face was white and pinched in the streetlight. "These people are my employers. Monsieur LoGrazie, the man I was on my way to meet was in on this, I am certain of that now. If they have decided I am expendable, then I must get back to my apartment."

"You're insane," Chris said. "It's obvious they'll have your apartment covered."

"Still," Milhaud insisted, "I must go. They will come for the *Prey Dauw*." He was already moving, and Chris was forced to follow him in order to continue the conversation. They hurried across the street, turned a corner onto the Avenue New York. "I have it, and my employers want it. I have refused to give it to them."

"Wait a minute," Chris said. "Just who are your employers?"

Loping into the shadows, Milhaud ignored him. "We're directly across the street from my apartment," he whispered. "I don't see anyone watching the entrance."

Chris, craning his neck in order to see in every direction, said, "It's impossible. They aren't stupid enough to ignore the possibility you'd head back here."

He signaled Milhaud and Morphée to stay where they were, then moved out of the shadows. He walked down the full length of the block, first along one side of the street, then doubled back on the other side. As he went, he peered into the darkened interiors of the parked cars. There was no one. Every so often he turned to look up at the apartment windows he was passing for any sign of a face, the stir of a curtain, or the glint of metal that would indicate a rifle. All the while he kept an eye out for the black BMW, but by the time he had returned to where Milhaud and Morphée were waiting, it had not appeared.

"You're right," he said. "I couldn't find anyone watching the house." Instead of reassuring him, his tour had disquieted him. Why hadn't someone been assigned to watch Milhaud's building? Something did not feel right. What?

Milhaud began to cross the street, and Chris pulled him back. "For God's sake, wait," he whispered. "They may already be up there in your apartment."

Milhaud looked at him with a grim expression. "If they are, I'll know about it." Then his eyes turned curious. "You saved me once, now you want to do it again. Why?"

"I love your daughter. I always have."

Milhaud waited a moment, then nodded. "Yes. I believe you do. But, unfortunately, Soutane and I are no longer family. She undoubtedly thinks I am dead and, believe me, it is better that she does."

"She has the right to know the truth."

There was a rueful smile on Milhaud's face. "My boy, I know

you mean well. But if she knew the whole truth, she would damn me with all her heart.''

''I can't believe that. You are her father. What have you done that she cannot forgive?''

Milhaud, half in and half out of the streetlight, appeared much as he had on that hot summer night in 1969 at his villa in Mougin. The overlays of darkness, like makeup, had smoothed out the lines that time and worry had etched into his face. Seeing him as he had been, Chris was reminded of his extraordinary strength of purpose.

''My daughter, as you no doubt know, is a Buddhist. As such, killing is abhorrent to her. I have killed with premeditation and anger. Do you think she could forgive that?''

''She herself has killed,'' Chris said. ''Her cousin Mun taught her, and she killed to protect him. The knowledge of what she has done is eating her up inside.''

''Ah, my poor child.'' He shook his head. ''And you think that will make a difference? No, no. Even if she could forgive what I have done, I cannot forgive myself. There is no penance I can perform to absolve me of the blood on my hands. I have no choice but to continue on the path I have set for myself.''

''Of course you have a choice.''

Milhaud shook his head. ''My boy, you know nothing about it. It is because of me that your brother is dead. He possessed the third and last piece of the Forest of Swords. Do you know of it?''

''Soutane explained it to me.''

Milhaud grunted. ''The mystical aspects, I am sure. But the practical application of the sword is still not fully known. It could very possibly be the only thing to unite all the opium warlords of the Golden Triangle under the banner of one person. Do you comprehend the nature of this threat?''

''Power and money,'' Chris said. ''It's what we all crave, even you, Monsieur Vosges.''

''No!'' Milhaud almost shouted it. ''You misunderstand, or you have been misled by my daughter, who surely never understood me or my motives. I only wanted freedom for the Cambodians, a complete break from the colonialism imposed on them by cruel and unthinking countrymen of mine . . . and yours.''

''So you turned intellectuals into radicals, and sold them weapons.''

''I had no choice! Don't you see? The process had advanced too far for reason. Armed force was the only answer. The imprint of colonialism was too deeply ingrained in those in power for the success of any alternative."

"But the result, Monsieur Vosges, was akin to genocide. You unleashed Pol Pot. How many Cambodians were senselessly slaughtered because of you?"

Milhaud shuddered, and Morphée put her arms around him. "Every night," he said, "I dream of them . . . of death. How could I have known how it would turn out? How could I have seen that Saloth Sar would have been transformed into a walking, living nightmare?"

"History," Chris said, "would have shown you the way, if only you had bothered to look. Greed rules mankind, not theory. The lust for power and money overrides the teachings of even the best-intentioned philosopher."

"But I taught only the path to freedom," Milhaud said miserably. "I cannot yet fathom what happened."

Chris wondered if all such philosophers down through history had been so thoroughly deluded. "You said before that it is because of you that Terry is dead. Did you order him murdered?"

"If I had," Milhaud asked, "would you be able to forgive me?"

"Did you?"

"No. His death was an accident."

"And what about the murders of Dominic Guarda, Al DeCordia? What about the attempt on my life?"

Milhaud stared at him. "What are you talking about?"

In the dim light it was difficult to be certain of his expression. "Monsieur Mabuse—Trangh—executed Dominic and DeCordia in the same way he murdered Terry. He decapitated them. Then, in New York, he came after me, and almost did the same to the woman who was with me."

"What is going on? I never authorized—"

"But you *were* working with Terry on the drug pipeline."

"Working with him? Why, no. We were, as you might call it, friendly rivals in the same business. Until, that is, I was contacted by Monsieur LoGrazie's group."

"Your employers?"

"Yes. At first I was convinced that they were Mafia. Then, because of a listening device I secreted in Monsieur LoGrazie's residence, I became aware that they were CIA masquerading as Mafia."

"CIA? Involved in a heroin pipeline?"

"Oh, yes. You are surprised? Well, they have been involved in drug smuggling ever since the war in Vietnam. I made a deal with two of their representatives who I rendezvoused with in Angkor Wat in 1969. One of the men was called the Magician. The other was your brother, Terry."

"Oh, Christ." Chris closed his eyes, suddenly dizzy. "No."

"But, my boy, I thought you would have known. You were his only brother, after all."

"I never knew . . . anything." The enormity of those words came crashing in on him. He felt tired, and so sad he wanted to cry. He took a deep breath, marshaling with a tremendous effort his thoughts. "You said you made a deal with the Magician and Terry, so I assume they bought your pipeline."

Milhaud nodded.

"What did they give you in return? Money?" Even as he asked the question, he was aware that part of him wanted to hide, desperate not to know.

"Oh, something far more valuable than money," Milhaud said. "After all, the pipeline was a source of never-ending money. There was only one reason I would have given it up. For a chance to assassinate Sihanouk. But when it was botched, I settled for arms. They provided me with a constant flow of weapons even my money could not get for me."

Chris was feeling sick to his stomach. "And these arms went straight to Pol Pot."

"To the Khmer Rouge, yes. As I said, my primary objective at that time was to assassinate Sihanouk. When that became unviable because of his ties into Peking, I settled for his ouster."

"What did the CIA want with a heroin pipeline?"

"I didn't ask."

"You didn't want to think about it, you mean."

"Possibly," Milhaud admitted. "But it hardly matters. They would never have told me."

"But later, when Terry and Mun were running the pipeline, surely you knew to whom the heroin was being distributed." It was of the utmost importance for Chris to understand this. Now it seemed, after all his hopes and speculations, after his faith in Terry's motives, he was to be proven wrong. Terry had become a drug smuggler, it was that simple. That truth seemed too horrible to contemplate.

"That was the one odd thing," Milhaud said. "I never did find out who was buying the heroin. I can tell you that it was none of the usual sources."

"I still don't understand," Chris said. "If Mr. LoGrazie is CIA and he wanted you to take control of Terry's pipeline . . . According to what you've told me, that pipeline was already the property of the CIA."

"I said only that it had been bought by the CIA in 1969. I don't know what happened in the interim. Perhaps the Magician and Terry sought to take it private; certainly they had a falling out of epic proportions, over what I cannot say."

"So the CIA hired you to get the pipeline back."

"Yes, in Operation White Tiger, though initially I was not aware of who they were. And the key—what they were truly desperate to acquire—was the *Prey Dauw*. With that talisman they can control all of the poppy production in the Golden Triangle."

"How would they have learned about the Forest of Swords?"

"The Magician. That was the name your brother gave Virgil."

Chris was watching the avenue for any sign of the black BMW. "The Magician wants all of us dead. Do you know why?"

Milhaud stirred. "It doesn't matter. Now we are all set upon this path. We have no choice but to follow it to the end."

"That's not true. It has been my experience," Chris said, impaling Milhaud with his gaze, "that people who claim they have no choice lack the courage to make it. If it will be painful for you to change, think of this: perhaps you are the one to help Soutane become whole again. You spoke before of penance. Wouldn't that be penance enough? Wouldn't that be sufficient to heal you?"

Milhaud tore his eyes away from Chris's. "We are wasting time," he said harshly. He turned to Morphée, pushed her farther back into the shadows. "Stay here," he said. "Whatever you do, don't move until we come back for you." Then he was running across the street. Despite the warnings inside his head, Chris went after him. "We must get the *Prey Dauw*." Milhaud unlocked the front door of the building. The garage area was pitch black, and he deliberately kept the light off. Their footsteps echoed eerily off the walls.

Upstairs, the rambling apartment was dark. Milhaud locked the door behind them. Here and there, pale wraithlike patches of light dappled the floorboards and carpets.

Milhaud cautiously led them on a circuitous route down hallways and around heavy furniture. He turned on no lights as he went, and Chris was obliged to keep close enough to touch him in order not to lose his way or bump into anything.

At the doorway to each room Milhaud paused as if sniffing like a dog to catch an intruder's scent. With each step they took it seemed to Chris as if the tension was increasing exponentially. He had begun to sweat, to peer into the darkest corners where he could not possibly see anyone lurking, as if his intuition would provide him with warning. Until, like a child afraid of the dark, he began to see movement, coiled and sinister, within every ill-defined shape and partial outline.

At last they came to Milhaud's study. It was accessible through open, double sliding doors. The two of them stood in the doorway, Chris trying to discern shapes in the dark, Milhaud concentrating intently without looking at anything at all.

They moved quickly into the room. Milhaud went immediately to his desk. While he did so, Chris stood at the windows that looked out onto the Seine and, across its expanse, the École Militaire and the Parc du Champ de Mars.

Bamboo shades covered the windows completely. Nevertheless, narrow strips of dim light seeped through. Chris moved closer, until his face was against the bamboo slats. In this position he was able to look down through the gaps at the Avenue New York.

He saw the black BMW double-parked. He could see exhaust curling; its motor was running.

Chris turned away, saw Milhaud with a gun in his hand. He was about to speak, but Milhaud waved him to silence. Milhaud pointed to a door in the room, opened it, and went through. Chris slipped in after him.

They were inside a storage closet. "The black BMW that followed you from Angkor Vat is downstairs," Chris whispered into the cramped space.

"I'm not surprised," Milhaud said in his ear. "Someone is in the apartment. They have come as I said they would to steal the Forest of Swords."

That interested Chris. He recalled that Milhaud had locked the door, but he had heard no sound as of a breaking lock. That meant whoever was in the apartment had gained entrance with a key.

He reached out, opening the closet door a fraction further so that their view of the office was of a more generous slice. It took in part of the open doorway, the area of Milhaud's desk, as well as a section of floor-to-ceiling bookcase.

He was about to ask Milhaud who might have a key to his front door when he became aware of a shadow filling the open doorway. Next to him he felt Milhaud tense, and could see him moving the pistol into position.

The figure stood for a moment, as if surveying a familiar environment. Then it crossed silently to Milhaud's desk and, leaning over, snapped on the etched-glass lamp on one corner.

By its light Chris recognized Trangh. Milhaud relaxed, and the gun lowered. He shifted position, about to stand up and perhaps emerge from the closet, when Trangh moved to the bookcase and, laying his hands flat against its surface, moved a portion of it away.

It was a hidden door, and as soon as it was open, Chris felt a new kind of tension filling Milhaud. Trangh was leaning into the interior of the open space, and now he emerged with an odd-looking triple-bladed sword.

"Merde!" Milhaud breathed. "He is taking the Forest of Swords!"

Thinking of the black BMW downstairs, Chris whispered, "Maybe he saw the car in the street and has come to move the sword in order to protect it."

"It was perfectly safe where it was," Milhaud said. "Christ, what a fool I've been. He has betrayed me." Chris saw the gun come up, aiming at the back of Trangh's head.

At the same instant it seemed, so many tiny pieces of the puzzle were falling into place. Now Chris knew why no one had been observing the apartment. No one had to because Trangh was their eyes and ears.

Trangh was working for Milhaud, the someone high up in the pipeline, but now it was clear he was secretly working for someone else. Who? Whoever had sent Trangh to kill Chris, whoever had set Milhaud up to be shot tonight, whoever was in the black BMW. Milhaud's employers?

Then Chris had it. "He's working for Marcus Gable!"

Milhaud turned his head for an instant. "Who?"

"Virgil."

"Yes! The Magician. It must be!" Milhaud sighted down the gun barrel. "He'll die for this!" His finger tightened on the trigger.

Chris, staring at Trangh rewrapping the Forest of Swords in chamois, was brought wholly back to their confrontation in the stable in Tourrette. He remembered what Seve had said. Trangh had murdered Terry, Dominic Guarda, and Al DeCordia. And in trying to murder Chris, he had maimed Alix.

And yet, when he had had another chance to kill Chris, he had not. Instead he had accepted Chris's bargain of Soutane's life for the dagger Terry had wanted to keep. Why?

Chris did not know, but he recognized in Trangh a mystery that he perhaps needed to solve in order to understand who and what he had become. Because it was clear to him that he was no longer the Christopher Haye who had stood in court defending a man who had then all but confessed his guilt to him. The Christopher Haye who had felt betrayed by the law he had sworn to uphold, helpless to enact a justice he knew had been mocked.

For a time he had been convinced that he had been slowly absorbing as if by osmosis his dead brother Terry's identity. That would have been simple enough to understand, and would have made a neat literary point. But ever since that night in the stable, he knew the truth was far more complex, as life was far more complex than any work of fiction could be.

He saw the muzzle of Milhaud's pistol aimed at Trangh, and in his mind rose the boyhood image of the stag in his rifle sights. It pawed through the snow, the steam rushing from its nostrils as its warm breath met the frigid winter air. He felt Terry's finger over his, making him squeeze the trigger against his will.

He saw that Trangh was like that stag, knew that if he allowed Trangh to die, he would never know, he would never come to understand what he had become. And somehow Terry would be gone from him forever without his ever being able to say goodbye.

This quest had begun to determine who had killed Terry and why, but it had become something far greater in scope and importance. It had become for Chris a personal journey toward a home he had never suspected he had, let alone believed that he would ever find.

Milhaud's finger was tightening on the trigger, and Chris twisted the gun out of his hand.

Ma Varada had said to Mun, "You will not die," and she was right. Mun, having used his powerful friends and considerable funds in Bangkok, walked off the jumbo jet onto French soil. It was Paris, not Nice, because Paris was where Ma Varada said the Magician was.

Paris or Vence, it did not matter to Mun. France no longer felt like home. His mind, his spirit were consumed with Sagaing. It had only been with an immense effort that he had been able to pull himself away from the city of prayer.

He would not have come back but for the Magician. He watched Ma Varada as they went through Immigration and Customs. She was wearing a high-fashion linen and silk suit, a knockoff of an Ungaro she had made for her in Bangkok. She had her hair cut short, in a very modern style. She wore snakeskin high-heel shoes from Charles Jourdan, a pair of iridescent green bracelets on her left wrist, and carried a snakeskin bag. Although it was well past midnight, she looked as fresh as when she had stepped onto the plane in Bangkok. It was impossible to believe that she was the same person Mun had saved from the punishment of General Kiu.

"Don't bother with a taxi," she said when they had cleared customs. "I had a friend bring my car to the airport lot."

It was a Citroën with a modified engine. She drove very hard and very fast. At this hour, traffic was almost nonexistent. Several times, Mun was obliged to hold onto the passenger handle as she whipped around the curves of the Périphérique. Ahead of them lay Paris, a soft and willing lady wrapped in sequins of light.

They entered the city via Porte de la Muette, heading east on the Avenue Henri Martin. They were in the Sixteenth arrondissement, a mainly residential area that, lately, had become quite chic.

Ma Varada turned right on the Rue Scheffer. They had to come around in order to gain access to the tiny Square Petrarque. A vehicle bar prevented her from driving into the private street. She pulled the Citroën into the curb at the side of a corner three-story house with a rather severe Neoclassic facade which was made of thick slabs of white stone. A small but ornate wrought-iron balcony dominated the second story, and a pair of imposing oval windows flanked like all-seeing eyes the maw of the front door, which was set rather deeply into the stonework. In the streetlights, the facade rose out of the shadows like a beacon or a reef. Mun wondered which one it would turn out to be.

As they got out, Mun could see that, were it not for some new apartment blocks, the upper levels would overlook the Place de Trocadéro and the stark, rather fascistic Palais. Once, of course, they had. They were three blocks from the Passy cemetery where heroes of the wars had found their eternal rest.

"The Magician is here," Ma Varada said.

Mun was tired and in pain. He knew this was not the time to force a confrontation with the Magician. His wound was healing quickly, which Ma Varada attributed to the blind man of Sagaing's elixir, but he was far from being recovered. There had been considerable tissue and muscle damage, and only time could complete the process of rehabilitation.

Mun also knew that time was one thing he did not have. Not when it came to the Magician. He had to be stopped now, before he gained possession of the *Prey Dauw*. Before he could command all the opium warlords. Before he took complete control of the

Shan. His power was already considerable on the Shan Plateau. He had somehow co-opted Admiral Jumbo, and it was conceivable that, despite persuasive orations to the contrary, he had done the same to General Kiu. Now Mun knew that the Magician and Terry had had the same plan: to unite all the warlords. But what each meant to do with that enormous power was so different.

Kiu or Jumbo, one or the other of the warlords had killed Mogok, and had tried to kill him and Ma Varada. Which one? Mun did not know. Only the Magician knew.

Abruptly, Mun laughed. It had occurred to him that it did not really matter who had tried to kill them. In the end it was the Magician who was pulling the strings.

Mun, looking up at the building, wished that Terry was here. He whispered a short prayer, then said, "All right. Let's go."

But Ma Varada pushed at his chest, went up the stone stairs alone. She stood on the landing, in full view of the video camera mounted on the stone and mortar ledge three feet above her head. With her back to him she rang the bell. In a moment she put her hand on the door handle and opened it inward.

"I don't want to see her," Milhaud said. "When she learns the truth, she will despise me and, knowing that, I will not be able to go on. Now, at least, I am insulated from her hatred; I can fool myself into believing that it does not exist."

Chris put down the phone and, misunderstanding the source of Milhaud's fear, said, "You're not giving her enough credit." He saw that Milhaud looked as terrified as Soutane had sounded when he had called her at the hotel.

"Chris, where have you been! I've been nearly frantic with worry!" She had almost shouted in her anxiety.

"To Porte de Choisy," he said. "While you and Seve were off having a *tête-à-tête*, I made a startling discovery."

"What? Did you find Trangh?"

"Yes and no. Are you sure you're interested in this?"

"For God's sake, Chris, tell me what's going on. Don't you understand that we both hurt. For a moment last night you made me forget my pain. I called out, forgetting that Terry was dead. But is that any reason to punish me further?"

Chris felt instantly ashamed of himself. Did he really need to know that he was more important to her than Terry had been? But how would he ever know? How could she ever prove it to him, even if she would want to?

"Chris, are you all right?"

"I want you and Seve to get over here right away," he said.

"Seve just passed out. He's still feeling the effects of Trangh's attack on him," Soutane had said. "We've had the doctor up. He's not going anywhere."

"Then you come," Chris had told her. "Do you have a pencil? Take down this address."

Now he watched the fear crawling across Milhaud's face, a hideous thing, and said, "It's too late. She's on her way."

"Then I will leave."

He turned to Morphée. "Can you do anything about this?"

Milhaud had insisted they come here, to Les Portes du Jade. It was, he said, the only place he felt safe. He had also insisted that as a security precaution they come separately. He had taken the métro; Chris had cycled across the Seine to the Left Bank.

Out the windows Chris could see part of the courtyard. The verdigris fountain was lighted, and he could make out the head of the dolphin that was the fountain's center, the mermaid's long hair, tangled as seaweed, wrapped around it. Beyond, the dark square of the Luxembourg Gardens was as still as death.

Morphée smiled at him. He had recognized her immediately as the woman who had been with Milhaud at Angkor Vat. "He will not leave," she said. "He dreams about his daughter. He even sees her in me." And she turned to look at Milhaud. "Did you think I wouldn't know that? I may not know what is in your mind, but I am always sure of what is in your heart."

Milhaud turned away from her, went to the window, staring out at the city. "This waiting," he said, "is like a little death."

"You'll survive," Morphée said. "Just as you've survived all the desolations of war."

She came up behind him, but he shrugged off her touch. "This is different. Don't you see? Soutane is my soul; she is part of me."

"You have lived so long without her."

"Not lived; hardly that." Chris could see the despair sculpt lines into Milhaud's face. "I have been dragging myself around like a creature who has gnawed off its own legs. My past has become so vivid, I hardly understand anything around me anymore. The present has become as gray and dark as a winter's evening; it is as dim as memory to me now." He started at the sound of a knock on the door to Morphée's apartment.

Chris opened the door. "Hello, Soutane."

She was dressed in black leggings and a form-fitting blouse. Over the leggings a sable-colored miniskirt hugged her hips and, barely, her thighs. She was wearing no makeup, but he didn't think that was why she looked pale.

"Chris, are—"

"Come on in."

She came across the threshold, and he stepped out of the way. She saw Milhaud from across the width of the room. He appeared rooted to the spot, scarcely able to breathe.

"Dear God," Soutane breathed. "Father?"

Chris could see that Milhaud wanted to nod, to open his mouth, and speak that one word he had been yearning to utter, *Daughter*. But he could do neither.

She went across the room and, without taking her eyes from her father's face, said, "Chris, what is this?"

"He calls himself Milhaud now, not Vosges."

It was as if he had delivered her a physical blow. She reeled backward, but it was Milhaud who winced. Morphée closed her eyes. "The man—" Soutane swallowed, was obliged to begin all over again. "Trangh works for my father?"

"Yes," Chris said. He felt like a translator at a delicate juncture of a superpower arms summit. "They met in Indochina in 1969."

"I saw in Trangh a soul lost in the madness of war." Milhaud had regained his voice. Perhaps it was the topic, a return to the territory of philosophy that had been his life, and was a comfort to him now. "He was the Magician's lackey, jumping at his every command. I could not stand how he was being degraded, like the Vietnamese and the Cambodians had been for more than a century, since we French had first visited them. I saw in him a way to perhaps redeem in some small measure the injustices heaped upon him and others like him by my people.

"So I took him under my wing, took him away from Virgil. I taught him to forget his colonialist past, I taught him to see a future filled with freedom."

"Freedom?" What was it, Chris asked himself, that suffused Soutane's face as she spoke? Was it horror or revulsion or some combination too complex to fathom? "Is that what you're calling murder? I can't believe your blood flows through my veins."

Milhaud turned helplessly toward Chris. "I failed with Trangh just as I failed with Pol Pot. It is as you said, I understand the theories, but I failed to comprehend their psyches. I was undone by their personalities, which I still cannot understand."

"It seems," Chris said, "that Trangh did not respond to his lessons. At some point he recontacted Virgil, and has been secretly working for him ever since. His orders to kill came from the Magician, not your father."

"It's true," Milhaud said quickly. "Trangh was supposed to buy *La Porte à la Nuit* from Terry Haye—that was all. But Terry tried to sell me a phony. He didn't think I'd know the difference, and he was right. But he did not know that Trangh worked for me, or that I would send him to inspect the dagger before completing the transaction.

"Trangh was one of very few people who had actually seen the Doorway to Night. He spotted the substitute right away, and everything followed from there."

"It seems clear now," Chris said, "that Trangh already had orders from the Magician to kill Terry, and this was the perfect excuse to do it without giving your father an inkling of what was really happening."

Soutane turned to M. Vosges. "Is this true?"

He nodded ruefully. "It appears to be. Yes."

"But why," Soutane said, "did you disappear, change your name, live your life as if I didn't exist?"

M. Vosges gave a quick glance in Morphée's direction before turning to look out the window.

"Father?"

He stirred, as if, sleeping, he was in the midst of a turbulent dream. "There is, I am afraid, no satisfactory answer."

Silence in the room. Chris looked from one to the other before his glance settled on Morphée. She was standing very still, her eyes on neither one, but somewhere else, as if having had an intimation of disaster, she had been compelled to observe its bloody face firsthand.

Soutane took a single step toward the figure by the window. "Do you seriously expect me to leave it at that? To fling myself into your arms, cover you with kisses, and tell you, 'It's all right. I forgive you.' "

It began as a bleak smile, but as he saw her expression, it withered as he put his fist up to his mouth into an embarrassed cough. The gesture was inadequate to hide his dread of her.

But Soutane, in her extreme agitation, appeared oblivious of her power over him. "Chris," she said, "I want to get out of here."

"I don't think that would be a good idea as yet." And when she turned to him, surprised and angry, "Monsieur Vosges's connection—however tenuous now—with Trangh may prove to be the edge we need to trap Trangh and bring us to the Magician." He shot her a look. "No matter what your current emotional state, I don't think you'll want to let this go."

Reluctantly, she nodded. "But I won't stay in the same room with him."

"Come, darling," Morphée said, taking her arm, "I'll make you comfortable elsewhere."

M. Vosges was about to protest, then, seeing the look on Morphée's face, thought better of it. His hand, which had been outstretched in supplication or in warning, fell to his side with a slap.

Morphée and Soutane went out the door of the apartment, and he said with great sadness, "She has destroyed my heart."

Chris, watching him closely, said, "She is involved in that, Monsieur Vosges, only to the extent that you have made it so."

•

Mun ran up the steps, ignoring the pain in his side, brushed past her into the vestibule. He turned to slam the door in her face, but she had already slipped inside with him. Had he wanted to exclude her now because he wanted her protected or because he still did not trust her?

He put a finger to his lips, made a motion with his hand for her to stay near the door. They were in a dimly lighted entryway. A crystal bowl filled with forsythia and dogwood, standard bearers of spring, occupied the top of a Louis XIV commode decorated as if it were a wedding cake with ormolu and fruitwood. A Flemish tapestry on the wall to their left was dark with feverish hunters, snapping dogs, a bloody stag at bay.

Ahead of them, a polished oak staircase up to the second floor. A light was on in the upper hallway and, against it, the knife-edged silhouette of a man rushed down the steps.

"Ma Varada?"

The Magician's voice brought in a rush of myriad of images and remembered incidents. Mun shook himself, signaled.

"Yes?" Was her tone defiant or resigned?

"Come upstairs."

Mun saw at the same time her mouthing to him one word, *Karma*.

He went, crossing as he did the distorted shadow which seemed to move with him away from the light.

Upstairs, he saw a man he did not recognize. The man was holding a Beretta automatic. "Hello, Mun," the Magician said. "I saw you when you got out of the car." Over his shoulder, a portrait of a soft man dressed in royal purple, a prince or a king, pink-cheeked and smug.

"What happened to you?" Mun said, though he could very well guess.

The Magician gestured with the Beretta, and Mun went down the hallway, past the portrait of overfed royalty, into a brightly painted room. A walnut clock ticked sonorously on a marble mantelpiece. A pair of windows like eyes overlooked the narrow street, and beyond, the militaristic statues of the Trocadéro.

On top of an ornate chest of drawers a very modern suitcase of parachute cloth was open, trousers and shirts piled in it. The Magician's clothes. Where was he going?

"I died," the Magician said, "and was born again. Life is really quite simple to create when you know the right people, and they have an unlimited amount of money."

"The CIA."

"Oh, good God." The Magician laughed. "No, no. The Company is run by a bunch of tight-asses who don't know the difference between money and influence. It's no different now than it was when I worked there. But that, dear Mun, was a long time ago."

Mun was thinking that they had given him the perfect face: Virgil could hide behind its expressionless exterior. When it moved, it was like elastic, responding to commands rather than emotions.

"I kissed the Company goodbye in 1972. Christ, but that was good. It felt like I had been constipated for four years, like I had been consigned to the inner ring of purgatory, which in 'Nam, I suppose I was."

"Where did you go?" Mun not staring directly at the Beretta, seeing the jungle, the stone of Angkor, the god Vishnu creating and destroying.

"Is that what you came here to find out, dear Mun? Jesus, I hope you're not that stupid."

The gun was not the source of death, it was the man. The Magician with his plastic face bore watching.

"It's true in the beginning I loved the CIA. But that was principally because I was naive. I believed them—and by extension myself—to be a modern incarnation of the Texas Rangers, with a history of nerve and grit. I thought in those days that the Company stood for something unique and important. After all, I knew the history of the OSS, the great things that organization did for America in World War Two."

Mun had to keep reminding himself of how dangerous this man was, of what he had done to Terry. His was an utterly benign face. When he smiled, it was impossible to believe that he could harm any living creature. It was prudent to keep in mind how full he was of the kind of power that Asians covet. He was centered, in full control of his energy. He was, in a way, far more Eastern now than he had ever been when Mun had been with him in Indochina.

"But I was wrong. Just as I was wrong in believing that we were over in 'Nam for good reasons. I found out that war was no longer being waged by generals or even the chiefs of staff. Vietnam was the president's baby.

"When did Nixon and Kissinger stop trusting the Congress, their own Cabinet members? I don't know, but since that time, no American president has given a shit for Congress or the people its members represent."

It was, Mun thought, as if he had gone somewhere and learned the secret of life. He was no longer concerned, as other Westerners were, about why we are all here.

"Not that I can completely blame them. What has the modern Congress done but line its own pockets? It enacts a tax-reform law and adds to it a rider giving all its members a raise. Senators and representatives whine because they're not told about top-secret CIA operations, and when they are briefed, they climb all over one another to break it first to the media. Political power is now measured in a perverse reflection of Hollywood megawatts: how many minutes you can wangle on TV.

"Are you getting all this, dear Mun, or is it too much for your poor Asian brain to comprehend?"

Mun said, "I see you for what you are. Your new face cannot hide you from me."

"I am the future," the Magician said. "Only I am clever enough to stop America from eating itself alive. For years the Japanese have been buying our corporate bonds. Now they are snatching our prime real estate and the companies housed on this property. America is being cut up piecemeal and our government has gone into a trance. The president is obsessed with power and covert operations, and the Congress with raping the taxpayers."

Then Mun understood the difference in the Magician. He was not afraid of death. Not as he had been in Vietnam, because he believed himself to be invincible, but because he had learned that life and death are entwined, that death is not the end, but the beginning.

"I left the Company because it was in chains to the bloodthirsty media hounds on Capitol Hill who wouldn't know an operational imperative from a Häagen-Dazs bar." Leaning against the mantel. He was, Mun saw, enjoying himself as much as he could enjoy anything.

"Since I've gone—well, independent, you might call it—I make my own decisions. I still have a boss, but I have my own agenda. He thinks one thing, and I know another. He's a little less stupid than the rest of them but still I doubt whether he'd condone what I'm doing. Like all of them he has become a prisoner of his own power."

"Who is he?" Thinking, who's kidding who? You can't be independent and have a boss at the same time.

The Magician grinned. "You'd like to know, I'll bet. But, then, you'd like to know the answers to so many secrets, dear Mun. You've been mucking around in the Shan, haven't you? Have you discovered my plan yet? But, no. Otherwise, you wouldn't be here now. You want to know who sold you and Terry Haye out, Admiral Jumbo or General Kiu. Well, you came to the wrong place. I do not dispense information, especially to a Cambodian who would just as soon see me dead."

"You had Terry murdered," Mun said. "Killing you would feel good."

"Why?" the Magician asked. "Don't tell me it's because it would feel like justice? You were nothing but Terry Haye's lapdog, just as Trangh was my lapdog. The only difference between the two of you is that Trangh still knows his place."

"You're a fool if you believe that."

"Yap, yap."

"Terry was my friend. My only friend."

The Magician turned the Beretta round, let it lie flat on his outstretched palm. "All right. If you are serious about taking your revenge, come here and kill me." Mun did not move. He knew a trap when he saw one. It was the same as approaching the enemy empty-handed, which the Magician had been good at in the days of the war. The idea behind it was greed. Greed made people careless, and in the war a careless person was a dead person.

"You were right to go to the Shan," the Magician said. "That's where it all stems from: money, power, life, and death. How many men, dear Mun, have died up there on that plateau because they could not tell one from the other?'' He laughed. The Beretta was still offered like poison to a rat. Mun ignored it.

''You're smart,'' the Magician said. ''You've gone the course. Even Terry couldn't do that.''

''Your hatred betrays you,'' Mun said. ''In the end it will destroy you. You who are consumed by sensual desires.''

The Magician laughed again. ''You're a good one to spout Buddhist tenets, dear killer Mun.''

''War creates its own necessities.''

''Bullshit!''

''Is that so? You more than most can understand what war makes of people. Death is nothing compared to the grotesqueries one remembers, the deformities of spirit visited on the firsthand survivors.''

''Cut the crap.''

''Do you remember,'' Mun said, ''the little girl crying so piteously? She was so helpless, so hopeless. Even with the VC grenade triggered under her arm. What do you remember about her, I wonder? The sound of her crying or the noise of the explosion when you shot her and set off the grenade? Personally, I remember both, so vividly I often believe it happened yesterday.''

''Shut up,'' the Magician said. He took the Beretta off his palm, aimed it at Mun. ''I should shoot you now.''

''I can't see why you wouldn't,'' Mun said. ''I'm as great a threat to you as Terry ever was.''

''Never.'' For the first time a sliver of emotion energized his face. ''Terry was the only man I ever trusted. He knew everything.''

''In the end that was the problem, wasn't it?''

The Magician nodded. ''He was as independent-minded as I was. When the crunch came, we were like two bighorn sheep butting heads. Both of us got hurt.''

''The crunch? What was that?''

''You mean he never told you? Well, that surprises me, at any rate. It was how he ended up with the pipeline into Admiral Jumbo, the one we'd gotten from Monsieur Vosges during the war.''

''The rendezvous at Angkor. The Khmer Rouge.''

''Mmm. The pipeline was like Terry's consolation prize when we parted company.''

''When he ended his involvement in your private group.''

''Yes. He threatened to expose us if we didn't let him go. Well, what could we do? He gave us a copy of a diary he had made—

names, RDV locations, matériel consigned and redirected. He said the original was well hidden. They said fuck it, let him go."

"But not you."

"I said it, too." The Magician smiled. "But I didn't mean it. I never lost track of him. I held him in my sights like a buck who needs maturing before being brought down."

"You were counting on him to improve the pipeline."

"Which with your help he did." Mun thought the Magician's hand must be getting tired holding up the Beretta for so long, but he wasn't of a mind to count on it. "Only thing I didn't count on was you two getting your own ideas as to where the heroin should end up. By the way, who *did* you sell the shit to?"

Mun thinking, General Kiu knew what they had done with the shit, but the Magician obviously did not. Now that was interesting. Did it mean that General Kiu had been telling Mun the truth, or that he was keeping secrets from the Magician? Mun said, "No one you ever heard of."

"But where did it all *go*? There was so much of it. Too much for me not to have heard something of its destination."

"Well, really, it's a puzzle."

The Magician's eyes, translucent with concentration, were like drops of wax on a tabletop. "I'll give you this, you're a hard sonuvabitch. You were a damn fine soldier, too."

It sounded to Mun like an epitaph, and now he concentrated not on the Magician's waxy face, which would tell him nothing, but on the forefinger of the right hand curled around the Beretta's trigger.

The sound of the gunshot, somewhere in the house, made Mun start.

"Easy there," the Magician said as if talking to a skittish animal. He smiled. "Did you think that Ma Varada would rescue you? Did you think I was alone in the house? I said I saw you from the window. Mr. LoGrazie, my connection with the private—the off-the-shelf—organization, has taken care of Ma Varada. Permanently. She, too, was independent-minded. At first I considered that an asset. But, gradually, as you no doubt understand, it became a liability. Too much contemplation inevitably leads to a questioning of the status quo, don't you think? Ma Varada had of late become restive. This end is best for her." All the time watching Mun's face for any signs of life, any hint that the verbal knives were finding a nerve or at least fertile ground.

Mun thought of returning to Sagaing with Ma Varada. He thought of heavily painted *stupas* of the temples, a cessation of desire which was necessary in order to attain nirvana. He thought of a lifetime of contemplation, of offering service to others, and of the Buddha's face through a mist of incense and cardamom.

But if all that were not possible, he would accept it. *Karma*. His desire for that new/old life, were it to dictate all his present actions, was in itself destructive.

"I did not know until this moment," he said, "whether she was lying to me or telling the truth."

He saw and enjoyed the flicker of anger as it passed across the Magician's face. The Magician disliked, as he had said, divulging secrets.

"It does not matter. In a moment it will be of no import to you."

Mun, feeling the encroachment of death, said, "You are doing me a service, perhaps the only good deed you have ever performed. In my next incarnation while I strive to atone for the sins of this life, I will struggle to do only good works."

The Magician frowned. But it wasn't, as Mun had first thought, at his words. The Magician's attention had turned toward the open doorway.

Ma Varada stood on the threshold, a Beretta, the twin of the one the magician held, pointed at him.

"Put it down" she said, "or I'll kill you."

"Mr. LoGrazie?"

"He was stupid and soft," Ma Varada said. "I hit him. Then I took his gun, opened his mouth, and put a bullet through his palate into his brain. Isn't that how you taught me to do it?"

The Magician nodded. He said, "Ma Varada?"

"Yes?"

He shot her without seeming to have moved the barrel of his Beretta. Ma Varada's eyes opened wide as she flew back, slamming into the far wall of the hallway. Blood blossomed over the spot where her heart used to pump.

"And that's another way," the Magician said.

Mun was already moving. The Magician must have seen him out of the corner of his eye because he, too, was in motion. But he wasn't fast enough. Mun, grimacing through the pain in his side, kicked out, the toe of his shoe catching the Magician in the groin.

The Magician fell to his knees, and Mun chopped him hard on the side of the neck. The nerve bundle went into complete dysfunction, and the Magician flopped on his side, temporarily paralyzed.

Mun snatched the Beretta and, turning the body over, jammed

the barrel as far as it would go into the yawning mouth. His finger tightened on the trigger.

He had thought of this moment often, dreamed about it constantly. In his dream he always thought of Terry, of evening the balance in the scales drawn between the ancient symbols of good and evil, Hanuman and Ravana. But now, since his brief stay in Sagaing, he knew that this decision was not for him to make. It was for the gods, not man, to even the balance of the scales.

More precisely, it was for Mun to contemplate, to do service and good works. It was not for Mun to kill. Killing was a sin which Mun could no longer commit. The Buddha had been quite correct. There was no such thing as the human soul, because the existence of a soul meant a kind of permanence. One's essence, Mun had been taught so long ago in the *kyaung*—the monastery school in Sagaing—and which he understood now in the most profound way, is eternally in flux.

This was the new Mun, rising out of the ashes of the old. He had no desire to kill, saw, moreover, no need to do so.

He let go of the Beretta, stood up. It lay in the Magician's mouth like a strange metallic rune or stigmata.

He went into the hallway and, beside the blood smear on the wall, checked Ma Varada, confirming what his instinct had told him, that she was dead. His fingertips touching her cheek, her lips, her eyelids. Her lashes were wet with tears.

Thinking of her hung upside down on General Kiu's crucifix, cutting her down, he meditated for a moment on the quality of her life, the nature of her rebirth. Then he returned to the room, went quickly through the suitcase, looking for some hint as to where the Magician was headed. He stared at the tickets, and nodded, thinking, Was there ever any doubt? Carefully, he searched the house for any sign of the *Prey Dauw*. There was none. Returning to the suitcase, he stared again at the tickets. After a moment he was no longer seeing anything in the room.

He heard the chanting, the brass gongs calling the faithful to prayer, and he, too, uttered a prayer. But whether it was for the Magician or for himself he did not know.

Diana opened her eyes and contemplated death. Was this what it was like, stuck in the position of your demise for all eternity? She prayed to God it was not so.

And He heard her supplication.

She took a shuddering, painful breath and knew she was alive. She tried to move, and screamed. The pain almost blinded her. She heard her heart beating, her lungs filling and deflating as loudly as if they were pumping rock 'n' roll rather than life.

She took a look around her. There was so much blood that she almost passed out again, fought against that because of the implicit danger: if she fell asleep again, she might never wake up.

She thought, How can I save myself?

For a moment her thoughts became entangled in the notion I have been shot and I'm hurt. How badly? Am I going to die?

Diana closed her eyes and took a deep breath. This is not going to help me, she told herself. Already she could feel the clammy edge of panic turning her mind into an inchoate mess, incapable of coherent reasoning. This is not the Way, she told herself firmly.

She opened her eyes and looked around the room. She noticed the bed first, its mildewy bedspread spattered with blood—her blood. Oh, God!

Took another deep, shuddering breath.

Beside the bed, the wood-grain night table. On it, the metal lamp, an ashtray, a black telephone.

The phone!

She needed to get to it. She tried to get up, found that she could not move. Her heart lurched painfully as she thought, I'm paralyzed! She was crying, the hot tears rolling down her cheeks, dropping onto her useless thighs.

Then the storm had passed, and she thought, You don't know anything at all. Stop thinking so much, and get to the goddamned phone!

She pushed away from the wall with the heel of her hand. It was crusty with dried blood. She flopped onto the ruined carpet, began to crawl like a snake.

Her heart beat fast, and the air seemed hot in her lungs. Every breath she took seemed like a burning spike in her insides. She used her elbows to drag herself along the carpet. The pain was terrible, but she gritted her teeth and edged forward. Until a lance of pain jerked her to a halt.

She lay on her side, panting. Colored lights sparked behind her eyes and, for a moment, she thought she had blacked out. Perhaps a breeze from the air conditioner revived her, or else she hadn't lost consciousness at all. In either case she knew she had to go on. But she couldn't. The pain was too great, and she could make no headway at all.

Then, as she rested her head on one outstretched arm, she glanced behind her, saw her feet, lying one atop the other as if dead, hooked at the ankle around the shaft of the brass standing lamp. She screamed then, out of rage and frustration, and because she had not known until she had looked.

For a moment, then, she lost her will. It was all too much for her, the pain and the shock and her blood. Wherever she looked she saw her blood, wherever she crawled it was through her blood.

Her heart was laboring so hard she was certain it was about to burst. A heart attack or a cerebral hemorrhage on top of all this—*boom!* she would be gone, just like that.

But I'm not gone, she told herself. I'm here! I'm alive!

And began again her arduous trek across the room. She reached back along her numb legs and, groaning, carefully lifted first one foot then the other from the base of the lamp. Then, twisting her torso, pressed her left elbow, then her right into the carpet, drawing her body along, tears of pain squeezing out from beneath her lids. Talking to herself, singing the lullabies she had heard as a child, trying to feel safe and warm, concentrating now on Seve, imagining him kissing her, imagining him asking her to marry him, walking down the aisle, saying their wedding vows, her belly being swollen with new life, her first glimpse of the baby, *their* baby, until her forehead hit the leg of the night table, and she reached up, pulling hard on the telephone cord.

Dialed 911, said, "Police Officer Diana Ming. I've been shot." Then she gave them the address of the hotel and Captain Kline's private number.

She must have passed out then, because the next thing she knew, she was on an EMS stretcher, and Joe Kline's concerned face was hovering over hers.

"Diana, can you hear me?"

She nodded, winced.

"Who did this to you? Did you see a face?"

There was a great deal of activity around her, just outside her field of vision. Then she became aware that she could not move her head.

"The doctors have immobilized you." Kline, seeing the expression on her white face, adding, "It's just a precaution."

"How bad?" Aware of Seve having said nearly the same thing, after he had been attacked on the roof in Chinatown.

"It's too soon to tell," Kline said. "Diana, do you know who did it?"

"Yes." Thinking, I must get to Seve.

"Who?"

"Captain, I need a phone." They had begun to move her.

"Later. You're going to the hospital."

Being rolled across the barren hotel room, she could only beseech him with her eyes. "It's a matter of life or death." She had to tell Seve what had happened, but most of all, she had to give him the name and address R&I had traced from the number she had gotten from Reed Parkes's mobile phone. Brad Wolff had died because of it, and so had Charlie Karnow and Randy Brooks. In the end she was the lucky one.

Joe Kline stared at her. She supposed he was wondering why she didn't tell him anything. Then he nodded. "I'll get the portable phone from my car. You can use it on the way in."

A voice from over her head, one of the EMS paramedics, said, "The doctor won't—"

"Fuck the doctor," Kline said. "You heard what she said. My people's needs come first."

Trangh found the Magician with the gun still in his mouth. He put aside what he had been carrying and, kneeling down, took it gently out of the Magician's mouth. Then he put his hand on either side of his neck. He located first the heart pulse in the carotid artery, and when he had calculated the beats per minute, he pressed the outside heel of his hand against the nerve meridian, getting a feel of that flow running from the heel to the tip of his middle finger.

The clock upon the mantel ticked off the minutes during which, crouched over the prostrate form, Trangh conjured the healing side of *pentjak-silat*.

All at once he tensed, feeling the beat pick up along the nerve meridian, and at that moment the Magician's eyes flew open. He grabbed Trangh by his shirtfront and stared at him so hard his head began to tremble. Then, as if some crisis had passed, he shivered.

"Just another fucking slant," he whispered, and let go of the material.

Trangh pushed pack on his heels, walked to the open suitcase, placed the long, chamois-wrapped package obliquely across the soft clothes.

The Magician rubbed the heels of his hands into his eye sockets as if awaking from a long slumber. "The sword is the key," he said. "It has always been everything. Milhaud was of use to us as long as he had two-thirds of the *Prey Dauw*. It took us all a long time to figure out that he had quite by accident come across two of the three pieces of the relic Mun had hidden in Angkor. Bandits, traders in stolen antiquities before they got into the drug trade, had dug them up. Not knowing what they were, they had them lying around. It was Milhaud's good fortune that he acquired them along with the pipeline he sold us.'' The Magician was sitting up, propped against a turned chair leg. He wiped the sweat off his face with his forearm. ''It is the real one this time.''

Trangh saw no point in answering. He knew that the sword meant nothing to him now. He knew that the gods of Angkor were stirring after centuries in limbo. He could feel the power beginning to shift in the world, had felt its first primordial glimmering at the precise moment he and Christopher Haye stood face-to-face in the stable in Tourrette. The knowledge shook him.

''Have you found a way to carry the sword through airport security?'' the Magician asked.

''It could not be simpler,'' Trangh said. ''I disassemble the blades. They are made of jade, so they will not register on the X-ray machines. Whatever metal there is is of no consequence.''

''What was that?'' The Magician had jerked erect.

Trangh turned to look at him.

The Magician, crouched and tense, said, ''Don't you hear it? Sounds like a voice crying.''

''I don't hear anything.''

''Yes. A young girl.''

''There is nothing.''

''Someone's in the house.''

Trangh said, ''Whoever is in the house is dead.''

The Magician's eyes swung around. ''You mean LoGrazie and the girl.'' He went across the room, into the hallway. ''I don't mean them, fool.'' He stared down at the body of Ma Varada. It was already beginning to stiffen. Her face was whiter than he had ever seen it. He squatted down and pulled her eyelids up. He stared hard into her fixed pupils.

''You're dead,'' he murmured. ''You're not crying.''

Abruptly, he became aware of Trangh standing over him and, as if embarrassed, he quickly stood up. ''I want to go through the house.''

''All dead,'' Trangh said, but in any event, followed him from one end of the house to the other. Except for the corpse of Mr. LoGrazie, there was no one else.

They ended up back in the sitting room, where the Magician's suitcase was almost full.

"You'll dispose of the bodies," the Magician said, "in the usual manner."

"If that is your wish," Trangh said, in such a tone that the Magician turned to look at him.

"What's with you?"

For a moment Trangh said nothing, then as if he himself were a god of Angkor stirring out of sleep, "Christopher Haye and Milhaud are together."

The Magician blinked. "Now that's interesting."

"Haye has hooked up with Seve Guarda."

"The Dancer." The Magician scowled. "You should have killed him in Doyers Street when you had the chance. You got me out of the building in time."

"If I had stayed any longer, I would be dead now."

"But so would Guarda," the Magician said. He closed the suitcase, zipped it up.

"I think we should go," Trangh said, "to where they are."

"They're together?"

"Christopher Haye and Milhaud are. Along with Milhaud's daughter."

That got the Magician's attention. "Time to destroy what's left of Milhaud's life, correct your lapses in judgment, and finish this whole business forever."

He smiled that cruel smile that was the sole holdover from when he had been Arnold Toth. "I will kill Soutane while her father watches. But—" He raised a forefinger. "I don't want him harmed, do you understand? I want him to understand, and to suffer, before I kill him."

Trangh looked at the man who had betrayed him, and felt neither anger nor hate. He felt, rather, a kind of satisfaction stealing over him. "I have suffered enough," he said, "to understand perfectly what you have in mind."

Outside, he got behind the wheel of the black BMW while the Magician came around, slipped into the passenger seat. He started up, and they backed down the narrow street.

Trangh concentrated on the road ahead of him. Lights spun off the polished hood and fenders of the BMW like daubs of paint thrown onto a blank canvas.

Which was, he thought with some surprise, what Paris seemed now to him to be. Each city he had been in had its own aura, a personification of man, god, or beast. Saigon had been a whore, Angkor a slumbering god, Pnompenh a demon's stronghold. New York was a machine, Nice a willing child, and Paris a willful grand dame, as perpetually young as it was perpetually wise.

Now Paris had become a blank slate, a *tabula rasa* upon which he was being given an opportunity to write his own beginning, middle, and end. To atone, as it were, for all the sins which he, as ultimately willful as this city once was, had committed.

The Seine was illumined by lighted barges, diamonds dancing on the crests of its tiny wavelets. As Trangh sped across the Pont d'Iéna and around the Eiffel Tower, he examined what was being offered to him. It was not freedom—not yet, anyway—but an opening of a path.

He was no longer aware of the being sitting beside him, no longer aware of the city, save as a vessel, a finite structure against which to pin his vision of the future.

As he increased his speed, he was suffused with ribbons of light, the linings of chrome and neon that had lain so long dormant beneath Paris's fashionable skirts. And this extraordinary light seemed to twist out of shape, to take on properties hitherto unknown in light, so that it coalesced into something resembling a trumpet call.

Glass was breaking, soundless and exhilarating, into one hundred million shards. The lights of night poured down like angels upon the jagged fragments until the reflections from the pain of their shattering illuminated the sky like the coming of a second sun.

Dimly, as he trod the accelerator to the floor, he heard a shouting, but it was as distant as if it were coming to him from another world. He ignored it. He was too old to take orders, too young to understand them.

He saw the night-black forest of the Luxembourg Gardens at the same moment he felt someone shaking him, shouting again in his ear. The muzzle of a gun was pressed to his right temple.

Then he jerked hard on the wheel and, tires screaming in protest, they were jumping the sidewalk, piercing the chain pedestrian guards, hurtling headlong toward the high black-and-gold iron fence close by the Medici Fountain, where the Greek Cyclops, Polyphemus, gazed hungrily down upon the mortality and grace of the human lovers, Acis and Galatea.

Immediately before impact, Trangh realized that, ever since he had first read *Crash*, this was how he had wanted to die. He had not merely *wished* it, but had actively desired it. All that had been missing was the reason for that death. No, not all, for above all, his death was impossible without faith. And, of course, all faith had been burned out of Trangh by the roiling napalm, devoured by the insatiable maw of war. Until, holding the whole *Prey Dauw* in his hands, he had unearthed the truth inside himself. How he had been manipulated by Virgil. Now, in destroying Virgil, he was satisfying both faith and reason.

Bright chrome, brittle glass, and fragile human flesh met with immense force the staunch iron fence which had, since the seventeenth century, guarded the environs adjacent to the palais Marie de Medici had built for her residence because she found the Louvre boring.

Trangh not only wanted to die, he was prepared for death. Far from being frightened of it, he was eager to ride *samsara*, the wheel of life, another notch, to discover what his next incarnation would be, and how he could use it to cleanse his essence of the accumulated filth of this one.

But it was not to be.

He awoke, bloody and bruised, to find himself staring at a constellation of winking lights and, embedded within it, a kernel of darkness relieved only by random splotches of deep red.

Then his head cleared completely and he realized that he was looking at the Magician, who had been thrown halfway through the BMW's windshield. Lying in the midst of a sea of shattered safety glass, the Magician dangled as if above a vast, unseen precipice.

The chrome rim had been ripped from its moorings by the impact and, like a greedy adder, had wrapped itself around the Magician's outflung left wrist. The slow drip of blood ticked off the minutes of shocked silence.

The Magician was dead, but he, Trangh, was not. Why?

Millions weep a fountain
Just in case of sunrise . . .

Staring at the body beside him, Trangh was struck by a thought so startling that it was as if he were bathed in white celestial light. He shivered, as understanding flooded over him.

He was never meant to die here, crashing into a black barrier, spangled with light. That was the Magician's fate, not his.

Trangh saw, in another moment of illumination, that he could not die yet. The process of his metamorphosis had just begun. It could not end until he again confronted Christopher Haye.

He unstrapped his seat belt and, leaning forward, ripped the Magician's jacket down the center seam. Beneath, he stripped the shirt off and used it to wipe himself. The stripes of cloth were almost sodden by the time he was through.

He searched around the seat and the foot-well for his *gunsen*, his iron war fan which he had taken because, remembering the loaded gun in the BMW's glove compartment that the Magician might make use of, he had thought it prudent to arm himself. But precious moments trying to find it were useless. Perhaps it had slipped out in the crash. He took one last hurried look around the mangled, bloody passenger compartment. Then he got out of the car and headed obliquely across the Place Edmond Rostand to the Boulevard Saint-Michel.

As he gained the sidewalk, he looked back. A lone car, passing along the street, had stopped. A driver got out and cautiously approached the wrecked BMW. He peered inside, and his head shot out as if stung by a swarm of bees. He looked around, and Trangh shrank back into the shadows of the buildings. Then, as other cars slowed, beginning to converge like carrion on the site, the driver ran to a phone box.

I burn.

Trangh moved hurriedly up the boulevard. The Magician had had the foresight to keep Milhaud under surveillance ever since Milhaud had proposed to double M. LoGrazie. Therefore, Trangh knew of both Morphée's existence and of Les Portes du Jade's location.

He turned, and saw its gates ahead. Everything was on fire now.

Someone was playing *"Desafinado,"* a Brazilian pop song from the sixties, when Seve arrived at Les Portes du Jade. It was strange, Seve could remember exactly where he had been and what he had been doing when he had first heard that song. Then, as now, João Gilberto had been singing it, her mellow contralto caressing the lyrics, making innocent love to the melody.

He had been in a sweaty, corrugated iron hooch with a Vietnamese girl named Sugar, who giggled every time he used her name. Afterward, when he had come home, and saw the otherwise screamingly funny Billy Wilder film *Some Like It Hot*, he thought of this Sugar every time Marilyn Monroe was on screen.

She was a thin, pathetic thing, who nevertheless danced the bossa nova with demonic skill. Where she learned it Seve had no idea.

He had asked her, and she had giggled. When they made love, which was often, she clung to him as if it meant something to her and, afterward, was reluctant for him to slither out of her.

Once, she told him that she was alive only when he was with her, and Seve somehow believed her.

He could have spent his free time with other, far more beautiful and fleshy women, but he always chose to be with Sugar. When he was with her, he often thought of his brother, Dominic. Already Dominic was reading the Bible when the others in the unit were drinking, whoring, and getting stoned. Dominic's moral rectitude in the face of Vietnam's malignant garden of earthly delights seemed to Seve noble. He admired his younger brother's strength and fortitude. He saw in Dominic a calm, a surety of purpose that was as reassuring as it was enviable.

The truth was that Seve was already feeling connected to that moral rectitude. The cop who later, stalking the dark underside of Manhattan, would hold the law before him like a lamp and a shield was born here in the filth and the insanity of a war that should never have been fought.

The truth was that Seve wanted more from Sugar than her body or even her company. He wanted without quite being aware of it to make of her something better. As Dominic wanted to save those who had been maimed by their time here, so did Seve want to save Sugar from the chaos into which her country had been plunged.

Of course, it was not possible.

As Dominic had said, God had turned his face away from this part of the world, and while He did, the devil ran rampant. Seve returned to Sugar's hooch one day, prepared to read to her from a tattered pocketbook of Chaucer he had extracted from the garbage in Ban Me Thuot. Many pages were torn or missing, but that did not faze him. Rather, he saw this as a challenge to create from his own mind the bridges that would successfully span the gaps in the great storyteller's work.

Sugar was sitting up on her poor straw mattress, but she did not answer his greeting, and she did not move as he came into the hooch.

He went to her, and saw that she was dead. There was no blood. She had not been killed or hurt in any way. There were no drugs evident, though he was fairly certain that she smoked marijuana and, when she could get it, smoked opium now and then.

She had simply died, as Americans pass away when the body

runs down at age seventy-nine or eighty-five. Sugar had been nineteen, the average age of the American soldier in Vietnam.

Seve had spent the night sitting by her side, reading Chaucer out loud, while softly in the background João Gilberto sang *"Desafinado"* from the tiny, tiny cassette player he had given her.

Now, as he entered the building on the Left Bank, it seemed to Seve as if so little time had passed since that moment. The strains of *"Desafinado"* drifting through the semidarkness echoed through the expansive courtyard. He saw, in front of him, the patinaed fountain, the dolphin and the mermaid locked in erotic embrace. The musical sound of the water mingled with Gilberto's voice.

No one had answered his knock. No one was in the courtyard now. He thought that it had been his good fortune that Soutane had been in his room when she had gotten the call from Chris. Of course, having been frantic about his whereabouts, she had instructed the hotel concierge to transfer any calls for her to Seve's room.

Ten minutes after she had left, and Seve feeling miserable, the phone had rung again. It was Diana. He had listened to her speak, part of him terrified for her, another part so proud of her. Still another absorbed each item of intelligence she was reporting.

When she had come to the name and address R&I had given her, the man Reed Parkes had been trying to phone when Diana had killed him, he said, "An unlisted car phone. So it's *the* Jason Craig. Someone not in the intelligence community at all."

"Yes and no." Her voice, so far away that he was straining to hear the inflection the mechanical means of transmission deadened. "Considering who he is. Chairman of ICC."

International Communications Conglomerate was the largest worldwide producer and operator of media networks, voice and data transmissions, commercial satellite relays. There wasn't a country in the world that did not in some fashion avail itself of ICC's technology. It was a true global organization. Jason Craig was not only the CEO of ICC, with seventy-five percent of the voting shares, he was the owner, answerable only nominally to a handpicked board of directors he controlled.

"Can one man actually be behind all this?" Seve knew what he was asking.

"You mean his own private intelligence-gathering army? His own worldwide drug network? Enough power to countermand the DEA, the CIA, *and* the president? I don't know." Abruptly, he could hear her exhaustion, even filtered through the transatlantic wire. "You tell me."

"Forget about it now," Seve said, trying at least for the moment to gain some distance, some kind of perspective on the mind-bending situation. "Just concentrate on getting well. Okay?"

"How can I forget it," Diana's voice said in his ear, "until I know you're safe?"

"I'll be fine."

"Will I see you soon?"

"Sure. Very soon," Seve had said. And then, "Diana? You did some helluva job."

"Thanks, boss." There was a pause. "I love you, Seve."

He swallowed. "I love you, too." And knew he wasn't just saying it. He had cradled the receiver, had looked at the address Soutane had written on the pad beside the telephone. Then he had hurriedly begun to dress.

Inside Les Portes du Jade, Seve looked around. Chris and Soutane. Where were they?

To his left the courtyard opened up into a lush garden filled with budding dew-covered spring flowers, azalea, jasmine, lilacs. To his right, a wide staircase. He went that way.

He was about to ascend when his eye fell on a doorway half hidden by the ornate bottom of the staircase. He went around and stood in front of it. The short hairs at the back of his neck stirred.

On the wooden door was painted in red a symbol he knew well: *phung hoang*, the Vietnamese phoenix. Trangh's talisman.

With a trembling hand Seve reached out. He brought his red-smeared fingertip to his nose, sniffed it. Blood. Dear God! Whose?

He pushed open the door, and entered the darkness beyond.

M. Vosges said, "She will never speak to me again."

Chris looked at him "It's certainly possible," he said. Then with an arched brow he uttered an ironic laugh. "Are you looking for sympathy?"

"No," M. Vosges said. "For forgiveness."

"Then I believe you've come to the wrong place."

"Have you no Christian charity?"

"Certainly," Chris said. "For those who deserve it."

"Who are you to make that determination," Milhaud said, "when judgment is the sole province of God?"

"Have you so suddenly gotten religion? How convenient."

"You would no doubt find it amusing if I told you that God led me to Indochina."

"You're quite right. I would."

"And yet that is precisely what I am telling you."

"Monsieur Vosges, you can tell me anything you want," Chris said, turning away to glance out the window. "It doesn't mean I have to listen."

"God will forgive you your inattention, but not your presumption to judge others."

He could just make out, down by the eastern gates of the Luxembourg Gardens, a cluster of cars. As he watched, blue flashing lights appeared. The police. No doubt an accident of some kind. He returned his attention to M. Vosges.

"Coming from you, a murderer and a drug runner, this self-righteousness is disgusting," Chris said.

"Really?" M. Vosges's head was trembling with emotion. "I was not aware that you and I were so well acquainted."

Chris watched the other for a moment. "I think I know all I need to about you."

"Ignorance," M. Vosges said, "is the cynosure of the fool." He stood in the center of the room. "The one thing you certainly are *not* is a fool." He crossed his arms over his chest. "Both Buddha and Vishnu were dying in Indochina by the time I arrived there. My countrymen had seen to that in their usual efficient manner. Then the communists set about vilifying God, and His son, Jesus Christ. The result was, of course, chaos.

"I wanted . . . I *needed* to do something about that."

"With that goal in mind," Chris said, "you should have been a Jesuit."

"Perhaps, in an earlier time, I would have been. But today—even two decades ago, this was true—the Jesuits have lost their power. And so has the Church as a whole. South America has become their battlefield, and both sides, it appears, are losing."

"South America is a long way from Indochina."

"Indeed it is." M. Vosges seemed calmer now, as if the simple act of being heard was for the moment at least Christian charity enough. "I fell upon the pipeline—the entrée to Admiral Jumbo—quite by accident. I had made a grave misjudgment in human nature and had run afoul of a gang of cutthroats and thieves. They made their living trafficking drugs—the amount when they told me was astonishing. And what were they doing with this money? Greedily scheming among themselves for a larger slice.

"I saw then a way both to escape them and to take with me the only thing of value they possessed. I connived with one clique against another, then secretly connived with still another against the first. I repeated this process over and over without being discovered. Avarice is a powerful fuel. They took very little time in devouring themselves, and when it was over, the victors were so weak that I had no difficulty in dispatching them into the same graves into which they had consigned their most recent adversaries.

"Do you know what I did with the profits of the pipeline?"

"You bought weaponry for Saloth Sar and the Khmer Rouge."

"Oh, eventually, yes, a percentage of the money went for revolutionary matériel. But before the Khmer Rouge there were teachers' salaries to pay, school buildings and supplies, Church property to purchase. And even after the Khmer Rouge came into being as a band of ragtag *maquis* hiding in the mountains, I did not stint on my education budget. It was far too important. Of course my teachers did not preach as the other French professors did that their country was the center of the world, and that the Vietnamese and the Khmer were eternally beholden to *pater noster*, France."

"What is it you want from me?" Chris asked. "I cannot absolve you of your sins. I am not a priest."

"Forgiveness from a man is all I ask," M. Vosges said.

Chris thought a long time before he said. "I'm sorry. I cannot give it."

M. Vosges looked for an instant quite stricken. He quickly recovered, even gave Chris a hint of a rueful smile. "It's all right."

Chris, looking out the window, saw a taxi pull up outside and a familiar figure get out.

"Jesus," he said, "Seve's here, after all."

"What? Seve Guarda, the American policeman?" M. Vosges walked to the window to look down, but Seve was already inside. He looked at Chris. "Are you sure? It's very dark."

"I'm sure."

M. Vosges's face was white. "He's discovered that I'm not dead, he knows who I am. He's come for me. I was always more afraid of Guarda than of your brother. Guarda's spirit was like iron, even back when he was working with the DEA in Burma."

"Do you really think that's why he's come when he said he wouldn't?"

"What other reason could there be?" M. Vosges said. He was clearly terrified.

"That," Chris told him, "is something I'm going to find out." He went out into the hallway, M. Vosges right behind him.

Seve went down a flight of steep stone stairs worn into concave shapes by time and use. For a moment he stood very still. His nostrils flared, and he almost coughed. And he was hurtling back twenty years. The air seemed laden with the same agglomeration of spices—lemon grass, chilies, fresh mint—and decomposition—blood, pus, fecal matter—that he associated with the war.

He went forward, bent in the crouch, half defensive, half aggressive, he had learned to employ in the steaming jungles, the soupy paddies.

"Dancer?"

Seve stopped.

"Is that you?"

Seve did not want to give his position away by speaking. War was in the air.

"Are you afraid," Trangh's voice whispered like the wind through the trees, "to reveal yourself? Are you afraid of me? Don't worry. I know where you are."

Seve began to sweat. A combination of the tension and the drugs the doctor had administered were working against him. His head throbbed, and an unpleasant lassitude gripped him. He felt his own adrenaline, pumped into his system by fear and excitement, trying to counteract it. There was a war going on inside him, too. He began to move, around pipes hissing with steam, conduits of wires like ganglia ripped open by trauma.

"Don't be afraid, Dancer." Trangh's voice wavered, a ghost in the darkness, reminding Seve of the seductive calls of the VC hidden in the jungle. "I know you seek the Magician. He's dead. I killed him in the most beautiful fashion, glass and light and sculptured metal pierced him in many ways. There was a great deal of blood."

Seve, moving still through the man-made jungle of the buildings bowels, considered whether Trangh was mad. Perhaps he had always been mad.

"It was you," he said at length, "who was working for the North."

"I was in harness," Trangh said, "to the South, and to the North. In my time I answered to both, and to none. Because, in the end, they are the same. There is no difference when avarice and fear pollute political ideals. Everything turns to poison, and no one is strong enough to stand against that hideous tide."

What he said, of course, made sense. But Seve realized that he did not care. He didn't give a shit what Trangh had done during the war, or for what reasons. He only knew that Trangh had murdered Dom, had taken his disgusting war fan and had sliced the crenellated blade through Dom's neck, severing flesh, muscle, arteries, and spinal column. Trangh had to be punished for that.

"You killed my brother." Scuttling forward, bent between steaming pipes, moving silently over stanchions, around plastic-wrapped cables. "I'm coming for you."

"I have already sinned too greatly; I do not wish to kill you," Trangh said from out of the darkness. "But I cannot die. Not yet." He wanted to say so much more, to tell the Dancer of his epiphany while holding the Forest of Swords, his revelation of white light inside the wrecked BMW, but he seemed inarticulate, as if his memory not of English words but of English concepts had deserted him. So he began to speak in Vietnamese. But his native tongue, so little used or heard by him, caused him to weep, to see sheets of oily flame, the conflagration that had been his ultimate undoing. With an audible snap he shut his mouth.

When Chris and M. Vosges reached the entryway, it was deserted.

"Perhaps he is in the garden," M. Vosges said.

But by that time Chris had seen the bloody sign on the wooden door.

"What is this?"

M. Vosges, coming up beside him, said, "It is a *phung hoang*, a Vietnamese phoenix. A sacred mythical creature said to be immortal."

"Trangh," Chris said, and opened the door.

They, too, descended into the darkness.

The smell of grease and rust stained the air. It was as close and fetid down there as a crypt. They reached the bottom of the stairs, and Chris, almost decapitating himself on a sharp metal outcropping that intruded into the space at head height, ducked and signaled M. Vosges to do the same.

"I know Trangh," M. Vosges said at the foot of the stone stairway. "Let me handle him."

"We know he no longer works for you," Chris said. "Perhaps he never did. He's already betrayed you once."

''Nevertheless,'' M. Vosges said, ''he is Vietnamese. I know what is in his mind, what is important to him.''

''Stay back.''

Chris recognized Seve's voice.

''What are you doing here?'' Chris asked. ''Soutane said—''

''You shouldn't have to ask,'' Seve said. ''You know why I'm here.''

''It looks as if Guarda has already found Trangh,'' M. Vosges said under his breath.

''Seve, we must take Trangh alive,'' Chris said. ''He's our only lead to the Magician.''

''I'm surprised to hear you talking like that,'' Seve said. ''Trangh killed your brother. He almost killed Alix.'' Chris heard something odd in Seve's voice, a guttural slur that made him sound almost feral.

''He'll pay for that, Seve,'' Chris said. He was sweating profusely. He was getting an inkling of Seve's thought processes. ''Come on.''

''I'm warning you,'' Seve said. ''Stay back. Trangh's mine. He killed Dom. Now he's gonna have to pay.''

Tried one last time. ''For Christ's sake, Seve, you're a cop. You can't—''

''Stay out of this, dammit! You haven't the stomach for it.''

''Come on!'' Chris whispered urgently to M. Vosges. ''We've got to move quickly now.''

''Nothing can be done quickly down here,'' M. Vosges pointed out. ''It's a maze of pipes and wire clusters. Even with the lights on, we'd have difficulty seeing where they are. We'd need a twelve-foot ladder to get above the networks for that.''

They used their ears, instead, letting the sounds guide them, their hands flat out in front of them to warn them of the low-hanging tangle of pipes and wire bundles.

''Hurry!'' Chris said. ''He'll kill Trangh if he can.''

''Or Trangh will kill him.''

''It does not matter that you no longer love him,'' Morphée said. ''I will love him enough for the two of us.''

Soutane, standing near the door of a suite down the hall from where they had been, said, ''I don't think I ever really learned to love him.'' In rich pools of light cast by lamps scattered about the room, she was studying Morphée as if the other woman was some kind of creature thought to be long extinct. "What I can't understand is, knowing what you do about him, how you can care for him at all?"

Morphée smiled in that way which people who did not know her took to be subservient. On the contrary, it was fecund with the inner peace she maintained. "Unlike you," she said, "I understand that human nature is both flawed and frail. If life has taught me one thing, it is that our struggle is not in seeking perfection, but in correcting our mistakes."

Without quite being aware of it, Soutane had moved as far away from Morphée as she could. In this far dark corner of the room she could see past the open door to the hallway, but she felt only marginally safer. She had an urge to take a drink, but there was no liquor in evidence, and she did not want to show that kind of weakness by asking Morphée to get her one.

"This is a whorehouse," Soutane said. "What does that make you?"

"I know what I am," Morphée said, moving through the lamplight like a wraith in a moonlit forest glade. "But it is important how you see me." Her voice was soft with no trace of anger or recrimination.

"Why?" On the other hand, Soutane's parts in this exchange were fairly barked out.

"I would have thought that obvious," Morphée said. "You are his daughter."

"Funny, I don't feel like his daughter."

"Ah, well, that is of course the tragedy of all this."

"Is that why you brought me in here? Did you think that you could change my mind?"

"I took you away from where you did not want to be," Morphée said, moving from darkness to light. "That is all."

"I don't believe you." Feeling cornered now, as Morphée came closer. "You think that you can somehow make me love my father."

That smile again. "Soutane, why can you not see what is so evident? You cannot learn something that is instinctual. It seems to me that though you say that you never loved your father, quite the opposite is true. I think you have always loved him. Over the years you merely learned to hate him."

"No, I—"

When Soutane saw Chris and her father hurrying past in the

hallway outside, she was already moving. She had by that time taken flight.

"I see him!"

Chris turned his head. "Which one? Seve?"

But M. Vosges was already moving. I can make it happen, he thought. I can put an end to this madness. I can perhaps atone for what I've done.

"Monsieur Mabuse," he whispered as he moved among the pipes and rods in the semidarkness. "Listen closely to me. I have come to save you. Believe me when I tell you that I forgive you for everyth—"

M. Vosges jerked up off the floor, tried to scream, but there was a hand clamping his throat. He could not speak; neither could he breathe. He stared into M. Mabuse's face. It was strained and pinched; a tiny blue vein bisecting his forehead pulsed as if with a malignant life of its own.

"Tu . . . me . . . pardonnes?" You forgive me? It was squeezed out with the highly aspirated syllables that came from incredulity. Trangh slammed M. Vosges so hard against a cluster of rusted pipes that his entire body danced like a marionette.

"Mon Dieu," M. Vosges managed to gasp before Trangh dropped him in a heap upon the oil- and grease-smeared concrete floor.

Trangh crouched over him, panting like an animal at bay. His eyes were wide and staring, and through his mind like a bright river of molten metal ran the words, *Sometimes I feel like a motherless child . . . a long, long way from my home. . . .*

"It is not for you to *forgive* me." As before, each word was squeezed out of his constricted larynx like poisoned bullets. "It is, rather, for me to forgive you. But forgiveness presupposes mercy." He reached out. "And I have none left inside me." Until his fingertips touched M. Vosges's chest just above his heart. "Your people burned all mercy out of my heart."

The fingers stiffened as M. Vosges watched with a kind of morbid fascination the formation of his own death. "You erased the memory of what mercy means from my soul." The nails, sharp as daggers, ripped M. Vosges's sweat-soaked shirt, pierced his skin.

"Now, after all you and your kind have done to us, in your supreme arrogance you expect me to be grateful for your forgiveness." Red rivulets running hot and sticky down his bony chest, dripped from the round bowl of his belly. "It is worthless." M.

Vosges, paralyzed by something more than fear, no doubt the last vestiges of *kebatinan* that was all that was left Trangh. He felt the pain as one hears the whistle of a train, still far-off but approaching with such speed that one cannot comprehend its method of motion.

"Worse, it is part of the cancer that has eaten us alive ever since you French set foot in my country." Trangh's stiffened fingers, all the weapon he required, plunged in a *juru* inward with a ferocity that matched the set of his face, his lips pulled back, baring his yellow teeth. "The only way to get rid of a cancer is to expunge it forever." Snapped by the force of the blow, M. Vosges's ribs broke, their ragged ends rending him like arrows shot from a bow. He arched up as blood fountained, running up Trangh's ridged wrist in a violent expiration of life.

Feeling neither satisfaction nor remorse, Trangh rose, felt simultaneously the Dancer's swift approach hard upon him, and instantly regretted his single-minded act of hollow vengeance because in those precious moments when he was concentrating on M. Vosges's demise he had lost track of the Dancer, and now he knew that there was no way to avoid their terminal confrontation.

His sadness lasted long after the bulk of the Dancer crashed into him, sending them both hurtling along the wall, past groups of steaming iron pipes and massive elbowed stanchions. Soon it was joined by his closest companion, despair. And it was the despair alone which allowed him to break away and stumble headlong into the looming darkness.

"Oh, Jesus," Chris breathed. Blood covered him as he knelt over M. Vosges. Not knowing where Trangh was or whether he would like a demon unexpectedly return, he pulled on M. Vosges, hooking his hands beneath the Frenchman's armpits, dragging him behind a cluster of scabrous metal switch boxes. It seemed to take a very long time. He could hear the thick raling of M. Vosges's breathing. Then he heard another noise, and tensed. Trangh!

"Chris?"

He caught a glimpse of Soutane poking her head this way and that, trying to find a way to get to him.

"Stay where you are," he called softly. "Trangh is near."

"Is my father with you?"

He looked down at M. Vosges. There was so much blood it was difficult to believe that he was still alive. But his eyes were open, looking up into Chris's face.

"Forgive me, Christopher, for I have sinned," he sighed.

Chris lifted his head off the floor.

"For nineteen years I have not had Confession. For nineteen years I have turned my eyes away from the sight of God. I would not have been able to bear his gaze because of what I did, out of passion, out of jealousy and rage. I murdered my wife, Celeste."

His sigh turned into a racking cough. "There. Now I have said it. Am I absolved, Christopher?"

"I—"

"Chris?" Soutane called. "Are you all right?"

"Yes."

"And my father?"

"He's with me."

He heard her coming, opened his mouth to tell her again to stay where she was, but knew it was useless. In a moment she was through the latticelike wall of the boxes and beside him. Her fearful eyes went from him to her father's prostrate form.

"Dear God! What happened?"

"Your father thought he could still control Trangh. He was wrong." He could feel her warmth; he longed to take her in his arms and hold her.

She looked down upon M. Vosges's face. "Can you be a stranger," she said, "and still be my father?" Of whom was she asking the question? Chris wondered.

He saw M. Vosges smile. "Father," he said distantly. "That's all I wanted."

It was a lie, of course, Chris thought. His whole life gave evidence of that. Or perhaps at the end it was not a lie at all. Perhaps he had undergone a conversion, not of faith but of substance. All his life M. Vosges had trusted in God to show him the way. In so doing, he had trusted in human beings, and had been betrayed by their baser nature. It had made him disillusioned with people, so that he had come solely to use them, even his wife and his daughter. If he had seen that at the end, surely that was a kind of redemption.

"He's gone, Soutane," he said, closing M. Vosges's eyes.

"And Trangh?"

"Somewhere in this maze. God alone knows where."

"That's right," Seve said, "keep quiet now. Quiet as a fucking mouse." He saw an image of Sugar, her thin body frozen on the filthy mattress, her insides withered from the ravages of the war.

"But your stillness won't save you, and neither will your words. If you feel remorse for what you've done, or if you don't, it's all the same to me." Creeping along amid a slush of oil and water and sweat. "You can't escape except by going through me, Trangh." Rats, squealing, fleeing from his progress. "Bastard. Fucking sonuvabitch. You killed Dom. A priest. A man of God, who never wished ill of anyone. You could pray for forgiveness from now till doomsday and it wouldn't mean jackshit. Do you understand me?"

"I think I do. Yes. I have seen you in the jungle. You are relentless. The Magician feared you almost as much as he feared Terry Haye."

"It just proves," Seve said, making his way around a massive crusted metal elbow joint, "how wrong you can be. Terry's dead, and I'm still here."

"I beg you to reconsider," Trangh said.

From the resonance of his voice Seve calculated how close they were: not more than two arm's lengths. Seve moving ever toward the source of the voice, thought of a phrase from 'Nam, "unknown and hostile," which described the VC night raids into American territory that his SLAM unit had been formed to exterminate. He could see how the term more or less applied to himself now.

Seve's mind had ceased to recall Dominic in any fashion other than as a disembodied head lying in a bower in New Canaan. The first moment of recognition when, being led outside the Holy Trinity Church, past the dense privet, already smelling strongly of growth and renewal, he had come upon the head of his brother, was akin to seeing the sun at midnight. His skin had crawled, and he had begun to hyperventilate. And then he had stifled an almost overwhelming urge to weep uncontrollably.

Dominic, the sickly child at birth, living for the first six weeks of life on the brink of death, taught boxing by their father as a form of physical therapy. And Seve given the unspoken trust of keeping Dom safe from harm. Seve, in New Canaan, staring down at his brother, knowing that he had failed.

He sniffed at the darkness and, like a hound on point, found his quarry. He slipped silently beneath a dripping pipe, rushed at Trangh in a burst of raw, unstoppable energy.

His callused hands, his corded forearms striking Dominic's murderer, acted like a powerful drug. The more he struck, the stronger Seve became. It was as if he had been transformed into an avenging angel. More, he felt the avenging might of the arcane God of

Abraham and Isaac flowing in his veins, the righteous anger that was in its way a self-fulfilling prophecy.

His body fairly sang with the exhilaration of its newfound freedom as it went about its revenging work, until there was nothing left inside Seve but his desire for retribution. Gone was the balance that had been the core of his decision making. Gone was his sense of justice, his need to be guided by the strict tenets of the law.

What, then, was left but the animal's blood lust that went beyond the imperatives of protection of self and of territory. When the written codes of God and man are abandoned, what remains but the footprint of the demon?

I beg you to reconsider.

Trangh wanted to say more. He wanted to tell the Dancer that he was both more and less than he had been when, on the rooftop on Doyers Street, they had last encountered one another. But he still, perhaps, lacked the understanding of what was taking place inside him to articulate it.

Instead, he said in an attempt to mollify Seve, "I have no quarrel with you."

His words had the opposite effect. Enraged, Seve leaped upon him, and they both went down.

Ever since he had told Seve, *Don't worry. I know where you are,* Trangh had been trying to summon *kebatinan*, that mystic state of *pentjak-silat*, where the world was revealed to him in its primitive state. In this he had been unsuccessful—it was as if M. Vosges had sucked the last of it out of him—and he had begun to feel the first touch of fear.

Instead of the rustling silence of the open field typical of *kebatinan*, he heard only the rising babble of the voices of the dead. The cataclysm that had roasted their bodies had not stilled their essences. They knew who Trangh was and what he had done as clearly as had Luong, who had destroyed herself instead of him so that he should never forget the memory of his sin.

Now, borne down by the weight of the other man, Trangh struggled to understand what was happening. He had had no intention of allowing the Dancer near him, had in fact been relying on *kebatinan* to protect him. He had not wanted to engage the Dancer. On the contrary, he had been desperately seeking a way to defuse the situation.

He had not wanted this. He had been waiting. For what?

He had written in his own leaking blood his sign upon the door to the basement for a reason. What had it been?

He had forgotten or he had never known. In which case he was lost and, surely, he might just as well have died along with the Magician in the crash.

Had that even happened? Of course it had! Trangh, struggling with the Dancer, was overcome by the memory of the crash: inside the BMW, swerving around the Place Edmond Rostand, the high iron fence rushing at him through the windshield. But he could not recall the instant of impact. He could see the Magician's body flung through the shattered glass, the metal strip rising, grasping his wrist in a perverse lover's embrace. But even this vivid memory failed to calm him. The truth was, Trangh was no longer certain of anything.

He used *jurus*, the percussive blows of his discipline. But either he had lost some strength in the crash or he had forgotten to which parts of the body they needed to be applied.

He was being inundated by heavy, two-handed blows about the head and chest. He felt pain, concentrated to cut it off, only to feel it renewed in another part of his body. He tasted blood in his mouth, and he thought that he had lost the vision in one eye.

He fought back as best he could, with his stiffened four fingers against the Dancer's solar plexus, the outer edges of his hands against the ribs, his curled knuckles against the forehead and ears. Nothing seemed to work. The pain was incessant, spreading.

And then, as if growing out of the luxuriant mass of Trangh's newfound despair, came the words of his *pentjak-silat* instructor: *When you have reached the end, you must return to where you began. Intense training by its very nature negates instinct. So many principles to hold in one's head! In the end you must let principles dissolve in the elemental river of your instincts.*

And this was how Trangh found the way to preserve his life: by turning around and employing the first *juru* he had been taught: the phoenix in the stone.

His torso reared up and, like a cobra spitting, the granite-hardened heel of his right hand struck Seve over his kidneys with such blinding speed Seve did not even have a chance to cry out.

Seve was only dimly aware that something was wrong when, abruptly stripped of strength, he slumped over, and a grayness like a mist at dawn filled his consciousness.

His enfeebled fingers continued to scrabble at the claw holds they had maintained on Trangh's flesh. He would not give up his obsession even as he was engulfed by a pain more terrible than he had ever known before. His spirit drew closer to Dominic's smiling face. A hand—that of Dominic's or of God's—beckoned to him, palm open, fingers slightly curled. He reached out, and was plunged into darkness.

"There," Chris said, pointing through the maze of pipes. "I see him."

"Seve!"

Soutane was right. Chris could see the two of them, Trangh and Seve, entwined. Then Trangh's torso twisted, and his head came up, questing. He saw Chris, and their eyes locked.

"He's badly hurt," Trangh said. He was addressing Chris alone. "He may be dead."

Chris had to pull Soutane back from running toward them. He had seen something in Trangh's eyes, something terrifying that made him wary.

"Stay back!"

Soutane stared at him. "But Seve! He could be—!"

"Do as I say!" Chris shouted. "I want you to get out of here."

"But—"

"Now!"

"Chris, I can't leave you—the both of you."

"Listen," he said, grabbing her. "If you come near Trangh now, he'll kill you."

"But you—"

"He won't kill me." Chris didn't know anything of the sort. He suspected something—but what? That Trangh would not want to break the connection between them? But what if it was only he, Chris, who felt the connection?

Soutane was very frightened. "What do you mean? How do you know?"

"Just trust me, Soutane, and we'll get out of this. Otherwise . . ."

She nodded. "All right. But I won't leave. I'm staying right here." She looked down at her father, then, leaning across his still chest, kissed Chris hard on the lips. "I'll be waiting for you."

"Whatever you do," he cautioned, "don't follow me."

He got slowly off his knees. His legs ached from the position he had been in. He stared at Trangh. ''I'm coming,'' he said. ''I want to take a look at Seve.''

''You don't want me. You want the Magician,'' Trangh said. ''He was killed in the crash.''

''What crash?''

''I crashed the BMW into the gate of Les Jardins de Luxembourg.'' Trangh looked quite dazed. ''He went through the windscreen.''

Chris felt an enormous sense of relief: Gable was dead. But at the same time he was acutely aware that Trangh could with one swipe of his hand snuff out his life. He was so frightened his heart seemed to be beating in his throat. He fought down a desire to gag and summoned up all his courage.

''I just want to see how Seve is,'' Chris said.

Trangh knew this for the lie it was, and he wondered briefly what he was going to do about it. Christopher was now able to reach Seve's waist. That meant he was within striking distance. Trangh knew that he should stop him now but, as Christopher resumed his approach, he did nothing but watch him. He could not tear his gaze from the other man's eyes. Not even when he reached out to put his hands on the Dancer's body and encountered Trangh's leg.

Trangh could see the pallor on the Dancer's face, but it was impossible for him to tell whether or not he was still breathing. Watching the play of emotions across Christopher's face, he said, ''Was he a friend of yours, the Dancer?''

''Dancer?''

''That is what the Magician named him when he recruited him for the unit in Vietnam. Because of how he liked to dance with the girls. It gave him a great deal of pleasure to move his body to the music, the Rolling Stones or even something old, with a bit of history to it, so he said. I've never understood. There is no such Vietnamese music. I hear Vietnamese music and I think of the war. I don't imagine that is what he meant, though, otherwise why would he have been dancing to it?''

Trangh, who hardly ever talked to a Westerner more than a sentence or two at a time, could not stop himself from talking now. Why?

''I remember wanting to understand what it was about the music that made him want to dance.''

''It was the beat.''

''What?''

Chris was looking at him as his hands, red with the Dancer's blood, felt for a pulse. "The rhythm. You know, one, two, *three*, one, two, *three*."

"I see girls perform," Trangh said. "Dance and perform like the ancient *aspara*, the celestial dancers of Angkor. But I don't understand it. Are they trying like the *apsara* to tell a story with their dancing?"

"He's breathing," Chris said, "but he's unconscious." He looked up into Trangh's face. "I'm going to roll him off you."

"No!"

Trangh could see Christopher squatting very still so close at hand. He seemed, like the Dancer, scarcely to breathe.

"I just," Chris said, "want to get him out of here. If he doesn't get to a hospital very soon he will surely die."

"I cannot permit that," Trangh said. "If you move him, I will kill you."

"You don't want to do that, Trangh," Chris said, getting his hands beneath Seve's body. He began to roll him off the Vietnamese.

Trangh's torso sprang forward, and with his iron fists, he jerked Chris toward him so close their noses were almost touching, so close Chris had to look from one eye to the other in order to see Trangh.

Trangh said, "I mean it," melting one fist into a flat wedge, sliding up against Chris's throat. "If I do this any harder, you will be unconscious in fifteen seconds, dead in twice that time. I hope to God you believe me."

Chris did, but he rolled Seve away. The pressure against his throat increased until he could no longer suck in air. The oxygen inside him was rapidly being used up. He began to asphyxiate. Still, he tried to drag Seve toward the staircase.

"Why are you doing this?" Trangh asked.

"I have put," Chris rasped in what thin voice was left him, "my trust in you."

"But *why*?" Trangh had begun to tremble.

"Because—" He had to stop. The effort just to make himself understood was immense. "Because you did not kill me when you could have. You gave me your word, and you honored it." He was getting dizzy. With the loss of oxygen sounds were echoing. "There is no one else I can put my trust in."

"Stop this!" Trangh cried, but he pulled his hand away from Chris's throat.

Chris almost collapsed. His head, bowed over Seve's body, quivered while his chest heaved in great gasps of air.

"I could still kill you."

"I know," Chris whispered hoarsely. "There was never any doubt." But when he had regained enough strength to lift his head up, he saw tears rolling down Trangh's cheeks.

"Let me take Seve to the other side of the stanchion so the people there can get him to a hospital."

Trangh reached out, grabbed Chris by the hand. Chris waited, unmoving. He knew instinctively that if he even tensed his wrist, Trangh would snap it like a dry twig.

"Listen to me. Listen to what I have to say, to why I am here. In the days of the war, when I knew your brother and the Dancer, I was indentured to the regimes of the North and the South. I spied, and spied upon the spies until I no longer knew who my true masters were. During that time I reported everything, and shut my mind to the consequences for either North or South. I was spent like an arrow asked by its archer to travel too great a distance, which therefore finds no target but the earth.

"I found the earth, but even it would not have me. I wanted to die, but I lived. While others far more deserving of life died at my feet by my hand.

"Our SLAM unit, the one commanded by the Magician, made annihilation runs into enemy territory. Often we went on foot. But just as often we were carried by helicopter. These were for the larger targets—whole villages where the North Vietnamese were dug in and, supposedly, secure. That was our job, you see, not only to kill but to destroy their sense of security.

"On those airborne forays it was my job to guide the pilots who did not know until we arrived at the target site where we were headed. I found the villages, and the 'copters would make their run, coming in low, firing, destroying.

"This one mission, we did the same. Everything was the same. We headed north, flying over the border, until we crested a rise and, beyond the line of trees, I saw my own village. I had been so caught up in the war that I had not realized . . . I did not know until it was too late. I had already given the pilot all he needed to know.

"We came in low, as always and, as always, we hung out the open sides of the 'copter firing our Soviet-made AK-47's, bazookas, whatever we had.

"I saw faces I knew, had grown up with, scattering in fear, being mowed mercilessly down, being blown apart or covered, screaming, with liquid fire.

"The screaming. I have never stopped hearing the screaming."

There was over them now that peculiar silence that comes in the aftermath of a firefight or a bombing run. Chris felt a residue of mutated energy, turning the stillness too bright and brittle, so that when it was broken the resulting sound hurt his ears.

"Trangh," he said, "there is a way out, a way to salvation for you."

"You're like all the rest!" Trangh cried. He jerked his hand away as if he had been holding flame, not flesh. "Like Monsieur Vosges and, in his own way, the Magician. Trying to bring me the redemption of a God I care nothing about. I don't want to be saved. I want to be free!"

And he was up, retreating into the shadows of the basement. Chris began to follow, calling out to Soutane to get Seve. He moved off, reaching the rear of the basement without seeing any sign of Trangh. For a moment he panicked, thinking that Trangh had somehow doubled back and was now on his way to where Soutane was.

Then he saw the darker splotch in the midst of the shadows and, reaching it, saw that it was an old, long-abandoned service opening in the floor. Beside it was a heavy round metal cover. He peered at it, reading what was printed on it with some difficulty. Then he pulled his head away, looked down into the hole. Below were the sewers of Paris.

He was about to descend when Soutane's voice stopped him.

"Chris! Are you crazy? Leave him down there. He'll drown or asphyxiate, who even cares? As long as you don't go down there. Hasn't enough harm been done already?"

"You don't understand, Soutane," Chris said softly. "Perhaps neither do I yet. But there is a connection between Trangh and me." He put one foot on the first rung of the vertical iron ladder, access to the first level of the sewers. "I felt it the moment we confronted each other in the stable in Tourrette. That mysterious connection is why he let you go, why he honored the bargain I made with him—your life for the Doorway to Night."

"Oh, Chris, how can you trust in something you don't understand?"

"Isn't that what always makes us afraid in life?" He looked at her. "I have to go."

"Why? For God's sake, Chris, come back." She was pleading

with him, rigid with fear for him. "There can only be destruction down there."

"You're wrong, Soutane," he said, stepping down one rung. "But if it makes you feel any better, pray for me."

"Don't you understand," she said bitterly, "that it's too late for prayer."

Chris climbed down. The rungs of the iron ladder were treacherous with condensation and slime. Once, his shoe slipped and he hung by his arms, his other leg bent painfully, until he could find purchase.

Halfway down, Trangh's voice rose to him. "Christopher, go back. If you come down here, you will die."

It's too late for prayer. Chris continued the descent.

All manner of smells assaulted him, salty, acrid, a viscous and suffocating miasma. When he reached the bottom, he could see, here and there, light burning, bare bulbs hung from flex strung along the glistening stone ceiling. From somewhere close at hand, a heavy dripping made its doleful presence felt. Farther off, quasi-musical sounds as of a rill or race.

Chris, peering this way and that, turned full around. Trangh hit him on the jaw, and he went down on his side.

"I warned you not to come down here," Trangh said, standing over him.

Chris looked up at him. He did not get up or even rub his jaw. He wanted to make no overt move. "You are not responsible for me, Trangh." With part of his mouth numb, his voice sounded odd. "On the contrary, I am responsible for you."

Trangh squatted beside him. His eyes seemed to burn from within his skull. "Why do you say that? Tell me?"

"When you killed Terry," Chris said, understanding it himself for the first time, "you killed a part of me."

Trangh had been feeling the stir of the ancient gods of Angkor. It was they, he was certain, who had provided him with his moments of revelation with the *Prey Dauw* and just before the crash. Now they gifted him with the knowledge for which he had been searching ever since Luong had cursed him by taking her own life.

He saw in a flash the path to his atonement and his freedom. "It is true what you say." He nodded his head. "But just as true is the fact that Terry lives on in you."

"You're wrong," Chris said. "I am not my brother. I never was."

"I knew Terry better than anyone, save perhaps Mun. What I

see in your eyes is what I saw in his. It is different, but the same. Different because in Terry I never understood what it was. I doubt very much whether Terry himself was aware of it."

"I don't know what you mean."

"But I think you do." Trangh shifted and, in so doing, saw the glint of something lying between them. He reached close to Chris, picked it up.

"Can it be? Is this Terry's knife?" There was a hint of wonder in his voice and, with this last revelation blinding him, a cessation of the screams of horror and agony that had been his incessant tormentors for more than two decades.

Chris took the stag folder from him, opened the blade. "It's my knife," he said. "Terry gave it to me as a Christmas gift one year. I threw it back in his face. We were no more than kids then, and I didn't understand. Because of him, I shot a stag in the forest. Terry wanted so much to be the hunter, to come home with a trophy. I have never forgotten that wanton death." He touched the scale with a fingertip. "This is made from that stag's antlers. It was Terry's way of trying to apologize, to atone, I suppose, for what he had made me do."

And Trangh, certain now that the ancient gods of Angkor were both awake and regaining all their awesome power, grasped both his freedom and Chris's hand at the same time.

With his strong fingers, his will guiding Chris, he pulled hard, straight toward himself, so that the six-inch blade buried itself to the hilt in his chest.

"No!"

Chris's cry echoed on and on down the endless subterranean corridors. He pulled the knife out as soon as Trangh let go.

Trangh smiled into the look of stricken horror on Chris's face. "Do not despair," he said. "Rejoice, instead. With help, you have killed twice. Both were innocent acts, and are therefore holy. You gave your brother what he wanted most on that Christmas afternoon, a gift only you could give. Your brother was like me: primitive. He lived his life according to a strict inner code of honor, one that he upheld all his life. In this gift to you he was in his way trying to tell you that. He gave you the knife not in atonement, but in friendship.

"Now you have given me my freedom, and it is all that I could ask for."

There was a great deal of blood, but Trangh still possessed enough strength to brush aside Chris's attempts to stem the flow. "I am at last free from desire. That is the answer we seek in life, all we can expect from it. To free us from desire."

He slipped a little in the slime, his strength failing him. Chris held him in his arms. His mind was still stunned at what had happened.

"If you understand this," Trangh said, "you possess everything of value."

His head lay on Chris's shoulder, and he felt very close to a peace he had thought beyond him. His faith had not been misplaced, and he thanked Buddha for this solitary blessing. He sighed, knew that his task was not yet completed. "Listen, Christopher." His voice was as ephemeral as moonlight. "Listen to me. I have much to tell you, and there is so little time."

When, at last, Trangh's eyes closed, Chris got up and, bent over, slung the body over his shoulder. He had no intention of letting Trangh rot here in the sewers.

With great difficulty he began to climb up the slimy ladder. It was not the weight but the awkwardness that made his progress slow. He was somehow glad of the burden he carried, as if every step he took with it brought him closer to Terry.

As he ascended, he wept. But it was not until much later that he understood why.

Soutane's face was the first he saw when he emerged from the sewer. The look of relief that flooded her as he appeared was all-consuming.

"Thank God!" She hugged him to her. "What happened down there?"

Chris felt someone shaking with profound emotion, and did not know whether it was himself or Soutane. The cops were not far behind, having answered Soutane's call. They swarmed over the basement like flies. Flashbulbs popped around the spreadeagled corpse of M. Vosges. Paramedics were busy loading Seve carefully onto a stretcher for the difficult trip up the stairs.

Chris stared hard into Seve's closed, bloody face, trying vainly to discern the ephemeral flutter of life beneath the pallid skin. As Seve was hoisted up the stairs, a pair of cactus-faced Parisian detectives began asking them questions. They did their best to answer, which was not at all easy. Who could believe their story?

The interrogation plodded on interminably. The detectives showed no willingness to let them go, until a young man in a navy-pinstripe suit arrived and, flashing credentials Chris couldn't see, went into a huddle with them. A moment later Chris and Soutane were informed that they were free to go.

"Qui êtes-vous?" Chris asked the man in the pinstripe suit. Who are you?

"Get out of my face, asshole," the man said in English. "Speak only when you're spoken to. What is your involvement with Marcus Gable?" His all-encompassing gaze made it clear that he was speaking to both Chris and Soutane.

Chris told him everything he knew, save what Trangh had revealed to him. The man in the pinstripe suit took Chris's statement with a micro-recorder. He said nothing other than to ask his terse, pointed questions in a noncommittal tone of voice that gave no clue as to his point of view. When they were done, he told them that they were free to go.

Outside, dawn was spreading across the rooftops of Paris, sunlight slowly finding its way down the wide avenues and boulevards. Down the narrow sidestreets the remnants of night still huddled in mean and grimy corners.

Chris pulled Soutane down the block. When they were out of sight of the building, he hailed a cab. Trangh had told Chris where he had put the Forest of Swords. He had also told him what he knew of the Magician's secrets, which was considerable, more than Gable had been aware. But not, unfortunately, for whom the Magician worked. Trangh had told Chris, however, that the man, whoever he was, was immensely powerful, that he controlled an independent, clandestine intelligence network. Having once broken free of him, the Magician had vowed never to return. But the man had become aware of the circumstances surrounding Linda Gable's death and, using that, had tried to coerce the Magician back into the fold. When the Magician refused, the man had made good his threat, manipulating the police to get Gable arrested, cutting though the judicial red tape to ensure a speedy trial. Which was when Marcus Gable had come to Chris. In the middle of the trial, with more damning evidence about to be delivered by agents of the man to the district attorney's office, Gable had capitulated, returning to the fold.

Chris told none of this to Soutane. He considered what Trangh had told him a sacred trust. Through Terry and Trangh, it had become his responsibility. To expose Soutane—or anyone else, for that matter—to the Magician's secrets would be to unfairly involve them in what did not necessarily concern them.

They arrived at Mr. LoGrazie's house at Square Petrarque, and found, as Trangh had said, the front door unlocked. Holding Soutane behind him, Chris kicked the door so that it swung inward. He peered into the gloomy interior, but could discern nothing. Certainly there was no movement.

They went cautiously inside. The hallway was awash with a sickly-sweet smell, as of a vast carpet of rotting vegetation. Soutane gagged, then put her hand over her face.

"Breathe through your mouth," Chris told her.

"Oh God, what is this?"

He did not want to tell her, and plowed grimly on through the dim corridor. Sunlight filtered in here or there between thick velvet curtains, unfastened shutters. The slender well-defined shards were like stalks of wheat, brilliantly illuminated on a summer's day.

Soutane gasped, and Chris looked where she was staring. There was fresh blood drying on the walls and floor in the second-floor hallway, but no bodies. Soutane wondered whose blood it might be. Though Chris knew, he did not tell her. He drew her onward to the base of the staircase, then he made her sit, signed to her to remain there. She opened her mouth to protest, and Chris put his forefinger across her lips. He shook his head, began to ascend. But almost at once he was aware of a presence behind him. He turned to see her following him. He was already halfway up and he knew he could not make her stay downstairs. He felt anxiety rising inside him. He wanted to get the *Prey Dauw* and get out of this enormous tomb as quickly as possible. He allowed her to catch up to him.

The suitcase was where Trangh had said it would be, lying open in the second room along the second-floor landing. "There it is!" Chris said, and was heading for it when in a blaze the lights came on.

He drew in a sharp breath. Beside him Soutane exhaled one word, *"Merde!"*

Standing in the doorway at the top of the stairs was Marcus Gable, the Magician. He was covered in blood, and was naked from the waist up. His trousers oozed blood upon the parquet floor, creating a dark and noisome puddle at his feet. The Magician was alive! How was this possible? Chris asked himself. Trangh had said that Gable had died in the car crash at the Luxembourg Gardens.

With mounting horror Chris began to understand that within moments Gable would be upon them; he would need a weapon. But there was nothing near to hand, and now there was no time.

He could see that Gable was standing hip-sprung. His left shoulder was lower than his right, and his left arm hung at his side as if it were made of lead. He was supporting himself with his right hip against the stair railing in order to take the weight off his left leg.

His face was streaked with bloody lines as if he had been raked by a tiger. What appeared to be a forest of tiny glass shards was embedded in the flesh of his cheeks, jaw, nose, forehead, and neck, so that when he moved, his face crackled with refracted light. Only his eyes had been spared in the cataclysm that had maimed him. Those eyes were the same intense blue that Chris remembered so well from the preindictment meetings in his office, the pretrial sessions in prison, and the posttrial dinner at the grill. He remembered how much scorn and contempt could be processed through those eyes, and wondered what emotion besides rage they now held.

"Shithead lawyer," Marcus Gable, the Magician, said, and thrust the muzzle of his pistol straight ahead of him. Chris ducked, just as Soutane lashed out with the toe of her boot. It struck Gable in the center of his face, sending him reeling back against the wall. The impact loosened his grip upon the gun, so that it flew from his hand, bouncing down the stairs to the ground floor.

Chris stared. Apparently the shards of the tempered windshield glass studding the Magician's face had, like bizarre sutures, been holding the flesh together, because Soutane's blow had the most extraordinary effect upon it. Marcus Gable's carefully reconstructed face was now a mass of bleeding flesh, as unrecognizable and inchoate as if it had never been molded by the sculptor's hand.

"Chris!" Soutane cried. "Look!" In the spot behind where Gable had been standing, leaning precariously against the wall, was the *Prey Dauw*. That was why he came back here, Chris thought, instead of following Trangh to Les Portes du Jade.

She made a move toward it, but the Magician had already regained his feet, and he struck her a blow with the back of his heavy hand. Soutane cried out and staggered against the balustrade where moments before the gun had dropped into the well of darkness.

Gable's hand grasped something that was stuck in his waistband. He withdrew it and, with a practiced flick of his wrist, fanned open the iron ribs that were more like blades of Trangh's *gunsen*. There were eight tines, each ending in a point as sharp as a razor. In their present horizontal position they resembled nothing so much as an eagle's spread talons as it dives for the kill.

The Magician now thrust the *gunsen* out in a flat arc so that Soutane was obliged to bend over backward in order to avoid being slashed. Laughing maniacally, Gable lunged forward and, with a scream, Soutane tumbled backward down into the inky blackness of the stairwell.

He turned on Chris. "You better run for your life, fucker."

Chris shouted wordlessly, leaping upon Gable's huge, slippery frame. The Magician roared in rage. His blue eyes seemed to be weeping crimson tears. It was like embracing an open grave. The cloying, oppressive stench of death was already upon him, turning the air powdery as if with clouds of nauseating pollen.

His mouth opened wide as if he were a tiger or a bear, and he shot his head forward on his thick neck. Chris jammed his elbow into Gable's mouth, forcing as much of it in as he could.

Gable tried to snap his jaws closed, but the bulk of Chris's elbow made it impossible. Instead, he bit through cloth, skin, and flesh with a kind of frantic energy.

Chris winced with the pain, kicked Gable in the stomach with his knee. Gable staggered, had to use the hand that clutched the war fan against the blood-spattered wall to steady himself.

Chris kicked him again, and Gable grunted, biting down harder, bringing tears of pain to Chris's eyes. At the same time the *gunsen* came flying at the top of Chris's head, the fluted fabric between the tines making a kind of high-pitched screaming like the squeal of a thousand bats circling in concert.

Using his free hand, Chris gripped the Magician's genitals with such force that the veins stood out on either side of Gable's bull neck. Chris became aware of an odd, hair-raising animal ululation that seemed to reverberate through his very bones. Blood flew from Gable's eyelashes and hair as he thrashed his head back and forth in a vain effort to rid himself of the excruciating pain.

Meanwhile, Chris was trying to use his upper torso to bend Gable's head back. They rolled, locked together, straining and in agony, until they fetched up against the balustrade over which Soutane had tumbled. Chris, momentarily on top, tried to push Gable's head through the space between two of the carved wooden uprights.

The Magician swiped at Chris's shoulder with the *gunsen*. He missed, but the iron tines slashed into the wood, severing two of the uprights as if they were sheaves of wheat.

Chris, because he had to twist away from the whirring blades, loosened his grip on the Magician, and Gable used the leverage of his hips to upend Chris, crunching him against the floor and, simultaneously, slamming his knee into Chris's kidney.

Chris let out a grunt, and Gable whipped his head back in an effort to free his jaws from the massed assault of muscle and bone.

In so doing, he flipped Chris upward, over his own supine form and into the damaged part of the balustrade.

The small of Chris's back smashed into the top of the balustrade, and the force of his weight combined with the cracked uprights to collapse the entire structure at that point.

Chris found himself half flung into the blackness of the stairwell. His back felt as if it had been broken, and all the wind had been torn from his lungs. He flopped like a fish out of water, his skin- and flesh-shredded elbow torn from the grip of Gable's mouth so precipitously he was certain the arm had been wrenched from its socket.

Gable, panting and bleeding, crouched over him, not so much as human figure but an elemental animal shape, hunched and malformed, some malefic precursor to man before human beings could stand erect and reason.

He stared down at his antagonist with a baleful expression and, reversing the *gunsen* in his hand, reared up, preparing with one titanic effort to bury the tines in the center of Chris's chest.

"Stop!"

The one word froze him, and he looked up, blinking back bloody tears, to see Soutane appearing up the stairs. She held his gun in the marksman's two-handed grip, her arms held rigidly out in front of her. The muzzle of the gun was aimed at him.

"Put it down!" she commanded. "Put it down now or I'll kill you!"

Gable recovered from his amazement at her existence—for in the heat of his monumental struggle with Chris he had forgotten her completely—and began to laugh. He knew that from her low angle she had no clear shot, that she was afraid of blowing the top of Chris's head off.

"I mean it!" Soutane said, advancing up the stairs, bettering her angle.

"You haven't got the guts," Gable said, and watched without blinking as she pulled the trigger.

Or, rather, tried to. It wouldn't fire. The battering the weapon had taken as it flew down the flight of steps had apparently jammed it.

"Fuck you!" Gable said, and turning his attention back to Chris, began his vertical strike downward at his chest.

"Jesus!" Soutane swore, and did the only thing she could do. She threw the gun at Gable.

She did not have time to consciously aim. Rather, she let her instincts guide her hand, and the weapon, somersaulting through the space between her and the Magician, struck the spot that was most central and the closest to her: the *gunsen*.

Gable swore as the blued steel cracked the knuckles of his good hand. The raised sight scored his skin as if it had been a knife blade, and blood spurted.

Chris had been trying to gather his resources. He was fighting heavy odds. Pain girdled him from the blow that his back had absorbed, and from his ripped elbow. In addition, he was having great difficulty getting air back into his lungs, which meant he had no strength. But this was not all. He was having to battle against his own nature. No matter his personal feelings, he did not want to kill Marcus Gable. It went against a nature that had been deeply ingrained in him from birth. He was a man who, above all, believed in the efficacy of man's laws. With Seve—and perhaps, though he did not want to believe it, with his brother, Terry, as well—he had seen the sad result of forsaking law, and he knew better than to follow that ruinous path. Nevertheless, he did not want to die.

Out of the corner of his eye he saw that Soutane, running full tilt, had gained the second-floor landing. She turned the corner, just as Gable wrapped his hands around Chris's throat and began to squeeze.

As Gable had moments before, Chris began to thrash from side to side, hoping that his violent movements would dislodge the Magician's lethal hold on him. Already he was beginning to gasp as all air was cut off. An amorphous blackness crept into the edges of his field of vision, so that he could no longer see Soutane or what she was doing.

Until, abruptly, Gable's hands came away and, with a roar, he twisted his torso, striking out at Soutane as she made a lunge for the *gunsen* that the Magician had let fall from his numbed hand.

He hit her heavily on the side of the head, and she groaned, going down in a heap. Gable, grinning like a death's head, rained blow after blow on her spine and rib cage. Chris, trapped below his dripping bulk, could hear the animal grunts he made with each effort.

It was too much. Law or no law, this was more than he could bear. He felt the adrenaline like a great fountaining of fireworks as the drug hit his bloodstream, and he was pumping at full throttle. He knew from his racing experience that it would not last long, that he would have only one chance, one last desperate moment to gain control of the situation before Marcus Gable would kill Soutane and turn his murderous attention back to Chris.

He did not think; he moved. His reaction was primal, the basis of every martial-arts discipline. The mind/no mind in flight cannot be tamed, therefore it cannot be vanquished.

Chris used the strongest part of him, his thighs, twisting and clamping, then wrenching in concert with the fulcrum of his hips, the place of *hara*, of energy, with such monstrous intrinsic force that Gable was thrown onto his back with a crack like a clap of thunder.

Nevertheless, Gable managed to thrust his good hand out, grab hold of Chris's shirtfront. Chris was jerked upright from his waist with teeth-chattering force. He almost passed out, sucked breath into his burning lungs in great drafts. Then he saw that the Magician had gathered up what Soutane had meant to use, Trangh's *gunsen*, and he thought, staring into Gable's manic face, This is it. It's over. I have nothing more. . . .

And then, gasping like a fish in air, his bulging eyes caught sight of the *Prey Dauw*. In the thunder of their hand-to-hand battle, the talisman had slipped down onto the floor, where it now lay hilt-first, just an arm's length away.

Chris made a grab for it and Gable, using his ruined hand to grasp Chris's hair, pulled him back. Gable screamed with the pain, and Chris kicked out, using his powerful thigh muscles, the flat of his shoe sole.

One chance, one last desperate moment . . .

And in that moment, as Gable's grip slipped in Chris's sweat-soaked hair, Chris extended himself fully. His hands settled around the hilt of the Forest of Swords. He lifted it, the triple blades traveling from light to dark and back again. He held it before him, angled toward Gable. And although he was certain that his last reserve of adrenaline had been dissipated, he nevertheless felt a renewal of strength. It was nothing like the jolt of an electric current, or even as he might have expected the familiar kinetic blockage of exhaustion as the adrenaline was pumped into his system. Rather, it was the most subtle form of galvanization, a river of dark silver from which he was being nurtured, his pain receding, his fatigue washed away altogether. His courage and his terror were simultaneously sustained.

The terrible, chilling laugh came again. "Idiot!" the Magician cried. "Those blades are jade. They have no real edge. As a weapon, that thing is useless!"

Crouching, sure of himself, he came at Chris with the spread war fan, its deadly tines tipped with fire as they passed through a spire of sunlight. His nostrils were flared as if he could already scent the kill, and his eyes were locked on Chris's face as if like a greedy vampire he were about to feed on the twilight of the life he was about to take.

Because of this, he failed to see Chris's kick until it was too late. The heel of Chris's shoe smashed into his left knee, spinning him around. Even so, he thought he had caught himself, the reflexes honed in the bloody jungles of Vietnam and Cambodia still protecting him. In opening up his stance to keep his balance, he skidded in a pool of his own blood and pitched violently forward.

Directly onto the outstretched jade blades of the *Prey Dauw*.

Gable had been right. The jade was not made to kill, but kill it could if its victim descended on it straight on, as Trangh had known when he had used the replica Doorway to Night, part of the *Prey Dauw*, to stab Terry.

Chris had stepped forward; his muscled arms were rigid as he sought to anticipate either absorbing a blow or delivering one himself, almost as if the sword itself were drawing him onward like a lodestone toward its mate. Gable fell upon Chris so quickly and with such force that all three blades passed completely through his massive body.

Chris grunted with surprise and effort. For a moment he was borne perilously backward. Then, as if the hilt of the *Prey Dauw* had abruptly become hot to the touch, he relinquished his grip upon it, and Marcus Gable fell to the floor.

Chris was already at Soutane's side, turned her gingerly over, stroking the hair back from her face. He saw that she was still breathing, said a silent prayer. As gently as he could, he felt for any broken bones. Once or twice she moaned as if in pain, and then her eyelids fluttered open.

"Chris!" Alarm thickened her voice.

"It's all right," he said soothingly. "Gable is dead."

"I tried, Chris. I tried."

"Shhh," he said, stroking her cheek in order to calm her. "I know." He smiled down at her. "How do you feel?"

She tried to sit up, winced, made it on the second attempt. She lifted her arms to his shoulders. "I want to get up."

"Soutane—"

"Up!"

And he rose, drew her into his arms. She came against him

immediately, as if the bones had melted in her legs. Her forehead dropped onto his chest, and he could feel her labored breathing. Then, with the considerable strength in her arms, she pushed him gently away. She stood for a moment, swaying slightly. Then she took the first steps toward where Gable lay. The flat of one hand was pressed against her side, but the color was fast returning to her face and, otherwise, she appeared unharmed.

"This son of a bitch," she said, touching him with the toe of her boot, "really was a kind of magician."

Chris saw Marcus Gable's face. His eyes, in death, were not turned upward, but rather downward to the earth. Or perhaps they were turned inward, to glimpse one last time the fantastic solipsistic soul that had evolved like a patient, multi-eyed spider in the center of its web.

Soutane, staring into his bloody face, shuddered heavily. So drawn to this evil visage was she that it was not until Chris, putting one shoe on Gable's meaty shoulder, pulled the Forest of Swords free of its human wreckage, that she breathed its name.

"The *Prey Dauw*."

Gripping it again, Chris felt a return of that subtle sensation, the connection with a bright, black river that spanned not fields and mountains but centuries, ages. Was it just his imagination, or something more? Would he, a pacifist, have been able to defeat Marcus Gable, the predator, without the *Prey Dauw*? Had this talisman, in the end, sought out the human black hole that Marcus Gable had become?

He blinked and looked around him. He saw Soutane standing over the corpse of Marcus Gable. He saw the blood-spattered walls, the slimy, sticky floor. He smelled the sickly-sweet stench of the open grave. All these things he had experienced before; they were quite familiar to him. Nevertheless, he had the distinct impression that now he experienced them in some subtly different form.

He stared at the jade blades, believing he saw movement there as one does when, dropping one's freshly baited line, one is aware of darting shapes beneath the dark, winking surface of a lake.

Before they left, he went through the house and, as Trangh had directed him, raided it of its well-hidden secrets.

Later, back at the hotel, after they had bathed and, using the first-aid paraphernalia they had picked up at a nearby pharmacy, had cleaned themselves up, Chris told her what he had to do. It seemed, oddly, as if he had known this all his life.

"Why must you go to the Shan?" she asked.

"Because that is where the Forest of Swords belongs."

She shook her head. "I don't understand. Destroy it. Bury it where no one will find it. Throw it in the Seine. Can't you just let it go? Have you truly become so much like your brother that you, too, are obsessed with the *Prey Dauw*?"

"Long ago when I met you I thought I was obsessed with finding the war," he said. "I had convinced myself that I was guilt-stricken at having run away from it when Terry had not. Years later I realized that it was Terry I had run away from, and I became even more guilt-stricken.

"Now, at last, I realize that Terry followed his heart and I followed mine. I came here, I met you, I fell in love, and I almost won the Tour de France. For many years I was certain that those events had shaped my entire life. Now I know how wrong I was.

"I'm not obsessed with the *Prey Dauw*. In fact, for the first time in my life, my mind could not be clearer. But I must find Mun, now, and talk to him. He holds the last part of the puzzle that was Terry. You see, Soutane, I came back here not to bury my brother, but to find him, and in finding him, find myself. I've lived inside a dream for so long, I had lost the ability to make myself happy. Since then, I've found out so much about Terry, and for that I'll always be grateful. But I also know that somehow it's not enough. It isn't over yet, and I can't go home until it is."

He saw her stiffen. "Home," she said softly. "Do you know where home is, Chris? Is it here in France, or in New York?"

In New York with Alix, was what she meant. An image of Alix flashed though his mind. "Is that an invitation, Soutane?" he said. "Because if it is I want you to understand fully what that means."

She turned away, unwilling or unable to reply. In a moment she said, "Just don't ask me to go with you. I've gone as far as I can. I'm spent, Chris. I'm done."

"I know," he said.

"Then don't go. Stay here with me. I need you."

"I'll just interfere with the rest you need."

Her eyes were incredulous. "My God, after all that has happened, it would be cruel to leave me now."

"I once told you," he said, "that my father was Welsh, from warrior stock. He used to quote an old Welsh saying he was fond of: 'Let all the blood be on the front of you.' If I don't go to the Shan, Soutane, there will be blood on my back."

She stared at him, wide-eyed. "I was right about you," she whispered. "You're quite mad."

He put an arm across her slender shoulders, wondered at the sadness he felt welling up inside him.

An hour later, after he and Soutane had returned from the hospital where Seve was recovering, he was talking to Alix on the phone. By then he had read the telex Max Steiner had sent him. Not trusting the hotel's operator with taking down a lengthy message, Steiner had outlined in his own words the nature of Alix's operation, the result, and the optimistic prognosis.

"Christopher," Alix said, "is that really you?"

"It's really me," he said, an unidentifiable emotion taking hold of him. "I'm sorry I'm not there."

"Max is taking good care of me. He got rid of my ex-husband, who had started hanging around. He got a court order to keep him away from Danny."

"Are you all right?"

"I'm fine." And to his relief she sounded it.

"You've been very brave."

"Me? I've been a basket case. Dick's reappearance really shook me up. Thank God for Max."

"He's a good friend."

"Yes. He is." Silence blossomed, of a sort that rose between intimates long parted. Were they both thinking of the distance that separated them, wondering with fearful anticipation what effect it had worked on their relationship?

"What about you?" Alix said at last. "Is it difficult there? I know you loved your brother."

"How did you know that?" he asked, astonished.

She gave a little laugh, and it sounded so good to him that he squeezed his eyes shut. "It was obvious, dummy." In the pause, the crackle of transoceanic static. When she spoke again, her voice had softened. "I hope you found whatever it was you were searching for."

Chris wondered about that. "It's almost over," he said, not understanding himself precisely what he meant by that.

"Have you—" Said impulsively, then cut off just as abruptly. She began again. "Christopher, I know I have no right to ask this," she said, "but when are you coming home? It seems like such a long time since I've seen you. I miss you terribly."

"Soon," he said, unable to bring himself to give her any other answer. Feeling the pull of that dark river of silver—wondering at what it promised. "I'll be home soon."

SPRING, PRESENT

SHAN STATE

Mun met Chris at Mingaladon Airport, twelve miles northwest of the city of Rangoon. Mun had been waiting there for a day and a half while, for one reason or another, Chris's BAC flight from Bangkok was delayed. That was nothing unusual for Burma. Chris's tourist visa was good for seven days, but he had been told not to let that concern him.

Without a word Mun slung Chris's suitcase into the back of a dust- and mud-covered jeep. The engine made a horrific roar, as if it had not been looked after or had an animal stuck in the distributor.

Three days later they had abandoned everything save sturdy canvas backpacks Mun had pulled from the rear of the jeep, and were halfway up the Shan. Their pace was slow, and they were obliged to stop often because of Mun's injury, and Chris's aches. Once a day because of the extreme heat and humidity, Chris applied disinfectant and clean bandages to his elbow.

Sometime during that first day Chris had said, "Trangh, the Magician, Monsieur Vosges. They're all dead." He had already told Mun that Milhaud was actually M. Vosges.

"And the Dancer?"

Chris had still not gotten used to Seve being spoken of by that name. "For a day he was suspended somewhere between life and death. He breathed, his heart beat, but that was all. We still don't know what Trangh did to him, but it hardly matters now. He'll recover. We spoke at length before I left."

"And my cousin?"

"Soutane is with him, in the hospital." He looked at his watch, checking the date. Actually, he was certain that Seve had already gotten himself released by now. "She's not alone there. She and Monsieur Vosges's mistress, Morphée, have become friends."

"Is it difficult for Soutane to be in Paris instead of being with you here?"

Chris thought about that for a long time before answering. "I'm not at all certain that she wanted to come."

"She is content, then, to look after the Dancer."

"No," Chris had said, "she is far from content. She did not want me to leave, and she did not perhaps want to come herself."

"Did she see the necessity of it?"

"Of my coming here? I don't know. I wonder now if she ever saw the sense in any of this. Her refusal to come to terms with who she is has crippled her."

"I created what she has become, Christopher," Mun said. "I live with her inner pain every day of my life. I had hoped, when you came back into her life, that her pain would end."

Climbing through the impossibly dense, triple-canopied jungle of the Shan, Chris wondered whether he would ever be home again. He wondered where home was. Was it in Nice with Soutane? Or in New York with Alix?

The Shan.

It stretched before him, reaching toward heaven.

On their second night out they were overtaken by a rainstorm of terrifying strength. Immense stabs of almost fluorescent lightning ringed the mountaintops, while thunderclaps with a physical presence beat upon the drum skin of the sky. Birds, folded-wing and trembling, cowered within the inadequate shelter of the jungle, while the treetops bent almost in half.

In the morning the sky was clean and bright, scoured by the storm.

"What about the Magician and Trangh?" Chris had asked. "Didn't you think they would follow you?"

"I didn't consider them," Mun said, by which he meant that he had known that they were already dead or near death. In their five days together Chris had already come to know Mun well enough to accept, if not to understand, his reliance on psychic auras.

In the cool of first light as they broke camp, Chris thought of Terry. Were they following a path that Terry had taken months or even weeks before? He imagined his brother's tanned, lined face, confident and strong, passing this way. Terry may have felt comfortable here in this sweat-soaked wilderness, but Chris certainly did not. He felt frightened by the alienness of the difficult terrain, was disturbed by the obvious lawlessness inside Burma.

Unconsciously, he touched the stag-bolstered folder that Terry had given him, as if it were an amulet that would protect him from unseen dangers. And Alix's voice slipped into his mind. *I love you madly,* she had said just before hanging up. And what had he said to that? Nothing. He turned that over in his mind all day, but at night he was so exhausted that he fell into a dreamless sleep as he had on the other nights of this trek.

On the fourth day of their trek Mun woke him two hours before dawn. "We must be more careful now," he said in a low voice as they set out in pitch blackness. "We have just crossed over into General Kiu's territory. There will be many patrols; there is much danger."

By the time they reached the extreme northeastern edge of General Kiu's territory, they had indeed seen four such patrols. Mun steered them clear each time. The atmosphere had changed considerably. There was a definite chill in the air. They were approximately ninety-seven miles from Mandalay, more than a half mile above sea level.

Just as the sun, a majestic red oblate disk, was rising, Mun led him onto a small rock promontory. Over the edge it was a long way down to the jungle floor.

Here, the earth was blackened, filled with powdered ash, as if a bonfire of prodigious size had been burning for months on end.

"You came to discover the truth about your brother," Mun said. "Here it is. Terry was coerced into joining the Magician's organization, but at least he did so somewhat on his own terms. He insisted on having complete and autonomous control over the opium pipeline they had wrested from Monsieur Vosges.

"That was agreed upon, but when the Magician discovered that Terry was pulling merely intelligence rather than profits from the pipeline, he threatened to take the network away.

"Terry gave the Magician copies of the diaries he had made on the organization's work—the originals of which he entrusted to me to disseminate in the event of his death."

"But why didn't you bring them to light when Terry was killed?" Chris asked.

"Because," Mun said, "I no longer had them. Trangh had stolen them." A wind was rising, and Mun braced himself against the bole of a weather-stunted tree. "When Terry left the organization, he came to me. He was determined to continue running the pipeline, and I decided to help him."

"Why?"

"Because," Mun said, "I believed in what he was doing."

Chris stared incredulously at him. "In feeding poison to kids?"

Mun shook his head. "I told you that I wanted to make certain you would come here, that merely telling you would not have been sufficient. You would have disbelieved me or, at the very least, doubted my word." He spread his hands. "Now you see the truth with your own eyes."

Chris looked around him at the scorched earth. Everywhere was ashes. "I don't understand."

Mun bent, scooped a handful of ash, let it pour through his fingers like sand through an hourglass. "This is what happened to the opium we purchased from Admiral Jumbo. This is the end of the pipeline."

Chris was in shock. "You *burned* it?"

"Yes. We took CIA funds, bought the opium, and destroyed it."

Chris was looking at him quizzically.

"The other half of the scheme was pure genius. Terry made a deal with the Communist Chinese. In return for destroying a set amount of opium per year they provided him with strategic and military intelligence concerning Russia that they had gleaned from their sources both in the north, at the border, and in Hong Kong.

"When Terry was with the CIA, he provided them with the intelligence. Later, when we were independent, we continued the arrangement, only on our terms. We made they pay through the nose."

Chris sat down on a part of the outcropping. This, then, was the secret, the end of his quest. Perhaps. He carefully unwrapped the *Prey Dauw*, in preparation for what? he wondered. He looked up at Mun. "But something happened."

Mun nodded. "For a long time we were in a position of great power. I suspect that it finally got to Terry. Suddenly, doing what we were doing wasn't enough for him. He wanted the Forest of Swords. He wanted to use it to control all the opium warlords, to unite them under one man: himself. And, in the process, he seemed determined to destroy the Magician."

"But why, after all that time? They seemed to have lived in an uneasy truce for so long."

"About two years ago the Magician became aware of you, who you were. In you he saw a way to get back the pipeline he felt Terry had stolen from him. He threatened Terry, and that set everything in motion."

"I can't believe that Terry was really going to sell the Doorway to Night to Monsieur Vosges."

"No," Mun said. "He wasn't. That's why he had the duplicate made up. I knew nothing about this, and would have fought him had I found out. Terry knew this, and did it secretly. We needed money. The CIA had reneged on their last payments. Budgetary problems, they said. Terry didn't believe them. Anyway, we needed the cash."

Chris turned away. He stared out into the nothingness suspended beyond the rock outcropping. All this had happened because Terry had wanted to protect him from Marcus Gable. My God, between them they managed to turn the world upside down.

For the first time Chris saw a glimmering, an intimation of the extent of the power at work here. He did not know whether to be terrified or exhilarated. And then, with a shivery start, he realized that this mixture of emotions was precisely what Terry must have once felt.

He got up, approached Mun. "Before he died, Trangh told me everything he knew about the Magician's setup. He knew all the keys but one: who the Magician was working for. But Seve's people found out who that is: Jason Craig, chairman of the board of International Communications Conglomerate. Trangh compiled records, taped conversations. They have enough evidence, with what I gave them, to indict him."

Mun looked at him. "An indictment is a long way from a conviction," he said. "Guys like Craig employ armies of lawyers full-time who are prepared for anything."

Chris was already shaking his head. "Who better than I would know that?" He grinned. "I used to be one of those lawyers. But I'm on the side of the angels now, Mun. I'll make sure Craig won't get off."

He turned into the sunlight. The toe of his boot stirred the ash, like black sand on the shores of oblivion. Here, at last, in the elemental jungle of Burma, Chris could feel Terry close beside him like an abiding presence. "You know," he said slowly, "before all this, I though I'd had it with the legal profession. Now I realized that it was the kind of lawyer I had become that I couldn't stand.

"I was all ego, Mun, eager to take on the impossible cases other lawyers wouldn't touch for fear of failure. I craved notoriety as if I were an addict. You know what Terry called me? *Le monstre sacré*. The superstar. And that's exactly what I was. I burned with an impossible brightness. I burned with ambition, and blinded myself to the kinds of people I took on as clients, telling myself that everyone is entitled to legal counsel and a proper defense. But really what I was doing was playing a game, a game where I outwitted the prosecution. This game had nothing to do with my clients, which was why it was so easy to blind myself to their evil. It had to do with me."

He saw, then, the terrible illusion of freedom. When most people spoke of freedom, they did so with the insular consciousness of "I." Freedom, though Chris like a child was just learning it, was pure ego, rampant selfishness. That was not what he wanted for himself.

It was a matter of choice. Chris's choice. He remembered reading somewhere that in Eden, Adam and Eve's choice had been that of self over God, arrogance over faith. Their choice was not as was normally supposed about blind obedience or righteous piety. His choice was very much the same because he had glimpsed the truth, that all choice was created at the same source.

At the end Trangh had spoken of faith, that faith was synonymous with an absence of desire—as it were, a pure spirit, as Mun wished now to be. Chris knew that he would never be a pure spirit; he was far too human to dream such godlike dreams. But he could be a better human being.

Your brother was like me: a primitive, Trangh had said. *He lived his life according to a strict inner code of honor, one that he upheld all his life*. Now Chris saw that it had been a stricter code of honor than he himself—the righteous brother!—had been able to muster. It was both a humbling and an exalting experience, for in this one moment of recognition, Chris had at last found his brother and himself. The circle was completed, and the first beginning tendrils of a kind of contentment began to steal over him like the onset of the sunrise.

All at once Chris realized that all this time he had been holding the *Prey Dauw*. The leaf-green jade blades seemed to glow with an inner light, but when he turned the talisman into the sunlight, the jade turned opaque, as black as night. Between his palms, the dark, shining river, pulling at him. It was like a drug: alluring, fascinating, multiplying its power to seduce like a skein twined by an unseen weaver. But he also recognized in its depths an alarming, inchoate danger, a path that, if not adeptly sidestepped, could strip him of all humanity.

"Mun, is the *Prey Dauw's* power real?"

Mun smiled. His face, free of care and worry lines, was burnished like the jade by the oblique early-morning light. "I suppose,'' he said, ''it depends who you speak to. Belief is an odd and complex region which has yet to be fully explored.''

Chris cocked his head. ''Is that a yes or a no?''

Mun looked at him. ''I am surprised you are asking. It is both, of course. The power of the *Prey Dauw* lies in the mind.''

Chris stared at the talisman, feeling—or supposing he felt—its limitless power. ''What will become of it now?''

''That is entirely up to you. It belongs to you. Yours is the power to wield, if you choose to.''

Chris was already shaking his head. ''No. Not me. It belongs to someone pure of spirit. I hardly qualify.'' He looked into Mun's open face. ''What should I do? I can't just bury it somewhere, that would be irresponsible. Won't you help me?''

Mun smiled. ''You must know, Chris, that you are not alone. You have Terry.'' He pressed his palm to the center of Chris's chest. ''Just here. In your heart. Perhaps he speaks to you.'' He gestured. ''Perhaps this place speaks to you. I can see that you have responded to the spirit of the Shan.''

His chest was warm where Mun had touched him, and he was very aware of his heartbeat. It was not only Terry he held inside him, but Alix as well. He had understood that the moment he came upon the ridge bathed in the sunshine of a new day.

What of Soutane? Mun had said, *I had hoped, when you came back into her life, that her pain would end*. But now Chris saw that it was not up to him to end Soutane's inner torment. Neither was it up to Mun. That kind of healing could only come from Soutane herself.

Soutane was part of his past. Her essence was encysted there beside the figure of himself as a youth, the two like images in a sepia-toned photograph. It was Alix who belonged to his present, whom this modern-day Christopher Haye missed and longed for.

''That was the other reason you brought me here, isn't it?'' he said. ''So I could have a chance to feel the world as Terry did.''

''I have accomplished what I wanted,'' Mun said. ''You have your answers, you have seen the truth. Now I must return to Sagaing. The Buddha calls me.''

Chris held out the Forest of Swords. ''I think, in the end, he knew you would be its guardian.''

''Who?'' But it was clear that Mun already knew.

''Trangh.'' Chris felt a great weight at the thought of the power he held in his hands. ''To be free from desire, he said. If you know that, you know everything.''

Mun had taken his eyes from Chris's. "The *Prey Dauw* is a great transmitter of power. In this land people would call you God or Lord or Master with it in your hand. The opium generals would prostrate themselves before you. You could have anything. Are you certain you want to give that up?"

Chris grinned as he placed the talisman in Mun's hands, the mesmerizing lapping of the dark, shining river fading. "I never had it," he said.

In a moment the two of them turned and, walking through the ashes, climbed down off the bare peak.

Up here, as elsewhere in the world, Chris knew, it was not in gaining the power that the danger lay. It was in allowing the power to destroy you.

He knew that from this day forward, he would never forget that. The old Christopher Haye never even would have dreamed of the concept, let alone have been on guard against it.

But this person who walked the Shan with such assurance was someone new. Chris was looking forward to getting to know him.

ABOUT THE AUTHOR

Eric V. Lustbader is the author of *Zero, Shan, Jian, Black Heart*, and *The Ninja*, all bestsellers. He lives in New York City and in Southampton, Long Island, with his wife, editor Victoria Schochet Lustbader.